NEW HAVEN PUBLIC LIBRARY
3 5000 09462 5653
P9-AQY-529

K. Michael Wright

Angelslayer

The Winnowing War

Medallion Press, Inc.
Printed in USA

DEDICATION:

For Buffy who always believed.

Published 2008 by Medallion Press, Inc.

The MEDALLION PRESS LOGO
is a registered trademark of Medallion Press, Inc.

Cover Illustration by Jeff Easley
Cover Design by Adam Mock
Book Design by James Tampa

Printed in the United States of America
Typeset in Adobe Jenson Pro
Title font set in Sloth and Parseltongue

Library of Congress Cataloging-in-Publication Data

Wright, K. Michael.
Angelslayer : the winnowing war / K . Michael Wright.
p. cm.
ISBN 978-1-933836-53-9 (alk. paper)
1. Angels--Fiction. 2. Spiritual warfare--Fiction. I. Title.
PS3623.R554A84 2008
813'.6--dc22
2008018228

10 9 8 7 6 5 4 3 2 1
First Edition

ACKNOWLEDGEMENTS:

Many thanks to Carrie Wright whose help as an editor and talent as a writer helped bring Angelslayer to life.

There were giants in the earth in those days; and also after that, when the sons of God came in unto the daughters of men, and they bare children to them, the same became mighty men, which were of old, men of renown.

King James Version of Genesis 6:4

Chapter One

Darke

An isle in the Southern Sea of Etlantis
Thirty years before Aeon's End, the first apocalypse of Earth

The sky was a slate gray when Darke's ship pulled into the island's cove. The waters of the lagoon could have been inked. Darke, the corsair, was a lean figure atop the forecastle; his black mantle flared in night's wind; his hair curled about the shoulders of his leather jerkin. His men were gathered. They were men hard of the sea.

At the forward ports, archers crouched, waiting. Amidships, the mighty crossbow, with its fifty-stone draw, was armed with an oaken bolt fitted with a heavy, rusted iron tip. At the cutwater strakes, the siphon jets of the flame throwers curled their fire breath against the prow.

In the lagoon across from them, an Etlantian galley rested. Rather, it once had been an Etlantian galley. Etlantian ships were brightly painted—red and blue, green and white. Solid plates of oraculum, the Etlantians' silver-red metal, always wreathed the top strakes; in the sun they could reflect the color of bright blood, but this ship was a brigand, with time eating slowly at the hull and sailcloth.

Darke's own ship was black and waxen. Its sails were designed light but strong, a sacred ashen color that had allowed the night runners of Captain Darke to cut the sea like shadow. Darke's ship could appear from nowhere—always at Darke's chosen time, always at Darke's chosen place, always with speed, and sometimes with such stealth that many an Etlantian had died in the sea never knowing he had been brought down by the Shadow Hawk, the last of the Tarshians—the giant killers, the raiders of Ishtar's horned moon.

However, this night Darke had not come for battle.

Storan stood beside his captain as the warship drew quietly into the deep of the lagoon. Storan was the helmsman. He had been with Darke from their youth, from the beginning when blue blood coursed through their veins, and they could as easily have sailed the stars as the sea. Storan was a bearlike figure with deep, dark eyes inset like a bull's beneath thorny brows. He had ill-kept, graying hair. His axe, a yawning blade well quenched of blood, was always at the ready, sheathed in a woven leather belt lashed against his muscled thigh.

There had been a time in memory's reach when Storan and Darke had sailed as lords of all Tarshish, the emerald cities of the Tarshians, but Etlantis had destroyed the cities of the Tarshians, laid them waste one by one, and now any Tarshians alive were raiders, hidden among the isles of the sea. They were becoming few, like carnivores that once ruled but now were being hunted for sport to extinction.

The world had changed since Darke first sailed. Most of all, the Etlantians, the sons of the angels, had changed. This last generation was like no other. Giants, some stood seven foot and more. Some were barely recognizable as human, and so they were called Nephilim, spawn of the fallen. Holy blood ran in their veins, but unholy flesh twisted them, drawing them into aeon's breath, the folding of time, the ending of all things.

The Etlantian galley in the lagoon was a large ship of the line. She had once been prime, a three-tiered craft, one-hundred oared, with four masts and a spar like a great spear, sheathed in oraculum that arched over a bull's-head ram. On her main deck were three catapults. Her sides were lashed with grappling planks, and bolt launchers ringed her bow ports like teeth. Her fire throwers were both fore and aft, but they were unlit, dripping an oily drool over the cutwater timbers.

She lay in the harbor like a fat-bellied whore, and yet, even then, her majesty still lingered in a shadow. This was not the ship of a Nephilim, of an angel's son, or even of an Etlantian prince—those born to the angels in olden times, who were often still honorable. This ship belonged to none of those. Though no emblems adorned her and no colors flew from her top masts, Darke could trust his instincts: this was the ship, not just of any angel but of a Named—Satariel, the lord of the Melachim, the sixth choir of the third star. This was a

Watcher's ship, the ship of a high-blood angel. He was here somewhere, waiting, just as he had promised.

Darke raised his hand.

"Lay back the oars!" Storan echoed the command.

The oars lifted in a single, powerful sweep and whined as they eased back against the oarlocks into their beds. Silence. Timber moaned as Darke's low, sleek warship circled slowly in idle current, keeping its distance from the Etlantian. Darke's ship looked like a black bird resting in the night.

Had he spotted Satariel's ship at sea, Darke would not have been sure whether to attack or to raise colors. It was said that Satariel had sunk more Etlantian timber than even he, and as evidence, the oraculum ram of the angel's ship was scarred like a well-used blade.

Storan, the muscled helmsman, studied the ship skeptically. "The bitch is at anchor, her oars in lock. If we struck her now, we could split her like a crab."

"I have come in truce," Darke said.

"You know as well as I that we are nothing but bait, Captain." Storan spat over the side. "So where is he? Where is this unholy bastard?"

Darke studied the lagoon. Storan was right; they were unprotected here. If this were a trap, the lagoon offered no protection. If Etlantian warships were to close on the mouth of the lagoon, death would follow in short breath.

"Drop anchor," Darke said quietly.

Storan shifted uneasily before giving the order. "Do not much like anchoring out here with our asses bared in moonlight like painted whores."

"Storan, if he is who he claims, we would be as dead as stone if he desired. So far, he's kept his word, which means he needs us for something. We've come this far; we may as well learn his purpose. You think?"

"You would rather not know what I think of all this, Captain." He turned. "Let out the stone!"

The anchor chain rumbled as the weighting stone splashed into the quiet waters.

There were times Darke could sense things, times he could feel a merchantman before she ever pulled onto the horizon. He could pick his way through the coral reefs of islands as if he knew their skin. And weeks ago, when a river ship had hailed alongside and its captain, an aged, withered giant—an Etlantian—had given him the scroll, something seemed to promise that it was no trick. The scroll was aged papyrus, and its edges had been dipped in blood. Darke broke the waxen seal with its bull's-horn signet. It had been an invitation, more likely a trap, but either way, it had fired his curiosity. Because of it, Darke had sailed to this island to see the face of an angel. He wanted to gaze on a being who had been roaming Earth since the dawn of man, a being whose eyes had withstood God's fire. Darke almost didn't care the cost.

"Where is it we are to meet him?" Storan asked.

Darke searched a moment and then pointed toward the dim light of a tent, beached to the lee of the Etlantian galley. Although barely visible, Darke had found it easily.

Darke's mother had laid a balm of nightshade and galbanum on his eyelids before the umbilical cord had been cut, and thus she named him Darke and promised vengeance of the night.

"There could be fifty men in those trees, Captain," Storan grizzled. "You said he would meet in the open. I name that alone breach of word. I say we try to kill him now and mark our names in the list of the damned."

"He is a dark angel of the holy choir; he might prove difficult to kill, Storan."

"I do not indulge beliefs of angels of light or of dark, nor do I care for choirs. I want a song; then, I will find me a whore with a sweet voice in a tavern somewhere."

"Not that kind of choir, I fear. This angel has slaughtered enough innocent blood to fill this lagoon." Darke turned and spoke quietly. "Bring me Danwyar."

Calls went out for Danwyar.

Darke searched his men. He needed a shore party, a small one. Anxious, Taran stood with his hand over the hilt of the double-edged iron he had taken off a Pelegasian breached at high sea. Taran was Darke's brother, though younger by twenty-two years, something of a mistake of birth on his mother's behalf. Taran was only ten and nine. He'd be a fine warrior someday, but that day would never be reached in the light of this sun. The sun of Darke, the star of this earth, now numbered its days carefully, and though he never spoke of it to his men, Darke knew the numbers. Taran would die too soon, ever to become the slayer for whom he had been named, his great-uncle, the lord of Anguar, Taran the Red.

Still, the boy was good. More kills than his years, and that by Darke's count alone. Who knew how many more in the scream of battle? The sword the boy had chosen was heavy and whetted with a taste for blood. Darke had seen him working it for long years now. That was not the reason Taran had been chosen; the reason was that the boy's only chance of surviving was to learn. This was to be one of those occasions where one either lived or more likely died—but it was certain one would learn something, something of critical importance.

"Taran, prepare a longboat."

Taran nodded and quickly dropped over the forecastle railing to begin paying out the longboat lines. Sometimes Darke wondered how he saw through the long, sandy hair so often in his eyes.

Danwyar had climbed the ladder to the forecastle and now waited silently. Danwyar was small and bald on the whole of his body from a disease that had caused his hair to fall out. If anything, it made him all the swifter. His bow and short sword moved like the tongue of a serpent, and he could see well enough to navigate by stars even though cloud cover would discourage the most seasoned pilot. He was descended of the princes of the second city of Tarshish, and his father had been Ryhall, the king of Ichnosh. Not only was he the named second of Darke, but also he was far and away the best man the captain had.

"You will take the helm, Danwyar," Darke said. "Anything proves wrong, gut the Etlantian. Sink her."

Danwyar nodded.

"Storan, you will come with me."

Storan merely chuckled. "You can kiss my sweet flowery ass on that," he said. No one could stop Storan from coming if the life of Darke, his king, was to be in danger.

"And Marsyas," Darke said.

Marsyas was full-blood Etlantian, ugly to begin with, and standing near seven foot. A blow had once split open his face, and he had been found among the dead of battle. Not a Nephilim, he was a lesser born—a third generation born. Nephilim were firstborn only, direct descendants of an angel. But

Marsyas had been born powerful, intelligent, and strong, and he had brought down ten men that battle. Darke kept his life, and Marsyas had sworn oath. It was said the children of Marsyas's generation, the third generation of the sons of the Angel's Isle, had fallen to the curse of Enoch such that only the meat and blood of men would quench them, but if the curse was with Marsyas, he kept his blood-taking to those who, in his own opinion, deserved to be drained. Darke always held his hand, as he would in a tight game of dice: there were bad Etlantians, but many were still good, many still men of lineage. Some of the older princes of the firstborn were of the light and so were, in Darke's mind, many of the angels. They had to be. They had been bred pure of God's blood; their eyes had seen God's light. Foolish men said they had fallen for woman, for the daughters of men, but Darke would hedge his bet on that.

Marsyas, though a third-generation descendant of the angels, was one of the best comrades Darke had met on this small world. He was as loyal as Storan.

Marsyas had but half a tongue. He could speak, but seldom did. In response to Darke's command, he only brought his big fist to his chest.

Darke was satisfied—Taran, Marsyas, and Storan—enough for a good killing, certainly enough for a chat with an angel.

In the longboat, they passed slowly beneath the stern of the angel's Etlantian galley. Dull light filtered through thick, semiopaque windows of the cabin structure. From the deep of the lagoon, it had looked abandoned, but now, along the top railings, figures watched them pass. They seemed to have no focus, no faces. They might have been nothing more than shadows.

Once past the Etlantian hull, the keel of Darke's longboat hit the sand. Storan and the boy leapt out, wading through warm water, to set the shoring blocks.

The four pirates assembled on the beach. The tent, lit by braziers from within, was down the shoreline some twenty yards. Storan let his thick fingers curl about the worn haft of his axe, but he did not draw it.

Darke looked to his brother. "Taran, you stay here with the boat. Should anything happen to us, try to get back to the ship to warn the others."

Taran nodded.

Darke, Marsyas, and Storan walked slowly along the water's edge. The only sound was that of the shallow surf. The trees and vegetation should have been humming with insects, but they were dark and silent. Near the brigantine ship and the single, unadorned tent in the sand, the foliage had begun to die. There was even a stink to it. From the corner of his eye, Darke noticed the body of a cormorant, lying on its back, its legs stiff, its head twisted full about, face into the sand. It seemed an odd sight.

Marsyas walked silently, without emotion, but the closer they got, the more nervous Storan became.

"Sweet and holy Goddess as my witness," Storan muttered. "I do not like this, Captain. My mother would tell us to turn back now, she would. I know that to speak to you at this moment will be no more productive than to piss in the wind, but there will be no good to come of this; I promise you that. 'Tis a bad season, this. I feel the turning in the air. We'd be coming into a storm not of this world."

"Are you going to talk the whole night, Storan?"

"Why? Will you listen to what I say?"

As the tent of the angel became clearer in the night, what appeared to have been black canvas was instead dark red, glistening slightly from the dull torchlight within. The smell of it was certain. It was coated in blood that had not yet dried. There were fields of slaughter that held this smell, this sour, slightly metallic taste. The stakes anchoring the tent's edges turned out to be leg bones, snapped at the kneecaps and driven into the sand. Darke would be damned if the tent had not been made wholly of the flesh and bone of men. Here and there were swatches of stiff human hair.

"Oh, lovely," remarked Storan. "Studied protocol, this angel. Takes people and makes tents of them."

"Stop here."

"I'm going to say something, Captain, going to say it once, then speak no more. Turn away from this. In the name of the Goddess who watches over us and blesses our ways, turn from this. Let us walk back to the dory and return to the ship."

Darke never took Storan's counsel lightly. In times of battle, Storan might joke or swear through his own and others' fear of dying, but always his advice was well founded, and this time his voice was deep and certain. He was correct, and Darke knew it, but everything that was correct was not necessarily right.

"I cannot do that, Storan," Darke said. "Sorry, friend. And there is worse news yet. You are to wait here, outside of the tent, both of you."

Marsyas nodded.

"Frogs fuck my liver and worms suck dry my balls to withered stones before I wait outside, letting you go in there and face some bastard mistake of Elyon's creation. I have been your left hand since you were born wet and naked, and I will not let you go in there alone, Captain. Maybe he has us here to chat, this angel, or maybe he just needs another tent, and you are the right size for it. Whatever his plan, you have two choices: kill me where I stand or allow me and my grandpa's axe to go in there with you."

"The angel gave me explicit terms, Storan."

"I give a flying shit in a hard wind."

Darke sighed. He glanced at Marsyas.

Marsyas nodded. "Noise," Marsyas grumbled with his broken tongue, "any bad noise, I come as well; otherwise, I stand here as commanded."

"Why can you not be as agreeable as Marsyas?" Darke asked Storan.

Storan smiled. "I am agreeable. I am agreeing to go in there and give this sweet, cunning bastard a kiss on his pimpled ass. If that is not agreeable, my mother taught me ill all these years."

The tales had always fascinated Darke, but he had never seen one—an angel who had fallen from the sky. It was said they were members of the choirs of Elyon, the Most High, said that they sang the *Holy-Holy-Holy* that created the Earth. However, by word of Enoch, all of them now were damned, though Darke did not really countenance Enochians. Elyon's business, in his opinion, had nothing to do with charity or damnation. The Lord of Hosts killed good men and made the wicked rich. Darke had little use for Enochian priests and their promise of Elyon's grace in this world.

Darke lifted the still damp parchment of human skin that was the tent's doorway. He expected a giant, as were the sons of angels, as were the Etlantians, as were the few Nephilim he had seen and killed; but then he remembered how his grandmother had told it: "They begot the giants, Little One; they were never giants themselves. They, as we, are the image and expression of Elyon, the Most High, but they were never meant to have children, you see. They are immortal. They need no children to continue as men do, so when they cohabitated with women, their offspring were cursed, and the mark of the curse was that all were giants so no man would mistake them for a child of Elyon."

However, seeing the creature sitting on a bronze throne inside the tent, Darke would never have guessed him to have been a star that stepped from heaven. He looked not only mortal in size and bearing but also far from beautiful, as the ancient legends claimed angels to be. To see an angel was to see perfection, but this angel had apparently been scourged by age.

Satariel was hideous: his hair was a sullied white, his pallid skin harrowed by wrinkles, his robes unclean, his smell rancid. His eyes were grayish blurs difficult to look into because of the ring of blinding light at the edges, but Darke defied his own fears and looked dead into them for a moment, a challenge, but it stung. He was forced to look away and was left confused, disoriented. The angel chuckled, an aged, whispery sound.

"Try not to look directly into my eyes unless I tell you to do so, mortal," he said carefully, in the language of men, with no hint of an ancient accent, nor did he use words known before the Earth was made.

His hands, where they rested on the arms of his chair, were no more than knotted claws covered with the thinnest of leathered flesh. In fact, but for this loose, scabbed, craggy skin, he was skeletal.

Storan knew enough not to speak; he had faced enough horrors to know when merely to step back and wait. Expressionless, axe sheathed, he kept his eyes directly ahead and unfocused. His interest here was only in his captain.

"Captain Darke," the angel mused. He then motioned Storan. "Here you are, but I do not remember agreeing to a second."

In response, Darke motioned toward some batlike creature the size of a dog standing near the leg of the angel's throne. "Why not? It appears you have one," Darke answered calmly. When mentioned by Darke, the creature crept under the table with a shudder and wet itself.

The white eyes of the angel shifted to Storan as if inviting a response, but Storan did not flinch.

"Should you want me to piss my leggings," Storan replied without moving, "you will damned well have to do more than sit there looking ugly."

"Quiet, Storan," Darke commanded sharply.

Satariel chuckled. "One thing Elyon granted humans—a sense of mirth. Even in the darkest hours. How droll I find you all." With an intelligent sigh, the angel leaned forward, the glow in his eyes dimmed.

"You may now look at me," the angel commanded.

When he did, Darke could feel his mind being probed as though cold fingers were touching.

"Enough," Darke swore when the searching brought a sting of pain.

Satariel smiled and withdrew the probe. "Do you know who I am, corsair?"

"You are the killer of ships, the Etlantian bastard angel common legends name Satariel. More than that, I know not. I keep little stock of myth."

"Then we shall not bore each other with lineage. I shall tell you why I have sent for you, Shadow-Hawk. It is all quite simple: I can obtain something you want, and you can obtain something I want; we exchange the two, and all is well under heaven. We sail our different ways and never meet again."

"What could you have that I would possibly desire?"

"Oh, many, many things. Things once tasted you could never resist. You would beg, drool, crawl, give yourself up to even the lowest of sexual acts just for another sniff. But I have in mind something less compulsive. In fact, it is a human—one much like you, one dragged from the sea five years ago, nearly drowned, barely alive. Of course the slavers who took him had no idea who he was. He was simply taken in netting with his drowning crew after the hull of his fabulous warship had been sundered, rived like splitting a common crab."

Darke flinched.

"What? You thought your son had died nobly battling some Nephilim prince? No, no, quite the opposite. His ship was rammed from a fog bank by lowly slavers. They do have their modest talents—slavers. It was all a very dishonorable affair. Your son and his mighty Tarshian marines who had brought down seven Etlantian galleys at high sea and killed countless raiders did not so much as have time to draw their swords.

"They were all sold to Etlantians. Most are dead now, worked to their graves. Your son proved exceptionally resilient to death. I suppose you can take pride in that, but he is without hope. You see, he works the oraculum mines. He is lowered each day into a narrow cavern of earth where he hacks at black rock—mining the Etlantians' precious red metal. He is nearly blind, pity . . . those piercing blue eyes."

"Enough. Make your point."

"I am making my point. Are you not paying attention? Your son is dying. He is not well nourished—the Etlantians do not feed slaves well—no profit in it, too easy to get more. Your son's liver is riddled with disease and his kidneys are failing—all from malnutrition. I might give him a single count of the moon more, but perhaps that is being generous. Had these fools who captured him known this was Lothian, the Tarshian emerald prince and son of Darke, you would, of course, have been offered ransom long ago, but your son has not revealed his identity to his captors. Perhaps this is to his credit, that he works himself to a sure death rather than disappoint his father. Unfortunately, these particular slavers are not much interested in the finer aspects of their craft. So, to sum up, once the Etlantians have drained his strength until he is no longer of use to them, they will let the Failures have him. The Failures always complain there is little meat on these specimens, but then again, they can always suck the marrow from the bones . . . or make soup."

Darke tightened his jaw.

"No need to be angry with me, Tarshian."

"I thought you were at war with the Etlantians. Why would they give you my son?"

The angel chuckled lightly. "You would not understand, but that is actually a very ironic way of putting it—me at war with them. But then, it is true I kill Etlantians whenever I find them, ill bred, well bred, even breeders. I have yet to kill one of my own brothers, but they tend to make themselves difficult to find lately. They fear me, you see."

"Why should they? You look just shy of a corpse."

"Come now, let us not insult each other. Have I insulted you? Have I?"

Darke did not answer.

"Although I suppose you have a point." The angel lifted his arm and shook the loose baggage of skin that once was his bicep. He sighed. "Once my brothers saw that I had begun to age, they believed I had fallen to Enoch's curse—which I suppose I have, which is all the more irritating since I never believed in Enoch or his ascendance to an audience with heaven. Nevertheless, my brothers believe it is communicable. Fear makes fools even of angels."

"Enough chat, Satariel. Get to the point."

"Ah, the point. Do you know of the Daath, those who claim they are descendants of the guardian of the ancient East of the Land, the literal bloodline of the archangel known by common tongue as Uriel?"

"I have heard of them—no more. I would not know for certain if they even exist."

"Oh, they exist, and you are going to find them. Gather your maps and your talented pilots, and plot your course through dark water to the land called Dove Cara. It can be found along the eastern continent, south, not far from the tip of Etlantis's fabled Mount Ammon. It is said the Daath were once troops of Etlantis. For nine hundred years they have been killers of one sort or another, and now even Etlantians hate them. So they kill Etlantians—how droll. Once you have found the Dove Cara, you will discover that there is a city above it, the fine castled city of the Daath, with its spires that remind one of the seventh star—the mothering star of Dannu. The city is called Terith-Aire, which translates something like Sky Dwelling. It is in their city that you will find their pure-blooded king. You see, since they sailed for Earth from the seventh star, the Daath have by faith kept their line of kings as pure as a breed of fine hounds. The hound I am most interested in is the scion of Uriel. I want him brought to me in sackcloth."

"I have no enmity for the Daath."

"Which makes you a logical choice. If I approached, they might suspect malevolence of some sort."

"You are an angel. Surely you can take what you want."

"The scion is well protected."

"Are you admitting there is something about them you fear?"

"No, I am admitting there is something about them for which I have no patience. Now, you will bring this holy scion to an island of my specification—alive. Remember, Tarshian, as capable as you and your marine slayers are, the Daath are far deadlier than they appear. They may look human, but the blood of an archangel flows through their veins, which makes them sometimes particularly lethal, especially those who have trained in the arcane arts of the Shadow Walkers. Let us pray you do not meet one of them. Our association would end abruptly, as would the lives of you and your comrades. But then, Shadow Walkers or not, this is no mean task I put before you, corsair. The armies of the Daath number four legions. Still, keep in mind that you need concern yourself only with one. I am told you are an excellent thief. It is why I summoned you."

"How will I know this scion?"

"You will know him because he will carry the mark of the father."

"And what mark is that?"

"You will know it when you see it. The sword never leaves his side; it is unmistakable. They say that once Uriel himself used it to guard Elyon's paradise at its eastern edge—the flaming sword that turned at once in all directions. I think it is all nonsense, personally."

"And what guarantee do I have that you will bring my son?"

"I do not proffer guarantees. I am no merchant, corsair." Satariel extended a parchment and what looked like a large, dirty rag. "The scroll—human parchment, my preference as you may have guessed—lists the island where the Daathan prince is to be delivered. And this is the sackcloth I want him wrapped in."

Darke stepped forward to take the scroll and cloth, but the bony hand of Satariel seized his wrist with the cold clammy touch of the dead, a solid, painful grip. The long, untrimmed nails bit into Darke's skin, spilling blood.

"You should take the time to learn whom you address," the angel whispered, close now, so close Darke had to look purposely away from the eyes, for they had suddenly brightened. "I am Satariel, prince of Orphanim, of the third emanation of Elyon's realm, Shabbathai, whose planet is Saturn. I was the bearer of the bull's head in the hour of Trisagion, the great *Holy-Holy-Holy*, which formed the Earth in its hour from the word of the Elohim. When next you come before me, you will kneel, and should you again have such insolence as to look into my eyes, I assure you that you will be blinded for life!"

He then released his grip, the nails leaving pricks of blood on Darke's wrist.

Darke stepped back. Angry, Storan shifted, hand on his axe.

"Do not even think it, Storan!" Darke snapped, without turning.

The angel chuckled. "Blood of mortals, Elyon's most curious craft. We have made covenant, Shadow Hawk—blood covenant." To emphasize this he licked Darke's blood off his long, curled nail.

"Now go," the angel said—a command, the voice no longer whispery. "Get out of my sight, mortal. And thank your pitiful Elyon and weak mothering star that I do not slay your second like a fat cow."

Storan snarled, but Darke grabbed his arm and dragged him from the tent.

"Let me go back in there, Captain!"

"The only thing you are doing is getting off this beach before he changes his mind," Darke commanded as he passed Marsyas, who fell in at his right flank.

Darke did not show it; his voice did not betray it, but he had been shaken far more than ever he had been in a lifetime of battles.

Chapter Two
The Disciple of Ishtar

The hidden island of Ophur in the Western Sea
The last city of the Tarshians

Whenever Darke and the others were gone this long and this far out to sea, a heavy, ever-deepening despair fell over Hyacinth with a weight that sometimes became unbearable. Of course, she was not alone. The island of Ophur, a volcanic cove of black sand where the last temples and buildings of the once mighty Tarshian kings still stood, was filled with women yearning for their men.

From a hillside, Hyacinth would watch them, what she called the widow women, because they feared the sea would take their beloved. Those left behind on the island had built tall wooden towers along the mountain's ridge where they could pace the walkways, their eyes always to the east, hoping to spot the approach of the ashen sail of Darke's warship, the last of what had once been a magnificent fleet.

On this voyage the women had waited and watched in vain, day after day, for what had become a full five count of moons—a long journey. Hyacinth wondered, watching them, what would happen if their men did not return. There were no other blackships of the Tarshians—only Darke's; there would be no warnings, no words, just empty sea, day after day. Their hearts would never learn the fate of their men.

Hyacinth gave her heart to no man. In a place unspoken inside her, she might always love Darke, but even then, her heart she kept her own. If by the cruel sun, Darke was never to return, Hyacinth would not mourn, she would simply move on, for that is what her love would have done—merely crossed over.

Hyacinth was not a Tarshian. She did not look like their women, most of whom were tall, with red hair and fair skin—starkly beautiful. It was said they were a race of kings and their queens whose bloodline had always been pure from the days of Adam and Yered. Hyacinth, however, was small and dark. Her hair was almost black, and tight curls often fell over her wide, rich brown eyes. Long ago, the captain had found her amid the ruins of a temple, unconscious, but still alive. She sometimes wondered, especially on days like this, when the men had been at sea for so long with no word, if perhaps it would have been better had the captain left her among the ruins of her people.

But with Darke she had developed keen and sharpened skills as a raider and a pirate. She had become deadly with her poisons, knives, and light crossbow. And Hyacinth was an enchantress, which made her invaluable. Her talents as a spell binder, though perhaps not unmatched, were certainly formidable. In battle she was as valued as the most hardened Tarshian marine, and she would give her life without question for her captain. On voyages, Hyacinth was rarely left behind, but this time Darke had done so without any explanation. It left her angry, but what could she do? He was at sea and she could only watch from the cliffs near the villa Taran had built her.

She had been raised in the village of Aravon, a coven of skilled sorcerers, future seers, and warlocks. But more than all spell binders, Aravon was an island of unmatched and unrivaled enchantresses—the most skilled and deft of any on earth. Hyacinth had just been growing into her talents when on a clear, shining day, they came—Etlantian raiders. They came swiftly, without warning: mighty warships, their sails embossed with the image of the bull. They descended like birds of prey; their prows hit the beachhead in a spray of sand; their gangplanks dropped, and horsemen swarmed the village. Despite the powers of the enchanters, these were firstborn Etlantian slayers and it was over quickly.

The Etlantian raiders hunted all humans, but more than any others, they searched out the covens of spell binders, especially the covens of Ishtar, the enchantresses.

Hyacinth had witnessed the death of all she had known and loved, and she had learned something that day. She had learned that there was no bottom to the depth of sadness Elyon granted His children; such sadness was as endless as the stars.

By the time Darke's blackship had found them, the village was only ash, embers, and death. It had been a fierce battle; many Etlantians had fallen, but of the magick casters, Darke found only one left alive, a small, dark-haired enchantress buried beneath cindered beams.

So it was that a child of Ishtar's horned moon came to dwell in Ophur, the last hidden outpost of the Tarshians.

When sailing with Darke, she was most alive, but those few times she was left behind were unbearable and she hated nothing more. Mysteriously, on this last voyage, Darke had not even consulted her. He had left in the night, under cover of darkness. As his absence stretched over five counts of the moon, her despair had become nearly intolerable. And worse, there was an unexplained dread that had taken hold of her. It was a fear she could not name, and it whispered an unspoken promise. Something was hunting them, Darke and the Tarshians. She felt it crawl over the winds and sky, but she could do nothing. It was deceptive, cunning, and more deadly than anything they had faced before. Why he had left her behind she could not fathom. If ever he had needed her, he needed her now.

Finally, she decided to take her fears—the dread of the hunter and the overpowering fear for her captain—and deceive them with a child's game. It may have seemed simple, but it would at least keep her from going mad.

So she turned to simple magick—children's magick. When she was a small girl, little Hyacinth had always had trouble sleeping indoors, especially in the stocky wooden huts of the magi who, despite their talents in spell binding, built plain and sometimes ominous huts of unfinished wood and great, ugly halls that looked like shadow castles. So, to help her, Hyacinth's mentor had taught her to capture the stars, how to bring them into her sleeping chambers. To Hyacinth, there was no greater comfort than the glittering wonder of the mothering sky.

They first melted sugar into thick, liquid goo, then, using tiny glass blowers, they formed hollow sugar globes, crystals so delicate they would often shatter at the slightest jar. What was amazing about the trick, something little Hyacinth could only watch before years of practice, was the way her mentor skillfully used a silver stylus to etch the single word of binding on the surface of each globe that would then become the crystal's incantation. Once finished, the orbs could be left in an open field overnight, and each time they would capture the sky and all its wonders whenever the Pleiades reached zenith.

Inside the crude hut where she slept at night, Hyacinth would break open a globe. The ceiling and walls would melt away, and a comforting blanket of stars would fold over them. She would study the sky until sleep overtook her. She learned all the named stars, all the patterns and formed creatures that danced across the night. Adding to the enchantment, like a voyager, she could sail among them, witnessing sights few even knew existed: spectacular variable stars laced with lightning that flashed a blinding blue-white; great, swollen red giants like rubies glittered; spinning stars left streamers of all colors as they swirled, even the darker ones, the stars that hid.

After Darke had been gone four counts of the moon, Hyacinth began to craft sugar globe after sugar globe. Each had to be flawless; each took hours to perfect, but time did not matter, time was on her side, as was patience. She was older now, and though forming sugar globes required little skill, the inscribing of the binding word that would transform the sugar crystal from candy to magick took deft and proficient concentration. Hyacinth was now able to work the stylus quickly, never once shattering the delicate crystal.

She worked deep in a mountain chamber carved long ago into the black rock of Ophur's dead volcano. She had no idea who had carved it, but it had become her hidden place, where no one would find her or interrupt her. Here she had collected all her treasures: manuscripts of rolled parchment, books with ancient bindings, jars and boxes of herbs, powders, and poisons. Also kept here were the many gifts Taran, Darke's younger brother, brought her from the sea. He knew she craved artifacts and pieces of delicate art, and he also knew that most of all she craved the books and scrolls of the ancient temples. She had so many now that she imagined her library might be unmatched, even among the temples of the followers of Enoch.

Once she had crafted the twelve orbs, she took them, one at a time, each dusk to the edge of the southern cliff that overlooked the deep blue of the Western Sea. Here, there was clear, uninterrupted sky. Eventually, each orb had captured a separate flawless image of the night sky.

In her cave, Hyacinth gathered the crystal globes with their captured skies, and whenever her angst became too much for her, she would star voyage. She would set a globe before her and break it open. The ceiling and walls, even the floor, spilled over, turning to a clear, unblemished sky of brilliant stars. Except for the silence, the lack of any animal sounds or sea or wind, she might have been sitting on that ridge, though her books, jars, and potions surrounded her, a few of them hovering midair beyond the cliff's edge.

And then she traveled. She would move through wondrous clouds that held endless color and sometimes travel vast expanses of darkness looking for anything at all that might be hidden there. It surprised her how much of the sky was empty when from Earth it seemed swarming with stars. She also found dark clouds of matter that seemed to have no purpose. They simply swirled, slowly, alive yet seemingly dead for they had no light. Hours Hyacinth would spend voyaging, her mind lost in the wonders she beheld and the misery of the long count of moons since she had seen the blackship of Darke, at least for a time, forgotten.

Chapter Three
The Book of Angels

Where are your walls?" a voice said, suddenly interrupting Hyacinth's concentration. She turned, excited, for it was not just any voice; it was Darke. He alone knew the path to her cave. He glanced down, calmly noticing that only stars and sky were bearing him up.

Hyacinth leapt to her feet and bounded into his arms, wrapping her legs about his waist.

Darke held her tightly. He wanted to kiss her, to squeeze her, but for all the years she had been with him, he had kept his feelings for her hidden.

"Captain," she whispered in his ear, "oh, Captain, how I have missed you!"

"As well, Little Flower."

He finally set her down, then searched the strange room hovering amid the stars. "What is all this?"

"You have been gone so long. I get lonely. The stars give me comfort."

Hyacinth knelt to crush her last orb. They were left in the pitch-dark of the cavern a moment, but with a wave of her hand the braziers and torches came alive. She lifted a shard from one of the broken orbs; it looked like tinted glass.

"Candy," she said, taking a bite. "Quite good. Like some?"

"Another time, perhaps."

"I will bag these, and you can pass them out to the children, but make no mention they are from the *witch*."

"That is not how they think of you, Hyacinth."

She didn't respond. She simply gathered the candy shards into a thin leather bag, stood, and tossed it, roughly, at the captain's face. He barely caught it and stared back, surprised.

Hyacinth's eyes flashed, suddenly angry.

"What?" he asked.

"Why did you leave me here without even telling me?" she shouted. "Why?"

"I could not have taken you, Hyacinth. There was no certainty I would return myself."

"So you believe I am better off left on this godless island with mourning widow women forever pacing their tower walkways? What kind of fate is that?"

"It was simply too dangerous, Hyacinth."

"I care of danger? You think I care? If ever you should die, Captain, it is my choice to die at your side! Do you understand?" She stepped closer, her brows narrowed fiercely. "Do you?" When he failed to respond, she roughly shoved him back with both palms. "What was there to be gained leaving me on this godless, stinking sulfur island?"

"Sometimes you have to trust me, Hyacinth."

"You ever do that to me again, and I swear . . . I will cause you true pain."

"I believe that."

"So why have you come to me? You left me behind for five counts of the moon; you could not care for me." She paced, waiting for a response her heart could accept, avoiding the captain's eyes. "I thought you did not like my cave."

He reached into his leather tunic and withdrew a folded parchment, its edges stained red. Hyacinth could tell that the blood was not merely for effect; the stain was a signet, and she could smell the blood—unordinary blood. Her heart leapt.

"This is an angel's epistle! You have made contact with one of the old ones!"

"*Old* is a good word for him."

"May I open it?"

"It is why I hiked up here to give it to you."

She quickly unfolded the parchment. "Human skin," she commented.

"He seems to have a penchant for that."

She studied it, fascinated. "A map. I sense a name. It is not printed, but it floats above the etchings like a scent. This is the blood of the angel Satariel." Her big, brown eyes suddenly flicked up. "And you have seen him—face to face!"

"You are quick, Little Flower."

She studied it further. "He has etched this in his own blood, which means he somehow took yours in exchange when he gave it to you. Am I mistaken?"

Darke displayed the punctures left by the angel's daggered nails.

"Captain! This is more than a map; it is a covenant sealed in blood! Not only that, but you are mortal. What could he possibly want so badly that he would enter into a blood covenant with a human?"

"I was hoping you could help me with that."

"Captain, do you even realize what you have done? He has bound you. A creature like Satariel does not make deals with mortals. He is malevolent; he has no good purpose in his heart, and his soul is hollow. When he is finished with you, he will destroy you, pure and simple. How many times must I tell you to take me with you?"

"Hyacinth, I know little of these so-called fallen angels, but I do know they despise the disciples of Ishtar, especially enchanters. If he had sensed a child of the horned moon among my crew, he might well have decided there should be one less spell binder in this world, regardless of the consequence."

"I could have hidden from him, veiled myself."

"I was not willing to take that chance. Now, will you calm down enough to answer a few questions?"

"What do you want to know? How he is going to boil you, or how he will slowly peel away your skin? How he is going to sever each limb before he lets you die a miserable death?"

"I had other questions in mind, actually. What do you know of a people called the Daath?"

"Why mention them?"

"Because he did."

"I know of them, but they are not people."

"What do you mean?"

"According to the Followers, the seers of Enoch who keep the scriptures of lineages, the Daath are not the blood of men. They are descended of an archangel, Uriel, and a goddess—the mirrored image of the mothering star of Dannu.

She is one star, a single being, but as with all of us, she bears a shadow, like the face from a mirror. The shadow of Dannu is called the Daath. She is cruel. She would birth slayers."

"All this according to the teaching of the Followers of Enoch?"

"This according to scripture and the Followers of Enoch are the only ones left who keep any scriptures alive. But I suspect the angels know all legends, all scripture. The angel Satariel would know their linage as clearly as any priest. Some call them star voyagers because it is believed they voyaged from the seventh star to Earth in the days of Yered. Others call them killer angels, because they are so deadly. Simply put, they are slayers. It is said they strike from nowhere without sound or warning. What does this angel want of them?"

"He did not say."

She glanced up, studying Darke slyly. "Tell me what this angel looked like. They are said to be ever young, ever beautiful. Did he shine with the light of stars? Was he perfect?" She did not wait for an answer. "No, he was hideous, was he not? This one has begun to age, and if my guess is true, his body was no more than a corpse, the only light left him the rings about the edges of his eyes."

"How could you guess that?"

"Because he has summoned a mortal to do his bidding. He is afraid, and the reason he is afraid is that he has begun to turn. He has lost the light; he has become one of the fallen."

"I do not understand."

"We need the book; it will clarify these things."

"What book?"

"The Book of the Seer. I will read from it. It speaks of the turning."

She walked to a far corner of her cave where she worked a spellbound lock, then slid back a panel. Inside was a small chamber lined in wolf fur, and resting on it, holding a faint reddish glow from its oraculum binding, was a book Darke recognized well. Two years ago he had sailed near an island whose inhabitants had recently been slaughtered by Etlantian raiders. It contained a temple, and the spires left intact marked it as a temple of the Followers of Enoch. This had been an island of priests, and the Etlantians hunted the priests of Enoch with a vengeance equal to that which they held for enchantresses of Ishtar. Darke and his crew went ashore to search for survivors—there were none. But Taran spotted the temple, and he knew what it might contain in its lower chambers—treasures Hyacinth would cherish. He always brought her gifts, gold, ancient artifacts, emeralds, diamonds, but nothing pleased her more than scrolls and books of knowledge. Before Darke could restrain him, Taran plunged into the still smoldering embers of the temple.

Danwyar had stepped to Darke's side, curious. "Why does he risk a burning temple? It could be a death trap down there."

"It is for Hyacinth. He is hoping for scrolls—the writings of Enoch. I think he believes one day he will discover a gift so enticing it will turn her heart."

"Perhaps you should explain to your young brother that the priestess has no heart to be turned."

"Oh, she has a heart; she just keeps it to herself."

They had waited anxiously and finally Taran emerged, singed in places, smoke still streaming from his hair and tunic, but tucked against his chest was what would become Hyacinth's greatest treasure. It was said there were only four in the entire world. Covered in Etlantian oraculum, sealed on all sides with spellbound locks, it was nothing less than the Book of Angels, often called the Book of Enoch, for it was written by the fabled seer's own hand.

When they had returned to Ophur, instead of kisses and attention, Hyacinth had hugged Taran, showered him with brief words of affection, and then disappeared for weeks into her hidden lair. Taran's heart was once again broken, but Darke knew it would heal by the time he spotted another treasure on another voyage. His devotion to her was hopeless.

Darke watched Hyacinth retrieve the sacred book from its enclave and sit down beside him. She carefully laid the tome on her lap. "Kneel beside me, Captain. Your answers are here—in the words of Enoch."

He did so. The book's outer covering was an unblemished sheath of the purest oraculum. Even more mystifying, there appeared no way to open it—no latches, no locks, no panels. It was perfectly smooth on all sides.

"Could you hand me that orange bottle over your shoulder," asked Hyacinth, "the one with the sparkling crystals?"

Darke searched and gave it to her.

"The Book of Angels can only be opened and read under the pure light of the full moon. Of course, we lack a moon, but we can summon what is just as effective—salamanders."

She poured the powder into her palm, then blew it outward and spoke words of binding in her sacred language. Though Darke never understood her incantations, he liked hearing them. She always spoke them as a kind of song or poem. The orange dust swirled to coalesce into three salamanders, floating midair. Their skin was wet, a silvery sheen. The salamanders' eyes were riveted on Hyacinth, waiting for her command.

"Give me moonlight, silver ones, and I shall reward you with cinnamon."

They seemed to have no problem with the offer and scampered up the walls onto the ceiling directly above. There they coiled tightly until they became an image of the moon. Their slivery skins then began to shimmer and soon the chamber was bathed in what seemed perfect moonlight. With a wave of her hand Hyacinth dimmed the braziers and torches.

Darke watched as her fingers worked locks now visible in a faint blue, much like soft flame.

She laid the book open. The pages were of gold, thin as foil. They looked fragile, yet were unblemished. The moonlight cast of the salamanders left letterings of soft flame on the smooth pages. Darke could not make out any of it.

"Do not bother trying," Hyacinth said, guessing his attempt. "The words were inscribed using the pure light of the mothering star—undecipherable without the stones."

"What stones?"

"I will show you." She turned to the back plate, where she slid open a panel. In a thin hollow lined with velvet rested two stones, one a dark-set ruby, the other a lighter shade of blue sapphire.

"Seer stones," she said.

"How do you work them?"

"They are worn."

She lifted them carefully. They had holders on the sides that unfolded, and she was able to slip them over her temples and curl the pliable metal about her ears. There was a crossbar that balanced on her nose. She looked up to

Darke, her big brown eyes now magnified in ruby and blue. He had to smile. She smiled back, then turned to the book. She expertly leafed through several of the golden foil pages.

"Only the stones make the letters plain. Each page holds three layers: the first deals with things of ordinary speaking—the Assiahian World; the second deals with principals and powers of the Earth—the Atziluthic World; and the last lies beneath and can be discerned only by seers and prophets. It is called the Braiatic World. I will read for you from the first layer, which contains the histories. When I am finished perhaps you will understand why you have been such an idiot to have sealed a deadly covenant with this fallen angel and why you should never, *ever* leave me behind again." She paused at a certain page, running a painted nail over the lettering. "I already know you have no faith in these words, Captain, so I challenge you simply to open your mind. The words of heaven, when spoken correctly, leave a tingle that runs down the back, a testament of their truth. These are the words of a seer, a man once lifted up to heaven, a man who has spoken with Elyon—the Light of Severity—He who cannot be named."

"Then why is He named? You called Him Elyon."

"Elyon is not a name; it simply means God."

"Then why not simply say God?"

"Simple people, the unlearned, do." She took a breath and began to read. "'These are the words of Enoch the son of Yered, the seventh of the first; named of the angels the Scribe; whose words will stand as testament of Aeon's End before the coming of the age of men.'"

She turned through more pages, gently but deftly. She had probably studied every letter and word of this book many times over. "I will read only what is useful, but some names must be spoken in their proper order or the words will be offended."

"A word can be offended?"

"They will fade until I will no longer be able to decipher them." She paused. "I will start here, at the point where the first angel stepped from heaven: 'And in the days of Yered there fell a single star from the sky and all the hosts of heaven wept.'"

Her finger paused on the word, and she stared at it, affected. "They called him the Beautiful One," she said, her voice a bit saddened. "He shined so brightly that he was known as the Light Bearer. He was one of the firstborn sons of Elyon, and he was the beloved of all. That he stepped from heaven to save Earth was the most noble of acts, a sacrifice. He risked everything for the sake of his father's children, that none would be lost, that not a single soul would fail to return to their father. His fall left a brilliant, fiery streak across the sky so magnificent that many called him the Son of the Morning. Some say that he rules still, there in Etlantis, the city he created, but that he dwells now in secret places. Many believe he is a savior—our savior. What do you think, Captain? Does it spark belief in you?"

"It seems to me a savior would be out hunting raiders instead of hiding among the Etlantians."

She turned more pages, her fingers skillfully skimming the words. "Here it speaks of the others who stepped from heaven to join the Light Bearer: 'Three was the number of their lords, and seven were their prefects, and two hundred was the number of the Watchers of heaven who joined them, and they were the Auphanim, the wheels, for they held the spheres of the firmament of the fixed stars.'"

She paused to use both hands to steady the stones from where they had begun to slip off her nose. "You cannot do it, Captain," she said, taking him off guard.

"Do what?"

"That which you are thinking."

"And what am I thinking?"

"That you can trick him—find a way to kill the angel Satariel."

"Why should I want to kill him? He has yet to cross me."

"It is useless to attempt to fool me, Captain. I know what you are planning. Just understand something: they cannot be killed. He would destroy you with but a word uttered. He is a living creature of the Elohim. As clever as you are, as quick as you are, he will slay you without a second's thought."

"Is he mentioned in there?"

"Yes, but I must speak the names of others before his."

"Hyacinth, I have been at sea for nearly half a year; I have no time to read through all the damned divine orders of whirling creatures."

"Patience, Captain. I will be brief." She took a breath and read on. "'This is the name of the second to step from the sky, the first to follow the Light Bearer: Azazel, the lord of the holy choir of the Auphanim. Once upon the Earth, Azazel looked about and saw the Earth was covered with humans. It was overrun with them, for in those days humans did not die. Thus, by his word, he named the years of men one hundred and twenty, after which they would become dust of the Earth from whence they came. Because of this, men would thenceforth live on only through women and the bearing of children. Therefore, men named him Ahriman, the Angel of Death.

"'He then taught men the making of swords and shields and all manner of weapons. He taught the crafting of tombs, crypts, and sepulchers, as well as the embalming of flesh, the draining of blood.'"

"So he named death, then provided the tools for tidying up."

"You jest, Captain. Have I not asked for reverence?"

"Sorry—just slipped out."

"It is good it is not Azazel you intend to challenge. He is the cruelest of all angels. No aging would you have found in him, no weakness, and neither would he have summoned a simple mortal to do his bidding."

"So in a way you are admitting Satariel—who summoned a *simple* mortal, me, to do his bidding—does have a weakness."

"You cannot kill him, Captain. He may be aged, he may be cursed of Enoch, but make no mistake: he is powerful beyond your dreams."

"Keep reading, Little Flower."

"'The third and final high lord to follow was named Arakiel, Earth of God. It was he who taught women the painting of their faces and the fashioning of bracelets and rings and all manner of adornment.'"

She paused, glancing at him with her own painted eyes, touching a finger to her cheek, bracelets rattling.

"You may continue, Hyacinth."

She sighed and turned back to the book. "'Because of the teaching of Arakiel, fornication multiplied in the land'—though Ophur, apparently, was spared of all fornication and even of kisses or any manner of affection."

"Hyacinth, I have a wife."

"I know, and she is tall and starkly beautiful and will always own your heart."

"Taran begs for your favor, Hyacinth. He adores you more than the sun."

"And I adore him, but my heart is already given."

He suspected her meaning, but said nothing that might encourage her.

She turned back to the pages. "'And those are the three who made covenant upon the mountain—the Light Bearer, their king; Azazel, their prince; and Arakiel, the singer. Thereafter, they called that mountain Ammon, which means "Oath of Binding."'"

"Ammon, the mountain of Etlantis?"

"The same."

"Why should these three need a covenant?"

"To hide themselves."

"From what?"

"Elyon. They were pure, spiritually pure. They were members of the choirs of the Seraphim; they sang in the great Trisagion—the Word that brought the world into being. More than this, they did not need women, for they were ever immortal. It was only from lust that they sealed the pact upon Mount Ammon, a pact to cohabitate with the daughters of men. Though they were angels of the Most High, they fell due to lust for trinkets and painted eyes."

"So, as with everything else, it all comes down to women."

"But think, Captain, is it not, in a certain sense, romantic? The angels looked upon the daughters of men and found them so beautiful that they laid down all they were, their honor, their glory, even their light, for that single taste."

"Romantic? Try idiotic. All they possessed—the power to create worlds—and they risked it all just to take a woman."

"Exactly as it reads: 'Thus the angels looked down upon the daughters of men and said to each other, "Let us choose, each to our own," and they lay with them. They then brought forth the firstborn, those born of Lillith and Astarte and Libet and many other daughters of men who then became Star Walker Queens, terrible to behold, for not only did they bear in their wombs the seed of angels, but also they were taught the secrets of creation—that their words, once uttered, were sealed in heaven; that their breath made real things spoken.

"'But their offspring, even many of their firstborn, were called Nephilim, for they were born giants, and Elyon caused this that they would never be mistaken for the children of men. In those days, many of the Nephilim were filled with the light of their fathers and ruled as men of renown.

"'But their seed was cursed and each generation became more corrupt than the last. Thus, the firstborn—the Nephilim—gave birth to the Emmin, the terrors, for they were cruel and had no compassion in their souls. With each generation the light of the angels continually dimmed until it was lost utterly.'" She lifted the seeing stones to rub her temples.

"Are they heavy?" asked Darke.

"Yes. We now live among the seventh generation of the angels. Those who believed Enoch, the Followers, claim the Emmin will be the last because they cannot reproduce. They are known as the Failures, for some are born without heads, some without arms, some without legs, some with but a single eye, some with too many eyes, like spiders, but all bearing the mark of shame, all grotesque."

She paused, remembering. "I saw one once—a Failure. It was no more than a face that crawled over the ground like a huge crab using its loose skin to pull itself along, groping with its mouth for food, its eyes wide and searching. The sorcerers of my village tried to kill it, but seeing them it swiftly moved into the trees, and for nights and nights we heard screams of animals being eaten."

She set the stones back in place and turned through several more pages. "The names of the lords I have now spoken. The rest I need not name, but the next who fell were those called prefects. Their number was seven. They were lesser beings, but nonetheless they were filled with the holy light of heaven and the knowledge of stars. We need reference only the one that interests you: 'Here names the seventh of the prefects, Satariel, he who bore the bull's head before Elyon, a high lord and singer of the choir of Melachim. He taught mankind the giving of signs and secret combinations, becoming the father of all sorcerers and fire speakers.'" She paused, looking up. "I remember something . . . from my early teachings."

"Which is?"

"He was known by the sorcerers of our village; some even admired him. As well, Satariel often traded slaves with the Pelegasians, who at times came to our village. We did not desire slaves, but their ships were often the only way to obtain supplies. The Pelegasians had a special name for this angel, as did our sorcerers: they called him Balberith."

Suddenly, she shivered as if a wind had struck. He saw her skin pale, saw her touch a hand to her chest and gasp.

"Hyacinth?"

"He heard me, Captain. He just heard me speak that name."

"How?"

"From wherever he is, he somehow pierced my heart to remind me, to let me know he is no fool." She looked up to Darke, her eyes clearly frightened. "Could you . . . could you hold me?"

He did, kneeling beside her, pulling her close, feeling helpless at her sudden fear.

"Is he listening still?" Darke asked.

"No, he cares little of us; he just wanted to put fear into me, and he did. Oh, Captain, you cannot go against him. He mocks us; he toys with us."

"Let him. I have not lived to be the last king of the Tarshians without reason. He may be an angel, but he knows little of my ways, and by threatening you, it is clear he knows me even less."

She rested her head against his shoulder a moment. "The fear he pierced through me was a promise, Captain, the whispered promise of an angel."

"And what did it say?"

"He is going to kill me. He just showed me my own death."

Darke sharply took her at arms' length. "Listen to me: I will not let that happen. I do not care his lineage or his list of names and titles, whether he is a lord or a prefect. Everything dies, even an angel, and we will find the way. The key must be this Daath he spoke of. Satariel wants him badly. Would any clue to why be hidden in this book?"

"Perhaps." She steadied herself and started turning through pages once more. "I do not fear death, Captain. It is the way he sent his probe. He poisoned it with fear; he weakened me. I am stronger than this. Do not believe I can be shaken so easily."

"I know you, Hyacinth; I have seen you in battle. I have no doubt of your courage."

Still, her hands trembled as she searched the pages, and he caught a tear fall over her cheek, one she ignored and one he pretended not to notice. It tore at his heart, and his anger flared. Time would come, this creature's powers aside, and in the Endgame, Darke would bring this bastard down.

"Here, these pages," she pointed. "Now I remember why the angels grew so angry and why they began to lose the light and become the fallen. When they realized their offspring would fail, that instead of ruling the Earth, their children would amount to nothing, they sent for the one human they trusted. He was Enoch. They knew him to be the seventh of the first, which means he was the seventh born of Adam, the first man. The angels trusted him; they called him the Scribe and believed him to be righteous. So they asked him to plead their cause before Elyon. And he did. It was the archangel Uriel who lifted Enoch through the many fiery pillars that support the heavens. Enoch beheld many wonders, but most glorious of all," she paused, "he looked upon the face of Elyon. I will read: 'And Elyon spoke, saying "Why have you come before me, Enoch?" And Enoch then pleaded the cause of the angels, that they were now repentant. He told Elyon they had stepped down from heaven only to help mankind, and Enoch pleaded that they and their children be spared His wrath.'"

"And Elyon's answer?"

"It was Azazel who met Enoch when he returned to the Earth. The Angel of Death asked what Elyon had said, and Enoch delivered Elyon's words: 'You are angels, sons of the Most High, and yet it is a man you send before me to speak in your stead? You have become fallen, and from this time forth, you will be cut off from the light of heaven. Yea, though once you walked as sons of gods, Bene ba Elohim, you shall die as men shall die, and your souls shall be imprisoned. You shall dwell in the deserts of Dua'el and in other desolate places where you shall be bound by the same fiery pillars that separate the depths of the Earth.

"'As for your offspring, even your firstborn, all will perish when the Earth passes through the abyss of Ain to be cleansed of your abominations. And until then, henceforth from this moment, no longer will they find nourishment in the fruits of the Earth, no longer shall the waters and sweet streams satiate their thirst: they shall be forced to drink the blood of men to give them life, to eat the flesh of men to give them strength.'"

"Sounds more as if Elyon's curse was against men," Darke cut in. "This is when it started, is it not—the raids, the wars? This is when the warships of Etlantis began to strip whole coastlines of villages, leaving only bones and ash, slaying even women, even children. And this is Elyon's curse against angels?"

"Yes. It is known as the curse of Enoch."

"Call me simple, but is it not men who fell, men who were burnt and tortured, drained of their blood? Is it not men who suffer this curse?"

"It is the angels' curse because, unlike the animals they had trapped or the water of streams from which they had drunk, men fight back. When they are threatened, men become slayers. And it was men such as you, Captain, the lionhearted, such as the Tarshians, who were among the first to strike back, to sink the warships of the Etlantians, and even to kill their princes."

"Yet far more innocents fell, whole villages of women and children! How can this be ordained of Elyon?"

"The souls of men return to heaven. The souls of the giants have no home; they are not of heaven, but are bound to Earth, and so they are doomed to become wanderers. They are left to scourge the Earth and are called the Uttuku. They will plague mankind until the final coming of the Son of Women in the Aeon of judgment, a time far from our own."

"So as well as sending the Etlantians against us, Elyon offers evil spirits as a bonus to drive sane men mad and tempt thieves and murderers. What a kind and loving God, Hyacinth. No wonder I take no comfort of priests."

"If we are not tested, Captain, how shall we ever grow?"

"Grow? I have watched my own brothers die in my arms! I have watched the cities of the Tarshians burn one by one until I am the last of my kind, and you tell me it is all for the sake of Elyon's pride?"

"Do not ever speak so against Him, Captain, I beg you."

"Believe what you will, Hyacinth. Myself, I shall not be found praying for light of a God who leaves His own children to suffer such horrors. Is there anything else? Anything worse this book has to offer? Or can it get any worse?"

"One more passage, the last riddle of your puzzle."

"Tell me, and then I must go walk the shores, calm my blood."

She nodded and turned through pages. Darke could no longer kneel beside her. He stood and began to pace, his hand on the hilt of his sword.

"Here," she said, "this is the last part you should know. 'And the Earth itself became so heavy with the bloodshed of the giants that she cried out to heaven, to the mothering stars and to the light of Elyon, and the Earth wept for the carnage and death that weighted upon her soul. Finally Elyon turned His face and He sent forth the Arsayalalyur to be His wrath, to answer the blood of the innocent.'"

"And where is this Arsayalalyur? When does he show his face? Once the last of us have perished?"

"The Arsayalalyur was sent long ago. Time in heaven is not as it is on Earth. Elyon sent the Arsayalalyur back into the days of Yered, when the Oath of Binding was uttered by the lords of the Watchers on Mount Ammon."

"Then this savior has been here all along?"

"Elyon's works are a mystery to men, but all He does is for us to return our souls to the light. Wait, I remember something, from my teachings. I remember something of the Arsayalalyur! Why did it not come to me sooner?"

"What?"

"The Arsayalalyur is known as the mark of the father, and the father is Uriel. It has been so long since I studied those words, forgive I did not remember sooner, but that it is, Captain—that is the key!"

"Explain."

"It is a sword. The Arsayalalyur is the sword of Uriel. In our words, made plain, it would be called the Angelslayer."

Darke paused. "You referred to it as the mark of the father?"

"Yes, and the father is Uriel—the archangel. And his children are the voyagers, the ones you mentioned first, sent in the day of Yered. Uriel's children are the Daath!"

"He spoke of that—the angel. He spoke of the mark of the father . . ."

"The one who carries the mark of the father is the Daathan king, for the sword of Uriel can never leave his side."

"Then you are telling me these Daath carry the one weapon that might make a difference, and yet they watch from the spires of their city as the children of men are slaughtered? And this is Elyon's wrath!"

"Captain, I beg you—"

"Enough of this book. I know all I need to know."

She reverently, rather sadly, closed the book. Darke turned, furious, but at the cavern's exit, he paused.

"Wait . . . have you any magick that could show me this supposed savior, this mighty Daathan king?"

"Yes . . . I may be able to do that."

She searched quickly through jars and potions until she found an enormous glass bulb, almost too big for her to lift. She set it in the floor, then lifted the top of the glass and laid it aside. The room filled with the stink of heavy musk. It was so strong it made Hyacinth sneeze.

"Forgive the smell," she said. "This is very old. It is called a flounder mushroom. See the way it grows on its side, as if it were hiding on the seafloor?"

"What good is it?"

"It is rare. I do not know how Taran managed to find it, but he explained he admired the round glass it grew in. Come. You will need to be close; the image will likely be tiny."

He walked over and knelt beside her.

"I sense you are angry with me, Captain."

"Not with you, Little Flower, never with you."

"Do not be angry with Elyon. We cannot hope to understand His ways, but—"

"No more talk of Elyon! Now what does this damned mushroom do?"

She lifted a flint and struck it with a quick flick of her wrist. The mushroom ignited instantly, a thick, greenish smoke billowing upward. The fungus quickly withered to black ash. She blew away the smoke and uttered quick words of binding over the ash. At first nothing happened.

Darke stared, impatient. "A burnt mushroom—that is the king?"

Hyacinth sighed. "Show us the scion of the Daath," she commanded. The ash instantly blossomed into a tiny vision of the tops of trees, oak mostly—a thick, massive stand of oak that looked as old as the Earth. Hyacinth stared at it a moment, puzzled.

"Nothing but trees," said Darke.

"*Will* you have patience, Captain?" she snapped, almost losing her own. She searched the trees carefully, finally lying on her side until she could peer beneath them. "Here," she said. "Here he is."

Agitated, Darke lay down beside her, so close he could smell her hair—its scent, of course, that of hyacinths.

"The figure there," she said. "Do you see him? I believe he is playing a lyre. He plays quite well, actually."

"A lyre player? A minstrel is the king of Daathan slayers so deadly they are called killer angels?"

"Yes, Captain, I sense truth; there is no mistake. You are looking at the scion of the Daath."

Darke stood brushing himself off. "Apparently you are right. I have made a deadly covenant, since it turns out my single possible strategy against this angel is a boy no older than you. I have as my secret weapon a deadly slayer who is going to strike from nowhere without sound or warning *with his lyre*! I need a walk. I need to smell the sea, get out of this damned musty dungeon."

He left without saying more, but Hyacinth had not even heard his last words. She was stricken, staring at the tiny figure. She was able to focus, move in closer, until she could see his face. He was, indeed, Daath. His skin bore a light blue tint, his hair, where it fell over his shoulders from under the hooded cloak, was braided, night-black. His face was the most beautiful she had ever seen. The song he played enchanted her with the power of a siren.

"Greetings, my little Angelslayer," she said. She reached into a pouch of her belt and from between her fingers she crushed a tincture of rosemary, grinding it to a powder that fell over the tiny oak trees. Hyacinth smiled as the lyre player looked up, puzzled at the light rain of red blossoms.

Chapter Four
Daathan

Lucania: a village near Terith-Aire, the capital city of the Daath

The skies were an unwashed blue as Adrea set her father's finest horse, the dappled gray stallion, at a gallop. She hugged the withers as the horse cleared the border fence just beyond the cottage and let the stallion run. It tossed its head back and muscled into a hard gallop. Adrea leaned into its wind. She loved to let him run, and though few would know it, she was one of the best riders in her village.

Later, far from her father's cottage, she saw a figure wave from a hillock. He started his mount at a trot, then broke into a gallop to catch up. She silently cursed. Her brother, Aeson, had found her. Probably he had been lying in wait for her. He knew she had been coming this way for days now, riding this same ridge, and he was far too curious to ignore what she might be up to. Aeson hugged the neck of his horse, riding bareback, and Adrea had to slow to let him catch her. He rode alongside her a moment, quiet, tumble-brown hair bouncing. Aeson was ten and three years.

"I thought you had cattle to feed, Aeson."

"They can forage for tubers."

"What about Lamachus?"

"He can forage for tubers, as well. I intend to spend a little time with my sister before she is sold."

"Aeson, I am not being—"

"Sold—like hung venison. I listened to them last night. You know the kind of things they said about you?"

"No, and I do not want to, but I get this feeling I am going to hear it anyway."

"Lamachus, he liked to bang his fist against the table when he said such things as 'good woman, Marcian!' and 'blood Galaglean' so I figured it would not be too much longer before they would be in to pick you for bugs and have a notch cut in your ear, mark you for milking." Aeson studied her for reaction.

"Things like this are done—tradition," she said.

"Maybe for others, but you are not ordinary. You are different from others, something in you, and they ought to know."

"That is silly, Aeson. I am no different from anyone else in Lucania."

"Maybe you do not know it, but I guess you never looked in your own eyes. I see it; I see who you are. They should not give you to just anyone."

"Have you not listened to Lamachus? Marcian is a captain; one of Quietus's veterans." She spoke in imitation of Lamachus's deep, gravely voice, "A hero of Tarchon Pass."

"Who could be your grandfather."

"But Aeson, he is rich. He is a horse breeder."

"Maybe being rich has a lot more to do with this than tradition."

Adrea didn't argue. The night before, the horse breeder had ridden up to the cottage with four men, all wearing the rust-red cloaks of Galaglean warriors. The men turned out to be the horseman's sons, his four eldest, and they never spoke, never even took off their helmets. They waited silently the whole time near the stockade.

"At least he is not a Daath," Aeson said.

"What should that matter?"

"You know why they brought us here, the Daath—what the wars were about. You know why they keep us. We are their breeding stock. They like the red hair and fair skin. I am surprised one has not taken you already."

"Those are just stories."

"What about Binnith? They rode in and took her—a cohort of them. Daathan riders, everyone saw. Are you going to argue that?"

"Binnith had been seeing one of them in secret, something you did not know. The Daath do not steal village girls. I believe Binnith merely wanted it to appear that way. Do you know whom her father planned to give her to? That toad, that meat merchant, Ragthart."

Still, Adrea knew that no one in Lucania trusted the Daath. Yet, instead of being wary of them, she was curiously drawn to them. They were striking. The few times she had seen them, she had been fascinated. They were tall, always handsome, and their hair—the way it was long and night-black, she could not help being curious. Those who passed through Lucania were mostly warriors, headed for the passages of Hericlon, a mountain stronghold to the north. They were all young men, but in their armor and shimmering cloaks they looked formidable, and by reputation, they were. Not even the Etlantians challenged the Daath. They were feared and respected.

Riding through the streets of her village in formation, their faces were stern, their demeanor austere. But once, Adrea had hidden behind sea meadow grass to spy on a group of them as they stopped to water their horses. They shed their stoicism and became boys, joking, laughing, even wrestling in the grass. There was no doubt that they were capable and adept as warriors, which left her a bit uncomfortable, but to be honest, the Daath attracted her far more than any of the boys of her village. It left a taint of guilt in her, as if she were betraying some unwritten code, but it was something she could not dismiss.

"I could smuggle you out of Lucania before the marriage," Aeson said.

"Smuggle me out?"

"I have a plan and I have saved up some bread cakes and cheese."

"And where will we go?"

"In Ishmia, there is no shortage of trader galleys leaving for the western seas, and all of them have need of able-bodied workers."

"I am a girl, Aeson."

"We could disguise that."

"You think so?"

He glanced at her, his look betraying that it might be difficult. "Yes. We are clever enough."

"So you believe we would be better off as seamen?"

"Maybe on some island or even onboard a ship, you might meet someone, someone worthy of you, instead of an aged captain of the gathering wars, older than Lamachus."

"On the other hand, my gender might be discovered, and I could end up in a brothel in some unsavory trading port. Things can be a lot worse than marrying a horse breeder."

"It is just that—you are gifted, Adrea, and Lamachus should know. He has no idea who you really are."

She didn't argue with that. Lamachus was truly thickheaded. They rode a time in silence, the tall grass brushing the horses' bellies. To Aeson's credit, Adrea had been trying to forget about last night, though it lingered like a bad dream. Marcian Antiope, the son of Ventnor of Galaglea, had a solemn, narrow face and a large nose. And he stuttered, which was something she would never have guessed of a veteran captain of Quietus, the Galaglean king.

Aeson suddenly pulled up on the reins. He searched the ground nervously. "Adrea, look here! What is this?"

Adrea glanced down. The tall grass had been scattered with red blossoms that were still tumbling in the light breeze. Oddly, they smelled like rosemary, though that could hardly be possible, not in this part of the woods. She glanced up. They were at the edge of the forest called the East of the Land. She came here often. The ancient trees never failed to stir something deep inside her, as if they were able to awaken a part of her that too often slept. It was said that long ago, beyond these trees to the west, the fiery sword of Uriel, the archangel of the seventh star, waited, always turning, always guarding the eastern edge of the place where Elyon first touched His finger to the Earth.

"That is the forbidden forest," Aeson muttered, suddenly realizing where they had ridden. "How did we get so close to the forest?"

"We rode up to it."

"We should not go any closer," he warned.

"Why?"

The East of the Land was mostly oak. There must have been thousands of oak in there, ancient guardians, heavy and solemn. And along the borders were other noble trees, like the tall aspen that reached for the sky, and quicksilver with its white bark. They were as old as the Earth, as old as life was old. Within them, shadows curled, and strangely, today the shadows were littered with red blossoms, stirring in the light wind. There was something about them, something unnatural; Adrea could sense it. She sensed many things, though she kept such thoughts her own. She knew one thing for certain: the blossoms were not of this forest, and though there was no explanation, she felt there was also no threat; rather, they seemed mischievous, leaving them all the more intriguing.

"We should leave, Adrea. Ride back before something happens."

"What could happen here? These are the ancient trees of legend. The oaks are protectors. We could be no safer."

"You think so? Well, do you see the shadows in there? Those shadows harbor Uttuku."

"Nonsense."

"Uttuku, hunting for flesh to inhabit. I have heard it said by more than a few."

"I come here often, and I assure you, little brother, not once have I been possessed of Uttuku. I look in those trees, and suddenly there seems so much more to life. Think of it, Aeson; this forest has witnessed it all, the ancient garden when it was still sacred. It has seen the coming of the angels and the first man to ever breathe life. Do you not feel the light still burning in these ancient trees?"

"No, and I am telling you we need to leave. Now."

"Sometimes—I do not know how to put it exactly—but sometimes I come here, and I feel as if life were so much more than marriages to horsemen or even Lamachus and his cattle. I feel something turning, as if the entire world is being drawn into its reason for being and that soon, not far from now, in a single star-fire moment, the limitless light will make itself known."

"Listen to me, Adrea. There is no sense in thinking like that, speaking deep things like that. You spend too much time listening to those wandering Beseers, the Followers of Enoch, and you know what Father thinks of them. Besides, what kind of name is the East of the Land? It makes no sense. The only thing special about these trees is that they are easy to get lost in."

"How would you know?"

"I have been lost in them; that is how I know."

"You have ridden in there? Alone?"

"Alone but for the heifer I had to chase down. She got in there, and it took nearly the whole day getting her out."

"You did not feel anything magical? It is said that within the East of the Land there still exists the sacred ladder, the passageway to the castle of Arianrod in the sky."

"No ladders. No castles. But there were plenty of snarled, thick roots that can catch horse hooves, plenty of sharp rocks, and lots of shadows that get so thick you can even lose the sunlight. If I felt anything unnatural, it was the Utuku watching; those shadows offer them a good place to hide. You should trust me. I know these things. And what is more, we should leave here before the sun gets any lower in the sky. We will barely make it back before sundown as it is."

She nodded, still staring at the trees. "We can leave," she said. She started to turn the reins when something caught her eye. She quickly searched the shadows, knowing what to look for, and there he was. A tingle flew down her back. He was carefully hidden, but it was clear he was letting himself be seen. Aeson had no clue, but this was the reason she had ridden up here every day for more than a week—to find the rider who kept always to the shadow, but watched her from the trees. She had never seen him clearly, but she sensed his eyes, something about him, something strange and fascinating.

"What is it?" asked Aeson.

The figure was so still the shadows almost swallowed him, but this time, unlike the others, she saw the flank of his horse, a glistening, silvered white. That was no shadow.

"What?" Aeson said again, this time pressing forward, searching. He must have seen the rider, as well, for he jerked back so suddenly his horse reared. Aeson was a good rider, but he was so startled he dropped the reins. He did manage an ungraceful dismount, only to stumble and fall on his back.

The look on Aeson's face made Adrea chuckle. "Are you all right?"

He scrambled to his feet. "Of course, I am all right."

Adrea leaned forward to catch the reins of Aeson's horse before it bolted, but he quickly snatched them back and nimbly leapt onto the horse's back. He composed himself, smoothing his hair into place.

"Stupid horse," he muttered.

"It was your horse's fault?"

"Must have gotten his foot stuck."

"In the grass?"

"Maybe it was a rat hole or something."

"So, you did not see anything in the trees?"

"Of course not." He hesitantly searched the forest's edge. "No," he affirmed with relief. "There is nothing in those trees at all."

Adrea looked back. The rider was gone, as though he had been no more than a trick of light.

"We must start back," Aeson insisted.

"Yes . . . of course."

"Even if we ride hard, we might not make it before sundown, and as you know that would leave Lamachus very anxious."

"Well, we would not want that, would we?"

"No, we would not."

A moment longer she searched the trees, but Aeson pulled up in front of her, blocking her view, watching her suspiciously. "Is there something here I should know about, Adrea?"

Adrea calmly smiled back. "No, Aeson; nothing here to worry about."

He cocked his head to the side and lowered one brow—mimicking the serious look he had so often seen on Lamachus's face.

Adrea laughed.

"What! What is funny?"

"Sometimes you are rather cute, Aeson."

"I am not cute. Girls are cute. I am . . ."

"Yes?"

"Agile. I am agile."

"As long as you manage to avoid rat holes."

"Adrea, we cannot wait any longer. We have to leave now!"

"Lead the way, agile Aeson, and I promise to follow."

Aeson galloped away, brown hair tossing, not looking back. Before she followed, she glanced once more to the forest, marveling at how the sun split through the shadows in streamers. She held her hand up, spreading her fingers in the sign of the word, the sign of greeting, then turned the reins and set the stallion at an easy lope.

†

Aeson was right about one thing; it was late when they made it back to the cabin, and Lamachus was there to watch them enter, his eyes narrowing on Adrea. He spoke to their mother, Camilla. "Could use a bit of warmed ale before bed, woman."

Camilla turned from the fire, giving Adrea and Aeson a warning glance of their father's mood as she poured ale in a clay goblet.

"And I did say bed," Lamachus emphasized, "which means you two are late."

"I was giving the stallion one last run, Father," said Adrea.

"And where were you running him? To the blessed Parminion Mountains?"

"We were out along the west road," answered Aeson.

"Believe I was talking to the girl."

"Well, I was with her, Father."

Lamachus grunted. "And that's supposed to offer me comfort?" His eyes remained on Adrea. "You have been letting that horse run a lot lately."

"I have had a lot to think about."

Lamachus sipped his ale. "Should keep in mind while you are 'thinking a lot' that people have gone to some considerable effort arranging things on your behalf."

"Not to worry, Father, I can scarce forget what is being arranged."

She stepped past him into her and Aeson's room, letting the woolskin coverlet fall into place behind her.

Lamachus ended up staring at Aeson. He was quick to notice Aeson's eyes dart away.

"What have you two been up to?"

"Got that fence mended in the north pasture," Aeson muttered.

"Ah? You say something?"

"Said I got that fence mended."

"What fence?"

"The one in the north pasture."

"Do not recall sending you to the north pasture today."

"You just told me to tend to things, so I did."

"Up north?"

"Yes."

"By way of the trees?"

"Trees? What trees? Oh, you mean the oaks?"

Lamachus glanced at Camilla, but she only shook her head.

"You ask me, she is scared of them," Aeson said.

"Scared of them, is she?" Lamachus responded.

"Yes. Seems that way to me."

"Explain this to me, boy."

"She thinks there are spirits and such in there—castles. The castle of Irum Rod."

Camilla chucked softly. "Arianrod, dear."

Lamachus grunted. "No more castles in those trees than there are between my middle toes. Boy, do you see my toes where they come out of my sandals here?"

"Yes, Father."

"You see any castles between them?"

"Was not me that said there was a castle; it was Adrea."

"Are you telling me your sister believes there are castles growing out of my middle toes?"

"No, I meant . . ."

"I want you both staying away from the north woods. Now, since you two are so smart, I will not need to be repeating all this, will I? She is up to something, and you should perhaps remind her I am not so slow as to be unaware."

"No. Certainly not. Well . . . good night then, Father."

Lamachus grunted and continued to eye him until Aeson was safely behind the door's coverlet.

Aeson found Adrea near the window, looking up at the moon, where it hid behind scattered clouds.

"You heard all that?" he asked.

Adrea nodded.

"We best not ride up there for a while. No need to anyway. Is there?"

Adrea knelt and whispered out the candlelight.

"Have you ever dreamed there was something more, Aeson? Something out there that would make our simple lives here seem meaningless?"

"Like what?"

"Have you ever heard of Aeon's End?"

"No, and I do not want to hear of it because I want to be able to sleep tonight."

"I study the sky from this window each night, and somehow it is different. The patterns of the star system I call the horsemen, it has changed. I cannot even say how, but those are the words of the Followers that say in the coming of the last days the stars will lose their way in the sky."

Aeson slid down and turned to pull the blanket over him, closing his eyes.

"We are all just asleep here, in our quiet little village," Adrea said. "The Daath as well, for that matter, in their mighty city. Sleeping just like us while the Earth begins to tilt and the words of the prophets begin to move across the sky. I do not know how to explain it all, but it is written, and I feel it, and I am not simply going to sleep through it like everyone else."

"What are you going to do?"

"I am not sure. Run away. Maybe."

"Really? You would do that?"

"Better than waiting here, doing nothing, missing it all."

"Missing what, Adrea?"

"The coming of prophecy—words and scripture as ancient as this Earth."

She glanced at him, but Aeson slipped farther into his blanket, his back to her, and soon pretended to be dozing. She turned to stare out the window. Something up there had possessed her, for several counts of the moon—ever since she had noticed a particularly brilliant star streak across the sky.

Moments later, Aeson was probably actually asleep. Lamachus worked him hard enough that he could often fall asleep the second his head touched the blanket. But Adrea could not sleep at all lately. She would stare for hours at the stars, something stirring inside her that almost wanted to make her scream.

Something out there was calling her, speaking her name, and she ached inside because she had no idea how to answer.

Chapter Five
The Little Fox

The beach of the Dove Cara, below the Daathan city of Terith-Aire

As the blackship from which he had just disembarked turned back to the sea, Rhywder slung his saddle over his horse and cinched it down. He paused to take a last glance at the darkened sails of the Pelegasian. She was a weathered old warship, but had he a choice, leaving with her would have offered far more comfort than what waited for him here. He paused to take a long drink from the wineskin of bloodroot that hung from his saddlebag. Behind him were the mighty cliffs of the Dove Cara; and above those cliffs, barely visible from where Rhywder stood, were the alabaster spires of Terith-Aire. It had been over a year that he had been at sea, longer since he had been in the city. Glancing up, it seemed something of a dream against the blue sky—that or a nightmare. The walls and towers of Terith-Aire, some said, Rhywder among the believers, were not of this world, but were crafted of voyagers from a distant star.

Rhywder pulled himself into the saddle. For whatever reason the warlord had summoned him, it wasn't going to be happy news, so Rhywder was going to enjoy his innocence as long as possible. He rode slow and easy in the saddle.

He did not look like a captain of the fabled Shadow Walkers. In ten centuries, only four humans had worn the plain, silver upper armband that was the signet of a Daathan Shadow Walker, and Rhywder was one of them. In the gathering wars he rode at the left hand of the Daathan king, Argolis. He was a ranger and a scout, as well as the most fierce and loyal protector of his king. Also, before she died, Rhywder's sister, Asteria, a seer and child of the mothering star of Dannu, had been Argolis's wife, the fifth queen of the Daath.

These days, Rhywder chose to travel unmarked. He looked like a lone, weary adventurer, down on his luck. His red hair was unkempt, as was his beard. His cloak, a fabled Daathan cloak, was so weathered it had lost its luster and was left gray and dusty. He preferred it this way, appearing as a road-weary wayfarer. He did not like being singled out or discovered. He had learned to keep his head low, dress as an ordinary adventurer—easier to avoid those looking for fame—and bringing down a Shadow Walker would be a prized mark.

Beyond, a hidden cavern led to the city above. It was ancient, secretly cut into the rock, and known only to a few. Here one first had to ride through tidal pools and beneath hanging moss, then duck to avoid low branches, wind through massive rocks, and wade into the deep water of the stream that ran from the eastern ridge to the sea. It was sweet water, this stream, always clean and clear. Rhywder was tempted to drop off and get a drink, maybe even splash some water in his face, but that seemed too much bother, so he kept riding. His horse had to swim some distance and then maneuver several sandbanks to reach the hidden, narrow cavern that curled off into darkness.

Things scampered here. They scampered because they could smell him, not simply the stink of a year at sea. They could smell who he was, what he was. Others they might have grizzled at; still others they might have eaten. They were a hoard of Etlantian Failures, and Enoch's curse had left them desperate for human blood or flesh. What could possibly have been Elyon's purpose in these savage miscreants, Rhywder had never fathomed. Sometimes they were nothing more than teeth and claws moving on stubs of legs.

He lit a small torch and anchored it in a side notch of his saddle. He saw some of them slipping into shadows from the light. He glanced at the wall of bones they had built at the entrance to the passageway. They had been working on it all these years. It was a wall made wholly of human bones, mostly thigh heads to smooth the facing. Skull caps were used to form words of binding—Etlantian words—all of them warnings for any who dared pass. Once again, this left Rhywder puzzled: not only had Elyon fashioned these pitiful creatures, but also He had given them intelligence sufficient to craft Etlantian incantations into bone walls. Rhywder had faith in Elyon; he would give his blood and had bound his soul to the Lord of Kings, but His ways left Rhywder endlessly bewildered.

From here the cavern was a long winding passageway to the top of the Dove Cara, emerging in the forest men called the East of the Land. It was an odd passageway, cut deep into the rock, sometimes well crafted into winding stairs a horse could easily climb, and other times so narrow it seemed the masons had grown lazy. Everywhere there were traps. Of course, Rhywder knew them all, but in the old days, during the gathering wars, when novices attempted the ascent, Rhywder would commonly pass bodies slowly being drained of blood. The curse of Enoch had turned human blood to precious nectar for these creatures, and they loved nothing more than to hang bodies and drain their blood into casks that were later sealed with wax and hidden in the dark recesses of the passageway.

Higher up were natural caverns, large and dripping with stalactites. The Daath had built row after row of recessed chambers in the catacombs. They were the burial places for Daathan royalty—kings and queens, those of noble blood, and warriors who had distinguished themselves in battle. Seven generations of Daath were buried here, among them his sister, laid in a golden sepulcher encrusted with diamonds. She had been called the Seer Child; her natural gifts of magic and her ability to peer into futures were unparalleled, even in the history of the mystical Daath.

The Daath, though originally descended of the archangel Uriel, were the mirror image of the mothering star, Dannu, the Goddess named Daath. The Daath had always chosen their queens from their sister tribe, the Lochlains. Though they were considered the children of men, it was said that the blood of Dannu in the Lochlains refined and purified the severity of Uriel's light. Otherwise, his descendants may have fallen victim to Enoch's curse, just as the offspring of the angels who swore upon Mount Ammon.

Though his sister's gifts had been legendary, Rhywder himself had but a few tricks, learned mostly of his grandmother. Rhywder's true magic was in his ability to keep his flat ass walking upright—that and granting him occasional uncanny luck at the tables of tavern bean games.

Riding past row after row of vaults in the labyrinthine catacomb reminded him of the processions of the fallen that he had attended in this chamber. The gathering wars had been meant to bring the tribes of Dannu under a single rule, and in truth, it had made them the most powerful standing legions on Earth. Even the Etlantians did not challenge the Daath and their followers. However, in the shadows of their dead, Rhywder wondered at the cost. So many had fallen in uniting the tribes of the Goddess; Argolis had slain nearly a third of their number.

Ahead was the first tomb built, carved into the natural rock and bearing, in gilt Etlantian lettering, the name of the first Daathan king, Righel of the Seventh Star. To most he was known simply as the Voyager. It was said he crossed the stars of heaven in the days of Yered, when the covenant was sealed by the angels upon Mount Ammon.

Waiting for Rhywder, standing near the lit braziers of Righel's tomb, was the warlord of the Daath, Eryian—the Eagle of Argolis. Even standing still, waiting, his bearing was intimidating. His every move was practiced and precise, nothing wasted. As a warrior he was unmatched; no one could cross swords with the Eagle. Eryian wore burnished silver Daathan armor, as well as one of the fabled Daathan cloaks, said to bear magical abilities.

The warlord's eyes were cruel in the dark of the cavern, lit only by flame, though in broad sunlight they could soften to a silvery blue and even, at times, look forgiving. Here, cloaked in his darkened armor, he looked nothing less than a wraith—as though he were a natural creature of the catacombs.

The warlord was Rhywder's high captain. Rhywder may have pledged his sword, his bow, his life to Argolis, but his honor and his heart he had pledged to this man, Eryian the Eagle.

He circled his mount before Eryian. It had been long since they had seen each other. Rhywder knew his own face had acquired a few wrinkles since they had last met, but the warlord had hardly aged at all. They were all like that. He had learned never to wager on the age of a Daath. Stoic as the warlord was, Rhywder dropped from his horse and stepped up to embrace the captain, squeezing him hard, even slapping him on the back. They had fought through white-knuckled terror and witnessed blood that could curl one's soul—their closeness was the kind of bond shared only among warriors.

Rhywder stepped back and grinned wide. Eryian did not. He wasn't a man for displaying emotions. Rhywder briefly wondered if it was all the dead of the gathering wars, all those souls on the captain's shoulders, for he had been its architect; he had persuaded Argolis to gather the tribes despite the terrible cost.

Before Righel's tomb was a basalt altar. Something had been laid out on its smooth, dark surface. It was a body. Rhywder did not look at it directly, but he knew its origin. He leaned back against the crypt near the warlord and crossed his arms, crossed his dusty, weathered boots.

"Do not tell me that is the same cloak you wore when you left here over a year ago," Eryian said dryly.

"This is the same cloak I wore when I left here over a year ago."

"Elyon's name, but you stink, Rhywder. Might you have thought to bathe before coming here?"

"What would be the logic in that? This is a catacomb. Everything here rots. Why should I not? Besides, your message said it was urgent, Captain."

"You no longer need call me that. We are merely brothers now. The gathering is long past."

"Know that; but you are still, and always will be, my Captain. Blood be blood, my lord, and time will never change that oath. What is so urgent? Ah, let me guess. Could it be this body I see laid out on Righel's altar?"

"This?" said Eryian. "No, this is your lunch, Little Fox, nicely roasted. You have been on the road so long—I acquired the best cuisine I could manage."

"My grateful thanks, Captain, but I've had lunch already." Rhywder smiled and patted his wineskin. "Still working on it, actually. The intent is not to stop until I fall on my face and sleep in my own spittle."

"A noble intent, Rhywder. Now, tell me what you know of the body."

"Ah, then you were merely joking about it being cuisine?"

"I understand you were the one who found it."

"Well, more as though they brought it to me. Someone let word out I was docked in Ishmia. I was bringing in acceptable slaves. You know—those with no home or chance to stay alive—children mostly. A few widowed women. I planned on selling them on Ishmia's pier."

"I thought you hated the very idea of selling slaves and, most of all, slavers themselves."

"In fact, Captain, this last voyage I laid seventeen slave ships into the deep of the ocean, along with their captains and crew. We lost some slaves; more than I would have wished, but you would certainly understand necessary casualties. I saved those I could, leaving the adults and able-bodied on free islands, but the fry—the wee ones—those were the ones I auctioned off in Ishmia."

"Why not simply give them away?"

"Unless a rich man pays for what he gains, he gives it no value. They were too young to simply let loose. They would die in the streets or be made whores or the like. I thought them better off in the homes of the rich."

"You know, I've forgotten how much you can talk once you get started."

"Then you talk. You can start by telling me why you have dragged my sorry ass all the way back here to the Dove. I rather had my thoughts on some deep water; raiders getting thick out there, fine hunting."

"I have already stated my reason—the body."

"What is there to say you wouldn't have guessed yourself?"

"Amuse me."

"All right, here is the story—they bring me this body. It is so tightly wrapped, it was clearly Unchurian work, cannot find body wrappers anywhere else that good. Besides, the wrappings were carved to the skin with the signet of their father. Rather we not speak his name openly, if you don't mind."

"Fine with me."

"So, I see that name inscribed on this body and I said to these fellows to take the body and burn it."

"What!"

"That's how I felt, knowing where it had come from. The Unchurians had floated it down the Ithen on a bamboo raft. From Hericlon. From the jungles, Captain. Just setting eyes on it was enough to determine I needed to know nothing more about this particular adventure. My adventuring days are over."

"You wouldn't call hunting down raiders at high sea adventure, then?"

"No, that I call sport. This, this wrapped and inscribed body, this was trouble. So I say to these fellows, burn this unholy piece of dung on the shore, then bring your priests and pray over it till dawn. Of course they ran away. So what I did then, I went out and hired some unsavory types—had them ship it here, to you. Seemed logical. You would know as well as I the intention of floating this body down the Ithen. Then I settled down to drinking for five or six days, and would have managed it had I not gotten your message on the second. Not that I was surprised. So I caught a Pelegasian blackship to the Dove and now here I am. I say we burn it. Smoke will be slow to air out, but shouldn't disturb the residents."

"You know we cannot do that."

"Elyon's name, Captain, just burn the damned thing! Have we not both had enough of this kind of trouble? For the love of God, can we not, just this once, be levelheaded about things and burn this poor fellow? You and I both know this means we are going to need to add a fresh edge on our killing blades, and the thing that bothers me about that—haven't we fought enough wars? We lost so many, Captain. We are a generation drained of blood. If you are going to tell me the gathering wars were just a prelude, then I say for the love of Elyon it is pissing unfair because we already did this! Understand me? We fought until there was nothing left us, gave Him our bone and blood and sweat, froze in the peaks of mountains, burned in traps, drowned in floods, and fell by the sword until surely we've given enough!"

"Something else you would rather do than kill bastards that need killing, Little Fox?"

Rhywder paused a moment to consider. "No. No, not really, I suppose. Guess not. Guess you have a point."

"Then tell me what you know about the body. Did you unwrap it?"

"Captain, unless they are warm, breathing, and female, I typically do not unwrap bodies—just a policy I have kept over the years. Your priests must have done this, and not a bad job, I might add, seeing how they've taken care not to pull off the burnt skin."

"You did not even look at her, did you?"

"Her? She's female? Ah, love of frogs, see, now right there is a just and good reason for burning. Just burn the poor bitch, Captain."

"First you are going to look her over, which is something you should have done in Ishmia without wasting three days."

Rhywder sighed, lifted his shoulder off the tomb, and started to walk around the body, studying it carefully.

"Ever seen a dead Nephilim come alive when the words of binding were spoken correctly by a sorcerer? Those cabbage-headed priests. The first thing they would have done—they would have started trying to incant the spells. That's why I sent the body here. Damn; the closest I have ever come to dying was in that village on the Weire coast when some priest started muttering out the incantations and cut into this Nephilim's corpse. Suddenly he gets one correct and I am meeting this fine, eight-foot gentleman of Etlantis when he comes back to life and sits upright."

Rhywder paused to rub one of the girl's slender fingers. "Big bastard, too. Had a two-headed axe embedded in his chest. The Nephilim found it handy, so he ripped it out, stood up, and started killing everyone in sight."

Rhywder paused, fingered a bit of the corpse's remaining hair. He circled and dropped back against the wall near Eryian, shivered, then spat to the side. "Name of Elyon, blessed be her soul."

"What can you tell me?"

"She wore a ring on her right index finger—my guess is it was a signet of the second legion. There, on the thigh a sword scabbard seared into the skin. Her backup weapon. She was a Daath. Carried a crossbow, would be my guess."

"How is that?"

"Quietus of Galaglea likes to train women to use a crossbow. The Etlantians always assume the women are easy prey until they find they have this new limb growing out of the center of their foreheads. My guess—she was a Daathan mercenary deployed in the jungles of Unchuria beyond Hericlon's gate."

"So she was killed by Etlantians?"

"No. This one was killed by Unchurians. *His* children."

"This angel we have chosen not to name out loud."

"He had such pure light they say his firstborn were much like you, not giants, almost human except for the tint of their skin. Reddish, dark in the sun. And since this angel is the architect of weapons and warfare, I would guess they are just about as deadly as your Daathan legions. And this poor lass, she must have taken out a score or so before they brought her down by a fire lance. They have paid her honor, sending her downstream as a message for us."

"What kind of message?"

"A warning."

"Why should he warn us?"

"Courtesy. After all, he taught men the craft of war; he would tend to follow protocol."

"Remind me of this death master."

"You know as much as I, Captain."

"Yes, but just remind me, if you would. Humor me."

"They say there was a squabble. Far before our time. I understand one of the three who swore the Oath of Ammon turned against the others. Something to do with a woman. Always ends up being over a woman, eh, Captain? So he left the mother city some centuries before our own. Who knows what he has wrought there in the far south."

"You haven't sailed there?"

"No one I know of has sailed that far south and returned, so anything I hear is no more than rumor."

"Why warn us?"

"War. He is letting us know he plans a preemptive strike against us."

"But would that make it not preemptive?"

"His message is secreted in symbols—clues. We might or might not have understood."

"Honor among the deadly."

"Yes. That would be my take of it. About one count of the moon back, I felt something ripple through the sky. You feel it, as well?"

Eryian nodded. There was actually nothing Rhywder could tell him he didn't already know. It had just been a long time since they had seen each other. This was no more than a chance for conversation.

"I think one of them lost the light," Rhywder went on. "One of them has turned. Probably aged, or is plagued by disease. It panicked him and so he tried to escape this future to another. All he managed to do was send a ripple outward through Earth and sky and in doing so close the time between us and Aeon's End. He drew it closer—his fate and ours. I've always believed it was coming, just never imagined I would live to see it. Probably still won't. But we can assume that if we felt it, so did our friend down south."

Eryian nodded. "Let's take a ride," he said.

"Why not. Oh, this poor lass. Perhaps you shouldn't burn her after all. She was a fighter if they honored her, and so should we. Even lay her to rest here, among the gallant."

"I'll see the priests take care of it."

Once outside the cavern, Rhywder and Eryian rode along the edge of the forest at the top of the Dove Cara. They rode in silence for a time, both with troubled thoughts.

"Tell me, Rhywder, if the angels are going to turn against us, why not the first of them, the Light Bearer?"

"He still believes himself to be our savior. He still believes the light of his heart can turn back the abyss."

Eryian nodded. They paused at the edge of the cliff where the wind of the Western Sea furled their cloaks.

The warlord stared solemnly at the curl of the ocean's edge where it dropped over the horizon. "I am going to ask you to find out precisely what waits in the jungle, Little Fox. I need you to know their numbers and how much time we have before they reach Hericlon."

Rhywder tightened his jaw. "Aye—thought as much."

"Sorry, my friend."

"Alone?"

"If anyone can get in there and out, it would be you. But I don't want you going in alone. I will send a chosen, a protector—someone who knows the shadows. He will meet you in the agora at sunup. Head south, stay light, move fast."

"You had best tell your protector to have his affairs in order before we leave."

"He is the type who keeps his affairs as simple as the haft of his axe."

Rhywder nodded. "Got a feeling about this one. Got a feeling this is the one that will finally get me killed."

"My experience is that you are not so easy to kill."

Rhywder drew a deep breath and sighed. "Least there is one night left to both find me a woman and get falling down drunk enough not to remember if she was ugly."

"Yes, you should use the night wisely."

Rhywder turned, a sad look in his quick, blue eyes, as if he might be bidding the captain farewell. He lifted his hand, spread fingers in the sign of the word. Eryian did the same.

"Light of Elyon go with you, good friend," said Eryian.

"As well, Captain . . . as well."

Rhywder pulled on the reins and started for the city. Eryian remained staring at the sea.

Chapter Six

Pagans

For Adrea, the morning had begun routinely. She finished the milking and then watched as Lamachus and Aeson headed off for the south fields where they were going to mark the newborns. She helped her mother with simple chores, and then quietly slipped to the stables and saddled the dappled gray.

She made certain she wasn't followed, even taking the far way around the upper pastures and then waiting nearly a degree of the sun before she moved on. No one was following. She thought of riding into the trees for cover, but though they inspired her, they were sacred, and she still hadn't built up the courage to go in. Yet someone had—the rider who had been watching her.

It was still early enough when she reached the edge of the forest that its colonnades were deep in shadow. There were shrill calls of far birds. She noticed that within the wood, so little sun got through the upper foliage that it left the ground nearly barren.

It was hushed in shadow and she rode slowly along the edge, waiting for the sun to at least get high enough to dispel the darker shadows before going in, but this was the spot she had seen the rider and the flank of his white horse.

She heard hooves from behind, and turned. Her heart jumped. It was Lamachus, coming at full gallop, his wild hair flared. He rode like the warrior he had once been. When he reached her, he circled, then pulled up beside her, sweaty, his horse breathing hard, the air still cool enough that puffs of breath misted from its nostrils.

"He going to meet you here?" said Lamachus, his dark eyes focusing a growing anger.

"No one is meeting me!"

"Where is he, then? Does he hide in the trees?!"

"Father, I was just riding."

"You been doing a bit too much riding lately. How long has this been going on?" He paused, his temper on the verge of breaking. "Answer me, girl!"

"There is nothing going on!"

He glanced at the forest, then rode forward a bit, lifting in the saddle. "You in there!" he screamed, and Lamachus had a thunderous voice that could echo. "Something you should know. I manage to lay hand on you, I will crack your skull from one side of your head to its other!"

"Father, this is ridiculous. There is no one there!"

"You keep back from my girl! Understand! Else we shall contend, Daath, and know this: I have downed more than a few Daath in my day."

"Father, there is no one there! I have never even met a Daath."

"Yes, well, this whole affair stinks of Daath. They take our women at will—have done so ever since the wars."

"No one knows that for certain. It is nothing but a rumor."

"Are you questioning me, girl?" He turned in the saddle, waiting, daring her.

"No. No, Father."

"They take what they want, the Daath, they always have, but not my girl, by God." He turned again to the forest. "You hear me!" he shouted. "Not my girl!"

Lamachus then turned and studied her carefully. "Worthless. He is worthless whoever he is. He has no grit—gutless—hides in the trees. Someone were to issue me that challenge, we would by God engage—hand to hand."

Adrea half-closed her eyes. "Father, this is nonsense."

"Let us make certain of that, shall we?" He leaned forward and wrenched the reins out of her hands. Adrea had to grab the mane of her horse as they bolted into a gallop. She had no idea where he was taking her, but she guessed it would not be pleasant. When Lamachus's temper broke, he was capable of anything.

Camilla was outside the cabin when they reached it, glancing up as they passed, she gave Adrea a look of concern. However, to Adrea's surprise,

Lamachus did not stop at the cottage; he rode on, full gallop, his horse grunting under his weight, the reins of Adrea's horse tight in his fat fist. He had not even glanced at Camilla. She followed them to the fence line with growing anxiety.

Eventually they wound their way through the village streets, hooves echoing against the stone. Lamachus was barely giving people time to step clear of his horse, and this was market season, the streets crowded. One vendor knocked over his cart in panic. Some of the shopkeepers, those who knew Adrea and her father, looked up with unease. They likely guessed what was happening, and even Adrea guessed, as well. They were heading for the shrine of Baal.

It was a small shrine of gypsum imported from Galaglea stone by stone when the Galagleans where relocated by force at the end of the gathering war. The shrine was maintained by the village's two priests and their gathering of women attendants.

The tribes of the goddess Dannu were united by the blood of their mothering star, but the Galaglean still paid worship to their ancestral god. He was no Elyon; rather an empty, hollow idol that graced the top of the shrine named Baal.

Adrea had never been able to pass the shrine without a shudder. When she was only four, her father had brought her to witness a sacrifice. Rains had come scarce that year, so the priests had slaughtered a young bull. Adrea would always remember the blood gutters running. They had given her endless nightmares.

Lamachus rode up, dropped from his winded horse, looped his reins over a hitching post, and walked up the gypsum stairway. He pounded a heavy fist on the oaken doors. The stone lintels looked rusted, stained from blood offerings. A priest appeared, his head shaved, his long robes black and unadorned. Lamachus spoke low, almost a whisper, indicating Adrea. The priest looked up sharply. He laid a hand on Lamachus's shoulder.

Adrea had the impulse to pull on the reins and launch her horse into a gallop. The gray would easily outrun Lamachus's heavy warhorse, but Lamachus would have pursued relentlessly, never giving up. He would end up pushing the warhorse so hard it would probably die of exhaustion. But Adrea was too old for this, and she was reaching the point where Lamachus was no longer going to force her to do anything.

When the priest reached her, he took her by one wrist, pulled her from the saddle, and hoisted her over his back. He strode up the steps, past Lamachus. There were people from the village watching and Adrea shuddered with embarrassment.

It was shadowy within. Only thin streamers of light managed to break through the triangular windows of the vaulted ceiling. Braziers on crow-legged tripods left everything in a reddish glow.

The women who pulled her onto the cold altar stone were old and wore hooded, black gowns, their faces hidden. They held her down, four of them, and two pulled her legs apart sharply. Adrea knew there was nothing to do but endure. She closed her eyes, willed her consciousness elsewhere as the priest knelt before her and lifted an oil lamp. His hand was cold and brutal as it probed. Adrea was then released. The priest escorted her to the doorway, pulled her into the sun, and there he looked to Lamachus and nodded.

She jerked away from the priest's grip, then quickly walked to her horse and mounted, taking up the reins. She watched Lamachus pull himself into the saddle. His beard was tangled, his eyes dark with their leathery wrinkles at the edges. When he turned to her, she slapped him sharply across the cheek. She had never slapped anyone before and did not know what to expect, but Lamachus only narrowed his brow with a sneer.

"You saw the hags, girl?"

She stared back defiantly, not answering.

"You betray this marriage, and by your mother's own blood, you will live life shaven and bitter as a servant before Baal."

Adrea said nothing. She hated him so in that moment. She'd never felt such hate, and tears fell across her cheek as she put the stallion into a gallop.

Aeson was in the east field, riding down a stray heifer. The heifer belonged to a Daath, the baron who lived in a palace east of the village, near the sea. Whisperings were that once he carried a war hammer and killed many in the gathering wars. Now he was old, had lost his hair, and had gotten fat—rare for a Daath. On the other hand, Lamachus, equal the baron's age, was still a warrior. Lamachus's cabled muscles still held their tone, and once Aeson had seen his father bring down a maddened bull barehanded with a double-fisted blow to its head. Lamachus could carve up the Daathan baron like a hind of boar for the spit if it came to that. Still, even though Lamachus had his own herd, for pay he also worked the baron's lands. Aeson worked them, as well, and Lamachus had always said the baron's cattle were to be treated as their own. That is how Lamachus had taught him, that if a job was to be done, it was to be done well or not at all.

Aeson ran the baron's heifer back through the fence, over the same broken top post she had gotten through twice before. Aeson had repaired it both times, but the cow had gotten the idea that its purpose in life was to knock this piece of fence apart. Cows lacked for brains, but they had incredible determination.

Aeson dismounted and pulled the top post back in place. This time he brought along braided leather thongs to make the lashings and pieces of pine to strengthen the center break. Next week, he would take an axe and ride the half-day journey to the high country to cut another top post. The forest of the East of the Land was, of course, much closer, but to cut a limb or a tree from the sacred trees was a sentence of death by law of the Daath, and Aeson had no doubt they carried out their laws without mercy. Besides, he respected Adrea's feelings for the forest, her reverence for it. He would have ridden the half-day journey with or without the Daathans' law.

He finished the last tie, then took the reins and mounted. As he turned his horse, he drew up with a gasp. Directly before him, mounted on a roan stallion, with veils and silvered hair, was a starkly beautiful woman. She had rich, blue eyes and painted lids and pale skin with a slight tint of blue as if she were cast in moonlight. It was a Daath! The bodice of her tunic was unlaced at the front. He had never before seen a woman so beautiful, and it sucked all the breath out of him and left him dizzy. All he could do was to stare as if frozen. Briefly, he wondered how she had gotten so close, without his hearing anything. It was said the Daath could do that, move without sound.

"You are the boy—Aeson?" she asked. She spoke an educated Daathan, her voice practiced and liquid clear. Aeson merely nodded. He watched in amazement as she reached delicate fingers with painted nails into her bodice and withdrew a small, silver cylinder. "This is for your sister, the red-hair. It is for her alone."

She leaned in her gilded saddle and folded the cylinder into his hand. Her hair brushed his bare shoulder, and the touch of her fingers over his sent a shiver down his back and a strange arousal that left his throat dry. She smiled, warmly, then turned the roan and set it at a gallop. Her silver hair streamed in flight and he watched as long as he could, until she vanished over a far hillock, back toward Terith-Aire.

Aeson looked down at the cylinder in wonder. It was pure silver, molded in images of laurel leaf. It bore an oak-wood stopper sealed on the edge in wax with the imprint of the eagle. Without thinking, his fingers started to break open the seal, but then he remembered—for the red-hair alone. With difficulty, he stowed the cylinder in his belt pouch. He had too many chores he needed to finish. There was no time ride back to the cottage and find Adrea, and he knew curiosity would curse him the whole day.

Aeson's last duty was pulling out a calf that had lodged in its mother's birth canal. The calf was dead, but so would be the mother if it was not pulled loose soon.

Lamachus tied a line of hemp about the forequarters of the dead calf, and Aeson tied the other end about the horn of Lamachus's saddle. Aeson would have used his own horse, but Lamachus had yet to give him a saddle, telling him he would become a better rider the more he rode bareback. Maybe he was right.

Near the ailing cow, Lamachus took stance. He shook out his huge arms, gripped the cow by its head, and wrestled it down. It moaned, struggling, but Lamachus was strong and the mother too weak to fight. Lamachus soon had the head pinned against his thigh, twisted to the side, all his weight against it. He shouted to Aeson, "Now, boy!"

Aeson spurred Lamachus's horse and the calf came out, hit the dirt, leaving a bloodied swath before Aeson pulled the horse to a halt. Aeson dropped out of the saddle and unlashed the rope, then turned and stared aghast.

The calf had two heads and it was lying in the dirt almost torn in half amid its blood and afterbirth, steaming in the cool air. Aeson couldn't move, almost couldn't breathe because the two misshapen heads were human. They were hairless, with dead, human eyes, foreheads that had sloped, wrinkled brows, and wide, thick noses. It made him want to heave but his panic bit deeper than the nausea. He also noticed their teeth—sharp teeth, not the kind of teeth you would find on a calf—teeth for shearing flesh.

Lamachus let loose the cow. It staggered off a ways to hang its head, breathing heavily. Lamachus cut the birth cord with his big knife and wiped the blade on the mother's coat. He then walked over to stand above the monster, shoving the blade through his belt.

"Good Lord," Lamachus muttered, "at least we can be thankful this thing did not survive its birth."

"That . . . is . . . it is a Failure, Father."

"Damned sure something failed, being as it has a second head growing out its ass."

Lamachus looked up, noticing the stark fear on his son's face.

"What," demanded Lamachus. "You have never seen a stillbirth before?"

"Father, look at the faces, they are human. Do you know what that means?"

"That they're damned ugly?"

"No, no, it means that . . . it means this is one of them."

"Them? What kind of *them?*"

"A Failure."

"Well, one would hardly think it's going to make a good milking cow."

"No, no, I mean it is born of a giant, a wanderer. They say some have been seen in these parts."

"Did you say a giant?"

"It has to be. How else could the faces be human?"

"You are telling me some Etlantian monster has journeyed all the way from the mother city just to fornicate with one of my cows?"

"Yes!"

"I have heard some odd things come out of you, boy, but this one is simply too strange for comment."

"But look at it! The teeth! Look at the teeth! You do know the curse of Enoch?"

"You listen to me, boy, this here, this is god-awful. It is a poor bastard breech two-headed calf, but nothing more, and there is no name for it other than pitiful. Now gather some kindling and burn it."

"What?"

"I said to burn it. Have you lost your hearing as well as your mind?"

"We have to get a priest. We have to get a priest up here, Father."

Lamachus's face went red. "What? Have you gone utterly mad? That damned half-witted priest would be slaughtering my cattle and cutting off privates from all my prime bulls before the sun could set. Lord spare us, just what I need, as if life were not already trial enough."

"One of the giants, a flesh eater, has been here and could still be here."

"Having sex with my cows? Boy, you speak another word, and you will be picking yourself up off the ground. Now gather what few senses you have, and once you've managed that, burn this miscarriage and say nothing more about it. Nothing! To anyone. Do you understand me?"

Aeson was still staring at the steaming blood and flesh.

"I said, did you understand me?"

He finally looked up. As terrifying as the stillbirth was, the expression on Lamachus's face was even more so. "Yes," Aeson answered quickly. "Yes, I heard you, Father."

"Good, good, that is progress. Hope. Now burn this thing, scatter its ashes, and then forget you ever saw it. In fact, best you forget the whole day; imagine you were too sick to get out of bed this morning."

Lamachus mounted, gave Aeson a stern glance of warning, then put his heels to his horse's sides and left at a gallop for the cottage.

Alone, Aeson stared at the mutation and felt sick in his stomach. He kept thinking it was going to move. He looked around at the hills, the far line of trees, fearing something might be watching; come for its child. When he turned back, the eyes of the face nearest him were open. They were dead, opaque eyes staring right at him, and he knew they had been closed moments before.

†

It was late when Aeson came home. He was blackened with ash and smelled of burnt flesh. Camilla looked up, astonished. She had bread cakes waiting, with goat's milk and cheese.

"Lord!" his mother exclaimed. "Aeson, have you been in a fire?"

Aeson nodded. He splashed water from the washbasin onto his face. "I had to burn something."

"You look exhausted."

Camilla glanced at Lamachus, who sat near the back wall in his oaken chair with a clay mug of grog on its armrest.

"You are working the boy too hard, Lamachus."

"Maybe I have not worked him hard enough. Seems he has got too much time to imagine on things that are nonsense."

"Father, we should have . . ." He paused, catching Lamachus's grim expression of warning.

"What?" dared Lamachus.

"Maybe we should have at least had it washed."

"What is he talking about?" asked Camilla.

"Not your concern, woman," Lamachus answered, shifting in his chair. "Your boy is soft in the head. Tell you what, Aeson, you return to the field, open your breech, and void your piss upon the ash. That should wash it, cleanse it, and curse it all in the same breath. Then our souls can rest the night in peace, ah? You think?"

Aeson stared back, solemn, but Lamachus just chuckled.

"Aye, boy, save us from these flesh-eating calves!" At this he chuckled harder.

"Lamachus, what on earth is this about?"

"It is about you, your daughter, and those damned seer-speakers wandering about filling up people's heads with idiotic ideas. Back in the old country, they would be stoned, which is what would happen to them here if not for the stinking Daath looking over our shoulders. I had a proper god when I fought in the battle of Anarch and I need not be trading him in for the drivel of the

Followers of Enoch, and if I should catch any of you listening to their babble, so help me you will regret it; promise you that. Aeson, my boy, I have some strong advice—you forget all this, go in and get some sleep. We have more than enough work tomorrow in that north field."

Aeson tightened his jaw, then turned for his room.

Before she could say anything, Lamachus looked to Camilla and narrowed his thick brows. She sighed and went back to washing the last of the dishes.

"He did not even get supper, Lamachus," she said.

"Something you brought on him. And no more! I am done with this nonsense, understand me? Followers of Enoch—I find one, I intend to break his nose just for giving me this day."

In his and Adrea's room, Aeson leaned against the wall and slid down it until he was sitting, staring across at Adrea. Her knees were drawn up to her chin, her arms folded around them, and her eyes swollen from crying.

"Adrea! Are you all right?"

"I am fine. And we can all be comforted I am still marketable."

Aeson narrowed his brow. "What did he do to you? I know he did something. What was it this time?"

"Nothing, Aeson. It was nothing."

"Someday I will be grown, and he will not make you cry ever again."

"He cannot help himself. He has seen a lot of war, a lot of men die, some of them his own brothers. It changes men. Maybe it would leave you with a short temper, as well. We need to learn to be forgiving. He is still our father."

Aeson sighed. Then, suddenly, it came to him. The cylinder! He had forgotten all about it. He scrambled to his knees and searched the pouch of his belt, panicked that it had been lost. "Ah, no . . . wait, here it is." He pulled it out, sighed in relief, and held it up. "See this?"

She didn't answer.

"A harlot gave me this. I was in the east pasture, the baron's land, fixing that same fence again—damn cow, maybe a rock to its head would fix that fence. But what happened is a harlot on a roan stallion came up and gave me this."

"Aeson, what are you talking about?"

"It is for you!"

"What is for me?"

"This!" He twirled the cylinder. It was embossed with etchings, and he was certain it was pure silver by the way the moonlight played on its surface. "The harlot, she had rings on every finger, and anklets of silver, and she smelled of myrrh. She knew you. She knew me by name and she called you the red-hair. She was Daathan, her hair was dyed silver—I guess they do that. And look here on the edge of this chamber; that is the seal of the eagle."

Adrea was now beside him and snatched it from his fingers before he could say anything more. "When did this happen?"

"This morning."

"And you waited until now to give it to me!"

"I had chores, and Lamachus was watching me all day."

Adrea studied the eagle signet with interest. "The rider of the wood," she whispered. Adrea closed her hand about the cylinder and crawled back to her bed mat. Aeson was watching, wide-eyed.

"All right, Aeson, you have given it to me. Thank you."

"Are you not going to open it?"

She hesitated. She would have preferred opening it when she was alone, but she could wait no more than Aeson could. She broke the waxen seal with her thumbnail and pried out the wooden stopper. A papyrus scroll spilled into her palm. She carefully unrolled it and studied the print. Aeson was pressed beside her.

"I am not that good with Etlantian script," she said, "but I can read most of it. These are directions—they say to go east, several leagues beyond the King's Highway. I know where that is. I have ridden there before."

"You have? You have ridden past the King's Highway on your own?"

Pointing to the scroll, Adrea continued, "Do not be silly; of course I have, many times. In fact, this is the cliff that borders the eastern edge of the ocean near the forest. This is the top of the Dove Cara! And here—this names a time, the first degree of sunrise tomorrow morning."

She stared at Aeson, amazed, who stared back with equal amazement.

"What are you going to do?" he gasped.

Her expression did not require an answer.

"You are going to do it! You are! Alone?"

"No, I will ask Lamachus to escort me. What? I suppose you would have me wait here hoping Marcian might drop by?"

Aeson gave it some thought, narrowing his most serious brow, and then looked up with an idea. "Lamachus will be watching your every move, especially in the morning, but perhaps I can give him something more important to watch. Something he would not have the choice of ignoring."

"Such as?"

"Leave that to me."

"You surprise me, Aeson. I would think you would warn me to stay away. What if it is a Daath planning to steal me?"

"You did not see the harlot—those rich veils, the bracelets, and the cylinder. That cylinder is pure silver. If it is a Daath, he is not an ordinary Daath. So I think you should go. But only on one condition."

"You are laying down conditions?"

"I follow you. I will be close—not that anyone will notice, however. I will use stealth."

"You are practiced at stealth, are you?"

"Yes. I practice all the time. Do you know how boring it can be pushing cattle all day? I am planning on becoming an able scout. You think I want to herd cattle all my life? I can stay hidden. Anything goes wrong, be assured I will not be far."

"Then I have little to worry of, do I? Just make sure of one thing: make sure Lamachus does not notice my leaving."

"I will make certain you are the last thing on Lamachus's mind." He grinned.

Chapter Seven

Agapenor

A tavern on the outskirts of Terith-Aire, that same night

Seven thick, bronze coins were slammed down onto a rough-hewn table and then mashed in place by a fat thumb. The pits smelled. The whole tavern smelled, but Agapenor had no choice. He was being called out.

"Seven!" bellowed Cindos, one of Agapenor's sergeants, invaluable in battle but utterly useless in peacetime. Cindos kept his thumb on his precious stack of coins and raised his fist in the air to stir the whole cavern into madness, which was working quite well. It was just the opposite reason Agapenor had come to the city. He had been hoping to find a quiet place to have a few drinks before shipping out in the morning, but that was definitely a dream lost now.

"Seven!" Cindos screamed again. "By God, I lay seven bronze on our man Agapenor!"

There were murmurs all about.

A Daathan warrior stepped forward. There was an entire contingent of Daath in the tavern, all members of the tenth cohort of the second legion. Agapenor had no idea how they had overtaken the tavern so quickly. When Agapenor and his five axemen had first come in, there were a few Galagleans and a scattering of Pelegasian seamen. Now it was wall to wall with Daath.

"Seven bronze?" the tall, lean Daathan captain said, smiling at Cindos. "Hardly a difficult wager, Galaglean—seven pieces of bronze. This is all you can say of your mighty commander?" The Daath cast a demeaning glance at Agapenor. The captain had narrow black eyes, almost like a cat. There was a time, back in the gathering wars, when Agapenor faced such eyes as those, in battle, and they still sent waves of rage through him. Insolent bastards.

The Daathan captain drew a solid gold piece out of his belt pouch and tossed it onto the table, dwarfing Cindos's bet.

"One gold on my man," the captain said flatly.

Cindos stared angrily. It was overbetting, meant to make a fool of him. One gold piece was more than Cindos drew in a full count of the moon. Agapenor laid a hand on Cindos's shoulder.

"Let it be, Cindos," Agapenor said. "We will find another tavern."

Cindos pulled away. He furiously kicked over a stool and banged his fist so hard on the table everything bounced up and came back down, mugs rolling off, mead spilling onto the already mead-sodden floor.

"I will make good, spear-chucker!" Cindos screamed into the Daathan's face. He looked about at his fellow axemen. "Well!" Cindos demanded. "This spear-chucker wagers gold! Do we answer him?"

"What is it, Cindos?" one of the Galagleans asked. "You have no money left?"

"Gods, no. Put all the money I have down because I got faith in my captain! What about the rest of you? This is Agapenor they have challenged! We going to let him down, my brothers?"

Agapenor gritted his teeth. He reached into his own belt and slammed a fistful of coins onto the table, some silver, some even gold. He really didn't give a damn.

The Galagleans shouted a heavy volley as Agapenor walked forward and dropped into the fighter's pit. It was hollowed-out barren earth, the floor and walls rock-hard clay scored well with blood. Agapenor unlatched his axe belt and tossed it to one of his men. Daath and Galagleans crowded about the pit, peering over each other's shoulders.

All Agapenor wanted of this night was a few drafts of ale and then home to his good woman; now he was sucked into some Daathan grappling match. He really just wanted to grab one of these blue-skinned bastards and crack his head open. The Daath had their day all right, but Agapenor could still break any one of them in half.

He reached behind his back, pulled out his backup dagger, tossed it to Cindos, then took a wide stance and waited, clenching and reclenching his fists.

Agapenor had been born big and it was said in the village where he lived that he nearly killed his mother coming out of her. By seven, he could lift tree posts barehanded, and by twelve he could wrestle cattle to the ground. By twenty, no man could mark time in an arena with the axeman. He was older now, a veteran, but far from being past his prime.

Still, even Agapenor was unprepared for this—a roar. He wrinkled his brow.

The Daath had all gathered closely about one side of the pit, and now they began to stomp their boots on the wooden floor, shouting, beating their fists against their breastplates.

"Here you are, Galaglean!" the captain cried. "My chosen champion!"

The Daath were wrestling with something—unstrapping leather cords. They threw it into the pit. It was a beast—a red-haired aberration of nature almost six and a half feet tall. More if it had been able to stand upright, but it was bent over. One arm dragged along the ground, a huge arm, while the second arm was the size of a boy's. This was an Etlantian Failure, one of the pitiful bastard children of the giants. It seemed he was part animal with the thick, bristled red hair on him. Agapenor had heard of such things in far places—seen them, as well—birth creatures of giants who had mated with animals.

"What in God's name be that?" screamed Cindos.

It had probably been trapped and caged, prodded and driven mad by the Daath for the sole purpose of winning tavern brawls. It staggered into the pit with crazed eyes.

"Its mother was a red ape," the captain shouted at Agapenor, "and its father a brainless giant, so you both have something in common, Galaglean!"

It roared, exposing canine teeth—a flesh eater—and slammed its big arm against the dirt wall causing a slight quake. Pebbles bounced off its huge, hairy shoulders. The monster had nearly brought down the wall with one blow, but Agapenor knew the worst of it would be the teeth—avoiding the teeth. They were razor sharp and stained with fresh blood. The Daath had probably just fed him a rat for effect.

There was cheering and laughter, but Agapenor was feeling some genuine concern. The face of the creature looked as if it might almost have been normal, but one side was melted, a sad-looking effect, as if it were permanently weeping.

It suddenly moaned out with a mockingly human voice, "Moooom!"

That startled Agapenor, the near human voice, but nothing bothered him more than those teeth. They were shearing teeth, like a shark's, staggered and uneven, bigger on the lower jaw than on the upper.

Agapenor noticed Cindos standing with dread in his eyes, and he guessed the dread was more for his wagered coin than for Agapenor's peril.

Agapenor circled wide. The beast tipped its head to the side and watched Agapenor through narrowed, little black eyes that were suspiciously intelligent.

"Tear off its head, Captain!" Cindos screamed. "It is just a simple ape, that is all, so tear off its head!"

There were screams and jeers, but Agapenor continued to circle, uncertain of his next move. He could be the one getting his head torn off—who knew what this thing was capable of?

The grotesque creature then screamed and leapt forward, using the knuckles of its one big arm to pivot off the wall. Agapenor ducked, rolled on his shoulder, and was quickly on his feet behind the creature, where he brought both his hands together and slammed his elbows into the ape's back—a hollow, heavy thud, all his weight into it. That would have brought down a human right there.

The creature reared, enraged, and its huge arm swung out of nowhere to catch Agapenor in the side of the head, slamming him against the dirt wall. Agapenor slumped a moment, stunned. God's blood—that was a hard blow. This bastard was strong. The beast then pivoted and struck with the little arm, the fist belting Agapenor with several quick jabs to the jaw, each knocking the Galaglean's head back.

About the pit, cheering erupted. The bar was going insane. Taverns loved a good fight. Fun for all.

Agapenor tried to clear space between him and the long arm only to find himself backed against the wall with nowhere to turn. The giant's hand reached across and wrapped about Agapenor's neck, sucking him into a hug as though they might be best of friends. The little hand dug into Agapenor's shoulder with sharp nails that drew blood. But what worried Agapenor—those teeth were about to go for his neck, and there was little time to get out of this. The grotesque creature was quite calm, taking its time choosing its bite. The grip about Agapenor's ribs was at any moment going to snap his bones like twigs. The little hand now curled over Agapenor's skull and yanked his head back, exposing a nice shank of neck. The beast was going to take a bite out of him as if he were a bread roll.

Agapenor screamed and brought both his fists up and back hard, slamming them against either side of the creature's head into the temples. The beast's head was bald and the skin surprisingly soft. The first blow seemed to have little effect other than to confuse it a bit. Agapenor's second double-fisted blow seemed to irritate the monster, but that was followed rapidly by a third, delivered so hard it would have cracked any human's head in half like a walnut. That had an effect. The creature reeled, stunned.

Agapenor was able to pull free. He turned to deliver several rapid side kicks to the beast's breadbasket—if it had a breadbasket. Those kicks should have brought the thing to its knees, but nothing, no effect. Agapenor paused and stepped back. The monster was holding both the big hand and the little hand over its ears, swaying, moaning.

"Maaaaa!" it suddenly cried, like a child who had been bullied.

This was pitiful. Godless. Agapenor had nothing against mutations; it wasn't their fault they were godless evil. He took hold of one edge of the pit and pulled himself out. Then he searched out the Daathan captain.

"Maaaaaa!"

The Daath was laughing so hard he was holding his gut.

Agapenor threw several men aside. Before the Daath could realize what was happening, he was grabbed by the front of his burnished silver breastplate, lifted into the air, and heaved headlong into the pit.

"I wrestle men, not grotesques, you silver prick!" Agapenor screamed.

The tavern had gone completely insane. Fights were breaking out, chairs were being smashed, windows knocked out. The bartender ducked beneath his table for cover. The tavern would likely not be standing in the morning. In the pit, the Daathan captain scrambled madly for the edge but a thick-fingered red hand seized him by his black hair, jerking him back in. His men were forced to leap into the pit, weapons drawn.

Agapenor snagged Cindos by the shoulder. "Get us out of here!" he shouted.

Cindos took precious seconds to snag all the coin he could from the table and then ducked out with the other Galagleans. The tavern was in such turmoil no one noticed the six big axemen spill out of the door and run.

Soon they were trudging uncertainly down a back-end Daathan street. The spires of the great castle behind them pierced the moon like some alien temple. The city always left Agapenor uneasy, as though it belonged somewhere else, not a part of the Earth he knew.

"We should go find us another tavern," Cindos said, stuffing coins in his belt pouches. "One without Daath crawling through it."

"We are in their city, Cindos. They are going to be hard to avoid. Besides, what we should do is get some sleep. The barge pulls off the west dock before sunup. You keep drinking like this; you are going to puke when we get out to sea."

"It is being sober that makes me puke. All I need is to keep drinking until I pass out and I will be upright and fit to sail come dawn."

Agapenor drew up, motioning the others. They had rounded a street corner and suddenly, blocking their path, were four mounted Daathan warriors. And they were not typical Daathan warriors. Agapenor caught a glimpse of a plain silver armband on one. Shadow Warriors—possibly the warlord's personal guard. Their horses alone were worth more than Agapenor could ever hope to make in ten lifetimes.

Their helms were capped in white horsehair. This wasn't about a tavern brawl. It smelled of trouble—bad trouble.

"Which of you is Agapenor, the axeman?"

Agapenor regarded them with suspicion. "That would be me," he growled.

One of them urged his horse forward and offered a scroll. Agapenor had no choice but to take it, though he would rather pull a tooth. Once he had the scroll in his hand, the four Daath turned in motion and the hooves of their horses clip-clopped away. Agapenor narrowed his brow. His men gathered about. The scroll was expensive papyrus, and the silver-wax seal bore the imprint of none other than Eryian, the Eagle of Argolis.

"What be this, Agapenor?" Cindos pressed.

"It is a scroll—sent of their warlord. That is the signet of Eryian himself."

"God's blood, what should he want with you?"

"One way to find out," Agapenor muttered, cracking the seal with his thumb.

Cindos pressed closer. "Well?"

"Trouble," Agapenor said. "This is bad trouble."

"What does it read?"

"Cindos, you idiot, you know I cannot read Daathan."

"Then how do you know it is trouble?"

"What? You think he had invited me to the king's ball? It smells of trouble; that's how I know—my mother did not raise me ignorant. I know what this intends."

Agapenor looked up, searching a moment, then started quickly across the street.

"You there!" he shouted. "Boy! Hold where you be!"

A Daathan youth froze in his tracks, turning to see six huge Galaglean axemen coming for him. His impulse was to run. He glanced in either direction, but it was no use; they had him surrounded. He stared with panicked eyes, and pressed back against the brick of the alley. When Agapenor reached him, he held the scroll opened before his face.

"Read this to me," he said.

The boy's voice caught on the first word, but he took a breath and started over.

"Agapenor . . . son of . . . son of Bauron . . . shall present himself in the agora of the city upon the morrow at dawn to Captain Rhywder of the Shadow Walkers. He is to be . . . to be . . ." The boy squinted. "Could you, ah . . . hold it still, please?"

"Motherless whores," Agapenor muttered. "What are they getting me into?" He steadied the scroll, pushing it nearly into the boy's face.

". . . to be fully fitted out and ready to ride," the boy finished.

"Ah, God's love of frogs." Agapenor moaned. He crumpled the scroll and stuffed it into his tunic. "Give the lad some coin."

He strode away, leaving it to Cindos to reluctantly give up a single bronze coin.

"But what's it mean, Agapenor?" Cindos said, hurrying to catch up.

"Means I should have stayed away from this city like I promised my mother when I was ten and two. She understood. 'Never trust them Daath, Gapey,' she told me, 'you stay away from them black hairs.' Ah, my mother, she were a God-lovin' woman."

Chapter Eight
Loch

Before sunrise, when Lamachus was still cutting wood, Aeson rode up at full gallop and circled his horse, anxious. Lamachus straightened up, one hand on his blessed aching back.

"What would be the matter with you, boy?"

"The east field! That same heifer broke through again! And this time she took the entire herd with her!"

"You told me that fence was bound!"

"It was. I tied it, roped it, everything I could think of, but somehow she broke through again! She is possessed! Perhaps of that spirit we birthed yesterday!"

Lamachus waited for no more. "I see you are as addle-headed today as you were the day before," he muttered, walking for the stockade. Moments later his big stallion burst out and leapt the fence. Lamachus spurred it into a hard gallop toward the east field where the baron's herds were kept. They were almost more important to him than his own stock.

"I will take the north hillock and the highway!" Aeson cried.

Aeson watched him ride off and smiled, although guilt tugged at him. There was a good, heavy day's work down there. Aeson had scattered those cows from there to the sea.

The place the author of the scroll had chosen was high, at the very edge of the

Dove Cara, where the thick trees of the forest reached the cliff side, which fell sharply to the sea, sixty feet below. The Dove Cara was a scar hacked into the rock, as if heaven's blade had cut through the edge of the East of the Land and left this bone of marbled granite. In fact, some said that in the angel wars of the Dawnshroud, long ago, that was exactly what had happened.

The shore below was a ring of crystal white sand. A cold wind was always present, always curling along the lip of the cliffs. As Adrea rode up, it cut the morning air with its chill.

This was far from the King's Highway, far from Adrea's village, beyond the reach of any protection, though she did not really feel the need for any. Adrea always had an inborn sense of things. Her grandmother had called these senses *the knowing*. Sometimes she had referred to it as the star knowledge, left her by blood of the mothering star, Dannu. Whatever it might be called, Adrea sensed no danger in answering the papyrus Aeson had brought tucked inside the silver scroll.

The forest seemed more primal here at the cliff's edge; it seemed to gather more shadows than the oaks near her village. Whatever had happened here, it had left a lingering malevolence.

Still, it drew her. She came here often; she rode along the edge of the cliff watching the sea. Aeson would have been right about these woods. They did contain Uttuku. The spirits hid in the forest's shadows, and there had been times when Adrea thought she had spotted them, gray shades swiftly darting. What she sensed of them, however, was not danger—not toward her anyway. It was more as if they were lost.

The view was utterly astonishing. Far out to the west was the edge of a misty island, a ring of far trees. She wanted to sail there, and she knew that beyond were other islands, even the city of Enoch and the temples of his Followers.

The water was dark blue, and it was cold because it was deep water—the cut that had formed the Dove Cara left a deep trench in the ocean, as well. This place was ancient, sacred, and whatever had happened here left spirits that stirred even to this day. She knew it was more than mere chance the rider of the wood had named this place for them to meet.

She turned toward the trees and then, quite suddenly, found herself staring at him. He was there, waiting for her. As always, he was slightly hidden in shadow, but this time he did not disappear. He waited for her. Adrea nudged her ankles against the gray's sides and slowly rode toward him. For the first time in her life, she entered the ancient forest that was the East of the Land, and as she had always expected, she felt the sprit of the trees, almost as if they recognized her. Something within Adrea changed as the shadows of the ancient oaks fell over her; she wasn't sure what it was, but she knew she had just stepped from the safety of the sleeping world into her destiny.

He was Daath; she recognized the skin, the dark hair. He was on a magnificent white mare whose bridle was golden and tasseled. He wore leather leggings, polished black boots, two very expensive crystal swords—a long double-edged at his left, and a second short sword through his belt at the right. From a back brace, the curl of a crossbow rose above his shoulder. His muscled chest was hairless, and his right upper shoulder was covered by a black tattoo that disappeared beneath the Daathan cloak. It was a phoenix rising from flame, the detail and workmanship magnificent.

She sensed a slight tension in him, something almost sad. Adrea had a gift of reading people, of picking up their feelings, even as they passed by, talking to one another. But this Daath was difficult to read; his feelings were confused. They were also hidden. His senses were as powerful as hers, and he was keeping himself guarded.

His face was sharply cut, his skin pale, tinted, as were all Daath, a slight blue. His night-black hair was braided in leather thongs, which dropped over his shoulders. She would not have called him handsome, rather she would have called him beautiful, as if an artist had crafted him from marble.

There was a sudden wind gust and his cloak blew across him, leaving him for the briefest moment nothing more than a shadow. There were Daathan warriors so highly trained, so skilled at their craft that they were called Shadow Walkers. They had gained their skill through a lifetime of training. They were slayers, and he was one of them, deceptively so, for he did not look severe or deadly.

Shadow Walkers were dedicated from birth, and once they were initiated into the cult, they bore a signet, a plain silver band on the upper arm. He wore one, and indeed, there was a precise, practiced edge to his every move.

When she drew alongside him, he bowed in the saddle.

"I must ask you to forgive all this intrigue."

"It has made things interesting. I like interesting."

"Were you expecting a Daath?" he said.

"Yes, I expected one. I have just never been this close to one."

"Is it a fright or a comfort?"

"By reputation, that would depend on your attitude toward me. I know I certainly would not wish to be your enemy. I find it comforting that you have gone to so much trouble to meet me."

"I am glad you came, and I assure you I could never think of you as an enemy. Allow me to introduce myself, Adrea of Lucania. My name is Lochlain. Those who know me well call me Loch, and you are welcome to do so."

This she had not guessed. That he was royalty was obvious, but it took her completely by surprise. "Lochlain? The son of Argolis—the king?"

"I thought it best simply to lay it out so that we then forget about it. I am not here as a prince. I came to meet you. I have watched you for so long. To see you this close . . ."

His eyes seemed almost human—a soft brown in the shadow light. And there was an odd, inexplicable sensation that she somehow had seen these eyes before. Then, she noticed a lyre hanging from the saddle against the white horse's flank. It was distinctive, silvered along the edges with intricately carved, dark, polished wood. He had left it there on purpose; he knew she would recognize it.

She had seen it before, and the sudden realization struck her. She looked up, astonished. "That lyre . . . you are the minstrel! The one who has played in my village these last weeks; the one I passed each morning I walked the path of the Water Bearer. That was you?

"Yes."

"You were always there so early, before the markets began. It puzzled me. The only ones to hear your songs were those preparing their shops or setting up their carts for the market crowds. You would have acquired much more coin if had you waited until midday."

"I was not interested in coin; I was interested in you, Adrea. The only one meant to hear my songs was you."

She stared at him a moment, moved by what he had said.

"You would not know," he added, "but I have searched a long time to find you."

"But why did you not say anything? Why play the minstrel?"

"I am a minstrel. More so than a warrior, despite these weapons I carry. I was born into a life I never chose, but it is one I must follow, regardless. At first I was silent because I had to be sure who you were; then, even after I was certain, oddly, I did not know what to say to you. Of course, there are many women in my court; however, I did not know quite how to approach you. I have never been shy with any women, ever. It was new to me, this feeling."

Adrea had met no greater royalty than the fat mayor of Lucania. To meet the prince of the Daath should have left her shaken, speechless, but she found herself oddly unaffected. She almost wondered if there were spell binding at work.

"Do you want your scroll back?" she asked.

"Please, keep it," he said. "I am told you are a Water Bearer of your village."

"Yes."

"From birth, or was it a calling?"

"From birth, my mother, my grandmother, all were Water Bearers."

Before the gathering wars, the Water Bearers had been born into the cult, passed from mother to daughter. But so many of Adrea's tribe had been lost in the war that most of those in her village now were newly initiated. To be a Water Bearer was to be a priestess, but Adrea at present was merely an apprentice. Every third day of the week she walked the path from her father's cabin to the well in the center of town. There were six Water Bearers in her village, and each morning they filled the village fountains and basins from the town well.

She had always guessed that being a blood descendant of the Water Bearers was what had given her *the knowing*, the senses she felt of people and things, such as the oaks of the forest. The feelings came to her quietly, whispered inside her. They whispered now that there was nothing to fear of this prince; still, he had been watching her for weeks, hidden in the trees—in a way, stalking her.

"So why have you been following me, Loch?" Adrea confronted him. "Why watch from the shadows of the forest? Why send secret scrolls by way of my brother? It could hardly be difficult for you simply to walk up and take me aside anytime you wished. After all, you are the Daathan prince."

"It was important I choose my timing carefully."

"Why?"

"That will take some explaining."

"Then, explain. I will not stop you."

"Not here; this is not the place."

"Then, where is?"

He motioned beyond the cliff. "Down there, that curl of white sand that borders the sea below us."

"The Dove Cara?"

"Yes."

"But that is more than a day's journey. We would have to circle almost to Ishmia and ride the shoreline. There are no pathways down this cliff side. Believe me; I have long searched for one."

"I have no doubt. But it so happens I know a secret passage. I can have you back before nightfall without alarming your father."

"My father? Why mention him?"

"He seems particularly concerned with your welfare."

"More with my dowry."

"Nonetheless, I do not wish to anger him further. It is better that we keep our meeting quiet."

"You mean secret?"

"For now."

She tightened her jaw. "I am no longer a little girl. I can do as I wish. Let us leave my father out of it."

"Very well."

"Go ahead. Show me this secret path, and I will follow."

"This way, then."

He turned and rode quickly through the trees. She spurred the dappled gray to keep up. Soon the forest grew deep, and the shadows thickened. They rode farther in than she would have ever ventured on her own, and she kept close to Loch's flank. Confident that she was an accomplished rider, he kept a quick pace.

"Oh, I almost forgot," she said. "A slight problem—my brother."

"I know. He has followed you all the way from your village. We expected that."

"We?"

"I have companions. They will intercept him. His day should prove to be somewhat interesting."

"He will not be hurt?"

"My promise."

They rode through an opening in the tangled branches of hemlock trees and beyond them into a shallow river before a waterfall. Loch then rode straight through its face. She tapped the gray's flank and leapt through, as well. It was a passage, a doorway. On the other side was a wide, spacious cavern with a pathway cut into the rock.

Aeson had managed to keep his distance from Adrea, careful to avoid giving the impression that he was pacing her, should any onlookers pay note. He considered himself skilled at stealth and planned one day to become a scout for the armies of Galaglea. He had good eyesight and was able to track his sister even though she was no more than a far dot.

When she neared the forest, however, he had no choice but to cross an open field where he would obviously be spotted by any who might be tracking her, as well. He slipped sideways, hugging his mount's right shoulder so that anyone watching from the north would see nothing more than a wandering horse without a rider.

The only problem was his father's hounds, Lamachus's herding hounds. They had followed him from the cabin and kept constantly at his heels. They would only serve to mark him.

"Damn," he swore, hanging from the side of the horse. "Go! Get!" he shouted. "Go home, you boneheads! You will get me caught!"

Finally, he gave up; at least they were keeping close and were not baying.

Eventually, he reached the cobbled road that was the King's Highway, the only roadway that cut through the forest of the East of the Land to the Daathan city of Terith-Aire.

Aeson was used to this light—early dawn; he worked it often, and so he was startled when four riders broke from the trees and had him instantly surrounded. He had been taken completely by surprise. His heart was pounding as he pulled himself upright. The hounds were baying for all they were worth.

These were Daathan warriors, with their darkened breastplates of burnished steel and light, silvery cloaks.

"You, boy! State who you are!" demanded one of them who seemed to have rank—a ring of silver studs on his shoulders. Aeson figured them for captain's tassels.

"I am . . . I am . . ."

"You seem uncertain."

"My name is Aeson."

"And these are attack hounds, Aeson?" the captain shouted over the baying.

"No, no," Aeson said, "they are just plain hounds—for herding."

"Shut them up."

"Quiet. Bobo, Runt! Both of you! Quiet! Quiet!"

They went on baying. They were loyal hounds. Only Lamachus could silence them.

"You are certain they are yours?"

"It is your horses. They are scared of your horses."

"Bobo! Runt!" the captain commanded. "Quiet!"

They stopped baying. Bobo sat on his haunches, his tongue lolling, exhausted.

"Now, boy, explain your purpose on this road."

"Me? Riding. I am just out for a ride."

"Do you always ride hanging sideways from your horse?"

"Oh, that. Practicing. Hoping to be a scout someday."

"Well, you have a distance to go, but that was fairly skilled riding for a boy."

"Thank you, sir."

"Perhaps too skilled for a mere boy. Skilled enough, I might suspect, for an assassin."

"Assassin?"

"Could be you are a scout, riding sideways in early dawn with expertly trained hounds Bobo and Runt, or you could be an assassin, creeping up on the city with ill intent. Archlon, seize him!"

"What?" gasped Aeson.

Archlon, who was huge, leaned forward and effortlessly snatched Aeson from his horse.

"Skinny rat," said Archlon. "Just what you would expect of an assassin."

"It is?" said Aeson, genuinely surprised.

"Assassins are always skinny," the captain said.

"But I am no assassin! I promise!"

"Clever assassins would do no less. Take him to the city, to the maiden's chamber. Stretch him out a bit."

"Wait! Wait, my sister!"

"I see no sister."

"My sister, she is alone—down there—she . . ."

"Alone?" said the captain. "Alone where?"

"Did I say alone?"

"You did."

"No, she is with someone, but I cannot leave her!"

"You indicated she was west, toward the woods?"

"No, I didn't indicate where she was at all."

"Well, not to worry, young Aeson," the captain smiled. "I will find her for you."

"You harm her and, and I swear I will hunt you down!"

"Seems he is an assassin, Captain," said Archlon.

"Plans to sic these attack hounds on me, no doubt."

"You touch my sister, and I will find you. I will make you pay!" Aeson shouted as Archlon rode off with him toward the city, hounds trailing.

Chapter Nine
The Captain Rhywder

The courtyard of Argolis's castle was built on the high, natural granite that capped the cliffs of the Dove Cara. The city was walled with timber and stone ramparts about its outer edges, but the cliff that overlooked the sea was dominated by the castle, a winding, pure white alabaster wonder with twisting, icelike crystal spires that reached to the sky. When the sun hit those spires just right, it would split into myriads of color. They said the castle was built long ago, in the days of Yered when the Daath first came to Earth, and not only was the outside unearthly, but the inside, as well. The castle's stairways and tunnels and rooms were like nothing found elsewhere in Rhywder's travels and he had traveled this mud ball a whole lot of years thus far.

Rhywder believed the voyagers built it, voyagers that sailed from the seventh star—that is what his grandmother told him and she was usually right about most things. Besides, those high-up crystal spires were smooth and unblemished after centuries and yet looked to be fashioned of nothing more than glass. No culture he knew of could manage that.

Sitting there, staring up at the Daathan castle, thinking how it was built by star voyagers, Rhywder had to ask himself: What happed to the ship? If they came in a ship that could sail stars, what had they done with it—misplaced it? Lost it in the woods? If he ever in this life or the next bumped into one of these voyagers, those would be the first words out of his lips: "So what did you do with the ship?" A star ship would sure make the trip south, which he was about to undertake, a whole lot easier.

Rhywder was sitting against the main fountain of the agora. In fact, he was sitting *in* the main fountain, letting the trickle of its cool water sooth his pounding head and run through his unclean beard. He had fulfilled his promise to get falling-down drunk and now he was paying for it. There was a woman involved, and he couldn't remember her face, just as he intended.

His tasseled boots were propped on his bedroll and saddle, which were sitting on the bricked edge of the fountain. His horse wandered not far. They had been together a long while, him and this horse; they knew each other well enough that there was little need for talking. The horse had heard nearly all his stories.

He marveled how the bottom of the well was a kind of silvery polished blue metal. He'd never found metal like that anywhere. Maybe it was the voyagers who brought it along. The center of the well, directly above where the water trickled over the top of his head, was a cluster of ice-spires, just like the spires of the castle. Voyager spires, that's what he called them.

What he really wanted to do, rather than go south and get killed in the jungles, was to sail off on a well-fitted warship and kill Etlantians at sea. They were stripping whole coastlines of villages these days, like eating fruit. He wanted badly to do some slaying, kill as many of these heartless bastards as possible. They ate children, something Rhywder could not abide. The Etlantians had gone bad, no other way to put it. Used to be there were honorable Etlantians. He'd known a few in his time, men he looked up to, men whose eyes held a strange light. But he had not seen one of those in a long time.

All that seemed left of the Etlantians now were these bastard child-eaters. They hunted in well-built, fast-running warships armored in oraculum that bore the rust-red bull's-head insignia of Etlantian raiders. To kill them you had to have a good, skilled, deadly crew that did not panic. That was what he really wanted to do, gather himself a pack of warships, stock them with the best fighters to be found, and start hunting. That stirred his blood even now, sitting here in this fountain. But it was not to be. He was going after a different kind of bastard.

Azazel. He let himself think the name straight out, damned be what might happen. If he wanted, let the high-blood bastard fly through the air and kill Rhywder right here, right in this fountain, just for thinking his name. Azazel was the common name of the angel lord, but it was one that should never be spoken aloud, for it was spellbound. All the names of the angel lords and prefects were spellbound. Speaking their names aloud was heard by them, even if they were a continent or an ocean away. Thinking their names—who knew? Likely they heard the thinking of their names, as well. On this particular morning, being as he had the happy task of venturing into the jungle in front of him, Rhywder just did not give a damn. *Azazel,* he thought again, defiantly. Azazel and his Unchurians—they would be found somewhere past Hericlon's gate. Of course, he could not argue, Eryian was right. Some poor bastard had to go down there and get a read of how many there were and how long before they were going to reach Hericlon.

Suddenly a deep, gravely voice cut into his thoughts.

"Be you the Captain Rhywder?"

He had to hold his hand over his forehead to get a look through the falling water. The big man on the horse in front of him was a shadow blocking out the sun, a huge axeman almost the size of an Etlantian. This had to be Eryian's chosen.

"Who is asking?" said Rhywder.

"What, you avoiding credit seekers or husbands?"

"Just want to know who is asking."

The axeman looked from one side to the other, then back to Rhywder. "Looks to me like I would be the only one here. Which would mean I am doing the asking."

"And . . . you are?"

"I am Agapenor. You are not dressed as any captain I ever met, so if you are one you had best speak up before I get irritated."

"What would happen if you got irritated?"

"Look, this is a simple question I am asking, and I need an answer. Be you the Captain Rhywder or not?"

Rhywder slowly pulled himself to his feet, stepped out of the cool water of the fountain, and lifted his saddle and bedroll off the brickwork. From here out it was going to be a miserable, long hard ride to Hericlon, and from there:

the jungles—nothing he hated worse than the jungles. He walked over, slung the saddle over his horse, and began to cinch it down.

"We will be moving dead south," Rhywder said. "*Dead* being an apt word all considered. We will be keeping a tight pace, as well, so I hope you have a good mount. You have everything in order? Check your rations? Kiss your woman farewell?" Rhywder cinched down the last strap and looked up.

The big Galaglean was right in front of him, dismounted. He seized the Little Fox by the front of his tunic and narrowed his gaze as he growled, "Be you the Captain Rhywder or be you not the Captain Rhywder?"

"I be the Captain Rhywder."

The big man paused. He seemed genuinely surprised. He released Rhywder's tunic as though his fingers were hard to manipulate. "My respectful apologies then, Captain. Just . . . a man needs be sure of things these days."

"We'll not argue that point."

Agapenor handed over the scroll that contained his orders. "I am Agapenor, first captain of the twelfth corps axemen under command of Argolis, king of the Daath, dispatched here by order of the warlord Eryian."

"I guessed."

Rhywder tossed the scroll. He pulled himself into the saddle. "Mount up, Agapenor, first captain of the twelfth; we have now been properly introduced."

Agapenor mounted, wadded up the reins of his horse. He had a large-built charger, one of Eryian's war-stock that took the man's weight well.

"I assume you made all last arrangements, just in case." Rhywder said. "Could turn out to be a tough ride we are about to engage."

"I look at you; I know well enough we are not off to fish for groupers. Yes, Captain, I got things arranged."

Rhywder set off at a lope and Agapenor fell in at his flank.

Chapter Ten

The Ring

At the entrance to the cavern, Loch turned the great mare whose hooves kept dancing, ready to bolt. "Once we go in from here," Loch said, "it is important to keep moving. The tunnels and catacombs in this place keep their own law."

"I will be at your flank."

He paused to light a torch. That's when Loch actually looked at her—really looked at her—wet from the waterfall, her lashes damp, her hair played out in curls. She wore only a herder's leather tunic and a buffed horsehair cloak, but it didn't matter. The full, rich, red hair and unmarred beauty overwhelmed everything about her. Guilt in him wondered if that was why he had brought her, because he was fascinated with her beauty. But he could not ignore the dreams of her, the memories, some of them intimate—her touch, her smell. And so often the dreams held the sting of losing her. He shoved the torch into a saddle brace at the shoulders.

"Follow, keep up."

"I will. I have no desire to be in this place unescorted."

He smiled at that, and then he slapped the reins and started off at a fast trot. The shadows were everywhere. He paid them no attention. As he pressed the horses to a gallop, he commanded any who might be in their path.

"Make way!" he shouted.

There was scampering.

"About to become steep," he told her without looking back, trusting that she was an able rider and could navigate the twisting path.

He turned a sharp corner and for a moment was out of sight. When she followed, she found it was hard rock, slick, wet in places with a pitched grade. This was taking all her skill; she would have fallen if the passage had not been wide enough for switchbacks.

When she reached the bottom and found him waiting for her, she had to draw the gray up and then turn to circle at his side.

"It is true what I have heard," he said. "You are a fantastic rider. I have never seen such a capable horsewoman."

"I thought you said we were to keep moving."

"We should . . . we will. I just . . . I had to admire your skill. Most need assistance down this incline. My compliments, Adrea."

"Most? Are you saying I am not the first you have guided down this path?"

"No, not the first."

"And these poor creatures, the things I see scurrying away in terror of you. What are they?"

"Far from poor creatures. If not for me, they would be at your throat."

"They know you?"

"Let us say they have not forgotten our first encounter." He paused, then stared openly. "What? Is something wrong?"

"No. I was just at a loss for words. Elyon's name, but you are beautiful."

There were echoes in the caverns behind them. One of them was a low, mournful wail, a word she could almost make out, as if it were human.

"My lord," she said, "might we keep moving?"

"Of course." He turned and broke into a hard gallop.

This time, it took all her talent to keep pace. There were times the torchlight reflected off the walls, and for some reason she noticed his night-black hair, the way it was so carefully braided with leather.

"Sharp corners ahead," he shouted. "Keep shy of the walls; they are laced with obsidian carved to rip horseflesh. You should keep well to my right flank."

"I am on your right flank."

He looked back. "Where did you learn to ride like this?"

"Since I could climb up onto one, I have been riding horses."

"It is evident. There are warriors I am certain you could leave in the dust confused and bewildered that a woman had just bested them."

"But not you?"

"No. Not me. Sorry, no disrespect intended."

"None taken."

He lifted his hand, and they slowed a bit. The torch revealed a wide cavern, as wide as a Galaglean mead hall, and though it was naturally formed and stalactites still dripped down onto stalagmites, there were also man-made catacombs with rows of massive granite slabs, some holding sarcophagi. Loch seemed to be slowing out of respect. She noticed that the lettering above the tombs was Etlantian.

At the end of the catacombs, he turned his horse about, pausing. "The path will narrow from here on. And I am sorry to say there are even more pitiful beasts below, bolder than the ones we passed above. Best we stay close together and move swiftly."

"Understood."

She leaned forward, her thighs gripping the dappled gray hard.

Loch flicked the end of his reins on his horse's rump and the white mare bolted into a quick flight. Adrea struggled to keep up with him.

"We will soon reach the lower bowels!" he shouted. "Some years ago a ship smashed into the rock off Dove Cara. Flotsam and jetsam spilled onto the beach, and some of it managed to crawl into the sunken caverns. Living things. They were Failures—the failed generation of the angels' offspring. What they all were doing on that ship, no one really knows, but there were plenty of them, an extraordinary variety of shapes and sizes and features. I have always guessed they were a carnival. In any event, they now make the bowels of the Earth below us their home, and we will have to ride through them. Make sure you show them you are unafraid."

"I will offer my bravest face. How big are they?"

"Some are as the offspring of the early generations, giants; others are smaller even than humans. There are all sorts and sizes, but no need to worry. I am known to them. But you should never try coming here without able escort."

"I have no intentions."

There were shapes scurrying among the shadows, fleeing the flickering light of the torch, but their skin was so pale that Adrea could sometimes make them out. She rode closer to Loch since they seemed itching to rush forward. There were sounds—clicking sounds, sliding sounds, sharp sounds like nails against rock. Once or twice, whispers echoed along the walls, and as before, they sounded human.

"Are you all right?" Loch asked, maintaining the steady pace.

"Yes."

He drew the long sword and shouted a brief war cry, causing lots of quick scatterings of creatures, grunting, running over each other to get out of the way. She saw one of them fleeing—a huge creature on two tiny legs, arms flailing.

"Someone with imagination should come down here and turn them into steady workers," Loch said.

"What do they eat? I have heard the Failures are all cursed, that they can only survive on human flesh and blood. There seem few humans to feed on down here."

"They set traps for passing barges, but apparently they can survive on fish if they have to. But as the curse grows stronger, I find more and more Failures dead of starvation. Even the firstborn of the angels have begun to thirst for human blood."

"What of you? What of the Daath? Are you not the seed of an archangel?"

"But we are not born of women; we are of the mothering star."

She thought of that—how he was not human, how he was what some disgruntled Galagleans, still bitter of the gathering wars, called *breeds*.

He pointed to a corner as they rode past. "Look there," he said.

She noticed a wall, built smooth and well fitted, floor to ceiling, with human bones, mostly thigh bones, but also the tops of skulls used to form symbols.

"Apparently the Failures are not stupid," he said. "Those are words."

She marveled. If they were intelligent enough to write on walls using the skull caps of the humans they'd managed to trap and eat, what could they do? And what purpose could Elyon have for such creatures?

"An underground river emerges just ahead," Loch said. "The horses will be doing a bit of swimming. Anything in your packs you would not want wet?"

"Nothing in my packs."

He urged his mare into the water and the horse went without hesitation, the water up to her neck as she started swimming. Adrea's dappled gray followed trustingly.

They crossed to the other side, then waded through clear, shallow water. Finally, they rode into the open, into what from ancient times had been called the Dove Cara. It was almost like still being in a cavern. All but three sides were high, sheer cliffs. The western edge opened to the dark purple of the Western Sea. She feared the lingering malevolence she had felt above might be even stronger here, but Adrea found her fears misplaced. It was simply too beautiful: high spires of sheer cliffs dripped in foliage and others spilled ribbons of white, crystal falls.

"I can promise we are alone here," Loch said. "In the Dawnshroud it was said that for nine hundred years the Etlantians tried to take this shore, but the sword of Uriel could not be breached. Even to this day, none dare land here. However, you and I, we need not fear; we both have in our veins the blood of Uriel—you through the mothering star of Dannu, and I, if it is to be believed, from the archangel himself."

"How often do you do this? Bring women down here?"

"Why do you ask?"

"Merely curious."

"I am not a womanizer. Not as it is whispered of me. I take comfort in women, but I do not exploit them. Still, there is no comparison. The others I have brought here were for companionship. You are here for a very different reason. You are a Water Bearer, a maid of the lake of Lochlain, where my mother was born and lived." He drew back on the reins and turned to her.

"Odd," he said.

"What?"

"I cannot read you. Most women, I can see through as if they were glass, but not you. Nothing. You must be very powerful."

"I have never thought of myself as powerful."

"You are also very brave."

"Brave? You said we came alone. What do I have to fear except you? Should I fear you, Loch?"

"Are you familiar with the Book of Angels?"

She nodded.

"There is a passage in the fourth chapter: 'In those days the stars shall forget their path, and the Earth will tilt, and all of time will begin to turn toward the mirrored abyss.' Are you familiar with it?"

"Since I was young I have listened to any singer, any Follower who passed through our village. Yes, I have heard these words."

"I have trained all my life to face the prophecy of that passage. What I am about to tell you, I bid you listen with the knowledge that was gifted you as a Water Bearer, as a child of Lochlain, the birthplace of my mother. You may have no idea how strong *the knowing* is in you, but it is very strong, and it will be only through that gift you will discern the truth of what I am about to tell you. Let your powers judge my words, and you will know I speak no lies."

That startled her, for she understood what he meant. All her life, she had been able to spot a lie, even when not directed to her, even when spoken from afar. The gift of seeing truth was strong in her, and the Daath knew it. It appeared he was about to depend upon it, which worried her a bit.

The wind off the sea seemed suddenly colder, and she stared at the dark blue waters, not really wanting to hear what he was about to tell her. Feelings, whisperings, they were coming at her swiftly, too swiftly, leaving her off balance. She began to wonder if coming had been a mistake after all.

"Before you say more," she asked, "can you tell me, Loch, if are you a Follower?"

"I believe in the truths given by my mother. Yes, Enoch is a seer, but his days are numbered, and his people cannot save this world. I would be his protector if I could reach him, but they will destroy Enoch, and his city will be left like an empty hole in the center of the deep. And you—you are a Follower?"

"Always."

"Yet, none have taught you to find them, the singers of Enoch. Your father made you swear an oath to stay away from them. Still, you went. And even though you are a Water Bearer, none of your so-called elders have invited you to counsel; no mentor has taken you aside to teach you of the secrets, have they?"

"Perhaps because I have not inquired."

"They fear you. They fear your eyes; they know you carry the light in you so strong it would blind them, so they pretend to keep you a mere initiate. But, in fact, they have nothing to teach you. Each day you grow in the light your ancients called the star knowledge. You do not know who you are. Let me guess; you have this sense you have been sleeping and you cannot wake up?"

"Perhaps . . ."

"This is why I have brought you here, to help you find yourself. For instance, your name, Adrea, means child of the wine dark sea. You were named for this water, the water out there, the dark, the deep of it. It is called by seafarers the terror water. Hundreds of ships have been lost in it, never to return." He stared a moment, his eyes no longer soft, growing more and more serious. "It is why you come alone to the cliffs so often, why you stare over the ocean searching for something you cannot name. You are kindred of this sea; it is your soul."

"How can you know such things? How can you know secrets I've never told a single person, not even my own mother?"

He fingered something about his neck. She noticed it for the first time, a ring on a silver chain. "I have been searching for you a long time. I have looked carefully, making certain always there were no mistakes. It is not me that knows these things about you, Adrea. My magic pales before yours. The ring led me to you." His eyes were now dark, intense. "It belonged to my mother. As she lay dying, she set it in my hand, curled my fingers about it. It has been my curse ever since. It has given me dreams, visions."

Adrea knew his mother was the last queen of the Daath, Asteria. She was the most famed of all Water Bearers. She was called the Little Seer, because she was small and frail. But Adrea knew, by faith, that she had been Elyon's chosen. Suddenly it struck her. She hadn't thought of him that way, but this was the son of a prophet.

"Come," he said, dropping from the horse. "Walk with me a time."

He helped her dismount, then let her reins dangle.

"Let them wander," he said.

"What about the creatures back in the cavern?"

"They know I am here; they will stay well hidden."

Adrea and Loch began to walk along the surf's edge, the beauty and wonder of the Dove Cara all about them like a mirage.

"Would it offend you if I spoke further of your powers?" he asked. "It seems no one has bothered telling you that you are not ordinary. Some know, some of your elders, but they have chosen to keep it secret. Perhaps they hope you will not discover it yourself."

"Why should they hope that?"

"Because their powers, in comparison, are no more than common tavern tricks."

"I still do not understand how you know me so well."

"You bear the blood of the archangel. Not as I. It does not tint your skin or give you night vision, but it courses through your veins; it runs through you like a pure, crystal stream. My knowing—my inner knowledge—comes from the Light of Severity, the burning light of Elyon, but yours is given of the mothering star, the *Light Whose Name Is Splendor.* That is our difference, why you are called human and why I am called a *breed.* Your knowledge, your sense of things, comes not from training, but directly from the blood of your ancestors. It is gifted."

"But why? My mother, though she walked the path of the Water Bearer, knew of no spell bindings or star knowledge," Adrea said.

"You do not mention your grandmother."

"She was different."

"Yes, very different. When I was young, I wondered the same of myself during my training, so much so I even fought heaven to understand why such feelings were in me. And we are left on our own. Like all of Elyon's chosen, we are simply thrown to the wind, like leaves—left to fight its currents. Any guidance we receive is useless to us. He leaves us to find our path alone. Yet, here you are, Adrea, knowing the names of stars that no one taught you, effortlessly following their paths, understanding secrets scholars spend a lifetime searching for."

She did not deny she knew the names of stars and that she understood things of which others seemed utterly unaware.

He reached behind to unlatch the silver chain about his neck. He let the ring it had secured fall into his hand. Adrea could not take her eyes off it. The capstone was a deep, dark purple like a diamond, and yet looked soft, palpable.

"She died four and ten years from this very day," Loch said. "It was why I chose it as the day I would bring you. Some say she died of illness, that she was frail always, even from birth. None of that is true. She was murdered. And this is not only her ring, but also the ring worn of five queens before her. It was forged from the light of the mothering star, Dannu. But on Earth it has always been known as the Ring of the Water Bearer. Before you, my mother was the last born seer of the Lake People, the Lochlains."

"Before me? But I am Galaglean. My father, Lamachus, he is the son of—"

"He has raised you his own, but he is not your father. Your father—a Lochlain, like your mother—fell in battle many years ago. Your mother and Lamachus chose not to tell you."

Adrea gasped. All he had said thus far had rung true, but this, that Lamachus was not her blood father—though it was not a lie, it did take away her breath for a moment. Maybe she had known, but she had been so young, and it had been so long, it was something that had slipped away. Yet, she knew he was speaking true. There was no Galaglean blood in her.

"I still do not understand how you could possibly know these things," she said, slightly angered.

"You cannot guess? The ring. I know because of the ring. For me, it has always spoken in dreams. I wear it about my neck, and the dreams have haunted me all my life. If I could have thrown this ring into the ocean, I would have. But I could not. It was all I had of her. All I had of you, if you choose to think of it that way.

"Your mother, her people—they were a proud race. They refused to give in to Argolis's demand that the tribes of Dannu be united. They cherished their separateness, and perhaps with good reason; their faith was pure. So the elders of the Lochlain chose to make a stand. They fought him, the greatest warrior on earth, and they but simple people of the lake. Yet Argolis believed his cause was the command of Elyon, and he delivered it without mercy. Either the tribes would be united, or they would be destroyed, and the Lochlains were almost completely wiped out. Your mother escaped with the Galagleans, taking you with her, hiding you. Perhaps that is why she has never told you of your true lineage. She hoped to protect you, but the truth be known, you and your mother are the last true Water Bearers living on this earth."

"But there are many in Lucania," Adrea countered

"Pretenders. They have no gifts of blood, but they struggle to keep their ancient faith alive. They initiate chosen girls into the cult. Your mother almost did not let you go, but she understood that to deny your blood would be to sin against the mothering star. Yet she never told you how strong is the blood that flows through your veins. She knows; she sees it in you, but she fears for you, as well. She did what she did to protect you."

"The Daath, I understand, have chosen only the kindred of the lake as their queens? For centuries. Only the Water Bearers," Adrea added.

"Yes. I have been told the reason is that the light of the mothering star leaves our own light less harsh, less cruel, and that each queen chosen purifies the blood of Uriel. Otherwise, we would become slayers, cruel and uncaring. The blood of your people has softened our mettle."

He stopped and presented her the ring.

"What?" she gasped.

"Take it."

"I . . . I cannot."

"Have you not been listening, Adrea? This ring belongs to you. Somewhere, inscribed in its shank, is your name, foretold ages ago."

She looked into his eyes. Loch was attempting to appear stern and hard, but Adrea saw something else, something that drew her—the part of the warrior-poet left broken by the death of his mother.

"One count of the moon ago," he continued, "something, someone made a failed attempt to create an opening in the fabric of time. You must have felt it, as well. I suspect it was one of the angels, one of their weakest. He must have lost the light and panicked, attempting a time rift that would allow him to escape this future to find another. But this fallen creature's failed incantation changed the course of all the Earth, moving everyone, everything closer to Aeon's End. The signs you have seen in the heavens mark the theft of years that otherwise were our last innocence, years meant to be ours—time we would have shared, grown to know each other, love each other naturally as we should have." He paused. "Take it."

"What?"

"Take the ring in your hand until it is warmed by your flesh. It will find you quickly, as if you were its child. And when that happens, look into the stone, and tell me what you see."

"Why should what I see matter in all this?"

His temper again flashed. "Not much matters, Adrea, only an entire living world—everything that exists in Assiah, the world of being. Forgive me, I should be kinder to you but this ring—it is no longer mine. It belongs to you now."

He touched her wrist, turned her hand, and placed the ring in her palm. He closed her fingers about it and continued to hold her hand while he studied her eyes.

"My mother's last request of me is fulfilled. Her dying words. *Find her, find the eleventh Water Bearer.*"

Instantly, Adrea felt the ring coming alive in her hand, warming to her skin—a careful touch, a woman's touch. It was *the knowing* that had whispered all these years inside her wakening, coming fully alive. It was the touch of Asteria; it was as if the light of the mothering star, Dannu, had touched Adrea's palm.

It came too quickly for her. Frightened, she pulled her hand away and opened her fingers. For a moment it looked so ordinary. The purple stone was turned to the side where, thankfully, she could not see into its center. But even the shank filled with light. She began to see visions.

"It is ancient," said Loch. "It is from the days of Dawnshroud. It has not connected with the light of the mothering star. It has been dark these many years."

"Loch, this frightens me."

"I know. It frightened me, as well, and when first the dreams spoke to me, I was but a boy nine years old. You are the one it has searched out, Adrea. Your touch alone has lit the script of the Pleiades."

She noticed the writing now, tiny, etched with perfection. She could not guess what visions threatened, but the touch of the shank whispered to her that in aeons past she had held this ring, and with that sudden knowledge, swift memories spilt through her, and she could not turn them back. They were memories of him—of Loch.

She had known him not only in this world but also in so many others. They had traveled together for Aaeons unspoken. In this life, the veil had cloaked the memories, but the power of the ring, locked inside for so long, melted the veil and memories fell like rain.

They had been lovers, voyagers; together they had sailed many stars. She remembered those ships, the star ships, how they were dark and swift, how they moved, soundless.

She drew in a sharp breath. It was madness. She wanted to throw the ring into the ocean.

"This . . . these things I feel," she said. "They cannot possibly be my memories; they must belong to someone else, other queens."

"Yours," he answered. "And you know it. No use in trying to run from it."

She looked up and remembered his face as if she hadn't seen it for years. She remembered him kind and gentle, but also fierce in battle, and she remembered that these same eyes had blackened and turned on her in fury—a temper as strong as her father's. He was like a fiery wind, unpredictable, and as much as she had loved him, she had also feared him.

They had always lived life amid fires, within tempests. Yet, despite her almost desperate fear, she knew he was all she had, and she knew as well that in her heart, throughout the aeons, she had cherished him despite the demons that raged within him.

Now she understood. She knew why he had been forced to find her and what it meant—the time that had been stolen by this rogue angel. For her and Loch, it was a lifetime stolen.

"Loch." She whispered, his name no longer strange to her, neither his name, nor his touch, nor his skin, nor his smell. "I . . . I cannot go on," she said. "It is all too much, too fast."

As she stared at him, tears flooded, tears for so many lives gone. How many times had she watched him die, clutched in her arms?

She closed her eyes, tight, as if to block the visions. "Take it back," she said. "Take it back now! I cannot bear these memories!"

"For me," he answered sadly, "they came always as dreams. There were many dreams, but dreams of you were the ones of comfort. When I was younger, you were often just this . . . this feminine presence, but your presence, it kept me strong—alive. Without your presence, so many times I would have failed had it not given me courage, a reason to hold on when reason held no sanity."

"And now?" she asked.

"What are you asking?"

"Now, Loch, what is it now? Are you weak or strong?"

"Neither. I am angry. Fear is meaningless; it does not change my path or my purpose."

"Lochlain, I know in times past I have been . . . I have been your salvation. Your safety—even your sole comfort. But it cannot be this time. I cannot save you, Loch."

"You think this is about protecting me? No, Adrea. You have gifts, but I see the future clearer than you. You could not possibly change what comes against me. It is not about that—we are both insignificant."

He didn't say more, but what he implied struck her, chilled her. She almost couldn't breathe. It could not be happening. This was all impossible!

"Adrea . . ."

She looked up. His eyes had softened somewhat, but they were intense, serious. "We must be sealed. It cannot wait." He motioned over his shoulder. Startled, she looked in the direction indicated and saw a horseman. The sight of him shivered through her like ice. He was a giant, an Etlantian, the scion of an angel. He waited at the far end of the Dove Cara, near the cliff, and he did not move or flinch; he simply watched them from a shining black steed.

"He is here to bear witness," Loch said. "He is an Etlantian, but from ancient time. The light is still with him. This one is a priest, a holy scion. His name is Sandalaphon. He carries a sunblade, the terrible weapon of an angel, and since the days of Uriel, since the Daath were sent of Elyon to this Earth, his sword has been the protector of our seed. He knows the reason I have brought you here."

"Sealed . . . you mean . . ."

"Adrea, I am so sorry. If I could, if heaven allowed, I would put this sword through my heart. Forgive me, but you must turn the ring now. You must look into the stone."

"No, I cannot do that."

"Search your heart."

She stared at him through her own tears. With the back of one hand she angrily wiped them away. "It cannot be me! None of this. It cannot be!"

He waited a moment before speaking further. "There is something else you must know."

"Something else! What else could there be?"

"When you look in the stone, you will open a passage to heaven that is known as the eye of Daath. The second it opens, others will see it—the angels, their minions. And when they do, in that instant they will send out ships. They will send out their winged ones, their fliers with their thousand eyes searching like screamers through the sky. They will hunt us. And if they find us, everything your people and my people have struggled for all these years, everything for which the Earth was intended, will be lost."

"Angels? Angels will hunt us? And how do we flee from angels?"

"Faith's Light."

Her breath came in short gasps now. "No, no, none of this can be happening."

She struggled to control the panic, and did, forcing it from her by simply screaming at the sky. She looked up to him and narrowed her brow, angry.

"You are wrong," she said. "He is wrong—that horseman. All of this is wrong, and if I must, I will prove it to you. I will look into your stone, and when I do you will see that someone, something, even heaven, if that is what speaks here—is wrong. I am not the one! So you can watch and when I do look in this stone of yours, you will know: I am not the *chosen*!"

She turned the shank and looked directly into the dark purple stone, dead into its center.

With a pulse, like an implosion, there was sudden silence, and everything was bathed in sheer light, light that should have been blinding, burning; light that should have been so intense that it should have melted skin and turned the sand to glass, but there was no pain, no heat. It was pure light, soft light.

And then the images rushed her; they flashed, blurred in lightning strokes that came so fast, so swiftly and furiously that she did not breathe at all, but she did see everything, every movement, every minute detail, a million, million images all in seconds.

And then, finally, the images stopped and the Dove Cara melted to a field of battle, but it was a battle that encircled the entire globe. It was like nothing she had ever witnessed or could even have imagined: the sword and axe flaying, arms cloven, men falling, screams, the thick smell of blood. A bull roared as its flesh was pierced, and a horse shrieked as it was sliced from one side to the other. Women wailed. Children cried out. Men's faces everywhere were twisted and ugly. Nothing here was beautiful or brave or glorious.

Then everything stilled—frozen. Nothing moved. Slowly, Adrea looked up. She saw the Seraphon, standing not far from her, and when he met his mother's eyes, in the flicker of an instant, a thousand, thousand souls screamed, and the angels wept as their sons died in their arms, and the light of Uriel's sword blinded everything, pierced all time as the Earth passed into the great and endless abyss of Ain, spilling into it like falling over a great waterfall of endless pillars streaming downward into nothingness.

When the vision finally ended, Adrea could not believe she was still standing, yet she was. The blue sky folded in above them, and they were once more standing in the calm white sand of the Dove Cara. Inside her, from her soul, her heart, a voice whispered. It was a soft voice and she knew whose voice it was. It was Dannu: the *Light Whose Name Is Splendor.*

Go now, child, walk in Elyon's blessing, Water Bearer, and be quick, child, cling with all you have to the thin, silver tendril that is Faith'sLight.

It was over. It had been more terrifying than anything she could ever have imagined. Tears streamed down her cheeks until there were no tears left. She fell into Loch's arms, hugging him. Her fingers dug into his back.

"It pierces like a knife," she whispered.

He held her tight, and she felt his own tears, wet and cold, as they touched her neck.

"It is true," she said, "all of it—everything. It is truth."

"Yes. Truth. I am but the willow. The final queen shall bear the oak."

She swallowed past the tight knot in her throat. "Do it," she said, not a request. "Do it now."

He shut his eyes tightly. He lifted his face to the heavens. "By the Boundless and Limitless Light I speak, by the Son of Women I speak, by the mirrored shadow of the Creator Star I take you, Adrea, forever, and for all of time."

She wept quietly through it all, as he took her, as he laid her in the sand. She wept as never she had wept before.

Chapter Eleven

Actors

In the courtyard beyond the castle, Aeson waited anxiously. He was surrounded by the same four warriors that had taken him that morning, but his day had been extraordinary. There were simply no words that could describe that particular day, but that was fine because it would be a day Aeson planned to never speak of to anyone. He felt such relief seeing Adrea coming toward him. Of course he was a bit embarrassed; surely she was going to have a good laugh, but at least it was Adrea. She could be trusted to keep a secret.

As they rode up to Aeson and the Daathan guards, Adrea at first did not realize who he was, even though Bobo and Runt were sitting at the heels of his horse. She was still filled with terrifying afterimages of the ring she had tucked in her belt pouch. She dared not keep it on her finger, not yet—even though Loch had told her to. It frightened her and so it remained in her belt pouch where its warmth was like a living thing against her skin.

After such visions it was good to know the world was still intact. It was dusk, cool, and riding through the streets of the Daathan city with its white spires was nothing short of ethereal. Then she realized the figure on the horse amid the guards they were approaching was actually Aeson. He was unharmed, but they had dressed him as royalty—the finest of royalty—as if he were about to attend a royal banquet or ball. The only problem—his clothes were of the wrong gender. They had dressed him as a girl.

"It looks as if they took him to the maiden's chamber," Loch said as they approached.

"What?"

"I must apologize for my companions; they have an odd sense of humor. I am sure they led him to believe the maiden's chamber contained something other than maidens—torture devices and such. But it actually is the residence of the, ah, the women of the palace."

"Your women?"

"Yes, once, but that has ended now. Be assured I have a single companion, here and ever after. Still, it looks as if the girls had a bit of fun with your little brother."

They drew up beside him and Loch nodded with respect. "You must be Aeson."

Aeson swallowed nervously, but attempted to answer unshaken. "Yes, and you are?"

"My name is Lochlain. I am the son of Argolis."

Aeson's face paled. He glanced to Adrea, even to the other guards, before looking back to Loch. "You are the prince?"

"Yes. Your sister will explain everything. You both need to be leaving, I'm afraid. I have promised your sister you would reach home before sundown."

Aeson nodded. "Yes, yes, a good idea. Our father, he has a short . . . what I mean is, he would be expecting us and he might be worried if we were . . . late."

Loch smiled at Adrea; she half-smiled back.

"Well, we cannot have that," said Loch.

It was strange, but part of Adrea didn't want to leave. She wanted to see the cottage, her mother, even Lamachus, but what she felt for Loch was something new for her, something she had never felt for anyone. She loved him. How odd. The morning before she hadn't known anything about him and now he was this someone she loved, this someone she couldn't live without. Her husband—this was her husband and a large part of her did not want to leave his side, even for one night. The ring's memories had so changed everything. She felt confused, lost between worlds.

Earlier, before they left the Dove Cara, Loch had explained why it was important to return home. He had told her that for now it was the only way to keep her safe—to hide her by letting it appear she was what she had been that morning before setting out to meet him—a maiden of Lucania, the daughter of a herdsman about to marry a horse breeder. Apparently, they would soon be hunted, now that she had opened the eye of Daath.

"We will hide you by pretending. The ring will help. It is not strong enough to hide you if any were close, but they are far from here and none were expecting what has happened this day. For now they can search using only their blind sight, the eyes they can send across the sky to find things hidden in far places. So what you do is pretend the day never happened."

"Pretend? You can explain to me how I pretend all this away?"

"I know it will not be easy. Myself, I have been trained to block my thoughts. Eryian, my master, he can hide himself standing right in front of you. I have learned a similar skill of mind, though my skill is that of a child's compared to his. Still, I know how to hide in thought. Think of it as it must have been when you played with dolls. Assuming you did such things. And do not forget, you must use the ring, you must let it teach you hiding."

"How?"

"Ask it—just will it to hide your thoughts. That is all I know to explain it. I never really understood how it works, how it does what it does. It belongs to a queen—it was never really mine. Mostly it teaches you. It has no secret powers, other than the power to teach. But I believe it can help you hide your thoughts, at least for one night."

"One night?"

"Yes. I have a ship fitted and a crew of marines. They are deadly, very capable. And the ship is a runner, built to move swift. The pilot is able to navigate deep water. Most pilots must keep near the shore, but he is talented, which makes him expensive, but then—as you might guess—coin is not a problem. Still, he is not so talented as to attempt running unfamiliar deep water at night. So we will hide in pretense until tomorrow's dawn."

"A ship? We are leaving tomorrow?" She was stunned, but he seemed to think little of it.

"There is no choice; we must become runners. Tomorrow we will vanish into the Western Sea."

She sighed. Before, such news would have left her panicked, but the ring had already taught her enough to understand. She was to leave everything. There was no choice in it. Her whole world had changed completely, so quickly it seemed already only a memory. It struck her with sadness, but at the same time, the horse breeder, he was to have taken her away, as well. Marcian Antiope was planning to take her to his land in Galaglea to the north. She would have rarely, if ever, seen her family again. How was this so different—other than the eyes of the angels even now soaring through the skies hunting for her?

"I am so sorry," he said.

"Are you?"

"Yes. It does not present the same problems to me, but for you, I can only imagine. And yes, Adrea, I am truly sorry."

She glanced downward with a sigh. None of this was his fault. If she had anyone to blame, it might be Elyon Himself, but since she was but a small girl, even from the time she had begun to understand her world, there had been this love for whatever or whomever He was, and it came from her heart and soul. It had never left her and never would.

She could tell Loch was struggling to make this as easy as he could for her, but how could he do that?

"The deep waters of the west will cloak us," he explained, "the same waters you have so often felt drawn to. It is because they are the realm of the Followers and the place where lies the island that bears the city of Enoch. Even the angels have trouble hunting those waters, seeing through them. The faith of Enoch obscures their sight."

"But did you not say the city of Enoch would be destroyed?"

"In time, but even then, I could be wrong. I have not studied the futures with devotion. Still, think about it, Adrea, if we can find him, who better to guide us than a prophet who has looked upon the very face of Elyon? We have the Western Sea to hide us and a prophet to tell us how to survive whatever must follow. And we have each other. We are neither of us ordinary, we will learn. Do not be frightened."

She nodded, but she was frightened, very frightened—she could almost picture them, the blind sight, the angel eyes that flew, searching, the hunters already hunting—not things easily dismissed.

Seeing her fear, his eyes went from brown to black; they changed as she watched, even their shape, narrowing. Suddenly, he was the Daath. The Shadow Walker had stepped into his skin. He looked less human now, but determined, strong, even assured. Perhaps he thought that was what she needed.

"They will not get to you," he said, a promise. "I am not going to let you be harmed, Adrea. I will protect you. Why else have I trained all my life if not for this?"

"I believe you, Loch."

"And the one in the dream, the reason we have joined, I will not let any harm come to him, either. You are both my charge, why I have been trained since birth, since I could walk or speak. Eryian, my master—every day of my life I have studied, trained. It is no mere illusion. I am a Shadow Walker, so now comes the time I walk the shadows, and you will walk them with me."

"Why not make our stand here, surrounded by the invincible legions of the Daath?"

"A legion can protect against armies, against satraps and kings and princes—but not assassins. If the shadows of the night want us, legions are useless against them. We must become runners."

"Forever?"

"Who can see forever? Let Faith's Light hold forever. We will focus on the path directly before us—and the path for now is that we become runners."

She took a long breath. He was being as careful as he could with her, but there was a vapor of anger running through him and she knew him well, from memories. She knew his anger could quickly become rage, though she understood it was not against her, the anger was from his frustration, how they had lost time, how their lives had literally been stolen.

"It will be as you say, Loch. I will start pretending now. Aeson and I, we need to be back before dark, and not let Lamachus get angst ridden and riled as he did yesterday."

"Yes, yes, it seems silly, considering all we face, but those are the kinds of thoughts you must put in your head. Use the ring, it will help."

She nodded.

"Tomorrow's dawn we leave for the protection of Enoch's sea."

"I will be ready."

"I am not certain exactly when I will come for you, but it will be early dawn, so stay near the cabin and keep watch."

"I will."

"And your good-byes . . ." he paused. "Let your heart speak them as you wish. I do not have family, but you—family is your world. I know how hard it must be. At least I can guess how hard."

"You have no family, Loch?"

"The warlord, but he has kept his distance. He cares, but is a strict master. Whatever his reasons, he has never gotten close. I guess emotions are not part of becoming a Shadow Walker."

"What about these girls? They say you have girls, women—people whisper of it."

"My harem?"

"Yes—are they not like family?"

"No. They are companions. And it is not as people say. I have kept myself pure. I just . . . they are friends, that is all. Finding me gone, I suppose some will weep. A few of them care. I keep them because I have always preferred the company of women, but I have never loved any of them. I have not loved anyone since the death of my mother."

"Why?"

"You cannot guess?"

"No."

"I have kept my mother's ring about my neck on that silver chain all my life. The reason I have loved no one is because of the girl in the dreams. The ring left her as real as flesh. I have loved only her, with all my heart. The Water Bearer. You. I have only loved you, Adrea."

She nodded. She well understood the power the ring had over memories.

"What about your father?"

"We will not talk about my father."

"Why?"

"Not ever. We do not even mention his name." He clenched his teeth. "I have no father," he swore. "Understood?"

"Very well, Loch. We will not speak of him."

He took a breath, burying some emotion. "When you speak your good-byes, one thing you must remember is that you cannot tell any of them the truth. Even your brother, no matter how close he is to you. No matter how much you trust him. You cannot leave any truths behind that can be traced. I am not you, but if it were my decision—I might just let them believe in this rumor that the Daath sneak into the village of Lucania and steal women, and it turns out you were one of them."

"But would that not be a truth?" she said and half-smiled, trying to ease his tension.

"I suppose you have a point," he said, but he did not smile. His emotions ran deep, she could tell he struggled hard to keep them in check—that being a minstrel turned warrior had never come easy for him. Emotion was something he would never be comfortable with.

"I will follow you, Loch," she said earnestly. "I know your heart as I know my own. But maybe you can tell me what to do with these images still screaming in my head?"

"Use the ring. Take it out of your belt and put it on your finger."

"Put it on my finger. Maybe I should just show it to Lamachus, point out how beautiful the stone is."

"I see what you mean. Maybe . . . perhaps you could wear gloves."

"Why did I not think? Of course, I wear gloves all the time." Finally, a smile from him. She took his hand. "I understand, Loch. I know my world has changed, that we must hide, we must become runners, and for tonight I must pretend. I trust you, I believe in you, so I will do my very best at pretending. And, in fact, I did play with dolls. It was not that long ago, I suppose."

"Good. The ring will help. It may even let you fool yourself, let you slip back into your familiar world—turn reality into a dream and make the dream reality. It did that for me on occasion, let me escape. Just pour your thoughts through the ring."

They returned through the caverns and back to Terith-Aire. But she did not realize it was Aeson they were riding up to until they had almost reached him. Once close, she had to smile because he made quite a pretty girl—hair in braids with lace and baby's breath flowers. He wore a rich, gilded bodice. His eyes were painted and he had on an expensive silk tunic and skirt. Those alone were worth more than her entire wardrobe.

"Do you know the way out of the city?" Loch asked him.

"Yes, certainly," he answered as if insulted.

"Then I will trust her to you."

"Fine. I mean thank you . . . your majesty."

Loch turned to Adrea. He held up his hand and spread his fingers in the sign of the word. She returned it, saddened that she was leaving him so soon. To love someone so true and so deep, it was a kind of madness. Perhaps in time that would change.

"Faith's Light," he said. He backed his horse away and nodded to Aeson. "Safe journey, Aeson."

"Thank you, your majesty."

Aeson pulled on the reins, turning the horse, and left at a gallop, anxious to be gone. Adrea paused only briefly before she turned to follow.

Once past the gates of the Daathan city, once away from the smell of them, Aeson slowed his pace and rode alongside Adrea at a lope so they could talk. He drew back his lip. "Maiden's chamber," he cursed. "They first threatened me as an assassin and threw me in this maiden's chamber where they told me the truth would be stretched out of me. But it turned out there was nothing in there but actual maidens, and they . . . they did this to me." He glanced at her.

"And you? What was it all about? What did he want with you?"

"I will explain when the time is right."

"He is planning to abduct you, is he not?"

"Do I look abducted?"

"No, but I saw the look in his eye. It was as if he already owned you. He is going to take you. Tell me I am wrong."

"As I said, I will explain in time."

"Why not now?"

"Because *now* is not a good time."

"Lochlain, son of Argolis—they spoke of him as if he were some god, his maidens. They told me they were his attendants, whatever that implies. I have heard that the Daathan prince is touched. You know, a little bit crazy. His women certainly are. What did you think? Is he touched?"

"Perhaps a bit."

"Well, I do not trust any of them, Adrea, not one of them. And look what they did to me! You should not trust them, either. He is a prince that keeps all those women like a stable of fine horses. He is most likely planning to add you as another mare. These Daath—Father is right, they are all mad." He glanced behind. "Are they following?"

"No, we are alone."

"I will not trust that until we are home beside the hearth."

Aeson was riding with grim determination, despite the fluttering, expensive veils. When they reached the northern pasture, he paused to think things over.

"We should split up," he decided.

"You think?"

"Yes, I will need to take the long way around, perhaps down past the stream where I can muddy myself up."

Adrea stared at him a moment, taken by the way they had painted his eyes, green malachite with the top of his lids dark, extending outward across his temples. She would like to try that herself.

"Stop staring at me," he demanded.

"I am just admiring the workmanship."

"You know, Father said the gathering was all a plot of the Daath. I think he is right. I think things were far better off when we were separate tribes, doing as we pleased."

"How would you know? You were not born yet."

"I just know. I am guessing. The gathering wars were a mistake. We were fine with our old ways."

"We still have our old ways, Aeson. The Daath have forced nothing on us."

"You are defending them now?"

"No, just pointing out they did not force their ways or their faith on any of the tribes; they merely united them."

Aeson paused, pulled a strand of baby's breath from his eyelid, and stared at it, puzzled. "What is this?"

"It is woven all through your hair."

"They have put flowers in my hair!"

"Along with gold filet. What did they do with your clothes?"

"I do not want to talk about what they did, at all, any of it. Is that all right with you?"

"Of course."

"In fact, it will be fine when I can wash this off, get back in my own clothes, and forget this day ever happened. Throw all this down some well."

"Perhaps you could save me the bodice?"

He lowered one brow, but this only made Adrea chuckle.

"You go straight for the cottage," he said. "I will circle around through the village and come over the west fence, try to crawl in the back window. Maybe I can sneak in and change clothes before Father spots me."

"Let us hope so."

"I find nothing about this humorous."

"Perhaps I should get you a hand mirror."

"Ha, very funny, it is all a big joke, I suppose."

"Just make sure as you circle through the village that none of the boys make ill advances toward you. Be very firm with them, Aeson."

"I can handle this. I have been in worse situations."

"All right, but take my word for it, some of these boys can be quite bold."

He gave her a last warning glance, turned the horse sharply, and started down the hill. She smiled watching him ride off, straight in the saddle, braided hair bouncing, veils streaming. But once he had gone, she felt sadness close over her. The memories were swiftly returning. She reached into her belt and slipped the ring over her finger, whispering to it in her mind, *hide me, return me to simple ways.*

Then she noticed something. It was a figure, far to the north, along the edge of the forest, watching. It was Sandalaphon, the protector of the Daath. She was one of them now. But the idea that she was to be their queen seemed impossible.

Aeson rode past the tall twisted oak that marked the east field, down its embankment, and started through a shallow stream below. He pulled up on the reins, and was about to dismount—at least wash some of the gunk off, when he openly gasped. "Oh, God . . ." he muttered silently.

Lamachus was coming directly toward him, moving slow, pushing several head of cattle before him. Aeson panicked, but there was nowhere to turn. All he could do was wait and hope. Maybe Lamachus wouldn't notice. But just in case, he began desperately trying to quickly think up some explanation.

As he passed, Aeson's father actually did not notice at first. Lamachus simply nodded with a curious glance, a glance one would offer an interesting stranger, and rode through the stream lazily. He looked pretty tired. His thinning hair was sweaty and tangled, his face was dusty. Poor Lamachus. He was so tired from finding all the baron's cattle that he hadn't even noticed a golden-fileted, painted trollop in the middle of his eastern field. Aeson held his breath.

Suddenly, Lamachus paused, pulling up on the reins. Slowly, he turned in the saddle, squinting. Then his mouth dropped open. He turned the horse sharply, splashed through the stream, and pulled up directly in front of Aeson, staring, astonished.

"Good God! Boy, is that you?"

Aeson swallowed, uncertain he had voice. "Yes, Father. It is me."

"Blessed mother of us all!"

"Am I ever glad to see you, Father."

"Explain that to me, boy."

"Well, this morning I . . . I was near the road looking for cows, when suddenly . . ." He paused a moment.

"Yes, yes—when suddenly?"

"When suddenly this caravan passed. Lots of painted wagons."

"A caravan?"

"Yes. Actors, I believe."

"Actors?"

Aeson nodded. "I think so. I first tried to outrun them. But they had fast horses."

"Actors with fast horses?"

"Yes. Surprising, is it not? You would not think acting paid that well."

"But why on God's good earth do you believe actors would run you down?"

"I wondered of that! I did!"

Lamachus curled his lip. "And?"

"Perhaps there were not enough actors. For their play, I mean. Perhaps it was just a very important play and they needed another. They were headed for Terith-Aire. Yes, thinking on it now, they must have needed another player very badly. For the part of a girl. Which is . . . which explains why they . . . ah . . . tied me up and did this to me."

Lamachus stared wide-eyed. His mouth parted but he said nothing.

"I know . . . it must sound odd, but—"

"Odd? Boy, that is the most amazing story I have ever heard and it makes no damned sense at all."

"No?"

"Not a shred of sense."

"I suppose not."

"But it is obvious what has happened here."

"It is?"

"Slavers."

"What?"

"Good God, they were slavers. Not actors!"

"You think so?"

"Well, of course I think so! God gave me a brain, though you must have stepped out of line to void your piss when they were being handed out! Think on it! If someone tied me up and painted me like a trollop, I would not for the love of frogs think actors had done it!"

"Ahhh . . ."

"Lord, boy, we all know good actors are hard to find, but to think they would kidnap villagers to play parts! God save us." Lamachus shook his head. "Must have been planning to sell you on the block. But how could the fools take you for a girl!"

Aeson thought this over. "Perhaps . . ."

Lamachus waited.

"Well . . . they knew I was not a girl, but—look at me."

"Indeed," Lamachus mumbled. "On my mother, you look fit to be married! God in heaven, I would marry you. You should kiss the earth, boy. Give thanks you have escaped!"

"Yes, indeed, I should."

"Had they sold you and some merchant discovered your private organs, he might have had them removed, God help you—or worse he might have preferred them." Lamachus slapped Aeson hard on the back. "You have done well! Outran slavers!"

"Yes—thank God."

"Let us for home, son. We have both had trial this day! Those damned brainless animals were all over the face of the sweet Earth! If they could have acquired a ship, they would have set off in search of a new world!" Lamachus turned the horse and started south. Aeson fell in behind.

Chapter Twelve
The Vale of Hericlon

Rhywder could smell the flesh burning before he even saw the black smoke. Flesh had a smell not easily forgotten. Once his patrol had ridden into a village where there were bodies burning in a huge pile, and though the smell of the burning pitch was strong, the smell of flesh was stronger.

"Burning ahead," the axeman observed, noting the thin stream of black smoke as it came into view.

Rhywder pulled up on the reins. The Galaglean drew alongside. "You see there," Agapenor said, "something burning."

Rhywder nodded. He searched the trees that lay to either side of them. Something here was not right—Rhywder felt a shiver run though him, a familiar shiver, something he had not felt in a long time.

They were in the Vale of Tears, the valley that lay before the mountain of Hericlon, the highest of Parminion's peaks. Hericlon held a narrow passage. North were the city-states of the Daath and the tribes of Dannu—homeland. South, beyond Hericlon's gate, were the jungles of Unchuria. Rhywder had been south but once or twice and never had he gone far. Unchuria, it was said, was a land ruled by the rogue angel lord Azazel. It was the home of things unknown, things such as the Uttuku.

Rhywder's grandmother had first told him of the Uttuku when he was a young boy. He enjoyed her tales of how the dead of the Nephilim, and of giants, were cursed to become wraiths, shadows that wandered always hungry but unable to eat, ever thirsty but unable to drink. Rarely, the stronger of them, the fallen of firstborn and pure-bloods, were powerful enough to take a mortal body, trapping the soul inside, and walk in its skin for years. He would stare wide-eyed whenever she spoke of them. But she explained that by far, most of them were weaker Uttuku, and were unable to inhabit bodies for long. After but a short time, a degree or so of the sun, human flesh would reject them so violently, it would begin to decompose.

Rhywder believed many of his grandmother's stories outright. But he always thought the tales of the Uttuku were for his amusement, stories she made up and told him at night when he had trouble sleeping. That was until the time, when he was south of the gate of Hericlon, in the jungles of Unchuria, where he witnessed an entire patrol of warriors, a cohort of Daathan shield-bearers, taken by Uttuku. At first the warriors turned upon each other in deadly battle. Rhywder had been far enough away that he felt safe, and though the others with him fled, he remained to watch, amazed. For a time they battled, but just as his grandmother had told him, eventually their flesh began to violently reject the Uttuku inside them. He watched as parts of men, arms and legs, swelled until they burst. He watched skin peel away in bloodied strips. They died screaming, twisting. Some cried in tongues and curses. The noblest managed to fall on their swords. The entire cohort had been lost, and they had been good men, hard men.

After that, Rhywder had journeyed south to an Unchurian town just to find a witch. They were said to carry warders against the Uttuku, and he found one that carried hers on a silver chain at her waist, a talisman of onyx with the bone of a white owl in its center, shaped as a mandrake. The Uttuku, the witch told him, would be drawn to the mandrake, and the onyx would deflect them into the night. Rhywder had killed the witch, for the witches of Unchuria did much evil among men. He had washed the talisman in the old hag's blood, making it even more powerful. After that he always carried it hitched against the inside of his sword belt, and he seldom gave it much thought. But it had suddenly begun to burn against his skin.

"What is it?" the axeman queried, growing impatient. "What is this? We praying? I am telling you that something is burning ahead."

"It is flesh," Rhywder said, keeping his eyes on the forest. It was getting dark, and the shadows were thickening.

"Aye, this I already know. What I am wondering is if we are going to investigate or just wait here, sniffing the air?"

"We are being watched," Rhywder said. "The trees, west."

Agapenor squinted. "How many?"

"Unknown."

"Since we are out here in open grass like fatted calves, what would you say we should do, Little Fox—you being the captain and a ranger and all?"

"Keep moving south as we have been, but with careful watch on our western flank."

Rhywder eased his horse forward, toward the smoke. He knew it was bait, but this far out in the open he figured he might just as well spring the trap.

Agapenor purposely kept back for a moment, letting the captain gain distance before he started forward slowly, weaving, keeping an eye on both the little red-haired bastard and the shadows to the west, as well. He had yet to form any certain opinion of this Shadow Walker captain who was a human. No human he had ever met had worn the armband of a Shadow Walker; he was not even aware the Daath allowed it. It meant this was no ordinary captain, but from the look of him, this Little Fox, as he let himself be called, might just as easily have been a drunkard or a homeless wanderer. The Daath were always composed, armored, straight in the saddle, their dreaded darkened swords and silvery cloaks marking them as high bloods. But this ranger, he seemed to care less how he looked, or smelled for that matter.

Still, he was right, something was watching. Agapenor sensed it creeping under his skin. Whatever it was, it was not natural, and the burning ahead of them was most surely a trap. Yet the captain rode straight into it, seemingly without a care. He knew things, this Little Fox, knew a lot of things he was not talking about. And by his manner alone, Agapenor guessed him to know witchery. From the moment they had met in the agora of Terith-Aire, Agapenor knew this to be a bad assignment. There were things ahead he could live his life out never knowing of and that would be just fine. But he had orders to keep this captain alive, and that was what he intended to do, though he knew from the start it was not going to be easy. As they closed on the stream of smoke, Agapenor loosened the tie of his axe, lifted it from the saddle thong, and laid the dark haft across his thigh. He sensed there would be cutting soon.

As they came over the rise, Rhywder noticed the smoke had nearly extinguished itself. It looked to be coming from an oddly shaped fire in the middle of grass that was still green. When they reached the spot, Rhywder circled his horse and looked down. The perfect impression of a man was seared into the grass, the grassy edges around it untouched, the flesh of the withered corpse within the impression nothing but black ash. White teeth mocked a rectus grin. Rhywder scanned the southern ridge. Beyond the tips of conifers, he could see the high, jutting peak of Hericlon, white against a gray sky. Hericlon's peak was always iced spires of black rock.

Agapenor joined him and stared down at the remains.

"He is just a plodder," Rhywder said.

"How is it you know that since all I see is ash and teeth?"

"Up there to the south, plow horse wandering alone."

Agapenor spotted it. "Ah."

"This plodder was spellbound."

"How do you mean that?"

"He has been seared into the ground by a spell that turned him to ash—not a simple spell. Somewhere not far must be a spell binder with considerable talent."

"And why do you think this spell binder went to all that trouble, since this is nothing more than a mere plodder?"

"The intent, my guess, was on luring us up here to have a look."

"Then you already figured out it was a trap?"

"You thought otherwise?"

"No, but I have been wondering why you chose to simply ride into it."

"The binder that baited this trap and whatever else has been watching us from those western trees had us the moment we entered the vale. Only choice I saw worthwhile was to engage them. See how clever they are."

Rhywder didn't hear the approach of the wolf. It crossed the grass soundlessly, and he didn't even sense it coming until the last moment when there was a soft-throated growl as it leapt from the ground. Uttuku. Rhywder fed the teeth his leather wristband, but it hit him so hard he was knocked from the saddle. He took hold of the muzzle as they fell, pulling the head back, but it was stronger than he expected. They rolled, struggling until the wolf was suddenly wrenched upward by the skin of its neck. Agapenor shook it so hard Rhywder heard the neck snap. The big man cast the body aside, looking irritated.

"Wolves have something against you, Captain?"

"No. Wolves have always been my friends."

"You have many friends of this sort for us to meet?"

Rhywder came to a crouch. "Looks like there are at least a few more," he answered.

They were coming quick; dark, swift shapes, darting silent through the tall grass.

"Quite a few," Agapenor said.

Rhywder swiftly grabbed a bladder of naphtha from his saddle, used his short sword to slit it open, and quickly spilled it in a line before them. From his belt he grabbed a sulfur bag. Pelegasians made them and Rhywder had found them useful more than once. They were laced with flint and when ripped open, the sparks ignited anything flammable. When it hit the line of naphtha, it erupted into a wall of fire. Wolves would have run from it, but these were Uttuku. Still, it was going to slow them down.

The boldest leapt through the thick flame without hesitation. Rhywder caught the first and rolled onto his back, sinking his short sword into the thorax, and heaved the body over his head.

Agapenor took a stance in front of Rhywder, both hands on his axe, and there he began to slay them. The axe hummed as it split heads, chests, anything that came near enough to cut. Agapenor made a sizable target, but not a single wolf got past his axe. For a big man he was amazingly swift, wielding the axe as agile as a sword. Rhywder began to understand why Eryian had chosen him. It left him with nothing to do but watch, propped on his elbows. One of the wolves tumbled over Rhywder's head, halved down its center in a cut so clean, the guts didn't spill until it hit the ground.

More reached them, but by this time the wolves were beginning to scream in pain. The Uttuku had been in the bodies too long. They had been lying in wait, and the fact that Rhywder and Agapenor had taken their time to slowly ride up the vale to the smoking body was now working to their advantage. Most of the Uttuku fell to ground, writhing in spasms as flesh and fur began to violently decay. Rhywder noticed one actually spinning on its hind legs, a macabre dance of pain as fur peeled off its sides and belly.

Agapenor watched them die, amazed at what he saw. One of them wailed like a woman as the fur shriveled off its face, leaving bloodied bone. When it was over, the big man turned to Rhywder and lowered one brow, a deeply troubled look on his face.

"What was that we just fought?" he asked incredulously.

"They were Uttuku."

"Explain Uttuku to me."

"Souls of slain giants. Some are strong; some weak. These were weaker. They were unable to hold the flesh on the bodies that long. Once an Uttuku is inside a body, the flesh tends to dry and decompose. There are stronger ones. I have heard some can possess a body for years, even decades."

"A sweet thought. I always believed souls left for heaven as my mother taught us when we were young."

"These are souls that have no heaven. The angels that gave them birth severed their bond with the light of Elyon. They were able to birth children and grant them eternal souls, but the curse of their death is to be bound to the Earth to plague mankind until the end of days."

"What a happy story. Where did you learn of these Uttuku?"

"My grandmother. Did not believe her for the longest time, but as you witnessed, turned out she was telling me the truth."

Agapenor shoved his axe through his belt. "Your grandmother a witch of some kind?"

"A priestess, what they call a Water Bearer."

"Yes, heard of those. Lochlains. Most of them were killed in the gathering wars, I understand. You a Lochlain?"

"I am."

"Explains a lot."

Rhywder wiped the blood off his sword, and sheathed it. "The more powerful Uttuku, the firstborn of angel lords and prefects, are able to grow their own bodies. They learned from their fathers the secrets of the bindings of roots. They grow their bodies from pods that spawn a particular kind of wood found nowhere else. Once it hardens it is strong as steel."

Rhywder whistled for his horse, which had run from the wolves and now wandered just south of them. The horse started back, taking its time, and Agapenor's followed behind.

"So," said Agapenor, "what you are saying is these already dead Nephilim walk about in bodies armored of wood strong as steel?"

"It is true. I know because I met one myself."

"You met one of these? Personal?"

"It got very personal, actually."

"And how did that work out?"

"I managed to kill him. Strange, but what haunted me ever since were his eyes—this soul in these black empty eyes. I still remember them, how they had this far light in them. What was troubling for me, I knew it to have once been the light of Elyon, the light of his father—an angel lord. That was truly the toughest fight I ever fought. I was so weary after that fight I did not get up for three days."

The horses reached them. Agapenor shoved his axe into the saddle scabbard before mounting. He watched Rhywder mount with a troubled look and waited for Rhywder to meet his eyes.

"Tell me something, Captain, just what is it they have sent you up here to find?"

"I am not dead certain, but I can assure you of one thing, we will know when we find it."

They started riding for the mountain whose peaks had snagged dark, ugly clouds. Rhywder knew they were clouds that had drifted from the south.

"Those we just killed," Rhywder went on, "they were trained. The Unchurians do that, train them as assassins. Unchurians are masters of all things dead."

"Ah, well, that will be a comfort for me," Agapenor mumbled, "seeing as Unchuria is where we are headed and I have this fondness for lifeless things, particularly if they can walk about and take over your body and make you rot like a dead rat."

Chapter Thirteen

Marcian

Adrea stepped into the cottage and closed the door. She had been lost in thought, and when she glanced up, she stared, startled. She had broken conversation and all faces turned toward her. Lamachus stood wide-eyed, clasping a mug of ale, beads of it on his thistle beard. Camilla stood near the hearth where she had been removing loaves from the stone oven. Aeson was on a corner stool holding a clay cup with both hands—he had replaced the veils and bodice with a filthy leather tunic, but he still looked pretty, for he hadn't gotten all of the curls and baby's breath out of his hair. But most surprising—in the center, standing just opposite Lamachus, was Captain Marcian Antiope of Galaglea. He stood tall, oddly handsome in the brazen cuirass and blue cloak that arched from his shoulders. On their plain cottage table was set a dark helm with ornate cheek guards. Only Marcian offered her a smile. There were two retainers with him—probably his sons. They also wore the blue and bronze of Galaglean warriors. They stood off to the side, and both looked away when she tried to meet their eyes.

"Good God," Lamachus muttered. "First the boy rides up dressed as a girl and now you coming in so late we were about to go off in search of you."

"The dapple gray may have twisted his ankle. I was not sure, but I had to walk him just in case. He has been favoring that ankle."

"Way you have been riding him these last days, surprised he has not collapsed from exhaustion."

"Well," Marcian cut in, "it is ba-barely dark. Not that late."

"Hello, Marcian," she said. "I would not have guessed you would be here."

"I-I came without a . . . a . . . announcement," he said.

Though words seemed difficult to him, he did not seem to mind struggling through them, and his stutters produced no emotional reaction.

Lamachus's face was flushed red, and she didn't meet his eyes. If not for Marcian, she would hardly have been able to ignore him, but in the presence of the horseman, Lamachus was forcing himself calm, though he seemed to tremble from the effort.

Her mother set the loaves on a wooden trencher. "Where have you been this late, Adrea?" she asked.

Almonds had been burnt in the incense bowl, and Adrea knew that was for special occasions only. The last of the smells was venison, which was cooking in herbs and butter. They must have been warned the captain was coming.

"I rode to the beach today," she said. "I did not realize it would be this long getting there and back."

"The beach!" bellowed Lamachus.

"I was thinking, Father, in Galaglea it would be long before I saw the ocean again. So I took one last ride. I am so sorry I am this late." She was careful to keep one hand over the ring, but Lamachus was too lost in controlling his temper to notice.

"She does have a-a point, Lamachus. There is no ocean in Galaglea."

"What you do not know, Marcian, is this girl has been riding that horse into the ground these last few days."

"Perhaps she has a lot on her mind," the captain suggested.

"Needed to see the ocean," Lamachus hissed through tight teeth. "My guess is . . ." He paused, as if only now realizing he was losing his temper again. "Well," he stammered, "you could be right, Marcian, she does have a lot to think about—marriage and leaving for Galaglea and all."

"Yes. It is a lot, indeed," Marcian said. "I was wondering, Lamachus, if-if I might borrow her."

Lamachus had a look of grief on his face.

"It will be for but a short time," the captain added, carefully. "I-I wanted to speak with her—alone."

"Alone?" Lamachus stood. "You know, Marcian, it is never a good idea to go speaking to a woman alone on an empty stomach, particularly this woman. Beyond that, I believe I would like a few *words* with her myself."

Marcian smiled. "Please," he said with simple firmness that seemed left over from being a commander.

Lamachus stared back, frustrated. "Certainly," he said.

"There is something I h-have meant to share with her. It should not take long."

"Well," Lamachus fidgeted. He set down his wine. "Suppose you ought to be able to talk to the girl. Being as you are about to wed her. Suppose it is logical."

"Good." Marcian set his hand tenderly on Adrea's shoulder and guided her to the door, but Lamachus was there ahead to open it.

"And, while you are speaking with her, Marcian, you might remind her that the next time she wants to be off to visit the ocean, she should tell her family so they are not left worrying half the night where she has gone."

"Lamachus," Camilla cautioned quietly.

Marcian motioned the doorway. Adrea smiled at him and at Lamachus as she stepped past.

Lamachus almost followed, but Camilla pulled him back. "Well," he grizzled, "just remember the smell of this venison is going to have my stomach turning." He tried a laugh, though it came out a bit false.

Marcian smiled and nodded.

Outside, she walked alone with him, and it wasn't until Marcian was well beyond the cottage before he spoke. "Your . . ." he paused, the words stuck for a moment. He took a breath and started over. "Your father seems strict with you."

"Yes. He is that."

"He must ca-care for you deeply. I would—a daughter like you."

She didn't respond. It was dark out, and glancing down, she noticed the ring had darkened, as well. It looked rather plain as though it understood the need to disguise itself. That surprised her.

He gestured to the horses and they walked slowly toward the stalls. "I was . . . here this day on dispatch. Hence the captain's tassels. I prefer to wear them as little as possible."

She glanced up. "Well, you do look impressive, Marcian."

He shook his head. "War is never impressive. Never think that. I am afraid these tales you father has probably told you of Captain Antiope—they are . . . a bit overdone. I am a breeder of horses like my father before me. I was pressed into the service of the king; I am no wa-warrior and never was one."

"Yet you are well known as the hero of Tarchon Pass."

"My bro-brother died there. It was rage. Rage does not make heroes." His eyes were serious on this point. They had paused and she noticed that his face was not at all as she remembered. Not so gaunt; rather it was handsome but for the nose. And the gray hair, it didn't leave him looking old as much as it lent him wisdom. Perhaps he would not have been all that difficult to live with. He was stroking the mane of one of his horses. "As you know, hardly able to forget I suppose, we are soon to be we-wed, Adrea."

She did not answer. He tenderly looked in her eyes. The horse nudged him for more attention and he continued to stroke its mane. "D-do you fear all of this? Me? My sons?" The two attendant warriors had been his sons.

"I know not what to think. I am anxious, but how could I help but be somewhat anxious?"

"Of course. You need n-not explain."

She nodded. "I have known only Lucania, my village, my father . . ." she paused, but strangely, as Loch had suggested, her world had slipped back into place, the day's memories had receded, left shadowy.

He was careful with his next question. "Be honest. Is it so hard that . . . that you would prefer I take my two sons and leave?"

She only shook her head, her eyes downcast. "No. If you sense anything, it is just that I was not expecting to see you tonight. I was surprised."

He nodded. He brushed a tangle of hair from her cheek, which surprised her. His stutter only made him appear shy; he wasn't shy at all.

"You are . . . a most beautiful girl, Adrea. Much too beautiful for me. I am old; I feel very much like a-a thief. All this seems wrong, but somehow . . . well, when it happened—when I approached the matchmaker . . . I surprised even myself." She couldn't meet his eyes, but it didn't matter. Marcian was gazing at the stars above the cottage. "Know that all this frightens me, as well," he said. "I have six sons . . . and you . . . you cause me to feel younger than any of them.

No more than a foolish, simple lad." There was a smile, but it slipped away. "I did not feel this way when first I wed. I felt . . . as if I was old. An old, wise man I was at ten and seven years. And now . . . I am as lost as a young boy. Interesting, these tricks of time."

"What was she like, Marcian?"

"She?"

"Your first wife."

There was a long silence. A shadow passed over him. She could tell the memory was hard and that he rarely spoke of it. "Simple," he finally answered. "She was . . . a soul to cherish."

Adrea nodded. "I understand."

"The war took her. The Daath set a blockade against Galaglea. She was taken by the same fever th-that—the same that took my son. I had named him August." He smiled briefly. "He had stark white hair like an old man. I have learned by it that we all must take wh-what is given. Elyon offers little explanation."

A slight sense of guilt brushed through her. She felt in him a deep love for the boy he called August. He must have been young, but he had been cherished, and merely saying his name had misted Marcian's eyes. She remembered Galaglea had withstood a long siege before giving into Argolis at the end of the gathering wars.

"You know when this all started?" he asked.

She shook her head, not looking up.

"I was riding though Lucania and I happened t-to see you among your father's stock. You were . . . were watching a mother clean her foal. And I thought—a thought from nowhere, unbidden—I thought: a son. For some unknown reason, something in me I-I really cannot explain. I saw you and remembered the eyes of little August, his shock of white hair." He paused, took a careful breath. "I have sons grown to men. All . . . all these long years and suddenly, seeing you that day, I thought of August. So that is the story." He lowered his eyes, perhaps misted with tears he hid well. "This feeling that if I had another son . . ." He broke off, lost for further words.

"You do not have to explain, Marcian. I believe I can understand." She touched fingers to his wrist. "It must have been hard. You are not that old, you know."

"You think so?"

"I do. Why should you not have a son if you feel this way? I see no reason."

He nodded, almost as if he were thankful there was no need to explain further.

"Marcian, I could ask no better. A captain, a horseman, a knight of my own land, honored of kings. If anything, in truth, I can only answer you that . . ." she paused, this time to choose her words carefully. "That I might be the one who is unworthy. Certainly not you."

His somber gray eyes lifted to study her.

"Impossible," he said.

Finally, he reached to finger the dangling bridle of the horse he had been stroking. The horses he had brought were all magnificent—four of them, coats shimmering. He was well known as a horse breeder, and he often sold warhorses to the Daath, many as fine as Loch's. This one was a black stallion, young, strong.

"I thought as long as I was going to be near Lucania this day," he said, "th-that I might bring a gift."

She gasped. "Oh, Marcian, you do not mean this horse? He is too magnificent, I could never accept—"

"If you are to be my wife, surely I can offer a gift."

"But he is so beautiful."

"Yes. He is of the fin-finest bloodstock in all Galaglea. I could sell him to the Daath for quite a sum. But I choose him as a gift. And you"—he looked in her eyes sternly—"you cannot refuse."

He offered her the reins. She paused, feeling suddenly guilty again.

"This has nothing to do with winning your favor," he added. "It is because he is to horses what you are t-to women."

The horse turned about, nipping at Marcian's hand, which must have offered too many apples and carrots. She noticed a white streak down the nose. Its eyes were keen and quick.

"He is beautiful, Marcian. I have no idea what to say."

"You have no need to say anything. He can outdistance any . . . any horse in the land. I promise. I have trained him" He tucked the reins into her palm. "I am afraid my youngest son, Lucian, has given him an osten-ostentatious name. Thunderbolt."

She smiled. "Seeing him, I would say it is a name that must fit him well."

"Why not . . . why not ride him?"

"Tonight?"

"It is a beautiful night. Yes, tonight. With me. Now."

She noticed the horse study her with suspicion. She stroked the hide of the strong neck. "But what of Lamachus's stomach?"

"We will let it grumble—with the rest of him."

Marcian rode a strong roan stallion. Past the fences, they rode at a lope. His breastplate glimmered in the moonlight, his long gray hair flayed in the wind. The black stallion he had given her was resisting her, letting her know he belonged to the horseman and she shouldn't be getting any ideas.

"Can we let them run?" she asked.

"I would love to."

He shook the reins and clicked his tongue. His roan stallion dropped into a run.

Thunderbolt paced him easily. They passed what seemed to be dozing cattle.

"Take hold," he shouted, "and we will let them full out!"

"Let them out?" Adrea whispered to herself, for already they were at a gallop, but Marcian leaned forward and his roan gained amazing speed. Thunderbolt needed no prompting to keep up. The horse lowered its head and its shoulders pumped in a hard gallop that could easily have rivaled the great white mare of Loch's. They were sailing over tall grass.

"He's so fast!" she shouted across to Marcian.

"He could leave me behind," Marcian shouted back. Finally, they slowed to a normal pace. Marcian smiled at her.

"Do you g-go to the ocean often?" Marcian asked.

"Hardly ever."

"I am afraid Galaglea is fa-far from the ocean. It is beautiful country, but far from the forest of the East of the Land and the ocean. I sense you are going to miss them both. Am I wrong?"

"No. I will miss a lot of things, but there is always much to be learned elsewhere I should guess."

She paused, pulling up on the reins; Thunderbolt resisted until Marcian stopped. Adrea tried to turn him; Thunderbolt snorted and pulled back toward the captain.

"He seems bent on following your every move," Adrea said.

"You have discovered that he has a mind of his own?"

"Oh, yes. But since we are to be horse and mistress, perhaps I should give him a taste of my mind—while he can still see you."

"Keep careful rein."

Adrea twisted the reins about and kicked Thunderbolt's sides with a shout. He bolted hard, but not smoothly, and had run only a short distance when he tried to force a turn on her. She straightened him out, firmly letting him know he had a new boss, but not with the reins or her body; she did it with her mind. She was able to feel through to him, able to assure him she would make a good mistress. He responded, he seemed to hear, and he demonstrated in a quick burst that he was easily the swiftest horse she had ever handled.

She was enjoying the wind in her hair when for a second the other world leaked through, the memories, knowing she was leaving in the morning. The ring was not completely effective. She slowed Thunderbolt, and turned him to ride back to Marcian. He was waiting patiently. She had a slight urge to let him know. He seemed so honorable, so kind. What she was going to do to him, despite her reasons, despite even Elyon's command, it still seemed wrong. If there were only a way she could tell him, but she knew she could say nothing, give no hint, and riding his magnificent gift left shame in her she couldn't easily dismiss.

Chapter Fourteen

Asteria

At first it was but a dream as dreams are made—disembodied sounds, images blurred, shadows that whispered, but then changed. It became real. It became as brilliant and alive as living itself. It must have been the kind of dreams Loch spoke of. She was even aware she was sleeping, and she marveled that it was all so real, so vivid.

She was in a winter forest, the trees and earth covered in virgin snow. Beyond, amid a stand of conifers, waited the lone figure of Argolis, the young king of the Daath—this was Asteria's Argolis, the conqueror.

And Adrea *was* the young queen; she was Asteria, mounted on a heavy, mountain-bred workhorse, crossing the vale toward him. She was wrapped in thick, white fur specked with gray. Despite the fur, she shivered from weakness and she was in pain, stinging pain across her back and sides. She knew what it was. She had been whipped, and the cuts still burned. She was so weak it was hard to stay in the saddle.

From the distance, she could see the cold-blue eyes of Argolis. He was astride a large, dark charger. Around the king's shoulders bristled a thick cloak of silver wolf's fur. His cuirass glimmered with a reddish hue. He seemed etched in blood cast from the east rising sun of the early dawn. In those days they called him the Silver King. He was young, but hardened beyond his years, his eyes commanding and as edged as the cutting blade of a sword.

How many had fallen before the shields of Argolis and his Eagle, the dreaded warlord Eryian? They had swept the land with the fire of conquerors, and Asteria dared not probe too deeply into what drove him, whether the gathering wars were truly inspired of Elyon's Light or whether they were the consequence of Argolis's own dark fury. But she was certain of one thing, she loved him. She loved this king and she had just sacrificed all she knew for him.

Even now, his warriors would be marching upon her own village, her own people. The burnished swords and darkened shields of the Daath would be glinting in the dawn's light as the armies of the Shadow Lords pressed through the snowbound forest, closing on the people of the lake slow and certain.

The villagers, Asteria's people, by now had dug pits, anchored slaying spikes, thrown up dirt ramparts. They would be gathered, faces set against fear, weapons readied. But it would be quick. The tribes of Hebe and Lochlain would be swept as chaff before the winnower's fire. Argolis was the winnower, and this was his season.

The night before, Asteria had tried, with all the spirits that spoke through her, to save them.

She had managed to gather the elders before the council fire one last time, but they were tense, their minds already hardened against her, especially the king of the Hebe, Tisias. The Hebe and Lochlain were brother tribes, but Tisias had taken rule several years before. He stood tall, wrapped in the dark of the bear's skin he had famously slain with a dagger in his youth. Capys was the last elder of the lake walkers, the Lochlains, but he was old now, and his voice was not as strong as Tisias. Still, all of them had come, one last time, to listen to Asteria. She was called the Seer Child. She stood before the fire and the eyes of the warriors, the commanders and elders watching, waiting for her words, though they seemed dark in the night, far from her. Somehow, before she had even spoken, she sensed she had lost them.

But Asteria was the true Water Bearer, the seer, and though she was but ten and four years, already she had prophesied. She had warned them of the famine of the sixth year of Toth, she had foretold the fire that swept the vale of Siris, and she had even predicted the death of Demandes, the elder, seven days before the snow leopard brought him down.

As she stood before them, her red hair—uncut from birth, long to her hips—fanned out in the fire's fury. She knew there was no chance of turning their hearts, but she had to try, even if hope was lost.

"Hear me!" she cried. "Sons of Hebe and Lochlain, take mark this night! Do not lift your hand against the Silver King! He is mighty and he comes with the legions of the Daath, but think not of his sword, for he seeks not your blood, but only your vow that you honor the tribes of heaven's queen, Dannu. He speaks true, soften your hearts, and think on what I tell you.

"Separate, we are weak. United, all the tribes of Dannu, us, the Daath, even the Galagleans, think how strong we could be. No more fighting tribe against tribe. We would stand as one. I tell you now that in the day of our children, we will need all the strength we can gather. In the day of our children, such powers will come against our tribes that if we remain scattered, bickering, we will be destroyed, and we will be no more. We must gather, it is spoken of Dannu, and it is spoken of Elyon. In the day that will come, the day of our children, we must stand as one tribe, one force!"

"Led by the Daath!" shouted Tisias, cutting her off. "Commanded by their king, knees bent."

"No, Tisias! It is not about pride. Can you not see, they were sent, long ago, they are here to be our sword and our spear! It is true they are born slayers, warriors of blood, but there comes a day when the Daath will be the first to stand against our enemies!"

"I have no enemy other than the Silver King," Tisias shouted back. "I see no other enemy before me!"

At that they shouted in unison, in agreement, some banging sword against shield.

"He is not your enemy, Tisias."

"And this told me by his lover."

She was stunned, stricken.

"Yes, we know! You have gone to him in the night. You have lain with him. Dare you deny my words?"

She had no answer. It was true; Argolis already had taken her as his wife. It was to have been a secret until the tribes had agreed to the terms, but someone had betrayed them. She knew who it was, not a Hebe, not a Lochlain, they had been betrayed by a Daath, a captain of one of Argolis's legions with ambitions of his own. It was bloodlust, and it fanned the flames behind her with an evil she had no power to turn.

They were shouting now, driven to frenzy, and Tisias urged them on. When old Capys, the elder of the Lochlains, tried to speak in her defense, Tisias swept him aside before he could utter a word.

"No more!" the king screamed. "No more of this blasphemy! You may once have held the light, Seer Child, but now you have betrayed both your goddess and your tribes! And it had been for him, for this Silver King, that you betray us. This council is at an end. Seize her! Take her now! Take the witch!"

Asteria backed away, and fear swept her. The heat of the fire seared her back, but Tisias's guards closed on her, and looking past them, she saw the rage in Tisias's eyes. He was filled with rage—an unnatural rage. It was lost. There was no hope here.

"Please," she whispered as they took her arms, pulling her forward. "Even if you believe I have somehow betrayed you, you cannot stand against him! You will all die! You cannot stand against the Daath! I plead for your lives!"

"Silence her," shouted Tisias.

One of the guards slapped her cheek, and it was then that her brother, Rhywder, leapt on the guard's back, pulling him down, kicking him in the ribs. He fought the others for a moment, as well. He was a fighter, he always had been, but he was quickly overwhelmed, and it was Tisias who finally grabbed him and struck him so hard he went down and did not get back up.

Before they dragged him off, as well, his brothers-in-arms, his kindred quickly pulled him away and out of sight. They were too busy with Asteria to bother following.

Asteria was stripped of her robes and the night was cold against her pale skin as they tied her to the tanning post, high, leaving her feet dangling. The leather lashing that bound her wrists were tight; they cut into her skin. She wept for them—the tears that fell were not for fear of what they were about to do, but were only for her people, for she had somehow failed them. With tomorrow's dawn they would foolishly face the swords of Argolis's legions.

The first sting of Tisias's whip cut deep. Her skin was tender, and the whip felt like a blade cutting.

"Witch!" he screamed. "Where is your Silver King now?"

The whip cracked again and Asteria almost cried out, but she did not care of the pain; it meant nothing. She pressed her cheek against the wood and let herself think of him, of Argolis. As the strokes cut, she let the memory of his eyes be the last she saw before consciousness slipped away.

She hung there in the night, as the fire dwindled. She would have frozen to death; she had been left to die, but when the others were gone, Rhywder and his kindred came for her. He pulled her down, wrapped her in furs. She looked up to see the youth that had gathered with him, twenty and eight, all young archers, Rhywder's closest kindred. They had trained together for as long as they had known each other.

"We follow you, my sister," Rhywder whispered, tears in his eyes over her pain. "We leave with you, even against our fathers. They would have let the night kill you. They have forgotten, you are their light and their voice. But we have not. Lead us to your Silver King, Asteria."

Rhywder lifted her onto a waiting horse and mounted his own. He drew up the reins, and together, what would be the last of the Lochlains to survive the gathering rode into the night.

When they reached the spot Asteria guided them to, the Little Fox and his companions waited to first let her cross the vale alone to Argolis, who had come as he had promised.

When she reached him, she drew her horse alongside and held up her hand, delicately, her fingers spread in the sign of the word. Argolis laid his hand against hers, curled his fingers into hers. He reached over and pulled her from her horse onto his own, holding her close against him. He looked across to the others.

"This is all?" he asked.

"Yes," she answered. "Only twenty and nine, my brother among them, but we are yours, my king. I am sorry, but someone betrayed us and Tisias gathers his forces against you."

Argolis nodded, sadly. He saw the rest were merely boys, but all armed with bow and sword, faces hardened—Lochlains. He needed more of them, they were valiant, the tribe of Lochlain; it was beyond sadness that so many of them would fall this dawn.

As he held her firm against him, Asteria glanced down and saw, briefly, a glint from his sword, the mark of the father, the sword called the Angelslayer, resting in its ivory scabbard against his thigh.

With the sight of it, the dream dissolved and Adrea found herself again standing in the midst of the battle, the same image that had swept her when she stood on the sand of the Dove Cara that afternoon. It was the image of a war that covered all the Earth, the screams, the smell of blood. It was all linked to the sword. The mark of the father.

Adrea found herself sitting up in her room, in the quiet of the cabin, breathless. She noticed Aeson awake, as well, staring at her, frightened.

There were heavy footsteps, and the goatskin was thrown back from the doorway. In its shadow stood Lamachus, his great axe gripped tight in his hand. He was poised as a warrior, searching the dark. He looked to Adrea.

"What is it, girl! What happened?"

She placed a hand against her breast, feeling weak, as Asteria had.

"Did something happen?" she asked.

"You did not hear your own scream?"

"I screamed?"

"Enough to turn the dead."

"It . . . it was just a nightmare, Father. Sorry that I awakened you."

"What could have made you scream that way?"

"I . . . I cannot remember."

"Well, that must be God's blessing, not remembering, considering it took a few years off my skin and I was in the other room." He relaxed, took a deep breath. "Well, at least you are all right." He started to turn, but paused. "You need anything? Milk? A bit of grog? Could help you sleep."

"No, I will be fine. Thank you, Father."

Lamachus nodded. He pulled the goatskin closed and she heard his bare feet pad back to his room. She looked to Aeson. The dream was still with her, clouding her thoughts. Looking down, she noticed the bloodstone of the ring had turned from purple to black, except it burned with a tiny, distant spark. She kept it covered from Aeson's sight.

"If you talk about nightmares, they lose their power," said Aeson. "Do you want to talk? I will stay awake."

"I will be fine, Aeson. Whatever it was, it is over now."

"Are you still afraid?"

She stared at him a moment, but nodded.

"Want me to sleep with you?"

She nodded again.

Aeson crawled over and curled into her blanket, nestling beside her, and was asleep almost as soon as he laid down his head. Adrea lifted her hand to look back at the ring. She felt no comfort from it this time, only a far, terrible fear and the death of too many souls to bear thinking of.

Chapter Fifteen
Hericlon's Gate

It is said of the ancients that the black mountain, Hericlon, was the first land to emerege from the primeval dark. Before the coming of the angels Hericlon captured the winter wind. Her spurs curled about the valley below, leaving the ground cold and raw. Her spires and crags were forever iced. A canyon cleft had been cut through to the south as though by the sword of God, with sheer rock walls of black-gray that blocked the sun.

In its center, the highest plateau of the pass, where the air chilled and all seasons moaned from the winds, there, the Etlantians built the mighty gate of Hericlon, spanning the width of the great canyon with gigantic, red-granite blocks.

Hericlon's gate rose eighty feet up the black rock. Steep stone stairways to either side ascended to the causeway. The battlement was of heavy stone, with archer ports and dark towers overlooking the passage south.

Hericlon's portcullis was unlike anything known, even of Etlantis. It was made of ancient bars of heavy, crimson Etlantian oraculum. Each oraculum beam was the width of two men and there was nothing on Earth that could pierce the portcullis when it was closed. In morning's light the red metal looked bathed in blood.

Below the gate, in the span of the passageway, blunt, squared-stone housing served as Hericlon's garrison for horses and seventy men.

Hericlon was stone upon stone, for no tree, no root, nor vine could find the sun. Hericlon was the stonework of gods. With her portcullis closed, Hericlon was impregnable.

From the moment the canyon cliffs began to rise to either side of him, Rhywder felt his skin crawl. The air was thick with what was called Hericlon's southwind, the cold that streamed down from the mountain's crags and spires. It moved through the pass, always a mournful cry, as if it were a memory of the wars of Dawnshroud, when it was built by the angels, separating the north of the Light Bearer from the south, claimed of Azazel. It was an ancient mark, a boundary as old as the Earth. As Rhywder and Agapenor rode into the canyon's yawning black walls, the axeman on instinct unlatched his axe and laid it over his thigh. It was as if they were leaving the world of light behind.

"What is that for?" asked Rhywder.

"Feel something," was all the axeman said.

Suddenly, a horse passed, riderless, eyes wide. It galloped madly, careening off the edge of one rock wall in a swerve to avoid them. A Galaglean saddle dragged behind, bouncing off the rock.

Rhywder drew his short sword and pulled up on the reins.

"Care, Agapenor."

"Aye," the big man answered, "as I just said—feel something. It would be just up ahead of us."

They continued, riding slow and carefully. When they rounded a corner, both paused. Sitting against the stone was a Galaglean warrior in full armor. He had drawn a dagger and was stabbing his own face. The dagger sank in and out, blood whipping, until the face was unrecognizable. The Galaglean finally stilled, relaxed, the bloodied dagger slipping from his fingers, and for a moment he almost looked relaxed, resting against the rock, but for the destroyed face and blood that spilled across his breastplate.

"Agapenor!" Rhywder screamed. "Get behind me! Now!"

Agapenor lost breath as the spirits came, jetting out of the bloodied corpse with screams to match the wind, four, then five, all gray shadows. Seeing Rhywder and Agapenor, they went for them, oval mouths agape, hands clawing.

Rhywder ripped the witch's amulet from his belt and held it before them. He kept a tight grip on the reins, but his horse reared as the wraiths collided with the amulet. It was as if Rhywder were blocking a blast of fire. They were repelled, soaring upward, some vanishing into the very face of the rock, others high into the chill, night air.

Rhywder latched the amulet back beneath his belt. He glanced to Agapenor, who was holding the reins of his horse in one fist and his axe in another.

"Yet more Uttuku?" Agapenor asked, rather calmly, considering.

Rhywder nodded.

"Those were weak or strong, would you say?"

"Strong; they were able to hold the flesh, walk it."

"How would you fight something like that, Captain?"

"Magick—such as the amulet I just used."

"What if one had no magick amulet?"

"Then you would likely be taken, but if they cannot find a mark quickly, it is said they are lost for many counts of the moon before they can strike again."

"Some comfort, eh?"

Rhywder eased his horse forward, and rode slowly, till the danger was past. Hericlon always left him uneasy.

"Things are off, not right. It has begun to turn."

"What has begun to turn? What are you saying?" Agapenor prodded.

"Endgame. The signs are in the skies, though I have tried hard to ignore them. If I were a Follower, a preacher of Enoch, I would tell you the Earth itself has tilted, that even time is a bit off course. It is the work of the angels, what they call *star knowledge*. Hard to explain, would not worry about it if I were you, Agapenor."

"I will try, Captain, though if not for you explaining it, I would not have it to think of in the first place."

"Some say I talk too much. Habit."

"Learning more each day with you, Little Fox. I was not thinking this adventure would turn out such an educational opportunity. So this is the passage of Hericlon? Never thought I would see it. Have to admit it is impressive."

"If nothing else, Hericlon does always impress."

"You say these Uttuku cannot take one whose heart is pure, is that true?"

"So it is said."

"Then why do you carry this amulet? Your heart is not pure, Little Fox?"

"There are a few things I have regretted in my time. How about yourself,

Agapenor? How would you figure your heart?"

"I suppose it is as pure as any other slayer who has spent most his life killing those that needed killing. But I do no whoring. I am true to my woman and I do not gamble or lie or steal. Who could say? Maybe my heart is pure, though I have no desire to put it to the test."

When the opening of the garrison and Hericlon's gate fell into view, Rhywder drew up a moment. He was surprised that the great portcullis was raised, like the mouth of a dragon—open. There were blue-cloaked Galaglean warriors atop the causeway and more guarding the huge windlass assemblies of cogs with their rings of thick chain. Even more disturbing, the passageway was cluttered with pyres burning. A score of them at least.

"This does not look good," Rhywder said.

"You think?"

Rhywder and Agapenor were shortly surrounded by a company of horsemen, javelins lifted, steel bows drawn. They parted to let a rider through, a captain by his shoulder tassels—a young Daath commander with a darkened silver breastplate and Daathan cloak.

"State who you are," the captain said boldly but hopelessly in soprano.

Agapenor grunted beside Rhywder.

"Have no fear, Captain," Rhywder touched the plain, silver armband on his upper right arm.

"A Shadow Walker!" the commander gasped.

"Would you mind lowering the tips of these arrows?" Rhywder asked calmly. "I would hate to think what might happen if one of your men got an itch."

The captain raised a gauntleted hand and the weapons lowered. The Galagleans he was commanding were to a man more experienced and capable than the young Daath, but that was the way of things in Terith-Aire.

"Elyon be thanked," the youth said with a sigh of relief. "One of our men has finally gotten through! You bring word from Argolis? Are they coming?"

"Who?"

"Reinforcements! I have sent ten men for reinforcements over the past fifteen days. Surely that is why you are here?"

Rhywder eased back in the saddle. There was fear in the young captain's eye, the kind that came of witchery and shadows.

"Sorry to disappoint you, but we would be just passing through."

"No, no, it cannot be. This is madness, we are trapped here. There had been no word, no sign any of them have even gotten past the vale."

"Not to dampen your spirits, but you might want to build one more pyre."

"What?"

"One of your men a few leagues back."

The young captain looked at the others. "They got Cragus! God, even Cragus did not make it."

"How far?" one of the Galagleans asked.

"Just behind us. You will only need two men; the canyon is safe for now."

At a motion, the guard and one other rode off, hooves echoing.

"Take us to your quarters, Captain," Rhywder said.

In the garrison's quarters, Anton—the Daath captain who was perhaps twenty and four years at most—poured himself some wine, his hands shaking as he brought the goblet to his lips and drained it. Agapenor tightened his jaw, shifting, uneasy.

"You were asking of the gate?" Anton muttered, refilling the goblet. "A good place, this gate. A good command if what you desire is to slowly drive yourself mad, day by day. Each night it has been getting worse. No sun. You believe that? I have not seen the sun in weeks." He drained the second goblet. "The nights are clear, but each morning, just as dawn comes, these dark clouds move in from the south. Even at midday, the shadows of the passage are so thick it is like an eternal night. It is as if something were designing this madness, and all with such care."

"Tell us about the pyres," Rhywder said.

"Love of Elyon. It happened this morning, not far past dawn, though who can say for sure since dawn no longer comes. Without warning, without reason, the Galagleans in the pass below the causeway just started killing each other. They were veterans, good men. All of the Galagleans I have left are hardened. The cowards have already deserted; all I have left are veterans of Quietus. All I know is I heard screaming, and when I stepped into the passage they had already started killing each other. Never seen anything like it, no one could stop them, they simply fought to the death."

"How many did you lose?"

"A full score, twenty and two men, all lying there dead—and not just dead but cut to pieces. It was savage: arms severed, guts spilled, pure carnage. The passage was covered in blood."

Thinking of it, a shiver swept through Anton. He started to pour another goblet, but Agapenor set the flagon of wine aside.

"You need to pay more attention to Captain Rhywder, and less to the wine," Agapenor said.

"Yes, sir. Sorry."

"You need me, Rhywder?" Agapenor asked. "Otherwise, I will be just outside. Feel the need to get some air."

Rhywder nodded. Agapenor ducked through the doorway to step outside, letting the door close behind him. Rhywder felt a bit sorry for the boy; he was obviously in over his head.

"You have some capable veterans out there, Captain. Would you like me to place one of them in command?"

"No, I admit I am shaken, but they listen to me. I have been in command here for seven counts of the moon. I am still capable."

"Good to know. So how long has this been going on?"

"What? Killing each other, you mean?"

"Yes."

"Only today. Can you explain any of it? Is it witchery? Some kind of spell binding we are under?"

"Anything else unordinary?"

"There are the screamers. I would not call them ordinary."

"Screamers?"

"They come every night now. Gray shades, they come down the passage screaming like I have never heard—high-pitched inhuman screams. Some of them pass right through the stone of the gate, other just fly overhead. I have no idea what they are. They do not seem to cause any harm, but it goes on sometimes all night. It has been weeks now. No one has been getting any sleep. I think some of the Galagleans are suggesting we drop the portcullis and try to get through the vale, get help. But there are others, some of the older commanders, who understand we need to hold. I have been relying on them."

"Has anything else passed through? Anything corporal?"

"Villagers. They were coming through in steady numbers a few weeks back. Some with carts for their dead. It is why we had left the portcullis raised, though the past few days they have slowed to a trickle. And those who do make it are burnt or wounded. Some have begged I send patrols out for their kindred. As if I have men to spare."

"Have they said what has been killing them?"

"Yes, they talk of mutations—giants, the monstrous ones. I believe they are referring to Failures, raiding parties of Failures. I am told they mostly come for blood. I have heard they hang the villagers upside down to drain them of blood for drinking."

"Any word of Unchurians?"

"You mean the ones like us, like the Daath, only red-skinned?"

"Yes. Do any of the villages say they have seen Unchurians?"

"No. No, I have heard nothing of Unchurians."

"So the only ones coming through the gate have been villagers?"

"Yes. Those and the screamers."

Rhywder nodded. "All right, I want you to listen to me, Anton. I need your full attention."

Anton nodded.

"Not long from now, there could be something coming against Hericlon from the south. It could be giants, Failures, possibly even Unchurians. They may come as raiding parties, but it is also possible Hericlon may be invaded."

"Are you saying we are at war?"

"Yes, it is possible the Unchurians will attack in force, but I doubt it will happen soon. I believe there is time to get word to Quietus in Galaglea. And keep in mind, this is Hericlon. With this gate you have enough men to hold back an entire army if it came to that. I doubt very much that will happen, but you and your men need to be aware that Hericlon must be held at all cost until help arrives. At all cost. So this is what you are going to do: you are going to drop the portcullis and once it is closed, you will open it for no one. Understand? No matter what comes, the gate remains closed."

Anton nodded. "What about villagers? Will they not need passage?"

"They will not be getting passage because it could be a trap. If you lift the gate, things can get through; if you keep the portcullis closed, this gate is nearly impregnable. From now on, from this point forth, you will lift it for no one. Tell the villagers to turn back and clear the passage or they will be killed. And if they do not listen and you have to, kill them. Trust nothing; trust no one. Keep the passage clear and the gate closed. Do you understand me?"

"Kill villagers?"

"Kill anything that tries to get through to the north. You cannot risk it. If Hericlon is breached, our homeland is at risk and that cannot happen. This gate is closed; this passage is no longer open to anyone."

"As you say, but—"

"Trust nothing, Anton! You can no longer take any chances; you are too few and there is too much at stake. The gate of Hericlon will remain closed. Do we understand each other?"

"Yes."

"How many men do you have left?"

"Thirty—thirty Galagleans."

"That is all?"

"We were seventy, but many of them deserted."

"You have veterans out there, warriors who will stand their ground. Gather them and make sure there are no more desertions. We will take some measures, get help from Galaglea, protect you from the Uttuku—"

"Uttuku? What are Uttuku?"

Rhywder sighed, shaking his head.

✝

Outside, more then ten Galagleans had gathered about the captain's quarters and were left staring at Agapenor. He could guess what was on their minds.

"Any of you wish to know what is happening here, just step up," said Agapenor. "Step up and ask."

One of them did, a large Galaglean, though not as large as Agapenor. "Can we leave this godless vale? Drop the gate and try to reach King Quietus in Galaglea? If we move in force instead of one or two at a time—"

Agapenor grabbed the warrior by his breastplate, knocked off his helmet, and whapped him in the side of his head. The Galaglean's knees buckled and Agapenor let him stagger to the side. "Now this man here—he did not ask the proper question. But any others of you that are curious and have other questions, step right up."

Anton stared at the Little Fox, horrified.

"You . . . you are going to leave, sir?"

"Yes."

"South? You are going into the southland, where they are being murdered and burned?"

"I am, but there are a few things I will do to help before I leave. Are your food stores intact?"

"Yes, the food stores are safe."

"Water wells?"

"The wells are fine, though the water seems darker. But no one has gotten sick."

"Good, good. Now, tomorrow at dawn, send a party of seven riders north, just to the edge of the vale, no farther. Along the foothills and the forest have them gather mandrake and garlic. There is garlic that grows along the edge of the western woods, and mandrake near the foothills. Have them gather as much as they can in a single trip."

"And what are we to do with it?"

"Every man wears at least one mandrake root about his neck, and all of you should wear wreaths of garlic cloves. Wear them day and night. The kind of creatures that killed your warriors today will often enter the mandrake before they enter a body. They are fooled by it, an old witch's trick."

"Yes, I understand—mandrake root and garlic."

"Tonight, once the moon reaches mid-sky, I want you to slay your fattest bull and speak Elyon's name over it. Take the blood and paint the lintels of your barracks. From the top of the gate's causeway, lower a wooden scaffold over the outer edge and paint the lettering of the gate's archway, making sure you cover every letter inscribed in the stone. Understand?"

"And will that help?"

"The screamers will stop coming."

Anton nodded. "Are . . . are you a priest?"

"Hardly. Now, I want you to bring me a rider, someone light and small. From your stockade select a black horse, the swiftest you have. Cut the neck of one of your laying hens and smear its blood into the coat of the horse, work it deep into the hide."

The boy stared back stricken. He nodded and stood, waiting.

"Do it; go, now, I do not have much more time!"

Anton rushed out of the quarters leaving the doorway open. Rhywder sighed, poured himself some wine. Anton was shouting orders. Agapenor ducked his head and stepped inside.

"What now, Captain?"

"We will be leaving south."

"And you are going to leave the gate in the hands of these fools?"

"With the portcullis closed, nothing will get through. It sounds as if there are nothing more than raiding parties out there. Failures and giants hunting blood. Nothing leads me to believe there is anything close enough to threaten Hericlon, at least not yet. They just need to get a runner through to Galaglea. Luckily, it is not that far."

Anton and two guards, both big Galagleans, entered with a boy, a young Daath, barely sixteen. Rhywder was encouraged to find the boy's hair was dyed silver. There was a brotherhood of young thieves in Ishmia who died their hair silver, and this boy was most probably one of them. At last a bit of luck—

he would at least be skilled at running, and probably was good with daggers. He was mostly skin and bone. Agapenor fingered one of the boy's arms and glanced to Anton.

"Food rations running low, Captain?"

"This boy is the cook's steward," answered Anton. "He is small and light, and he is a good rider. He just does not eat much. His name is Cathus."

"There a reason you do not eat, Cathus?" asked Agapenor.

"I eat," the boy answered. "When I am hungry, I eat."

"He will do fine," Rhywder said. "Strip him of the tunic."

Cathus was given no time to protest. His tunic was pulled up over his head. Rhywder unlatched the witch's talisman from his belt and set it against the boy's ribs, strapping it in place with a strip of leather.

"Do not remove this," Rhywder warned him.

The boy half-nodded.

"Give him back his tunic. Fit him with leather armor and give him a short sword before he leaves."

"Leaves?" the boy said. "I am going to leave?"

"You know your way to Galaglea?"

"Yes."

"That is where you are going."

Rhywder fished a small pouch from his belt and gave it to the boy.

"Eat some of those."

The boy pulled out crumpled, white flower petals. "What are they?"

"They will make you bold. Keep eating them every few hours."

The boy folded a couple into his mouth, chewing.

"Now listen careful, boy, if you see a specter, a wraith of the night, there is no need to fear it; the talisman I strapped to your chest will protect you. But if you see a man, if you see any riders—outrun them. We are giving you a fast horse, and using a bit of witchery to make him even faster. Let us hope no one finds you, but should it happen, you are light, your horse is fast, and speed will be your only prayer, understand?"

The boy nodded.

"Keep moving. Do not ride in the open, stay out of the Vale of Tears, circle to the west, near the trees, until you reach the flooded quarry. Once clear of the quarry, find yourself a shallow crossing along the river Ithen, and then head for Galaglea. If you have to, ride this horse into the ground, but get to Galaglea; understand?"

The boy nodded. They were strapping on leather armor. Anton handed the boy a scabbard and a short sword.

Rhywder pulled a papyrus scroll from Anton's table and wrote upon it. He folded it, used Anton's candle to seal the edge, and pressed the signet of his ring into the wax. He stuffed the papyrus into the boy's tunic. "That is for Quietus, the king of the Galagleans. Since he is a king, he should not be difficult to find. Show that paper to anyone who asks to see it. Any questions?"

The boy shook his head.

"Good. You just ride for all you are worth until you reach the wooden ramparts of Galaglea. Now, go, boy. Elyon's Light be with you and Godspeed." Rhywder slapped him on the back.

The boy nodded at Rhywder and stepped into the night.

Agapenor grunted. "That boy will never reach daylight, let alone Galaglea."

"We have given him a good horse and he is a thief, which means he can ride and use a blade. Have a bit of faith, Agapenor." Rhywder turned to give Anton a grim look. "I may or may not return, but whether you see me again or not, remember one thing: the gate remains closed."

"It will," Anton assured him.

As they left Anton's quarters and walked for the horses, Agapenor chuckled. "It looks as if all is well, Captain Rhywder of Lochlain. The Goddess smiles on you this night. You have sent a noble champion sure to reach Quietus in Galaglea, and you have a bold Daathan warrior and these fearless Galagleans left to hold the gate of Hericlon against all of Unchuria. No worries that I can see."

"None that I can think of, either, my friend," Rhywder answered, pulling himself into the saddle. "Let us find out what is waiting in the splendid swamplands due south."

"I will try not to wet myself from anticipation."

Chapter Sixteen

Axeman

It was before sunup, the dawn's mist still on the ground. Aeson and Lamachus had set out already to cut timber for a new fence beam so Adrea did not worry of having to explain Loch's appearance. She had thought of saying good-bye to Aeson, and that night she almost did, but all she managed was to cry, so she decided to send an epistle later on, words of farewell by papyrus.

Adrea searched from the house, from behind the fence. She was packed, everything stowed and ready. Thunderbolt was saddled and she searched the skies, worried. She had thought over taking the horseman's gift or leaving the stallion behind, but finally decided to take him. He was swift, he would be useful, but that was not her reason. She knew enough of Marcian's nature that she believed he would want her to keep the horse.

She had said nothing to her mother. There would be too many tears, so she decided on a letter for her, as well, and perhaps one for Lamachus, who would never forgive her this.

Aeson helped Lamachus lash the last of the newly cut fence posts onto the side of the packhorse with strips of leather. They only needed one, actually, but there was no reason not to stock up—posts were laid to either side of the horse, enough to last a season of moons. Aeson would have ridden farther to the south, far past the sacred woods of the East of the Land, but Lamachus had found a small stand of wood that was separate by nearly a quarter of a league.

Some would consider it too close; call it a part of the forest, and Aeson worried, but Lamachus told him this wood was safe to cut. It was new wood, he reasoned, since it was not part of the ancient trees, what could be the harm of it? They worked in the dark, cutting and shaping. Lamachus was determined to get the baron's fence solid before night and that meant a lot of riding, so they had come out early. Aeson kept staring into the shadows of the East of the Land. He kept thinking they were just too close, but he realized it was something else crawling beneath his skin. He began to have the certain feeling that in the deep shadows of the ancient wood something was stirring. He even thought for a moment he saw something indistinct, maybe no more than gray mist, but after seeing it he could not get it out of his head. Something was in the forest, something watching them, but how could he explain to Lamachus he was afraid? That they needed to forget about the posts and leave? There was no possible way, so instead Aeson worked as hard and fast as he could.

"You need not kill yourself, boy," Lamachus said at one point. "We have time."

"Just feel energetic, Father."

He was trimming off limbs with single blows, working quickly. But the eyes, the thing watching them, waiting in the shadows of the East of the Land—it did not move, it had found what it was seeking, and Aeson figured it had been seeking them. Aeson was almost in a panic, but he could think of nothing to say that would do anything but provoke Lamachus.

Besides, Lamachus seemed burdened himself. It had been with him all morning, since leaving the cabin, this heaviness—sadness. It was an odd emotion for Lamachus to carry.

Usually he was telling stories or talking of the wars, but this morning he had hardly spoken and once or twice he had sighed, heavily. Once he paused, holding his axe, looking to Aeson.

"You think I have ever been good to her, boy?"

"Adrea, you mean?"

"Her whole life—I ever been good to her?"

"Of course, Father."

"You know, son, I have loved that girl. When she was little and I would toss her into the air and she would screech with delight, ah, did I ever love her. But she grew and things—somehow they changed. I no longer knew how to speak to her, what to say to her. But lately, well, lately I been downright mean. And wrong, not trusting her. Marcian saw that. Just wrong."

"It is the pressure of knowing she is leaving, Father; it weighs on all of us."

"Aye, but then I think to myself, I been cold with her my whole life. Now it is ending, she will be leaving, and I cannot go back, make things different. God, why could I not have given the girl a hug now and then, why not tell her what has been in my heart? But no, I've just been hard on her, thinking it is a hard life and she best just learn that truth. It is the war did this to me. Stripped so much out of me. Hard was all it left me."

"She knows you love her, Father."

He sighed, cinching down the last strap.

"Well—that should do it, you think?"

"Plenty. Enough for spring and even summer, I figure."

"You worked damned hard, guess that is why we are done so early."

He shoved his axe in the saddle thong. Aeson was anxious to leave, he had already mounted, but for a moment Lamachus just stood there, staring off at the dim predawn sky.

"No matter how I think it, though," he said, "what I come up with is that I have been a bastard to her, Aeson, pure and simple. She is a good girl; she has not been betraying me, not that girl. She has a heart in her that is pure, always has been. What is the matter with me, son?"

"It is simply your nature, Father, being firm. She will be fine; she is strong." Aeson wanted to tell him to mount up, to get out of there. His skin was crawling. He couldn't remember ever being this frightened.

Lamachus sighed, deeply. He finally circled around and mounted his horse. "Well," he said sadly, "still a bit of time left, I suppose. Maybe I can make it right, not much, but maybe just a bit right. You think?"

Suddenly Lamachus turned to the east, toward the forest. He had spotted something in the trees. He had been a warrior and his eyes were quick. Whatever he spotted, it startled him. His mouth dropped open from what he saw.

Aeson turned, breathless.

They came swiftly, no warning, not a sound. It happened so fast neither Lamachus nor Aeson had any time to react. Lamachus pulled back so hard his horse reared, but they came like the wind, twisting out of the shadows. First they soared high and then dove straight for Lamachus.

"Father!" Aeson screamed.

All Aeson made out were gray shapes, shades, hands with groping fingers, open mouths moaning, some screaming, some of them women. They slammed into Lamachus, one after the other, like blows from a hammer, jerking him from one side to the other. How many there were, Aeson could not count, but they dove in and they did not come out.

"Father!"

Silence.

Lamachus was on his horse, barely gripping the reins, head hanging. For a moment, Aeson thought he was just going to fall, drop off. Aeson started forward to help, but paused because Lamachus slowly looked up, his manner strange, jerky. Aeson gasped. Lamachus had no eyes. They were gone, just holes there, covered by a kind of damp mesh and behind them a glow, like greenish coals burning.

Aeson backed his horse away. He was terrified, but still he raised his right hand, spread his fingers in the sign of the word. "Elyon's light before us!" he shouted. "Elyon's Light protect us!"

He was there; Loch was there at the fence. How he could appear out of nowhere on his enormous white stallion astonished Adrea. She had the ring tucked away in the folds of her tunic. After the dreams, knowing how many were going to die of the Seraphon, of her son, she wanted no more dreams. If she died, maybe, it was for the better. She knew if the Seraphon lived to reach manhood, many, many would die. Countless would die. The entire world would twist in an agony of death. How could the death of so many be asked? How could Elyon bless such dreams?

"It is time," Loch said.

"I am ready." She pulled Thunderbolt, equipped for travel, from the barn. All that was left was to cinch down the haversacks and bedroll.

She paused, seeing her mother in the doorway. It was early, and Camilla had not needed to make breakfast since Lamachus and Aeson had both left when it was still dark, so Adrea had held to the faint hope her mother would take the opportunity to sleep later than usual. But she was there now, and she knew. Sshe glanced from Adrea to Loch and back again. Adrea walked to her slowly, gave her a hug, and as she did, whispered in her mother's ear.

"Elyon's Light, dear mother, but I must leave now. I will not come back. Perhaps . . . perhaps you can tell them good-bye for me."

Camilla said nothing, but one or two tears fell as she watched her daughter turn and walk back to Thunderbolt. Loch backed his mount far enough to leap the fence. He rode to Adrea's side and dismounted to help her tie things down. He glanced at her mother only briefly, but Adrea could tell he had nothing to say. What could he say?

"The others?" he asked Adrea quietly.

"Left early to cut timber," answered Adrea.

"Just as well, Adrea, it would not be easy leaving them if they here watching."

He took the leather straps of her bedroll from her hands. "Let me do this." He cinched it down. "Know that I am so sorry."

"This has to be. We both understand what has to be."

"So why do I feel such shame? I feel like a damned thief."

"This is my choice, Loch. My choice to follow. Anywhere you go, I will be with you—you are no thief; you are my husband."

She looked past him, a sharp chill cutting through her at what she saw. Loch turned to see what had shocked her. It was a figure, galloping from the east across the fields, hair streaming, moving fast.

It was her father. The big man was coming at a thunderous gallop. It was too fast to be natural. There was something very strange—the horse looked to be almost flying.

"Go!" shouted Camilla. "Run, go! Before he can get here, Adrea."

Loch stared at the figure, alarmed. "Something is not right," he said.

"He looks angry," said Adrea. "Mother is right; we should just leave.

Certainly we can outrun him?"

Loch shook his head. "I do not think so."

"What do you mean? He has nothing but that old warhorse; he could not possibly keep up with . . ." She lost her words. Loch was right. He was moving like the wind, closing on them impossibly fast.

"I do not think that is your father, Adrea. It may look like him, but it is not."

"Where is Aeson?" Adrea asked. "I do not see Aeson."

"Mount up and be ready to run," he ordered. "I will make a stand to intercept him. It may be I will have to kill him, Adrea, but know that it is not your father. I fear your father is already dead, or would be soon no matter what happens."

Unexpectedly, once Lamachus had cleared the fence line and was on the road to the house, he pulled up on the reins and came at them slowly, the horse's breath steaming from the hard run.

Lamachus reached the edge of the cottage and brought the horse to a stop. He sat staring at the two of them calmly.

"What is this?" Lamachus said harshly, but his voice was strange, as if it were ten voices, all washed out and whispery. "I thought as much as this," he said. His head moved unnaturally, turning to Adrea. She gasped. His eyes! "This is your lover, is it not?" the voices said.

It was not Adrea's father, Loch knew that. Perhaps she understood, perhaps the ring had given her knowledge to know the power of the Uttuku, but Loch knew enough to even see them, inside the man; gray wraiths were writhing in him. It was painful, such possession, both for the body of the possessed and the Uttuku, but these were strong, first- and second-born dead—ancients. They could hold this body a long time without the flesh withering. He could see them clear enough to notice that as they moved inside they were speaking with each other, voices neither Adrea nor her mother would hear. The language was ancient, pre-Etlantian.

"Stay back," Loch commanded. He began to clear distance between himself and Adrea. "Whatever you do, both of you stay clear."

He knew that if they guessed who she was, what she bore, the Uttuku would go for Adrea, but they were being influenced by the emotions of their host, Lamachus, his suspicions for so long now confirmed—it affected even the Uttuku, and as Loch hoped, their rage for now focused on him as the first target.

"You are correct," Loch said, to provoke the rage even further. "We are lovers, the two of us. You have been deceived, old man."

The Uttuku could not help but absorb Lamachus's rage. The glow of their eyes became intense. He had stirred confusion in them. It was going to be one of his few advantages. He let the moist mesh of the empty eyes focus on him and stared back defiant, as if he could care less.

"Yes—it is me you want. To get to her, you must first come through me."

The eyes studied him without passion, the face frozen, no emotion. The spirits within were arguing with one another until finally they focused. All had now turned on Loch.

"Ohhh," said the voices. "We intend to, scion of Daath."

Taking Loch completely off guard, Lamachus suddenly drew a short sword from his belt and flung it. Loch had not even seen the blade. He was thinking of the big axe hanging against the horse's flank. The Uttuku moved swiftly. Loch barely had time to step clear. He twisted, the blade passing over his shoulder close enough to cut into the leather of his tunic above the breastplate. That was too close—he had never seen anyone move so fast. He realized this was not going to be an easy kill.

Adrea screamed.

"Stay back, Adrea!" shouted Loch, seeing her lift the reins. "Just stay back!"

The voices all chuckled at once.

Loch drew both his swords and took a stance. Lamachus dropped from the horse and without ceremony advanced. He had the big axe in one hand, angled to the side, and as a warrior he apparently carried still a buckler as well, for it was in his other hand, its face spiked with a lance tip, its edges sharp as a sword. He was not moving like the old man he was, but instead he moved with a powerful stride. There was no guessing the Uttukus' strength. He closed quickly, and when the axeman engaged, he wielded both weapons with deadly skill. Loch threw each blow aside, blocking everything that was thrown at him, but as quick as Loch was, as fast as he moved, he was not going to be able to dodge such blows for long.

The buckler sliced across his cheek. Loch spun in the dirt and as his long sword blocked the axe, he passed close enough to cut through Lamachus's leather tunic, leaving a gash in his side below the ribs deep enough to spill a line of rich blood.

Adrea watched in horror, unable to do anything. Camilla stood frozen in the doorway of the cabin.

The hilt of Loch's sword slammed into the stocky haft of the axe as it came down in an overhead blow, and Loch planted a side kick hard enough to stagger the big man. Loch then took his opportunity and drove in hard, both swords spinning, but the Uttuku countered deftly. They were able to anticipate his every move, moves Loch had perfected through years of training. Still, he was able for the moment to keep the Uttuku on defense, even driving them back, nearly off balance. That he managed this infuriated them, which was good—their anger was also Loch's weapon—the more they lost their temper, the more mistakes they were going to make. He needed only one.

"Slow for ancients," Loch taunted.

They were enraged and he was able to continue pressing them, continually driving them back. Even though they were countering every skilled blow, at least they were not able to turn the fight and attack. They snarled and hissed. Loch could see they were on the verge of losing focus, but somehow were able to move as one, continuing to fight with amazing fury. Still, all he needed was one slip, one slight opening. If he saw it, his instinct would take the death thrust and the Uttuku would be forced to leave the body. They needed the soul and heartbeat of the human they held prisoner. They could not wield a dead body. Loch managed another cut, this one slicing deep into the thick muscle of Lamachus's arm.

They became livid that he was able to score another wound. They screamed through tight teeth, infuriated. They had enough, they were ancients, they had lived centuries, and this was but a Daath before them. He could see them focus, taking in their rage, and finally they turned the fight, attacking with incredible power and speed.

Loch was suddenly being forced to use every ounce of skill and knowledge he possessed just to ward off their aim. The axe sliced through the air with a heavy whistling sound, the shield just as deadly, sideways, then upward, ever unpredictable. Each blow they chose was a deathblow if not blocked. When the fight had first begun, Loch had felt certain he could take them. Now he was simply staying alive. Even then, he continued to search for any opening, the slightest pause, anything.

Adrea slipped the ring over her finger, tried to learn from it some way of helping. She was watching the battle helplessly—the blades slicing, clanging, moving so fast it seemed impossible. She had never imagined men could fight with such speed and power, and watching she was amazed Loch was even able to keep blocking. But he did; he spun, ducked, twisted, and moved at times in such unexpected directions that the creature that was once her father would be thrown off its pace, but always it found him, drove him farther back, never slowing. There were moments when Loch, with the aid of the silvery Daathan cloak whipping, actually seemed to vanish. It was the legendary move of a Shadow Walker, and it seemed fantastic, but whatever was in Lamachus was able to outguess him, turn each time in the direction Loch dodged.

She saw movement from behind them, coming from the field Lamachus had ridden out of. It was another horse—Aeson's! It was coming at a gallop, but sadly, it was riderless..

Lamachus continued driving Loch back, the numbing hiss of the buckler followed by the heavy hum of the axe. Loch parried, blocked, back stepped, parried again, but even Adrea could see it would only be a matter of time. As good as he was, Loch could not possibly outmatch the strength and speed of this creature.

"Lamachus!" Loch shouted. She guessed he was trying to reach through to her father, past the creatures possessing him. "Lamachus, fight them! I do not want to kill you!"

"Oh, but we sooo want to kill you," the Uttuku all hissed back, chuckling, unaffected.

Adrea pulled a dagger from a sheath in her saddle. She readied it, but she had never thrown a dagger in her life. She tried to aim, but they were moving too fast, spinning one way, then another. If she were to throw this dagger it could as easily hit Loch as Lamachus.

She hardly noticed the riderless horse had now reached the fence and was coming toward the cabin at a steady trot. Then she saw a hand—Aeson, he was stealth riding! He was sideways, hanging from the horse's neck, out of Lamachus's line of sight.

Lamachus was momentarily distracted by the approaching horse and Loch took advantage of the slight pause. He spun low beneath the axe and his short sword stabbed into Lamachus's leg, a deep thrust near the groin. Blood sprayed outward. The axeman only snarled and turned on Loch with renewed fury, one heavy blow after another. Loch could barely hold him off and Adrea guessed the creature was using the last of its power, all it had, everything it possessed now focusing on killing Loch. She knew something about the kind of cut Loch had made; that it was fatal, and that the creature was running out of blood and life. His heavy axe was relentless, furious, coming downward, sideways, oblique, too swift to follow. Still, each blow was blocked by one of Loch's swords.

The horse came up behind them. The creature was focused solely, utterly on killing Loch; the Uttuku did not even see the figure leap atop the horse, and from there onto Lamachus's back, wrapping one arm about his thick neck to hang on. Lamachus tried to heave him off while still attacking Loch, but Aeson drove a dagger deep into the muscled neck, hard, burying it almost to the hilt. Finally, something had taken effect.

As Lamachus's body staggered, Loch stepped forward and drove a swift death thrust, into the heart and out, his blade like the flicker of a serpent's tongue.

It was over. The Uttuku swarmed out of Lamachus's chest. At first they frantically searched for a mark, another body; but it was not Loch, he was Daath and pure; nor was it Adrea; nor could they take Camilla, she was a Water Bearer, her heart too pure. Without a mark, they screamed and flew skyward, soaring, vanishing with screeches and cries.

Lamachus's body dropped to its knees. The buckler and axe fell away. His head sagged and he fell backward, into Aeson's arms.

Loch stood, for the moment too exhausted to even move.

Adrea rushed past them to reach Aeson, but when she got to him, she saw that though he held his father in his arms, his head was limp, his eyes sagged. Aeson was barely alive. She then saw the wound in him. Whatever had cut him had pierced through to his back where fresh blood trickled down his side. He was soaked in his own blood, coated in it. He had ridden up to them already dead, with life barely in him for his one last move, a move she had seen him practice so many times in the fields, leaping from the side to the back of his horse and bragging how he would some day be a good scout, the best.

Aeson couldn't lift his head, but he was able to move his eyes. They turned in his head, looking to Adrea.

"I . . . I saved you," Aeson whispered. "You and him, did I not?"

She wrapped her arms about his neck. "You did, Aeson! You saved us."

"Scout in me . . . after . . . after all . . ."

"Much more, much more in you than anyone could ever ask."

He half-smiled at her, and then he collapsed. Lamachus rolled to lay face-down beside his son. Aeson's body stilled, his face staring blankly upward at the sky.

Adrea cried out, tears streaming as she reached forward and pulled his lids closed.

Their mother reached them, crouching at her son's side. Camilla cried out and pulled Aeson's body into her lap, stroking his hair.

Adrea backed away, horrified.

"Go!" Camilla said. "He has given you time with the last of his blood. What if there are more of them? Go with your man, Adrea. Run, both of you."

Loch led Thunderbolt and helped Adrea into the saddle, then mounted the white stallion.

"My sorrow, good woman," he said, turning the horse.

Adrea and Loch then turned and set off at a gallop, leaping the fencing.

Camilla watched them until they were out of sight.

Passing through the trees of the East of the Land, Adrea and Loch drew up when they reached the center of a circle of ancient standing stones. It seemed a place he knew well, a place he felt safe enough to pause. He curled a fist against his thigh.

"We should keep riding," she said, "keep moving, should we not?"

"Yes."

"Then why do you wait?"

He didn't answer right away. He searched the trees. "I am not certain of my path. Perhaps it is better I draw them off, leave you. This is a place of power, this circle of stone. Creatures such as the Uttuku cannot even cross into it, and here you are also hidden, eyes cannot see you. If I head west, they will follow me."

"And then what? What do I do, wait here forever?"

He glanced at her.

"I know things, Loch; I have learned quickly, the ring has taught me just as you said. They are hunting us—not just Uttuku, but others, riders, assassins. Loch, I can see the near future. What you suggest, it will fail and you will die for nothing."

"Do you see any path that will not fail? The ship is due north and west. It is not far, your horse is easily as fast as mine—we could reach it. There are brief covers of wood, but we will have no choice but to cross at least two open fields."

"All I see is that we die. I am sorry, my love. I see these futures like shadows, images. I see choice, but all of them end in the same way. We die. Not long from now."

"There are many futures, and there is a path! This cannot end here! It will not."

"Can you command time? All I see, all the ring tells me, is that they will kill us and they will kill the child in me. I see nothing else, Loch."

"I do. I see light. We will follow it, take my path." He met her eyes. "I do not believe it is over, Adrea. I will find a way through. Now, we ride forward and when we reach the edge of the sacred trees, we must cross the field just beyond it. There is a patchwork of woods and farms. Just beyond them, an inland river is where the ship waits. In the open field, you stay close. I will ride hard and unpredictable—just stay with me."

He touched her hand, her cheek, and then she watched his eyes darken, and the Shadow Walker came into him like someone stepping into his skin. It was the other she loved, the soft brown eyes. She wondered, briefly, if she would see them again.

He looked skyward. "They may be close; they may not. It comes time to run the gauntlet."

"I am with you, Loch!"

"Elyon's Light guide us."

He started off at a good clip, breaking into a gallop. As she followed at his side, Adrea searched through the shadows of the forest. Nothing in them, she could tell. She was learning quickly, more and more, but somehow she felt them running out of time in this world, and she knew that if that happened, it could mean the end of all worlds.

"Hard and fast," Loch said, emerging from the trees at full gallop. He shouted, urging the horse even more speed. His stallion was fast. It was good she had chosen Thunderbolt; nothing in Lamachus's stables could have kept up with the white charger, but Marcian's stallion kept at his side easily. They streamed through tall wheat, moving faster than ever she had before. They would be hard to catch, she knew that much, but still the fear remained, *the knowing* in her that all paths led to an ending from which there was no escape. She trusted Loch. Perhaps he knew more; perhaps he knew something she didn't.

She glanced back. She was shocked to find there were riders coming for them, that they had already been found. There were at least six, moving in a swift line obliquely from the west.

Loch and Adrea would easily outrun them. These were perhaps two of the finest horses anywhere. Before the riders could close on them enough to draw their bows, Loch and Adrea had crossed the open field and reached the woods beyond it. They tore into them, into their shadows and cover. She noticed, glancing behind, that oddly, the riders in pursuit slowed up. They did not even enter the woods. It could only mean something else waited on the other side.

In the trees, Loch's path wove tightly; he rode low on the horse, hugging the neck. "They have nothing that can touch us in deep water," he shouted. "If we reach the warship, there are bowmen and catapults to protect us. We will be safe! Just one more field to cross. Only one more open field and we have made it!"

But tears streamed across Adrea's cheek. She did not know if the tears were for Aeson and her father, or if they were for her and Loch. She felt something closing now as though it was bearing down from the sky. Only one more clearing, but her new knowledge, the ring and its power, told her that whatever closed on them now was something they could not outrun.

Loch broke from the trees hugging the neck of his horse, full gallop, and they went for the river, everything they had now, every muscle and sinew into this hard, pumping run, both horses side by side, close. It was there; she could see the river beyond. They were tearing through a field of dried cornstalks, and ahead of them she noticed the top of the ship's highest mast. But then her heart sunk. Flames were curling up the mast. The ship was burning. It had already been taken. Loch saw the same thing; he reared the horse, knowing they had ridden into a trap. The white stallion whinnied, rearing as Loch circled him, searching for a direction.

"The sea!" he shouted. "We make a run west for the sea!"

They turned, breaking into a gallop, but archers rose not far from them, standing up out of the rows of corn. They had been lying in wait. Missiles flew in swift exchange, and both horses went down.

Loch's white stallion dropped hard. When it struck the ground, its chin was shattered, the neck as well, and the horse rolled. Loch had managed to throw himself aside.

Thunderbolt was stronger, quicker. For seconds, he seemed to dodge the arrows; he pressed for the end of the clearing, determined. When he dropped, he came down sideways. It seemed he was straining to protect his rider. His body slid through the cornstalks as arrows thudded into his back and shoulders. Adrea was thrown clear, landing behind him. She rolled, turned, and quickly crawled to the cover of Thunderbolt's belly. The arrows were heavy, zinging over her head, others striking Thunderbolt. He grunted with each strike and then she felt the moment his spirit finally left him. He had not wanted to die. He had fought to the last with everything he had.

Loch crouched in the grass, spotting Thunderbolt's body. He ran for them, arrows whispering about him, but he was somehow able to dodge. He spun, the cloak working its magick, and momentarily he vanished. When he reappeared, he was diving over Thunderbolt's body. He turned and crawled up beside her.

"This is not finished," he said, defying logic. He wasn't giving up.

"Loch . . ."

"Yes?"

"I love you. I mean, we know that we have always loved, but I am not speaking of memories. I speak of here and now. I love you. Just in case we do not make it, I wanted you to know."

He stared at her, touched by what she said, but the Shadow Walker was in his eyes, and he watched her with an inhuman gaze. "It is not over," the Daath insisted. "Nothing is ending here. This is not finished. They still have to come through me."

"I pray you speak true, Loch."

He turned, drawing his swords. "You have the gift of a seer now, and you use it well. But even the most gifted of seers have been wrong on occasion."

Horse hooves—coming for them, fast, hard.

"Sounds like five or more," Loch said. "They are few in number, these assassins. It is how they managed to get this far north, by being few. I believe these are the archers—they will not be as well trained in close kills. I will take them down."

He handed her a dagger. "This is not to fight with. If somehow they manage to get past me, if they kill me, put this through your heart. End it there."

She nodded. By the sound of their hooves, the horsemen were now spreading out.

"And I have always loved you," he said, "even if I do not remember all your names." He took a breath. His eyes were dark as an eclipsed moon. He was waiting, his swords clutched, timing his attack.

"Faith's Light, Lochlain of the Daath."

"Faith's Light, Water Bearer."

With a scream he stood, leapt the dead husk of Thunderbolt, and ran, weapons tucked against his chest. Once he had cleared enough distance from her, he dropped into a back stance, swords whipping, poised to either side. "Here!" he shouted. "Here I am! Come welcome death!" He waited emotionless as they turned and closed on him.

He first took out the neck of a horse, leaving it to tumble, crushing its rider. He next severed a horse's leg below the knee. It went down hard. As the third rider reached him, Loch leapt high, spinning, slicing open the horse's throat, then quickly stabbing the rider through the inner thigh with his short sword.

He dropped low. The fourth horseman was fast on the other's heels. This Unchurian managed to strike Loch with a heavy morning star, knocking him aside. Loch's armor had protected him, barely dented. On his feet, Loch sheathed his swords and reached behind his back to draw two daggers. As the horseman turned to maneuver for a kill, Loch's first knife sank into his throat, the tip out the back of his neck. The rider dropped.

Loch then killed the horse, a knife to its throat, as well.

No more, not for the moment—there were no riders, no archers, all was quiet.

"You do not think we might have used that horse?" Adrea asked, still crouched behind Thunderbolt.

"No. On horseback we merely make better targets at this point. The tall corn is our cover for now."

He searched, crouched and waiting. She carefully stepped around Thunderbolt and came to his side.

Everything was still for a moment and then, from the tangled wood near the shore, there came a single rider. Unlike the others, he came slow and easy, as if time did not matter. He did not wear armor; rather he had an outer skeleton of hard, darkened wood. It covered his face, his legs, arms, even fingers. He wore a blue cloak, cut in strips to drop between dark, leathery wings. This was the firstborn of a prefect—a Nephilim that had abandoned his own body to house himself in one grown from the thorn wood ancient spell binders had created. Loch had heard of these creatures, but never had he seen one. The polished wood looked hard as stone.

"Run," Loch said.

"What?"

"Get out of here! Run! Now!"

Loch growled and charged the rider, building speed as he ran, head down, nothing in his mind but to attack. He leapt when he reached the horse, swinging up and behind the rider to bury his short sword into the chest at an angle, piercing an opening through the bone armor. He rode the Nephilim to the ground as they both went over the side of the horse. When they hit the ground, Loch was on top and continued to plunge his short sword deeper. Loch then stood, drawing his long sword, and as the giant started to rise, he slammed the pommel into the eye socket.

The Nephilim did not even seem to care of the wounds. He knocked the sword aside, took Loch by one shoulder, and threw him as though he were weightless. Loch hit the ground hard, sliding on his back. The Nephilim flung a dagger sideways, not bothering to even check his aim. It pierced Loch's breastplate in the shoulder and for the moment, he went down.

In a single beat of its wings, the Nephilim was suddenly close enough to touch Adrea. But at first he did not try. He simply stared at her, taken, as if he wished to admire her beauty. One eye socket was crushed by Loch's blow, but both of them held a dark, distant light she could barely make out—the soul of the Nephilim.

Over his shoulder, Adrea noticed Loch come to his knees and wrench the dagger from his shoulder where it had lodged mostly in his armor. On his feet, he soundlessly moved for his sword.

The Nephilim touched her hair.

Loch was running for them, his long sword against his chest, but the creature did not look back; instead he seemed to tip his head, noticing something. He looked to Adrea's stomach.

When Loch reached them, the beast simply snarled. He turned to knock the long sword aside with a sweep of his hand. He twisted to the side, grabbing

Loch by one arm, and threw him over his shoulder, slamming him so hard into the ground that Loch did not get up or even move.

Now the Nephilim could take his time. He stepped back toward Adrea, started to reach for her—but Adrea had laid the tip of Loch's knife against the vein in her throat.

"Touch me and I am dead. You will have no life to suck. I deny you."

"Cut your pretty throat," he said, his voice a harsh whisper, distorted. "It will be disheartening, but I have the life I came in search of. I will kill this one, his father is already dead, and the last scion of the Daath is in you. It is over; it ends now."

She tried to stab at her abdomen, but this creature moved far swifter than she. He slapped the dagger from her hand. He grabbed her hair, drew a sword, and was about to behead her when suddenly there was a pulse, a burst of some kind, like nothing Adrea had seen before. It was pure and white and focused. The Nephilim simply turned into shadow, then scattered as dust in the light wind from the ocean.

Adrea turned to see the Etlantian named Sandalaphon behind her on a huge horse. He was watching her, sheathing a sword whose blade was still pulsing with a silver-blue.

He looked at her only a moment, then rode past toward Loch. Adrea felt something from him—she sensed it. The creature he had just slain was once his brother. He had just killed one of his own—a light bearer's child.

"No shame, Loch," the giant said sternly as Loch moaned, slowly struggling to get to his feet. "You did all you could. He would have proved hard to kill for anyone."

Loch was able to stand, breathing with difficulty until he pried off his dented armor and threw it aside. He looked around for a corpse.

"Where is he?" asked Loch. "The Nephilim?"

"Slain," Sandalaphon said. "He is dust. His spirit—who can say? You had no chance, Lochlain. He was a firstborn son of a prefect. He would have killed you both and taken the child."

"His father?" asked Loch.

"His father was my father," Sandalaphon answered. "They did not yet realize there was a child. This one just slain, he discovered the scion, but only when he was near enough to smell the girl. Until then he was unaware. But his senses were keen, strong; others may now know what he saw.

"Assassins moved through this land from the south, they were few in number, but they spread out and chose their targets carefully. They meant to wipe out the bloodline of Uriel by killing both you and your father. They failed to take you, and though you will still be hunted, for now you are safe. But know something, prince of Daath; they have slain your father. Argolis is dead."

There was only slight emotion in Loch's face over his father's death. He seemed determined not to care, but his eyes were no longer black. They softened.

"Many will soon move against the Daath," Sandalaphon said. "It begins. Azazel comes with his armies against your people from the south of Hericlon—he comes with many. But do not fear the sea, as well. I suspect Eryian will learn enough to move his legions for the south. But if they find this girl, none of it that will matter."

"Then what?" asked Loch. "Hide her? Where?"

"It is not possible to hide her in this world. They see everything in this world and shortly they are all going to realize what has occurred. You have taken a queen that opened the eye of Daath. No one expected that. Not even me."

"Then what are we to do?"

"I can think of only one thing to try. I must take her and attempt to jump time. If I can, I will open but a small rift, one barely felt, and find a future so closely parallel to this that it will intercept, fuse, become one."

"That happens?"

"It can be done. I know that is difficult to understand, but that is the way of the star knowledge. There are things I cannot fully explain. It will be difficult, even for me, and it is possible I will fail. But I see no other path. Even if I were to remain, try to protect her, they would get past me. The only chance we have is for me to attempt a star walk.

"I will leave you as bait, but even you will not know my destination. I am sorry. If I fail, you may not be able to find her, even in all of time, but then if I fail, all will fail, Aeon's End will swallow this Earth, this universe, everything you see or know."

"You are certain of this?"

"I am certain."

Loch noticed tears streaming down Adrea's cheeks.

"I am sorry—I know you have both only now found each other. But it must be done, and it must be now; we cannot delay."

"Now?" asked Loch. "This moment?"

"The powers that seek out the scion of Uriel are stronger than even you imagine. We cannot wait. It must be now. Which leaves you both to say good-bye."

Loch turned to her. His eyes were burning and if he let his emotions out, he might have found words for her, but all he could do was offer his hand in the sign. When her fingers touched his, he pulled her close; he pulled her hard against him and held her for all he was worth. No tears came. Perhaps he had no tears, but he clung to her because he would need to remember this, the feel of her, the smell of her.

"Good-bye, my love," she whispered in his ear.

He stepped back. She stared at him, lines of tears down her cheeks.

Sandalaphon bent in the saddle and lifted her, pulled her against his chest.

"You have done well, scion of Uriel. You fought as a lion. Faith's Light, kindred."

Loch swallowed past the knot in his throat and turned away. He did not want to see them vanish. He closed his eyes, head lowered. He felt something pass through him, like a cold, soft wind. The earth around him shivered slightly, and then quiet closed in. He shivered, sadness moving through him like rain as he slowly turned. They were gone. There was nothing there but the dead Unchurians and fallen horses.

He had been alone before, but never so utterly. He could no longer feel her, not her flesh, not her soul, not her spirit. He no longer even had the ring to give him dreams of her. It was as though she had vanished utterly from his world. Perhaps forever.

He walked through the field, steeling himself against the sadness, tightly drawing in his emotion and forcing it deep where it could not affect him. He began a run, keeping an easy, steady pace toward Terith-Aire. It was a far distance, but he thought of nothing as he ran; he left his mind as empty as the sky.

Chapter Seventeen

Runner

It had been a far journey from the gate of Hericlon to Galaglea for Cathus. It was like nothing he had known. But after four days, he was still alive. One would not have guessed by looking at his emaciated form, but Cathus the thief was very good at staying alive.

He had ridden as Rhywder had commanded. He had pressed down the twisting passes of Hericlon and about the edge of the Vale of Tears. Once or twice he passed through something insubstantial, a mist like it was formed of gnats, but he continued to ride. He did not look back. His fear of the night mounted until it became as fears often did, until it melted into itself, numbness, a resignation. If something was going to happen, then so be it. His father had taught him that before he was killed in a tavern bar, leaving Cathus homeless.

Cathus was ten and five years. He had lied about his age to join the Daathan legions, but in these days, the Daath cared little of names or ages; there were garrisons in far lands that housed many youths who had simply run away. And Cathus had been running all his life. He had grown in the twisted streets of the rich port city of Ishmia. He had never known father or mother. How he had reached an age where he could steal and eat, he did not remember.

The first night of Cathus's ride from Hericlon passed without event. Cathus had circled the quarry, and though it was wide and deep and stank of swampland, still it was quiet. He kept along the trees, his shield over his shoulder, one hand always on his dagger.

He had slept the day curled under a fallen log, his horse given heaps of pulled grass and tied to a sapling in a gully. With nightfall he rode on. It was the second night when things grew difficult. It was not long before he found he was pursued—not by demons or spirits or haunting or screaming winds, but riders. If you see a man, him you fear, the Little Fox had told him.

Looking back, he saw them coming through the trees, six or more—Unchurians.

Cathus was good at running away, and they had given him an agile, quick horse. He took a twisting, deceptive run through the trees, keeping low. Cathus decided perhaps his ability to fade into shadow had something to do with the rooster's blood they had smeared into the hide of the horse. It had seemed idiotic as he had watched the big Galagleans painting the hide with rooster blood from a bucket, but now Cathus understood it was the reason he was able to outride his pursuers the entire night.

At first light, the trees ran out. There was a long stretch of clear ground before the lake of the Ithen, and here they killed his horse. Cathus was certain they had meant to kill him, but the javelin, dark-wrought with a heavy, barbed tip, dropped low and lanced the horse's underbelly. Cathus dove over the mane and hit the ground in a roll. He sprang to his feet. The riders were closing on him at full gallop, spears and even axes at the ready. Cathus gasped and did a full-out run for the waters of the lake. He wasn't going to reach a shallow crossing below as the captain had told him, but the lake was his only chance.

Cathus's long sinewy legs stretched their limit, going hard, his straggly hair blown back as javelins and arrows sang about him.

"Elyon's Light be with me!" Cathus screamed aloud, taking his longest strides. "Elyon be my shield. I know I done many wrong things, but forgive me now, save me now!" He ran in switchbacks, losing precious distance, but never giving them a direct target for their terrible spears. One soared past his ears with a scream.

They were closing. It would all be over soon. The thunder sound of hooves was bearing down on him. He was never going to make it. Cathus urged speed to his legs. He closed his eyes and threw his head back, and he ran as he had never run in his life. He felt that if a wind could catch him from the back, he could have flown. He hit the dark water still running, wildly high-stepping, and dove headlong. With a gulp he was under, and he swam deep. Though he was winded, he swam hard, keeping as much underwater as he could. When he broke the surface, frantic for air, arrows immediately zinged through the water about him. Cathus dove under again, stroking beneath the waters like fish must do all their lives. He broke the surface and this time glanced back. They were still mounted, dark riders, searching along the shoreline. But they didn't wish to swim and possibly they didn't deem him worth the trouble. They watched from the banks, then one turned, then another, and they rode slowly back for the trees.

Cathus swam the entire length of Ithen Lake. It was a hard swim. If he had the horse he could have ridden past the point where the Galagleans had dammed the river that formed the lake long ago, and found a shallow crossing. But now he had no choice other than a long swim.

At times he rested, rolling onto his back and doing a lazy stroke while he caught his breath. The water of the old quarry was very, very deep. No one alive knew how deep. It was black and he imagined creatures lying on the slimy bottom watching him with jelly eyes.

When finally he staggered onto dry land, it was midmorning, and his legs and arms were rubbery and aching. He stood a moment, swooning. He glanced down to find the scroll was useless mush. He pulled it out and spread it on a rock very, very carefully. The print was still legible—the ink was water-resistant—but he would have to let the paper dry or it would become pulp. There was a hollow in the rock, out of the sun, and he crawled in to wait. There he fell asleep.

From ages of sleeping in treacherous alleys and gutters and beneath wharves, Cathus had learned to keep an ear awake for sounds. Thus, his eyes flicked suddenly open when he heard the air stir. A horse danced. A hand lifted the scroll from the rock. From beneath the rock, Cathus saw the rider. He was tall in the saddle. Long, straight hair fell over his shoulder. It was black, but for a lock of it, to the left, which was a silvery sheen. Cathus screamed and leapt to his feet. There were trees to the right, and Cathus ran for them, gasping. For a moment the rider didn't pursue, but then he turned the reins and the horse galloped with heavy hooves.

Cathus was a good runner, but he could not outrun a horse. He would in moments be dead. At the very moment he felt the rider close, some weapon rising for the back of his neck, Cathus dove for the earth, rolling. The rider brought his horse about. Sharp hooves assailed the earth about Cathus as he rolled one direction, then another. The rider finally snarled, then dropped off the horse. Cathus scrambled to his feet and ducked the arc of a sword blade, then dove to tackle the Unchurian's feet. The rider had not expected this, especially from an emaciated boy. They rolled in the dirt. The Unchurian was strong, he would have killed Cathus easily, but Cathus had one skill that had kept him these years in the streets as a vagrant. He knew how to use a dagger. Cathus stabbed the assassin between the ribs, stabbing and stabbing and stabbing.

When Cathus struggled away and looked down, he was amazed, for he must have stabbed the Unchurian six or seven times. Blood was everywhere. His head was dizzy from sheer terror.

The Unchurian was not dead. He had propped himself on one elbow and lifted his own hand from his gut to study the dripping blood. He looked to Cathus, stunned. "You little whelp-shit," he snarled. Then, he fell over and died.

Cathus looked at the horse. As he started for the reins, it reared and attacked him. A hoof hit his shoulder, and Cathus staggered. The horse reared and came for him again. Cathus dove to the side and rolled into the body of the Unchurian. Seeing the assassin's long sword in the dirt he scrambled, grabbing the hilt with both hands. On his knees, he screamed, slashing at the horse. He thrust the blade deep into the horse's chest. It almost fell over him, but Cathus scrambled out of the way.

The rest of the day, Cathus ran. Surely he was as good a runner as any champion in the games, keeping measured pace. Surely, the day would come when bards would tell of the great run of Cathus. He could imagine many of the verses already.

When finally he reached Galaglea, Cathus felt like a bird that had died, its corpse blown in the wind. He was so spent; he staggered, exhausted, past thick-built, wooden houses and halls. Galaglea was a land of thick timber, and they liked to leave the outside of their buildings unfinished with the bark still on the wood.

The palace of the king, Quietus the Falcon, was a great wooden hall, and

Cathus made his way wearily through its great oaken pillars. It was a night of feasting and the king and his lords were gathered, but as Cathus entered, he was immediately seized by guards and thrown into a hole in the earth. Heavy bars were dropped, and his cries fell on deaf ears.

"I must see the Falcon! I have come from Hericlon! I have swum the Ithen Lake. I have run all the way to Galaglea! Someone must hear me!"

He was left in the hole for hours, but he kept screaming, he never stopped, and someone must have become irritated, because finally a big Galaglean guard came to reach in and pull him out with a yank. He was dragged to the king, right into the big mead hall, right past the lords of Galaglea, who were having their meal, smelly from shanks of pig and flagons of sour mead.

Quietus, the Falcon of Galaglea, was a huge man with a large head and a mane of thick, shaggy hair. His red beard of stiff hairs fell to his chest. Cathus was held before the king by two Galagleans, who held both his arms, his legs sagging. He hadn't even tried to use them since he had nearly run them off his body and was so nearly starved he was sure he couldn't walk.

"This be the waif?" Quietus said, setting down his clay mug and looking to Cathus.

"This is he, my lord."

"Boy, I have been told you keep screaming that you have run all the way from Hericlon. That true?"

"No, I had a horse part of the way. It was smeared in chicken blood. But I swam the Ithen Lake and ran all the way from there in one day."

"Why for the love of God would you smear your horse in chicken blood?"

"It was the Daath ordered that, my lord Quietus."

"What Daath? Explain me this."

"He called himself Rhywder, the Little Fox."

Quietus drew back with a start. He glanced at one of the big captains beside him, then back to Cathus. "Can you prove me this, boy?"

"He pressed his ring signet into the scroll I carry."

Quietus stretched forth his hand. "Hand me the scroll."

Cathus looked down and gasped. "Oh, lord, oh, Elyon's name, I . . . I forgot it! I left it on the rock."

"You ran all the way here from Hericlon to give me a scroll but you forgot to bring it along?" Quietus looked wide-eyed and many Galagleans chuckled.

"I wouldn't have forgot it if I hadn't been attacked, my lord."

"Who attacked you?"

"An Unchurian assassin."

"Where?"

"Beyond the lake, my lord."

"Unchurians are killed on sight at Hericlon, boy. How did one get beyond to reach you at the lake?"

"They are getting through. They have raided the villages and mines to the south of Hericlon, they have slaughtered and burned villagers, they are blood drinkers, flesh eaters. Some even eat children, my lord. I hear the whole of the south has fallen."

Quietus raised a thorny brow. "That is not possible, boy. The Unchurian south of Hericlon live in trees and hunt ground rats."

"These are different."

"Explain me this."

"The one I killed . . ."

"You killed one!"

"Yes, my lord, with my dagger. I kilt him. I cut up his stomach good. He was tall, not like Unchurian, and part of his hair was silver."

Quietus stared at him a moment.

"Which part?"

"A strand to the right; his hair was all black but for the silver strand."

Quietus glanced at one of his captain. "The mark of a firstborn," he said, "could only have come from the deep south. How would the boy know that?"

The captain shook his head.

Quietus eyed Cathus skeptically. "Bah, can't believe a word of this. Take him. Throw him back in the hole."

Cathus gulped as they turned to drag him off.

"Wait," Quietus said.

Cathus was wrenched around once more to face Quietus.

"Say the name of my century captain, boy, who be stationed at Hericlon."

"Craigus, my lord, but he has been killed now."

"What?"

"They most have been killed. We have only thirty left to man the gate. The one named Craigus, he hacked out his own face with a dagger. It is said he was taken by evil spirits, the Uttuku."

Quietus narrowed his brows. "Boy would not make up such a tale; how would he even know of Uttuku being so young and thin as a bird? Something wrong here." Quietus glanced to the captain beside him. "What you make of this, Rathon?"

"Seems a good liar if a liar he is, but I fear I smell the truth, my lord. Hericlon is in trouble, and how would he know the name of Rhywder, a boy like this?"

The entire hall of men was silent as Quietus closed his eyes in what Cathus imagined to be heavy, deep thought. In short time, Cathus was either to be thrown in the hole or written of in books by bards and sung of by minstrels for his heroic run. He waited, breathless, until Quietus finally looked up.

"Damned with it. I can't decide," Quietus said. "But we march on Hericlon if for no other reason than to smell horseflesh and to strap on weapons once more." He stood, raised a fist. "For Hericlon!" he shouted.

The Galagleans all screamed in response.

"Gather yourselves up and speak to your womenfolk!" Quietus shouted above them. "We march in tomorrow for the gate!"

Great cries went up. The nobles stood and screamed. Knives were driven into the great, oaken tables. Clay mugs were smashed against the walls, dripping grog. Quietus stormed out of the hall, and his lords followed him. In moments the entire hall was emptied of Galagleans. Cathus stood alone but for a gathering of children who were playing with a wooden hoop. Cathus crawled onto the table, squatted before a large wooden platter of massacred pig, and began to stuff himself. He considered Galagleans, as a race, wholly insane, but they could roast a good pig.

Chapter Eighteen
Unchurians

Agapenor gazed at Rhywder. The Little Fox was turning two rabbits on a spit over a low fire. He had lured the small beasts from their hole by crouching at the entrance and making whispering sounds through his hands that implied he spoke rabbit.

"You have a woman, Little Fox?" Agapenor asked. "Some redhead bint in the city who marks each day until you return? Or perhaps a village maid who warms her bed with stones when the Little Fox is not about?"

Rhywder looked up. He lifted a sizzling, well-cooked rabbit and tossed it, spit and all. Agapenor caught the sizzling flesh in his fist and held it, even though the hot juice was dripping. He grinned.

"I was going to mention it might be hot," Rhywder said. "Looks like I need not bother."

"It is calluses," Agapenor said, tearing away a rabbit leg. "Calluses build up. You work the stakes with a heavy axe, years pass, your hand becomes like leather." He sucked the meat off one leg and it left white and clean. "So, you have any women, Rhywder?"

"No."

"Why not?"

"Let us just say that I do not keep women and leave it at that."

"Ah . . . one of those kind." A second cleaned leg bone was tossed. "Would not have thought that of you."

Rhywder paused. "No, Agapenor, I *prefer* women. I just do not keep them. They tend to follow you around, cook you things. Become a bother."

Rhywder carefully broke off a hind leg of rabbit and bit off a chunk of meat. In contrast, watching Rhywder with bemusement, Agapenor took the remainder of his small rabbit, opened his mouth wide, wider, and with some effort managed to stuff the entire body into his mouth. There was a wide grin across the puffed-out cheeks as he began to chew, with difficulty at first, crunching. Apparently it was all for Rhywder's amusement.

Rhywder had to wince.

"I have but one woman," Agapenor said when he could talk, after pulling out chunks of spine and tossing them. "One woman—a full-blooded woman whose bottom I can hold in both my hands." He held out his big hands in demonstration of the indicated size. "One woman! What do you think of that, Little Fox?"

"That is a big woman."

"Children, as well. My woman bore me twelve fat children."

The axeman continually amazed him. "How many, did you say?"

"Nine of them boys, all strong; three of them wee girls. Ah, God, but I do love the wee girls more, curse me but I do. I oft think of them when I find myself in godless places such as this one you have brought me to presently."

He pulled a bone from his mouth that had been cleaned and sucked white as a newly formed tooth. He studied it a moment, admiring his work, then tossed it. "I wish to know where we are. Tell me."

Agapenor lifted a wineskin and tore off the cork. He tipped his head back, drinking until the last drop was gone, and tossed the empty skin.

They were camped beneath tangled mangrove roots, near a swamp whose smell threatened to become odious if the wind shifted, but would hide them well from any scouting parties. Insects bearing certain disease were thick in the air. They rubbed themselves down with garlic cream to ward off bugs. And after a day of sweat against the garlic, the Galaglean smelt like a decaying elephant. Rhywder was keeping well upwind of him.

They crisscrossed jungle. Dusk, the day before, they had come upon an abandoned camp. They had ridden through it awestruck. Bones riddled the ground from feeding, and the underbrush had been trampled to mud all around. Agapenor had paused.

"You notice most of these bones look human?"

"They are human—my guess, the majority of these bones are gathered villagers. I think these were giants, probably Failures that came through here living Enoch's curse, flesh and blood needed to sustain them."

In a grove, Rhywder found an altar strewn with rotting hearts. He was used to seeing altar stone sheathed in rotting blood, but this one was weathered and clean. Instead it was littered with scores of hearts that were left nothing but tight little knots, like peach pits. They had obviously had the blood completely sucked out of them.

Whatever caused the carnage was close; Rhywder and Agapenor moved cautiously. They had ridden fairly deep in and when Rhywder found them, the tracks were swinging north toward Hericlon. They were moving slow, foraging as they went, gorging on villages. But they were moving in a meandering pattern, swinging wide before turning northward, which was how he and Agapenor had ended up behind them.

The stars were out, the moon nearly full, and they had not eaten in days, so Rhywder had chosen to take a chance with a fire. The thicket was good cover and the stink of the swamp would mask the smell of cooking. He imagined Agapenor was close to starving from eating roots and berries. Hot food would replenish them both.

"I am not entirely sure where we are," Rhywder finally answered. "But no worries, I can always find my way out. By the stars we are farther east of Hericlon than I expected."

"You read stars?"

Rhywder nodded.

"Where is it you learn all these secret things?"

"I travel a lot. And my grandmother, she had star knowledge, she was gifted, taught me things when I was young."

"So why do they call you Little Fox?"

"My sister did that. Asteria. She called me Little Fox because I was small as a lad."

"Well, at least you have a sister. A mother maybe? Have a mother?"

"Both dead."

"Ah. Pity for you. Father?"

Rhywder shook his head.

"You have no one who is family?"

"Nephew."

"Tell me of the nephew."

"Strange boy. He never talked that much growing up. So what are we doing, here, Agapenor? Why all the questions?"

"We be having a chat, Captain. We should be sharing some mead, but you seem to have forgot to bring any."

"Perhaps I should have packed four or five mules for you."

"Perhaps, since this red wine of yours tastes like pissed vinegar."

"You should know—having finished it off."

"Tell me of these Unchurian. Are the tracks we have been following—Unchurian?"

"Yes, I believe so."

"Any secrets you know of them, as you did the Uttuku?"

"Once, I was aboard a Pelegasian and its captain sailed southward farther than I have ever been. He kept out to sea, but he was a bold son of a whore, and he came close enough to shore get a look at Unchurian cities along the shore. The cities were red stone, square and blunt, built one on top of the other like blocks, until they were stacked high as mountains. Ugly cities, no beauty to them, all of them stained the dull color of dried blood. It is said there are many more of them in the deserts of desolation, Du'ldu. No man I have ever met has returned from that place, Du'ldu. They say it lies on the edge of the Earth, the kingdom of the death lord."

"So they are numerous, these Unchurian?"

"The death lord moved south centuries ago—splitting with Etlantis. Over a woman, I understand. Always such matters seem to have a woman at their core—you ever notice that?"

"Makes logical sense if you ponder it."

"As far as the cities in the far south, the deserts, no man knows their number. You can find Unchurian settlements not far from where we are now, just minor villages in the jungles. But the truth be known, all land south of the gate of Hericlon belongs to the death lord and the Unchurian, which is why the Galagleans were blessed fools to be crossing over to start settlements and villages."

"Forget that I am a Galaglean myself, Captain?"

"No, and you would be likely to take your women and all your children and start a settlement here yourself if you were a plodder."

Agapenor grunted, not sure if he was insulted. "So these Unchurian were born of an angel, were they?"

"The angel who named death. We can speak that name, death lord, it is not spellbound as his other names. He is the one that bore the nation of Unchuria."

"But they are not giants, I understand."

"He was an angel lord; their blood is pure. They were once archangels, those named as lords. Unlike the others who fell to Earth, lesser angels, the blood of the angel lords were pure, and even though the death lord had sinned and taken mortal women as his brides, his blood was so pure, his bond with heaven so strong that for many generations his children were almost like men. Like the Daath, not human exactly, but neither were they giants. That time is past now. No man has ever returned from the southern deserts of Du'ldu to say, but according to the seers and priests of Enoch, he has fallen. The tether that bonded the death lord to heaven for so long, even for centuries after his sin, has finally withered. He now bears monsters, giants, Failures, just as the lesser angels. He has become one of the fallen. But the nations of Unchuria were his firstborn. They age like patriarchs, centuries old—which leaves them deadly warriors."

Rhywder was about to say more when he heard something. He motioned silence, drew his dagger, but never had a chance to throw it.

A naked Unchurian, the very topic of their conversation, leapt from the mangrove roots for Agapenor. He was painted in yellow and blue markings. Agapenor grabbed the Unchurian and slammed him into the ground, hoisted his weight, and brought a knee into the man's chest with a crunch. He peeled the Unchurian's knife away, breaking fingers. When the Unchurian started to scream, Agapenor hammered in the face. The body of the Unchurian shivered and lay still. The nose was driven into the back of his skull.

"You see this, Rhywder?"

Rhywder could only stare, amazed.

"This man is painted! What are these?"

"Signets, incantations, pay them no mind."

"You mean you can read the bastard?"

"Yes. Step back from him, Agapenor."

"What is he? Not human—his eyes look more like a jungle cat than a human. Skin not painted is reddish. Speak of them, Rhywder, this would be an Unchurian! Am I right?"

"Yes."

"He was not that quick for having lived centuries and bearing such a reputation as they do."

"I believe you took him utterly by surprise."

"The tops of his feet are painted with the heads of blue salamanders. Seems a lot of work to go to, to paint a man like that."

"Burn him."

"As asked," said Agapenor.

He grabbed the body by an arm and leg and heaved him into the fire. He kicked in more shredded wood that would burn quickly. Soon the Unchurian's skin caught fire and started to sizzle.

"Hate that smell," grumbled Agapenor.

Rhywder drew back. He wanted nothing of spellbound incantations, but as the Unchurian burned, Rhywder saw names in the swirls of the smoke. Surprisingly, they were not spells; there was nothing alarming except for the fact these were names Rhywder had rarely seen. Valefar, Abigan, Bathim, Sarganatanas—they were the vulgar names of the fallen, the Watchers, but names used only by the Pelegasians who sailed the southern isles and the merchant cities of Weire. They were not meant so much as magick as they were devotion to the one who had painted them. This priest had not been sent to kill; he was not hunting Rhywder or Agapenor. It was more likely this was just a simple priest, most probably gathering roots and herbs for his poisons.

Suddenly, before Rhywder could turn from it, a sacred name curled from the smoke. It had been painted in devotion by the priest, but it was spellbound. Rhywder tried blocking it, but the name still managed to press through his thoughts. It was Mictlan, a true name of Azazel, but it was a name used only in the far, deep south, in the desert cities, never in the north. It was Azazel who, by a spoken word, created death, and that was the literal meaning of Mictlan: death speaker. What startled Rhywder was that as soon as the name had gotten in his thoughts, he did not feel the angel listening; instead the spell sunk into him, sending chills. It left him acutely aware there was something was close, threatening, terrifying.

"You all right, Captain?"

Rhywder looked up. "Yes. That was a priest. Possibly why he was so easily killed."

"A priest, yet he comes at us with a knife? They have brave priests."

"He is far from home. The words on him, they were words you would never find this far north; he is from the deserts of Du'ldu. He has never seen our kind. My guess is he mistook us for plodders."

"Serious error on his part."

"That it was. Problem is, he would not be traveling alone. The raiding party we have been tracking, they must be closer than I guessed. You wait here, Agapenor, I am going to range a bit, see what I can see. Keep these horses alive. If any warriors discover you, they will take the horses. You, they will save for the blood drinkers. The blood of a human your size would be as valuable as keg of grog would be to you. So keep the horses alive. We will move out as soon as I return."

"Simple enough."

"Put out the fire—this priest is burnt enough. Wait in the dark, keep hidden in this thicket, and keep still."

"Understood." Agapenor used his boot to stomp out and scatter the last of the fire, smothering it with the moist, swampland dirt. The priest's body was a smoldering lump. Agapenor walked to the horses and unlatched his axe.

Rhywder splashed through knee-high swamp to a high, dead oak. The swamp had slain the tree, but it still reached barren fingers to the sky, the remnant of a former forest giant, the highest tree in miles. He scaled it swiftly, adrenaline charged, until he reached the top. There, his heart stilled, and his breath caught in his throat. He had found the dread that the priest's painted spell had inspired. It was not at all what he expected. The land beyond was dotted with a thousand fires—fires that covered the horizon, the hills, the plains, as far as he could see. They were like stars spread over the land. Despite what he had just told Agapenor, to Rhywder's astonishment, they were here, the armies of Du'ldu, armies unknown and unnumbered. Anything this large would move slowly, but if they managed to breach Hericlon's gate, it would mean annihilation.

Something whispered his name.

He turned. There was something small crouched on a limb next to him. It had tiny eyes of pitted stones and leathery skin—overlaid with a wooden skeleton. Perhaps it was an Uttuku body, but nothing like he had ever seen before. Suddenly it hissed and a tiny claw swiped across Rhywder's cheek, cutting a line of blood. It took him by surprise. Rhywder fell. His fall was broken occasionally by branches and he was able to twist, catching enough of them to land unharmed on his feet.

The shadows seemed to climb slowly, painfully down from the trees and pocket all about Agapenor. He swore it was almost a tangible thing. The horses began to stir. One suddenly jerked its head and screamed, twisting, but Agapenor pulled sharply down on the reins, holding tight. Something flew overhead, its wing beat like the slap of leather being tanned.

"Goddess be near," Agapenor whispered. He kept between the horses, ready for anything. When he heard someone coming through the bush, straight for him, he readied his axe.

"It is me, Rhywder," the Little Fox said. Agapenor relaxed.

Rhywder vaulted into the saddle, then took up the reins. "Mount up, Agapenor—something to show you."

From the hillock overlooking an Unchurian camp, Rhywder and the axeman kept to the shadows. Agapenor stared in awe. A shadow crossed his face like a cold wind, as it had Rhywder's when he was crouched in the tree.

"Sweet Mother of us all," moaned Agapenor. "We are all dead, Captain. Their fires have no number. You go on now, let the others know. Me, I believe I will go down and introduce myself."

Rhywder caught his arm. "Winter is coming, Agapenor."

Agapenor paused. "What should we care of winter?"

"Hericlon is impassable in winter. If Hericlon is held until the snows, no more than a single count of the moon from now, the Daath and the kindred will have a season to prepare. In a season, we could even escape to the Western Sea."

Agapenor searched the thousands of fires beyond the hillock. "For Hericlon, then."

Rhywder galloped at Agapenor's side. They thundered between jagged rock, through the thick of trees and vine. They circled about the edge of a clearing, keeping to shadows. Rhywder thought he knew a clear path to Hericlon, but it was as though the jungles had shifted. He swore he was following the same pathway back, but soon nothing looked familiar as if the thickets were closing around them, and eventually they found their way north blocked. Rhywder drew up on the reins, his horse dancing for a moment as he searched. The jungle thickets could be so dense at times there was no way to press through them. The only passage offered before them was a gaping hole dripping in moss. It looked like a mouth waiting, like something that might swallow them. At least this was a road; wagon wheels leaving gutted tracks snaked beneath the moss.

"Looks awfully tight going in there."

"I do not see a lot of other choices to continue north. Pretend it is plodder road through the thicket."

"Pretending has helped you before?"

"Works well until you find out otherwise."

Agapenor urged his horse forward and they rode carefully across the clearing and into the shadows of the mossy arch.

Rhywder knew the jungle. He had felt his way through foliage denser than this, but never had the darkness seemed so thick. The air itself seemed to crawl across his skin, damp and thick. They were soon riding slow, searching their way each step, enveloped in dark fog. Rhywder could hardly make out trees only a few feet away.

"This is impossible," muttered Agapenor. "It is another trap."

"We are moving north—that is good enough for now."

"How would you know? You see stars through this?"

"I sense north. It is a talent, taught me of my grandmother."

"Way I feel right now, I wish your grandmother were here with us."

There was a scream, not human. A piercing howl. The trees shook violently. Rhywder looked up. Dropping from the high foliage were howlers. Howlers never hunted humans in packs. Uttuku again, just as the wolves, coming fast, only this time they had not lain in wait. The Uttuku had fresh bodies a long way from decomposing.

"Kill them quick, Agapenor!"

"You saying I should not be gentle?"

Agapenor ripped his axe free. Rhywder reared his horse as one clamped onto his shoulder with picket white teeth. He stabbed it in the back until it dropped off. Two others hit him so hard he went over the flanks. On the ground, he saw the neck of his horse shorn open. As his old friend dropped to its knees, struggling, he noticed one of the creatures clinging to its side, desperately sucking blood from a severed vein.

He heard Agapenor growling as he slew.

A howler rushed Rhywder, moving so quickly it managed to rip out a swath of flesh from his thigh. It left hot, burning pain. Rhywder swore, coming to his knees, then broke the howler's sternum with the pommel of the short sword. He slit the throat of another. He stabbed the face of one clawing up his leg. One he grabbed by the head and wrenched back, breaking the neck. And that was it. The killing had been quick. There had been no shortage of howlers; they had simply been easy kills.

Agapenor knelt over mounds of bodies beside his dead horse. His tunic was nearly torn away; there were gouges and scratches everywhere. The axeman still clutched his weapon in one sticky, bloodied hand, but his other hand was cupped over one eye. Blood streamed between the fingers.

"Bastards took my eye," Agapenor hissed through clenched teeth. "I been through motherless dark and killed giants and Nephilim alike, yet it is a damned monkey is what gets my eye!"

Rhywder came to his side and steadied him. "We have to stop that blood, Agapenor." He wadded a torn strip of cloth and stuffed it into Agapenor's empty socket, feeling the skull cavity as he did. Agapenor moaned slightly and started to reach up, but Rhywder pushed his hand away. He wound the rest of the cloth about Agapenor's head and tied off the end.

"No worries, friend," said Rhywder. "I know a good stone worker in a village east of Galaglea. Best you can find. He can cut you an eye from onyx and sapphire that will leave you the envy of all."

Agapenor studied him a moment. "You say that as though you believe we are getting out of this thicket alive."

"We are." Rhywder helped Agapenor to his feet. "I have seen worse than this."

"Not I, Captain, not I. We are two and behind us is an army like the sands of the endless sea. They smelled us, you and I both know it. If I were a wagering sort, my guess is there would be heavy odds against us making it through this glade alive."

"We continue moving north. Forget everything else. Besides, if you were the wagering sort, you would have learned to never think on the odds." He grabbed Agapenor's arm and pulled him forward.

"Worse than this," the big man muttered. "You tell me you seen worse than this?"

"Try to keep focused. West and north there was a Galaglean village—horses."

"Something wrong in me. Some manner of feeling crawling through me like I am coming unhinged."

"It was your eye—hard thing, losing an eye. Stay with me, Agapenor, we keep due north until we find open ground."

"Aye, open ground. Would not mind dying if it were open ground. Or a forest. Forest is good dying ground. But this here, a stinking motherless jungle? Somehow it is Elyon's amusement I get to die in a place like this?"

"Nobody is going to die." Rhywder paused to pull a wad of coca leaves from one of the pockets of his belt. "Here, suck hard on this—steadies your nerves."

Agapenor stuffed it in his cheek. "Never needed anything to steady my nerves afore. There is something unnatural in me, Little Fox. Was those damned monkeys, left some manner of curse working in me."

Suddenly there was singing—women, voices rhythmic and smooth that seemed to float through the air.

Agapenor drew up, stunned at what he was hearing.

Rhywder quickly grabbed the big man's shoulder. "Ignore that, understand? Do not listen."

He turned Agapenor and looked dead into his remaining eye. "Stay with me, Agapenor, stay with me."

Agapenor half-nodded. "Aye . . ."

"We just keep moving! Block it out, do not listen."

Agapenor stumbled a few feet, then just stared into the dark. "But . . . can you not hear that, Rhywder?"

"Agapenor, you are being spellbound. Listen to me!" He shook Agapenor and the axeman finally looked down at him. "Try to keep your mind on something, anything else. Just keep moving; keep your mind on moving north and nothing else!"

He managed to jerk Agapenor back into a run, but after a bit the big man pulled free and stopped once more. It was useless. His remaining eye was glossed over—he was gone.

The lure began to work into Rhywder, as well. It was a choir well taught, well schooled, all young voices, girls. Rhywder was slowly being spellbound, and even though he fought with all the magick he knew, the song twisted through his brain like worms. He glanced up. The fog was gone. Above, the horned moon of Dannu's last harvest was bright and mid-sky. This was the night of sabbat. It was sacred to all those who practiced Ishtar's arts, to the Followers of Enoch as well, but here in the south, the sabbat's song was twisted into mockery and the voices were lacing every word with a siren enchantment. They worked in the names of the fallen, all in vulgar tongue: Abaddon, Asmodeus, Astaroth, Leviathan, Semyazza. And in the background of the vulgar names, one singer whose voice was pure and light as fresh rain sang over and over the known name of Azazel.

"You wait here," said Agapenor. "I shall come back for you." He began to push forward through the bushes toward the singing as if he were walking blind.

"Agapenor, wait!" Rhywder circled around in front of him, trying to push him back, while desperately fighting the spell himself. "Those are not girls you hear, they are"—Rhywder paused, unsteady, the song working through him—"witches," he stammered, "siren song—it is a siren song . . ."

Agapenor was now out of sight—vanished into the dark.

Rhywder could no longer feel the pain of his wounds from the howlers. The song swept away all gloom of dark and stilled the whisper of the jungle. It had even begun to arouse him. He turned and started in its direction. Whatever it was, it would help; it would give him rest, and he needed rest so badly. But even then, as he walked, he tried to use the edge of his sword to keep from fully being spellbound, slicing through his palm, hoping the sting of pain would wake him, but the lithe voices were numbing all his thoughts and promising sweet balm.

He stepped into a large, circular clearing hewn out of the jungle. A bonfire raged, sending sparks into the night. Women were gathered, singing, moving as though the summer wind had taught them the dance. They were naked, oiled—long, night-black hair. Light red skin. Perfect, every one, as beautiful as anything he had ever seen. He was wrong, there was no danger here. They welcomed him, lured him closer, their arms waving, fingers beckoning.

"Come, Little Fox." They knew his name!

With a screech, one dropped onto his back. The suddenness of it jolted him, and Rhywder was able to break the spell just as her teeth came for his throat. Rhywder took hold of her arm, slammed her into the ground, and planted his blade through her left breast. He stood, pulling the blade free, flinging blood. More were coming, some tumbling, others dancing, spinning as they came for him. He could hear Agapenor screaming.

He knew the intent now, the spell was broken, all these Unchurian women wanted was his blood. They thirsted madly for human blood, and the blood of warriors was the richest of all. The blood of the valiant was like the finest, richest wine to them.

Close, they rushed him. Rhywder was able to kill two before he was seized, arm and leg. To keep them from getting the sword, he shoved it through his armband, anchored against his lower arm.

He was being carried by girls toward the fire. He noticed their painted eyes, their naked shoulders. One hissed at him, catlike. Her lips were full and bloodred, her teeth a brilliant white, the canines elongated, fanged.

Rhywder glanced skyward. The moon was at its zenith. Communio—they had timed their feeding to the mid-sky communion of the sabbat.

There came times to die, but this wasn't one of them.

He drew breath and began to fight for all he was worth. He kicked one foot free and rammed it into a pretty face, knocking the girl back, blood flushing from her button nose. He twisted, jerking free of their hold. He almost got to his feet, but they overwhelmed him again and this time threw him to the ground. One tore open the front of his tunic. Another, on her knees, came over him, her soft, puffy lips parting his, sensuous and hot. She snipped his bottom lip with her razor teeth, chuckling a little girl's laugh. He glanced to see one sliding down between his legs, mouth agape. That sight gave him inhuman strength.

Rhywder screamed and heaved two of them off him. Another he grabbed by the hair and flung to the side. He slammed at them with fists, shook them off until he managed to get to his knees. He pulled his blade free and started killing—ripping through windpipes, breasts, eyes, anything he could strike that would be effective. They finally managed to pin his sword arm, but though they tried to get his sword, he clung to the blade so tightly his fingers might have been welded to the bloodied leather wrap of the hilt. New teeth sunk into his neck from behind. One bit into his thigh and began to suck. The sucking stung with sharp, sweet pain, though at the same time it infused him with an opiatelike drug he almost welcomed.

All the singing had stopped. It was feeding time now.

Teeth were shearing through Rhywder's skin everywhere, his legs, arms, sides. It was truly not the way he wanted to die. He looked to the heavens and whispered the name of the mothering star; he called out to the *Light Whose Name Is Splendor.*

Suddenly, the Galaglean appeared above him, bloodied, teeth marks riddling his skin everywhere, one arm chewed off, half his right leg gone with gouges and teeth marks spilling rich blood, but still he was still strong. He pulled a girl off Rhywder, flinging her high and tumbling her into the night. He grabbed the hair of another, snapping the neck. He stomped in the back of a third, cracking the spine like a dry branch. He thrust out a hand.

"Take hold!" he commanded.

Rhywder grasped Agapenor's wrist and was wrenched up and thrown clear. He hit the ground and quickly sprung to his feet.

"Now run, you little bastard!" Agapenor screamed.

Rhywder did—he ran. He heard them bringing Agapenor down, but he could not help and he did not look back.

He found himself wildly leaping through the thicket, crashing through the brush, racing blindly through trees and creepers. There was a sound of pattering feet and whispered snarling. He glanced behind. They were coming for him—many on all fours. He was not going to outrun them—but he had managed one trick. He had managed to keep hold of his short sword and he ran with it tucked against his chest.

Chapter Nineteen

Albino

Krysis waited at the white painted fence Eryian had built them seven years ago. He had purposely chosen rough wood stakes instead of smoothed ones, and he had oiled it and then let the winters, spring rains, and white summer sun paint it. Now it seemed just a part of the forest at the edge of the cabin. Eryian had built the cabin himself and beside it, moorings and dock works, built from the wooden beams of a slaver ship he had once taken at high sea—at the time sailing with Rhywder.

He was young then, Eryian. It was just before the gathering wars, just before he left with Argolis for the northland. His face had been unfairly handsome. Krysis sometimes thought he was embarrassed of it, the way some women looked at him. Though everything about him spoke otherwise, Eryian had always insisted he was nothing extraordinary, that in other circumstances he might have been a cobbler, or a blacksmith, no more warlord than a land plodder. In fact, while his liege, Argolis, lived in the stone and timber castle of Terith-Aire, overlooking the sea, Eryian had found a far piece of land near a quiet bay nestled into the thick forest northwest of the city. Of course, Krysis spent long months never seeing him, raising Eryian's son. When he did return, she could sometimes watch soul and lifeblood return to him as he shed the warlord and let himself look out his eyes at her. He loved her, she knew that. He let himself be almost human when alone with her and she knew he did that nowhere else.

"One day I will not leave, Krysis," he would often tell her, nights, alone with Little Eryian asleep. "One day, much like an ordinary day, I will ride back and we will become plodders—same as you might find digging potatoes on the outskirts of the East of the Land."

"I am pleased, Eryian—although I am not going to hold my breath."

It was as though he had heard nothing sarcastic. He nodded, continued on. "Plain weft, hunter's weft, maybe a bit soiled—that instead of armor. My bow, perhaps I will keep it. And throwing knives. The rest of it I will leave behind."

"Your sword?"

"Into the sea, my love, into the ocean."

He smiled, stared at her a moment through the dark blue-ice of his eyes, eyes that no matter how they laughed or how they sparkled alone with her, still held beneath them a death veil. The ice eyes of Eryian were like the cutting edge of a sword—always holding a certain promise.

And this night, waiting for him as the storm came in hard from the south, Krysis felt a claw in her chest. She had felt it since morning. She tried not to look too concerned as night drew on, but she had began to pace Eryian's rough-hewn porch and then Little Eryian had finally taken notice. He had stepped past her to stare down the rough dirt path that led to the forest.

"What is wrong, Mother?" he demanded in a stern voice.

"Nothing, Little Eryian. I was just worried of the storm."

He turned the pale, whitish eyes on her with unnerving effect. Even now, with Little Eryian seven years and eight months, she still could not get used to his eyes. He had been born albino. He was like a marble sculpture, perfect in every way, and the piercing white eyes could unnerve even Eryian's warriors.

"It is Father, is it not? Something is happening—something not yet, but something coming."

She started to shake her head, but as he could with most people, Little Eryian had already seen through her. He lifted his bow from beside the door and slung his quiver over his shoulder.

"I am going for the city. If Father is in trouble, I can help. I will saddle the stallion."

He was almost off the porch, but she spun him about and held him firmly by his shoulders, kneeling to look in his eyes. "Little Eryian, listen to me—if your father, the Eagle of Argolis, is in trouble, then you, my seven-year-young lad, will stay here, beside your mother."

He studied her carefully. "You are afraid? Is that how you mean it?"

She nodded. "Yes, very afraid."

"Then I will stay."

"Thank you, Little Eryian. Now, do me a favor and tell old Cathyis to weather down your father's ship. I sense this storm is going to be harsh."

"Yes, Mother."

Little Eryian dropped over the railing. Watching him walk down the pathway, Krysis felt a tug at her heart. Time was turning, she knew that. Something was closing on them, and it was so heavy, so dark she could even not imagine what it could be.

Chapter Twenty
Silvery Eagle

Eryian had few memories of his past. It was something he never spoke of, something he had kept secret from all but his king. As he watched a storm forming from the south, standing on a high tower of the castle, he wondered once more why all his memories before joining with Argolis twenty and five years ago were shadowy, whispery images so obscure they made no sense. An injury or disease might have explained it, but Eryian knew this was something else, something of the star knowledge. It was *the knowing* that veiled his past.

It left him with no idea where he had acquired his deadly skills. He had no memory of learning or training, no memories of war, fighting, or slaughter, and yet he had come to Argolis unequaled as a slayer. Argolis had suggested to Eryian that he might be a firstborn—that his memories were veiled because his past was so deep in the beginnings. But none of the scions of Uriel lived as the patriarchs or the Nephilim—ageless for centuries—nor were there any such legends concerning the Daath. But then, eventually Eryian wondered who he really was. In the two and one-half decades they had been together, while Argolis's hair had silvered and his face had grown creases, Eryian looked barely older, than the day they had met.

It seemed strange that time could move so quickly. It was only two and a half decades ago when the dark season of the gathering wars had begun. Mars was ascendant and the Blue Stars were at their zenith the day Argolis had gathered his vast armies upon the plains of Terith-Aire. There, the king had named Eryian, almost a stranger among them, their warlord, second only to himself in matters of war and state. Argolis told the people that day that Eryian had been sent in time of need, and those words had never been questioned. There was a mystique that lay over the warlord ever since. Argolis had selected him over all the armies of the Daath on faith alone. But it seemed Argolis' faith was not unfounded.

Eryian had formed the Daath into the feared legions of Shadow Warriors they had now become. In mock battles before the wide, hilly rages and open land of Parminion's foothills he had prepared them in mock battles. He had organized the numbers of their armies. They were natural slayers, deadly by instinct alone, but Eryian had formed them into tight-knit units, taught them to deploy and fight as cohorts, each giving allegiance to their individual captains and leaders. He had taught the cavalry how to work the flanks of a battle, taught the shieldbearers how to quickly build and man defenses, taught the axemen how to fight uphill, the engineers how to construct deep river crossings, and the marines how to deploy against an enemy on soft sand. But more than anything, Eryian had taught the Daathan warriors how to die well.

In fact, after the gathering wars had ended, Eryian would have valued a single Daathan legion the equivalent of three Etlantian, and the Etlantians had armies that had fought since time had begun.

It was Eryian, as well, who formed and trained the King's Guard, elite warriors he named Shadow Walkers. Eryian had chosen the strongest of the Daath, selecting only the valiant. He then taught them skills no other warriors on Earth possessed.

There were silkworms that grew in certain parts of the East of the Land. Eryian had taught the warriors, not their maids or women, but the warriors themselves how to weave the silvery threads into exact, bound patterns that formed signets capable of capturing the power of the word they symbolized. He then taught the Shadow Walkers how these cloaks were used, how to perform with dexterity the precise, adept movements that took years to perfect. They gave the elite warriors the ability to literally vanish for seconds at a time. It seemed a small thing, but in battle it was a valuable and deadly asset. Yet, Eryian had no idea where he had learned these secrets, how he had known to even find the worms of the forest that spawned the silvery thread.

It was Eryian who told Argolis the tribes of Dannu must be gathered as one, no matter the cost, no matter the price. Once he had named Eryian his Eagle, Argolis had never questioned his judgment or counsel. The king unleashed the newly formed Daathan legions upon their own kindred, the blood tribes of the goddess Dannu, their mothering star. What became known as the gathering wars lasted eight long years. They were years that would leave a swath of blood across the homeland, a stain that would ever linger in the shadow of innocents lost. Yet, there had been no choice. Eryian understood deep within there would come a time in the future when the Daath and their kindred tribes could no longer be scattered, fighting for dominance, or squabbling over the rights to pitiful fields or streams as they had for centuries. Eryian's knowledge was certain. A day in the future was coming when a storm would gather against these people, a storm so dark and powerful that if they were not united as one force, they would be swept as chaff before the winnower's blade.

Eryian never questioned the source of his knowledge. It was connected like a silvery tether to the seventh star of the Pleiades and to the Light of Severity that was Elyon. Yet he could not explain how he had come by it, for he remembered no mentors, no priests. He had never studied scriptures or pondered lineages or histories. It was *the knowing* inside him. It unveiled secrets within him that even wandering prophets of Enoch that Eryian occasionally had brought to the palace to question could only guess at.

Who was he? And why had he been delivered to these people, strangers to him, even though by their skin and eyes they were obviously his own blood. He searched the heavens from the parapet of the castle, demanding answers. He had done all that was asked of him; he had followed every charge given him. He had raised up a king, Argolis, and had given him the finest warriors in the world to stand against the dark he had known would one day come against them. But that day was no longer coming, it had arrived, and ironically, Argolis had become its first casualty.

Eryian watched the storm with angry eyes, how it slowly turned, how it seemed to have drawn in the night, gathering it, coalescing into a slowly turning mass of black clouds. Eryian recognized it for what it was—no ordinary storm. He clearly saw the tails and streamers of the whirlers, the living beings that followed the path of their angel lords. And what troubled him the most was that his own memories, shadowy as they were, held an image of this angel's eyes as vivid and lucid as his own reflected in a mirror. Yet it did not include the memory of when or where he had met the death lord whose given name of the choirs of heaven was Azazel. He knew this living creature to be an ancient enemy—but how ancient? And why?

There were no answers. Eryian could only watch the whirlers from afar, knowing these were the winds of what would be remembered by mankind as the winnowing war. Azazel and his children were moving slowly for Hericlon. Only their numbers slowed them. Moving such vast armies took time, even for Azazel. Yet, if he managed to breach the gate, the battle that would follow would not be one of conquest—it would be a war of annihilation. Eryian had not believed he would live to see it, let alone be left with the charge of once more leading them.

He held a slight hope that Rhywder had gotten through in time to learn the threat, to know its numbers, to guage how close the armies of Du'ldu had gotten to the ancient mountain passage. And if Rhywder had been as adept as Eryian knew him to be, the Little Fox would have dispatched messengers for Galaglea where Quietus, the obtuse king who called himself the Falcon, would be able to marshal his two legions for Hericlon. He was within two days' striking distance of the gate. In truth, the obstinate Galaglean king was their only hope. If Hericlon could be held until the winter snows struck the Parminions, even Azazel could not cross, at least not with his children, his unknown armies that were without number. But Eryian knew that reaching Hericlon after winter's fall was an error Azazel would certainly never make. That he would make any error at all seemed unthinkable and yet—in a way, the mighty lord of death had already made at least one.

The assassins Azazel had sent this day were deft and skilled. They must have been carefully chosen, and their mission was to have taken out the scions of the Daath. If Azazel had succeeded in eliminating the seed of Uriel, he would have severed the root that bore the archangel's lineage on Earth. Prophecy itself would have died on its withering vine. But Azazel had failed. One still lived. The boy, Loch, had survived. Earlier, he had reached Terith-Aire from the north, bloodied, weary, but alive. Still, Loch was young and had never seen, let alone waged, a war. It was as if both Elyon and His fallen son, Azazel, were toying with them all. Perhaps that was the truest answer in the end. Perhaps it was all a game played of star lords and those who walked heaven's rim, including Elyon Himself.

Eryian turned from the causeway and down a flight of stairs to the king's chamber below. There he sprawled in a high-backed chair, watching the shadows of the hearth fire play on the marble wall. There was no solace. Here the shadow of Argolis's death closed in on him like a haunting. He despised the emotion it left in him, both the piercing sadness of a fallen brother and the rage that he had been unable to prevent it. Rage was fuel in war, in battle, but if it turned, it could also mean a warrior's death. It overrode even a warrior's highly trained instincts of survival.

Eryian's cuirass was stained of Argolis's blood and in the quiet of the room, the sounds whispered like ghosts; the screams of horses; the swift, stinging hum of an arrow's flight. For a moment he wondered if it had been personal, if Azazel were not grinning at him from the south, taunting him—*you live to suffer your agony and rage while your king is sealed along with the others in their fine tombs beneath Terith-Aire.*

Eryian heard voices from the hallway, and then a single thud on the door.

"Enter," he said.

The doors swung open. It was the boy, Lochlain. He was stained with blood. It was clear the fight he had waged had been desperate, yet the boy bore no serious wounds. One of his shoulders looked bad, but all Loch had done was to tuck wrappings beneath his tunic against the bleeding. Eryian had taught the young scion well. Those were no ordinary assassins that had come against the prince; they had been handpicked to eliminate something no less than an angel, and yet, here he was, barely scratched. Eryian almost wished he could have witnessed the fight.

He had trained Loch, not by order of the king, not by any orders—it had been something of a project he had become obsessed with over the years. This lad might well be considered Eryian's personal work of art.

When his mother had died, the boy had stopped speaking. He had completely withdrawn from the world, blaming Argolis for the death, and perhaps he was not wrong. Politics had become thickly complicated at the end of the war. There was some evidence that the king had no choice but to sacrifice even the women he loved—though it was far from proven. Eryian wasn't certain himself how she had died, other than it was poison that took her. The boy had withdrawn so far into the shadows that Eryian had decided he was lost. Should it matter if he took the emotionally crippled youth and instead of watching him waste into shadow, craft him into the perfect slayer? It became a project that soon obsessed Eryian, but one he kept secret, which was fine with the boy. If Lochlain had any inbreed talent, it was that of keeping secrets. Even Argolis wasn't aware—that or he took no interest.

Eryian had good material to work with; the boy's blood was pure and one could feel the fires of Uriel's light flowing through him—as quiet and withdrawn as he was. And there was ample fuel—hatred, a simmering deep hatred Eryian was able to nurse to its full potential. He had worked the boy for years; in fact, he had worked Lochlain his entire life, teaching him everything Eryian knew, every trick, every sly move. Loch had taken to the training with unspoken passion. He spoke little, he never smiled, but he listened to every word, studied every move with keen, quick eyes that missed nothing. Indeed, Eryian had been able to craft a very capable, very deadly slayer. The boy had been a minstrel when his mother was alive, and would have likely become some kind of distant poet-king, but Eryian had changed all that—molded him, turned him from a lyre player into a Shadow Walker of remarkable skill and alacrity. In fact, presently Lochlain's only weakness was his youth, but given battle, such as he had seen this day, the youth in him would quickly burn off. If he lived long enough, Eryian's project might well become the deadliest warrior alive. But Eryian believed that would take more years than the boy had to live. Considering the climate, considering the storms working over the skies of the south, it was unlikely Loch would age long enough for his skills to fully ferment.

Though they had worked together intensely, even intimately, Eryian had made certain they shared little emotion. A slayer had no need for emotion, none whatsoever. It was a weakness. If there were a way to eviscerate emotion from his warriors, Eryian would have done it. No doubt Azazel had been able to accomplish just that—bred it out of them probably.

Presently, stepping into the room, the boy showed no emotion whatsoever. Though Eryian could easily read most men, Lochlain blocked any clue. If there was sadness, anger, frustration, none of it showed in his face or his manner. Eryian almost wanted to smile, almost wished there were someone here he could share his achievement with. Perhaps it was cruel, what he had done, molding this boy into a killer. He wondered, in the back of his mind, what had become of the poet—if he was even still alive, buried somewhere deep within the Shadow Walker.

Loch's night-black hair was tangled and bloodied, but still tied in leather braids. His scabbard was empty. Oddly, in his belt was a Nephilim's dagger, and not just any Nephilim's dagger. The giant's name was inscribed on the black ivory hilt. It startled Eryian. Agrarel. It was the name of the firstborn of an angel lord. As remarkable and skilled as Eryian had crafted the young scion, Agrarel had lived seven hundred years, a mark too deadly to have died at Loch's hand. Yet, curiously, there was the firstborn's dagger, shoved though the boy's sword belt. Eryian wanted to ask, but he wouldn't and he guessed, as well, the boy wasn't going to offer any explanation.

"We should talk, warlord."

Eryian nodded to the guards. They stepped back, closed the doors.

"Anything you have to tell me?" Loch asked.

"Those who attacked your father are dead. Two-score Unchurian assassins, all of them archers, though archers with varied and perfected skills. They have been hunted down and eliminated."

"As well as those I killed near the river?"

"Including them, exactly two score; their leader prefers even numbers."

"Really? And how do you know that?"

"I am not certain, but I know. There are no assassins left alive in the shadow of Terith-Aire, or even within the East of the Land. The death lord's gamble appears to have failed."

"The death lord?"

Eryian nodded. He noticed the chain bearing Asteria's ring was no longer about the boy's neck. What Eryian had heard of the girl must have borne some truth, though he doubted it would be easily obtained. He had taught Loch to keep such matters his own. But if what his captains had told him was the truth, where was the girl?

"How is it you managed to survive, warlord?" Loch asked.

Eryian tightened his gaze, but offered no response. He knew Loch used the question as a dagger.

"I have a question a bit more relevant," Eryian countered. "Where is the girl?"

"What girl?"

"The young Galaglean," Eryian pressed. "The Water Bearer."

"No idea what you are speaking of . . . oh, wait, yes, there was the harlot, from the village south, Lucania. She was with me this morning. She did not survive."

"You are telling me the girl is dead?"

Loch nodded.

Eryian knew there was something hidden in Loch's answer, yet at the same time he sensed it was not a lie. Eryian attempted to learn more, but the boy's mind blocked his probe as effectively as a stone wall. Ironically, it was Eryian's own training working against him. It left him frustrated, but also, proud.

"Our people are out there," Loch said, "gathered in the streets. Hundreds of them."

"They have just lost their king."

"Am I to address them from the parapet or gather them in the square? What?"

"Eventually you should speak to them. They are your people now, Lochlain. But for today, I have told them everything they need to know. They were gathered in the agora. They understand Argolis is dead; they assumed I was all they had left. My men are spreading the word now that you have survived. They still have a king."

"What comfort that must give them, since they have no idea who I am. Most of them believe I am *touched*, as they put it."

"Is that not how you wished it? To remain a mystery?"

"I suppose."

"It turns out you have done well. If anything, they fear you. You can gain their trust in time. I have noticed that if you wish, you can be quite persuasive."

Loch crossed to the table of urns and searched over them. "My uncle Rhywder often spoke of a certain wine. Bloodroot. Which would it be?"

"Tyrinian wine—it is in the black urn."

Loch lifted an empty wineskin from his shoulder and poured from the dolphin flagon until he had filled the skin. He took a long drink. "Must be hard for you, Eryian," he said, "losing a king."

"As it should be losing a father."

"He was never a father. You of all people should know that." Loch dropped back against the throne's platform, propped one knee. "How did these two-score Unchurian assassins reach Terith-Aire?"

"By being few. Through Hericlon, two, three at a time. Most probably disguised as villagers. The assassins were unusual in one respect; all of them were from the land unknown, Du'ldu."

"They came that far? Just to kill me and my father?"

"If Azazel had taken out the two living scions of Uriel, it would have been victory. Tidy. He might not have even bothered with breaching the gate."

"You mean he would have gone home?"

"Destroy the scion: Azazel ends the prophecy, that simple."

"Azazel—you do not fear speaking his spellbound name?"

"I do not fear him or any of his names. I fear what he brings—his sons. He is moving with them gathered for Hericlon."

"Can you hold the gate?"

"Only if I reach it in time."

"How did they come this far so quickly? Is not Du'ldu at the ends of the Earth? He must have been on the march for many counts of the moon, and yet we knew nothing?"

"He is a high lord of the holy choir of the Auphanim; does it actually surprise you he can cross his own lands in stealth?"

"I suppose you have a point. What is our next move?"

"You are now the king, Lochlain. Our next move is whatever you tell us it is."

"I am hardly their king, lineage aside. In Elyon's name, you and I both know I cannot lead them in battle, it would be foolish. I can ride at their front, show my face to the enemy, raise my sword as a beacon for your Shadow Warriors to follow. But you are their warlord—they followed you through a war that nearly halved their number. Those that survived are now gathered. The Daath are your right arm; the others trust you without question. They will follow you through the abyss of Ain."

"Loch, you cannot—"

"I am not their king!" Loch snarled. "In time, whatever is left us, it could change. But currently I am nothing more than a symbol, and not one they trust. If such a day comes, I will grow old, pass out edicts, do what is needed, but that is going to take far more than a speech in the agora. For now and until I say otherwise, those people out there—they are *your* people. As your king I name you counselor as well as warlord. I will do so before them in the square tomorrow. If not in name, then in authority, you are their leader. Are we understood?"

"You seem to have no difficulty at all with command. Understood, my liege."

"So what is our next move, counselor?"

"My men march for Hericlon at dawn; they assemble as we speak. The tribal warriors to the north will be gathered as soon as riders can reach them. The snow walkers of Aragon will never cross Parminion's western passage in time to be of any use. That leaves the two legions of Quietus. The Galagleans are close enough to reach Hericlon. If they have been warned, there is still hope. But should Quietus face Azazel alone, even with the gate beneath him, I have little faith he can hold for long. Which means our fate lies with the Daathan legions. It is a week's pressed march at best. However, should we make it, I can hold Hericlon until winter, and with winter we will survive. Azazel cannot cross, no matter his numbers. So we play a very desperate gamble and *that* is our next move."

Loch leaned his head back. He took another long drink. Eryian was impressed, bloodroot was strong wine, it struck most men quickly, but the boy did not seem the slightest bit unsteady. He guessed it was his uncle Rhywder's blood in him.

"What about the sea?" Loch asked.

"The Unchurian have never been seamen; they build no warships and very few merchant vessels. As far as I know they have no fleet remotely capable of assault from the sea."

"Do not ignore the sea. I was given that warning."

Eryian nodded; he did not need to question the source. "Very well, we have seven warships in Ishmia. I will send a rider tonight; they can be deployed along the coast by tomorrow's dawn. I am certain nothing greater than a raiding party can threaten us. The Etlantians own all waters west and north, and right now they need us as much as we need them. The Light Bearer is no ally of Azazel."

Loch nodded with a sigh. "Good enough." Loch glanced at Eryian, offered the wineskin, which Eryian declined.

"You are certain? I would think your heart would be heavy this night, warlord."

"It is."

Loch took another drink himself. "So then," he said, "it has finally come to pass. The legends spoken for seven centuries, the curse of the covenant sealed upon the stone of Ammon. It begins with this—a weak attempt to sever the root of Uriel's seed and now the unknown armies of Du'ldu moving against the Daath. I understand that in latter days this will be known as the winnowing war. Do I speak truth, warlord?"

"You speak prophecy. I have yet to be certain prophecy and truth are the same."

"Whichever, I doubt either of us is going to see the end of this."

"I cannot argue that point."

Though Eryian had never taught Loch of destiny or the spoken legends, he guessed the boy was as well versed as any, having borne the ring of the Water Bearer about his neck for so many years.

"One small matter," said Eryian. "At dawn your father's tomb will be closed. Do you wish to see the body?"

"Why? Seal it."

"Very well."

"Burn it. Drop it in the sea."

Eryian stood. Perhaps the wine was taking effect. "I should leave, my king. I should return home. My wife and child may have heard of the assassination and would have no idea if I am alive or dead."

"Of course, but before you go . . ." Loch turned and pointed the wineskin's golden lip to Argolis's oaken bed. On its coverlet rested a scabbard.

"My father's sword," Loch said. "Were you even going to mention it?"

"It is your sword now, and there is nothing I can say of it that you do not already know."

Loch tossed the wineskin aside. He walked to stand over the scabbard, studying it for a moment. It was black ivory and carved intricately with precise, minute images of horses at full gallop, some enhanced by thin veneers of silver. The edges were darkly stained, polished oak.

"The sword the ancients called the Arsayalalyur," Loch said. "By word of the seers, it is now bound to me blood and soul. Is that true, warlord?"

"You know it is true, Loch."

"The mark of the father. Uriel's blade. The same that guarded the East of the Land, ever turning in all directions with the fire of severity, the light of Elyon's gaze. Yes, I know all these things, these sayings, but I have seen that weapon in my father's hand. I have seen him lift it high in parades of honor for all the people to look upon, and having seen his fingers about its hilt, I no longer believe it is legend or prophecy. It is merely a weapon. This cannot possibly be the sword of an archangel. What about you, warlord? Did you ever ponder it was no more than a prop?"

"It is not ordinary. I have felt something being near it. I will admit your father did not seem to draw its power. I cannot say why."

"Because it is not a sunblade. If ever Uriel's sword was once in our possession, it has been lost. This is nothing more than an elaborate copy, if not an outright travesty. Either that or my father did not carry the blood of Uriel in his veins. And if he was not Uriel's scion, well—neither am I."

"I have no answers for you, Loch. The sword has always been a mystery to me. Your father did change the texture of the blade."

"How so?"

"It was silver when you saw it held in parades, am I right?"

"And—"

"If you draw it from the scabbard you will understand. But there is one thing I can say. If such a blade as the sword of Uriel did exist, a sunblade forged of the seventh star, then it would exist beyond faith."

"What do you mean by that?"

"That it would be what it is whether you or I, or even your father, believed or did not believe."

Loch stared at Eryian a moment, considering.

"Always the master. Always the teacher."

"You did ask."

"Yes. Well, simple enough to find out, is it not?"

Without further hesitation Loch lifted the scabbard. He avoided the hilt on purpose and grasped one cross guard to pull it clear of the scabbard enough to clutch the flange. He then pulled the sword out of it black velvet lining and tossed the scabbard aside. Eryian hadn't expected that. He had never seen Loch so much as glance in the sword's direction when it was his father's, but the boy knew not to touch the hilt. He was not as certain it was a prop as he implied.

Loch carefully lifted the double-edged blade against the fire of the hearth, turning it.

"Weighted, but light for a broadsword," he commented.

The blade was clear, and the hearth's flame slid off it watery as if reflected from glass.

"I have not seen it like this," Loch said. "It could be simple glass."

"Not simple. It bears no imperfection of any kind, not a scratch, not a nick."

"Like the spires."

"How do you mean?" Eryian asked.

"The high spires of the castle. I have never seen them close up, but from parts of the causeway you can see them clearly. Seven centuries and they are flawless, no effects of weather. Dirt and even dust never cling to their side. Have you noticed that?"

"I haven't, but I suppose you are right."

Eryian guessed Loch was talking merely to cover his apprehension. The sword of Uriel left him uneasy; still, even with the effects of nearly a skin of wine in him, he remained calm as he carefully traced the elaborate etchings of the black ivory hilt. He paused short of touching the purple bloodstone of the pommel. It was like a diamond, but at the same time it looked soft to the touch. Eryian knew Loch would recognize it as the same stone set into the crown of his mother's ring. Yet, the pommel of Uriel's sword promised far more power, and Loch's mere proximity had ignited a soft, inner glow deep within its core.

Silver serpents curled about the inner black ivory of the hilt, carved so intricately their scales glittered. They formed finger notches that were said to mold to the sword's owner. The heads of each serpent bore tiny, red diamond eyes and curled fanged teeth of the same purple stone as the pommel. The teeth sunk into the pommel from seven sides—not merely anchoring it, but melding with it, and like veins, lines of purple curled through each serpent, vanishing into the mount of the cross guards. They ensured that anyone who gripped the hilt would also touch the pommel's stone.

Eryian found himself as fascinated as Loch, and he watched as the pommel seemed to smell the boy's blood, its inner light stirring, as though there were far, tiny stars deep within. Argolis had produced no such effect. His son, however, seemed to be awakening Uriel's sword from a long slumber. Loch was the sixth king of the Daath. Prophecy spoke there would be only seven.

Loch finally curled his hand about the hilt, letting his fingers slip into its mold. The blade flashed a glimmering, metallic silver. Eryian watched breathless as blood was drawn through the skin of Loch's palm. He knew what was happening, but he had never guessed it would happen to Loch. It left him stunned, realizing that the sixth king of the Daath was about to light the blade of Uriel. The blood turned the pommel a deeper red, then curled through the veins of the serpents and into the metallic sheen of the flange, where it coalesced in a swirl of bright red. Without warning, a lightning pulse burst through the blade. The entire room was engulfed in a brilliant white flash, so vivid and pure that for seconds it blinded Eryian. It took some moments before the room slowly came back into focus, as if it were cooling down, though there had been no sensation of heat. When the room was again normal, the blade had returned to its smooth, crystal glass.

Loch was breathing carefully, though he did not seem so much surprised as he was fascinated. Eryian understood what had just happened, but he had been taken by surprise. He would not have guessed the boy's blood to have been that strong.

"Any speculations?" Loch said, calmly.

"Only one and it is not speculation. I speak of the eye of Daath."

"Yes, I know all of it. It has been seared into my blood through dreams that have haunted me since I first touched the ring. The mirrored image of Dannu, as real as the Goddess—but separate, distinct. She is the mothering star of our people, unlike any other—yet you speak of her almost as if she were to be feared."

"You have already opened the eye of Daath. Tell me that is not truth."

For a moment, Loch ignored him. He sheathed the sword, dropping it back on the bed's thick coverlet.

"How could you feel the need to hide anything from me?" Eryian pressed. "You do not trust me? As long as you have known me, you still find a need to hide truth? Just tell me, Loch. You made that young Water Bearer the sixth queen of the Daath."

"That is your assumption."

"I make no assumptions. What I cannot understand is why you would deceive me."

Loch turned to stare at Eryian coldly. The anger in him, the fuel Eryian had used to mold the Shadow Walker, was close to the surface, simmering like fire running over coals.

"Tell me to my face the eye has not been opened," Eryian demanded. "I know as well as you what moves in the heavens. Tell me!"

"I have spoken no lies. In this world, her soul no longer breathes. She is gone. But you are correct, warlord. The eye of Daath is open. Her mirrored light now spills from heaven."

"Then we have loosened the curse of Ammon's covenant."

"No—I have. This is on me; it always was on me. Like shattering stone I have released her wrath—a shadow that will pass through the Earth, touching us all, men, angels, their Watchers and prefects, even the mighty lords of the choir, and all their children born of the Star Walker Queens. And when it is over, the Seraphon will walk the Earth at last. We will be all out of prophecies."

Eryian tightened his jaw. "Anything else you have kept hidden?"

"You think I know? What do I know, Eryian? Sometimes I feel I know nothing at all. Sometimes I believe I do not have the slightest idea what is happening, why I feel the things I do, the emotions that rip through me. Why was I driven to find her? Why does she mean so much to me? And why was she taken so quickly? If all this was meant to be, how could I have lost her having barely found her? You tell me, Eryian! You tell me."

Eryian finally got the true emotion he had been seeking. It spilled from Loch, a deep sorrow, a piercing sadness. Eryian glanced down, away from the intensity of the boy's eyes. He had not even guessed, he had never thought of what it meant to Loch, the sadness that had crushed him twice, first his mother and now this girl. He did not understand how, but the love Loch had for her was as strong as what he felt for Krysis. For the first time Eryian had the impulse to touch him, even hold him, as if he was a son, but he only watched, shaken by what he felt.

"I . . . I am sorry, Loch," he said quietly, but with true sincerity.

"Did you not say you needed to leave, warlord? Something about your family?"

Eryian half-bowed, then strode to the door and knocked for the guards. He glanced to Loch one last time, but all he could offer was to let his own emotion spill through his eyes, something he had done for no man, something he knew Loch would not miss.

Once Eryian was gone, the guards closed the heavy doors behind him.

Chapter Twenty-One

Pirates

In the black night, the single ashore boat from Darke's ship was but a shadow as it cut through whitecaps. The seven in the boat kept low and all of them wore cloaks that were the same dark-gray as the storm clouds above. Storan manned the oars, his cloak thrown back over his shoulders and the great muscles of his arms straining with each stroke. Darke crouched near the bow, searching the face of the cliff that rose before them. The tide had come in, but not just any tide, a rare tide. A tide this deep filled the Dove Cara only twice each year, covering the white sand high enough to bear an ashore boat all the way to the cliff side. Darke had learned about the high tide expensively, paying a Pelegasian captain handsomely for the information. It turned out the timing was perfect, this particular night, the sabbat of the autumn equinox, just happened to be one of the two. But such coincidence did not surprise him. Satariel had known well the timing of this rare tide. It was probably linked to some prophecy, just as everything else about this damned mission.

Darke had never been in this place. The hard, slate-gray granite rose sharply upward, and above it, he could make out the lighted spires of a city unlike any he had seen before. Above to the left he could also make out the dark shapes of the fabled trees that were the forest known as the East of the Land. There was myth to this place; he could feel it, land all about that was marked with legend as ancient as the Earth, but Darke put that out of his mind. He had a job to do, a difficult one, and should he make the slightest error, none of them would ever see Ophur or the Western Sea that was their home again.

Darke raised his hand and Storan laid back the oars. They were close enough. The crossbow machine was too heavy for a man to lift, so it had been set in the bottom of the longboat and lashed against the gunwales. Danwyar the Bald crouched behind it. The heavy iron beams were straining at their torsion. As the marksman adjusted his aim, the crossbow trembled. Danwyar centered along the bolt's shaft, checking the angle carefully until he was satisfied. He then eased back and gripped the trigger release. The tip of the crossbow's bolt was a heavy iron grappling hook, and in the bottom of the stern, a long line of triple-bound hemp was coiled.

"Take hold," Danwyar said quietly. The crossbow launched with a heavy *whang*. The recoil lifted the bow out of the water and dropped it back down with a heavy splash. The grappling hook soared into the night, arching, then dropped over a peaked crag midway up where it caught on a spur, anchoring. Danwyar quickly pulled in slack. When it came taut, Storan helped to pull the longboat hand over hand until they were at the base of the cliff. There they tied off.

Darke stood and shouldered a smaller grappling bolt loaded in a heavy crossbow. He took a solid grip of the hemp, tested it with a jerk, and began climbing up the black rock. There was a mist of rain from the heavy storm that was drawing black fingers across the sky bearing from the south. Occasionally the sky would flicker blue lightning fingers through the black clouds. It was no ordinary storm. It was the kind of storm most sailors would have avoided at all cost, but it was just one other thing Darke put out of his mind as he ascended the sheer rock face of the Dove Cara.

Behind, the others followed. The lightest, the priestess, came last.

When Darke reached the crag, he paused and leaned back to brace himself against the rock. He lifted the heavy crossbow. Above, he could see the edge of the Daathan's stone wall. It was not difficult to make out, for it was white alabaster. Along the causeway were archer ports, and every so often covered towers. He fired the bolt. The hook sailed high, trailing its rope. It was wrapped in linen and when it dropped against the causeway's stone, there was almost no sound. Darke tested it and began to climb.

When he reached the alabaster wall, the captain pulled himself over the edge and dropped nimbly, silently onto the wide causeway. He lifted the crossbow and this time loaded it with a plain, feathered silver bolt. Across from him was one of the towers and in it a guard, a tall Daath who was yet to turn this way, his cloak wrapped about him against the chill of the wind. There was no sound when the bolt sheared through the warrior's throat. The Daath crumpled into the tower. It was the first cold blood Darke had ever taken in his life and the taste of it soured in him, but that was yet another thing he put out of his mind. Warriors lived and died by blood; it was their profession—at least this was no innocent.

Darke crouched against the stone and waited. The wind moaned as it streamed through the causeway ports. There was a touch to Darke's shoulder, and he turned to see Hyacinth crouch beside him, the last over the edge, her brown eyes flashing. They were gathered—the seven of them. Storan was at Darke's left. Danwyar was training his steel arrows on the causeway to the south.

"Well, that was a damned long climb," Storan muttered in a whisper. Darke secretly knew how much Storan hated heights.

Hyacinth had already gone to work. She crouched and withdrew a gray sachet from the folds of her cloak. Close against the wall, protected from the wind, she sprinkled red ocher. Darke heard Storan moan—the big helmsman hated magick of all kinds.

She lifted a small bottle with a cork stopper and stared at the tiny creature within. "Show us the scion of the Daath and you are free! The wind is yours!"

Hyacinth held the bottle over the ocher and dropped it. When it shattered, the creature sprang upward but could not soar; captured in a reddish smoke bubble. She looked to Hyacinth, and then spun in a tight circle, like a dancer, weaving an image of the castle that soon took on substance until it was a tiny, ghostlike replica. The creature turned on its wing and followed along the causeway, past the tower where Darke had slain the guard, then down a stairway and through a vaulted window. Wings a blur, she flew down stone hallways. She paused at a corner long enough for Darke to mark the fixture on the wall—a double set of crossed torches whose holders were shaped as serpent's tails. The sylph took wing down another hall, and then a third. She turned swiftly down miniature phantom steps, and finally paused in a wide hallway. Here a line of silver torches burned from gold brackets. The creature moved only slightly down the hallway to pause before a set of heavy, double oaken doors. They were closed and guards were to either side. The sylph, hovering, finally turned to the priestess, waiting.

"We have seen the king's chamber," Hyacinth said.

She waved her hand through the smoke, breaking it open, and watched as the creature soared into the wind.

"We suppose to remember that?" Storan said.

"I will," Danwyar assured them, angling his silver bow to the side. "Follow."

With Danwyar in the lead, the seven ran, hunched over, across the causeway and down the stairway of the tower where the Daathan guard lay slumped in the corner, his helmet askew.

Once inside, they moved through shadows without sound. Storan reached up and snuffed each torch as they passed. When they stepped about one corner, they came suddenly face to face with three Daathan warriors. There was a moment's stunned hesitation between both parties.

The warriors drew quick weapons. Darke high-stepped and cut down the first. Before the others could move, Hyacinth and Danwyar's bolts whispered. Danwyar's arrows were quick thuds, close enough to pierce the armor. Hyacinth wore a small crossbow strapped to her wrist. She had designed it herself, could aim by guiding her hand, and loaded it always with poisons. The three Daath had been brought down with hardly a sound.

Darke paused to admire their armor, so thin and light, darkened silver, and their skin, pale, bloodless, tinted almost blue.

"Not so tough," Storan muttered. "These so-called vampire Daath—not so tough to kill, you ask me."

"They are not vampires," Hyacinth corrected him. "Who told you that?"

"Who cares? My point is they die quick as any other."

"Make no mistake," whispered Darke, "they are deadly killers. If we are discovered without surprising them, as we did these, none of us are getting out of here alive."

At Darke's signal, Danwyar went ahead. At each corner, he braced, turned with bow drawn, then kept going if it was clear. They reached a branch. At one point a hallway split to the left, then, a few feet beyond, it turned right.

Danwyar motioned he would cover the left—the first branch, and singled Rathe, a quick pirate who wore only light leather armor and was an expert with daggers, to check the right before they moved on.

Rathe crouched, moving forward swiftly. As he turned the corner, before he ever realized what had happened, he found himself walking straight into the warlord of the Daath—Eryian, the Eagle of Argolis. The warlord's surprise was a flick of hesitation before his heavy sword cleared its sheath. Rathe had not even touched the hilt of his many daggers when his chest was opened. He was then beheaded. In seconds both arms were shorn off.

Stunned, Darke saw Rathe's torso, stripped of limbs, stagger back into the wall. He knew the manner of the kill had been for effect, to strike terror. And it worked; even though Darke had seen deathly slaughter, a chill ran through him.

Darke drew sword. As the warlord came around the corner, closing on him, he was like a shadow. Suddenly he unfolded—two, three of him—all exactly alike, mirrored images. Darke had heard of it, but had never seen it done. It was effective.

Storan shifted to Darke's left, clutching his axe.

In the last instant, the mirrors vanished as Eryian closed for the kill—choosing Darke as his target. Darke was an able, cunning swordsman, and he blocked the first blow of the warlord's blade, though barely. It struck so solid that it numbed Darke's wrist, nearly dislodging his sword.

Darke staggered, and for the first time in his life found himself desperately trying not to die. The warlord's sword hummed as it moved. At times it phased out of focus, splintering into three, then four swords. Darke guessed each one true by the sword's path, but he knew he could not keep this up long. The lord of the Tarshians had never met his match, but he knew if it were but him and this warlord, he would not survive. Even now, with his men to either side, in moments this Daath was going to slay him. One blow sent him staggering, off balance. The next thrust was for the death, but it was blocked by one of Darke's men, Kerrian, who threw himself into the sword's path. Kerrian's head was perfectly sliced down the center and laid open to either side. The warlord's every strike was meant to inspire terror.

The Daath moved past Kerrian, still coming for Darke. The warlord's blade met the shank of Storan's axe so solidly the weapon was knocked from Storan's hands. It was the first time Storan had ever been disarmed. It seemed impossible. Sensing the big man's strength and threat, the Daath's sword went for Storan's throat, but just short of the blow he was forced back by a rapid series of steel arrows.

Danwyar fired his missiles swiftly—feeding them into the silver short bow one after the other in rapid succession.

Hyacinth slid to the floor on her stomach, crouched at Darke's thigh, and laying her small crossbow over her left arm for aim, fired, her teeth bared in a snarl. It was her captain the Daath was coming for, and her aim was certain.

The warlord had twisted from the path of each of Danwyar's missiles with amazing speed, stepping sideways, then back, then against the wall. One of Danwyar's shafts managed to graze his armor with a singing clank, but that was as close as Danwyar came. It was Hyacinth's small bolt that brought the warlord down.

Eryian turned for the kill, but paused, surprised by what was happening inside him. Hyacinth's bolt was lodged in the side of his neck, near a vital vein, but not lethal. It was the poison that had stopped him. The warlord stared at all of them in disbelief, then stepped back and finally dropped against the wall behind him, sliding down until he was sitting, his sword still in his hand, one knee bent. It looked as though he was merely resting. Hyacinth was a master of poisons and this one moved more quickly than any viper's. It was magick, aided by Hyacinth's best poison spell, swifter than lightning. The pirates could actually see it move through the Daathan's blood, the vessels in his neck turning purple as the poison sunk deeper.

"Mothering son of whores!" the big axeman snarled, lifting his axe from the stone, still enraged that he had been disarmed. He was turning for the kill, but Danwyar stepped in his path, blocking him.

"This one is mine," Danwyar said. He walked calmly toward the Daath, leveled his crossbow, the bolt inches from the heart.

With a tight screech, Hyacinth kicked the crossbow out of Danwyar's hand, then spun to kick him again, throwing him back from the warlord.

Danwyar barely maintained his composure, holding his now bruised wrist. "What in the—"

"My poison will let him sleep!" she fired at him. "What need to kill him, Danwyar? Are we killers now?" She looked at the rest of them. She turned to Eryian. "Besides, he is simply too magnificent to kill." She took a moment to admire his dark, ice-blue eyes.

"Are we listening to women now?" Storan swore. "This—this *thing* just took out two of our men!"

"Would you have done any different for your king?" Hyacinth snapped back at him. She had poised herself in front of the Daath, daring any of them to try to pass.

Danwyar retrieved his crossbow and turned to Darke for a decision.

"She is right on one count," the captain said. "This is not our mark. Leave him."

"Captain, if he wakes up—"

"He is awake, Danwyar," Hyacinth snipped.

It was true. Eryian was watching them.

"He just cannot move, though in a few moments he will have a long, peaceful sleep." Hyacinth turned to the warlord and waved good-bye.

"Keep moving," Darke ordered.

"What if we meet another like that?" Storan grizzled as they followed Danwyar down the next hallway.

"There *are* no others like that," answered Darke. "That was Eryian, the Walker of Shadows."

The Tarshians moved on, leaving Eryian breathing slowly, trying to fight the poison still working through him. Finally, his eyes closed and he slept, as Hyacinth had predicted.

They had reached the final stairway. Darke came to the edge first. He held up his hand. "The king's chamber is below us," he said. "The guards will be quick, deadly."

"Then let us not give them any opportunities," said Danwyar.

He took the point. Hyacinth moved quickly to the opposite side, her crossbow ready.

Darke lifted the heavy crossbow off his back and stepped down just behind and between them.

When the pirates came about the corner, there was a swift exchange. Danwyar dropped to his knees, sliding on the stone as he fired rapidly, one, two, three—four steel shafts ripping from the catgut of his bow. Hyacinth spun about a corner, leveled her aim, and fired into the eye of one guard. As the Daath twisted, Darke's heavy bolt went through his chest and out the back. Both guards lay in their blood. It had been soundless.

The Tarshians gathered before the heavy double doors of the king's chamber. Darke reloaded. Storan took position on his left, axe clutched with both hands. Hyacinth crouched near Darke, loaded her special bolt—light, hollow. She pulled off the moss that kept the poison moist. The poison that had taken down the warlord would have killed any human instantly, possibly would have killed a Daath. This poison was different; it had several effects, but none of them lethal. As all her poisons, it was spellbound to work swiftly. She briefly wondered if she should have made it stronger; the warlord had proven the Daath were resistant to poison. As a backup, she readied a second bolt and pinned it in the side notch of her small crossbow. She leveled it over her left arm, ready.

Danwyar's drew a silver shaft to the string and pulled it taut.

"Take out the doors, Storan," Darke whispered.

Storan brought the huge axe into the center of the doors, smashing through to break the crossbar. He kicked them open with a heavy boot.

It was quick. Though the room was dark, the king was on the bed, sitting against the headboard. He had not been sleeping and as the doors flung open he reached for something beside him, but Danwyar's steel bolt anchored his right hand through the palm to the back of the headboard. The shot had been a precise one. Danwyar did not want what might be the king's sword hand badly injured. He had sunk the thin bolt dead center, between the bones.

Hyacinth quickly fired her crossbow. The tiny bolt lodged in Loch's neck, just below his chin. It had pink feathers and was so small it was no more than a dart.

Darke felt a shiver. As adept at poisons as she was, the sleeper potion in Hyacinth's dart wasn't taking. The Daath snarled, curled his fingers back, and ripped his hand free, sheering off the feathers of Danwyar's arrow. Hyacinth, careful to control her panic, quickly reloaded. It was but a breath before her second bolt hit the king, directly beneath the first, but in that time, Loch had lifted something nearby.

Darke took breath, leveling the heavy crossbow at the Daath's heart. This Daath moved quickly. He was not even going to chance a disarming shot; if things went wrong, the Daath would die first.

The king, however, moved as quick and stealthily as had the warlord. But all he lifted was a double-edged sword. Darke did not fire; none of his men were even close. How could a broadsword pose any danger? Darke only briefly saw the blade—crystal, like glass.

Then it flashed.

Danwyar took a step back, blinded. Darke had somehow instinctually guarded his eyes, and Hyacinth, beside him, was shielded from a direct blast, but Storan took its full brunt and staggered like a drunken bull until he collided with the wall behind him.

Hyacinth looked up. Loch was fading fast. She dared not use another bolt; it could prove too strong. He would surely sleep, but he might not wake. She was startled that he looked her directly in the eye. He lids were sagging, his breaths short.

Darke was still ready to fire, but he took the chance the sleeper darts would take effect. The light had been blinding, but not lethal. In the brief seconds that passed, he realized the king was staring at Hyacinth. He was nearly unconscious, but the eye didn't close. Darke wasn't going to take the chance; he started to squeeze off the trigger when suddenly a second pulse flashed from the sword's crystal blade.

Darke's bolt fired, but soared upward through the ceiling as the pirates were hit with pure light that tossed them like leaves in a wind. Darke was thrown against the stone behind him, hard enough that the wind was knocked from him and he dropped, nearly unconscious. Hyacinth was lighter; she was sent spinning and hit the wall the same as Darke, but as she fell to the floor, she landed in a crouch, like a cat. Storan was already against the wall. He did have enough sense to shield his eyes, but his head was slammed against the stone. Danwyar had managed to throw himself behind the doorway, out of the light's path.

On his knees, swearing, Darke reloaded the crossbow, but when he took aim, the Daath was no longer moving. Darke wondered, briefly, why they were still alive. The last burst, if it had been stronger, could have easily killed them. Darke saw the king's eyes slowly close. His head dropped forward.

"He is out," Hyacinth said. "You can take him now."

The sword dropped from the king's hand. It struck the marble floor and spun, as if alive, emitting flashes of colors, until it finally cooled. The blade looked like cold glass, as fragile as a goblet.

"Be thanking the Goddess once out of here," Storan muttered, his hands waving in front of his eyes until he reached the doorway. "I'm going to be blind now, Danwyar?"

"No. It is wearing off. Go shoulder the king."

Storan felt his way along the wall. "Logical asking me, since I am the one cannot see my hand before my face."

"I am no better off," Danwyar said, edging into the room carefully, waiting for the effect to fade.

Hyacinth took Storan's hand and guided him to Loch. She watched carefully as Storan lifted him. The Daath's face was aquiline, beautiful, perfect. As Storan hoisted him onto his big shoulder, for a brief moment, the king's eyes fell open. They were staring at Hyacinth, but he was not conscious. His eyes, however, were brilliant, filled with a strange light, inhuman but fantastic, as if stars might spill through them. She gasped openly.

"Angelslayer," she whispered.

The eyes closed. Storan had him secured on his shoulder and looked about, his sight finally returning. "At last," he muttered. "Never wished to be blind, that be certain."

Danwyar looked at the king's face. "Is there a mistake here, Hyacinth? He is no older than you! You are telling me this is the king of the Daath? The conqueror of the fabled gathering wars!"

"This is the scion, Danwyar! You want to go search for another—go ahead, I am sure we have time. You think, Captain?"

"We are getting out of here," Darke commanded.

"Wait!" Hyacinth hissed. "The sword! The sword!"

They paused. Danwyar turned. He touched it carefully before lifting it. He found the sheath, shoved in the blade, and dropped the belt over his shoulder.

"Go," Darke said. "Danwyar, take point."

Danwyar ran at a crouch, bow loaded. Storan, hunched over with the body, followed behind. Darke made a quick search behind them. They had not been discovered. He ran with Hyacinth sprinting at his side.

Chapter Twenty-Two
Sunblade

Deep water, the Western Sea of Enoch

From the forecastle, Darke watched the horizon. At first, he feared a storm of lashing wind and rain, but the farther he sailed into it, leaving the shore of the Dove Cara behind them, the more he realized it was nothing like any storm he had known. There were winds lashing, and the seas had been whipped to crests as high as six feet, but luckily they were coming at him head-on, from the storm's center, which was due west, fitting the directions of the map. The storm seemed to be spreading outward as he watched, like a living thing, and now and then it flashed with deep veins of purple lightning lacing the black clouds.

"Elyon's name," muttered Danwyar, "what be this we are sailing into, Captain?"

"I feel confident we will discover that in due course, Danwyar. Slow to half."

"Half the speed!" shouted Danwyar, his command echoed to the stern where the rower's drummer slowed his beat.

"Bring in the main mast."

"Drop the main!" Danwyar commanded in a strained voice used to shouting.

Danwyar then stepped beside Darke, setting his hands on the forecastle railing. "No rain; clouds like that and no rain."

"I do not think they are clouds," Darke said.

"How do you mean that?"

"See how they slowly spin, how they seem to crawl across the night sky like fingers over the stars? You ever seen clouds do that, Danwyar?"

Danwyar shook his head. "Due west, those clouds are over the mark on that map. Of course, you know that."

Darke did not comment.

Danwyar studied the clouds, troubled, but something else seemed to be on his mind. He glanced to the captain, worried. "You all right, Captain?"

"Why? Should I not be?"

"Just that . . . I wanted to say, I know you feel it."

"What?"

"Cold blood. That first one, his back to you—"

"Keep your mind on this sky, Danwyar, as well as these waves."

"You should have let me take him out."

"Why? Would that make his blood any less damning? We did what we did, and we have both learned by now there is little use in looking back."

They both had to grip the railing as the ship pierced a particularly high wave. The wave rolled over them with a hard slap of cold spray.

"I have been thinking on this, Captain." Danwyar said.

"And?"

"Things have changed. You still believe we should sail into this?"

"What has changed?"

"The king of the Daath, he fought several wars. It is said he united all his tribes, hard fought, the gathering wars."

"I have heard."

"Whoever is it down in our hold, it is for certain not Argolis, king of the Daath. The little witch has made a mistake. I know you hesitate admitting, bearing a fondness for her—"

"Who told you that?"

"I am just trying to say that if we did have Argolis, maybe then we might have some kind of chance, not much of a chance, but something. Enough to spit on. As things stand now, we have no chance here whatsoever. So as second, I am saying we are damned fools, and you know and I know this angel is going to kill us and not even think about it the next morning."

"Anything more?"

"How do you mean?"

"Such as suggesting we turn back for Ophur. Run maybe?"

"I never spoke of turning."

"No? If you were me, standing where I am—this ship yours—are you going to tell me you would hold course into that storm?"

"It is not my place to say."

"I am asking you to say; in fact, I am telling to say."

"Why? You intend to listen to me if I do?"

"How would you call it, Danwyar?"

"I never would have taken the parchment from that river giant in the first place. He was a low thief and a child killer, and I would have pinned his stinking parchment through his heart with his own dagger."

"You would not have read it first?"

"No."

"You will never make a good liar, Danwyar. Pray you never have to lie your way out of some tight spot."

"Fine. Say what you wish. Only problem I have had since leaving shore is I am not sure how much I want to die, or you, or any of us, but that is what we are about to do. Die."

"It was bound to happen. Did your mother never explain that?"

"That boy down there—twenty years old, I would guess."

"I would say closer to twenty and five."

"Ah, well, twenty and five. Now I can sleep tonight."

"Keep the ice in your veins, Danwyar. We have fought with odds against us before this."

"Not these odds."

"We will find a way to turn them, my friend. Have them lay back first tier oars, these waves are coming higher. When you have done that, bring me the priestess. I will be in my cabin."

Danwyar turned, dropped from the forecastle to stride the midwalk. The sea broke over the gunwales as he did. They were cutting crests able to sink them easily if Storan slipped on the tilling oar, but the helmsman's grip was always firm.

"Lay back first tier," Danwyar cried. "Latch and seal!"

✝

In Darke's cabin, Hyacinth made herself comfortable, sitting on his sleeping cot, using it as though it were a swing. Danwyar had joined them, closing the door against the spray of the sea. It was a strange quiet, the winds outside howling.

"Some of that wine," Hyacinth said, "the Tyrinian bloodroot. That would go nicely right now."

"Yes," said Danwyar, "and we will have to break out some goat cheese, as well. Berries maybe."

"I would not turn down berries."

"Hyacinth," Darke said, keeping his attention on the maps spread over the table before him as an oil lamp swung to and fro above. "Tell Danwyar about those clouds, what you might have read in that book of yours."

She was all too eager. "Those are called whirlers, Danwyar. They are like dark stars with tails spinning, whipping in and out of each other. They were called the thousand eyes, the mirrors of Elyon. If you stare at them for a long time, right into them without turning away, you can spot the eyes, watching back at you, living things."

"What a comfort. I will have to give that a try."

Darke looked up from the map. "In all your books, your scrolls, anything at all about how to kill one of these bastards?"

"Captain, you cannot kill them. They do not die."

"There," said Danwyar. "A bit of reason. A little sanity. It is almost refreshing."

"However," she added, "we do have an Angelslayer down in that stinking bilge-soaked cage. He might know a bit about angels. Would you think?"

"Danwyar is worried he is a little young to be the Daathan king. Any thoughts on that?"

"He is young, but that is the scion. I have not erred. I am certain."

Danwyar sighed, shaking his head.

"Something to say, Danwyar?" she asked.

"No. You are certain. What is there any one of us could say further?"

"Good. Now, let me down there, Captain. Let me mind walk him."

Danwyar shook his bald head. "Yes. Pit our entire fate on witchery."

"Witchery?" said Hyacinth. "You really should be more careful how you put things, Danwyar," she added, wriggling her fingers. Each nail bore a different poison. "Why not calm down and think all this over carefully."

"Calm down and think," Danwyar said, irritated. "Of course, why have I not thought of that myself?"

"I will put it simple for you, Danwyar—we not only have the fabled scion of the Daath, we have the mark of the father."

"And what is that?"

"The sword," Darke answered.

"The captain remembers," Hyacinth said. "It is named of Enoch the Arsayalalyur. They say in the time of Yered that Elyon looked down and took pity and sent the Daath and the mark of the father, the Arsayalalyur to stand in the day that comes, in the time the Earth nears Aeon's End."

"Scriptures," muttered Danwyar.

"Truths," counted Hyacinth. "That is the sword of an archangel. Uriel. A sunblade of the Pleiades, the same that left the scar cut into the rock of the East of the Land they call the Dove Cara. You saw it? It was hard to miss—the huge cleft cut into the stone beneath Terith-Aire."

"She has a point, Danwyar," Darke said.

"So we send her down there and soon have all the answers we need?"

"Cannot hurt," said the captain.

"I recall one occasion she mind-ripped some poor bastard who could not stand for three days afterward. What if we need him still able to stand up?"

"If he is so weak she can rip through him that easily," said Darke, "then we truly have made a mistake; he is no scion of the Daath. Hyacinth, go do what you do."

"Let the witch tell us all how to live through whirlers and angel eyes."

Hyacinth offered Danwyar a downturned brow. "What did you just call me? Do you really wish to keep prodding me? *Danwyar the Bald?* Do you?"

Danwyar didn't respond. Hyacinth brushed past his shoulder as she stepped into the night. Darke paused to glance at Danwyar with half a grin.

"One day, my friend, you are going to push her too far."

Loch found he was tightly bound in triple-meshed hemp, strong, tied with such precision it was eating skillfully into his flesh. He ignored the pain; it held no interest. But he did let himself pay attention to the oncoming storm. It was curious. It was whipping the sea into high waves, and the warship was cutting through them like a spear, leaving him struggling against sickness. He had not spent time on ships. The Tarshians that had taken him were not only able to navigate deep water, a rare skill in itself, but they were also able to do so in high seas that would swallow most warships like a stone. He guessed this to be the one they called the Shadow Hawk, the Tarshian named Darke. These were no ordinary seamen. But, as well, this was no ordinary storm. It was a storm without thunder, yet he saw the distinct blue veins of lightning flickering through the beams of the top hatch, which could only mean one thing. A degree of the moon earlier, he had been facing the death lord of the south, Azazel, with armies that had no number any man could name.

Now, suddenly his world had once again turned direction. He still faced an angel, for the flickers of lightning were distinctive. But this one bore out to sea, and it was the Western Sea, which could only mean he was a rogue; he kept on the move. A rogue of Etlantis. Loch could almost sense his name, but he could feel him. He was weaker than Azazel, but this was an angel of the choir, far more powerful than the pirates who were sailing down the throat of his storm.

He turned with interest when the latch of his cage clicked, turning, and the doorway dropped open. A girl, the priestess who had hit him with the sleeper darts, squeezed past his bound feet, then locked them both inside and set the key in her bodice, between her breasts. Water spilled through the top hatch in icy streams and the spray kept Loch soaked, but he let it keep his mind sharp.

"I have heard the Daath are resistant to cold," she said. "Apparently it is true."

The priestess before him was seaworthy; she could ride the waves easier than he could; she bore no signs of the sickness he felt welling up inside. And she was also used to the cold seawater, though she shivered when a spray of it hit them directly, pouring from the hatchway above. For a while, all she did was crouch across from him, watching. She lifted her small fingernail.

"One wrong move," she said, "and it is nighttime, Prince."

"How many wrong moves do you believe I am capable of? The only things left unbound are my eyebrows."

"Yes. They have treated you like a piece of meat. Who tied you up this way? It was Storan, wasn't it? He is a pig. Does it hurt?"

"It is not supposed to hurt?"

"Here, I can help."

She crawled over and used the nail of her small finger as a lancet to make a tiny cut in his lower lip, then laid her second finger, and what was under its nail, over the blood pressing tight.

"Feel it?"

He nodded. It did, in fact, hit him hard—a warm, heavy euphoria. It was a powerful opiate. "If you do not mind, that is enough," he said, turning his head away.

"Very well."

He laid his head back against the hard, wet wood. The effects were instant, and while it was sweet relief to be out of pain, it was no longer as easy to think or concentrate. "I did not ask to be put to sleep," he said.

"You should sleep, actually. While there is time. You will need all the strength you have, I would imagine. For now we are in no danger, Darke can navigate these seas, high as they are, and we are far from the storm you see though the hatchway. It is deceptive; it looks close and yet it is at least a day or more from us. It is an angel's storm, but you know that, do you not? Yes. You know a lot, more than I, possibly. At least we can hope."

"You are saying you people know what you are sailing into?"

"Of course we know. Do you think you are aboard a Pelegasian merchantman's ship? This is the warship of Darke, once the lord of all the emerald cities of Tarshish."

"Then you are Tarshians?"

"They are. Not me."

"But apparently all of you are mad. You sail into the eyes of an angel."

She crawled over to him, brushed her fingers though his thick black hair. "Why did you let us take you?" she asked, innocently.

"Let you?"

She kneeled close to him. She had a scent, hyacinths. Her eyes were a beautiful, rich brown. It bothered him that her potion was not only an opiate; it was also heavily laced with aphrodisiac. She was difficult to ignore.

"I was there," she said, "in the castle. You know that, you met my eyes. I watched as you sent the second burst of light through the sword of Uriel. You could have stopped us; you could have killed us all. Why did you not?"

He studied her, but didn't answer.

"We might just as well be open with each other. It is a small ship, and we will be together now for at least a count of time. Why not kill us?"

"Something to learn of you, not certain what is it yet," he said.

He wanted to tell her to move back—her powder was crawling through him like fingers across his skin—but he did not want to give her the clue her potion had been effective. Her eyes were painted in dark lines and accented by malachite on her upper lids, much like they had painted poor Aeson in what now seemed a world away. Her lips were a rich red of her own blood. He recognized many of the rings on her fingers. She was a priestess of Ishtar. Her tightly curled locks of dark hair fell down her back and dark shoulders, wreathing her face.

"I am called Hyacinth."

"But you are no Tarshian."

"Of course not. I told you that. If you were to sail the Western Sea, off the southern tip of the continent of Mu, you would find many of us. I am going to call you Lochlain—I like it better than the other names you have, such as the son of Argolis or the king of the Daath. I want you to remain still, relaxed; I am not going to harm you."

"Harm me?"

"It might even prove pleasant."

There was nothing he could do to stop her; he was bound too tightly. She gently laid her head against his chest. Her hands slid up slowly, sliding over his shoulders until her fingers curled into his hair on either side of his head.

Before he could block her, before he even realized what she was attempting, she was inside him. She moved through his memories far too quickly for even Loch to counter, and he was trained at blocking his thoughts, turning away such mind probes.

It was said that every skilled magi learns but one true spell in a lifetime. Some could gain the skill to stop a heart, others could master fire like commanding wind; they could become healers, even able, it was rumored, to bring life to the dead. And though a skilled spell binder could practice much magick and become proficient in a number of arts and bindings, human witches could become true masters of but one, for such power took a lifetime or more to learn. There were, of course, Star Walker Queens who learned the stark knowledge of angels and Nephilim; but this was a girl, a mortal, and a young one at that. Obviously, this was her mastery, because Loch himself had practiced the art and she easily outmaneuvered him, moving much too quickly for his mind to block. She countered his ever move, almost as if she were enjoying herself, so light and swift that it was like a dance. He could almost picture her turning in cat steps, leaping, moving effortlessly through his every memory, every thought, until she was done with him. Finished, she had crawled back to crouch in the corner, though he did not remember her moving away. She had sent shivers all through him, not just in his head, but through his skin, his body.

"Do you have a name for what you just did?" he asked.

"I only know it in my native tongue; it would sound nonsense to you, but it mostly means *rape*. It is a lot like being raped. I can make it hurt if ever I wish. You are skilled. I was surprised, you attempted to block me, and better than any I have engaged before. The band on your arm. A Shadow Walker. You have been well trained. Most of my kind would have been unable to read you at all."

She paused, watching him curiously for a time. "Odd," she said.

"What?"

"That the Daath would choose a red-haired milkmaid as their queen."

Her words had taken him by surprise. "Do not speak of her again," Loch warned with a voice that even the priestess could not ignore.

"Understood, your majesty." She gestured with a wave of her hands.

"You are talented, priestess, but you are not as capable as you think. You see the surface, but you miss the depths. As for any questions you have, since you went to the trouble of raping me, answer them yourself."

She paused. "You have a temper."

"You have no idea."

"Oh, but I do. One more question, if you wouldn't mind, just curiosity in me. You have always cursed yourself over it, hated yourself, but do you actually believe you could have stopped them? Only nine years old?"

He forced himself still, keeping his anger beneath the surface, but his eyes grew black, inhuman.

"What are you trying to do, priestess?"

"Those were the two daggers nearest your heart. I needed to know if you could be easily broken."

"And are you finished?"

"Yes. You handle yourself very well. Exceptionally well. Is this how they teach all Shadow Walkers? To not feel even the most tender pain?" She paused a moment. Something in her eyes changed. For some reason, whoever she was, she let herself through into her eyes. He thought he saw them mist. She wasn't hiding; her feelings were honest. It left him confused. "What I just did was very cruel. Try to forgive me."

He said nothing. He left his eyes dark, inhuman.

"The red-hair especially. Such loss you feel. It leaves me saddened—no one has ever or will ever love me that way. I wonder of its taste. You are truly a king. I will mock you no more, Shadow Walker."

She watched him carefully now, but he did not let her emotions stir him, though he had to curse the potion she had left swimming through his blood. He wanted to look away from her eyes as a tear dropped quietly across her cheek, but he was going to betray no weakness.

"You want me to leave, do you not?"

"You should have what you came for."

"Curiously, I do not. I came to learn how to kill an angel, but though you are a Shadow Walker, you have taken little blood."

"He cannot be killed—the one your captain is hunting. He is prefect by his smell; with a word he could leave us all dust and wind. You should tell this Captain Darke to turn back."

"That would be useless."

"Then we are going to die, priestess."

"Those we are with—they know, as the Daath, how to die well, if it is any comfort."

"It is not. My people need me. I am of no use to you. Let me free; I can reach the shore from here."

"In these waves? They would take you like a stone."

As if to prove her point, the ship rose nearly vertical, then dropped to slam back into the sea before pulling out of the wave.

"I could stay here . . . with you," she said tenderly. "If you wish."

"Why?"

She shrugged—no answer. She crawled to the hatch, but paused before closing it. "If you need anything, if you are in too much pain, merely kick against the door. When they come, ask for Hyacinth." Her dark brown eyes studied him a moment longer, then the hatch closed and the key clicked as the lock turned.

Chapter Twenty-Three

Satrina

Lamech shielded his eyes against the sun and lifted his foot off the beam of his plough, pulling up on the reins of his oxen. A figure had just staggered from the thicket bordering his grain field. He was not tall, but was powerfully built. He was naked but for a shredded tunic tied to his waist and a rope through which he had shoved a short sword. He was bloody, blood dried all over him, over his face and eyes.

The hounds spotted him and charged, baying at full cry. The figure, startled, stopped short and looked up. Lamech saw the short sword flicker. Lamech was running, leaping furrows.

"No! No, do not kill my dogs! Please! Wait!"

The figure paused, staring at Lamech, then at the hounds that were nipping at him, snarling, surrounding him.

"Please! Do not kill them!"

"You want them—call them off, plodder!" snarled the stranger.

"Dogs! Dogs!" Lamech screamed, waving his arms.

It was not working—his dogs were ignoring Lamech.

"Back off!" Rhywder snapped in sharp command and at this the hounds stopped baying. Most dropped onto their haunches and waited for Rhywder to say more, as if they were his dogs now, but Rhywder just dropped to his knees, then passed out. One of the hounds stepped forward to lick his cheek.

†

Rhywder laid half-conscious. It seemed he could smell stew and bread baking, and it seemed he heard voices. He had been dreaming of his sister; they were running through fields, poppy fields in bloom, but then like a dark cloud invading, consciousness returned in a painful, aching fog that slowly came into focus. He had no idea where he was. He found himself lying on a table staring up at a cabin's ceiling. A well-built cabin, actually, the jointed work was with skill, sealed with pitch against moisture.

For the last seven days, Rhywder had run through jungle, winded, weakened from loss of blood and sleep. He had been delirious, but he had kept running. He remembered now, thinking he had to reach Hericlon, he had to reach the gate, he could stop for nothing, sleep nor pain.

Then he remembered the night the women had caught him in a streambed. He killed them all, screaming, working the short sword, his back against the stream's bank so they could not outmaneuver him. He slew relentlessly, with angled, quick kills—they never managed to overwhelm him or pin him down. They simply could not get past his blade. That he had clung to his short sword had saved his life. He worked the blade so hard he had to switch hands, his right arm wearing out. His left was weaker, not as skilled, but he had trained to fight with either hand and he continued killing until finally, Elyon's grace was with him and there were no more. The last image left of them was a young girl's head as it bounced down the river rocks.

He blinked, awake. He was staring at a girl. She was pretty, with gentle brown hair and long lashes that capped violet eyes. She was dipping a cloth into a porcelain bowl that curled in steam. When she turned she drew back with a start.

"Lamech—he wakes!" she exclaimed.

The plodder, minus his hounds, appeared beside her. He didn't go well with the girl—a plodder with dull eyes and calloused hands. This girl did not look anything like that should have belonged to Lamech, but then, here in these villages beyond the gate, some wives were bought from Galaglea without ever knowing their destination—if so, Lamech was lucky, she was not hard at all to look upon.

"Can you hear me?" Lamech asked.

"Yes," Rhywder answered.

"We believe you are a madman. Are you mad? Is this the lunar effect working upon you, making you mutter words of wolves and howlers and cats?"

"Moon does get to me at times."

"So I surmised when I saw you come from the wood! One like you came once before from that wood—walked upon four feet like a dog and died of a fever two days later."

"You are saying I was walking on four feet?"

"No, but look at you, you have lost blood to hundreds of savage bites. They are all over you, all of them from small teeth. Weasels perhaps?"

Rhywder paused, staring at the girl. She offered a simple smile.

"Where am I?" he asked.

"Euphoria," the man answered.

"What did you say?"

"Euphoria."

"You have named a stinking hole in the jungle Euphoria?"

"This is not jungle."

"We are near the mountains," explained the girl. "It is fair pasture land."

"Exactly," confirmed the plodder. "In fact, it was a vast meadow when we happened upon it. Lots of trees for building; it was almost perfect, a joy to behold, hence we named it Euphoria."

Rhywder dropped off the table. "You say I am near Hericlon?"

The girl offered a wineskin. "Drink," she urged. "It is fresh spring water. You need liquids."

"Thank you, but tell me first—how close to Hericlon?"

"Less than a day's ride," the girl said. She held the wineskin, insistent. He thought again it was damned odd a girl this remarkable would be housed with a fool plodder.

"Thanks," Rhywder said, drinking long and hard, then handing her back the skin. "I will need a horse. You have a horse?"

She shook her head.

"I do," answered Lamech.

"Bring it, plodder. And get your people together—leave now for Hericlon.

If you are lucky you can reach the gate before the armies reach you. I will have them raise the gate to get your people through, but there is very little time, so you must all move quickly. I will ride ahead; I have a warning to deliver to the homeland."

"Armies?" Lamech asked, arching a brow. "What armies?"

"Unchurian armies, about ten hundred, hundred thousand Unchurian armies—and that might even be a shy estimate."

"Impossible. Unchurians live in the trees. We have scared most of them off long ago."

"Bushmen are not Unchurian. You have never met an Unchurian, old man, and let us pray we can keep it that way because if you do not get your people out of here, you are going to be their sustenance. They crave both human blood and flesh." Rhywder glanced down. "I am naked—"

"I have been cleansing your wounds," the girl said calmly. "Every day, in fact. I have them under control, but many of them continue to fester."

"Satrina is trained in herbs and cures," the man added. "You are lucky. You would surely have died."

"Satrina," Rhywder said, "that is your name?"

She nodded.

"Pretty name."

"Thank you. I have drawn much pus, but it is laudable pus, a sign that your body is fighting back. You were strong; others might have died. The worst of your wounds I seared with hot oil. It will leave scars, but the wounds are cleaned. You did not feel the pain since you were unconscious."

Rhywder nodded. "I am grateful. Excuse me a moment . . ."

He took the horsehair blanket off the table he had been lying on, grabbed his short sword, which was nearby, and cut a hole through the center.

"You have anything like a belt?" he asked, pulling the blanket over his head.

She handed him a long, purple scarf. He tied it around his waist, cinched it tight, and shoved his sword through it. "I want the best horse you can find, light, fast," he told the plodder. "And throw in a breechcloth, if you would not mind. I have never fancied riding with naked thigh."

"Neither have I," the girl said. "The burns . . ."

Rhywder glanced at her. She smiled back.

"Ignore him, Satrina, he is mad."

"What if he is telling the truth, Lamech?" she asked, keeping her eyes on Rhywder. A little flirtatious, he thought, considering her husband was but feet away.

"I know a madman when I see one."

"So do I, but I believe you are wrong. In fact, we should listen to every word he speaks because this one bears the mark of a Shadow Walker—he wears the silver armband."

"It can easily be faked. What would an elite warrior be doing fleeing naked through the jungle?"

"But what if it is not faked? He speaks of armies, moving for Hericlon, a lot of armies."

"That is impossible. There are not even cities within thousands of leagues. Only jungle. He is mad, Satrina, he—"

Rhywder grabbed Lamech by the front of his tunic, then slammed him against the wall. "If I hear anymore, I am going to lose my temper, plodder. Now, you listen to me, you simple bastard. There were enough Unchurians on my trail to leave this village ash and fodder in a heartbeat! I am trying to save your pitiful life! Now get me a horse. After I ride, you and your woman gather weapons and prepare your people to ride for Hericlon or you will be feeding worms before sundown."

"It is already sundown," Lamech said.

"Already sundown . . ."

"Yes."

"How long have I been unconscious?"

"One day before this," the girl answered, "and now till dusk of the next."

Rhywder felt a stab of panic. "Elyon's grace," he whispered as he stepped past them. He walked over and kicked open the door so hard it snapped the leather hinges. Rhywder stepped out of the cabin. The sun was low, and the shadows were long.

"Have there been riders?"

He glanced back into the cabin. "Satrina, have there been riders?"

She shook her head, looking a bit alarmed.

"You broke my door," Lamech moaned.

"You, Satrina! Come!" Rhywder said.

The girl started forward, but Lamech laid a hand on her shoulder. Satrina pulled away sharply and walked to stand beside Rhywder.

"What do you need, Shadow Walker?" she said.

"How many people are in this village?"

"There are fifty men. Many women and children."

"There are more to come next season," Lamech said from inside.

Rhywder turned an angry eye on him. "One more word from you, plodder, and I will shove your tongue down your throat. Understood?"

The man backed farther into the shadows.

Rhywder turned to the girl. "Get us both horses. We will try to gather in as many of these villagers as we can and find someone capable of leading you."

"That would be Urich, he is the leader of this village."

"He will do. If your people can reach Hericlon before the Unchurians overtake you, it is possible you might be safe, at least for the winter—provided Hericlon still stands."

"Why do you not lead us? You are a Shadow Walker."

"I have to ride ahead—there is little time, I must move with all speed."

Rhywder watched children chase a wobbly wooden wheel down a wagon-scarred road. Chickens were all over. Gardens.

The girl suddenly grabbed Rhywder's arm, pointing. "Look!"

From the line of trees above Lamech's cabin burst a host of riders. They came with thunder and heavy horses, cloaks flared, a hundred and more. Rhywder recognized them immediately; they were high-blood Unchurians, a raiding party. They would not be interested in blood; they came to spread terror. They fanned out, trampling the gathered stalks of harvest wheat.

Rhywder grabbed the girl, pulling her into the cabin. All that was left of Lamech was his ass as he crawled through the back window.

"What are you doing with a frog like that?" he asked.

"Cooking for him."

"Then you would know if there is a cellar."

She nodded, but her attention was focused past him, through the doorway where an arrow looked as if it had been sucked into a villager, throwing him into rows of dry, brittle cornstalks. Arrows now whistled everywhere. A woman screamed, twisting to clutch at a feather shaft imbedded in her back as if it were a bug biting.

Rhywder grabbed Satrina by the shoulders. "A cellar! A fruit bin! Anything!"

She nodded, though still staring through the doorway. A woman was beheaded by an axe as the rider swiftly passed by. Headless, her body, for a moment, continued running on its own.

Rhywder noticed something in the floor. He kicked away a footstool, threw the table aside, and threw open the floor planking by its ringed latch. All he could see was darkness below, but he threw her in. She vanished with a shriek.

"Stay in there!"

He turned, ripping a bow and quiver of darts from where they were mounted over the hearth, ran through the doorway, and dropped to a crouch in the shadows of the porch.

"Elyon, I deliver you these souls," he whispered, his arrow taking quick marks. He was not killing Unchurians; he was killing the villagers. He was first searching out the children. If there was time, he would take women, as well. He dropped children one after the other.

He put a bolt through a little girl, through her back, and it tore at his heart to see her blond hair fly as she fell. His next arrow passed through the neck of a young boy who had been staring at the riders, curious. They spotted him now. Unchurians broke off toward Rhywder; the rest were, as Rhywder feared, keeping the villagers alive for torture.

Suddenly a warrior dropped off of the roof timbers, onto the porch, directly in front of him with a scream. Rhywder sunk his arrow through the Unchurian's sternum and he dropped to the ground with a puff of dust.

"Damn idiot," Rhywder muttered.

Another came from the side. He was mounted, cloak flaring as he vaulted his horse onto the porch. Rhywder rolled back into the cabin. He brought an arrow to the string, but the horseman reached the doorway quickly. He rode in, ducking beneath the lintel. Rhywder fired the bolt into the Unchurian's cheek at an angle that went through the left eye.

Now the horse came at him, hooves flailing. Rhywder rolled to the side, then crouched and quickly jabbed in and out of the heart with his short sword. A wooden chair exploded beneath the horse's weight as it fell to the side, but the animal also collided against several supporting beams. They cracked. The roof moaned. Rhywder looked up with a gasp. Just as it caved in, Rhywder was barely able to dive in the cellar.

It was an alarmingly long drop. Surprised, he struck water with a splash. It was wide, a stream, with considerable current. Rhywder would have been swept under by its force had not the girl grabbed his horsehair tunic and pulled him back up. He came out of the water breathless, drenched, and blinked at her, stunned.

"A well?" he asked. "I threw you into a well?"

"It is better than burning."

"Burning?"

She pointed and he glanced up. He was surprised to see flames had quickly taken hold; they were roiling over the wood above the well's opening.

"The casks of naphtha must have spilled and sparked a fire."

"Why would you have naphtha?"

"Lamech used it to burn trees in the early spring to clear more fields for planting."

"And the fool kept it in your cabin?"

"He did."

There was a heavy moan and Rhywder pulled her back against the muddy wall as debris crashed downward. Mostly it was broken chunks of flaming wood. Rhywder was able to shove them under and let the current take them.

He leaned back against the cut rock, letting the cold water numb out some of the stinging pain left from bites.

"Might be best you just stay here with me," she said.

"By rights I should climb back up, see if I can help anyone."

"With a fire above us? Please stay. They are killing everyone. You will but die up there unless you wait for them to move on. You are brave, but you are only one. They are many."

He paused. She had a point. "Sorry about your man."

"Why would these Unchurians do this? What have we done to them? I did not even know they existed. Why kill all our people?"

"It is not your fight; it is ours, the Daath. They are here to spread terror, let the word reach the homeland and the gate of what is coming for them."

There was a scream from above and she clenched her eyes against the sounds. Rhywder stared at her a moment. She was pressed against the rock, soaked. He knew that wasn't the place or time to notice, but she had fine tits.

"What do we do now?" she asked, opening her eyes. They were near tears, though for a girl she was holding up well, better than most women he had known.

"Nothing for a time. I suppose we have no choice but to wait. Know any good stories?"

She shook her head.

"No problem. I have a few."

Deep into the night, when the girl had fallen asleep against his shoulder, Rhywder finally looked up. It was almost dawn. The fires of the village that had raged all night were out now; there was only lingering black smoke. Earlier there had been figures moving, still more screams, but now everything had died down to moans. The Unchurians had left, and they had not eaten the flesh; they had reaped terror and moved on. It was a cruel way of waging war, but one that Argolis himself had used on occasion to force surrender of a village.

He noticed her bright eyes blink open. "Is it over?" she asked.

"Yes."

"Are you all right, Shadow Walker?"

"I am fine."

"But you do not look well."

"I feel like my skin is blistering—as you said—something to do with letting out pus."

"More than pus. There was poison in you. That or the bites were from very foul teeth."

"Foul they were."

"I wanted you to know that I do not mind that you threw me in here. You did not realize it was deep."

"No. I did not."

"At least the cool waters have eased your fever. That is very helpful. I hope you live. You are brave and good."

"Fairly brave yourself," he said.

"No, not me, I was terrified. Am terrified."

"Terrified has nothing to do with being brave."

A dim shaft of light highlighted her face; it almost left her looking in her teens, though he knew she was older. It was the button nose and the leftover light spray of freckles.

"Are we going to die?" she asked.

"We are not dead yet, which is good enough. Death—dying, it's not that important."

"How do you mean?"

"It is a passage. Dying young, like you, would almost be a blessing."

"I am thirty and two, Shadow Warrior."

Rhywder was surprised. Shocked. "Really?"

"Yes."

"Thirty and two? Almost as old as me. How is it you look so young?"

"Only the shadows down here, I am sure. They must be playing tricks."

She glanced up and shivered slightly, not from cold, but from fear. Above, floating black smoke was lit in a dim, red hue by the first light of dawn. He carefully put his arm around her.

"Whenever I am afraid, very afraid, I often think of what my grandmother once told me. She said one night, showing me the stars, the moon, the clouds—she told me that all of it, everything we saw—was not real. The world, she said, the Earth, it is all an illusion."

"And *that* comforts you?"

"It is more the thought that this is what Elyon has created, this is how He meant it to be, a winnowing. Within the world, terror is very real. These are the killing fields—the places of harvest. They send us here from the Blue Stars—leaving no memories of home, drawing a veil over our eyes, but the purpose is the harvest, the reaping."

"And what is it you believe Elyon is harvesting?"

"The valiant. I believe that is His harvest. The good, the valiant. But my point is that death is leaving the illusion for the real, for home. Never fear death. Think of it as going home, Satrina."

She nodded. "I suppose that could be comfort."

Rhywder stepped into the center, the shaft of dusk's light falling over him. He took hold of the rope that held the well bucket, testing its strength. It had been anchored to a rock just below the lip of the well, which was their luck. It had not burned.

"I will go up first. With this rope, it should not be hard. Understand, though, things above are not likely to be pretty."

"But the terror is all an illusion, correct?" she reminded him.

"Yes. All an illusion." He took a tight grip of the rope. "When I reach the top, wrap the rope about your waist, take hold, and then I will pull you up. When you get to the top, I want you to do something."

"What is that?"

"Keep your eyes on me. Do not look around. I have had the pleasure of terror such as this—we are old acquaintances—but there is no good in you looking around. Agreed?"

She nodded.

Rhywder began to climb. When he reached the top, he knelt for a moment, head spinning. He was impossibly weak. If they were found, he knew he would not last long in a fight. Finally, he surveyed what was left of Euphoria. Fires still burned. Smoke drifted like fog. Living villagers were impaled and set in various positions, hundreds of them—even infants. It meant the firstborn Unchurians were of such pure blood that the curse of Enoch had not taken them. They were going to be deadly opponents, centuries old.

He turned. "Ready?" he whispered.

"Ready," came an answer from below.

He hauled her up quickly, hand over hand until he could grip her wrist.

He helped her over the edge, and immediately put both hands on her shoulders, turning her so that her eyes met only his. She was a bit older than he thought, but her face was so fresh and pretty, she could easily have been twenty. It was a face he could get used to looking at, and such thoughts puzzled him, considering their circumstances.

"Satrina."

"Yes?"

"This is what we are going to do—we are going to walk through the embers to the end of the village. Do not look around. Just keep your eyes on me, understand?"

Satrina nodded, frightened.

Rhywder stood, took her hand, and started over the embers carefully. Some of them were still hot. He pushed aside fatigue and began walking fast, long-striding, and she was running to keep up when suddenly she let loose of his hand. He turned. She was staring at an impaled body. The legs had no feet; they had been severed. The man was gagging as the spike kept pushing against the roof of his mouth. Impalement, if performed with skill, could take as much as two days to kill a man. This one was still alive.

"Tenron!" she gasped, recognizing him.

"Ah, Elyon's blessed name," Rhywder said, drawing his short sword. He slammed it up through the heart of Tenron, then out. He wiped the blood on the man's tunic.

"Eyes on me, Satrina. Only me." He grabbed her arm and pulled her away, walking quickly.

"Should we not try to help any of the others? There could be others like Tenron—still not dead."

"That would be a kindness, but we have no time. Those riders were spreading terror. Behind them will be the main armies of the Unchurians. The armies move much slower, but should they reach us, there will be nowhere to hide."

"But wait!"

He wrenched her arm, pulling her along. "We have no time, Satrina. We cannot stop for anything!"

"Not even a horse?"

He stopped. He looked past her, catching movement—a horse wandering idly up the hill.

"Damn, a horse. Yes, we could use that horse. Just shut your eyes. Do not move, wait right here."

"All right."

Rhywder crouched and carefully ran for the horse, his feet soundless. When he was close, it reared its head, shook out the mane—the night had left it clearly terrified. Spooked, it was about to bolt, but Rhywder held up his hands, fingers spread, palms outward. "Wait," he urged with practiced tone. The horse paused. "Careful, boy, easy on . . . we need each other, my friend." Rhywder leaned forward slowly and carefully managed to take the dangling reins.

He rode back for Satrina who was waiting as though it were winter, arms wrapped about her shoulders, eyes clenched tight. She opened them slowly and looked up.

"Did . . . did you just talk to this horse?" she asked.

"Yes."

"You can talk to horses?"

"Anyone can talk to horses. It is getting them to listen that is the trick."

They had ridden through the day, but as the night sky began to draw down, he could see Hericlon's peak ahead of them, like a far, ice finger. Rhywder was by now having trouble staying in the saddle.

Satrina had notched her hands into his belt, laying her head against his back, and drifted in and out of half sleep.

He was finding it a struggle just to keep from losing consciousness. He kept the horse at a steady pace, but it was getting hard to stay focused. Whatever poison was in him, it played images through his mind, such as his sister when he was young. Asteria. She had been filled with such light. When she was born, he remembered that people would not look in her eyes. They were black, like night, and she was small, baldheaded. The Asteria child could turn and look right through someone's soul. He had seen adults actually back away. His mother had told Rhywder that it was because the veil was still thin with her. It was why Asteria still saw heaven and knew its secrets.

"She will not speak until she forgets them," his mother had told him.

And indeed, Asteria had not spoken for many years. When she did speak, her sentences were fully formed, and still, despite the precaution, it seemed to Rhywder Asteria had remained filled with Elyon's secrets. Even in the end, when she struggled so against the twisted intrigues of politics that eventually got her killed, it had always seemed that Asteria could, if she wished, part the veil with her delicate, long fingers and casually speak with Elyon.

He watched the sky wash with purple into an image of the sea and upon it a pale shadow of the last ship he had sailed—the stained, weathered strakes; the oiled, darkened sail. He could hear the waters; he could see the oars dip like great wings to fling the sea in a spray. They had hunted slavers, Pelegasians who had become wanton butchers to obtain flesh for the markets of Etlantis and Weire, which were flourishing these days. Rhywder had captained the blackship, moving like a shadow of death at night, striking from nowhere to take out the slaver galleys.

Rhywder jerked up. Things had momentarily grayed out. He had nearly fallen from the horse.

There was a far rumbling of thunder. A storm front was coming in from the south. When he turned, it struck him. They were not ordinary clouds. He had never seen a storm like this. He continued to stare, wondering if this was another delusion, but it seemed he could see eyes in the dark clouds, a thousand eyes swirling.

Rhywder didn't feel himself fall from the horse until the ground struck him. He had landed on his back, the wind knocked out of him. He moaned and slowly turned onto his back, lifting himself onto his elbows.

Satrina had quickly dropped off the saddle to crouch beside him. She wiped sweat from his forehead with the hem of her skirt.

He caught a glint of her thigh and wondered of himself. The middle of nowhere, death crawling after them, but still he noticed how she had legs like a dancer. It was impossible she was thirty and two.

"Poor Shadow Walker," she said. "This is the poison in you."

"Bitches."

"What bitches?"

"The ones that bit me."

"You mean the animals that attacked you were female?"

"Aye, the kind I always knew were out there somewhere."

"You are speaking strangely."

"No more than usual. Help me up, I have to get back in the saddle."

"You should rest, Shadow Walker."

"Name is Rhywder."

"What?"

"My name. Rhywder. You can stop calling me Shadow Walker. I am Rhywder, the Little Fox of Lochlain."

She nodded. "Whatever your name, you cannot keep going. You are pale. Why not sit here and take a short rest?"

He used her shoulder to pull himself up, kneeling. And then—he just stared at her, suddenly caught in her eyes. Maybe it was an effect of the poison, but her wide, quick violet eyes framed in the tangles of her red-brown hair—they just drew him in. She seemed so out of place here. Like a bright child in the darkest nightmare.

She reached forward and touched his brow. "Ah, this is good, Rhywder."

"What is good?"

"Your forehead—your fever has broken into a cold sweat."

"You think?"

She nodded.

"Then why do I feel so strange?"

"A cold sweat will do that to you. Flushes you all over, like little fingers running over your skin. Do you feel that?"

"More or less. Possibly why I keep staring at you."

"The good thing is, the sweat means the poison has passed through your blood. You should start to get better now. And you were strong, so I believe you will recover quickly. As long as you do not drink your own urine," she added with a smile, a bit of humor.

"I have always made that a strict rule, never to . . . to drink my own—" He tightened his jaw, staring. "Love of God you are . . ."

"I am what?"

"Just simply beautiful."

She blinked, startled. "Why, thank you. And, since you mention it—so are you."

He narrowed a brow. "So I am what?"

"You are beautiful, as well."

"No, no. You see me walk into a tavern, beautiful is not what should come to mind."

She reached carefully to smooth back the tangles of his red hair, though he pulled away as she did. "And you have such kind eyes."

"Pardon, but in this same tavern, kind is not what you should think in seeing my eyes."

"I suppose I have never visited this tavern."

He moaned and pulled himself to his feet. She stood, her hand taking his arm to steady him.

"Where is the horse?" he stammered.

Satrina turned, searching. "There he is." She motioned, waving her hand. "Here, horse!"

"What are you doing?"

"Talking to him. Like you did. Come. Over here. Come, horse."

"It does not work that way."

"Well . . . yes, it does."

Rhywder turned, stunned to see the animal obediently walking toward them. It lowered its head beside Satrina and shook out the bridle.

"Ready, then?" She handed him the reins. "Hold these."

"Why?"

Satrina hoisted herself into the saddle. She gripped the horn and leaned over, taking the reins. She then stretched out a hand.

"What are you doing?" Rhywder asked.

"I will get us to Hericlon. I know the way. Take hold."

He just stared at her, confused.

"What? You have never let a woman guide your horse? That is pretty silly, you know. Take hold."

He frowned, but let her help pull him into the saddle behind her. She took each of his hands and wrapped his arms tight about her waist.

"Wait," he said, "I can at least take the reins."

She firmly placed his hands back on her stomach. "Not wise. You are falling off the horse. I am rested. Be brave, Rhywder, Little Fox of Lochlain."

"Excuse me? Be brave?"

"No need to be afraid of a little help. Hold tight," Satrina shouted, kicking the horse's side. They were soon at a gallop. "Hericlon is not far."

Rhywder found he had to grip her waist tight as she leaned into the gallop. Apparently, she really had ridden horses before.

Chapter Twenty-Four

Krysis

At first Eryian thought he was waking from a dream, but then he quickly realized the images of the pirates were memories. What surprised him was remembering that it was not the captain—a capable swordsman—nor his protector, the big axeman who had stopped his attack. What had brought Eryian down was the girl. He had not even seen her, crouched beneath the thigh of her captain. The sting of the girl's dart was quick, but her choice of poison was strange. As he woke, it still left a slight opiate effect, calming and pleasant. It seemed a very odd choice for raiders. He remembered briefly catching her eyes, how they had glimmered with excitement.

He looked about slowly, surprised to find he was in his own room, the familiar worn wood of the walls, the tapestry that Krysis, his wife, had hung on the far wall. She had brought it from the island of Etlantis, her one treasure—picturing a white horse moving alone through dark green forest. She had always said it made her think of him. As the fog of sleep began to wear off, Eryian tried to get up, but as he did, he felt fingers touch his cheek and turned to see Krysis's light golden hair and crystal blue eyes. She was Lochlain, not one of the magick users, but certainly one of the pretty ones, one of those who had followed the queen to Argolis on the morning of the slaughter. If anything had burdened him over the years, it was the slaughter of the Lochlains. Had they not been sworn to follow the rule of a bullheaded foolish king from the tribe of Hebe, they would all have lived.

"Be still, Eryian. It is over now."

When he tried to get up nonetheless, she placed her palm firmly against his chest and pushed him back down. "There is nothing you can do," she said. Her eyes were firm.

"What has happened?" he asked.

"They brought you home. They seemed certain you would die, but you have only been asleep. You looked peaceful."

"They were pirates—Tarshians. There was only one Tarshian blackship left hunting the open sea and that was Darke. They called him the Shadow Hawk."

"Yes, Tillantus told me they were raiders; he did not guess their names, however."

"What possible reason could that have had in the castle of Terith-Aire?" He glanced to her when she didn't answer straightaway. "Have they been killed—the raiders?"

Krysis paused. "No," she said. She pulled a strand of golden hair from her high cheekbone, looking down.

"Then what? What did they want? What did they do?"

"They . . . they took the king, Eryian; they took Lochlain."

"What?"

"Lochlain, Asteria's son. They have kidnapped him. The pirates had a ship waiting below the cliffs. Tillantus sent one of our warships in pursuit, but it was night and this pirate you mentioned, he sailed straight into deep water. He did not even keep to the shoreline, though a storm was threatening, and I am told his blackship was far too quick. None could keep up with him, and the night swallowed all sight of him. They are still hunting, but Tillantus tells me there is little hope."

"Tillantus is here?"

"No, he rode out to see if you lived. He has returned to the castle. He said to leave you word if you awakened that the legions would continue to assemble. Nothing would change in their orders, but you may as well rest until dawn."

Eryian eased back against the oaken headboard. "They took the boy? Are you certain?"

"That is what he said, yes. I should thank these pirates if I saw them, Eryian."

He glanced to her. "Thank them? For what, in Elyon's name?"

"The poison they used, it merely put you to sleep."

Eryian nodded. "Apparently they had a witch—a pretty little witch at that. She would be the one you would need to thank."

"And the king, Lochlain, they did not kill him. They merely stole him."

"We have moved from assassins to thieves."

"Tarshians, you say. Are they not Etlantian killers?"

"Yes."

"Then perhaps someone hired them."

He smiled at her. "You always have been clever, Krysis. Yes, someone hired them. But whoever it was, he does not have a party planned for the king, I can assure you of that. Did Tillantus say if they left the sword?"

"Argolis's sword?"

Eryian nodded.

"No. He mentioned nothing of it."

"I have to get back to the palace, Krysis. Help me up."

"I will not," she snapped. "You are not going anywhere until you have your strength back."

"That should not be a problem. She merely drugged me. I have barely been scratched. How long has it been?"

"It is late night. Someone has been waiting outside the door ever since they brought you. Is it all right to let him in?"

Eryian nodded. "I seem to be fine."

She opened the door and not surprisingly Little Eryian was waiting, as though he had been listening through the door, which no doubt he had, though the wood was thick. His white eyes turned to his father, and he walked soberly to Eryian's bedside, studying him.

"I told Mother you were not harmed. But how did they manage to put you to sleep, Father?"

"It was a woman did that, Little Eryian."

The boy stared back amazed. "A woman? How? Can you explain it to me?"

"Women are always difficult to explain, little one."

Little Eryian glanced at his mother, but she only smiled.

"She used a small crossbow," Eryian told the boy. "Custom-made, mounted on her wrist. Her dart was tipped with balm, a poison, but one that merely put me to sleep."

"Why did she not kill you?"

"A good question."

"Was she fast with the dart?"

"Very."

"Do you think she was faster than I would have been, say, with a dagger?"

"No. She was fast, but I think what helped her the most was that she was small. I did not see her until it was too late."

"They were pirates."

"Yes. How did you know?"

"I imagined them. I saw a captain with dark eyes. And there is another I imagine as well, but he is . . . far. Him I do not understand. He is very hard to see, this one. I think the reason I cannot envision him is that he is too powerful. He burns with many fires and each fire has a hundred eyes. Did you sense him, Father? Was he with them?"

"No, but you describe an angel. Odd. It could not be the death lord. It would make no sense. He would have killed the boy. This is another."

"If you wish, Father, I believe I could lead you to this one. I could track him. We would need fast ships. He lies west and north, bearing far out to deep water. But if I tried, I believe I could find him."

Little Eryian stared a moment with his focused, white eyes as if the being he described were on the other side of the room. As a hunter, Little Eryian, even so young, was unmatched. He had gained his instincts from birth, the ability to see through anyone's thoughts and even envision events far from him. The few times they had hunted game, Little Eryian had tracked by instinct, never looking to the ground, never bothering with signs, just slowly closing on the game they pursued. Eryian had no doubt that if he applied himself, the boy could, indeed, track an angel. Of course, Eryian would never allow it, but it gave him the clue he needed. Bearing out to sea, north and west, it could only be a fallen, and not one in league with Etlantis. That left one obvious choice—Satariel, the prefect of the choir of Melachim. He had panicked and had hired the most capable and able thief on the planet.

There was no need to try to follow—it would drain resources, but beyond that, Eryian felt Loch was in prophecy's grip. The king was deadly and he learned quickly. Azazel could kill Loch without a thought, but this one, a prefect was weakened and panicked; perhaps there was reason to it. He was certainly capable of killing the king, but the timing of things left Eryian wondering. He again thought of the games heaven played. It must be amusing, watching from above. With Azazel bearing from the south, Eryian had no choice but to leave Lochlain in Elyon's hands.

"No, Little Eryian. It is not yet time to hunt the Watchers, but in your day, when you are older, things may be different."

Little Eryian nodded.

He looked to Krysis. "I am strong enough to ride. I must learn more. The kingdom and all allies north of Hericlon are threatened. I cannot rest; there is just no time."

She sighed, but consented. "When will I see you again?"

He stared at her, troubled. Krysis lowered her gaze. She knew the answer might well be never.

"Whatever happens," Eryian said, "we must fight with Faith's Light, my love. Bid me Godspeed. If I am able, I shall return."

She steeled her eyes and nodded, but a tear escaped.

He first rode to the castle, where he was met by the guard of the Seventh Cohort, the Shadow Walkers. He made his way inside quickly.

Eryian stepped into the king's chambers and paused, searching for clues. Guards had fanned to the lintels at his flanks and Tillantus, the high captain and commander of the first legion of the Daath, stepped in beside him. Tillantus had been in the rear guard when the assassins had come for Argolis, and presently, Eryian was grateful to have the big warrior still alive. After Eryian, Tillantus was now second in command of the armies of Daath, for that matter, the entire kingdom. He was a Shadow Walker of the old school, a weathered veteran who had been as loyal as blood to Argolis and would be the same to Eryian.

"Headboard," Tillantus said. "Single bolt through the hand, but little blood. They must have been experts; they intended to get him out of here without harming him. From the way the feathers are shredded off, I suspect it was the boy pulled his own hand free."

Eryian nodded. He noticed a crack in the marble floor near the bed, veined in black, the edges seared. Loch had fired the blade of Uriel. He stepped forward to study it. He also noticed the silver bolt lodged deep in the headboard, stained with Loch's blood. He suspected the witch's poison had put Loch to sleep as it had him, but if Loch had managed to bring the sword to life, why had he not killed them? Loch had guessed something. For whatever reason, the boy had let himself be taken. Eryian would say nothing of it. There were those who might think the king chose to be abducted rather than face the storms of the southland—but Eryian knew otherwise. It was *the knowing* in Loch that had spoken. There was purpose in what had happened here.

"I cannot understand why they would take the king," Tillantus grumbled. "Should we be expecting a ransom offer, for the love of Elyon?"

Eryian shook his head. "They did not come for money or jewels."

"What then, my lord?"

"I suspect someone wanted to know if Loch's blood could light the sunblade—or perhaps ensure it could not."

Tillantus knelt near the singed crack and touched his finger to the blackened rock. "Do you think, then, Argolis's sword caused this?"

"I do."

"God's blood. I saw that the sword was missing, but I thought it was you that had it."

"No. It is all connected, Tillantus. Since the death of Argolis, all that we watch unfold is covenant. It is as though we are merely spectators allowed to watch prophecies unveil themselves."

"Aye."

"This pirate had a well-fitted ship, did he?"

"Seen nothing like it. I watched from the top of the Dove and the ship vanished into the night like shadow in wind. I could send more ships in search by dawn; we have six anchored in Ishmia."

"No, leave them anchored. I know what the boy meant now."

"My lord?"

"Nothing, he mentioned watching the sea. I suppose he sensed what we now know."

"He was odd—knew hidden things. You could see it in him," Tillantus added.

"However, no need to send warships, the boy can take care of this on his own."

"Very well. I will say, I do hope to see him again. Some do not trust in him, but he was strong, with an inner light. I will pray for his safe return."

"Do that. In the meantime, we have enough to concern ourselves with."

"Aye, that is fact."

"The legions?"

"Ready to march, my lord."

"First sign of dawn you will leave for the hillock above Ishmia, overlooking the river Ithen. I will meet you there," Eryian directed.

"Meet us?"

"Something I must take care of."

"Alone?"

"I need no one slowing me down. I will not be long, by the time you have reached the river Ithen, I will have caught up with you."

"Aye, my lord."

"Hope for word from the Little Fox; he should return from the southland soon if he is to return at all."

"We will keep a careful eye, my lord."

Eryian wondered of him briefly. He loved Rhywder as a brother; it would not be easy to learn he had fallen. But if anyone could keep Hericlon in the hands of the Daath long enough to save the gate, it would be Rhywder. He noticed Tillantus watching, waiting for any command.

"It would seem we are all out of kings," Eryian said.

"Aye, grown short of them. An odd thing. However, be assured, the lords of the Daath follow your word now. We may be out of kings, but we are not shy of blood warriors capable of holding against the winds of the abyss of Ain should it be required."

Eryian nodded. "One more thing—we need a swift rider for Galaglea.

The Little Fox may have already sent word to Quietus, and the hour is late if he has not, but there is no reason to leave stones unturned."

"Aye, the Galagleans for Hericlon. But pray we get there before they blunder. Never have put much stock in a Galaglean's ability to think and ride a horse at the same time."

"Leave only a cohort to guard the city. The sixth of the second legion will do. I sense Terith-Aire in no danger with the Etlantians to our north, holding the seas, as well. We can safely focus all our strength against the south."

"I would agree."

"However, as a precaution, wherever you move the second legion, ensure the chosen are with them, always in their center, the Seventh Cohort of Shadow Walkers as their guardians. Leave their protection to no one else."

"As you speak, my lord, they have been gathered."

The chosen were the seventy and seven children of the pure-blooded Daath. In times of threat or war, they were always taken from their families and protected by Shadow Walkers against all possible enemies. The Walkers held talismans against Uttuku, and one of them was worth twenty of any ordinary warrior. They were trained since the gathering wars, and there were no guardians deadlier. When the children were under their protection, not only were they surrounded by the seventh, but they were also placed in the center of the second Daathan legion. If anything wished to reach them, not only would they have to drive through the first and then the second legions of the Daath, but then they would face the Seventh Cohort of the Shadow Warriors, the most elite guardians ever gathered.

"I trust you can manage without me a day or two, Tillantus?"

"You can trust in me, my lord. We will reach Ishmia and the river Ithen. Do not fear the chosen. However, my lord, are certain you wish to do whatever this is you have in mind alone? There are Walkers I could send with you that would certainly not slow you down. I bear no comfort with you traveling alone. These are not ordinary times we face."

"I make a small target, Tillantus, both swift and dangerous. Do not fear for me; I will be back before you are certain I have left. Until then, assume you are in sole command; Tillantus; assume you are king."

"Aye, my lord." Tillantus drew a fist to his chest and bowed his head as Eryian strode past. "Godspeed, my lord. Faith's Light!"

"Her light with you, as well, Captain."

Chapter Twenty-Five
Star Spire

That night, Eryian rode.

Leirn was the farthest northern outpost of the Daath, and he rode past it when the moon had reached its zenith. There were small glimmers of fire in hearths from a few of the huddled houses, but most were dark. Dogs bayed as he crossed one field, and the owner of the cottage burst through the door, axe in hand, but Eryian moved unseen.

He didn't follow the narrow wagon road beyond Leirn, but kept far to the right of it. The country beyond was mostly flat and offered only an occasional tree or scrub as a barrier. There were sand-swept crescent dunes and far to the right were skeletal buttes.

Eryian's horse flew, low, sleek, the hooves steady but well trained and in the soft dirt almost silent.

He guessed it was near to dawn when he spotted riders—four, riding in formation toward him. Eryian slowed and studied them as they closed straight on, dark shapes against the deep purple hue of sky.

They began to gallop. He saw a broadsword lifted from its scabbard. One unlatched a heavy, double-bladed axe. Unchurian. He sensed they had actually come from the sea, for he knew any that had crossed Hericlon had been killed and there was no logical reason for them to have come this far south. Perhaps they had taken a Pelegasian merchantman. It bothered him thinking they were seaborne more than it bothered him he would have to kill them.

Eryian galloped directly for them.

The assassins spread out.

He drew his sword only in the last moment, just as they were about to clash, Eryian pulled up on the reins and turned the horse sharply. It danced sideways into them. He opened the throat of the lead axeman as the Unchurian veered to keep from colliding with Eryian's horse. Eryian then dropped off his mount and crouched.

The other three circled. Eryian took the reins of the fallen warrior's mount and pulled it close to his own. One of them closed, sword drawn, and Eryian slipped beneath the belly of the assassin's horse, then behind the flanks where he grabbed a wad of dark cloak, and wrenched the warrior out the saddle, thrusting his sword in and out of the backplate. It was heavy armor and penetrating it had taken more strength than he would have guessed.

The other two realized they had chosen a wrong mark. Just as they turned, Eryian dropped one with a dagger through the neck. For the other he had to unsheathe his bow from the saddle, string it, then steady his aim due to the distance, but to make it difficult, he put the shaft directly through the base of the man's skull. The Unchurian dropped backward and it seemed a long time before he stopped rolling.

Eryian unstrung the bow and shoved it into the saddle sheath, troubled that there were four relatively minor assassins moving on Terith-Aire from the south. Their mission was probably meant to spread as much unease and terror as possible. Staring at one of the bodies, he was sure of it; they had meant to secret themselves in the city, killing from city streets at night, leaving grizzly offerings until they were finally trapped and killed. He kicked the body over. The side of the dead assasin's forehead was branded, as were all of the warriors from Du'ldu. The brand was a tightening swirl, the flesh pressed outward, making it look like something glued on. The swirl was an ancient mark of the angels, representing the whirlers, the angel eyes. It could be found in caves and ancient rock. He mounted and paused a moment, his horse dancing restless.

Something else was in the wind, not close, but Eryian sensed it. This one was different, skilled. Even the warlord was going to have to watch his back now. It irritated him. He did not wish to waste time killing hunters from Du'ldu.

As Eryian rode, the arid plains of the north were quiet. Odd, but he felt Azazel watching, not as if the angel were at all close, but watching from far.

Eryian watched back, defiant, letting him know by thought he wasn't fooled by the eyes that followed. If ever they met, angel or not, Eryian would leave a mark not easily forgotten. In response he heard a whispering chuckle. Why did he know this one? What was the history? Eryian tried once more, in vain, for the next few degrees of the night, to pierce the muddied veil of his past. It was real, images that moved like they were painted by some poorly skilled artist, but nothing he could make out clearly.

There were men who prayed. The seers, some of them, claimed to learn from Elyon, through a whispered voice, truths and warnings and even found comfort in knowing their Creator, but Eryian had never prayed. He was tempted. If seers could speak with Elyon, why should he not be able to, as he had done nothing in his life but follow the charges given him. He could ask that this fog be lifted, allowing him to remember his past. It had never bothered him this way before, so why was it getting to him now?

When dawn came, he rode until he found a small group of palms. He tied off the horse and stretched out for a light, troubled sleep. When the dreams came, he tried to pull out of them, tried to awaken, but they sucked him inward as if he had been caught in a net, dragged into them, and once more he was riding down a shadowy road that soon focused. It was washed in a hot, white sun and Eryian was with the king's hunting party once again. There was laughter, murmuring, the clatter of horse gear and weapons.

Eryian rode point, possibly the only one in the entire party that was not drunk. They rode in loose formation. These were all of the King's Guard, the first cohort of the Shadow Walkers, deft and able, but on this day they laughed, and there were women with them, some held in the saddles of the Walkers, others riding beside them. As they approached a wooded stretch of road east of a plodder's farm, Eryian pulled up on the reins, slowing. Something he didn't like, something hiding from him possibly, but if it was, it was doing an excellent job. Eryian tried to sense anything, any true danger, but the woods ahead were quiet. Perhaps that was all that bothered him, how they were so quiet. No birds, no animals, no wind in the leaves. It was a small clot of yew and oak, and it did not stretch far. To either side was high wheat grass. Eryian raised his fist and the column came to a halt.

Tillantus pulled up beside him, the big man concerned at the pause. He had a girl in his saddle. He dwarfed her, his big arm about her waist. She looked like a child clutched against his sweated tunic. He frowned at Eryian.

"Something wrong? Or you just pausing to sniff the air?" He was almost drunk enough to fall off his horse, and he shoved his special black leather wineskin at Eryian forcefully. "We will be at the castle in short time and you have not taken a single drink all afternoon. Love of Elyon, this was to be an easy day. It is at the king's command we drink."

"You know I do not drink, Tillantus."

"Damned odd for it, too. Why anyone would choose not to drink the whole of their lives?" The thought troubled Tillantus enough that he took a long drink himself to compensate.

"I want you to ride back; keep close to Argolis. Keep your shield ready."

Tillantus searched the trees. "For what? It is still daylight half a league from the city. Are we afraid we might be robbed?"

The girl chuckled. She couldn't have been more than ten and seven, Tillantus forty and six. He had always had this taste for young ones. He once told Eryian it was why he chose not to marry. The freedom of having whomever he wished without being bothered about it was well worth having to cook his own food.

"Give me five men, Tillantus, Rownan among them. Put some able shieldbearers behind the king . . . some at his flanks, as well."

"What is it? You see something?"

Eryian shook his head.

"Smell something? God's blood, if that stand of wood gives you a problem we can ride east and around it, though I cannot imagine why we should."

"We can do that, Captain, but I do not think it is necessary. Just taking precautions is all. Humor me."

"Aye." Tillantus turned his horse and shouted commands. "We are all of us going to humor the captain now!" he shouted. "Rownan, you and four men ride ahead into that stretch of wood at Eryian's flank. Ergon, you take some shieldbearers and stay close to the king. You women, you take the flanks here in the center."

There was considerable laughter over that.

Eryian turned in the saddle to look back to Argolis. He was in the rear. There were two women at his side, and the warrior king who was feared beyond any man alive was chuckling with them, curling his fingers through one's rich blond hair.

As Eryian rode forward with five of his guard, the dreaded Rownan at his right, he at least felt better about shadows. There had been a growing ill ease in him all through the hunt, but the king and the others had sensed nothing. Earlier, when Argolis had trapped a boar in a rock cleft and closed on foot with a single dagger for the kill, Eryian had suddenly dropped the animal with a crossbow bolt. Argolis turned with a baffled look on his face.

"Something about that boar did not look right," Eryian said, drawing heavy laughter from all of them.

"Assassin boar!" one of the Walkers had shouted.

Midway through the trees, Eryian began to wonder of himself. There was no movement; nothing stirred. Then he heard the low whisper of arrows, and it cut through him like a blade. He turned in the saddle, sword drawn, but anything he could possibly do was going to be too late. He could not have sensed these shadows even if he had ridden over one—they had trained their whole lives for this one, single moment. The arrows came thick, humming like insects, boring into the staggered line of warriors and their women. Tillantus's horse reared as darts sunk into its flanks and sides. The big man was thrown, and the only one to take the hits was the girl with him. She screamed, twisting in midair as shafts ripped through her. Eryian dropped from his horse and ran for the king with his shield over his right shoulder.

"Argolis!" he screamed.

Those men not hit by arrows turned their mounts and attacked, ripping into the trees without command. The Walkers about the king were slaughtered; the rain of darts was heavy, almost a solid mass. Tillantus vaulted onto a horse and set off at hard gallop into the trees, his heavy broadsword in his huge hand.

When the Shadow Walkers reached them, which took mere seconds, the Unchurian assassins made no attempt to fight back; they had already accomplished their mission. Dying meant nothing to them.

Eryian ran, dodging the last of the arrows. The shieldbearers that lay about Argolis were literally feathered in dark shafts, like the quills of porcupines. Argolis was on his side. Eryian dropped to his knees, cast aside his shield. It was over; the slaughter in the woods had ended, though the Shadow Walkers continued to search.

Eryian and Argolis had been through many years together, all they had lived, the blood, the kinship they had shared . . . it had ended without ceremony. Argolis was dead, his eyes open, but empty. No last words, nothing. Eryian moaned and began to pull a shaft from Argolis's chest as though it might have mattered.

Eryian woke suddenly with quick breaths. He cursed the dreams. They had come almost every time he fell asleep since the king's death, except for the sleep of the little witch's poison. He knelt for a moment, trying to calm himself, letting the white sun of midday wake him.

He looked up. Something in the distance had moved. It was far, and the horizon was an unsteady image of heat simmering. It had only been a flicker of movement, but he knew he was no longer alone. He sensed nothing and though he could feel nothing at the moment, he knew. It was an assassin, but one deeply skilled at stealth. The assassin had vanished, even as Eryian had caught a glimpse of the movement.

"Come ahead, then," Eryian whispered, still angry from the dream. He would welcome killing another assassin—a skilled one. It might make it easer to sleep when next he did. He gathered his gear and mounted.

Eryian kept a steady pace through the dunes. At one point he noticed a curl of sand that had drifted to twenty feet and looked so much like a wave it could easily have broken into foam. Eryian rode calmly, occasionally checking his flank. Whatever followed, it knew shadows as well as he did, an expert, which gave him comfort. Though he had not much farther to go, at least he had something to help time pass.

Eryian rode through the night, keeping the horse at an easy lope, but nothing closed on him. The rider kept back, and it was close to dawn when Eryian reached the end of the dunes. At the top of a hillock thick in cedar and foxtail grass he tied his horse, out of sight and smell. He found a vantage point that offered a good view. He had time to wait. He planned to catch the legions at the river Ithen before they turned east for Hericlon, but he had been making good time, and he could waste a bit now. Eryian sat back against a tree and drew his cloak about his shoulder, then faded into the shadow. Someone could have been four feet away and not have noticed him. For a long time nothing stirred—only a small gathering of gazelle that wandered slowly and gracefully out near the sea. It was beautiful country. If a man rode to the tops of the higher hills not far to the east, and from there, he could see the tip of Mount Ammon on a clear day.

The sun was nearly midpoint in the sky when he finally caught movement. The rider seemed to come out of the heat waves as though he had simply materialized—excellent, he was amazingly hard to follow. He moved carefully, weaving in and out of sight in the distance. He was good, too good to have been an ordinary warrior. Eryian guessed him to be first generation, which meant he may have lived as much as seven hundred years. He wondered what a life lived that long would be like. Were there still memories from the first days? His first woman, his first child? He rode with gifted stealth, silent and steady, never leaving himself open for long. The hood of his gray-black cloak was dropped back and only occasionally did he glance to the ground to track. He most probably tracked best by smell, but the wind was against Eryian right now, and he wasn't that far from his last bath. Long, straight hair fell across the Unchurian's broad shoulders, night-black but for a streak of silver to one edge. He remembered now, the streak of silver. All of the elite had it, the first- and second-born. It was their mark, like the silver band of a Shadow Walker, only this was natural, not dyed, but given of the angel by breeding to those who were gifted with the death lord's blessing. Azazel might even know this one's name. The Unchurian's careful movements, his secrecy—he was easily the equal of a Daathan Walker. If not by whatever accident that had alerted Eryian, he might have been a problem.

As he drew nearer, Eryian could smell the blood of the angel in him. It was a pure-blood. It seemed almost touched with heaven's light. Whatever the light of Elyon was, it had strange ways. Eryian had more than once sensed the light in a Nephilim. Though the creatures had turned long ago, though their hearts were evil, the light often still burned in them, a distant memory left in their blood from their father's lineage.

At one point, the Unchurian turned against the sun and Eryian caught a glimpse of his skin. It was reddish, as were all Unchurian, but this one had for some reason chosen to become a blood drinker. It left his skin a darker sheen. That explained his being so far south and tracking Eryian. He was a loner, a wanderer, and probably had been to sea. He hunted humans, and he did so alone or, at times, with Etlantians. The firstborn of such a high lord of the angels such as Azazel were only blood drinkers by choice; they were still able to resist the curse of Enoch if they chose to because their blood was pure enough to resist. Eventually, all of them, all the children of the angels would fall to Enoch's curse, but this one had done so by choice.

At one point the Unchurian paused and seemed to look directly at Eryian. He remained like that, perfectly still, the waves of heat occasionally blurring his image. A human, even an ordinary Daath, could sit where Eryian was and search for all he was worth and still not spot the rider. But for all his talent, the Unchurian still failed to sense Eryian. It was because Eryian had been here so long, moving not a single muscle but to breathe or blink, that he had blended into the tree he leaned against. The Unchurian chose to move on, closing. In that moment the contest was over—if ever a contest it had been. There remained only the kill. Eryian noticed a bow, already strung, strapped over one shoulder and a scabbard against the rider's left thigh. There was a small axe lashed to the saddle blanket, hanging over the flank and a row of daggers in a dagger sheath across his chest. Eryian wondered how many this one had killed. Far more than he. Could it have been thousands?

The Unchurian began to ascend the hillock, weaving in and out of the few trees here. He rode calm, eased back, one hand resting on his thigh and the other holding the reins loosely. Once or twice the rider's eyes would drop to the ground, scanning tracks, but mostly they searched the trees about him carefully.

Again he looked directly at Eryian, but still missed him, even this close.

Finally, when the Unchurian was within range, Eryian slowly stood, his cloak falling open. He knew that to the Unchurian he had just appeared out of pure, thin air. The Unchurian instantly froze, hand near his throwing axe, the fingers touching the hilt. Eryian was certain he could move fast, he could fling that small axe in a second's breath, and anyone but Eryian would be already dead, no matter the surprise of the sudden appearance. Eryian met his gaze, but the Unchurian watched back with steeled, dark eyes—no emotion, just a calm acceptance. Perhaps after living so many years, death offered an allure.

Eryian dropped swiftly to a crouch. The rider twisted, rearing his horse. His axe flung, but Eryian twisted sideways, feeling the wind of it as it passed. The Unchurian dropped over the saddle as the spooked horse ran. The assassin pulled himself across the ground and propped his back against a cedar trunk, watching Eryian. There was a slight gurgling sound with each labored breath. Eryian's dagger was in his throat, just to the side of his larynx, but in the back of his throat it had pierced his spine. Most of his body was paralyzed.

"You are good," the Unchurian said. "The best I have ever seen."

Eryian nodded, crouching eye level, not far from the Unchurian. "Did he send you, or did you pick up the scent on your own?"

The Unchurian stared back a moment, drew what was a difficult breath. "I ride alone. I feel him sometimes, but I have not been there for many centuries. He wants you. He wants you badly. Tell me, Daath, why such interest in you?"

"I was hoping you could tell me."

Blood spilled in a slow line from the corner of the Unchurian's lip. "If you would be kind, out of respect, a clean kill? I have no desire to die slow."

"How many more follow me?" Eryian asked.

"Nothing living follows you now."

Eryian nodded. He walked forward. When he was close he studied the dark eyes a moment longer. They watched back fearless, waiting.

"How many years have you walked this Earth?" Eryian asked.

"Six hundred seventy."

Eryian lifted his boot and set it against the hilt. He pressed his weight forward slowly, until the pressure sheared the windpipe with a pop. The Unchurian struggled only briefly before his eyes stilled.

As streamers of morning cut the sky, Eryian reached the sea. He pulled the horse up on a black rock ridge, the sea crashing below. He stared across waters, to the west. She was there, far against the horizon—the ice peaks of Etlantis's mountains brushing the far sky, shrouded in mist, the tallest of the Ammon. He turned the horse and slowly made his way down the hillside, then rode along the white sand toward the village. It was untouched, in all this time. Etlantis, war, famine, and fear, all had passed this village by as if it were on another planet. Elyon protected them; perhaps they were far more favored by heaven than any Daath.

This was Eryian's first known memory, reaching this shore. Just out to sea was a spire of black rock, barely visible from here. It was from that rock that Eryian had first come. He remembered clearly gliding in a shallow craft for this very shore. He remembered the villagers, and he remembered how he had a distinct sense of purpose—he came without fear, understanding, even though he came without memories. He knew the land about him. He knew that south along the coast lay a city of Daath, their first city, their capital. He also knew of the ancient forest whose trees had once beheld the face of Elyon. He remembered that day clearly, and he thought it odd now, watching as the small village grew closer, how he had come so unafraid, so certain of himself. It was not until later in his life that he became disturbed and searched for reasons why, tried to understand. The day he had first touched this shore it was possible he knew things he did not know now. Though all that had gone before was lost to him, he still remembered the day with clarity, and coming back was somewhat like returning to an old home, as if a mother waited somewhere to welcome him. The spire out to sea beyond this shore was a part of the veil that covered his past. It was only through *the knowing* that he understood to come here. It had called. He was still not sure why, but he had answered, and he had returned. He did know that the spire was linked somehow to the homeland, one far and distant for the rock that lay out to sea was not of this Earth.

There were girls working on the beach, bringing in fishnets, and when they saw Eryian ride toward them and dismount, their nets were dropped and cries and laughter went up as they ran for him.

Eryian soon found himself encircled by giggling young girls. They wore wraps of white weft about their waists, slit up their thighs. Their breasts were bare. Certainly they did not know who he was, but riders occasionally came through here, and strangers were always welcomed. Somehow, Elyon protected them from blood drinkers. That was a kindness, Eryian thought, for Etlantis and the rogue warships that often left her shores to hunt flesh seemed ignorant of the small village less than a day's journey from the island.

Eyrian stood taller then any of them by a head and shoulder. He smiled. Eryian had never learned the tongue—he had no idea what they were saying.

A party of warriors approached from the village huts that curled about the emerald lagoon. It seemed almost otherworldly here. The tall cliffs that ringed the village were black, stained with vine and moss, but the sand was as white as milk. He noticed a fat woman of impossible proportions gazing down from a village wicker tower with what seemed to be savage intent.

The leader, Danaoi, Eryian knew from before, and the look on his face left no doubt that Danaoi remembered him as well, though they had known each other only one day. There were probably tales of Eryian's coming still left in this village. Danaoi was flanked by his warriors; his once-proud dark hair was now gray, but still flowing in braids that fell over his shoulders. Eryian lifted his hand in the sign of the word and the king returned the same. The king then gestured to an old woman who had hurried out of one of the huts. When Eryian turned to her, she bowed.

"Well-come," she offered, toothless, in careful Daathan.

Eryian snapped the shoulder buckles of his darkened silver breastplate, then lifted it and the accompanying back plate in the air.

"For Danaoi," he shouted for all to hear and handed it to the king. The king stared at the breastplate as if it were a priceless treasure. He traced the silver eagle, then nodded and let one of his warriors hold it, walking about, circling to display it for the others who marveled in whispers of awe.

"I seek passage," Eryian then told the old woman. He motioned to the far finger of dark rock that could be seen where the edge of the ocean curled over the horizon.

"The forbidden place," the old woman whispered. "The place they say you once came from, they speak it still, the sacred spire."

"Yes," Eryian answered.

She studied him carefully. "Passage is yours, Silver Eagle." She then motioned, speaking quickly. Danaoi held up a fist, shouting commands, and instantly runners were sprinting to the beach. A girl took Eryian's hand and led him down the white sand to a narrow, painted reed ship that was being shoved into the warm waters. Before she left him she spoke words Eryian truly wished he could have understood.

Five rowers were soon propelling him swiftly across blue-green waters, oars sweeping the sea quick and strong. Beside him, Danoi grinned and stood proud as the prow cut the blue waters.

Here the sea was different than it was off the shores off the city. It was emerald and at times clear as glass crystal. Gazing over the side, Eryian could see fish gliding sleek among the coral. Danaoi spoke to him, pointing, and Eryian turned to see the humps of dolphins arch, then disappear below the water.

The reed boat was moving quickly, the rowers were strong, but it was half a day before the crystal spire lifted into the sky and the circle of black stone at its base began to emerge from the sea.

Seeing it, Eryian felt the shiver of *the knowing*. If he could peel it back, he would remember this place, he would remember who had anchored it here in the coral blue of the ocean. *The knowing* was always close, whispering, but never did it speak all truth, only parts of truth. He had come here twice before. Both times the crystal spire had called him, and he had answered. He knew this time was to be its final call. He had felt its pulse shortly after Argolis had died.

The villagers did not know how to dock the craft, and they stared at the high spire in awe. It was black from the shore, but closer, it was crystalline, and slightly transparent. He knew they would never have ventured this close without him. Even if they had, they would not have found it. Eryian had heard stories of Etlantian ships, skilled seamen, who had tried to close on the spire, and though it seemed almost within reach, always it would vanish. The closer they came, the more it would seem to recede until they would find themselves lost in ocean and sky and it would take days to find their way home. Over the years, seamen had learned to avoid the spire; it was whispered to be the sea's illusion, witchery.

"Stop here," Eryian said quietly.

The villagers nodded, finding a shallow ramp cut into the rock. The crystal did not reflect sunlight, but rather swallowed it. The ocean about its edge stilled, perfectly calm, leaving a glasslike surface, and the villagers stared amazed at the reflection of themselves and their small boat on the water.

Eryian stepped over the gunwale onto the crystal surface. His boots made no sound as he walked, for the rock, though it appeared hard and black, was actually soft to the touch. It was the touch of aganon, the same stone that was found in the pommel of sunblades. Aganon overlaid the spire like a skin. There was no doorway, but as Eryian approached, the skin of the spire opened, soundless. Without the sensation of passing through a portal or doorway, he found himself inside. Though he did not allow himself to ponder it—even briefly—he knew this was no rock, no island. It was a ship—a star ship, once his own—and its name was Righel Seven.

The world of the ocean and clouds vanished and stars opened like a flower unfolding, spilling the rich, glittering milk of the star stream that moved like waters above him. Part of him was overcome with wonder, but another part, the deeper part, where *the knowing* lived, felt the gentle kiss of home and with it, sadness and longing. Eryian remembered something, how each time he came here, he had felt sadness. The floor was a perfect mirrored crystal. It reminded him of the blade of Argolis's sword, and he thought now how once, kneeling to touch it, his finger against the stone had caused a shiver of light to spill through it.

In the center of the crystal was a black pedestal that held a polished, silvery-black container. It could have been a child's casket. As Eryian walked toward it, the area about the pedestal spilled with blue light, welcoming him. As he touched the lid there was a song, a far, distant song, a choir that whispered him calm. He had not come for the sword during the gathering wars.

The wars had been against their own blood and it had not yet been time. He never thought of it being here, resting here, and he had never believed it would call him. But the storm that came against them was the reason the sword had rested here so long. Not just in the years of Eryian's memory, but far beyond. It had been here centuries. He knew, in fact, it had rested in this place since the time of Yered.

He opened the lid. Lying within what seemed to be living tissue was a sunblade. Like the Arsayalalyur, it was able to harness the fires of a distant star. Though his memories were fogged, he knew this blade well. It was the sword of Righel, the firstborn son of the mother star that was the mirror, Daath, and the archangel Uriel. Like the Arsayalalyur, the pommel, hilt, and cross guards were entwined with serpents laced with the purple stone of the pommel—the philosopher's stone, the egg, or pelican as it was sometimes called. The blade was aganon, the same metal that formed the skin of the spire. It was smooth, unblemished glass. As he reached in and touched the hilt, purified light spilled through the room, not blinding, merely lighting it in a soft glow. The touch moved through him and he felt the connection, a touch from the light of the mothering star, Dannu, the *Light Whose Name Is Splendor.*

Eryian reverently lifted the blade from the coffinlike container. He lifted it high, pointed its crystal tip toward the sky dome, directly at the cluster of Blue Stars, the seven sisters. Home. Eryian let the blade drink his blood, and as he watched it swirl through the crystal, remembering the image of Loch's blood reaching the flange. He had always known how a sunblade drew the blood of its user; he had just never guessed that Lochlain was the one. He had thought the blade would be no different for Loch than it had been for his father. Eryian's blood turned the blade a dark, silvery red.

"Amon-Omen-Diamon," Eryian commanded—words he knew, though their meaning he kept almost on purpose from his consciousness. The blade responded with a sharp thunder crack as a pure silver pulse focused and streamed from the tip of the sword into the sky dome, into the stars, into the sky. The dome was no illusion; it focused on the sky, seeing it far from Earth, but the bolt that left the tip of Righel's sword soared through the heavens until it struck the seventh star of the Pleiades.

It was the signet: the signal. Though Eryian did not fully understand who was listening, he felt them answer. His call was heard. They had waited five hundred years—now they would come. Unnamed memories threatened, and suddenly he understood the veil, why it was there. He had brought it upon himself. It was spellbound, and Eryian had spoken the words of its binding. He slowly knelt, lowering the sword, bowing his head. For a moment he remained still, breathing carefully. He remembered without remembering, without seeing or touching the light that swam about him, but he wept knowing it would never be again, knowing that the end of the sadness he felt in this moment would soon become the end of all he knew.

When the villagers had seen the burst of light from the spire, the pulse that shattered sound with an eagle's scream and soared to vanish into the sky, they had fallen to their knees. Most had covered their eyes, but Danaoi stared breathless at the sky above them and watched as the bolt opened a pathway through to heaven. Though it was daylight, for an instant, stars spilled through and seemed somehow closer to the Earth than the night sky had ever been. With a blink, the opening closed and Danaoi knew the hush that followed was sacred. The villagers gasped, for the Silver Warrior was standing before them. He had vanished into the dark spire and now he had returned the same way, without a door or opening of any kind. He carried something he did not have when he entered, a magnificent scabbard and a hilt of dark ivory laced with veins of diamond. Danaoi had never seen anything like it, and he stared, amazed, even drawn to touch it though never would he have done so.

The Silver Warrior stepped into the boat.

"Row for home, Danaoi," he said.

Chapter Twenty-Six
Death Ship

When Darke's ship finally sighted the angel's island, it was a dark knob, a fist of black rock, and the waters about it were stained, as though it were melting. From afar it looked like a pustule of the leathered, blue ocean's surface. Nothing grew there. The rock was onyx black, at times rising in high, airless spires like temples. One edge facing the sea was sheer, a mile high, without blemish.

As they came about its edge, there was a bay curled into the muddied waters. Something was caught there, and the suddenness of it, the color, stunned Darke. It was a ship.

"Closer," he said. "Sail for the bay."

Storan put his weight against the tilling oar.

The sky was smooth, gray, windless, and quiet. The waves had little ruffle to them. As they closed, the ship caught in the bay grew clearer. It was a huge ship, an Etlantian fleet of the line, three tiered and well kept, its paint still bright, the plates of its oraculum shielding intact and repaired where they had been damaged. Until recently, it had been used and functional. Now it lay keeled to its starboard side. Its waterline was thick with slime and carbuncles, but she looked undamaged from the bottom.

This was not the ship of Satariel. His had been dull and ashen, the paint of its colors peeling, the sails shredded until they could barely hold wind. This ship was a fleet ship that had not long ago been at high sail.

"Bring her about, Storan."

Danwyar, who had been watching from the bow, sprinted to them. He clambered over the stern railing and came up to stand beside the captain.

"Weigh starboard oar!" Storan called quietly.

As they came about, Darke realized the entire exposed side of the Etlantian was gripped by huge slabs of rock. It looked—from the distance where shadows were more easily shaped—as though a hand had sunk jagged fingers into the Etlantian's deck and wale. Her main mast had sundered and her painted sail lay washing in the currents of the bay like colored foam.

"Weigh oars!" Darke cried. "Lower the anchor stone!"

Danwyar then drew back. "That ship, Captain—I believe we know her well."

"Aye," Darke answered, finally seeing the captain's signet over the shattered glass of the stern quarters. It was an ostrich.

"Euryathides." Darke said.

"Who is Euryathides?" Hyacinth asked from the railing where she stood, watching.

"He would be the Etlantian who captured Darke's son, Lothian," Storan explained. "But how has he gotten on this godless island and been destroyed? This could be some kind of trick, Captain. A lure."

"And we are the fish it baits," said Danwyar.

"Why is he familiar to you?" asked Hyacinth.

"Euryathides is a high captain of the Etlantians, a firstborn Nephilim. He was once a great commander, admired by many. He helped the humans settle much of the eastern continent of Mu and he was our ally, our friend. When he turned, it was without warning. He killed many before it was realized he was no longer valiant, that he had become fallen, his light was lost, and he made a very brutal killer. When it became apparent he was sinking galleons and merchantmen, slaughtering their crews, the Tarshians were asked to hunt him down. We had at that time lost many of our cities to the Etlantians, but we were still strong. Our blackships swarmed the Western Sea where Euryathides was terrorizing settlements. He had become both a slaver and a blood drinker. He left settlements stripped. He knew us well, knew of our ports, our cities, knew our ships and crews. More than any other, it was Euryathides who sacked and burned the emerald cities of the Tarshians. This ship was his command ship; with as many as thirty warships sailing at his side, there was no stopping him. We fought back, and we damaged them. They lost many, but in the end there were only two of us. Darke and Lothian."

"Enough of history, Danwyar."

"There is no more to tell, Captain. You warned Lothian, but we both know he must have found Euryathides and he went in alone. According to Satariel, they were not killed for their blood, instead they were taken as slaves. Oraculum has nearly been mined out, the mines still working are deep pit, the metal far underground. The dust and darkness kill mortals; they kill Etlantians, as well, but as long as there are slaves to be gathered, the Etlantians will continue to dig it out of the Earth."

"Then he is your greatest enemy," Hyacinth said. "And someone has spared you his destruction."

"Aye," said Storan, "and in no natural way."

"Satariel has done you a favor, then?"

"Satariel has crushed Euryathides's ship," answered Darke. "I doubt it was as a favor to us."

"Yet it is curious."

"And personal," added Danwyar.

Darke dropped down the ladder and went into his cabin. He came out tying on the scabbard of the Daathan's sword. The pirates gathered about. "I will take a single ashore boat."

He searched the faces of his men. He knew this time it would not be as the last. It was likely few of the men he picked would make it back; still, his choices were not much different.

"Taran," he said, and the young pirate stepped forward, nodding, already equipped with sword, his buckler over his shoulder.

"Storan."

"I am ready, Captain."

"Danwyar."

Danwyar nodded. He had already gathered his weapons. Darke searched the others.

"Marsyas," he said. As though he had known, Marsyas the Etlantian slid his arm through the strap of his heavy iron shield, dropping it over his back. The war hammer he carried was already hanging from his belt. He stared up through his mutilated face and nodded.

Darke searched further. Two more, at most.

"Gryn," Darke said. Gryn nodded his shaggy head. He was an oarsman, built large, with massive shoulders. Gryn was not particularly adept at weapons, but he could move the ashore boat swifter than any man Darke had, and his strength left him capable with the heavy, black double-edged iron he carried.

Darke turned. He found Hyacinth standing beside him, wearing a small breastplate, her crossbows loaded and her belt of daggers all with moss-grown sheaths to keep their poison.

Darke shook his head. "No."

"I am going."

"It is a death trap, Hyacinth."

"And I choose to die with you, Captain."

"I cannot allow that."

"Captain, I can go in your boat, or I can swim ashore, but I am going with you. Besides, I am not a Tarshian. I am not actually under your command. I will go where I wish."

"Hyacinth . . ."

"You choose any one of your big men, muscles in their fingernails," she shouted, eyes fired, "and I will lay him at your feet in a breath. I have more poisons than I have names for. If you die, Captain, I die!"

There was a moment's silence.

"Try backhanding the little bint up the side of her head," Storan grunted.

"She is not giving you a choice, Captain." Danwyar said. "As you knew she would not. You let your feeling get in the way of judgment; considering her particular talents it is foolish to leave her behind."

"One more, then," Darke said, searching. "The count should be seven." Darke searched the decks, then glanced upward. The Rat was waiting in the nest. He was not even looking toward deck, but was searching the wreckage of the Etlantian ship, fascinated.

Ten years ago they had pulled him from the sea where he was found clinging half-dead to a splinter of ship's whaling. He had been burnt over most of his body. He still screamed at night.

"Fire Rat!" Darke called.

"That mindless lizard?" Storan complained.

At the mention of his name, Fire Rat perked up. His bones often seemed to have no flesh—his skin could have been a fabrication of scarred, tanned leathers, but one side of his head had long hair, tangled and yellow as gold. He wasn't pretty, but he could see a ship on the horizon before its masts had cleared the skyline, and he was good with fire. Amazingly good. In all battles, Fire Rat handled the siphons of the flame throwers like they were his children.

Rat slithered quickly down the mainmast, then dropped the last few feet and vanished into a hatchway. Belowdecks he set about rummaging and clanking as he picked through his things.

"We shall need the king in the angel's sackcloth," Darke said. "Storan, Marsyas, you tend to that. Cut his cords and warn him the angel wants his skin. Give him a weapon and shield."

"Are we giving him the sunblade?" Danwyar asked.

"I shall carry it for now. Give the king a double-edged iron."

Storan grumbled. "And when we give the bastard a sword and shield, how do we stop him from killing us before we get him in the sack?"

"He will cooperate, Storan," Hyacinth answered.

Storan glanced at her and grunted. He turned, Marsyas following.

Fire Rat emerged from the lower deck, his bare feet pounding across the wood. He crouched like a hunchback with a load of tightly wrapped, waxed goat's bags. Each bag was filled with flint and a mixture of sulfur powders and rock. He had learned to use fire from the Etlantians and was as good at it as any Darke had known. In fact, he lived for fire. Rat found all his materials on his own. They had scarcely reached landfall when the he was over the edge, returning past dark, laden with nets of seemingly worthless oddments. And for his skins, Rat could spot a goat on an island before most could see land.

It occurred to Darke that his shore party was something short of a circus. So be it. He was a pirate now. Once it had been different. Once men would have known him by different names, but those times had bled away, and the blood between then and now was deep enough to sail a longship through.

He turned to study the Etlantian ship. Darke knew Euryathides was far too cunning to have sailed into the bay of an uncharted island, which this was. It was an island that had not been here even days before. Even if he had been curious of it, Euryathides would have anchored offshore, sent in longboats. But the longboats still dangled from their davits.

"Where are the bodies?" Danwyar puzzled, also studying the ship. "I see no bodies."

Darke had been wondering the same. An Etlantian war galley would carry nearly two hundred men full crew.

Loch was jerked out of a cold, dreamless sleep. Storan had thrown open the hatchway, eyed the king, then grabbed him by an ankle and wrenched him out of the hold.

"Here you come, you royal bastard! Watch your head!"

Loch's head thudded resoundingly on the deck.

Storan paused. "Ah, shame, Marsyas, we banged his head."

Storan crouched, drew his dagger, and began cutting through the ropes. Loch glanced at Marsyas—noticing the eye with its lizard lash.

The ropes had been so tight, it was as though his skin was being sliced open to let him out.

"We be cutting you loose, boy!" Storan announced as he cut through the last ropes.

Loch slowly got to his feet. Pain was everywhere. He shook out his arms, but his joints and muscles were so stiff it was difficult at first to even stand. "I suppose I should thank you."

"Do not thank me. None of this was ever my idea. Here." Storan tossed him a leather belt with a heavy sword in its wooden scabbard. "Put that on. We are going to hold court with a godless angel who long ago forgot his mother's name and the captain says to arm you."

"Then you have found the angel?" Loch said, pulling on the belt.

"Found an island that stinks of him, though he has not personally greeted us as yet. He knows your name, boy, now what you think of that? Asked specifically for you. Endlessly odd how things play out, is it not?"

Loch buckled his belt. They had sailed through to the center of the storm. Like the eye of a hurricane, the skies here were quiet. He still found it incredible the Tarshians were going to face an angel. It was like walking to their deaths, but they seemed to care little of it. Satariel. It came to him without thinking; the angel was Satariel, of the choir of the Melachim, but there was something else. The angel had turned; he had not only fallen, but he had begun to age. It made sense, it came to him—Satariel the angel had panicked and had hired a thief to bring him. Just as Azazel, he was going to attempt to sever the root of the Daath. Azazel was a high lord, the equivalent of an archangel, yet his assassins had failed. Now the Tarshians had walked into an angel's death trap, and Loch wondered if a fallen, weakened angel who was no more than a coward would succeed where a high lord of the choirs had failed. Satariel might be hurting, but he was easily capable of killing them all.

Storan threw a bronzed shield so hard Loch barely caught it before it hit his face.

"Shield for you."

"You know, of course, you are all going to die," Loch said.

"You have opinions, you can share them with the captain. You wish to know what I think, Daath—knowing we are all about to die is no news whatsoever. Now . . ." Storan motioned to Marsyas. The big monster lifted an ash-cloth sack from his shoulder, then held it open.

"Step in the sack," Storan ordered.

"What?"

"In you go. Goddess be blessed, but it so turns out the angel has asked for you in sackcloth and we have not come all this way to disappoint the unholy bastard. Now, get in."

Loch glanced at the monstrous Etlantian. There was little use in fighting; they were in the middle of nowhere and even if he killed every Tarshian and miscreant about the captain's ship, he would still be stranded on the angel's island. He stepped into the sack, and the Etlantian pulled it over this head, then tied off the top rope.

He felt Storan grab the weft. The pirate's dagger came close to Loch's face as two holes were cut, sawing out little circles. Through them, Loch saw Storan step back and tilt his head.

"See, I am not a bad person at all, I have cut some eye holes for you. You can thank me later. Pick him up, Marsyas, and let us go see what kind of party the angel has arranged for us."

Chapter Twenty-Seven
Angel's Island

Hyacinth watched with a tingle as Loch was lowered into the longboat with her and the others. Storan had apparently cut holes for his eyes, and Hyacinth noticed a curl of night-black hair.

The longboat shifted as Marsyas and Gryn pulled against the looms of the oars, pulling away from the ship. They began for the shore of the dark island. Men from the blackship's railing watched silently. Hyacinth knew the captain had chosen this small crew carefully. She wondered briefly why he hadn't taken more men, but that was his way. At high sea, all the crewmen were warriors; even the rowers became spearmen and archers. But any time he went ashore, he did so in small, handpicked groups.

She had always found Marsyas curious. She had never mind-walked him, but she had probed and all she found was pure anguish and what might be called a thirsting wait.

Next to him was Gryn, the rower, thick with muscle, weighted heavy and hard. On the looms he pulled the ship through the waters as though it were gliding.

Behind Gryn, in the stern, was Fire Rat. He squatted against the gunwale watching the water curl beneath the ship. He suddenly pulled a net, attached it to a short stick, and looped it over the side.

"Elyon's name," said Storan, "we are not fishing here!"

The Fire Rat ignored him, but when he caught a wriggling fish, Storan slapped it, stick and all, out of his hands.

"Why did you do that?" Taran asked. "Maybe he was hungry."

"It is sad, but we are not here for lunch."

Taran set his hand on Hyacinth's thigh, to reassure her. He was big, he was good with the sword, and he would fight like heaven's fire for her, but she was little comforted. If not for the Angelslayer in his sackcloth, Hyacinth would be certain they faced nothing here but a quick death. Her only real hope was Loch. Though she knew he wasn't aware of any certain way to kill an angel, there was a power in him she had found in no other she had ever mind walked before. He was not only unique, he was gifted of heaven's light far more than even the seers and priests she had known.

"Tell me, priestess," Danwyar said, "do you feel him—this bastard angel Satariel—there waiting for us?"

She turned, scanning the island. "I feel nothing here that lives, Danwyar."

"Bring her hard about," Darke said. "Keel her in the sand, in line with the pavilion."

Hyacinth stood, searching. A red pavilion flapped in a light breeze, far up on the black dirt of the island. It was the only thing of color. Behind it, the high black spires looked like something they had seen in the Daathan city, or even in a high church of the followers of Enoch found in the western islands. It seemed an odd choice the angel had made in design. She wondered if one were able to travel stars and to visit whatever planets circled the seventh star of the Pleiades, if the same spires could also be found, if perhaps they were the spires of voyagers.

"Another happy red pavilion," Storan mused. "Wonder if the blood has dried yet."

Danwyar dropped into the muddied waters, and from the stern, Storan did the same, the water up to his shoulders. They shoved the keel hard into the sand. Hyacinth expected cold waters, but as she splashed into them, she found them warm and viscous.

They gathered on the black sand of the shore. Very fine, beautiful black sand. She almost wanted to gather some. Gryn drove a long, deep stake into it using the pommel of his sword and tied off the longboat. Marsyas dropped into the water and helped Darke hoist Loch over his huge shoulder.

They were within sight of the Etlantian ship. It was just off the shoreline—half in the water, half out. Darke took the time to walk along the beach, studying it.

The Etlantians built their ships double-skinned, their whaling thick strakes of purest cedar; and the ribbing, transoms, and keels were of solid oak. They were ships not easily sunk. With a ship of the line such as this, the sides, between the ribbing, and even the bottom were overlaid with plates of oraculum that could withstand the stoutest ram of a warship. All the plates of Euryathides's ship were in good condition, few of them even worn, which meant he kept his ship always in perfect repair. The four projectiles of rock that from the bay resembled fingers, pierced through the upper wales leaving cedar strakes split open to bleed a pale yellow color where it broke through the thick paint of the exterior. Darke saw the lower tier of rowers' thwarts, all of them empty, the oars ripped free of their thole-pins. There were broken oars scattered about in the sand and floating in the shallow surf. The main deck was clean. Lines hung silent in the light wind. The blood casks of naphtha for the fire throwers were full, leaking tar rivulets down their sides. The ship had been taken quickly without even the slightest warning.

"See anything, Captain?" Danwyar asked.

"One thing I do not see—survivors."

Darke returned. He took the time to study the pavilion up the beachhead about a league's distance.

"May as well discover why we are here," the captain said, starting toward it.

Storan fell in at the captain's left, Danwyar to the right.

The tent flaps of the pavilion were open, fluttering in the silent wind. Within was the dark image of a man. He seemed to be the only thing inside, a single figure sitting on a square black stone.

To the rear, Marsyas trudged with a silent Loch balanced over his muscled shoulder, Gryn beside him, and Taran keeping the flank covered, watching behind them as they walked.

They were halfway up the beachhead when suddenly Danwyar noticed something.

"Look about us," he said. "Mounds, fresh-turned earth. Believe we found the crew."

Darke paused. Both to the left and the right were orderly mounds planted in the black dirt. They had been following what was almost a path up the middle of them.

Danwyar lifted his already loaded bow, leveled it off, and buried a shaft into the center of a mound. In recoil, a human hand reared from the earth, fingers groping. It was a giant, an Etlantian of the second or third generation.

Hyacinth, near it, did a quick back step.

The hand fell limp.

"Thought you said you sensed nothing living, priestess," said Danwyar. "That one seemed to have some life in him."

"No life, although I would not dismiss some manner of spell binding."

"Might be best we take the time to kill them all twice before going farther, perhaps it would eliminate any spells."

"Or perhaps it wouldn't and we waste the afternoon," answered Darke. "Leave them. Let us move on and see what waits in the pavilion."

Danwyar gripped the shaft of his arrow and wrenched it free and reloaded.

Darke continued on toward the pavilion. He pulled his cloak back and withdrew the Daathan sunblade. It seemed strange, wielding a sword of glass. It looked fragile, as if it were used against anything of substance it would simply shatter. However, it was perfectly weighted. It was a double-edged broadsword but unlike other broadswords, which required a good deal of strength to use and having the disadvantage of wearing out its user quickly, the sunblade was much lighter, about the weight of a typical long sword, much easier to wield and not nearly as strenuous.

In truth, Darke had kept the sword only to see if the Daath had any salt in him. If this were his blade, a sunblade of lineage, nothing would stop him from taking it back given the least opportunity. The captain didn't plan on making it difficult if the boy tried, but he did want to see how quickly the Daath moved. If this one moved anywhere near as fast as his warlord, perhaps they had a chance in all this. He was well aware the most probable outcome of this expedition would be their death. The only chance they really had, the gamble Darke had taken with his own and his crew's lives, was that the Daath would be more than he looked. He was well built and solid, but too young to be astute in battle, with pale blue skin that made him look almost sickly. However, the king did wear one of the plain, darkened silver armbands the Daath used to mark their elite, those they called Shadow Walkers. He must have had some training to have obtained it. Darke doubted warriors as deft and proud as the Daath handed out such armbands without discretion.

Darke took a stance before the pavilion and angled the Angelslayer's sword. The angel hadn't taken the time to use a human to construct the pavilion this time. It was ordinary silken red with golden borders, rich, but not extravagant.

The priestess crouched to his left and stood ready beside him, if anything she was fraught with anticipation. She was going to take a position near the Daath when Storan set him down. She had far more faith in the Daath than did Darke, but then he had not walked in the king's skin. This time Hyacinth had brought along a different crossbow, made from her own drawings by a Pelegasian artisan who had heavily overcharged Darke, thought perhaps it was worth it. It had a bolt feeder that could auto-load and fire ten small bolts at a time. It was light, small enough for her to wield with one hand, and was constructed of polished yew. To either side were two chambers loaded with bolts that could be snapped in place when the top chamber was empty, giving her thirty shots with hardly a reload. With her array of poisons, in tight quarters, it was amazingly effective.

Danwyar took position at Darke's right. He held his bow to the side, near his hip, one of the silver arrows loaded and at the ready. They were hardwood arrows on the inside, but Danwyar took the time to coat them in silver so they always left his mark on the kills. He had two scabbards full of them, one on either hip.

Storan stepped to Darke's left as shieldbearer. He would cover Darke's sword arm, as well as use the heavy axe with his right. It was more of a two-handed axe, and eventually, whenever Storan's arm began to wear out, he would toss the shield and use both hands. Either way, he was ever his king's guardian. In tight battle nothing had ever gotten past his shield or his axe.

Taran kept back a few steps from the rest, along with Marsyas, to guard the rear. The Rat was a ranger. He never fought in tight quarters with the others, but ranged for the best position to use his fire bags and daggers. The daggers would burst to flame when he flung them, and he refused to show anyone the secret of his mixture that flamed just from being thrown.

"Set the Daath well in front of us," Darke said. "He is, after all, our offering."

Marsyas set Loch on his feet, still bagged, in front of the pavilion. The Etlantian then stepped to the right and drew his war hammer. Hyacinth quickly moved to Loch's right.

"Hyacinth, back with the others."

"I will take my chances here," she answered. Again she made it clear that though she had the privileges of being one of his crew, she was no Tarshian and not someone he could command. It had often amused Darke, though this time it irritated him.

All of the crew took their fighting stances, ready. Inside the sack, Loch was moving. He unsheathed the sword and slipped the shield off his back.

"Satariel!" Darke cried. His voice echoed away into the black rock.

From within the pavilion came a cackle. It could have been an old woman.

"I have your scion," Darke said.

"Is he sacked?" asked the voice.

"He is sacked. Where is my son?"

"Here—with me. But first, we deal with the Daath."

"He is in the sack, as you asked."

The pavilion's silk burst into flame. It had no purpose but to distract them. The real threat was the ground directly before Loch. It erupted, flinging bits of black earth and rock; something was rearing up out of the Earth.

Hyacinth took a few steps back, leveling her crossbow, which left Loch the only one before the emerging creature.

Loch finally moved, and as Darke had hoped, he moved very quickly. His sword slit open the sackcloth. He turned, used a wrist grip, twisting the sword out of Darke's hand. Darke doubted he could have resisted even if he tried; his wrist shot a burst of pain up his arm. He had made the move so quickly, Storan hadn't even had time to react, though Danwyar's arrow tip tracked him, and could have easily taken him out. Loch tossed Darke the double-edged iron.

A scaled hydra reared from the black earth and was coming to life, separating into three serpentine heads, weaving deceptively among each other. Its focus seemed to be Loch alone, as if the others were not even present.

"My apologies, Captain," Loch shouted, taking a stance before the hydra, "no offense—we are all in this together."

"None taken," answered Darke.

"God's blood," Storan moaned. "Any of you see the hydra? Is this really a good time to chat?"

"The rest of you keep back," Loch said. "The blood is like acid."

"Aye, majesty," grizzled Storan. "We will be careful as we can be!"

Each of the three heads flickered tongues wrapped in tiny cords of flame. They all wove in different directions, striking for Loch, but the Shadow Walker effortlessly dodged them.

Darke watched with interest. Loch was making it look simple, but he knew it was not; this was no ordinary beast, and was feared by most men as one of the deadliest serpents known. Danwyar was about to fire, searching out the hydra's heart, but Darke set a hand over his wrist, lowering the bow.

"Love of Elyon, will you kill the damn thing!" Storan shouted.

Loch grasped the hilt. The blade of aganon flashed from crystal to a searing white, as if it had been held over coals for hours. The king tracked the hydra's movement a moment longer, dodging the strikes, then stepped forward and severed all three heads in a matter of seconds, the sword flashing, heads spinning into the air. Each stump immediately began to sprout new growth, green/gold snouts pushing out of the blood that boiled about the severed flesh. When the blood hit the ground below it sizzled, the acid sinking burn marks through the black rock. Loch slammed the flat of the blade over the stumps one at a time. The blade was obviously very hot; with barely any pressure it instantly seared each stump to a thick, blackened scar. He had to hack off the last head a second time for it had nearly reached maturity. When the last stump was seared, he stepped back and watched. The body, spellbound to begin with, shivered, withering quickly, collapsing, leaving what looked to be freshly shed snakeskin. Scrambling, Hyacinth gathered the scattered teeth and crammed them into a deerskin bag at her hip.

"Suppose he has proven some worth, Captain," observed Storan.

"I mean your captain no offense by taking the sword, helmsman, but we must use every advantage. The angel has laced this island with traps. He is a coward. He only watches from the distance. His traps, however, will prove very deadly—watch all directions and ignore nothing that moves or shifts."

Darke was staring at the figure seated on a dark stump of rock in the ashes of the pavilion as it slowly lifted its head, looking up. It was the face of Lothian. The angel had done as he promised, he had delivered Darke's son. Lothian wore one of his old leather jerkins, worn and stained, and wide, looped boots Darke recognized. He also wore his Tarshian sword in the sheath Darke had hand-carved from leather and reinforced with silver studs. Long, rust-brown hair fell over the shoulders. But there the illusion of normalcy ended. His eyes were gone, and he was searching blindly. They had been torn out only recently. Blood streaked his cheeks. But it would not have made any difference. His skin was leathery and tight against the bone. He was nothing more than a corpse, weeks old.

"Who is there?" the figure asked. Lothian's voice—still strong. "Father, is that you?"

"I am here, my son, do not move."

"It is you! But do you not know this bastard has laid a trap, many a trap, Father? You should never have come for me. I am not worth the lives of you and your crew. There is no way off this island."

"What has he done to you?"

Danwyar was crouched, searching for any target, anything that moved. Marsyas had stepped back and turned in every direction, searching behind them. Hyacinth remained near Loch, and Taran had positioned himself on her left to protect her, the shadow of his oval shield over her shoulder.

Loch watched the figure in the pavilion carefully.

"Tell me what has happened to you, Lothian," Darke said.

"I know not. A curse spellbound of the Watcher. He took my eyes this morning, using only the nails of his fingers. He has enjoyed himself for seven days as I watched my skin wither just as his is withered. I believe I am dead, days dead, and yet my soul is bound to my body and will not ascend. As well, the dying of my body has been such pain it is beyond endurance."

"Help him, Loch," said Darke. "Break the binding; give him heaven."

"I will, Captain. All of you please stay back."

Loch stepped over the withered skin of the hydra. Winds stirred as he walked across the charred platform of the pavilion. The head of Lothian studied Loch with its melted eyes, as a blind man searches.

"I feel you. I can sense you. Who are you, warrior?"

"I am Daath, a Shadow Walker, Lothian. Take faith—your pain will soon end."

One hand of the corpse gripped the arm of the throne; fingers gripping, stretched out and gripping again, over and over. The empty eyes tried to follow Loch as he stepped back and to the side, studying Lothian carefully. Loch finally stepped directly in front of the pirate and with a flick of the sunblade, sliced opened the chest cavity. Lothian cried out as his chest spilt and gaped wide, the shrunken muscles and skin pulling open the ribs. It was dead, all of it but the nerves, which continued to feed the poor Tarshian pain. Near the edges of the ribs, his skin curled back like rolled papyrus. The lungs were withered, the bowels dried as a rope, knotted along its edges. The organs were black and shrunken. There was no blood; everything was so dry it looked ready to crumble like ash—except for the heart. The heart was being kept red and blue and alive; beating strong, as it had in life. Curled about it was a small, green serpent. Seeing Loch, it reared its head, flicking a bright red tongue with a hiss.

There was a whispering chuckle that swiftly circled them like wind, coming from different directions at once—the angel mocking Darke. The captain tried not to let it affect him, but it did, his lip curled in a snarl.

Without hesitation, Loch lopped off the serpent's head with a slice of the Angelslayer's tip. As the tiny serpent fell away, Lothian moaned and instantly his corpse collapsed. It sagged to one side, dropped to the platform, finally lifeless, the rags of clothing fluttering in the wind.

"Sorry for your loss," said Loch, stepping back, "but his soul ascends; he returns home."

"Wait," said Hyacinth. She crept closer to where Lothian lay on his side. The body was still, but the jaw was working. The ribs were spreading outward, the organs swelling. The brain matter was growing so quickly it was squeezing through the orbitals of the eyes.

"Something spawns," the priestess warned.

Loch took her shoulder and pulled her away, shoving her behind him.

"Going to be a circus soon," said Storan, "courtesy of this Star Walker prick."

Darke threw his head back. "Satariel!" he cried, furious. "Face us! Where are you, coward? You are an angel! We are mortal; dare you not show yourself? Face me, you bastard!"

There was a growing sound of humming, like insects. Hyacinth backed away, close to Darke's leg. Loch watched the dried organs swell, growing, wriggling. He stepped carefully.

"Take up shields," he warned, angling the one given him toward the corpse. It was a large oval shield, thankfully in this situation more than a buckler.

Taran lifted his large oval shield and pulled Hyacinth to his side, covering them both.

"You know what this is, Daath?" asked Darke.

"I do not, but it will be like hail coming at us. Guard exposed flesh."

Loch stepped near Danwyar, who still searched with the tip of his bow.

"That will do you little good," said Loch.

Danwyar glanced at him, irritated, but with the bow still strung, he angled it to the side with one hand and pulled his buckler from his back.

"Guess is it good we brought you along," he commented.

"Much better to have never come," Loch answered. "He has little interest in you. It is doubtful he would even have hunted you. He is obsessed only with his own fate."

"Does anyone think it best we leave this pavilion?" asked Danwyar, "or maybe we wait for lunch and some wine?"

"Back step slowly," said Darke, "shields at the ready."

Lothian's spleen was the first to split open. What looked to be blood became thirty to sixty small winged creatures, fat as bumblebees, red as pomegranate seeds. They closed on Loch first, since he was foremost. He brought his shield up, crouched behind it. The pirates continued to back away. Loch looked to be turning back fire. As they struck his shield they splattered with bloody explosions.

Those that spilled past Loch streamed for the others. The Tarshians were quick, their shields blocking the fliers, but occasionally one of them caught flesh. One hit Marsyas's shoulder and bore in, whirling, drilling. He snatched it with his fingers and ripped it out, throwing it aside.

But they seemed little interested in the pirates, or in Loch. They continued streaming, and it was Danwyar who first noticed their objective.

"The mounds!" he cried. "They are going for the Etlantian dead—they are not even interested in us."

"Quicken your pace," Darke commanded. "Loch! Get out of there. Keep with us."

Loch did; keeping his shield over his shoulder, he ran to catch them. All of Lothian's organs had swollen to bursting now. The air was filled with the swarms of fat fliers. They soared over and around the Tarshians, still colliding with shields and taking any flesh they could find. Gryn swore as one hit the back of his hand, then bore through and kept going, leaving a bloodied hole.

One hit Darke's thigh, and Hyacinth was close enough to pick it out with the tip of her dagger. Once they caught the smell of the buried Etlantians, they seemed to be of one mind. They avoided the pirates and began going for the buried mounds, each choosing a different mound, hitting the dirt with splats and puffs of earth, and whirling as they bore downward.

"They have no further interest in us, Captain!" Danwyar screamed.

"For the ship!" shouted Darke. "Keep together, circle, guard all sides, but double-time for the shore!"

In a pack, keeping together, shields surrounding them, they were quickly moving through the rows of planted corpses.

"Break and run?" Danwyar queried.

"No," countered Darke. "It is what he expects. Keep together."

They moved in a group, all but Fire Rat; he chose distance. He had no shield, no weapons except for a long-bladed dagger and the rope that served as his belt, and so he ran, sprinting, his bags bouncing off his back. To use his weapons effectively, he needed distance.

Suddenly he paused. His path was blocked. A pustule shot up out of the ground, then blossomed quickly, shooting skyward in mere seconds, first a short bush of thorny branches, then stretching limbs for the sun, arching upward like a man standing from a squat. The Fire Rat was taken, mesmerized—he had to see what happened.

They were sprouting everywhere; the hundreds of Euryathides crew were all blooming into thorny bushes that tore through the earth and soared skyward as if someone had sped up the growth of trees or plants. Green leaves, bark, vines wrapping around the stems at they rose up. Darke and the others were moving through the middle of them.

"Get as far past these as we can!" Darke shouted. "But keep together."

"Those in front, those between us and the ship, they will surround us if they break open!" Danwyar cried.

"I know, but we keep together. If we break and run, we will be shredded."

"Your captain speaks best," Loch cut in, "they would prefer us piecemeal."

"And who do you speak for, Daath?" interrupted Storan, irritated.

"He speaks for us all," answered Hyacinth. "Listen to him, he reads time, he senses spirit, do not mock his words, Storan."

"These are known as pod growers," Loch said," but they are spellbound to develop twenty times their rate. They will shortly bear fruit."

"Rat," Darke shouted, spotting him. "Get out of there!"

Fire Rat was ahead of them, but he could only stare, amazed as the pod soared to the height of a giant, the size of an Etlantian. He never had been right in the head and presently, his curiosity had overcome all reason.

The wooden bushes were reaching seven, eight, ten feet now. The same heights of Euryathides's crew.

"They are about to bloom," Loch warned. "Be ready."

"Rat," cried Darke once more, "get away from there!"

"You have seen these?" Danwyar said as he sidestepped quickly. Danwyar was keeping his shield up, his other hand pinning an arrow to the bow, angled downward.

"Only matured. I do not know what will come from these pods, but I sense they are almost complete."

Fire Rat screeched, finally leaping away, colliding with Marsyas as the group reached him. The pod before him had split open and inside was a quivering, jellylike creature whose organs, eyes, and brain were all contained in a viscous fluid that seemed to be hardening even as Rat watched. Rat broke and ran on his own to clear distance for his naphtha bags.

They had made it through the center, and though pods all around them were splitting open, there were far more of them behind than in front. It seemed a short distance to the beach and the ashore boat, but it was not going to be easily reached; there were scores of pods breaking open between here and there.

Rat had cleared the mounds and turned to run backward, readying his bags, watching as the thorn pustules broke open. He saw one of the first giants emerge. The beast was a shivering globule of pale flesh somehow held together in the shape of an Etlantian—naked, pink, with muscle wrapped in thin cords and webworks of veins. On the outside something was quickly forming, a yellowish outer cover of ill-shaped bone, almost wobbly bone, though it seemed to be quickly hardening into separate plates: chest plates, back plates, arm and leg plates. All the outermost flesh was becoming a kind of rubbery armor.

Once free of the pod, the giant moved with amazing speed. Rat was down the beach, far ahead of the others, reading his bags, and it was Gryn the creature first spotted and leapt for. It was able to leap into near flight. Gryn screamed as a torn claw came down on him, and had he not stepped back quickly it would have torn open his chest; even still it left gaping slashes. Though the muscles and rubbery plates were almost gelatinous, the fingers were all heavy, dark claws of thorns, the size of a dagger, curved and razor sharp. Gryn was cut open, but he had mettle; he was no coward quick to panic, and he brought his heavy broadsword over his head and literally halved the creature down the center from the top of its head. It split apart, and the two sides fell outward then hit the ground in a splash of mucus and blood-meshed sacs.

There were hundreds popping open with cracks and snaps as the thorn plants split in their centers to release their wobbly, gelatinous spawn. The giants stepped free of their wooden wombs to search for food, needing blood and flesh badly. Like newborn calves, their legs and arms were at first unsteady and they moved in lurching strides, aided by wings sprouting from their ankles. Amazingly, the wings helped them leap so they were airborne for seconds, though when they landed, their legs were so unsteady in the beginning that many went down, spastically.

From all sides they were starting to swarm. Luckily, the pirates had gotten through most of the open graves, close enough to the beach to offer hope. But there were thorn pods still in front of them bursting open.

"Keep tight; head for the beach," commanded Darke. "Storan, Marsyas, carve out our path should they block it!"

Storan switched with Danwyar, taking position on Darke's left.

The crackling sound of the thorn plants opening was loud, like logs snapping and splitting everywhere. The angel had made a comedy of his trap. Once matured, pod creatures were invincible warriors, but newly born, they walked in unsteady staggers, arms reeling. They came heaving their way toward the pirates, making sounds, moaning as though they were talking with one another, but all of it high-pitched wails and gibberish.

"Mother of us all," Storan swore at the sight of them.

They were Euryathides's full crew, with oarsmen, and they would have numbered nearly two hundred. Luckily, the pirates had made it far enough down the beach that the majority were to the rear, but the plan seemed to have been to surround them. Many of them did not have pure blood in their veins. Consequently, some could not control the newly formed muscle and bone, and they emerged from their pods only to rupture in sprays of jellylike globs.

"Back to back!" Darke screamed as the creatures finally were able to move in with focus, leaping and lurching in quivering steps. Their bodies were like jelly, but their hands and teeth were hardwood thorns, and as rubbery as they were, they were incredibly strong. When the first one reached Loch, he slammed the buckler into its face, expecting it to be thrown back, but it proved surprising resilient, its hand swiping for his face so Loch brought the sword low, shearing through both legs. The creature dropped with a maniacal howl and a splash of viscous fluid and blood.

They were at first coming two or three at a time, and the pirates were taking them out with heavy weapons. All bore axes, double-edged irons, heavy bucklers and shields, and as they came two and three at a time, they were shorn open or smashed by Marsyas's hammer.

Danwyar used arrows through the eyes. The silver missiles splashed into the eyeballs and out the back of the heads with a splat and the creatures would scream and spin, wildly waving their arms. They were halted in their tracks, but never did they die quickly.

The wails, cries, and childlike bawls were unnerving as the creatures were smashed, shorn open, and sliced in pieces.

But they were also developing quickly. Hardening. The plates of what would become hardened thorn wood armor were yellow and spongy, but with each moment, each second, they were darkening and taking on coppicelike hardness more difficult to cut.

"This is simple, mindless madness," Storan shouted, shearing through glob after glob.

"Shield to shield—press for the shore!" Darke commanded. "And do not underestimate them—if they reach you, they will tear you apart!"

Darke slammed his shield sideways through the face of a creature. All the Tarshian shields were steel-edged. He sliced through just above the eyes, but even brainless, the beast kept coming, still swiping at him, snarling with a gurgle. Darke used his sword, in and out of the chest, until it finally screeched and spun, slipping to the ground where it writhed with sounds as though it were a terrified child.

Hyacinth stayed beside Loch with Taran to her right. Taran was using sword and shield to ward off anything that came near Hyacinth, hardly protecting himself. He had already taken blows to his back and sides, but he dodged them effectively enough that none were deep or lethal. He used his heavy, black double-edged sword in the same cut over and over to guard his right. He swiped through guts, their softer midsections, cutting deep enough that they fell over backward, snapping the rubbery spines or sometimes dragging their bodies as their legs continued their wobbly assault, harmlessly bumping and slamming into Taran's side until they lost control, spilling ooze across the rock.

The ground, mostly rock and dirt, had become slippery. It was difficult moving quickly without sliding, but these were pirates, used to heaving seas, all but Loch. He was finding it maddening, sometimes sliding backward instead of running, other times nearly falling.

Hyacinth moved backward half-crouched. Just as Danwyar, she was firing her tiny missiles into their eyes, upward through the tops of their heads, which were hardening as each moment passed and would catch the tips long enough to take the poison. The poison would often discolor their blood, swirling through their brains—orange, yellow, brown, sometimes a rich purple or dark blue.

One of them, feeling the poison, began whirling in a circle, its arms flailing and waving in what might have been a practiced dance until it finally dropped to a writhing mass on the black rock.

"He plays with us," Hyacinth said to Loch, "toys with us while he laughs somewhere."

Even though the ashore boat was close, there were now enough matured pod beasts that they had slowed the rapid retreat. The pirates were still steadily moving for shore, but Marsyas and Storan were doing all the work, hacking their way through, the heavy axe and the big Etlantian's war hammer working as if cutting through a thick jungle.

Hyacinth continued piercing eyes. At least when her bolts went through they stopped in their tracks.

"How many bolts do you have left?" asked Loch.

"Ten and four."

"Kill sparingly. Let me and your protector Taran take the brunt of them."

She obeyed, keeping the small crossbow at the ready, but waiting to choose her mark only when they were too close to her or Loch.

The path to the sea was finally blocked by a mass of them. The pirates for the moment found themselves surrounded, fighting on all sides. Marsyas's hammer took off heads one after the other, and Storan found his axe worked through the midsections.

Loch finally let the sword suck blood from his palm. It surged in pain up his arm and through his head, but the sword finally came to life, spilling light. Almost immediately they backed off, covering their eyes, some even screeching or screaming, and ran, arms waving above them in terror.

Hyacinth gasped. "They fear you," she said.

"They fear the sword."

Darke was busy killing, but he turned to see the Daath, poised and ready. The monsters gathered in a frightened mass before him; those behind them pressing forward, but those in front terrified by the humming light slashing into them, ripping them open, spilling out the fluids and blood and guts.

"To the front," Darke cried, "Loch, move to the front, cut a path to the sea."

Loch back stepped.

"Marsyas, cover Hyacinth!" he commanded.

Loch and Marsyas stepped past each other. From Marsyas's side they immediately came forward. There were perhaps hundreds back here. Marsyas prepared to slay, though he was exhausted, weary to the point of collapsing.

Loch stepped forward, separating from the others slightly, letting blood into the hilt. The sword readily drank, as if it were thankful. Like quenching thirst it sucked hard until the sting of blood slipping through his skin made his head light, while at the same time bolts of pain shot up his arm, through his shoulder, into his head with hammer blows. He let out a thin ribbon of blue light, focusing past the pain to move the blade slowly from right to left. The flowing, weaving ribbon of light cut hot and searing through legs, midsections, chests—anything it struck. All of creatures within sight of Loch were thrown into a wild panic. The ones in front desperately tried to run, only to slam into those behind.

The pirates needed clear passage to the ashore boat. Loch's arm was nearly paralyzed with pain, but he dropped a moment to one knee, lowered his head, and let the Angelslayer take a solid stream of his blood, granting it all it wished. Pain ripped into him, screaming, searing pain as blood tore through the skin of his palm and even streamed from the vessels in his wrist, sucking into the hilt and then through the blade. Darke saw a vessel in Loch's temple burst open, spewing blood into his hair. With a deafening crack of thunder, a blue bolt of light left the tip of the Angelslayer and spread out as it moved toward the giants. They were screaming in wild panic, throwing themselves back, but the light continued coming for them, widening, until it was like a wave rolling. It slammed into the thorn beasts, flinging them in all directions, tearing their flesh to shreds, their fluids spraying as they were blown into pieces. When it was over, the creatures were cleared all the way to the shore. A path to the boat had been opened. The ground before it was drenched in shredded flesh, vicious fluids, and bloodied debris.

The pain ripping through Loch was unbearable. It left things blurry. He ignored it, standing.

"I will take the rear now," he said to Darke. "Go for the boat!"

He turned and moved for the rear. He was nearly blind with pain, but he forced the Shadow Walker to see through it. He kept his balance, kept his focus. He let the blade cool down, and as he did some of the pain began to abate.

Taran, Marsyas, and Danwyar had been left to hold off hundreds closing on the rear. Now the light of the Angelslayer backed them off as Loch stepped past the captain to Hyacinth's side.

Darke glanced to the waterline; it was cleared, but just as he turned, a pod creature caught him in the shoulder, shearing away a chunk of flesh. Darke hissed, furious, and sliced him open, sideways from the midsection through the top of his head, but they were getting harder to cut; they were maturing. As they dried, their exoskeleton was taking on dimension, forming a coating of armor that by now was almost thick as leather.

Suddenly a circle of whispered chuckling swirled around them like wind. It was the angel, watching his circus, amused.

"Double-time for the shore," Darke commanded, "and hold the sides and flanks. We must still stay together—but move! Move!"

They were moving quickly now. It seemed close, the ashore boat, they could have sprinted to it in minutes, but they were being pressed too hard from the side and rear. If they turned to spring, those to the rear would be caught and torn to pieces.

Taran cried out. He had been fighting hard, his sword arcing and thrusting with deadly mark, shearing arms, legs, guts, slashing through faces. He had killed countless numbers of them, but a giant had suddenly stepped around the edge of his shield, moving with speed unlike the others, and this one sank thorny, arced teeth of hard thorn wood into the muscle of Taran's lower neck and shoulder, then ripped away a chunk large enough for the creature to step back, chew, and swallow. Taran's sword ripped through his gut as he did, but blood flushed across Taran's chest and his head was left leaning sideways.

"No!!" shrieked Hyacinth, whirling to send two bolts ripping into the giants coming at the weakened Taran, smelling his blood. She sunk her bolts through the eye sockets, and the pod beasts reeled in confusion, blocking those behind. One wailed, clutching for its eye as the poison visibly swarmed through its head, through the pink tissue of its brain.

But the smell of blood was strong and it drew them with renewed vigor. From the left another got close enough to grab Taran's shoulder with thorn claws, about to tear off Taran's arm. A bolt of light pulsed through the monster, igniting him like a torch before he exploded in bits of flesh and slop. The thorn claws were left lodged in Taran's shoulder, along with a piece of the arm above the elbow that flapped as Taran continued to fight, wielding the broadsword to protect Hyacinth at his side.

Loch hissed. Each time he fired the sword, an arc of pain ripped through his arm and up his neck. The sword caused a split in the veins in the back of his hand. As blood spilled from the wound, it was quickly taken by the sword. The Angelslayer seemed to crave Loch's blood as badly as the thorn giants, and it drew in the blood from the split veins in his hand in tiny streams, like rain being driven by wind. The blade rippled in fire now, a deep orange-red. The stream of fire roared as it streamed into the creatures. Loch gasped, sucking for air; it was out of his control; the sword was sucking in the blood from the wound without slowing.

For a moment he almost blacked out, but then he dropped to one knee and lifted the blade, using the pain and loss of blood to level off the stream of fire, letting it tear into them. The thorned beasts screamed. Some tried to turn and run. Panic spread as Loch swung the screaming swath of flame from one side to the other, shearing most in half, bursting others open, turning some into pillars of fire that caught others aflame as they ran through the crowded giants howling. At one point he kept it leveled straight and the stream of pure fire sunk deeper and deeper through them, killing dozens, as if cutting a roadway through the midst of them..

But he could barely focus, barely keep him eyes open. The loss of blood was tapping his strength, leaving him so weak he felt as he if were about to collapse inward, just like one of the creatures whose bloodline failed to hold their bodies. Suddenly, Loch's arm began to jerk in spasms and the light from the blade came in pulses, uncontrolled bursts of energy destroying everything they struck. Loch was unable to hold either the bursts or train their direction. At one point a solid, blue, crackling bolt of light spread in a wide, shimmering arc, imploding as many as fifteen at once, like a heavy blade ripping a deep swath through their fleshy outer layers.

"He cannot stop!" Hyacinth cried. "Help him; he cannot stop!"

Loch dropped his head back, growling through tight teeth as the pain overwhelmed him. His head was near to bursting; every muscle and tendon of his body was screaming. He managed to keep the sword level and he knew he was still slaying from the screams he could hear, but his head was tipped back and all he could see was sky graying—he was losing his vision.

Lightning crackled from the top of his shoulder, shooting out of his skin and twirling down his arm and forearm. When it struck the hilt, it flew outward in star-fire bursts blindly striking anything in their path. A wide burst of white light tore a deep gash in the black rock, ripping through the feet of giants, but doing more damage to the rock than any flesh. Amazingly, the rock bled. Red, rich blood spilled from the gash, as if it were skin itself and beneath was blood and veins. Another misfired bolt exploded a spire with a crack and the shards of crystal spun into the sky in fiery streamers.

"Help him!" Hyacinth screamed again.

Darke had reached Loch's side, swearing. He stepped in front of Loch and grabbed his hand where it held the hilt. Fire ran up the captain's arm, it even seared the flesh on the back of Darke's hand, but he continued to hold. He slammed his boot into the Daath's chest, knocking him back and ripping the sword free of Loch's grip.

Darke screamed in pain. It was sucking blood from him, as well, and for a moment it continued ejecting a stream of fire that Darke could not control. It soared skyward, high into the night like an eruption. Finally, it ran dry. The blade stopped taking Darke's blood. The captain hissed in obvious pain, backing away to turn for the boat.

"For the boat, everyone!" he screamed.

He ran with the sword to the side. The Angelslayer continued to glow, swimming in a myriad of colors, all metallic, red, blue, white diamond. Darke refused to drop it. He held though the hilt was burning the flesh of his palm.

"Run! Move! Move!" he shouted.

Loch's out-of-control fire bursts had, for the moment, cleared the monsters from the rear and flanks. Some remained on the side, but they hesitated to attack. All were still spooked, like children who had witnessed a horrifying event.

"Storan, take the king!"

Storan yanked Loch up so hard and so quickly, it seemed he almost tore off Loch's arm doing so. He threw Loch's limp body over his shoulder and ran for the shore. Marsyas wrapped Taran's arm about his neck and pulled him along as they ran. Taran was trying to run himself, but one leg was dragging behind. The left half of his body was paralyzed, and his sword fell away, his hand no longer able to hold it.

The thorn beasts were re-forming again, overcoming their fears. They had also hardened. The outer shells of armor was a darker yellow, the color of polished yew. They finally gathered their courage and began their strange leaping, half-flying pursuit of the pirates, closing once more on the rear.

"Move! Move!" cried Darke, urging them on. They were clear for the shore, but the flanks were closing on Storan and Marsyas.

As he ran, stepping sideways, Danwyar continued to feed bolts into his bow. They were close to the beach, and he was keeping nothing in reserve; each shot was for a head. None of his bolts missed. Most of Danwyar's shafts pierced through since the flesh and outer shells were still soft, but they were maturing rapidly enough that many of the exoskeletons were hard enough to catch the darts, leaving them lodged in the foreheads. These staggered blindly about. None of the creatures dropped quickly from Danwyar's bolts; they all took moments to die, even though the shots were all lethal and eventually they dropped. When his last dart was spent, Danwyar shoved his arm through the bowstring, slung it over his back, and ripped free his short sword.

Some of the giants were reaching the flanks, and though he was shouldering Loch, Storan still slew with the axe, and to his rear, any that drew close to

Marsyas's hammer had their heads smashed like bursting melons.

Hyacinth suddenly cried out, "Help me! Help me now!" With her crossbow and knives spent, she had been trying to dislodge her short sword from a sternum bone that had hardened enough to clasp it tight. The wood-beast had grabbed her and was leaning to shear her neck.

Gryn leaped over a fallen beast and with a warrior's cry he beheaded the giant. When that wasn't enough, the claws still going for the little priestess, Gryn sheared off the arm. Hyacinth staggered out of the monster's grip.

But as Gryn turned there were as many as five or six on him. He slashed through two of them before one finally ripped open his entire shoulder. His sword arm fell to the ground. The giant leaned down and shoved his face into Gryn's open chest to suck in the vitals as if they were the most succulent of fruit.

No one could help. Horrified, Hyacinth had no choice but to turn and run for the others.

One of them stepped behind and curled his hand over Gryn's head, sinking the dagger fingers into his eyes, ripping off the top of the skull to slurp out the brains.

Fire Rat was waging a war of his own. He had chosen his position not far from the boat and as the Tarshians fled from the giants, he was launching his bladder bags against their right flank. Already there were clusters of burning lumps where he had struck. His bags were all about him. He grabbed another and spun it over his head, gaining momentum, then let it fly. It went just over Gryn's headless shoulder. One of them feeding on him looked up in time for the rocks attached to the tether lines of Rat's bladder bag to catch his throat. The bag whipped in circles around and around the creature's neck until it struck the side of its head and Rat's fire chemicals erupted outward, spewing wide and high and raining over dozens. Every monster feeding on Gryn was now aflame; some were trying to run fast enough to suck the flame out, but they eventually fell, melting inward.

Rat spun another bladder over his head, and aiming carefully, he sent it spinning into a group of them closing on the captain's right. It caught a monster's head and when the bag erupted, even Darke and Storan had to shield themselves from the heat wave and the shower of flaming naphtha. It had been close, but it freed passage to the boat.

The exoskeleton bodies were maturing enough that now only the high blood of Euryathides's crew could maintain them. The firstborn were forming the hardened plates of armor and taking on the look of the Nephilim that had attacked Loch and Adrea. Others, however, did not have the pure blood required to preserve and hold the mature body's integrity. They would falter, their legs wobbling, their arms groping madly for balance before they fell. Their skin and armor plating would quickly decompose, rejecting the host spirit just as dematerializing Uttuku.

Rat looked down and was shocked to find he was out of bags. When he looked back up, ten to fifteen monsters were closing on him, and they came with amazing speed. They were using the wings at their ankles to leap into the air, flying for stretches, using their arms to guide the flight. Rat was about to be overtaken. He ran for the boat. He was small, but his legs were long and they stretched in a wild, lanky run, his head thrown back, his long, flaxen gold hair flying behind him, but the giants were hop-flying and some were almost in reach, the clawed fingers reaching for his neck and shoulders. Seeing how close they were, he ran all the harder, giving it everything he had. In panic he cried out in his own tongue.

"Galaaaack!"

Marsyas heard and turned. Seeing the little Rat about to become victuals for these giants, he snarled.

"Danwyar," he mumbled through his half tongue. When Danwyar turned, Marsyas heaved Taran into his arms, then turned and ran, his heavy boots pounding the hard rock. He lifted his war hammer, swinging it over his head.

As Fire Rat flew past him, Marsyas, the Etlantian waded into Rat's attackers, stopping them in their tracks, his deadly hammer smashing into heads and chests. They turned on the giant instead, forgetting the little Rat in favor of the meat offered of a fully grown Etlantian. But their cuisine proved deadly. One of the leapers was coming down directly on top of Marsyas, arms outstretched and claws ready to shred, but the Etlantian's war hammer punched through his gut and out his back with a splatter of blood and ooze. Marsyas had to rip his hammer free as the fluids and vitals splashed into his face. He took stance, gripped the hammer with both hands, and took them on, cleaving in heads, taking out midsections and chests. For a moment none of them could get past the singing war hammer, it ripped through them all, and Marsyas hammered them into a mound of mush all about his feet. But there were too many. Finally a claw ripped away the good side of his face, the good eye, the side almost handsome when it was turned in the right direction. As his hammer arm was ripped off and fed upon, they swarmed over him, delighted with the sizable feast.

Danwyar was helping Taran, who was trying to run, dragging his leg. "I am okay, I'll keep up," Taran said, but his words were slurred and his head hung sideways against his shoulder.

They finally reached the boat.

"Get aboard and get us out of here!" cried Darke.

Storan hurled Loch's body over the gunwale near the prow post, then turned to take up stance, axe ready if any closed in as the rest boarded. A few of the giants reached them, but none got past Storan's axe though he was nearly spent, his axe arm almost useless as rubber.

Darke helped Danwyar hoist Taran over the edge, then took Hyacinth's wrist and hurled her over as if she were a child.

"Go!" he shouted at Danwyar.

"You go, Captain. I do not leave this beach until you are aboard!"

Darke gave him a frustrated glance but took hold of the prow post and stepped up a whaling strip and over the edge.

"Let us get out of here, Storan," Danwyar cried.

"Aye," Storan agreed. The beasts were rushing for them, leaping, flying, but there was barely time for Storan and Danwyar to heave their shoulders into the sides of the boat and shove the keel out of the sand. Half-running, boots slipping in the sand, they pushed the boat into deep water. The beasts were just behind, reaching for them. Danwyar planted one of his last daggers in the forehead of one as Storan clambered over the edge. Danwyar took hold of the gunwale with one hand and hurled himself over the edge. The two of them immediately took up the oars, lifting them high into the air, then back down where they slammed into the dark water and took hold of the sea like clawed hands to pull the boat with a lurch swiftly into the deep. Darke stepped to the prow. A number of thorn-beasts lined up along the shore and stared, watching with uncertainty.

As the boat swiftly pulled into deep water, both Storan and Danwyar at the oars, the others, all but Darke, lay strewn in the bottom. Hyacinth crawled over to Loch, worried. A vessel had split open in his neck, not a vital one, but he was losing blood. She tore a swath of cotton from her skirt and wrapped it about his neck, tying it off with enough pressure to stop the bleeding. She found another vessel opened at his temple and she pressed her palm against it to let the blood clot. So much blood had soaked into his black hair it was matted against the side of his face. The sword had come very close to killing him. He was barely breathing.

Fire Rat lay against one side, breathless from his desperate run. He had put everything into it and now sucked air like he was drowning.

Taran was lying on his side awkwardly; facedown, one arm twisted beneath him, his head turned upward to the side. He saw Hyacinth, but only his eyes moved to her. Even then, through all that was happening, most of his body paralyzed, he still grinned out of half his face. "Don woory," he slurred, "we make it!" His blood was forming a thick pool to either side of the keel.

"Oh, Taran," she said sadly, quietly beneath her breath.

Danwyar and Storan wrenched in time against the looms with such strength, the stern was lifted out of the water slightly with each surge. They were clear; the shore was quickly receding. Hyacinth spoke quick words over Gryn and poor Marsyas, who had almost reached the boat when he turned to save the Rat. At least the Etlantians' sadness had ended. She sensed his whole life had been hard, the whole of it bitter. His spirit had surely found the path through heaven; he had died valiantly, despite his being a Nephilim. Of course, he was cursed to remain bound to the Earth, but she prayed the light of the mothering star he might be forgiven.

The captain was watching the shore. He slammed his fist against the prow post. "Damn," he swore bitterly. "God's blood, they can swim."

Hyacinth looked up. Though they had hesitated at first, uncertain, one or two of the high bloods, the stronger firstborn, had waded into the water, then leapt to a dive and began swimming. Seeing they could do this, other weaker ones followed. In moments, scores of them were coming through the water. Moments mattered because the older they got, second by second, the stronger they were growing and the harder their armor was forming. There must have been many firstborn among Euryathides's crew. Not all of them had entered the water. Some of lesser blood remained behind, looking uncertain and wobbly, confused. Their bodies would soon fail them, collapse, and swiftly decompose.

Those swimming moved slowly at first, but learned quickly until they were moving fast through the water. Hyacinth swore she saw webs forming between the clawed fingers as their hands lifted and fell with their strokes. The bodies of the creatures apparently adapted to their environment instantly. These were turning into water beasts. And this was the last of them, the strongest, the firstborn of Euryathides's crew. Euryathides had been a Nephilim born of the Light Bearer of Etlantis, and many of his crew were his sons, born first generation, six hundred years ago. They would eventually become minions, with wooden armor as hard as steel and were said to be nearly impossible to kill. The thorn-wood of their bodies, soft when the battle had begun, was being cooled and hardened by the waters. They were moving faster and faster; they were actually, unbelievably, going to catch up with the ashore boat, even though Storan and Danwyar were putting all they had into the looms.

The nightmare had still not ended. She felt a slight stab of panic and wondered why Elyon would allow them to fail. Why let this, His chosen Angelslayer, fall now, when they were so close? He lay unconscious, unable to help them. How could Elyon allow this to happen?

Though the thorn creatures were not numerous, there was a least a score, all of them quickly growing strong. They would be hard to kill now. They were nearly matured minions, the name given the pod growers, the powerful firstborn who used the thorn wood as their bodies.

"Mother of us all," Storan swore. "Cannot we get a single edge? Has heaven no mercy? We have killed scores of these motherless bastards; we have sacrificed Gryn and even Marsyas. Young Taran lies here bleeding; surely he gave his all. Even the Daath, he did his utmost, and he the chosen of Elyon. And now, now we find they can swim as fast as we can row? There is no mercy; Elyon's Light is no more than the hearth fire of a whore's coven."

"Watch your words, Storan," warned Hyacinth, "even now, even here. Speak not against Him."

"You tell us, little witch, you tell us all how His goodness will spare us yet. Some miracle to come down from the stars!"

Hyacinth looked to Taran; his head was rocking with the motion of the oars, he was still lying in the awkward position he had landed in when thrown into the boat. He was near death, so near Hyacinth could see his spirit hovering near the surface. He had been so kind to her, all the many things he had brought from far shores. All the risks he had taken just to bring her a book or a scroll. And he had hoped, in his short life, how he had hoped someday she would love him, never knowing her heart was already given to the captain. Tears were close as she crawled to him. Seeing her near, he attempted the half smile once more as though he had no idea his spirit was close to parting. She straightened out his limbs, giving him dignity where he lay. She pulled him against her where she could stroke his hair on the side where she guessed he still had feeling. "I love you, Taran," she whispered, and her eyes stung, tears finally spilled. "Shall always love you."

His eyes turned up to her. How long had he waited to hear those words? She had never given them, not even in jest. At least they finally gave him the strength to let go. She watched his spirit lift, slip upward into the heavens. She pulled down his eyelids and laid his head gently aside. He was one of the valiant; he would go now to the mothering star, to home.

Darke watched, amazed as the twenty or so creatures left alive closed in on the longboat. They could have easily killed these twenty or so on the beach when they first spawned, but now he could see the backs and layers of shielding on them had hardened. They were not yet fully mature, but nearly so. It would be like piercing copper or tin, but the kills would be harder and twenty of them were enough to cause havoc should they reach the boat. Twenty were enough to kill them considering they were only five now, the Daath lying useless, unconscious and Rat of little help without his fire accruements.

"Captain," said an exhausted Storan, wrenching on the looms, his thinning hair matted in sweat. "You think these bastards are actually going to reach us?"

"Possible, my friend."

"Gods's blood, but that is just blessed unfair. The Goddess is just damned unfair in this."

"Hyacinth!"

"Here, Captain."

"The Daath?"

"He is very weak, Captain. Even if I were to wake him, lighting the sword would surely kill him."

Darke nodded.

"So it be," Darke said, "but we are not yet finished. When the bastards reach this boat, we are going to kill them. Understand? All of you hear me? We will slay them like we have slain Etlantians before. We have not, by Elyon's Light, fought this hard and this far to die now."

The thorn beasts had learned to swim so well, they left wakes behind them.

"You got anything in you," Darke said, "either of you, row harder. We will be within missile range of the ship within moments."

"We got no harder, Captain," moaned Storan.

Amazingly, one had reached them. It clawed up the prow post and roared—no more wailing, no more shrieks, this was the hardened roar of a warrior. Darke stepped back to ram his broadsword in and out of the face. The beast dropped away.

A claw suddenly grabbed Fire Rat from behind, jerked him into the water. He was gone with a gulp.

"Damn!" screamed Darke. "Damn it, no! We need the Rat—we will be facing the angel's ship, and we will have no one to man the throwers. I am going after him."

"Captain!" Storan swore bitterly.

But Darke threw aside his long sword, grabbed a short blade, and leapt into the water. Now Storan stood, giving up the oars.

"Elyon look down on us!" Storan cried. "In the name of all we have done, You look down on us now! You will not let this happen!" He ripped his heavy axe from the bottom of the boat. "Damned fool," he muttered, "going after that pitiful creature! I am coming, Captain!" With a warrior's cry, he leapt over the gunwale, hitting the water with a splash.

Danwyar dropped the oar. He stood, staring, not knowing what to do. He understood, unlike the others, there was no chance in the waters with them; they had adapted as water beasts now. "I got two daggers," he said to Hyacinth, taking one from his back. "You?"

"Nothing, Danwyar."

"It has been good knowing you, little witch," he said. He flung the first dagger, no doubt straight and true and took the other from his back sheath, leaving it empty.

Hyacinth finally turned, seized Loch by the temples, and looked deep into his face, his skin pale almost to white. He was nearly dead, and this was likely going to kill him, but there was nothing left for them. They would die anyway. "Arsayalalyur!" she spoke in old tongue.

His eyes flicked open. Hyacinth closed her own, then let herself in him; she bled half her life into his, giving him strength, but she held control of his body. It was pitifully weak, but she was able to move.

Danwyar was about to leap into the waters, do what he could even hand to hand against them, when he saw Hyacinth drop into the bottom of the boat. He watched stunned as slowly, the Daath sat up. He moved strangely, as though the air was dense, but his hand curled about the hilt of the Angelslayer and slowly, with difficulty, he stood. He turned to stare over the side of the ship where the others were fighting in a froth of blood and seawater.

✝

The sea, the sky, everything seemed to be spinning and out of focus. Loch found himself looking over the edge of the boat, incensed with panic. It was not his panic, it was the priestess, she was in him, and not only was she in his thoughts, but she was moving his body, his legs and arms. She had literally given him life, a part of her own life, giving his body strength to move. Briefly he noticed her body lying in the bottom of the boat, near Taran. She looked dead, but she was in him; she was searching through his eyes.

There was fighting. As heavy as he and his axe were, Storan was still able to plant it into the head of a beast about to rip open the captain. Darke was stabbing another in the face with a short sword as he clutched the Rat in one hand. Coming at them were a host of the thorn beasts, and they were strong; they would shred all of them like tender meat. The priestess lifted the Angelslayer with both hands wrapped tightly about the hilt. She leveled it off. With a scream, she blew away a monster about to overtake Storan. Loch did not feel the pain; she was blocking it from him, taking it herself somehow.

She searched with the tip of the Angelslayer, showing him there were many, all of them closing at once.

"I cannot do this part," he heard her voice as clearly as if she were standing beside him. "But you must kill them. Kill them all at once, Lochlain! It is all you have left, a single pulse. Do it now! Do it now!"

A hand behind the captain was lifting. Storan was wrestling with another, still clutching his axe.

When the bolt discharged from the tip of Uriel's blade, it was like a sky storm rippling over the waters; it spread outward, separating into lightninglike serpents searching in a dozen or more directions, all at once, simultaneously, they struck every target. Heads exploded with whaps and pops, some with cracks of thunder, explosions blew sprays of sea and blood into the air.

The water was left murky, and there was a smell as though the air itself had just been burnt, but it was over, there were no more; every beast had been utterly destroyed.

Loch had fallen to his knees. He could no longer hold the sword; it had dropped from his hands.

Storan swam for the boat, through foam and ooze. His axe was tossed in and Danwyar helped him over the side. He was shredded with claws and teeth marks, as was Darke. The captain took hold of the gunwale with one hand, then heaved the Rat over the side and pulled himself over last.

Storan was lying in the bottom awash in seawater and blood, so tired he could do nothing but struggle for breath. Then he saw Danwyar.

"Captain alive?" he muttered, weakly.

Danwyar didn't answer at first; he looked to Darke, where the captain had propped himself against the prow post. His chest was an open gash, blood flowing over his stomach and legs. The captain was pale, his eyes barely focused; his life was spilling out of him.

"I said, is the captain alive?!" Storan repeated, forcefully.

"Yes," Danwyar said, though it would not be for long.

Danwyar then watched amazed as the Daath slowly, painfully crawled toward Darke as if he were struggling through terrible pain. He slowly lifted the sword. He was so weak; the sword was shaking, trembling so badly he could barely hold it. Still, he laid it over the captain's bloodied chest wound.

"Oh, Captain . . ." her small voice whispered inside Loch's head. She then spoke words he did not understand, a binding spell of her own language, but she sent it through the sword. A gentle energy trundled down his arm, but when it touched the blade it surged, and for a second the blade came alive, as brilliant as the sun, then died down to glass crystal. Darke's body was jolted, but when Hyacinth lowered the sword, the wound left as only a scar across his chest, completely healed.

Loch's head and body, in every muscle and sinew, every joint, even his skin, was simmering in waves of pain. He would have screamed except his body was not his own. The priestess finally dropped the sword. She crawled back to kneel over her own body. "Like this," she whispered inside him, touching his fingers to either side of her face, against the temples. "Like this, Loch, you and I, one. We were one beneath the stars. Part of me will always now be you. Pray I live."

A jolt passed through him, and she was gone. She took the terrible pain with her. Her brown eyes flew open and she gasped. The pain was possibly more than she expected. She cried out, arched her back, and clenched her hands into fists. Crouched on one knee, Loch pulled her against him, held her tight. She wrapped one arm weakly about his neck, then fell unconscious. He feared greatly she would die, but she was still breathing, her head lying against his shoulder.

Darke stood.

"She alive?" he asked.

"I think she will live. She gave much of her life to heal you, Captain, and some to heal me too; the little she had saved for herself has left her weak. As well she took the pain—that is why she passed out. If she lives on her own, she should wake with a degree of the moon or less. The pain fades once the sword is still."

"And if she dies?"

"She will not. I will take the sword and die first."

Darke glanced to Danwyar.

The ship was near, closing alongside. A rope ladder tumbled over her starboard side.

"You first, Captain," Danwyar said.

"No," he answered. "The Daath goes first."

Loch glanced at him. He stood, lifting Hyacinth in both arms. He let Danwyar take her. He started up the rope. Danwyar put the priestess over one shoulder and climbed until Loch reached to help him, lifting Hyacinth.

Storan lifted Taran's body, hoisted him up, and climbed the rope. The Fire Rat was next and Darke came last.

Behind them, something was happening to the island. It was falling inward. Huge pieces of its rock were crumbling. The sea had begun to boil about them with waves of steam rising as though they were in a cauldron. The angel wasn't finished.

Chapter Twenty-Eight
Dragon

Darke took grip of a halyard and looked over the starboard beam. They had been moving away from the island at full oars, the beat of the oar master's drum pounding rhythmically and the oars lifting and falling like wings. The island was gone. It had sunk, and the ocean all about was a cauldron, seeping inward. As seawater hit the molten core, a huge, frothing pillar of fire and steam tore upward into the sky, streaming yellow-red.

"Take shields!" Darke screamed.

The heat came at them fierce. Men leapt to the starboard gunwale, ripping shields from where they hung over the edge. Loch lifted one of the oval faces and threw the priestess, now awake but weak, behind him. She had pulled through, but she was barely able to hold to consciousness. Fire hit them. It roared over the deck and passed, striking everything as it did. The Fire Rat stared into it breathless, never lifting a hand to protect himself. His skin was singed, but the hardened scar of his face was hardly affected.

Then it was past.

A pirate dropped, charred and smoking, over the gunwale. Fire Rat staggered, breathless, but his body had somehow adapted to fire. No one knew his origins, perhaps there was some manner of spell binding involved, but fire and the Rat were well acquainted.

From the boiling waters of the hole in the sea, a great wave was rising, rolling outward toward them.

"Hard to lee!" Darke screamed. "Lay into the looms! Stay the mainmast!"

Lines sang as they soared through their staying rings, dropping the mast into its crutch.

Storan took hold of the tilling oar. "Hard over!" he cried, his muscles straining as he brought all his weight against the tilling oar to turn the ship into the current. If the wave took them from the side, they would be swamped.

"Give way starboard oar!" Darke cried.

The command was echoed below. The port oars lifted and swung back. The prow turned about to meet the gathering wave, but the timing was seconds from piercing the wave or sinking. The wave had become a wall of water gaining strength as it rumbled toward them. It was enough to take them. Possibly enough to take them prow-first, toss them like a leaf in the wind.

"Lay hold!" Darke screamed, coiling a rope about his wrist. "Anything you can grab, she will hit us hard!"

Loch curled his arm about a side cleat, and pulled Hyacinth against him, gripping her so tight she could barely breathe.

The serpent head of the prow was defiant as it rode the current, upward, into the center. Dark, purple water; a sheer wall of it. They continued to climb, but the tip of the curl was still far. At one point they were almost completely vertical, near to going over backward. Then the ram pierced a hole beneath the curl and they tore through. The prow soared, as they punched a hole and the wave rolled beneath and over them. For a scant second they were hanging midair. They dropped, steep. The keel hit the sea so hard much of the ship was for seconds underwater. It was almost long enough to take enough sea to sink them, but the blackship broke surface and water gushed from the scuppers. They were undamaged, and nearly everything on the ship was lashed tight, all but men. Loch could see the captain had lost two or three of his crew.

A second wave struck, the prow sending wide sprays to either side as it cut through, water spilling across the decks, but lethal danger was past, the waves were diminishing.

Darke was still on the forecastle, as if all he had faced was a harsh wind.

Beyond, where the island once lay, there was now a wall of steam rising. The blackship spun a moment as the seas calmed and the oars were still laid back. Storan eased off the rudder and lowered himself onto one knee, winded. For the moment direction did not matter; he let the ship turn. What did matter was the helmsman had lost so much blood in battle he was not only weak, but his sight was fading and he was feeling close to fainting.

The wall of steam was slowly fading. In its place was a ship. It was the lord of the choir of Melachim, the seventh of the angel prefects, Satariel.

"Elyon be our armor," Storan whispered weakly.

Darke stepped forward, leaning over the rail near the prow post, amazed to see the angel's ship literally rising out of the sea from the steam of the sunken island.

"To the oars!" he screamed. "Hard into the oars! Helmsmen! Hard about to port! Face that bastard!"

"Damn," Storan hissed, stepping up to lean into the loom of the tiller. "Captain, may I remind you that is a three-tiered Etlantian whore of the sea!"

"I know what she is, helmsman."

The oars of Darke's ship lifted like wings and dug hard into the waters, first spinning them to port, then both sides lifted and pulled the sleek blackship forward with a surge. The pace beat slow at first, to gain direction, then stepped up, the oars keeping pace until they were at full attack speed. The emerald eyes of the serpent's head that was Darke's ram glittered as it rose from the waters, curling back sprays of the sea to either side.

Darke turned to Loch. "Shadow Walker—up here! I want that bastard to see who you are."

Loch glanced to Hyacinth first. "Are you all right, able to hold on yourself?"

"I am fine, Loch, my strength returns quickly. My blood grows stronger each passing moment."

From the forecastle a wind gathered as they pulled through the waters. Loch climbed up to stand beside the captain. He laid his hand on the hilt of his sheathed sword, but offered it no blood. He had learned to control when it took blood and when it didn't.

"Keep her sheathed," Darke said. "It is draining you like bloodletting. Keep her sheathed."

"Through it all, Captain?"

"Aye, what I want the coward to see is you. You have not the strength to contest him."

"The bastard's turning about!" cried Storan.

"I can see that," Darke shouted back.

Loch stared as the painted prow of the huge Etlantian ship turned. It may have been gray and ragged, but it looked imposing and mighty as the distance between them started to narrow.

The oars of the Etlantian lifted with a mechanical motion, three tiers of them, well oiled, moving in unison, up swift, then into the dark waters, taking hold. The Etlantian prow, sheathed in crimson oraculum, surged with the force of the oars, lifting out of the water. Loch could see the dim fire of the throwers flickering through their ports to either side of the Etlantian's bow. From the forecastle, he could see wraithlike figures of giants gathered, holding shields, javelins ready.

"She is three-tiered," shouted Storan. "She will rain down all manner of fire from the sky if we pass her close in!"

"Keep your concerns on holding your course, helmsman."

Darke turned. He looked to Fire Rat standing beside him, watching the approach of the angel's ship with utter awe.

"Light the throwers," Darke said.

The Fire Rat literally gasped with zeal and leapt over the forecastle railing, scrambling through a hatchway. He was about to do the one thing he had lived his entire pitiful life to do.

"Man the catapults!" Darke cried.

"Mothering star, your light be our shield," Storan prayed. "Let us not go alone, good lady; give us your grace and protection."

"Take up shields!" Darke screamed.

"She's coming straight on, Captain!" Storan called.

"I can see that, helmsman."

"Damn it all, but we cannot take her straight on!"

"And she cannot take us. The angel fears his slayer! Danwyar!"

"I am here, Captain!"

"Bring the catapult about! Take out the forecastle and a few of those highborn Nephilim bastards when I give word!"

Fire Rat came from the lower deck, pulling the end ropes of goat bags, black from pitch and oil. He left them beside the catapult and then ran maniacally for more.

The angel's ship was gathering speed, closing fast, peeling back the sea about the prow in frothed curls, moving twice, maybe three times as fast as Darke. She was not a warship. Rather, the angel manned a ship of the line, heavily weighted, yet the sheer muscle behind her three tiers of oars was that of highblood giants, the sons of the angel, centuries old and as skilled as their age. Though Darke's ship was faster, the angel's was heavy and powerful. The ship's bull's-head ram—the ancient symbol of Etlantis, of which the angel was once a prince—lifted from the water like a beast. If it managed to strike Darke's ship, even graze its side, the solid oraculum, with its great horns like mighty spears, would tear anything they caught asunder.

"Daathan, get yourself a shield," Darke said.

"Call me Loch," he answered, sliding his arm through the buckler strap of a large oval shield tossed to him by one of the crew. For a moment Darke met his eye. If their circumstance was uncertain, the bond they had formed of mutual respect had overcome it.

As the distance closed, the Etlantian ship looked huge—a mountain tearing through the sea. It was so close it blocked out the sky, a ship as big as a city closing on them, the drumbeat in its belly hammering with an eerie promise of death waiting. On the high forecastle, giants were manning the prow with spear and arrow and crossbows. Her fire throwers were lit and dripping fire like splats of orange-gold blood hitting the water.

Darke knew he had never faced giants as these. They were every one of them a chosen, everyone a firstborn, all of them a Nephilim. Two hundred sons of the angel. In battles he had faced as many as ten or twelve Nephilim hunting in packs, but here, aboard this ship, were minimally two hundred.

Loch stared at the faces near the prow. One caught his eye and held his gaze, the eyes lit an ice-blue, like stars, the face below the helm weathered and angry. At first Loch had thought this was a Nephilim staring him down as a dare, but suddenly he realized it was the angel himself, Satariel.

"Hard starboard!" Darke cried.

Storan swore and heaved all his weight into the tilling oar, the spikes of his boots digging into the deck. He growled with the effort, the muscles in his neck bulging in cords.

"Lay back and lock port oars!" Darke screamed. In the final seconds, Darke's blackship, far more maneuverable than the angel's, was set to veer sideways, barely slipping past a head on clash.

"Catapult!" Darke cried just as they closed.

Danwyar rode the catapult as his men swung it about. Danwyar aimed the arm hard back to send his weapon almost vertical. He cut the braided torsion ropes just as the two ships closed. He braced against the recoil of the heavy arm as it slammed into the crossbeam. Fire Rat's bags soared high, wobbly, straight up, spreading out. They slammed into the railing and prow post of the forecastle. The strike was dead-on, exploding in a rain of fire, along with the Rat's special mixture of spiked iron balls, spear tips, and twisted, sharpened iron scraps. It sprayed the Nephilim preparing to launch their arrows and spears against Darke's ship as it passed below; it even struck the angel himself. It was deadly and would have taken out a score of ordinary Etlantians, but these were all Nephilim, and few would have dropped. However, the strike did throw their aims into disarray and their missiles went wild, soaring over the ship, striking the sea, the railing, hitting blind and missing nearly all the crew, though one or two cried out, taking hits.

"Shields!" Darke screamed.

The shadow of the angel's ship fell over them. With a mighty roar the fire-throwers off the Etlantian's bow exploded in a blast that curled over the railing and forecastle of Darke's ship. It hit the face of Darke's shield and peeled back as he knelt behind it. Loch used a large oval shield to guard both himself and Hyacinth as they crouched behind it. The heat striking the shield's face burned against the skin of his forearm where he gripped the straps.

Parts of the deck caught flame, but all of Darke's ship was waxed against fire strikes.

Storan screamed, red-faced, heaving all his weight into the tilling oar for the tight swerve while still keeping a shield over one shoulder. The horns of the bull's-head ram were high out of the water, eager to catch his rear, so as soon as the bow cleared the ram he moved his hand to shift and pull away the stern.

Darke wanted his blackship at the very edge of the Etlantian. It was a move they had perfected, but Storan was weakened and it took all he had to maneuver the rudder. Both ships were cutting through the waters at full speed, in a spray of sea.

The blackship barely slipped past the dark red horns of the angel's ram, so close the left horn screeched as it left a scar across the hull near the stern.

Arrows rained thick from the gun ports of the Etlantian ship, and Danwyar dove for the cover of the catapult base. One of his men went down with a scream.

Darke stood, lowering his shield.

As Darke's ship slipped past the bull's ram it purposefully slammed into the lower tier oars of the dragon's port side, snapping their timber, wiping them out with blow after blow of the prow post and port side of the blackship. The pirates were destroying the port oars of Satariel's ship like cutting saplings.

"Loch," he said, "stand, lower your shield, bare yourself."

"Captain," cried Hyacinth, "he will be killed!"

"I think not, I do not believe the angel dares; he fears the sword—fears prophecy."

Loch stepped forward and held his shield to one side. He did draw the Angelslayer and let it take his blood, the blade flashing white-hot.

Red-faced, the veins in his neck standing out, Darke screamed at the angel, "Here is your Slayer, you bastard! You told me to bring him—here he is, Satariel! Kill him yourself!"

From above, the angel's eyes were still following Loch. Loch wasn't sure of the captain's intent, but he did sense Darke's gamble was correct; the angel would hesitate, seeing the sword of Uriel, he was left uncertain. Even from the distance, Loch could see it. In the last second, seeing Satariel make his move, Loch touched the blade against the oval Tarshian shield, leaving its metal simmering with a covering of white fire.

Loch bore into the angel's eyes with his own. It was as if the distance between them had closed. He could clearly see the angel's dark blue eyes, and with his own black and defiant, he used Eryian's teachings and stared back fearless and defiant, body and soul. As the angel lifted his hand, Loch brought the shield about. With a sizzling crack that left an ozone smell, a midnight-blue bolt of light struck the face of the Tarshian shield, but did not pierce through—the Angelslayer's light left it strengthened. But Loch had no chance to return fire. The angel's bolt hit so hard, Loch was thrown into the air. He struck the railing of the starboard bulwark, his skin, his whole body sizzling with energy. He disappeared over the railing's edge.

"No!" Hyacinth screamed and ran for the bulwark.

Darke threw his own shield aside and lifted a javelin. As they passed below the bow of the angel's ship he flung it—not for the angel, he had no hope of slaying an angel, but he chose a firstborn standing next to the Watcher and his spear pierced the giant's throat, below the larynx and out the back of the neck. Even for a Nephilim, it was a lethal blow. The Nephilim arched his back and fell, dropping out of sight.

Hyacinth climbed nearly over the railing, clinging to its side, searching below for Loch. He was there. He hung from a swifter rope with one hand, his sword in the other, but he looked barely conscious. Darke turned to her.

"He is here, alive," she cried. "Someone help!"

"Get the king aboard," Darke commanded. He then screamed below to the Rat. "Fire the throwers!"

Below deck, Fire Rat crouched at the loom of the bellows. He stoked them hard back, and the siphons sucked in seawater where it curled back in against the bow, creating a suction and letting loose a stream of fire from the nozzle of the thrower. The thrower jet extended through a port at the edge of the bow and the Rat had modified it. Unlike most ships, he could swivel the jet, aim it in different directions. Using his feet against the bulwark for leverage, with both hands on the harness he had constructed, Rat angled the jet of fire directly into the hull of the Etlantian ship as they passed only a few feet from the side. The thrower was roaring, and Fire Rat screamed along with it, throwing his head back and using all his strength to keep it centered directly into the heavy strakes of the Etlantian hull. This is what the captain had saved him for, and this is what he would deliver. A flaming scar. If the wood of the angel's ship had not been proofed against fire, it would have burned the entire port side, but the oraculum plating protected the upper wales. Still, a long, deep gash ripped through the side of Satariel's ship; at times it was so focused it pierced the hull, striking rowers who screamed as the naphtha spilled over them.

The hulls of the two ships slammed together with a crack of wood as Darke's oars continued to press from the port side and Storan guided the collisions, timing them. The ships veered apart, but Rat kept the thrower trained on target. His fire cut a straight line of black, curling flame up the side of Satariel's galley.

Hyacinth had cast a rope to Loch. He caught it. He had sheathed the sword, but he was weak, and he could barely hold the line she had thrown. Fearing he might black out, he wrapped it about his waist and curled his wrist through it, as well, so he would not be left hanging as if he were a fish being reeled in.

Hyacinth was trying to pull him up, but all she could do was tug at the line. A muscled Tarshian came to her aid and hauled Loch in.

Loch held as they pulled him up. It was with difficultly that he kept himself conscious. The lightning stroke had ripped through him with paralyzing pain. His skin, everywhere, was still flickered and sparking with tendrils of blue light, burning as they continued to ripple in coils about his arms and chest. He dropped his head back, teeth clenched against the pain.

Belowdecks, Fire Rat screamed as the flames of his own jets were curling back against him in a spray, but the Rat held, both feet, against the wood of the bulwark. He wore hardened, waxed leathers, even a hood protecting his face to the nose, holes for his eyes. The fire bursts curling back on him were burning through most of the leathered armor, searing more of Rat's already scarred flesh, but Rat held. He was in his moment; the searing heat seemed to bring him to life as he screamed, swiveling the jet against the beams opposite.

The hulls separated wide. Storan then threw his weight into the rudder and slammed them back against each other, this time with force. One section of the gunwale of Darke's ship cracked and sent splinters flying. But the fire jets of the Rat had weakened Satariel's hull so badly the blow crushed in a vertical sanction, splitting a hull section, all the way to the waterline. Satariel's ship would take on seawater. It would be quickly repaired, of course, but the angel would from now on know his ship had been pierced through, had taken on sea, and by a mortal. As well, he would never quite erase the blackened, deep scar Rat's throwers had burned through the entire length of his port side.

From the stern, Storan screamed as a javelin lanced through his side. "Too much to ask, my lady," he muttered to himself as the pain burned thorough his side. It wasn't deep, he still held the tilling oar fast, but he continued to complain. "Clawed, eaten, and now lanced—just to let you know, I have not much left in me to keep alive, my lady."

The top of Darke's prow post, with its serpent head and emerald eyes, was sundered by a thick oar of the Etlantian ship. The serpent head spun wide and dropped into the sea.

Darke stepped down from the prow; the two ships were almost past each other. He backed carefully to Hyacinth's side where she sat against the bulwark. Loch was slumped beside her, still conscious. Darke crouched and glanced at the priestess who gave him a hard look in return.

They were finally pulling free of Satariel's ship, and Darke had left her crippled, sundering the port oars. If it were anyone but the angel, he would have circled for a center strike and split the weakened bulwarks open with his ram, but he was certain the firepower would overwhelm him if he tried. He was content for now having crippled a Watcher, a Star Walker, a prefect of the choir. No other mortal in history had done an angel such damage. It wasn't over. The angel would certainly repair and then begin to hunt Darke for all he was worth, but the moment tasted sweet. He had clashed with the three-tiered Etlantian monster, and his blackship had left a scar to always be remembered.

"That was reckless, Captain," Hyacinth scorned, "standing the king in the open to take a full strike of the angel. He could have been killed! What were you thinking?"

"That Satariel fears Uriel's sword like a child fears wraiths of the night."

"What if he had not!"

"Then your Daath would be dead."

Loch looked up. He met Darke's eyes with a half smile.

"What?" queried Darke.

"Just that you remind me of someone, Captain."

"Anyone I know?"

"I would doubt."

Darke nodded. "This was all a study of you, your majesty. He was gathering what he needed to know before he attempted a kill. It is why he has gone to all this trouble, the island, my son as a prop, Euryathides's crew in an attempt to take us out from a distance—the angel was not ready to face you. It was obvious." He glanced to Hyacinth. They were pulling free of the angel's ship. Darke had completely disabled Satariel. Unless he had magick, he wasn't going to follow.

"I see your eyes flash, Little Flower."

"Do you really?"

"He could not have attempted a death strike; he feared Uriel's sword, you would see it in him."

"What I think, Captain, is that you were guessing. All along. This has been nothing more than another bean game to you, and at its end you risked Lochlain's life just on the chance the angel would not kill him!"

"So it is Lochlain now?" Darke said, amused. He stood, watching them pull away from Satariel's wounded ship, watching the Nephilim staring back from the helm as he sailed for deep water, leaving the angel crippled.

"He was in no danger," Darke assured her without looking back. "I have been a gambler all my life—I know when to hold and when to play, and the angel was bluffing, mark me, he was bluffing all along." He sighed, eyes narrowing. "Problem we have now, I think he has finished bluffing. He is not dead and it is for certain he will hunt us. The next time we meet, it will be for the kill, no holds, nothing in reserve. His games are over now." He glanced to Loch. "Is the innate ability to regenerate quickly a Daathan trait?"

"So they say."

"Let us hope, your majesty."

He motioned toward Satariel's ship. "Something we have learned, as well. See there, his ship is crippled, but it appears there is nothing he can do about it. He has no magick to repair the oars and turn about, or he would try to take us not at sea. He has lost many of his powers. He is almost left mortal in many ways. Keep it in mind when next you face him, Daath."

"I will, Captain."

Darke turned and walked away. The fact that Loch's skin was still occasionally sizzled with blue star fire seemed not to bother him, but Hyacinth did not leave Loch's side, and she kept her hand over his forearm where it rested on his thigh, letting the remaining crackles of light spill across her, as well, one of them wrapping up the side of her arm.

"I have never been angry with him before," she said quietly.

"He was right, Hyacinth, he made no wrong moves," Loch answered.

"Hard oar!" Darke cried, stepping up the forecastle railing. "Lift the main mast! We head for home."

The oars unfolded from where they had been laid back against the hull, and hit water in a spray. The mast soared upward, the sail billowing as it was angled to the wind.

Darke's own ship was still ablaze, both midships and the stern where Storan still crouched, hanging off the tilling more than guiding it. But the fires were being extinguished and the torn stay lines replaced.

"Let out the sheet! Bring her in against the wind!" Darke cried. "More speed to the oars; let us put some distance from the bastard."

The oars master stepped up his cadence below, and they were soon moving swiftly through the sea, peeling back white water.

Chapter Twenty-Nine
Hericlon

The bodies in the high passage of Hericlon, near the gate, were at least two weeks old. Rhywder guessed they had fallen here not long after he had left the gate. The smell of rotting flesh was stifling. Rhywder reached forward to touch Satrina's hand as she reined in the horse. It danced, eyes wide.

"Oh, Elyon's grace," Satrina gasped, seeing the death before them.

Rhywder dropped off the horse, drawing his short sword. He circled, studying the fallen. He recognized one body, propped upright against the edge of Hericlon's rock. It was the young captain, Anoric. His face was now stretched, leathered skin, mouth open in an oval wail, the eyes empty shadows.

"Have the Unchurians been here?" Satrina whispered. "The terror spreaders?"

"No. These are weeks dead. More."

"Who killed them, then?"

"I believe they killed each other."

"Why would they do that?"

"I do not know. But we are lucky in one thing; no raiding parties or Unchurian hunters have yet reached the gate. The portcullis is open, and she is manned by dead alone, but she is still ours."

"What do we do now?"

"Simple, we close the damned gate."

He took the reins and walked the horse forward. The dark gray, cyclopean blocks of the Etlantian gate were shadowy and quiet as they passed beneath it. He looked up at the jaws of the portcullis—its line of teeth waiting to drop, aged but flawless, solid oraculum. The garrison's yards were emptied and dark. Rhywder paused, tingling when he saw the winch assembly. There had been terrible slaughter over it. Bodies were literally hacked in pieces and strewn at its base. Rhywder stopped, Satrina beside him.

"I think we are alone. They have fought each other to the last. No survivors."

He studied the heavy, rusted chain stretching to the high portholes of the stone facing. The links of the chain were as large as a man's arm. "We are going to drop the gate."

"Can we do it alone?"

"Gravity will help us."

Rhywder walked slowly about the bodies and hoisted himself onto the winch assembly. The assembly was a large wooden base with complex machinery of great wooden cogs. He saw what had stopped the gate from lowering. An axe blade had been driven into the cogs of the main wheel, between the teeth. The massive wheel had crumpled the axe like thin plate. Rhywder looked up, following the line of the heavy chain.

"This will not be easy," he muttered. "We are going to have to slacken the chain enough to pull this axe free. Come up here, Satrina."

Rhywder studied the platform carefully. The torsion bearings were still holding. To lower the gate slowly, it normally took three men manning the winch handle, since it was built for an ancient giant, but Rhywder only had to pull it back enough to lift weight off the axe keeping the rest of the teeth from shearing away.

He spat on his hands and slid his palms around one link, taking hold. Satrina had pulled herself up onto the platform and took position beside him.

"When I tell you to pull that axe head out, pull it! Then get clear quickly, this thing may lose control."

"But how can you lift the gate, Rhywder? It is not very heavy."

"It is. But I am very strong."

Rhywder braced himself, slammed his boots against the sanctions to either side and putting all his strength into the release lever. He wrenched back with everything he had, every muscle in his body, both feet braced for leverage. He threw his head back, his teeth clenched. The muscles of his arms bulged, the cords of his neck strained like cables, his face red. One cog began to lift, slowly. He screamed, pulling harder—all he had left, but the axe blade shivered.

Satrina sprang forward and grabbed the broken stub of the axe haft just as Rhywder's feet slipped. The heavy, ironclad wheel slammed back down with a thud and instantly the teeth of the cog wheels sheared as it spun, the full weight of Hericlon's portcullis ripping it to pieces.

Rhywder tackled Satrina, and they went over the edge of the platform.

As the portcullis of Hericlon fell, its metal pulleys within the stone screamed, the chain tearing across it in full flight. The portcullis dropped with a warm wind, gaining momentum.

When it hit, the earth rippled in response. Rhywder looked up. The bottom bar of the portcullis was driven hard into the earth; small mounds of rubble were thrown up and the spikes had buried themselves deep, all the way to the first crossbeam. The chain was still clattering inside the winch assembly.

He stood and helped her to her feet.

"Oh, no," she muttered.

"What?"

She pointed.

The horse was dancing, nervous—on the other side of the bars.

"Damn!" Rhywder swore. "Why did you let him leave on that side!"

"Me?"

"You are the one has a relationship with him! Calling him over, here horse, come horse. Why not tell him to stay on this side of damned gate?"

"You talked to him first, why did you not tell him!"

"Because I was lifting a three-ton portcullis!"

"You cannot lift three tons, Rhywder."

"Well, I did!"

"You used the levers. Do you think I am an idiot?"

"One of us is an idiot because now we no longer have a horse!"

She arched a brow. "Technically we still have him. We just cannot use him."

"He will be eaten by nightfall." Rhywder paused now to give her a proper, warning glance, but it had no effect at all. "You know, for a woman, you have a rather sharp tongue."

"And you can say that with certainty, can you?"

"What do you mean?"

"I am beginning to think you do not have much experience with women."

"I have got experience!"

"Really?"

"Plenty of it."

"And how much silver did all this experience cost?"

"Look, I have had other things occupying me these years, so I give a damn what the cost."

"Obviously."

"And that means something?"

"Everything means something, Rhywder."

"That's enough. No more speaking. We have lost the horse; now we are afoot."

"And it is my fault."

"That is correct. Now be quiet while I think."

"Very well," she answered. "I will stop talking and you can think all night if you want."

He nodded. "All right, then." He stepped back. He turned, stared at the gate. At length he glanced back at her.

"What?" she said. "I am not saying a word!"

"You are watching me."

"You cannot think when I am watching you?" She sighed, frustrated. "Fine." She turned. "I will watch him, then." She stared at a Galaglean whose face was peeling shreds of skin. She shivered from the sight.

"I know what we need," Rhywder said.

"What?"

"What we need is a good fire."

Rhywder and Satrina sat against a wall in the commander's quarters, watching the winch assembly burn through the garrison window. Rhywder had dropped the crossbeam over the door and had thrown a table up against it. He was chewing on a strip of dried meat. He glanced at her, cut off a piece, and offered it.

"I am not hungry."

"Eat it anyway," he said, tossing it into her lap.

He then slid down the wall and eased his head back. Satrina was amazed at how quickly he fell asleep. She guessed that warriors learned how to sleep quickly, anywhere. But she had never been a warrior. She remained for some time watching the winches burn. The fire cast shadowy figures up the side of the canyon wall. She tried the dried leathery meat. It was salty, much like eating a sandal thong, but he was right, she hadn't eaten in a long time.

With morning's light, Rhywder woke her. The winch assembly was ash and charred embers, except for the chain and metal wheels, which were still glowing red. As they stepped into the morning air, it was chill—a winter chill. Below, in the valleys, it was only last harvest, but here it was already cold and bitter.

They began walking down the canyon, the wind following. Morning's light was welcome as it trickled down the jagged walls, but it had no strength.

They had not gone far when Rhywder pulled her aside quickly, drawing them both into shadow. Footfall echoed ahead of them.

Coming up the canyon from the north side were some thirty youth—one of the tribes of Dannu. They wore leather jerkins and thick, fur-wrapped boots. A few axes dangled from wide belts. They were healthy stock, with streaming white hair and sun-darkened skin. Rhywder recognized the features as common to the southern mountain tribes who lived north of Hericlon. He himself had descended from such a tribe, though his tribe had been higher up in the mountain near the famous lake of Lochlain. Rhywder stepped suddenly from the shadow, directly before them.

Soundless they crouched and a number of obsidian-tipped arrows centered on Rhywder. He lifted his hand and offered the sign of the word.

"Calm," he said. "I am a friend."

One of them raised his hand, returning the sign, although somewhat wary. The boy was tall and well built, and despite his youth, his expression was steeled. His hair was long and white, falling over muscled shoulders. "Who are you?" he asked.

"I am kin. I am of the tribe of Lochlain."

"Lochlain—" one of the boys whispered.

"The people of Lochlain were slain by the Eagle of Argolis," the leader said, "none of them live."

"I live. I am the Walker of the Lake, as well as many others. There are a number of king's guard who were Lochlain. You may have heard of me. I am called Rhywder, the Little Fox, the Walker of the Lake." Rhywder tapped his armband—the signet they should all recognize.

The boy gasped. "That is the armband of a Shadow Walker!"

"Correct."

"If you are a Shadow Walker, why are you dressed like this?"

Rhywder was still wearing the horsehair tunic he had fashioned in Satrina's cabin. "My clothes were ripped apart by witches."

There was silence a moment. The leader glanced to the others, then back. "Prove you are the Little Fox or we will kill you."

Rhywder puzzled over that a moment. He stepped back and did a series of agile somersaults. When he finished he waved his arms as an actor might and smiled.

"What?" said the youth. "What was that?"

"Only the Little Fox can do that."

The boys looked about at each other, uncertain.

"Do we believe him, then?" one of them asked.

"We will believe him," the leader said. "He is either who he says he is, or a very poor circus performer. I am going to take him at his word." He then stepped forward, bowing. "I am Ranulf. We are a tribe of Dannu, the mothering goddess of our kindred, if you are Lochlain as you claim."

"You are correct, Ranulf. I am honored to meet you."

"Our seer-speakers commanded us to go to the mountain of Hericlon. We have gathered weapons, and we have come. Mostly, we are good with the bow, but we can use sword and shield, as well."

Rhywder studied them.

"And you are young."

"Our elders are slain. Monsters, Failures of the giants. Most of our fathers had died fighting them. We are all that is left but the women and little ones who are left hoping we find what is killing us before they strike again. They seem to come for blood, to drink our blood. My queen believes they are coming through the gate unimpeded."

"They were. But Hericlon is now a fortress; the portcullis is dropped and will not rise again for a long stretch of time. I will take command of you boys. You, the speaker, Ranulf, I name you captain. Now come, we are going to defend the gate of Hericlon against the coming of the worst of your nightmares and beyond. We will not be bored. And before we die, we may learn something."

They had been warned by their high priest, and by the look of their faces, many had already been told the cost might include their lives, yet they had come, for behind them were their mothers and younger brothers and sisters, all they had. They tensed suddenly, angling their bows upon Satrina as she stepped from the shadows. The bows slowly lowered. The leader stared, amazed.

"This is Satrina," Rhywder said.

The boy bowed. "My lady," he said reverently.

"She is no lady," said Rhywder. "Just a plodder's wife."

"I am nobody's wife, Rhywder."

"You mean—but what about the plodder?"

"He purchased my deed for one year. I was his cook."

"Deed! By Elyon's name, are you saying you were a slave?"

She shrugged. "I was a slave. Now I am . . . with you. Free, I suppose. I doubt Lamech still holds my bond."

"How did a woman like you come to be a slave?"

"To pay off my father's gambling debts. He lost a few too many bean games. He faced one year's servitude, so he traded me to the Pelegasians. The plodder found me on the blocks in Ishmia when he came for his yearly supplies."

"And the fool hired you as a cook?"

"Why not? I cook well."

"Just, well, let us say if it had been me, cooking would not have been my first thought in making your purchase."

"Of course. I suppose you 'purchase' quite a few women, do you not, Little Fox?"

"There is that sharp tongue on you again."

"I keep it in my mouth for arrogant types like you. And what exactly leads you to believe I am not a lady? I could have been a lady. What if my father was a big fat lord?"

"If he were a big fat lord, he should have been able to pay off his bean game debts."

"He could have been playing with other big fat lords. Very highly regarded bean games, wagering everything they had—horses, castles, daughters who are fine young ladies—"

"For the love of frogs, I cannot believe I am standing here in the very shadows of Hericlon's vale with an Unchurian army breathing down my ass debating whether lords play highly wagered bean games. I think you are the most unnerving woman I have ever met."

"For a Shadow Walker, you are rather easily unnerved, are you not?"

"All right, that is quite enough."

"Is it?"

"Yes, besides, we are here as an example to these boys. So enough from you. Not another word, understand?" She started to speak, but he stepped closer. "Not *another* word." He waited, daring her. Satrina only batted her pretty eyes. "Good. Now—go stand over there."

She backed up. "Here? Oops—a word."

"Just stand back while I talk to these boys. They have journeyed a long ways; they no doubt have questions and do not need a woman confusing things."

She backed to the wall.

"Good, that will do."

She nodded.

"All right then. Now . . ." Rhywder turned and composed himself. It was only then he realized the youth had all been watching, intrigued. "Ignore her,"

Rhywder commanded. "Just pay her no attention. Understand?"

"Yes, my lord," Ranulf answered for the others.

"And for Elyon's name, do not ask her questions!"

"Yes, sir."

"Now, how many are you?"

"We are thirty, my lord."

"Thirty. Horses? Any with horses?"

The boy turned, motioning. From the rear, one led two horses by the reins.

Rhywder nodded. "Two. You have brought two horses?"

"They—the monsters, they killed a lot of the horses. Most we left with our mothers in case we fail and they must flee the village."

"I see."

Rhywder looked back down the canyon. The wind moaned out of it, threatening, and the boys of the village stared down its shadows, uneasy.

"What am I to call you boys?"

"We are Kerrigans. Our people are the tribe of Kerrigan, once a great king."

"Well, Kerrigans, your seer-speaker knew the stars well. The gate was in danger and was left open, letting unnamed evil through from the south. We are going to stop that from happening for now. Sooner or later we are bound to have all sorts of company—either from the south or the Galagleans reaching us from the north."

"The Galagleans are coming?"

"If Elyon has been kind, they are."

Chapter Thirty

Firstling

When Quietus had crossed the river Ithen, he had his priest find a stone for sacrifice. The air was chill for being so early in the season, and the Falcon could see his breath as his men gathered about. The firstling fought the priest, which Quietus considered good. The priest's cowl fell back as he caught the head and wrenched upward, cutting the throat sharply with an onyx blade.

Marcian watched, unemotional. They were on high ground now. The tips of pines covered the distant valley.

"By the lords of the seventh star," the priest cried, "and through the blood of kings, give us this hour!" The priest lifted a goblet of blood. It steamed in the cool air. Quietus stepped forward and brought the cup to his lips. Such offerings were considered pagan by the Daath and even the other tribes of Dannu, who were Followers as a rule. But this was ancient tradition of one of the greatest of all kinds, and Quietus drank heavily, then turned and offered it to his captains. He watched as they drank. He watched Marcian as he lifted the cup, knowing that Marcian was, like his young wife, now one of the Followers of Enoch. But he drank as the others did, taking strength into his marrow. Still, Quietus sensed something amiss in the Captain of the Horsemen. Antiope was hiding something.

The fire was seeded with oblation of the calf's blood. The meat would be divided among the captains. It was time for bloodletting, even if it was to be the primitive Unchurian villagers of the south. A hunt was welcome—vengeance of any fallen Galagleans was welcome, as well.

"Release the herald," Quietus said.

"Aye, my lord," said the priest. He lifted the black cage of the falcon. The bird within waited with dark eyes for the latch to fall and then dutifully stepped onto Quietus's arm. Quietus stroked the neck.

"Let them know I am come," he whispered.

The wings unfolded and with a screech, the bird circled into the chill air.

Chapter Thirty-One
Messenger

Rhywder strode along the causeway, studying the cleft of the canyon beyond. He turned and watched a corpse rise from the causeway rock, lashed about a briarwood stake, rotted hands tied to a javelin haft, the breastplate and helmet covering most of the dried or rotted skin. In the towers, skeletal archers searched the canyon with what seemed intent and purpose. The blue cloaks of the Galagleans waved in the canyon winds once more; the causeway looked well manned.

As Rhywder paced, he noticed Satrina catch up to walk beside him. He tried to ignore her—not that he did not like her company; he had, in fact, begun to discover an unnerving fondness for her—but right now he was on watch, with the southern passage to focus on, and for some reason, this woman seemed able to unhinge his focus with little effort.

"See any Unchurians?" she asked.

"Our lives are hanging by a thin cord and you sound as if we might be strolling a marketplace."

"Not really. I dread going to market." She lifted a wineskin from her shoulder. "Like some mead?"

He paused, uncertain.

"It is garrison stock," she said. "Strange ways these Galagleans have. There are barrels of it—no wine, love of Elyon, not even water barrels—just barley and endless kegs of this soupy, sour mead."

"You make it sound so appealing." He snatched the skin, and tossed it to one of the youths, who caught it, startled.

"Have a drink," he told the boy, then turned back to her. "Now—if you would, Satrina, I would like you to return to the garrison."

"Why?"

"I am not used to giving reasons when I ask something of someone."

"Even a woman? You order women around, as well?"

"I give orders because it is my calling and my rank."

"*Rank* is a good word for this task; the smell up here is overpowering."

"Satrina, a number of these boys are observing."

"And? This means?"

"They need to know I am their commander—that I *command*, you get my meaning?"

"Sorry, Rhywder, boys or no, you do not yet command me. Besides, there is nothing whatsoever to do down there."

"And you think there will be something to do up here?"

"You are up here."

"What does that have to do with anything?"

"At least there is someone to talk to over the age of ten and six. This passage is quiet enough, nothing out there at all. Why would you not have time to talk a bit?"

"The Unchurians are eventually going to attempt to take this gate."

"Ah, which explains the reason for this overwhelming smell of all the week-old corpses; you are attempting to fool anyone coming from the south."

"And attempting to make us look more frightening than we actually are—you, me and thirty youth whose oldest, the captain, is ten and eight."

She glanced at the skeletal half-fleshed faces of the Galagleans. "Frightening they are, Rhywder, especially if the Unchurian have keen eyesight."

"The idea, actually, is to appear more numerous. They are meant to look alive, Satrina."

"More makeup. Maybe some wigs. You have little skill in theatrical arts, Little Fox?"

"Nor have I needed any."

"Until now. Presently it might prove useful."

"They stand upright; they wield weapons. Good enough for me. The passage is eighty feet below us."

"Good, as well—and lucky for us the wind is coming from the south and not toward it."

"Yes, all good things. Now, if you carefully consider my objective of convincing anyone approaching from the south the gate is still held by the Galagleans, then you would understand without my having to explain it that a woman up here chatting with them is not helpful."

"That is utterly silly. Galagleans do not cohabit with women? Is that what you are saying? I have never met a Galaglean turn down the opportunity to spend time with a woman, and I have known not a few of them in my day."

"I am saying they do not train women to man their battlements."

"Who would think I am here to man the battlements? Perhaps I am here for amusement, some company. Could get lonely up here, truth be spoken; this passage is the most god-awful place I have ever been to. Who thought it up?"

"Etlantians, and they created it for the purpose of life over death, with life the preference—and pray Elyon we are granted such a preference."

"You pray to Elyon?"

"I did not say that."

"Yes, you did."

"Satrina—"

"And as for having a woman up here, we could ask these strong silent types who are losing most of their skin, and if they could answer, I seriously doubt they would mind my being here at all."

"If you were to ask and they were able to answer, they could explain what women are good for: raising children, cooking—your specialty worth an entire year's gambling debt—cleaning up, and otherwise keeping to themselves."

"You forgot something the Galagleans would have placed at the top of their list."

"That, as well—but there are young lads about."

"Rhywder, you do not know the first thing about women. Not in the slightest. Why bother even trying to fool me?"

"I am not trying to fool you. I am trying to fool the Unchurians, and if they see you standing here chatting, it could compromise everything I have been working on all morning. You think it was easy getting these bastards to look deadly?"

"Did you say dead or deadly?"

"Satrina—"

"Besides, I have spent time in military outposts, and I am not as innocent as you assume. Your idea is just silly. These poor creatures were once full-blooded Galaglean. I assure you they would not give a damn about a woman disturbing their 'battlements.' In fact, they would be trading rude jokes and having a good laugh. Likely, they would ask me to dance. Do you want me to dance for realism's sake, since that is your objective?"

The boys at the archer ports waited, eager for Rhywder's answer.

"No."

"Really? You have not seen me dance. I am quite good, you know. And look about, some of these guardians of the gate still have active flesh and blood. Let us ask them. Boys, have you ever seen a Pelegasian bar dance?"

Out of fear of Rhywder, most of them did not answer, but one of them to the rear said, "No, ma'am, we have never seen a bar dance."

"We have never seen a bar," another added.

"Then I think you should be treated to a dance. What do you think, boys?"

They could not hide their answer, despite Rhywder's grim look.

"Here we go then," Satrina said. "I will need some clapping, pretend there is music, some flutes, a lyre or two, even a barrel drum. Ready? Let's clap now." She started them off leading them in cadence before Rhywder could complain.

Legs kicking high, spinning as her skirt swirled, Satrina did a lively Pelegasian bar dance, of which Rhywder had seen many. She lacked a bar to be on top of, but she was not at all lack for legs or cleavage, and even Rhywder had to admit she was an excellent bar dancer, perhaps one with a little too much experience, leaving Rhywder to wonder even further about her past. A cook, a dancer as good as any well-tuned harlot, a rich gambling lord for a father, and a face as innocent as fresh rain. Then there was her sharp tongue and an accent indicating she was well schooled, probably raised in the upper quarters of a larger city, either Etlantis or Terith-Aire. She was no village girl. The boys were breathless as she lifted her skirt to kick her legs high with a yelp that would have brought heavy howling and applause in a good dockside tavern.

"You have to be in a big bar," she said to the boys, "packed with lots of smelly Pelegasians and merchants who have been stuck at sea for whole counts of the moon without sight of a woman. By now there would be cheering and clapping and I'd have coins all about my feet to collect later. Fact is," she added with a spin, "if these fellows propped on sticks did not have their faces rotting off, they'd be banging their shields and stomping their feet in time with your clapping." She glanced to Rhywder. "Even here on the battlements," she added.

"You have made your point," Rhywder said calmly. "I suggest you stop before these poor boys are unable to sleep for a week."

Satrina stopped the dance with a last twirl and stared at Rhywder, grinning with her hands on her hips.

"Where exactly are you from?" he asked.

"My father was a lord of the mother city. He raised his fortune selling tapestry hangings, the best you could find in all the Western Sea."

"A rich father, yet you dance like a—"

She waited for his wording, since he was so sensitive of his "lads."

"Like a well-trained dancer."

"I have had to make my way using all my talents, Rhywder. As I said, my father was a hopeless gambler and unskilled at it, as well." She glanced at one of the corpses. "You know, the smell here is just too much. I suppose I will return to the garrison. When should I expect you?"

"Expect me?"

"Back, to your captain's quarters, which I have cleaned and which smells vastly the opposite of this causeway battlement."

"I would tell you if I knew."

"Gets awfully boring down there. Tell you what, answer me a few questions and I might feel more satisfied about leaving, giving you some things to think over."

"About me?"

"Of course."

"Why do you want to know about me?"

"I like you."

There were snickers. They were, after all, just kids.

"You actually want me to answer questions?"

"Yes. Questions I think up."

"And then you will leave?"

"You and your decaying troops can guard over the passage without a woman in sight."

"Very well, I will grant you two questions."

"Three."

"Fine. Three."

She paused, thinking. "All right. First question. Have you ever had a lover? And I do not mean some hired bar wench at the end of a hard day—I mean an actual lover whom you spent more than a night with?"

"And this is relevant because?"

"Because it is my first question."

"If you must know, I like women. I like them a lot. Life would be a damned sight less bearable without them. But as for being attached to one—and boys, since you are all listening—not advised. They tend to be clingy. Start thinking they can tell you what to do, how much you can drink, how long you can stay out at night. That sort of thing. Not recommended, lads."

"So the answer is no?"

"Yes, the answer is no."

"Okay, second question—I have three, correct?"

"You do."

"Tell me about your mother."

"Her, I lost her when I was young. I cannot remember her face." Rhywder paused as a gust of wind caught and swelled from the south. He sniffed it for Unchurian scent. "I used to think I missed her, but how could that be? I was only six. I cannot even remember her name."

"That is sad."

"Yes, it is sad. One more and you are out of questions. Use it wisely, Satrina."

"I will. Let me think. Ah, last question: how do you feel about children?"

"I dislike children."

She sighed. "I am certain that is a lie, Rhywder."

"I am not lying, I am telling you straight out. I dislike children."

"No, I think you like them just fine, in fact, on occasion, visiting some married friend, I image you playing with them. You have, have you not? Tossed the ball. Chased hoops. Deny it, swearing honestly as you are."

"I have not sworn anything."

"Well—are you denying it or not?"

"Very well, on occasion I put up with them. But I have limited patience. So then, all out of questions now."

"Guess I am."

"You are."

"Guess I will leave then."

"Good-bye, Satrina, it has been nice talking."

"Really?"

"I suppose it has. Let us not make it a habit, however, particularly on the battlements."

"All right."

She walked backward a moment, smiling, then turned for the stairways. Rhywder watched her leave, watched her walk, the way she swayed. Curious creature, she was. More curious than he had encountered in a long while. He found it amazing he had pulled her out of a well in a tiny village of idiotic Galagleans trying to plant crops and wheat in the southern land of the death lord. He was even more surprised she was an Etlantian. There were several human enclaves clustered about the mother city of Etlantis. They were well protected under the care of the Light Bearer for now, but he wondered how long before Enoch's curse would turn on them, as well.

Rhywder looked up at the approach of Ranulf. He had just come up the dark stone stairs from below and seemed pressed with purpose.

"Captain," Ranulf said respectfully.

"Yes?"

"It is a message. A carrier bird. He circled and landed near the stockade where we have drawn in our horses. This was in its leglet."

Rhywder took the tiny scroll and carefully unrolled it. "Was the bird a falcon?"

"Yes, my lord."

"The cook's steward must have reached Galaglea—amazing, though I did give him every chance I could manage. This is the signet of Quietus. He would have sent this dispatch once he had crossed the Ithen. He is close, then. Hear that, lads! Good news—Quietus is on the march. He will drag along at least a full legion."

"How close?" asked Ranulf.

"From the Ithen, a day or perhaps two—depends on whether or not he presses the march. Quietus tends to be excitable. We should expect them soon, which is Elyon's grace. A legion behind this gate, it can hold until Eryian arrives with Daathan troops. Over the fires tonight, we should celebrate, find the best victuals we can manage and perhaps, though you are lads, drain a bit of this Galaglean grog. If Eryian reaches Hericlon with Daath, we will hold through winter. There could be no better news."

"I think the mountain will ice early this year, my lord," Ranulf responded. "There are already drifts from the upper peaks."

"That is good, Ranulf. It may just be possible things are not as grim as I imagined. If this turns out well, you boys will be remembered in song, I shall see to it. You are brave making this stand, only thirty of you, sent by your mothers and the seer of your tribe. I will see to it even if I pay the minstrels myself—how you stood to hold the Unchurians in a dreadful hour."

The boys grinned among themselves.

Rhywder suddenly paused, noticing the passage south. "Speak of them," he muttered.

Three horsemen had turned the bend, riding slowly toward the gate, abreast. When they reached the shadow of Hericlon, they stopped. They were Unchurian. The center rider was a highborn, the hair black but for a streak of brilliant silver down the left side. A horse snorted, shaking its mane; the bridle clattered with a faint echo. They were firstborn, all of them possibly Nephilim of the death lord, not giants, but centuries old and deadly at their craft. Why send three such deadly killers? Rhywder did not like the smell of this at all. He searched the passage beyond, but it was quiet.

The highborn to the right bore shoulder brooches fashioned in salamander heads—perhaps a captain. It seemed reckless to Rhywder; the Unchurian must have been unaware he was manning the causeway presently. The handsome Nephilim slowly raised his right hand. His palm spread in the sign of the word—which Rhywder found too offensive to dismiss. It was the signet of Elyon's grace and light. The hand of an Unchurian mocked it. Rhywder curled back his lip, temper rising. When Ranulf started to lift his hand in answer, Rhywder caught his wrist sharply, pulling it down.

Rhywder whispered through tight teeth. "Have one of your archers kill him—the one who made the sign of the word."

"Sir!"

"Do it! Now!"

Ranulf turned, nodded toward the right tower. In it, one of the youths stood. He was tall and slender, and Rhywder had given him a Galaglean cloak. He leveled his bow. The arrow whistled soundless and pierced the Unchurian's breastplate with a *whrang*. The Unchurian swayed, but kept in his saddle, so the youth, obeying orders, sank two more shafts. Finally the captain fell to lie facedown in the dirt, the tips of arrow shafts pushed out his back plate. Wind blew his dark cloak over the back of his head.

The second highborn stared down at his captain's body. He looked back up. "We came in peace!" the Unchurian shouted. "Even offering the sign of greeting!"

"I have witnessed your greetings firsthand, highborn. Tell your death lord he can drink my piss!"

He spoke quietly to Ranulf. "Now the one on the left."

Ranulf grimaced, but nodded to the same archer. The boy's arrow sang once more, his mark this time through the neck, taking out the horseman quickly.

"Stay away from my gate!" Rhywder shouted at the last Unchurian.

The Unchurian circled his spooked horse to keep it in rein. "Ah, your gate. We are coming for your gate! Here, you mark the path of the sun. When it has passed the shadow of the canyon, your gate will be ours. I thank you for your offer of piss, however, my lord Azazel prefers flesh—which we will take." He rose in the saddle. "And you," he said, pointing to Ranulf, "you boy, shall be the first."

He then twisted hard on the reins and galloped away. Ranulf shuddered, backing away from the edge. There was a faint whistle and suddenly, as though someone had yanked him from behind, Ranulf jerked from a tug at his neck. He staggered, off balance, and dropped over an archer's port.

He heard Satrina scream. She had just come up the stairs again.

He ran for her. An arrow struck the stone near his foot; he felt the spark of the arrow's iron tip. He grabbed Satrina, jerking her into a run, then threw her and dove beside her to the cover of the causeway wall. A second arrow whispered past as he did.

"What are you doing here! You said you were returning to the garrison!" he shouted.

"I . . . I was coming to . . ." she paused, wordless, staring at the bloodstain left strewn across the stone where Ranulf had been hit. "They killed that boy, Rhywder."

"They intend to kill more than him," Rhywder said, holding her close against him by one arm. He searched upward. It was almost impossible to see where the arrows were coming from. The rock above them was sheer, but an archer had apparently scaled it from the southern side and found a pocket in which to hide.

The siege had begun.

Chapter Thirty-Two

Against the wall!" Rhywder cried. The youths scrambled. An arrow sank into the head of a Galaglean corpse, through the visor, and Rhywder stared, amazed as the briarwood stand wobbled, then toppled over. The corpse lay on its side against the rock. Rhywder held his breath. A second arrow buried itself into another propped-up Galaglean in the tower. The corpse shivered, then stilled, still standing. Before a breath, another arrow passed through the ribs and skittered up the rock of Hericlon. Then a third and then nothing. Other Galagleans were clearly in view, but the archer was no longer taking dummy bait.

"Damn," Rhywder swore. He paused, then glanced to Satrina. "Listen to me, Satrina. I am going to draw out his fire. When I do, you run for it. Take the west stairway; it is the most hidden from above. When you get to the courtyard, find a horse and ride north. You have got to find Quietus. The Galagleans are close. We will hold as long as we can, but you need to tell the Falcon the Unchurians are coming and we are going to need help, as fast as he can move his men and horses."

"Rhywder . . ."

"For the love of Elyon, Satrina, this is no time to argue! When the time comes, you run! Do as I say!"

She nodded, swallowing.

Rhywder glanced to the left and right. The youths were pressed against the stone.

Rhywder crept slowly along the wall, Satrina following, until he was close enough to speak to the boy in the west tower, the archer who had taken mark at Ranulf's order. The boy was not much past ten and four years.

"Your name?"

"Aedan."

"You know these rocks very well, Aedan?"

"I know Hericlon as well as any rock, my lord."

"Can you climb?"

"Yes, my lord."

"That dagger in your belt—can you use it?"

"I can, my lord."

"As you may have guessed, there is an archer in those rocks, somewhere straight above us. I want you to climb up there and kill him, Aedan."

The boy nodded. He stepped back, then looked up, through the tower port. Hericlon's side was smooth rock, there were few handholds, but Aedan laid his bow aside, then lifted off the quiver and set it aside, as well. Clearly he was frightened, his hands trembling, but without hesitation, he stepped off onto the edge of the tower, found a hold on a fissure of rock, then began to climb, slowly.

Rhywder remained crouched against the battlement. He lifted a large, oval Galaglean shield. Its face was pierced, a hole torn through the bronze plate.

"Listen to me!" he shouted to the other youths. "I am going to draw fire from above. Mark the path of the arrows, especially any of you to the east. He is somewhere on the western cliffside, so look for a cove, an outcropping of rock, something he is able to crouch on. When I give the word, fire back in force. The girl has to reach the canyon alive. The archer up there will try to prevent that from happening."

He turned. Satrina was close, waiting.

"You keep moving," he said. "Do not stop, not an instant, not for anything."

"How can I just leave you here, Rhywder?"

"That is not important any longer. If this gate falls, Satrina, we will all die—the cities, the villages—all our people. You have got to find Quietus; nothing else matters."

"I will find him, then. But you, you just stay alive, Rhywder."

Rhywder slid his hand through the leather arm brace behind the shield and glanced over his shoulder to the sky. "Satrina," he said, softer, "I want you to know . . ." He paused, then caught her eyes for a moment. "I want you to know I have liked you better than I have liked most women."

She stared back a moment, touched a finger to his cheek. "And I have liked you better than I have liked most women, too, Rhywder."

Rhywder half-smiled but then grew serious. "Elyon's faith be with you, Satrina. Godspeed!"

"I will be back, Rhywder. Stay alive."

"Aye."

Rhywder drew a breath and stepped into the light. He turned and quickly brought the shield upward. An arrow thunked into the wood of the shield's face. Satrina gasped.

"Picked a good spot," Rhywder shouted upward at the rock face of Hericlon. "I cannot see you at all. Hidden yourself well, have you not? Care to introduce yourself?" Rhywder lowered the shield, taunting him. The arrow came out of the black rock itself, from shadows. Rhywder spun sideways, angling the shield, making it appear as though he were catching arrow for sport.

"Take mark, lads," he said, watching the rock. "Watch for his next dart—then make your guess and stagger your shots, keep your fire steady from wherever you see his arrow fly."

No sooner had he spoken than another bolt skittered past his leg. The young archers turned, crouched, still keeping close to the battlements, and began to fire upward.

"Now, Satrina! Run!"

Rhywder then threw open both arms, baring himself, and started dancing backward across the causeway.

"Right here, you eagle-eyed son of a whore! Here I be!"

An arrow whispered death past his ear. Rhywder kept dancing backward, as though there might be music. He even started to sing.

"Oh, my mother were a tavern wench, and my father were a bastard's son!" An arrow kissed the skin of his thigh as it passed. "His thirst one night he came to quench and I was made 'fore the day was done!"

The youth's arrows were dissolving everywhere into the rock above.

"Run, Satrina! Run!"

An arrow came whispering straight and true, and Rhywder spun to catch it in the face of the shield. Its tip wedged through, intent on reaching his head. This time, Rhywder had seen the path.

"He is left of the sun!" Rhywder cried. "The high ledge a degree left of the sun almost exactly midway up! You can see the darkness he crouches in, a cavern!"

Another arrow flew, but this was not aimed for Rhywder. It angled against the side in a steep shot for Satrina, who had now reached the stairway and leapt down it, hair flying.

"Hey!" Rhywder shouted, throwing aside the shield. "Forget the girl! Here! I am naked! Prime meat! Take me out, you suckile frog!" Rhywder couldn't dodge the next shot. He hit the stone rolling, but the arrow still caught his side. The shaft snapped in him as he rolled over it.

"Bitch," he hissed, backing into the cover of the causeway edge. He scrambled to squat and quickly ripped the broken tip free. Flinging it, he scanned the wound. It was a lucky graze. It would burn, but it wasn't deep enough to cause much trouble. "Any more holes in me," he said to a youth nearby, "I will soon leak like a badly sown Galaglean mead skin." He used his short sword to cut away a strip from his horsehair tunic. "You get a hole in your leathers, last person you want stitching it would be a Galaglean. But if the bastard ever offers to cook you up a pig, do not turn down the offer. They make good pig." Rhywder cinched the tie about his wound.

The boy said quietly, "We are not to be leaving this causeway this day, are we, Captain?"

"Never toss the first stone on your grave, boy. Leave that for the ravens."

Rhywder checked the angle of the sun. Daylight was closing. In the narrow passage, it would come early. If the Unchurians were going to make a move, it had to be soon. "Can you hear me, boys?"

Most shouted back.

"I want each of you, for this moment, to think on your mothers. Boys like you, coming here—taking this stand. By Elyon's grace, that kind of mettle . . . your mothers gave you that. Courage."

Rhywder stepped from the edge, circling to grab the shield, and then came to a crouch behind it.

An arrow sang past him, angled over the causeway of the gate.

"It is fathers give us grit and anger, but it is our mothers give us courage," he shouted, dodging another. "We suck it down in our blood from the womb. Without our mothers, we'd all wet ourselves and run like gutter rats right now. You boys be proud."

Another one crossed the causeway in a slant. It was a screamer—the arrow's tip had been borne out, and air whistling shrilly just for its effect on the nerves. Rhywder glanced over the port. Satrina was running for the horses, and the screamer seemed to be searching her by scent—but she was too far now, the shot dropped short.

Rhywder threw the sword aside, quickly brought a bow up, aimed, then fired.

He was not sure if he took mark, but no more arrows came.

Rhywder heard the hoofbeats of Satrina's horse from below as she was clearing the edge of the garrison passage. But there was another sound now, deeper, a rumble.

He turned to the south passage, looking over the causeway. He had seen many things in his time, but this still made him shiver. For a moment he just stared.

"What is it, my lord?" asked one of the lads.

Rhywder glanced at the boy.

"Against the battlements!" Rhywder screamed. He leapt toward the causeway's ports. The young Kerrigans also scrambled to crouch tightly against the gray stone of the ports. They had been well trained. The rumble from the passage grew steadily. Something so heavy they could feel it through the rock of Hericlon's passage. There was a sharp, high-pitched whining, a sound Rhywder could not place, but that made him think of a cat being skinned still alive.

"There is some company on approach, boys." Rhywder shoved proper weapons through his belt. "We have any supper to offer? They have surely been marching all day. Probably be coming hungry."

He paused, catching several of their eyes.

"Well?"

"Aye," answered one. He pulled a silver arrow to a stiff-gut bowstring. "Our mothers would not have us here without sending the Unchurians their supper."

Rhywder let himself laugh aloud.

"Hear that," he screamed, throwing his head back, the muscles in his neck stretched. "You hear that, you mutant bastards! We got supper waiting! Hot and dipped in your favorite sauce!" He spit on the tip of his own first arrow.

There was light, nervous chuckling among the youth.

Rhywder then swallowed against the fear in his gut, and quickly stepped into an archer's port.

Machinery was coming up the passage, into the clearing of the gateway. They were tall towers, so high they were wobbly, with huge wooden wheels cut of massive trees. With the eastern sun going down behind them, they were left high, leaning silhouettes of assault towers, looking any moment as if they might topple, but with so many tiers, they would be able to breach even the gate of Hericlon.

There was a heavy thud against the causeway face. Pebbles bounced, spilling over the ports. A catapult had just sent a heavy rock against the wall, striking it so hard, bits of it were flung over the causeway in a spray of shrapnel.

"We will know Elyon this day, boys. You remember that," he said. Monsters. Everywhere, on the towers. He could see them massed in the upper tiers, miscreants, Failures being sent in as fodder. If only the Unchurians knew there were but thirty lads manning the ports and causeway of Hericlon.

"Make yourselves ready," Rhywder screamed. He pulled the bow taut while there was distance and took out a huge lump of flesh that made no sense, human or animal. It dropped over the edge of the tower, tumbling through the air, just a mass of flesh, here and there an arm or two.

Aedan had inched his way up the rock, using what notches he could find—but now he froze, looking below. In the canyon were towers, siege craft, and massive giants, misshapen beasts of all kinds, except they all bore human skin and faces, some with arms and legs, others grown in ways he had never imagined.

Aedan looked away. He knew there was movement up just below in the crevice he had managed to climb above. The man who called himself the Little Fox had injured the archer, but there was still movement from the narrow crevice, he could still fire down on the causeway, so at least Aedan assured himself his climb had not been for nothing. He drew his dagger, and clamped it in his teeth. He saw the tip of an arrow, angled for the causeway—so close he could almost grab it.

The singing below came up the wall of the canyon like a festival. The human beasts were hollering in a strange song, being led on by drum keepers, so eerie and inhuman it left chills through him. It was as though he were no longer on Earth, but some other planet, some dark and terrible dream.

Aedan moved—he stopped thinking and twisted, spinning full around to drop onto the edge of the crevice, his blade now between his fingers, barely crouched on the crevice edge. His mind only comprehended what happened afterward. The Unchurian was wounded, barely drawing the arrow taut, but he had been trying to hit the captain. Aedan threw his knife, but the Unchurian was quick. The arrow this close just went through Aedan, he hardly felt it, a tug, no more. He caught the edge just before he fell; clinging, he crawled up and over the side, then eased back against the rock. Sitting across from him as though they were pals was the Unchurian with Aedan's knife hilt through his forehead. He looked down at himself. There was a small round hole through his side, leaking blood slowly.

"Ready?" Rhywder shouted.

He glanced down the row of them. Some were speaking their last prayers. Others were weeping outright, but all clutched their weapons, ready.

Rhywder noticed there had been elephants down, driven by winged minions, mounted in great wooden chairs. He had never seen that before. It was a circus coming. There were singers, women dancing naked before the towers, as they slowly rumbled up the canyon, and all of them were singing, the miscreants and mutants hopelessly off-key and mutilating the words, but singing along with the others. The tall towers weaved like drunken sentinels. The

Failures were too stupid to even know why they had been lined in rows at the fronts of the towers.

"Man the ports!" Rhywder cried. "Ready your bows! We will fire on them with all we have. Give their number no mind, it matters not, what matters is that we fight for our kindred this day!"

The youths drew their arrows, ready.

"Fire, let them have it!" cried Rhywder.

The Little Fox and the line of youth all fired arrow after arrow as the big towers closed on them. Their quivers at their sides, they fed their bows quickly.

Things were dropping from the towers—ill-formed giants, Failures, the last generation of Azazel's children.

"Look for the humans," he shouted, "the human-looking ones. Kill them if you see any!"

And Rhywder did. It reminded him of a Daath, the way he moved, turned to aim a catapult. With Rhywder's arrow through his forehead, the Unchurian dropped back and from his catapult seat, arms dangling.

The towers were about to breach.

"Shields!" Rhywder cried, taking one himself, crouching. Many of the Failures were armed with bows. Arrows honed in like insects, quick, spraying everywhere, without aim. One boy cried out, then staggered, screaming. Arrows wrenched him off the stone and literally flung him into the air above the garrison.

"Crossbows!" Rhywder cried.

They quickly lifted loaded crossbows.

"Fire into their faces!"

It was no less than a few feet now. Soon they would be within range to drop the ramps. Rhywder put the bolt through the head of a horseman. The hinges were being dropped away from the gangplanks. He saw one of the Failures howling to the sky, circling a war hammer over his head.

"Behind your shields," Rhywder cried. He took a breath, ignoring the madness in his head from what he had just seen.

"Take up swords!"

He glanced down the line of them, either direction, in the moments that were left.

"They will breach at the ports!" Rhywder shouted over the rumble and drums and singing.

The causeway shook again, hammered by a series of powerful catapult blows. He watched as a gray, square catapult stone sailed overhead, missing the wall. It seemed to tumble slowly though the air as if for a moment time had slowed. There came times to die, and this was one of them.

"We will see the face of Elyon this day, lads, for all of you, all of us, we die valiant. When you reach home, welcome the light! That is what I intend, to kiss the light!"

Another catapult slammed, this one rocking them all. Rhywder angled his sword, crouched.

"On my word—"

The gangplanks fell, slamming onto the ports.

"Attack!"

Rhywder charged the gangplank. He slew. His sword and shield were a blur and when one sword lodged, he drew another. Then an axe. Then a long dagger, and finally the short sword he had been given by Argolis when first he joined the Daath. It was like no other, fashioned after the hilt of Uriel's sword, black ivory laced with silver serpents entwining the cross guards.

The youth were simply slaughtered. He saw one being eaten, lifted, arms and legs dangling as a giant mutation gnawed into his neck and shoulder.

For a time the Little Fox of the Lochlain held them on the gangplank, killed them, slew them like a working day, bodies falling to either side, some monstrous, some not. Finally, when he began to tire, when Rhywder knew it was almost ended, he pulled in the last of his life's energy and screamed, a warrior's cry, a death cry, and slit one final throat.

Chapter Thirty-Three
Galagleans

The Falcon rode at the head of his armies in a chariot pulled by four dark horses. The rich, blue mantle of the Galagleans flew high in the wind. His shoulders and neck were wreathed in black horsehair, and his helm bore rams' horns. They had finally reached the shadow of Hericlon. He had pressed the men to their limit, moving his armies up the valley toward the mountain.

Just behind Quietus were the Champions, mounted veterans scarred of battle, trained in far garrisons, and weaned on the gathering wars. He had always kept the Champions strong. They had never fallen. Quietus did not consider the final surrender of Galaglea a failure of warriors; it was his word, to spare lives, to put an end to madness, though in his head the madness still raged. He hated all Daath with a deep vengeful hatred.

"A woman," one of the Champions shouted, pulling his horse up alongside Quietus's chariot.

"What!"

The Champion pointed a gloved hand. Quietus was amazed. From the mouth of Hericlon's canyon came a lone rider—a girl with long reddish hair and naked legs. Her mount was galloping straight for them. Quietus raised his fist. His Captains called a halt. The Falcon watched in stunned silence as the girl rode up to them. The horse reared as she turned it about.

"Are you are the Falcon?" she cried.

"I am!" Quietus shouted back.

"Attack! Hericlon is under siege!"

She then whipped the reins against the horse's neck, turning back, galloping for the canyon as though she were going to mount the attack without them.

Quietus drew his sword.

"Follow that she-bitch!" he cried, launching his chariot horses. The Champions shouted, drawing weapons, spurning their mounts to fan out at the flanks of their king—fifty horses, bearing down upon the canyon in heavy thunder.

As he saw the Falcon and his Champions began to pull away at full gallop, Marcian Antiope drew his sword and held it high. He was captain of the Second Century Calvary, fifty strong. Though they were called centuries to match the divisions of Galaglean foot legions, the horse were ten cohorts, half-centuries actually, but as did the Daath, they were called centuries. Marcian's column commander circled his mount, waiting to echo his captain's orders.

"Second Century!" Marcian shouted, lifting his sword for those in the rear to see. "Ahead, full charge!"

He leveled the sword, sinking his heels into the sides of his horse. His command was echoed down the line, and the fifty horsemen of the Galaglean's second cavalry, with Marcian in the lead, streamed across the Vale of Tears for Hericlon's passage at full gallop, the formation spreading out to maintain top speed. Marcian could hear something, even beyond the sound of the Champions' hooves. He could hear rumblings from the canyon. It was as though the mountain itself were murmuring.

Marcian, with his swiftest horsemen, the first cohort, began to pull away from the main body, closing the gap between himself and the Champions.

Behind them, the two legions of Galaglea pressed forward at double-march. Quietus, finding a war to engage, had brought all his troops, every veteran, every elite nobleman, every solider and apprentice, down to cadets in training, all the armies of the second largest of Dannu's gathered tribes had been gathered by Quietus for the assault on Hericlon.

Marcian knew the king fully intended to take the battle into the southern jungles to avenge the colonies that had been attacked by the heathen Unchurian. The king believed it would be a quick and simple war, over in weeks, but he relished the thought of returning to battle, even a short one. However, Marcian also knew it made no sense. The villages of Unchurian were small. They actually were heathen, without hardly any relation to their homeland of the south. Marcian, however, knew different. There could be no reason for them to scour the Galaglean settlements and attack the gate of Hericlon. This had to do with the angel of the far southern deserts. It was said the numbers of his children had never been counted. No one had said anything of it, but Marcian knew, his wife had warned him, this was to do with prophecy and it balanced on the thin edge of the ending of all things.

Satrina galloped into the canyon. She clutched the mane, leaning forward, close against the neck, when suddenly, with a scream, something tackled her. She heard a flap of leathery wings, but never really saw what had thrown her over the flanks. She hit, rolling along the side of the canyon wall. She struggled to come to her feet, trying to fight it off, and for a moment saw its face, skeletal, the bone arching above the eyes. It reached a claw and then vanished, sucked beneath the hooves of the mounted Champions of Quietus's cavalry as they swept past. Satrina's own horse was carried away as the Champions passed, as well, their hooves deafening. Satrina had been forgotten, and she pressed herself against the canyon wall for fear of being trampled. They were truly terrible to behold, large men, heavy armor, weapons bristling, their bred horses like beasts of flight.

"Someone take me!" she cried. "Someone take my hand!" She gasped, jerking her hand back, as one of them galloped so close she was almost sucked beneath the hooves to suffer the same fate as the winged beast. She saw the king's chariot, thundering amid his horsemen. He rode in the car like a madman. He had thrown aside his helmet and his long gray hair streamed wild. He was red-faced, his neck muscles stretched like cables as he lashed the whip against his horses.

As Falcon drove his sweating horses, he felt no chill. From beyond, at what must have been the mighty gate, there came a furious roar, a roar of thousands, and though echoed by distance, there was no mistaking the sound. Hericlon had fallen. There was a brief moment when Quietus wondered how it could have been, that if they had taken the gate, it could never have been the village Unchurians of the south, hardly capable of even threatening the Galaglean settlements. It was possible this was actually a full-blown war he was riding into. The thought surged through his veins, leaving him adrenaline-charged.

Suddenly the wind of his advance through the canyon was split by the echoing roar of an unhuman beast. It reared upon hind legs in the pass before them, more than ten feet high. Its head was the face of a man, but there were fifteen, maybe twenty huge, muscled arms groping with clawed fingers.

Falcon's lead horses were thrown into panic. The chariot's harness bar snapped, and the center shaft staved into the earth. The car was thrown forward, slamming into the beast, knocking the animal back. All arms wrapped about both the chariot and Falcon, but the blow had been so solid, the beast fell forward, its gut and chest caved in. Quietus, the king of Galaglea, vanished beneath him.

Insane with fury, the Champions circled and dismounted. They leapt upon the creature and with sword and axe began hacking through bone and blood, tearing a hole through its back. They hacked through flesh and bone until finally they were able to pull Quietus out as if he were being given birth. The Falcon gasped for air, bloodied, covered in visceral guts and flesh. He struggled to his feet, steadied himself a moment, then looked up.

"A horse!" Falcon screamed.

A Champion dismounted, and Falcon took the reins, vaulted into the saddle. He spurred the horse into a gallop, drawing his sword and pointing forward. The Champions fell in at his flanks.

As he rode, Quietus wiped the blood from his eyes. When he turned the final bend of the canyon and the clearing of the garrison court as well as the great gate of Hericlon fell into view, he brought the horse up so sharply, it reared, and the Falcon stared, scarcely believing his eyes.

Men swarmed over Hericlon as though they were ants, as though the gate were no more than an overturned log being consumed by warms of voracious termites. The numbers of them took Falcon's breath. Amazingly, the gate was still closed, though he could see even more of them behind it. In fact, an army waited beyond the gate, trapped behind its thick, oraculum bars. The creatures pouring over the walls were of all shapes and size; they were like rivers of bare white flesh. Falcon twisted the reins and held his sword high.

"Champions!" he cried, then bolted forward, lifting his bloodied sword high. His Champions fanned out beside him in a phalanx. Dull, black iron tips of their lances lowered. They came like a wall of missiles. As they closed, those filling the passageway did not turn in defense, they had no shields to raise, no swords or spears, they were all of the last generation Failures of an angel, and seeing the Falcon charging, they were thrown into panic. Those that found the room to do so fled.

The Champions had passed and Satrina was running. She ran past the carnage of blood and body parts and dead horses. But then she spotted something. It was in the stomach of a huge, horrid creature with seemingly an endless supply of arms. It hung from a shred of skin in the back, near the area of its heart. The hilt was black ivory and about it were intertwined silver serpents. It was Rhywder's short sword.

"No!" she screamed.

She leapt atop the bloodied flesh and wrenched the sword free just as Marcian and the Second Century came about the corner. Marcian halted a moment, for it seemed this girl had brought down this huge creature, pulling a sword out of the heart from behind. She did not look a warrior, and though the creature had been hacked to pieces, the killing blow was obviously hers. It seemed impossible. When she spotted him, the girl did not ask permission; she leapt from the creature's flesh onto the back of Marcian's horse.

"Go!" she shouted. "Go, run!"

Marcian motioned and they thundered onward.

As the garrison fell into view, just as Falcon had done, Marcian paused, turning his horse sideways, dancing a moment, as he stared at the impossible. The Falcon had driven a massive wedge into a virtual wall of flesh and now in close quarters, they were slaying with axe and sword.

Marcian's second, an able warrior named Riuel, pulled up at his side.

"Goddess bless us," Riuel muttered, "I have never seen such a sight."

"It appears we are about to engage heaven's miscarriage!" Marcian cried. "Those are not warriors; they are mostly the last generation of an angel, Failures."

"So it appears, my lord," Riuel said. He turned in his saddle and lifted his sword as a mark. "Second Century! Prepare to engage!"

Marcian locked his cheek guards in place. He slipped his hand through a buckler.

"Hold tight, woman," he said, having no idea who she could be. He leaned forward, drawing his sword, and whispered his horse speed, kicking his heels into its sides. The cavalry of the Second Century Galagleans spread out to either side. They lifted their lances, anchoring them into the saddle sheaths at their horse's flanks, and lowered the heavy iron tips as they closed for the kill. One hundred mounted Galagleans were about to slam into the madness swirling at the bottom of the gate.

The mass of flesh, the seventh generation of the angel, finally began to group at the commands of their officers and rushed the left flank of the Champions, only to find they were being closed on by hundreds of horsemen and even more lances. Screaming, they ran in all directions, and most were slain with lances through their backs.

Marcian's horse drove into the thick of them, and once his lance lodged through a huge creature whose head had no neck, he drew his sword and began to slay from side to side. He cleaved flesh like the gathering of a harvest. None of them fought back. It seemed madness; it was madness. He severed a spine with a clean sweep. The flesh seemed soft, too easily cut—they had no armor, no shields. Behind him, the girl had come to her knees in the saddle, gripping his back plate with one hand as she stabbed at the creatures using a fine, Daathan short sword. She screamed, as fevered as any warrior, but she was no Daath. When his mount reared as it slammed into a wall of massed flesh, Marcian turned in the saddle, barely catching her before she went over the flanks.

Marcian found he had broken off from the others and waded in deep. With twenty horses and the girl, he found himself pressed against the miscreants and turned to see they closed off his rear. They had grown more capable as he neared the gate. Some were armored, and were turning to attack, armed with axe and spear. They were being closed on from all sides.

"Dismount!" Marcian cried.

The horsemen dropped from their mounts and angled swords, using their horses as protection. They drew inward, forming a tight circle, shields out, swords to the side. Marcian threw the girl behind him where she crouched in their center, her short sword, which had slain beasts, angled and bloody.

These were giants, fourth, fifth generation, fairly capable fighters. The game had suddenly shifted. As the giants pressed past the horses, stepping over corpses beneath them, Marcian and his Galagleans fought them back. Though they were seven and ten feet tall, they were not trained warriors. They fought poorly; their only strength was their numbers. For every one killed, two more would appear. To his left, Riuel fought in stance, efficiently slaying anything that drew near, as were Marcian's other men. Amazing, enough had swarmed the passage that the horsemen behind Marcian were now wading through flesh like cutting through jungle to reach him. One of his men grunted, taking a pike through his side. Its tip was barbed and caught in him in the gut, but there were so many he was then jerked back into them and beheaded. They roared as if scoring a victory. One giant wearing a misshapen bronze chest plate as if he had been given a poor man's armor, tore off the Galaglean's blue cloak and waved it for the others to see that the Galagleans could be killed, even by these, the lessers.

Marcian heard the main body of the cavalry coming—the screams of dying as his men were piercing through to reach him. They were the Galaglean captains of the old guard, and they had fought in hard and bitter campaigns. Such memories were not forgotten in a lifetime. They efficiently closed in with thrusting pikes and long swords, cutting a wide path through human flesh. As they reached Marcian, bodies were trampled so thick, the rock of Hericlon's floor could barely been seen, and getting over and past slain debris was a nagging offense. The angel's spawn were braver now, thicker, though no match for the Galaglean warriors who had reached them. The angel had taught them well, however, for they fed themselves to axe and sword, caring nothing that they were being slaughtered, making their slaughter in itself the impediment. Marcian began to feel his skin crawl from it. He had fought valiant battles, but this was madness and it seemed somehow an odd, cruel mockery of war. Even if they were misshapen, even if they were demon spawn, their faces were human, their cries were lanced with pain, and their blood was red.

The he noticed—for the first time—the base of Hericlon's gate. There was a hive of activity. It reminded him of a thick fur of bees swarming over their hives at work. There were hundreds all laboring at once, working on every part of the gate's machinery, rebuilding the winch assembly of the portcullis at an unbelievable pace. Freshly cut pylons were been thrown up and a series of pulleys and cogs were cut on the spot and quickly fitted to bearings. Scraps of cut wood, chunks of discarded beams, were scattered as the assembly rose almost as if it were spellbound magick, as if it were assembling itself. Somehow they had gotten the heaving, thick chains out of the gate's pathways that tunneled deep into the black rock and were threading them into the spokes and cogs and gears, hammering and winching them down into place. The workers were frenzied; they moved as if they were driven mad, as if invisible lashings were driving them at their tasks. They were the size of humans, but their skin was reddish in hue, their hair long and night-black. These were Unchurians, spawn of the angel, but they had not been trained as warriors. They were workers—mechanics, machinists, engineers—and they were moving at a fantastic pace, frantic—it was a frenzy of commotion and movement. Some were crawling on hands and knees over the top supporting beams, tightening the lashing.

His men were fighting about him, continually slaying, but Marcian was searching, trying to tease out the puzzle. Where were the warriors? Where was the core of the legendary Unchurian firstborn of the vast southern desert cities, the uncounted of Du'ldu?

He realized that someone must have utterly destroyed the winch assembly; he even saw trampled ash. It had been burnt to the ground. Someone had tried to ensure the gate would not be raised—someone who had the sense to realize what could come through it. So Marcian looked past the frenzied assembly to the gate of Hericlon, the thick bars of oraculum that was the portcullis, and there he found the prime, the Unchurian firstborn. They were waiting behind the bars, pressed against them, and deep into the passage south were endless numbers of them, enough to tear into the armies of Galaglea, enough to possibly take the legions that were now pressing up at full run from the vale.

Suddenly it all made sense. Instead of sending warriors, once the gate had been taken, the angel had poured workers over the stairways of Hericlon's causeway, hundreds, even thousands. He noticed they had torn apart the housing of the garrison to get wood. He even saw trees being carried hand over hand down the stairway that had been torn from the forested area just past the southern passages. There were enough workers here to build a city in a day. If they finished the assembly and raised the gate, there would be no turning the prime slayers of the angel, the dreaded legendary armies of Du'ldu that no man had seen or encountered in centuries, those who were called the unknowns, trained and equipped by the angel that named and crafted death itself.

Quietus had fought toward the captain's quarters and the housing and stockades. He and his Champions were surrounded by giants, holding them off—pinned back against the rock of Hericlon. He had not even looked toward the gate's machinery on the opposite side of the passage. His Champions were slaughtering, as was their trade, and no doubt the king of Galaglea was shouting on their victory, for he had not yet realized he was slaying a virtually endless supply of fodder the angel had sent against him almost as a joke.

Some riders were ignoring Marcian's commands and moving for the rescue of their king, not realizing that the caliber of their enemy was such that Quietus's Champions, some of the finest slayers in the world, could hold back all day, and into the next without losing a single armored warrior.

"Captain Riuel!" Marcian shouted.

"Sir!"

"The gate! Fight toward the gate! Send word to your captains! Everything we have against the gate assembly! If they raise the portcullis, all the armies of the south will pour through like a flood!"

"But, my lord—Quietus is surrounded!"

"Leave him; he is in no danger! Damn it, man, if they raise that portcullis the slayers of Du'ldu will pour into this chasm and then we will know what it means to be surrounded!"

Riuel himself studied what waited beyond the red metal of the gate.

"That portcullis lifts, we will all die!" Marcian said, driving in the point. "Even the legionaries will be unable to turn them back. They will come like a flood released of the abyss of Ain!"

Marcian lifted himself in the saddle and raised his sword high. "With me! All of you!" he cried. "Against the gate assembly!"

Cohorts of both the first and second commands finally turned to join Marcian. Riuel and his captains echoed the command. Marcian now turned toward the gate, driving forward, slaying in downward arcs and stabs. As the cavalry pushed them back, the Unchurian Failures and workers filling the passage were breaking into utter panic. Most were unarmed and wore no armor; there was only naked flesh but for breechclouts and cotton tunics. They began to scatter before the whispered axe and sword. But even as Marcian made his way toward the assembly, he could see the heavy iron of the portcullis shivering.

They had been working at such a pace, with endless workers, that already the chains were threaded; the cogs and winches were taking hold, the teeth were already turning. What would normally take weeks to reassemble had been rebuilt in half a day. And should they succeed, the prime of the angel's army waited to answer the slaughter of flesh that was being trampled into the garrison rock.

"Elyon's Light," Marcian whispered, for the chain work was moaning with the strain, taking up slack as it was fed into the machinery—the portcullis could begin to rise any moment, and between his men and the platform were a mass of workers, a sheer army of them, a barrier of flesh and bone holding the back the blue cloaks of the cavalry.

"Javelin!" Marcian screamed, turning his mount and lifting his sword as a marker. A cohort of horsemen dropped from their mounts and took up their spears. Marcian leveled his sword, pointing the direction. "The winch assemblage! Stop them now!"

The Galaglean spearmen ran, hoisting javelins, marking their aim, and launching them in an arch. The heavy iron-tipped pikes of the Galaglean ripped into flesh, tore through bodies, dropping workers on all sides. One lanced the worker who was at the winch that wound the thick chain and fed it into the main gears that would raise the portcullis. He disappeared, over the platform's edge, and the portcullis slumped back to the ground.

The assemblage workers had been annihilated; they were but bodies littered, lying in their own blood, spears lancing them. But in mere moments they were soon replaced. From behind, from the stairways, from the side, they swarmed back over the gate works, lifting tools, bolting down armatures. Almost within seconds, tools were once again hammering, wrenches working, strengthening the machine.

"Again!" Marcian cried.

Once more workers were lanced, the spears arching over the flesh between the Galagleans and the platform, then dropping like dark rain, and once again, workers were scattered, pierced, lanced, and thrown back. The work stopped. For heartbeats. And then more and more workers leapt to the platform, now hopping over bodies and slipping in blood, but the hammering and winches began once more working, and a muscled Unchurian laid into the heavy winching beam, rotating the handle, bringing the chains taut against the portcullis. From the opposite side, a second winching handle was in operation, and now both sides were being reeled in at once.

Marcian swore under his breath.

"Take that damned assembly and hold it!" Marcian commanded.

Marcian's horsemen pressed inward, slaying Unchurian fodder, hacking through flesh and bone until the pile of bodies made it difficult for the horses to keep moving.

"Dismount and fight to the platform!" Marcian shouted.

Marcian watched as his men dropped from their horses and, lifting axe and sword, began to carve out a hole through the virtual wall of unarmored flesh as if it were some macabre woodworking project, as if the bone and flesh, the heads rolling, were chips and chunks of wood flying as the cuts were being made. He could almost hear the angel chuckling over it; in fact, he wondered if he did, if above the screams of dying and the wails of utter terror from the unarmed workers, he could not hear a chuckle; as if he were in a tavern where building laughter inevitably followed a good joke.

"Riuel," Marcian said to his second, whose single bladed axe was working from side to side, spraying blood with each strike.

"My lord," Riuel shouted back. His face was covered in blood such that at times he had to wipe the gloved gauntlets over his eyes to clear them.

"Make sure all commanders understand! We take the assembly!"

"Captains of Galaglea!" Riuel screamed. "Take this damned motherless machine out! Echo my command!"

Riuel lifted himself high in the saddle, raising his bloodied sword as a mark.

"All to the assembly!" Marcian heard other captains echo.

"Every warrior against the machinery!" he heard from deeper in the ranks.

Foot by foot they were closing on the high wooden platform that held the machinery.

Marcian remained on horseback as a mark for the others, slaying from side to side, but his arm was growing rubbery and weak from the constant slaughter. His shoulder was racked in pain from each downswing. He was too old for this now. Perhaps as a young man, when he had found the Tarchon Passage; but now—now he felt old and weary, engaged in utter madness.

A worker threw both hands over his face just as Marcian's blade sliced through them and cut fingers flinging outward, the blade sinking deep through the eyes in a sideways slash.

The Unchurian's body didn't fall; it just slumped back against the terrified wall of angel spawn behind him, one eyeball swinging from its nerve root. Never before had he wanted to weep to heaven to stop this, but he had no choice; he had to press onward.

"Pull them back; throw the bodies from our path!" he cried, infuriated.

Thus far, only the cavalry were pressing against the wall of flesh. Marcian heard footfalls and turned in the saddle to see the legionnaires had finally reached the garrison ground—the first thousand of Quietus's troops. They were exhausted, breathless from their pressed run up the slopes of Hericlon's vale, but no sooner did they reach the garrison ground, then mounted captains shouted them on, pointing their swords and directing them toward the platform assembly. Without a moment's rest, they continued their run. They spread out, forming into cohorts, phalanx formation, as their pike lowered. A wall of spears was now closing on the machinery of Hericlon at full run. The unarmed workers of the angel were thrown into utter, unabated panic, clawing over each other, fighting desperately to find an escape from the wall of heavy, cast-iron tips.

Yet, despite the madness, the gate continued to rise. It had enough clearance that Unchurian warriors, armored firstborn, Nephilim, were able to crawl beneath and run to the assemblage, throwing workers out of their path, leaping onto the platform edge facing the Galagleans until soon it was surrounded by a wall of shields. The shields were oblong, oraculum-plated, and all bore the coiled serpent. But these were the children of the lord of death and the serpents ready to strike, and though their eyes were set in flashing red stone, they were skeletal.

"Clear ground for the pikemen!" Marcian ordered.

The weary, blood-soaked cavalry pulled back from the line, pulling their horses sideways to the gaps between the openings of the phalanxes.

"For the love of Elyon," Marcian shouted as the sweated, weary legionnaires passed at full run, "take out that motherless damned machine!"

They Galaglean phalanxes struck the flesh and fodder, obliterating them. The pikes were soon embedded so deep into flesh and bone they were abandoned. Bucklers, sword, axe, and war hammers began their work. Hundreds of Galagleans formed in squads of cohorts now closed against the few Unchurian prime that guarded the edge of the assembly platform. With the sheer weight of their charge, using the fallen bodies of workers and a ramp up to the assembly, the Galagleans finally slammed into true Unchurian warriors. The most savage fighting Marcian had ever witnessed in his day took place. The Unchurians actually, for the moment, held back ten times their number, fighting like the demons they were. These were the firstborn, the sons of the angel, many seven centuries old, and they fought like the lords of the dead that they were, killing ten, fifteen for each of them that finally dropped. Yet, as skilled as they were, the numbers against them were overwhelming.

Just before the assembly was finally and blessedly overtaken, Marcian saw a rider on a massive horse lower himself enough to squeeze between the bottom teeth. He was unlike any warrior Marcian had seen. He was far from human. His skeleton was on the outside, bloodred, hardened and polished like the finest wood. It formed red armor that sheathed his entire body. His eyes blazed like coals burning from the hardened helm that was both armor and his literal face. Horns like a bull's curled from his temples. Tips of leathered wings arched above his shoulders between slits in his bloodred cloak. He lifted a war hammer and began to slay, working his way into the Galagleans about him, killing everything in sight. In his other hand, his buckler was no less a weapon, edged so effectively it beheaded those that closed on his left with wide, swift strokes that cut through to the chine. Marcian watched, chilled, as if there had not been enough madness, as if the day had not yet had its share of insanity. In mere moments this creature had slaughtered a dozen men. But he was not moving for the machinery; he did not seem to even care of it. His objective was somewhere else, and briefly Marcian wondered what it could be.

The Galaglean legionnaires finally overwhelmed the platform. The last of the Nephilim standing surrounded the winch operators and continued on fighting in a desperate, furious struggle as the operators continued working the winches, the gate continuing, beyond all reason and sanity, to rise. Finally, a muscled axeman turned his attention to the great center gear mechanism and began hacking at its teeth, blow after blow, like a tree cutter working the forest until finally it snapped, triggering a chain reaction. The wooden teeth sheared away with a rickety sound, flinging bits of wood and debris into the air. The chain jerked some of the Unchurians hauling it upward, flinging them as the weight of the portcullis fell. Those warriors that had been squeezing beneath it were crushed into the ground, vanishing beneath the thick, heavy oraculum as its teeth sunk back into their holes.

The last of the Unchurian guardians fell, and the winch operators were hacked to pieces in furious vengeance. Marcian stared at the massive, unbelievable mounds of bodies and flesh, blood, and bone surrounding the platform on all sides as the assembly tore itself to pieces, breaking apart. Marcian closed his eyes, weary from the sight, and realized he was past his time for this. Had he not witnessed in his day enough death that now he should see such a circus of carnage that it defied imagination? His sword arm felt numbed, so worn out from killing that he just let it drop from his fingers, not caring if he ever found it again. Living through the gathering wars alone had taken his soul. Losing all he had and loved had left him for all the years of his life saddened and broken. But now this. Even more death, more slaughter, this time a carnival of it, a tavern joke, the slaying of the unarmed like the killing of so many children weeping as they were decimated by the sword and axe.

He lowered his head, weary, wondering, briefly, of the god he had prayed to all his life, seeking to answer the sorrows of his hearts. But what god was this? How was it that Elyon allowed such a travesty of all that was true and good to take place? How could He simply turn His face from such madness? Marcian felt so weary his soul was no more than dust waiting to be blown in the wind.

Satrina had kept with the Galagleans, to the rear. She continued searching, but hope had almost faded. How could Rhywder have ever survived this? There was no chance. Her heart failed her and tears fell freely across her cheeks as she stood weary and confused, warriors rushing past her for the gate, at times knocking her from their path. She looked up to see a rider on a massive horse hewing his way through the Galagleans as though they were no more than children. He was mercilessly slaughtering them—a single rider and no Galaglean could even reach past his buckler and hammer. Blood sprayed as Galagleans fell and a rider pressed through them, his path littered by their blue cloaks soaked in their own blood.

She knew of these. Her father had told her of them. They were Nephilim, high-blood firstborn who had slain their own bodies to craft new ones grown from pods that spawned a certain wood able to form arms and legs and sheath them all in exoskeletons hard as steel. Just the sight of him chilled her through to her bone. What looked to be his helm, with red iron horns, was, in fact, his face. He was driving forward, searching, but for what? The machinery had been destroyed, all hope of lifting the gate was ended, yet this one continued slaying with purpose. She noticed within his skeletal helm, the faint flow of his eyes as they continued to seek.

He was passing right by her, close enough to shear her neck open with the buckler, and Satrina did not even step back. She had lost all hope. If Rhywder was dead, what use was there? The creature almost seemed to hear her thought. It paused and the head slowly turned to her, almost a mechanical movement, and the faint glow of the eyes bore into hers. She felt him stab through her mind, a probe; it struck with blinding pain as he searched her memories. He slew a warrior coming at his side, knocking Satrina out of the way to have his throat opened. The Unchurian crushed another, beheaded a huge axeman with the edge of his buckler, kicked in the chest of a legionnaire who charged him from the side.

He finally turned from Satrina's eyes and the probing stopped, leaving her head throbbing as if he had just worked his fingers through her brain. But he had found what he wanted, and he turned with renewed purpose. She followed his gaze. There were tall pikes near the wall of the gate. She noticed bodies hanging from them upside down, tied to the tip of the pikes. She realized these were many of the boys who had been defending the gate. Their hands and feet were bound and carefully selected cuts in their necks were letting blood steadily drip into casks below.

Rhywder had spoken of this, how there were blood drinkers who collected human blood like fermenting fine wine, how it was something of an art with them, how they needed to collect the blood slowly, mixing it properly with the seasonings in the casks. A good brew took time, Rhywder had told her. And she remembered something else, the blood drinkers needed to collect the blood at just the right moment, while their victims were still alive!

The minion killed a Galaglean who leapt for him like it was an annoyance and turned his heavily armored horse toward the pikes, picking up his pace, continuing to slay, but now driving in a line for the pike and hanging boys.

Satrina then gasped. One was not a boy. One was Rhywder! The monster had sensed Rhywder's lifeblood through her eyes, and now he moved with a single purpose. The Galagleans would eventually bring him down; as omnipotent as he seemed, there were simply too many warriors filling the passage for him to survive much longer, but that mattered little to him. He had only one objective: the creature was going to kill Rhywder—Rhywder the Lochlain, the Walker of the Lake, the valiant one—and Satrina had virtually pointed him out for the beast.

Rhywder was hanging upside down from a briarwood post, his feet and hands lashed tightly. Cuts in his neck let his blood drip in steady splats into a keg below him, letting it mix and brew with the seasonings.

Satrina scrambled to her feet, lifting Rhywder's short sword.

"Someone help me!" she screamed. She ran and leapt for the minion's horse, but he anticipated, turned in the saddle, and his boot slammed into Satrina's chest. She was thrown high, the wind knocked from her, and when she hit the bloodied ground, the sky and commotion about her for a moment went gray.

The Galagleans not only had heard Satrina's cries; they had already lost hosts of their own to this single rider. Scores of Galagleans swarmed him. A lance pierced through the minion's underarm—a place where the bone-armor did not cover—but the dark rider ripped it away, even tearing the sinew that held one wing. The wing hung askew. He reared the huge horse, slew a Galaglean axeman in his way, crushed the head of another, but one arm wasn't working well so he cast the buckler aside, and used only the hammer, swiftly from one side to the other. He pushed his horse onward. Not much farther to Rhywder.

"Nooo!" Satrina screamed, scrambling to her feet. "Stop him! Stop him!"

Two more leapt at him from either side. The first he killed with a crushing blow of the axe. With his boot, he kicked the chin of the second so hard the neck snapped.

Satrina ran for him, clutching Rhywder's short sword tight in one fist. She was coming from behind this time and perhaps his senses were not as keen. She was, after all, merely a woman and there were armored warriors coming at him from all sides.

He killed yet another Galaglean, then cast aside his war hammer. From a back scabbard, he lifted a heavy iron crossbow. This was for Rhywder. As only Satrina knew, Rhywder was his single target. One bolt was all he needed, and he had used the hammer to clear ground for him, giving him time, and he lifted the crossbow, already loaded with a heavy bolt that would rip any man in half. The only thing he ignored was Satrina, leaping onto the back of his horse. He leveled off the crossbow, using his arm to steady the aim, lowering the oraculum tip on Rhywder's midsection, even ignoring a lance that buried deep between a break in the armor near his ribs with a heavy thud.

Satrina was no warrior. She had never fought in a battle in her life. But none of that even crossed her mind. The huge horse was big enough that she could crouch behind the upturned back brace of the minion's saddle, and with all her strength, she plunged Rhywder's sword into the only opening she could find, a break in the plated armor beneath the back of the head, just below the skull. It allowed him to look up or down, and it also allowed Satrina to plunge Rhywder's short sword deep, angled upward. She screamed with the effort, throwing all her weight into it, feeling it drive past the spine, feeling it pierce something round and almost soft until she was able to drive it in all the way. Only the crossbars of the hilt stopped Rhywder's sword from vanishing into the brain of the creature.

The crossbow's bolt soared upward, blind. The Unchurian arched his back, roaring, furious. He twisted roughly, throwing Satrina from the back of the horse as he reached, clutching for the hilt of Rhywder's sword. But Satrina had buried it deeply, and even as his armored fingers searched desperately, they were beginning to falter.

Lying on her back, to the side of his horse, she briefly saw the look on his face as he struggled to dislodge Rhywder's sword, a look of utter astonishment, a look of complete disbelief. And in the last moment, before he dropped over the flanks, his eyes even connected with hers, swearing at her, damning her as he fell.

Satrina had to dive to the side, crawl under his horse, then run for Rhywder.

Behind her, the Galagleans overwhelmed the struggling Nephilim, falling on him and hacking into him with savage revenge. He had left a trail of their best from the gate to where he had fallen, a litter of blue cloaks and fallen shields. She saw an arm torn free and flung into the air, the same arm that had wielded the war hammer that had caved in so many Galaglean heads.

When she reached Rhywder's side, she first grabbed a fallen dagger, then leapt to catch the post and quickly scaled it. She cut the cords that bound his feet, pulled him to the side where they would miss the cask of his blood still brewing with its strange smell of seasonings, and fell with him, rolling on the rock ground of Hericlon. She propped herself against Hericlon's wall and cut away the rest of the bindings, freeing his hands. She then cut through the hem of her skirt and tore away binding to wrap about the lances in his neck, putting pressure against them to stop the bleeding. Sitting beside him, she held him tight, his head lying on her shoulder. He was still alive, breathing, even stirring. She curled her hand about his and held it in her lap.

There were others being cut down, as well—five or six of the boys who had been selected for blood draining, as well. Apparently, the blood drinkers were picky, it looked as though they had selected the best fit, the most muscular and handsome of the boys, and were slowly draining them of living blood. The blood drinkers would have had no reason to suspect the gate was that same day going to be swarmed by Galagleans.

Rhywder slowly came to. He shook his head, ran his fingers through his hair, and looked about, disoriented. He then leaned back and turned to find Satrina sitting beside him. He believed it was a dream, none of it could have been reality, but a strange blood-soaked, chaotic dream in which he and Satrina were sitting against the rock of Hericlon's gate. He then noticed the tall pike and remembered being hoisted up, tied to it; how the priest, the blood drinker, had so carefully cut the right lashes in his neck to drip his blood out at the proper rate. There was simply no explanation from that moment to this, sitting here held by Satrina. She smiled, seeing he was conscious. He had to blink and look again, making sure it was real.

"Satrina?"

"I brought them," she said, "just as you ordered. I brought the Galagleans." She was bloodied all over, but not blood of her own. He could see no injuries, and it was truly her, it was Satrina, violet eyes quick and alive, the Cupid's bow lips, the button nose, and her expression was as if not that much had happened, as if everything were fine, just fine.

He coughed, still difficult to breathe. "How?"

"I told their fat king with his chariot and horses to come save you. I was not going to let you die, Rhywder. I will not let you die. At all. Ever. Do you hear me? Not here, not anywhere. You are staying with me now. You are mine, so get used to it."

He nodded, still troubled by disbelief.

"Promise me! Say you will stay alive from now on!"

"I . . . I promise, Satrina," he said weakly. "You have my word." He stared at the keg that contained much of his blood, realizing his head was light as a bubble.

Rhywder looked up to find a tall, bloodied Galaglean, helmet still on. He bore wounds and had obviously seen bitter fighting.

"This man helped me," Satrina said. "But I do not know his name."

"I am Marcian." He held out Rhywder's short sword, cleaned of blood. "Your sword, my lady."

"Thank you," she said, taking the sword by the hilt.

"You left it embedded in the Nephilim's neck, but I thought you might want it back. It is a sword of a Shadow Walker." He then noticed Rhywder's armband. "Yours, perhaps?"

Rhywder nodded. He saw by the tassels on the man's shoulders this was a horse captain; in fact, he knew this man. He was the captain of the Galaglean Second Century Calvary. He remembered the name and the face from the legendary battle of Tarchon Pass. He had met the captain that day, both during and after the fighting. It was a hard day to forget.

"I remember you," Rhywder said. "Antiope, am I right?"

"You are, but I am afraid I do not know your name."

"Rhywder. We met at Tarchon Pass."

Marcian stared at him a moment, then nodded. "Of course. I do know of you, Rhywder the Lochlain, Walker of the Lake. You were here then? Before we came—you defended the gate?"

"I did."

"With a handful of boys?"

"Uncommon boys. Did any survive?"

"A few, as were, still being drained of blood. So then, I am guessing it was you who burned the machinery?"

"Yes. It remains burned, I pray?"

Marcian sighed. "Rebuilt, but now destroyed. With much difficulty and bloodshed that will haunt my dreams for months to come. They still did not leave—the Unchurian prime, they watched us through the gate. I assembled archers along the length of the portcullis and ordered them to fire directly into the Unchurian. They were left with the choice of dying or retreating. You would be amazed at the number of dead that lay beyond that portcullis. They have no fear of dying."

"They have been taught well, Captain—by a lord for whom death is an art."

"Tell me, Rhywder, is this your woman?"

Rhywder glanced at Satrina, her eyes so innocent, even here, with carnage all about them. Satrina waited for his answer with more anticipation than Marcian.

"Yes," Rhywder answered. "Yes, this is my woman."

"Whoever you are, you need be proud this day. I can say with all honesty I have never seen such a warrior. She wears a skirt and yet, with your sword she killed a nameless beast nearly fifteen feet high with scores of arms bearing hands of five-inch claws. And, as well on her own, she brought down a Nephilim minion, armored of wood stronger than steel, but she put your sword to its hilt into the back of its brain."

Rhywder stared at Satrina, amazed. Satrina grinned back and shrugged her shoulders.

Chapter Thirty-Four
Violet Eyes

For the second time Rhywder lifted from a dark fog of pain, opening his eyes to look up—there she was. Again. Impossible, but there she was—using a cloth to clean his wounds much as she was doing when he saw her for the first time. She quickly noticed he was awake.

"Rhywder!"

"How it is possible you are here? We were about to be overwhelmed; the armies of the Unchurian, they took us all. How could it be possible I am still alive, looking in your eyes, Satrina?"

"I told you all this. I brought the Galagleans, and you were correct, it was a good idea. They are all very good at killing things—especially when there are hundreds and hundreds of them. So they became very incensed and they just simply killed everything in sight, Rhywder. The whole passage became a bucket of blood and dead Unchurians. And speaking of blood, the Unchurians, they were draining yours into a wine cask—draining it slowly so it could mix with the seasonings, just as you said they sometimes do. They were planning to have a party drinking the blood of those brave boys and yours, as well. It was all spoiled by my inviting the Galagleans."

Rhywder slowly lifted his hand. He found he could wiggle his fingers. "I thought I was paralyzed."

"You were stunned. They have huge beasts with stingers, the Unchurians. They cut off the stingers, then use them as daggers to stun their victims. It made it easier for them to tie you up and make the proper cuts for your blood draining. Apparently if you are alive and breathing air, your blood has a finer quality in the wine making."

"How do you know these things?"

"The captain learned about it by asking around. Marcian, you remember him?"

"Oh, yes . . ."

"Apparently, among the blood drinkers, those cursed of Enoch, human blood is made into the finest of wines. By using different seasonings and rates of mixing with living blood, they create different wines for different palates. There are priests among them who do nothing else but make and perfect these wines, can you imagine that? Is it not awful?"

Rhywder remembered very little, but he did remember being astonished when, instead of throwing him over the side or killing him by sword, they instead lifted him and brought him hand over hand, over the plank, down the stairs.

Rhywder turned the memories away and focused on Satrina's violet eyes. There he saw a whole different world, one that left him with feelings he had never felt before.

"I have something for the pain. Do you need it?"

He shook his head and murmured, "Your eyes . . . all I need."

A tear ringed the edge of Satrina's lash. "You were almost dead," she told him. "I do not know what I would have done had you died, Rhywder. I have come to love you deeply, I fear."

Past her shoulder, Rhywder saw the tent flap thrown open and a large bearded warrior step through, flanked by two captains. They seemed to fill the tent, and Satrina crouched at Rhywder's side.

The Galaglean king eyed her with an incredulous look, then turned to Rhywder.

"I know you," Quietus said. "You are the Lochlain, name of Rhywder. The Shadow Walker of Argolis and once brother of the queen."

"Yes. And you are Quietus."

"We have met?"

"I have seen you once or twice. You present a figure hard to forget."

"You, as well, Little Fox. Are you fully conscious, Walker of the Lake?"

"I believe so."

"There is word that when your people reach you that you are to be named the king of the Daath."

"What?"

"Argolis is dead. His son is missing, dead as well, it is assumed. The closest blood they have to the Daathan throne is you, the brother to Asteria, uncle of the son of Argolis. So then, by blood, I have been told, you are now to be their king, Rhywder of Lochlain. All that lacks is the ceremony and the naming. Of course there would be Daath required for that, but in principle, I suppose we now speak king to king."

Quietus brought a fist to his chest, as well as his guards.

Rhywder was stunned. Argolis was dead? The boy, as well? All the years, all the blood, the gathering wars, the death of Asteria, an entire era had ended. He found it hard to believe.

"Eryian, the warlord?" Rhywder asked.

"Alive, assembling now. A week or less he should reach the vale. I will let your wench keep you, my lord, but should you require anything whatsoever, my men will be outside your tent."

"She is no wench," Rhywder said clearly. "She is a lady."

"Of course, my lord, I meant no disrespect. Just that . . . the manner in which she fought, there are no ladies I have ever known could fight like her, but of course, my lord. My lady."

He bowed to both before the three of them left.

Alone, Rhywder slowly turned his eyes on Satrina as the tent flaps were being tied off. "Help . . . help me to my knees," he whispered.

She gripped his shoulder and Rhywder pulled himself to his knees, shakily. The ground swayed a moment, but he used her to steady himself, weakly gripping her shoulders. He looked into the deep, soft, violet eyes, as though they might be the only light in the room.

"You loved your king?" she said.

"Perhaps."

"I think you did. By the look in your eye, you did. I am sorry for your loss."

He gently touched her cheek, then pulled her against him and held her tight. The warmth of her, the smell of her, he never imagined a woman could stir such feelings.

Chapter Thirty-Five
Ophur

Ophur was hidden. It rested deep in the purple water of the Western Sea, open sea, but hidden sea, shrouded in fog. Once, some race had carved puzzles through the coral that surrounded Ophur. Any ship that did not know the route would find its hull shredded, and occasionally the Tarshians would find the wreckage of ships that had sunk. There were never survivors; sharks kept the waters about Ophur scoured.

This was the last city of the Tarshians. There were no others. Loch watched in wonder as they glided past beds of coral through a gray fog. There was sacredness here, a quiet, only the oars sounding as they sifted the waters. As suddenly, as though they had appeared from nothingness, outcroppings of rock would pass the hull, and in such moments the oars folded back against the upper strakes and the ship glided past smooth and quiet. They passed beneath a bridge of black rock that slowly emerged from the fog, and atop it stood warriors, watching silently, holding oval shields embossed with the emblem of the entwined serpent.

No sooner had they passed beneath the bridge than sun broke through and a crystal bay unfolded. As the ship glided into it, the prow post looked beheaded; bleeding white wood from the oiled stock where the serpent head had been sheared by an Etlantian oar. Darke's ship looked more battered and scarred than it had ever been.

"Ophur!" Hyacinth whispered beside him.

The island of Ophur was a volcano, and the cone rose into the clouds. Upon its spurs, nestled into the cove, were buildings of alabaster and limestone, many coated in an emerald green, beautiful in the sunlight. They were once called the Emerald Kings, the Tarshians, and they had not always been enemies of Etlantis, not until the turning had begun and the curse of Enoch had caused the villages along the coastline of the continent of Mu to be stripped and burned. Only then had the wars against the Etlantians started. That was seven years ago.

In contrast to the silence of passing through the mist, cries now went up from shore, and as Darke's ship drifted along the shallow waters and white crystal sand, people thronged: men, women, and children. From everywhere they came, racing along the shore, shouting, cheering. Darke stood upon the forecastle. He looked over his people silently, the expression on his face weathered, hardened; but slowly, hearing their calls, Darke held forth his hand, fingers wide in the sign of the word, and they cheered even more.

Loch had never seen such honor paid a king. Argolis had always returned with almost silence. Too many dead in Argolis's campaigns. His was a necessary war, but there were no cheers for the gathering that came to Terith-Aire when Loch was young. Whenever the seers called for a gathering, it could only mean an even greater war, an even greater threat, would soon follow. In the day of Argolis, it was only a far threat, for Eryian had told them it would come in a future time. But the future was now.

There were minstrels below on the sand that had made their way through the crowds, and they played horns fashioned of wood, flutes, as well as lyres. He recognized something of the melody and even the tune. Songs from different shores, yet they had a shared beginning, for they were the songs of a distant star.

The ship keeled amid the sand, and several of the men leapt over the side to clutch stay ropes and haul her up against the mooring posts. Darke lifted his hand to motion for silence.

Carried on their shields, the dead were brought. Taran was the first, his sword laid over his chest. Others followed, lowered down by ropes and taken by black-robed priests.

Hyacinth lowered her head upon seeing Taran. With his sword over his chest, his arms folded, the boy looked noble in death. Loch noticed she quickly brushed away a tear as though it were an irritant. The boy, Taran, must have mattered to her. He certainly had fought for the little priestess with all his life and spirit, as Loch would have fought for Adrea. Taran had laid down his life for Hyacinth and yet, with tears brushed away, when finally the priestess looked up, there was no hint of emotion. But then, she was an enchantress; she could show any emotion she wished on demand.

Storan heaved a rope ladder over the bulwark. It unrolled and clattered against the hull. Storan stood aside to let his captain pass.

Darke descended slowly. Upon the beach, he gathered his people who waded into the waters to reach him, then walked up the shore with him. They loved him. These people, they loved rather than feared their king. Loch had never before seen love given a king. Argolis had ruled with a steel hand, even, Loch believed, letting his own queen be killed to solidify the throne and the kingdom.

A few, mostly the poets, scholars, and elders, did not follow with the commoners. They had remained to see the other. They knew Darke returned with the ones some called the voyagers, because it was said they had come in the time of Yered. They traveled from the Blue Stars the common people called the Pleiades. Their kings were always said to have known the star knowledge, and their blood was of an archangel, though they appeared human. It was this reason so many were staring at him openly, some with reverence, and others with guarded judgment.

Storan laid a hand upon Loch's shoulder. "You are next, your majesty. They know who you are; they wait for you."

"I guessed as much."

"Might give them a nod or two; let them know we are united, friends now."

"Are we friends, Storan?"

"Men who taste death in battle are bonded in ways beyond mere friendship. The Tarshians bear no ill against the Daath; if ever your people, we will honor them. Now go, let them see the king of the Daath."

They watched silently as he descended. Ironically, it was quite like the way people watched his father return, with awe, even fear at his coming. Loch descended the rope and dropped into the sand. When he turned, he was not sure what to do. He had never been schooled in the art of being a king—he had no idea what to say to these people. The crowd was quiet and hushed as the Tarshians gathered to see the Daath. He was most thankful when Hyacinth dropped down beside him.

"It is him!" she shouted. "He is all they say he is, for I have seen him turn back the fire of an angel. This, who comes, is the prophecy, the Arsayalalyur foretold of Enoch."

A moment longer they were quiet, but quiet was not the way of the Tarshians, and when Hyacinth shouted, "Welcome him!" they broke out in cheering.

"Thank you," he said quietly.

"Of course," she answered.

"Now, could you get me out of here?"

"Follow."

She parted them, making a pathway through. Some were silent as he passed, but others cheered and leapt and there were even dancers spinning. But the robed ones, the scholars, they watched him as if he had stepped from the very pages of myth.

As Loch passed the minstrels who had gathered, they at once began playing the song of Elyon, the song of the Limitless Light. It was one he had always, every day he saw her in the village, played for Adrea.

Chapter Thirty-Six
Star Voyager

There was a heavy sound of surf from the rocky knoll when Taran's villa fell into view. A wind, cold and stark off the shore, left an icy mist among the thick conifers. Loch had never seen land like this. He had known forest, but that was mostly oak. The villa was built into the buttress of a rock cliff.

"Yours?" he asked, impressed.

"The boy, the one who died."

"He built it for you, then?"

She nodded.

"He must have been very skilled, a master, and I do not say that lightly."

Maybe a mist crossed her eyes, but she willed it gone. This was an enchantress. She could make you see what you wanted to see.

The villa was built of thick wood and mortar and blended perfectly with the tall evergreens and gray spine of the volcano that made up the island's spire. In Terith-Aire, such a craftsman as this would seldom have been given a sword. Artisans were highly valued. But he understood there were few Tarshians; they had all of them become raiders.

A servant came to meet them, but scurried away at an impatient gesture from Hyacinth. The stone walkway was lined with pomegranate trees—not native to the island.

"Where would these trees have come from?"

"Taran, again. He brought and planted them. They are from the mother island."

"He brought you trees?"

She nodded, sadly.

At the villa, Hyacinth lifted the crossbar, then pushed open a heavy oaken door. Loch followed her through hallways adorned in hanging armor and icons of all religions: a golden calf; a bearded hawk; the serpent, lord of seas; the shining Etlantian Apollo—whose name among the common people was Light Bringer and was said to been the first to come, the first to step down from the heavens. A savior. Some of these items were priceless.

Loch and Hyacinth were both bloodied. Any servants who saw them seemed uncertain, but Hyacinth quickly waved them off if they attempted to approach.

"Who has the taste in artifacts?" asked Loch.

"The dead boy."

"Did you care for him?"

"Of course, I did."

"Did you love him?"

"What is love? These people believing in love—just give them time and they all wake up."

"Perhaps, but this boy, as you keep referring to him, as if his name is now forgotten—I believe he loved you deeply."

"You said of your red-hair to speak of her no more. Can I ask the same?"

"If you wish."

"I wish. He is gone. Yes, he was kind and he loved me and he brought me gifts from all over the world, everywhere they sailed. He was precious, but he did not survive. They nearly tore off his head. I grieve, but he is gone. And so is the red-hair! I know you believe she is all you will ever know, all you will ever bleed for—your last breath hers. You are still here, alive, and though it seems blasphemy to think it, there are still others who could know you. Perhaps, by some chance of fate, even one like me."

"You?"

"It is possible."

"Why do you say such a thing?"

"Because she is a weakness in you and you let it drain your strength. You feed it your soul. Who am I to say, but right now, perhaps—weakness is not what you should dwell on. It could be the angel is the kind that seeks out every weakness he can find."

"What does it matter? Satariel is going to kill me if that is his aim. You saw what he did. The only mystery is why he held back. Why he did not finish it when he had the chance?"

"Really? If he wishes, you die, and it is that simple? Yet, here you are. Did you not see his face? He fears you more than his grave. If it is all that simple, then why all these legends of the Angelslayer?"

"People need their legends. They need to believe, pretend in faith, pretend there is more, but as you say of lovers, eventually they wake up."

A strong scent of spices struck them as Hyacinth threw open a set of double copper doorways. They stepped into an oval room where servants were pouring the last urns of hot water into an octagonal bath. The servants quickly slipped away. Silver dolphins, carefully wrought, continued to pour water in fountains as the flames of the hearth danced on their polished surface.

"Your bath," Hyacinth said.

"I do not recall asking for a bath."

"You are bloodied and you have wounds. The waters are treated; they will help heal you."

"Ah, yes, I almost forgot, you are a priestess of Ishtar, well practiced in the healing arts."

"For many of my sisters, yes, though I practiced other arts. I may be better at poisons, but these waters, the herbs and oils, are effective in healing fresh wounds."

"You say you are not practiced at the art, yet you brought your captain from the brink of death."

"That was your blood and your sword. I merely guided your hand."

"The sword can heal?"

"It can even bring back life from the dead, or so say its legend. You do not know the legends of your own legacy, the mark of the father, the sword of Uriel? But then, as you say, what need of legends and pretense?"

Loch looked over the flowing waters of the bath. "You are as bloodied and wounded as I. Since I am stronger and heal of my own nature, you should take this bath. I would like to walk the ledge beyond the villa, past the pomegranate trees. Look over the view of the Western Sea."

"Why would you want to do that?"

"I have other things to ponder than a bath."

From behind, she kicked him so suddenly Loch fell headlong into the steaming water. He came to his feet and then gave her a look out of dead black eyes that was admittedly a bit frightening.

"Do you dislike me?" she asked, simply.

"Listen," he said, firmly, "Hyacinth, skin walker, enchanter, whatever you wish to be—do you think for a moment we are going to survive this? He is an angel of the choir, and if I cannot figure out how to slay him, then all these people, this emerald village, your captain—not to mention you, Hyacinth—all of you will die. But you are like some schoolgirl. Like it is a game we play here!"

"It is always a game, but that does not answer the question. Do you dislike me?"

"I would like you fine—in a different world, different place."

"One without her, you mean."

"She is more to me than you know."

"Wrong. I know everything about you, Lochlain."

"I could have blocked your probes."

"You tried, and each time I had already moved on, learning all I wished. Do you care to test me? Have me guess your secrets?"

"You did not seem to pick up that we are in his shadow, that you Tarshians have drawn out a Watcher of the heavens and that I cannot save you."

"I am not a Tarshian, and I knew all this before my captain even chose to steal you from your palace. Of course, it was all a trap. The Watcher wants you dead. But do not forget it is Darke that has drawn out the Watcher, not you. Use your training, Shadow Walker. Focus on something else. You weaken yourself."

"Hyacinth, we have little time. Whatever he struck me with, lightning, star fire, had he not held back, that alone could have ended it."

"And there lies the point. Can you not see? He could easily have killed you. Flick his lash—the scion of the Daath has left nothing but a cinder of history. And yet—here you are. Alive. How very odd. *Obtuse*—that is a good word for you. You see the stone in font of you and all its square angles, but alas, you fail to see the crack though its center."

"Which is?"

"That he fears you. He failed to take you on his island; he failed to kill you from the forecastle even when you faced him eye to eye. Even now he takes his time closing on us. His ship was left slowly turning in the waters, crippled as if he were mortal. He is weak; all you need is to take faith instead of tossing it aside as pretense from which we will all wake up. That is not how you have lived your life. Why throw it aside now? Because you lost her? All because of her, you chose to fall on your sword?"

He stared back, but said nothing.

"And these lives, they are not on your shoulders. No one believes or expects you to save them, Loch. They knew; they are gamblers. To them, this is just another gamble, one with a thin edge, but it is what they do—it is how they have lived their lives. Darke knew he was an angel. The captain knew his powers were beyond imagining. It is his fault you are even here, and if any lives hang in the balance, their weight is on his shoulders, including yours. What you must do is turn your mind from these things. They cloud your thinking. Close it off for a time. Rest, regain your strength. Your strength, your skill . . . your courage."

"I have not lost courage."

"You weaken yourself. The more you dwell on the eyes of the Watcher, the more they weaken you. Lochlain, if only you knew who you actually were! If what you need right now is faith, then look in my eyes, take mine. I believe in you. I have since the moment they lifted you from your chamber. Your head fell back, your eyes for a moment fell open, and it was as if the stars were about to spill through them. What is it your people say? Faith's Light, is that not it?" She paused, her eyes hardening. "Faith's Light, Lochlain! Forget the Watcher. You are not weak. Think of the blood you lost, and rest, let the waters soothe your wounds and put your mind on something else."

Loch studied her. She had a point. Perhaps she was more clever than he gave her credit for. Of one thing he was certain; she was unlike any woman he had known before. He did not want to look in her eyes; he wanted to remember only Adrea. But the priestess was right. Adrea was gone.

"So then," she continued, "instead of brooding over the sea or searching for the magick spellbound shard that will destroy him—it is time to forget him. Forget he even exists. Let the moment and the waters heal you. Gain strength. The thrust that becomes a kill has no thought; it is simply executed. Your warlord taught you that, did he not? When the time comes, you will know. To dwell on it now is but to weaken your courage."

She waded into the water and unlatched his breastplate and back plate, lifting them over his head, laying them on the edge of the bath. She did not remove his leather jerkin, but she did take an urn and wash what wounds were exposed. She lifted the braids from his hair and pulled her fingers through it. His eyes were no longer black; they had warmed to a softer brown, almost looking human.

"I will tell you a secret, Daath," she said, stepping back to strip off her own armor, but not stopping there, pulling off her leathers, as well. "All your life you have known what was coming. You have magick in you, enough to see futures, and you have seen your own, a gift few of us are granted. You have honed your skill with ever fiber and sinew and muscle you have. But in the end, to do what you must do, you need to let go. Simply let go."

Naked, she now stood opposite him. She began to wash some of her wounds. As she did, she noticed from the corner of her eye that he watched. He was not as icy as his skin sometimes looked; there was human blood in him.

"We are dancing on the edge of a blade at the end of time itself, Lochlain. The world is no longer following rules as it once did—all the rules have broken apart." She moved closer. "Let her go, just for now." Hyacinth shook out her hair, then stood, thigh-high in the water. She had never stood naked before a man in her life. But he did not study her body, only her eyes.

She ran her finger down his cheek. She unlatched the first tie of his leather tunic.

"This cannot help," he said.

She snapped a second tie. "Do you know that I have shown myself to no man and yet you have not even looked at me? Just my eyes. Why? Are you afraid?"

"You stir something deep inside me, Hyacinth. I cannot deny I am drawn to you in a way I do not understand—but you cannot be the future I choose."

"Then let me be the moment you choose."

He slowly, purposely shook his head. "I am sorry."

She studied his eyes a bit longer.

"You are certain?"

He paused, nodded.

She turned and walked up the stairs out of the bath, lifted a robe, then left the doors to the bath open as she slowly walked into the shadows of the villa, not looking back.

Hyacinth sat alone in one of Taran's huge side bed chairs, curled into it, wearing a black silk tunic. On her lap—the star book. She wasn't reading, just marveling over the golden, tissue-thin pages of the Book of Enoch. The doors opened without announcement. He stared at her a moment, uncertain.

"I suppose you knew I would come," he said.

"Do not suppose anything of me, Daath. I am not like the women you have a taste for."

"I have a question."

"You are here—ask."

"It is you. You are the question. Who are you? Why do lure me?"

"I know what I am and who I am, but really—do not trouble yourself with me—it is not me you need. Not me you want. It is any woman who might soothe the pain of her loss. You almost fear nothing, not the night, not the angel, not even your own self-doubt. The only thing you fear in this moment is being alone."

He did not argue.

"So then stay with me. Just sleep. Sleep this night by my side."

As they lay on the bearskins, shafts of moonlight falling, he held her lightly against him. He let himself feel something for her; he didn't understand it or care to. It was just there, the feel of her, the smell of her. She shielded sorrow, left quiet comfort. There could be nothing wrong in that.

"Of titles the legends have for you," she said quietly, not turning, "do you know my most favorite?"

He waited.

"The wanderer—the Voyager. Star Voyager. That is who you are, Loch, the lone voyager of the night. It is your true strength."

He stared out the window at the passing moon. His strength. Alone. It somehow made sense—he had always been afraid of being alone and yet, what he had to face, in the end, he knew he must face alone. Still, this night, he kept his arms about her, kept her warmth against him—he let her take his fears.

Chapter Thirty-Seven
The Fall of Hericlon

Rhywder stood alongside Marcian on the causeway. They had patrolled the gate of Hericlon for two days now and in all that time Marcian ached to tell him. After all, one should not keep secrets from a king, and this one—the Walker of the Lake, as some called him—he was not ordinary among men. Marcian finally decided to trust the Lochlain. If anyone on this Earth could be trusted with what he knew, this was the man. Marcian even thought for a moment it was the only purpose they had reached the causeway; to save the one they called the Little Fox, to give them this small time on the causeway. His secret had been a burden like a sin, but it was sadness he could no longer bear. Finally, he walked up to the stone causeway wall next to Rhywder and paused there a moment looking over the deep canyon beyond them. It seemed odd the man who by all word and purpose was king of the Daath was not one himself.

Rhywder now wore Daathan armor, which he seemed used to, the mantle, the ash-gray cloak that made his movements indistinct sometimes as he paced. Some called them shadow cloaks. He noticed the insignia on Rhywder's bared arm, the plain silver band of Argolis's Shadow Walkers.

"My lord," Marcian said quietly, perhaps too quietly, for Rhywder did not even seem to hear him.

"Two days!" shouted the Little Fox. "Two days and nothing! What does he wait for, by the sacrosanct name of the Goddess, why does he wait?"

"I do not understand your anxiety," Marcian said, putting aside his message for the moment. "They are all very dead down there."

"Other than those that died beyond the gate by your archers, hardly a single firstborn is among them, anyone notice?"

"I suppose you are correct."

"Like dumping mud on us before pouring out the hot oil. Fodder used up, now the armies of the Unchurian are all waiting, the most powerful warriors we have ever faced, waiting just beyond that bend! But why does he not come!"

"The gate is lowered. How could they pass through?"

"He could fold this gate like you fold a parchment."

"We do not speak *his* name?"

"You speak his name, you give him power; you speak his name, and he can look into your mind like a hawk can spot a mouse. Never say his name, remember that."

"I will."

"Your men, as well. If fools among us whisper of named Watchers, tell them to keep their thoughts to themselves."

"Certainly, my lord."

"At least the gate is destroyed. Still—makes no sense he has not moved on us."

"You have not heard of Quietus's plans?"

"What plans?"

"Even now he rebuilds the cogs and machinery. He plans to open the gate."

"What?"

"He wants to lead the Champions through. He speaks of vengeance."

Rhywder quickly crossed to the Galaglean side of the causeway and looked down. It did not take him long to discover the workers.

"That is madness."

"It will be difficult dissuading him, my lord."

"Then kill him."

"What?"

"You or I—before he sets that machinery into place."

"But, my lord . . ."

"Choose now, Antiope. You or me?"

"My lord, he is my king."

"Then I will kill him, but this gate never rises from the Earth again."

"It is for vengeance. The Champions, all they want is another war. In a way, Quietus has outlived his time—as have I, for that matter. The blood of Tarchon Pass never really washes, does it?"

"It is blood on all our souls."

"My lord, there is something I must tell you."

Rhywder turned, waited.

"We cannot be overheard."

"Your message is for me?"

"It concerns the Daath. You are quite possibly their king. It is something I have kept hidden deep, even from my own thoughts, my own imagination."

"Yes?"

Marcian suddenly paused as if stricken. It was Satrina, walking toward them, wearing skirts and purple veils, all of them accenting her eyes. She carried no weapons. She had long ago given Rhywder back his short sword. Odd, Rhywder thought, that the sight of Satrina and her veils would leave this fearless Galaglean commander looking as if he had lost his train of thought in the middle of the battle.

"What is this, Satrina?" Rhywder asked.

"Breakfast, the best I can find—on its way up."

"I do not even in dreams recall asking you to bring up breakfast."

She looked also to Marcian. "Marcian."

"Good . . . mor-morning," Marcian said.

Rhywder glanced at him. It had sounded like he stuttered. He turned back to Satrina. "I am on watch, Satrina."

"Yes, I know that. I know all about how women are not supposed to be on the battlements; we went over that before."

"To no avail, apparently."

"You have not been down from here in two days, Rhywder. You have to eat sometime. Marcian, do you not agree? He should have some breakfast, should he not?"

"It co-could not hurt . . . Rhy-Rhywder."

Rhywder stared at him a moment, narrowed a brow. That was a stutter.

He was an awesome warrior, but women left him weak. It was typical. It was the problem with women in the first place.

Rhywder turned and attempted to be firm. "I cannot eat here, Satrina."

"This is just corn mush; it is all these Galagleans have. Before all they had was sour mead and they brought kegs and kegs more, but of food, this is it. Corn mush. I tried to make it edible with spices."

Her servant girls were setting up a table. Rhywder could hardly believe his eyes. He noticed looks from the Galagleans, this time living Galagleans. He prayed to Elyon she would not attempt to demonstrate how they would enjoy some dancing.

"In order for me to eat that," Rhywder said calmly, remembering now why it was that a proper warrior should not let women get attachments to them, "then there would have to be enough corn mush for every man on this bridge."

"But they come down off the causeway. They get their own—I see them, they come down from watch and boys carrying mush about in wooden pots are always there to serve them. You are special in that you have not left this causeway since it has been retaken. You did not even come down to sleep, I noticed."

"There are more Unchurians out that than I have numbers to count, Satrina, and sooner or later—"

"Which is why I slept alone. Still, you have to eat, and look here, I did find an apple. Actually, Marcian, since I knew you were the high captain on the causeway, I brought enough for you, as well, though I could only find one apple."

"That . . . I . . . It was not necessary."

The man had somewhere, sometime in his life been traumatized by women, for he was nervous as a cat in a canoe headed for the falls.

The two girls finished their setup: a small table, two stools, fairly nice, all told. Satrina sprinkled herbs over the top of the goat's milk and mush. Goblets filled with Galaglean mead were set out, as well.

Satrina smiled. "Very good girls, we can leave now."

They begin to walk across the causeway toward the stairs.

"Satrina, come back and take your mush with you!"

Satrina kept walking. She turned the causeway and descended without looking back. Rhywder stared after her a moment, then glanced at Marcian.

"She does have one point," said Marcian. "I have been worried myself. You have not left the battlements and not only should you eat her mush and her rare apple, but you should get some sleep, as well, my lord. We are guarding against a formidable evil. If you weaken yourself without sleep or food, what good does that accomplish?"

No stutter now, Rhywder noted. He deeply wanted to ask what these women had done to the poor man, but refrained.

"Now that you mention it, Antiope, those fellows down there, below the gate, the ones with all the arrows in them, they haven't had breakfast, either, so . . ." Rhywder stepped forward and heaved the table over the battlements. "Let them have some mush." The stools followed. "In case they want to sit as they have their mush."

Rhywder noticed, though he said nothing, that Marcian's expression bore the slightest hint of disapproval.

"Tell you something, Antiope; it has to do with principle, all this mush business. These women, as I am sure I need not explain to you, guessing your past, need to understand their place. Am I right or not?"

Marcian hesitated. "I suppose . . ."

"I have been without a woman for thirty-eight years, and now, for the love of frogs, is the wrong time to begin getting soft. The nations of the Unchurians waiting to hang us from posts and drain our blood for wine, and she comes up with breakfast! Women! I tell you, give them the slightest notion you care for them and they take over your life. Bloody start feeding you mush on the battlements! Well, not me. By God and whore's blood! No woman—*no serving wench woman*—is going to put a tail on my ass."

Rhywder stared over the southern pass, breathing heavily, having made his point. No one met his eye. All remained sober. But inside, though he tried his best, he had not convinced himself, and he wished secretly he could have the table and mush and apple back.

"Now," Rhywder said quietly, collecting himself, "this thing on your mind that concerns the Daath—though let me make it clear I am not their king, and as soon as there is opportunity I will make it known to them—now is as good a time as any to speak of it."

Marcian looked to either side. "Perhaps over against the side, my lord."

"My ear alone, you mean?"

"Aye."

"Good enough."

Rhywder walked to the other side of the causeway, put his hands behind his back, and stared down at the garrison. He tried to spot Satrina, looking for the blue veils, but did not find her.

"So, what would you have to tell me about the Daath? Understand you supply them with the finest of horseflesh."

"I sell them horses, yes, but this is about a woman."

"Ah."

"I some months ago was in a village near the Daathan village of Lucania. Are you aware of it?"

"They settled it with captives after the gathering wars. I understand mostly Galaglean, but the few remaining people of my tribe, as well, the Lake People, Lochlains. Quaint village as I recall. Rumors that the Daath occasionally steal their women from that village. Must have their women well trained there, you think?"

"I am no Daath, but I can attest they do have exceptionally beautiful woman in that village, but it was not just her beauty, something else, something of the heart in her."

Rhywder glanced at him, growing curious now.

"I cannot explain. No one believed, I am sure, but it was nothing to do with lust. I am not that kind of man, and age has left me even more so. The thing of it is, I lost a child in the wars, during the siege of Galaglea, when they hurled the diseased corpses over the walls and the fevers took. I lost my wife and a wee boy with white hair. His name was August because he seemed so wise with his white hair."

"Just to mention, that siege was never my idea, Antiope. I stood opposed, but by then Argolis had changed; he had become a hard man."

"No need to explain, I only brought it up to mention my boy. I watched him crawl, even saw him began to talk, then I buried him. But I wander—my point is that I saw this girl one day in the village of Lucania and suddenly this idea springs up in me: one more child, one more. I am forty and two, not young. Perhaps it was wrong, my thinking, but as if some madness had struck me, I approached her father, made an offer, a very generous one. It was set to happen, the wedding, but something went wrong the day she was to arrive. They only came to tell me the father was dead and the girl missing. I was ashamed of ever entering into it all, somehow as if it were my fault."

"Nothing in your story as yet inspires shame, Antiope. So how does this involve the Daath?"

"It was only weeks before we were called here. I was in the upper field, feeding the herd. I am afraid I name them. Anyway, I was there calling out their names when . . . when all I can say is, it was as if the air and the earth and time itself split open, like a knife cutting open skin. I have never seen anything like it, and doubt I ever will again. And from this opening there came a horseman. He was Etlantian. I believe him to have been a Nephilim but, unlike most, he was true of heart. There was a glow to his eyes that left me certain of that. Whoever he was, I sensed he was still connected to the heavens and the Blue Stars we call home. Without speaking, before I could even react, he turned the glow of his eyes upon me and set my mind at rest. I felt—it was like standing before a being of heaven's grace."

Marcian paused and glanced to Rhywder.

"Keep talking, Marcian, I have seen such beings. I have traveled far in my day."

"Yes, you seem to understand things. In the saddle with him was the girl, the one I told you of, from the village. Her name is Adrea, and she truly is a beautiful girl, long fire-red hair, though it is her heart that leaves her so exceptional. I was nearly overcome, I had no words, all I could do was stare, utterly amazed. I had seen her only days before, to give her a present before the wedding. What stunned me was that this girl, Adrea, she was pregnant. She was full term, about to have a child. I know that is impossible. She was a vir-vir—"

"Virgin."

"Yes, but days before, and now—near birthing." He paused, staring down at the garrison. "If you find my story too much to believe, I can understand, but I swear of its truth."

"I believe you, Marcian. You witnessed a time jump. It can be done only by those beings who understand the star knowledge, and this rider you speak of, his name is Sandalaphon."

"Yes! How did you know?"

"I know things, Marcian. Go on, I am listening."

"He told me, as you just stated, that his name was Sandalaphon, a protector of the Daath, and that was all I needed to understand of him. He explained many things to me, and it seemed, oddly, he did so without words, as if his knowledge, the things he knew, passed from him to my mind. He told me that he was giving me the power to hide all that he had said, that no normal being would ever discern I knew these things, these secrets he revealed, but that a time would come when I would find the man to tell these things to. I believe you are that man."

He paused a moment. Rhywder did not respond; he simply waited for the Galaglean to continue, but already he was guessing what the man was going to say. It made sense; it fit all that was happening. It explained a great deal. The eye of Daath had been opened. The battle for this gate was more than an ordinary war; it was the fulfillment of prophecy. It was the winnowing. Rhywder felt a shiver. He never believed he would witness the days of the winnowing wars.

"The things I say next, my lord—"

"I understand, Marcian, the things you say next would be hard for many to understand, but you can trust in me. Tell me what the Nephilim said to you."

"First, he took my sorrow, for I had loved this girl deeply. In the short time I had known her, I loved her like a daughter. I know that sounds odd, that I would marry a daughter, but that is how I felt toward her. She owned a piece of my heart and that she had lain with another would have brought me pain, but he took that pain; he took my sorrow. He told me that this girl now carried in her womb the scion of Uriel, the Archangel of the Seventh Choir, the one who held the fiery sword before the East of the Land."

Rhywder nodded.

"You believe, then?"

"I do. The girl, Adrea, was she a Water Bearer?"

"Aye, an exceptional one; she knew things. When I first met her, of course,

I thought her only the daughter of a cattleman, but this girl, she is filled with such knowledge that to think of it now almost brings tears to my eyes, knowing I am here, and she is far away, remembering how much I miss her."

"You have told no one."

"I have never spoken of it until now, this very moment."

Suddenly Rhywder felt something. It was like a cold wave flushing through him, and it left his skin shivering. He turned to look south, alarmed. He realized what had just happened.

"My lord?" asked Marcian.

"You were right in telling me, Marcian, but I fear . . ." he paused, wincing. It was happening swiftly, he could hear rumblings, and then he saw the sky. Whirlers. The eyes, the thousands of eyes. He was there, Azazel.

"What is happening?" Marcian said, also alarmed. "Is that a storm?"

"Much worse."

A whispered chuckle swarmed around them both, and Marcian turned searching, alarmed.

"What was that?" the Galaglean asked. "Did you hear it?"

"I heard, and so did he. I fear he was listening, Marcian."

"Who?"

"Azazel, the angel of death. Elyon save us—"

Suddenly, without warning, a powerful stone blew and struck just beneath the causeway where Rhywder and Marcian stood. It hit so hard, the mighty bridgework of Hericlon itself swayed outward. Before them, in the passage south, there were catapults. Scores of them, filling the passageway, and they were unlike any Rhywder had seen before, built massive, not of wood, but of oraculum.

"Name of the Goddess," whispered Marcian.

"He was listening as if he stood beside us," Rhywder said. "This is why he has been waiting!"

Another stone struck, and the causeway trembled along its length, leaving them off balance.

"Rhywder!" He heard a scream and turned. Satrina was running for him.

Another struck, and this time the stonework along the southern edge was broken loose. The Galagleans had lifted spear and bow, but the catapults were out of range, and even then, their operators were protected by massive sheets of oraculum.

Satrina reached his side. "I felt something," she said, "so cold, it went through my skin and—"

She broke off, seeing the catapults launch a dozen huge stones at once. She grabbed Rhywder's arm as they struck. The causeway heaved, thrown back by the blows. Rhywder could hardly believe the massive ancient stonework of Hericlon could ever be shaken. Two or three archers where thrown over the ports; others knocked to the stone of the causeway.

"By the name of Elyon, what have I done?" moaned Marcian.

"It is not your fault," Rhywder answered.

"But what can we do?"

"There come certain times to die, Marcian, and I fear this is one of them. Satrina, get out of here!"

"I am not leaving you!"

Rhywder could only watch the southern passage helplessly. The whirlers of the angel spilled among the catapults. He was there, out there among them. It was like a darkness beyond dark, a black night moving for them. The same sounds as the last siege broke through the air, the singing, the beating of drums. The catapults vanished in the whirlers. He had never seen them close, the eyes in them, watching. There was movement in the darkness, the snort of horses, a thunderous clatter; the Unchurians were gathering. It was happening too fast.

"Both of you, both of you, run!" Marcian said. "Do you hear me, Rhywder, Little Fox of Lochlain? If it was you I was meant to find, you must run! You must find her, save her! Go, now, we will hold against the onslaught!"

They had to grip the stone as another volley of the catapult struck. Satrina stumbled, almost falling, but he caught her arm.

"You cannot hold, Marcian, he will drop this gate but moments from now. Time is lost us."

"We are Galagleans. We have held Hericlon for seven centuries! No army has ever breached Hericlon."

"There has never been an army like this one," Rhywder said.

The chanting rose, solemn. It might once have been a song of angels: words of the choir, the spellbound words of heaven.

Satrina grabbed his arm. "Rhywder, there are fast horses below."

Another blow struck, and the entire causeway swung outward as if it were nothing more than a rope bridge. Men lost their footing and were tossed into the night. Others managed to grip the causeway wall. Rhywder held Satrina by the waist.

"She is right!" screamed Marcian. "I know it is not your nature, but you must run; you must find her! Save her!"

Rhywder glanced at him. He looked to the stairways.

Winds struck, like the torrents of a hurricane off the coast. They assailed the causeway so savagely, many of the guards were hurled over the edge into the air with screams.

Marcian grabbed Rhywder by both arms. "I love that girl with all my heart and all my soul," he screamed above the winds, "and the child, as well. Go, Shadow Walker, you are named his protector! Run! You have to save them. Somehow, we will hold this damned gate!"

"Galaglean, we are both about to die."

"No! I see it in your eyes. Elyon is with you, Walker of the Lake. He names you; He chooses you. You cannot fail them! You are the one, his protector! Now, go!"

Rhywder gritted his teeth. "Damn!" he swore, grabbing Satrina's arm. They both ran for the stairway.

Marcian turned. "Archers to the ports, steady, hold steady to the rock and wait for the mark!" Then the fire against the ancient gate of Hericlon came like a hailstorm from heaven. The gate had stood in this valley since the days of Dawnshroud. It was nearly immortal, built during a time of war when the Earth was still being formed. Its rock was the rock of the very Trisagion, the song of the choirs that brought the Earth into being out of the abyss. It was as ancient as heaven was ancient, but the heavy volley of hard iron-laced missiles that next struck its face seemed as if they had been hurled from the stars.

Marcian stared into it in disbelief, but then, there was little he no longer believed. Elyon was real, the scriptures, the tales of the seers they called the mad wanderers of Enoch—it was all truth. Prophecy was bearing down on them, and it had been written before the Earth was ever formed. It was an angel of the fallen coming against them now, Azazel. He knew that name; he remembered Azazel was the one who spoke death and death became the fate of men. The chants of the angel's warriors rose even above the winds as if to lay a signet over this chapter, this page of the ending. He cared nothing of dying, really. Even as his first captain screamed, vanishing into a flaming iron rock so molten it splashed, burning Marcian's cheek, even then he did not fear dying, and he spent the last moments of his life praying not for himself, not for his men, not for Hericlon, but only for her and the child.

"I found the Protector, my lord—now You must protect him. He must reach her, and only Your will can make it so."

A huge stone, fired like a meteor, ripped away the portion of the causeway Marcian had been standing on. He vanished, and the entire rampart began to buckle inward, folding. As the center went down, the weight of the massive portcullis fell, sucking in the causeway with it.

Rhywder thought they were almost going to make it. They had reached the side stairways, and even if the gate fell, the stairways were cut out of the rock of Hericlon itself.

They would surely hold, he had thought, but they did not. As the heavy ancient stone of the causeway beneath their feet gave way, it pulled whole sections of the stairway from the side of Hericlon's face. It was over. This was over, but he did grab Satrina by the waist, even as the stone beneath his feet reeled upward, buckling before it dropped. He threw her into the standing stone tower, also cut out of the rock face of the mountain.

And then there was nothing beneath Rhywder's feet. He should have been falling, but instead he was hanging, swaying, and looking up, he was astonished to see she had hold of his wrist with both her hands.

"Satrina, you cannot bear my weight! Let me go!"

"You fall; I fall! What is the difference? Instead of telling me how little you fear death, help, for God's sake, help me!"

He did. He was desperately trying to clamber up the face of the stone, but it curled under him in a bowl, and there was little grip for his feet.

"Satrina, just let me go! Save yourself!"

"No! Either you make it over this bastion, or we both drop into the cauldron below."

And it was a cauldron, for stone and the oraculum of the portcullis were raining down upon the passageway, and the mountain itself was shaking as if in a quake. Smoke and debris boiled upward in billows of dust.

He kicked off a boot, then the other. With bare feet he gained some grip, though little. Satrina was being pulled over the edge. She was on her belly on the stone, holding with both hands, fighting to stay in the tower.

The roar of Hericlon's fall was deafening. Through the plumes of debris and dust he could hardly see her.

Satrina then grabbed a chain, one used to haul up buckets from below. It was wrapped about a pulley and its end was a claw. Satrina held Rhywder by one hand and hurled it, wrapping it about a stone column of the tower, and then jerked it tight. She lifted the hook, swinging it.

Rhywder was about to pry her hand loose, let himself drop. She would be left in the tower, but there was the far chance she would somehow survive. At least a chance. Suddenly he howled in pain, something had pierced through his arm. She let go, but instead of falling, he was now swinging from a hooked chain that was threatening to rip out the back of his left arm. He was hooked like a fish.

Satrina slammed both feet against the edge of the tower and began hauling in the chain; hand over hand, using the pulley. It took all her strength. She screeched through tightened teeth, the muscles in her neck strained. Rhywder's right hand finally grasped hold of the tower's edge. He snarled and hurled himself over, landing on top of her, and they lay there for a moment, both breathing heavily.

"How . . . how did you do that?" Rhywder gasped.

"My father was a fisherman," she said, sweated, equally out of breath. "He taught me to hook fish."

"I thought he was a rich lord."

"A fisherman cannot be rich?"

He turned to the side, holding her tight, and looked into the deep violet eyes with their long lashes. "You," he gasped in pain, "you are some woman."

"I am, Rhywder, and as I swore, I am keeping you alive."

Below, there was a tremendous shout of victory, thousands of voices strong, tens of thousands, more. Hericlon was gone forever. The villages, the cities of the Daath, all the tribes of the Dannu, now lay before the dark that took the gate like sheep before a gathering of wolves. The Galagleans were fighting to the death, but it would soon be over. Rhywder felt tears in his eyes for them—not just the Galagleans dying down below, but all their people. There would be nothing to stop him now; Azazel would sweep over the north like a dark storm. No power on Earth could turn him back.

"Rhywder," Satrina whispered in his ear.

"Yes?"

"I know now that I love you. I thought it, but then—it has been such a short time, how does one love in such a short time? But the answer does not matter, because I love you more than I have ever loved anyone."

Rhywder stared in her eyes. Tears welled in both their eyes.

"Me," he answered, "I have never loved anything, nor ever expected to, but if this is what it feels like, it leaves me without words. So I guess I love you, as well, Satrina. I guess I love you with all I have in me." He then took a tight breath against gritted teeth. "Now, can we get this damned hook out of my arm?"

Chapter Thirty-Eight
The Watcher

Loch suddenly came awake. It was as though a cold wind had struck, but when he opened his eyes, the room was quiet, dark. He sat up. Hyacinth came to a crouch beside him, sensing the same thing—a whisper, as though someone had been close, almost close enough to touch. She searched the room, frightened.

"We are not alone," she said. She turned to him as a cold breath of ice passed through them. She laid a hand to her breast and gasped.

"Look!" she said, pointing to his scabbard.

Uriel's sword was still in its sheath of carved black ivory, but against the lip, the flange and blade were breathing a pulse of soft blue light. He looked to Hyacinth, and he saw panic in her dark brown eyes.

"I did not think it would come this quickly," she said. "It is him. Satariel has come, and this time he will not be denied."

A tremor moved beneath the floorboards. The walls and icons of Taran's house shook, dust spilled from the ceiling, but Hyacinth did not even seem to notice, her eyes remained on him.

"You stay here," he said, quickly pulling on his armor.

"Impossible. You know me well enough."

He took her at arms' length. "Hyacinth, I do not know how to kill this bastard, and I fear for you," he said, searching her eyes. His own were a warm brown, not the Shadow Walker, but the human, the warm blood of the Water Bearer. "I care for you. I do not want you to die here. Stay back, Hyacinth. You said it last night, I must face this alone."

"Listen to me first. There is something I sense, something you must understand."

"What?"

"I wish I could explain it, what I feel, what I sense, but all I know to say is that to kill him, you must let go, Loch. The Shadow Walker cannot defeat the Watcher of heaven; it is something else in you. Remember that."

He pulled on the shadowy Daathan cloak as he stood. "I will try, but there is no time left to outguess this. I am going to find him, and if I can, I will slay him. Do not try to follow me. If he sees you, he will kill you. He will use you against me, just as you warned me of Adrea. You cannot help me in this. As you said, I am the Wanderer, and this is a path I must walk alone. Good-bye, Little Flower."

He leaned forward and kissed her, as he had wanted to the night before in the baths. He then turned, and as his cloak flared, he disappeared.

She ran to the door, searching, but he was nowhere to be seen. It was as if he had vanished into the dark of the early dawn.

"Loch!" she cried, desperate, but there came no answer.

From the rock bridge that spanned the narrow neck of the lagoon that led into the cove of Ophur, two archers stared, amazed, as flame curled from the volcano's shadow. It had never been active—dead all these years. Even the crater was ash and silent; a smell of sulfur, but little else. Now billows of black smoke poured into the sky, and flames licked upward. The natural rock bridge they were standing on began to tremble. Rumblers were passing through the island. One of the archers then pointed, pulling his bow from his back, but there was little the two guardians of Ophur could do. The ship sailing toward them, coming out of the dark of night and the natural fog of the island was like a mountain. The massive prow post rose to nearly the height of the bridge. The hull was sheathed in weathered planks of oraculum. In seven centuries, no ship had ever found the Ophur. Some had tried, many had been found smashed upon the corals and beaten by the sea, but this one, with its ashen sails and its heavy bull's-head ram, smoothly parted the black waters as it slowly closed on them. It almost seemed to know the course as well as Darke. Lamps burned from either side of the bow, and yet they seemed to swallow the light of early dawn—even drink it. The sail was ragged, but the red stain of the bull's head of Etlantis was still visible, as well as another image above—a circled cross.

From the forecastle of the huge ship, a catapult launched. Its flaming iron ball struck the center of the natural black stone. Chunks of rock and debris rained down, but before the waters could even still, the prow of the angel's ship cut through them. The Etlantian galley then sailed for the inland lagoon of Ophur—its natural harbor. The shore was surrounded by the city; the emerald houses, the temples, and colonnaded buildings waited. The angel's ship came silently but for a curl of seawater at its prow and the flap of the worn sails from the warm winds blowing from the volcano that lit the early dawn in an eerie glow.

Darke held his horse in rein. He had been waiting, and now he watched from a grove of olives, with shimmering leaves that tossed in the sudden warm wind swirling upward from the volcano's flame. The emerald paint of the buildings and temples were bathed in the burn of the mountain's fire. Its rumble beneath their feet threatened to burst into a quake, but he guessed that would not happen. He guessed the fires, the rumbles of the mountain, all were for atmosphere—effect. It had been the same on the angel's island, the volcanic rock molded in spires like the finest cathedrals of the Followers. Satariel had a taste for theatrics.

Darke watched without emotion as the massive ship sailed out of the early dawn's night for the center beach, taking its time as if to appreciate the view of the fabled, hidden lagoon of Ophur. There were four, maybe five Tarshian blackships at anchor in the lagoon. Perhaps for sport, they were being pelted by the heavy catapults and ballistae of the Etlantian. One of them exploded in flame from the fire jet of the Etlantian's prow, which launched a stream of naphtha into the blackship's midsection.

Darke's own ship was well hidden. He had not really expected to live through this, but he hoped his ship might. It had served well these many years, it was a fast and reliable hunter, and maybe someday it would be found, marveled over. Certainly, if he wanted, the angel could find it and sink it, but the Etlantian would first have to circle the island and navigate even more labyrinths carved in the thick coral.

For a brief moment, considering the battle in which he was about to engage, Darke wondered how much of the angel's celestial powers were lost. How close he had come to being human. He thought of what Hyacinth had read of Enoch: *Yea, though once you walked as sons of gods, Bene ha Elohim, you shall die as men shall die.* In the time of first coming, the time of the oath of binding upon the mountain of Etlantis, the angels had been creators, fashioners of worlds, the walkers of the stars and darkness, but how far had Satariel come from such power over the centuries since he had turned from heaven's light.

The ground trembled, this time a quake splitting open a rift that slithered like a snake through the ground, shattering two or three houses to either side of him. But the houses were empty. The only humans on this beach were warriors. The women and children had all been hidden.

Darke really did not expect to prevail in this; he even doubted the Daath would prevail—the boy was fearless, but too young, too inexperienced, and the sword had nearly killed him on the island. Their only chance was that Enoch's curse had worked upon the angel to such an extent that he was no longer immortal. Even then, it would be no simple kill. Satariel came with his sons.

But Darke was determined that at least Ophur would cost them. These were the Tarshians, the raiders of Ishtar's horned moon that had fought Etlantians all their lives. Once they had ruled the seven kingdoms of the Western Sea, and for seven hundred years they had been killing Etlantians. It had come down to this, one final city, one final stand, and even though it was an angel of the holy choirs that was about to take the shore of the island, even for the Watcher, this would be no simple kill.

As another crack in the earth snaked almost beneath Storan's horse and his big roan reared, Storan drew in on the reins and calmed the animal. The horses of Ophur were practiced for battle, but cracks in the earth and the threatening rumble of the island's volcano were not part of their training.

Though Darke did not expect to live through this night, there was hope at least for his seed, the very last of the Tarshians on the face of the Earth—for these he had prayed Elyon for survival, and during the night, his men had taken them to a cave hidden so well it could hardly be worth the angel's trouble to search. After this aged, riddled creature had killed his Daathan scion, what interest would he have in searching the island further? Still, it worried him. As the moments closed before battle, it was the only thing on Darke's mind.

"You are certain the women and children are safe?" he asked Storan once more, not even letting himself think or speak of a location, knowing his thoughts could no longer be trusted as his own.

"Aye, Captain," answered Storan, "hidden well. Your woman, I might add, was most difficult of all. Claimed she should be here, with you and that sword she carries. Nearly had to bind her hand and foot."

"But you, of course, convinced her to remain with the others?"

"I told her if the Tarshians lost their king, at least they deserved to look to their queen for guidance. She seemed not to argue with that. Good woman, she is, wish I had known such a woman in my years."

"Perhaps you will. It is not over yet, Storan."

"Not yet, but I do understand that on that ship are firstborn. Not a single inbreed, not a single weakened generation—no Failures; no fourth, third, or even second birthing. These are said to be all high-blood Nephilim. Is that not sweet? Perhaps we cannot kill this withered old bastard—but we can by Elyon's grace winnow his firstborn seed. Hope that stabs at his heart in the end."

"I doubt he has a heart," said Danwyar from Darke's left. Danwyar slowly lifted his silver bow from his back and calmly threaded it with one of his poison-treated silver arrows. The arrows, the daggers, even the spears of the Tarshians were all treated with poisons taught them of the little priestess. She was damned gifted with poison. It was an irony—the secret of the Tarshians in their final hour was nothing more than the moss-dampened poisons of a little witch no older than twenty and two years.

Storan rubbed dirt in his hands and curled one hard about the leather wrappings of his axe haft. "You know what I am thinking, Captain? I am thinking this monster ship—just another Etlantian. No more, just another high-blood bastard believes himself to own the sea. Well, no one owns her, though this one has been courting her a damned long time, I suppose."

"He might have even created her," answered Darke.

Storan just spat to the side. "Piss that he ever created a pea. Nonetheless, my point is that these coming for us, they are Etlantians—just like the hundreds we have laid in the deep. Do not know about the angel, but the others, firstborn or not, we know they bleed, their flesh slices open, their bones break, and perhaps they are damned hard to kill, but by the Goddess's breath and my mother's blessing, have we not put down more of these bastards than any Etlantian slayers on this planet?"

"That we have, my good friend."

"We have done this world a service, by Elyon's grace. Done it a service. So on this godless dawn we will do it one more job and take a few more of these high-bloods with us to the otherworld. I will admit, I'd rather be tangling with them at sea, but this will do. So that was my thinking on it—this here, it is just another killing time."

Darke took a breath. His sword was still sheathed. His mount stirred, restless, shaking out its mane—sensing the danger. Killing time, Darke thought—just another killing time—and this one would probably include the Tarshian warriors, as well. He did not fear death. He held no hope on the babblings of Enochian priests over what waited beyond; that Elyon's Light would be there like a tunnel opening through time. What he had seen of death left him believing it was just a swallowing of life. No maidens, no beams of starlight to herald them as warriors fallen on fields of battle. It was an end to things—nothing more. And that was fine. They had done well with their lives. They had fought unspeakable darkness. Perhaps, at least, there was purpose to that. They had killed raiders that raped and burned and ate even children. That had to be a good thing—Elyon's heaven waiting or not.

It ended there, but then—all things ended eventually.

When the Etlantian ship reached the shore of white, glittering sand, the gleaming oraculum bull's-head ram plowed into it, spraying it outward. And then, for a moment—nothing. Just still and quiet, the warm waters of the lagoon lapping at its hull, lamplights burning from both fore and aft, as well as top lights high in the nests of the masts—but Darke was struck how they did not seem to flicker with the light of this Earth, this planet; it seemed the angel burned the light of his home star in his lamps, and like him, it was dim, shadowy.

And just as still, just as quiet and waiting, were the hundreds of Darke's warriors hidden among the foliage and buildings of Ophur. No hearth fires burned—the island looked deserted.

A drawbridge dropped open from the ship's hull, well weighted in heavy strakes of wood and brass linings. It slammed into the sand and sea, water sprayed, the ground shook, and immediately, almost before it had touched down, the Etlantians came on heavy horse, weapons drawn—Etlantians as Darke had never seen. Storan was right—Nephilim, all of them. Their armor was a dark-worked version of oraculum that was the rust-red color of dried blood. Their cloaks were red, also, but worn, dusty, as if they had never traded them for new ones. Their weapons swallowed light—it was as if the swords and morning stars and war hammers were burning, but instead of giving off a glow, they swallowed the light about them, leaving a void, a shadowy nothingness. Darke had never seen weapons like that. In other times, other fights, he would have fixed himself on the thought of taking one for his own.

The Nephilim fanned out as they hit the sand, then separated and rode in groups of three, outward in all directions, for the city. He might have expected hundreds, but there were no more than twenty or thirty raiders here, and although the emerald building looked utterly abandoned, it was as if they were not fooled in the slightest. Their horses were large chargers bred on the island of Etlantis to bear the weight of the giants. But Darke had fought mostly at sea, and he was taken with the thunderous blows of their heavy hooves. So these were the sons of the angel. There were few, but if they were as deadly as they looked, they just as well had been hundreds. Still, considering Satariel and his flair for the dramatic, perhaps it was more show than deadly. All wore helmets, but the eyes behind them glowed as though backlit, sometimes the clear blue of new stars, sometimes a shimmering white, the same burn as that given off by the lamps of the ship. He had seen Nephilim before. Their souls always shone through their eyes.

"Elyon's Light be with us, brothers," Storan prayed—rare for the helmsman.

Darke held up his hand. It was a signal for his hidden warriors. Not over yet, all this. They were impressive, these sons of the angel, but now they would face the deadliest giant killers living—Tarshians.

Darke dropped his hand, the signal.

Below, in the tiers of the city, Darke's men attacked. They rode out from behind taverns, whorehouses, and temples. They launched their attack on sleek, swift horses, weapons readied.

The Etlantians fanned out, each group of three choosing a target. The first of Darke's men was killed by a swift, solid blow of a war hammer that caved in his chest, splintering the bone. Another fell, his face cloven, blood spilling rich. A Tarshian horse was lifted off its front hooves and thrown back as a heavy axe sheared open its chest. One Etlantian dropped, with a poisoned javelin through his breastplate. Here and there an Etlantian fell, but the pirates were being hewn down like chaff. It was more than theater—the angel's sons were as deadly as they looked.

Darke drew his sword, lifting it, and spurned his charger forward. Storan came at his flank, leaning into the gallop, teeth clenched and a low growl in his throat.

Danwyar rode to Darke's left. He gripped the flanks of his horse tight with bared knees, reins in his teeth, and leveled off his bow.

Across the clearing, from the burning city, five of the angel's sons spotted them and turned to engage. Darke noticed how their red-black breastplates curled upward, emphasizing the broad, powerful shoulders. One bore a helm of curled ram's horns of tarnished gold.

Storan lifted his axe and started it spinning with a heavy song.

Darke killed the first Etlantian with a flicker thrust of his sword, through the side armor, angled for the heart. It was a move he had practiced for years, and it never failed him. His sword was also oily with Hyacinth's poisons. He turned quickly for another kill, but an Etlantian coming at full gallop hit him in the chest with a flail, and Darke went over the flanks, swearing as he hit the ground. He had never been struck that hard.

Storan sheared off a wrist, and when the Etlantian drew back, reaching for a second weapon with his remaining hand, Storan opened his gut, a swift, heavy arc through the oraculum. Storan's axe was like no other, and gutting the famed oraculum armor was his fondest killing stroke. As the Etlantian fell, Storan wrenched the reins about hard and dug his spiked heels into the sides of his horse, pursuing another.

Danwyar's horse came off a slight hillock, leaping past an Etlantian. He did not even turn to look back as he left a darkened silver shaft buried in the Nephilim's eye, through the fine, carved helmet. The edge of the helmet had stripped off the white quill feathers. The Nephilim spun, but the poison was taking hold quickly. He slumped forward as if he were drunk.

Darke came to his feet. He ducked the hiss of a curved blade and cut through the quarter-flank of the Etlantian's horse as it passed. He vaulted into the saddle of his own horse, turning it about. The giant had landed on his feet as his charger went down, but Darke simply flung a dagger—no ceremony to it, burying its poison in the Nephilim's throat. He coughed like he was catching a cold, and just as Danwyar's bolt, the poison worked slowly at first, then hit hard. The Nephilim turned his horse for the counterattack, but then fell sideways out of the saddle. His helmet rolled as he hit the ground.

Fire Rat killed differently than the others. He rode well, a small, quick mount that the big Etlantians could hardly keep track of, and each time he passed one, he would fling a goat's bag of naphtha. They were weighted with heavy stones and rope that wrapped about the giant's necks until the bags struck and exploded in wreaths of searing white flame—the Rat's own special recipes, sometimes brilliant white, sometimes orange, other times even blue flame, but all equally deadly, wreathing heads and helmets and melting flesh to its bone. One he flung about a horse's neck, a larger bag that exploded in a roar that swam outward, enveloping both the giant and his charger. As well bred as they were, even Nephilim did not like to burn, and the warrior screamed furiously as his face melted in his helmet.

Hyacinth stared over the city below, watching in stunned silence. Some of the big Etlantians were dying, but the tide was turning fast. Not only was the fabled Emerald city of Ophur in flames, but the angel's sons were beginning to kill the legendary sea raiders like cattle being slaughtered for a feast. She felt her breath grow short, seeing warriors dying that she believed invincible, warriors she never thought she would see fall in battle.

"Loch . . ." she said, turning, still searching for him. Gone. He had vanished, making it impossible for her to follow. She ran to the edge of the butte. "Loch!" she cried. The sound of hooves turned riders toward her, Etlantians—they had reached even the edge of the knoll where Taran's villa was built, and seeing her, they came as a group of five, thundering up the side of the hill that led to Taran's villa, coming directly for her. Hyacinth gasped and started running for the trees.

Danwyar was riding one down when unexpectedly, the Etlantian turned and flung a killing axe from his side. There was no time to dodge. The axe head sheared through Danwyar's upper arm, through muscle and bone, then spun away into the dark. He had just lost the use of one arm, but he ignored it, galloping after the giant as if nothing had happened, reaching over his shoulder to draw his crossbow. But his cherished silver bow fell to the ground.

He put the bolt through the oraculum breastplate with a solid ponk, anchoring it through the heart. The giant arched his back, and Danwyar had to drop from his saddle. He could not use the crossbow and guide the horse at the same time. He turned, then suddenly felt his blood run cold. Four riders were closing on him. He had been killing hard and fast, dodging, outflanking—the silver arrows had taken down seven Nephilim. Perhaps that was why they were finally noticing the swift-moving archer. He used his thigh to prop the crossbow and shoved in another bolt. This was not going to last long. Hard to reload with one hand.

He remained calm, centering his crossbow and waiting. He needed closer range. He wondered if he could get two. That would be a good end to things, bring down two more with just one arm. As the first drew close enough he watched the heavy crossbow bolt sink dead center through the opening in the helmet. That went upward into the brain and even a firstborn could not ignore it—the Etlantian went over the flanks, armor breaking away from him as he hit the ground rolling.

"Goddess be kind," Danwyar whispered, trying to get one more bolt in. One more—that would be satisfying. He lifted the crossbow, loaded, but they caught him.

A javelin struck Danwyar in the stomach. It could easily have been a death thrust, but purposely it only tore through into his guts, a slow kill. He tried to lift the crossbow, but his strength was failing too quickly and it slipped from his hand. Three of them circled him as he hit the ground on his back. One passed by at a gallop and wrenched the javelin free, ripping away flesh and blood through Danwyar's leathers.

"Giving you honor, slayer," one said in a deep voice, pulling his horse to a stop and staring down at the Tarshian. He then lifted a chained hook, spinning it and anchored the point through Danwyar's good arm. Another Etlantian anchored his leg. The hooks burned as they ripped into his flesh, and when they were attached, the riders brought the chains taut. Now his last leg. He hissed through tight teeth. He was going to be quartered; another was approaching from the right.

"Piss on you all!" he screamed. "Piss on you and piss on your mothers, you godless sons of whores!"

"They have got Danwyar!" Storan cried, seeing four horsemen about the little archer. He wrenched hard on the reins, turning his big horse so sharply it nearly spilled him, but then launched into a heavy, muscled gallop after Danwyar. He angled his axe for the strike.

Storan heard Danwyar's cry. They ripped limbs off him. It was more than

Storan could take. His eyes went red with blood.

Darke saw Storan's attack, but could not help. He had killed one highborn, but a second did something unexpected; he leapt from the horse and tackled Darke. When they hit the ground, the weight of the giant crushed the air from him, but before he was pinned, Darke managed to roll sideways, clearing enough distance to pull a dagger. Apparently the Etlantian had meant to beat him to death, no weapon drawn—just fists. Darke's dagger went upward under his chin. The giant went at it, managed to rip it out, caring nothing of the blood, but the poison then took hold and the Nephilim seemed to pause as though troubled, then fell forward on one hand, head hanging, and finally dropped completely.

Darke came to his knees, searching for his horse.

Storan guessed Danwyar already dead—he was a torso now. It brought tears of pure fury to the big helmsman's eyes. He would, in Elyon's blessed name, take out a few of these bastards, so help him, but then one of them turned. Time seemed to slow, everything slowed, and Storan clearly saw the eyes of this one—as if they drew him in. All the eyes of the Nephilim had a kind of light to them, but this one was different. He wore no helmet, his hair was white and ashen, and his eyes were black, as if they were holes in his head, but the thing about them was the feeling stars were about to spill through, as if these eyes opened through to heaven. It was not a highborn. This was the angel, and those eyes caused even Storan's to give a moment's pause, a second's flicker, and then he continued to charge forward with a battle cry, coming straight for the Watcher, straight for the bastard fallen from the stars as if this were going to be no different than any other kill.

Darke saw it; he was too far to do anything to help, though it would not have mattered.

The angel first drove Storan's horse mad. It reared, twisting, and Storan was thrown, though the big axeman did not seem to even care. He managed to land on his feet and kept coming, unfazed, at full run, axe ready, his war cry echoing into the early dawn, promising fury.

The angel seemed only amused, he watched Storan with interest before he calmly drew what looked to be a pure crystal sword from its sheath and leveled the tip. It was like the Daath's blade, a sunblade.

But it fired nothing more than a small pulse, like a stone of tight, fixed light. It unceremoniously pierced Storan's heart, blowing through the armor of the backplate. Storan was thrown back. He slid in the dirt until he lay still, eyes open face twisted to the side.

Darke lowered his head and curled his hand to a fist on his knee. He let the cold tear that fell across his cheek turn deep in his gut as he focused but contained his rage. When he looked up, he saw the angel and three of his sons turn and ride slowly north. They hadn't noticed him—maybe they didn't care, Darke never having been their target. They were going for the knoll, for Taran's villa, as if no one needed to explain how to find the Daath.

Darke held back a moment, then vaulted onto his horse. No more of them around. Killing mostly done now. Few screams—battle cries still from below, but it was over. Finished. All the years of struggle against the Etlantians, seven hundred years of it, and the last fight ended so quickly, it almost seemed without climax.

Darke turned the reins and started following the angel and his sons, but not at a gallop. He paced them, keeping to the shadows.

He passed Storan's body and did not look down. But when he reached Danwyar he paused, circling the horse. Danwyar's eyes were still open. They blinked. He was still alive. Tough little bastard, he was. Always had been. Danwyar looked up to his captain once more.

"Guess I lost that last one," Danwyar whispered, weakly. "But you keep going—find the Daath—make certain that unholy bastard angel gets taken out, you do that, Captain, you do that."

"My word on it," Darke answered as he unsheathed a dagger from his the belt over his back.

"A good fight," Danwyar said, blood drooling from the corner of his mouth. "Ending was written, but damned good fight, you think?"

"That it was. See you in the otherland, my brother." Darke planted the dagger into Danwyar's heart and watched the eyes quickly fade lifeless.

Darke turned the mount and continued pacing the angel, keeping his thoughts inward, keeping everything hidden now.

Hyacinth ran. The five horsemen had reached the plateau, and now they were easily going to catch her before she could reach the cover of the trees. Then, quite suddenly, there was a star-fire crack and one of them went down, violently flung off his horse, hitting the ground so hard she heard bones cracking. She saw him—Loch, standing near the trees. His face was cold, expressionless. He killed them, one by one, though she could see each bolt he fired from the sword rocked his body. It sucked blood and pain; she knew that from feeling it when she was inside him.

The last of the Etlantians tried to reach him, galloping hard, axe raised. Loch calmly let him get close, welcoming him. There was a dead coldness in Loch's eyes, no hint of the calm brown eyes she had seen the night before—they were now black as night and no longer human, but almost the eyes of a cat. Just as the Etlantian let out his war cry, close enough for the strike, Loch's blade fired a blast that tore off the Nephilim's head. The giant road past, axe still poised, and it was some moments before the body even fell from its mount.

She noticed Loch was bleeding. He hadn't been touched—none of them had reached him, but a line of blood streamed down his cheek from a split vessel near his right eye. The sword was going to suck out his life; he had measured the strikes—he had to pace himself—and she wanted to tell him, warn him, but he merely looked at her a moment.

"Stay back, Hyacinth," he said. "It will be over soon."

He then turned and started down the granite stairway that led to the city. There was a plaza just below Taran's villa, surrounded by conifers. She saw four riders slowly moving for it from the south, and one of the riders, the one in the center—though he wore similar armor and the same dull red cloak as the others—bore himself different. He wore no helmet and she realized, seeing the white hair, sensing him, that he was the angel. This time there was no fear in Satariel. She sensed he had come to merely get it done with, finish it.

Fire Rat sprinted hard through the shadow of the trees toward the last he had seen of his captain. Behind him, the body of a Nephilim was twisting in circles, burning. As powerful as they were, these firstborn, they really seemed to hate burning; it seemed to throw them into utter rage. Even if they lived, they would have no skin or eyes or hair. But Fire Rat had no more bags—no more bags of naphtha, no more hollowed knives with their flint and sulfur detonators. He had nothing left but his frail, ragged body and his thin legs as he ran full-out after his king, panting in measured breaths.

On the smooth, round stonework of the plaza, Satariel brought his horse to a halt. It danced a moment on the stone. The three firstborn with him drew up on either flank. There they waited for the Daath as he walked down a pathway, then about the edge of a granite wall. It was an overlook, with a view of the city below that was now a view of bodies and fire. When Loch reached the plaza, he stepped into the light, then stopped near the edge of the back wall, finished in limestone, and calmly met the angel's eyes. He showed no emotion, no clue to what was inside. If Eryian had taught him anything, he had taught him to keep his thoughts, his intent, always hidden.

Hyacinth reached him, slightly out of breath.

"You do not mind well, do you, Hyacinth?" Loch said.

"Not this time," she answered.

"Hyacinth," said the angel. "I have always liked them—the way the bulbs can wait decades and still grow to full bloom."

She said nothing, her eyes narrowed, her crossbow angled to the side, loaded with her most potent poison.

Satariel studied her a moment longer, then said quietly, "Kill her, Aragel."

One of the firstborn started forward, slowly.

As Loch began to lift the sword, Hyacinth laid her hand over his. "No," she whispered. "Save your blood. I can take him, Loch. Just let him a bit closer."

She waited, keeping the small crossbow with its six loads loose and ready. But when the firstborn named Aragel was halfway across the plaza, he paused, turning at a sound from the forest. It was Darke, coming at a full gallop. The firstborn seemed almost curious, watching from beneath his smoked helm with bright, ice-blue eyes as the Tarshian burst from the trees, hooves clattering on the stone of the plaza. Aragel did not even bother to draw his sword until Darke was almost on him. In the final second, Aragel's sword cleared the scabbard in a song, a dark, burnished oraculum blade, well used, moving in a blur—as did Darke's. Their blades rang out, slamming into each other as the horses collided, rearing, circling. As others, Darke saw the surprise in the Etlantian's eyes—that a mortal could move this quick, this deadly. He ducked, letting the firstborn's blade slice over his shoulder and used his side thrust, through the leather ties of the oraculum armor. In and out, with a serpent's flicker, Darke's long sword pierced the heart. For a moment it had little effect; Aragel was lifting his sword for another strike, but then he paused, drew a startled breath, then fell over the side of his horse, his armor clanking as it hit the stone.

Darke turned toward the angel. Satariel stared at his son's body a moment with a look of disgust before lifting his gaze to Darke.

"Still alive," he mused. "You truly vex me, Tarshian. But the girl dies now."

Moving swiftly, with a flick of his wrist, the angel flung something from his side, a small spinning disk of silvery light.

"No!" screamed Darke.

Hyacinth had no time to react. The disk swiped soundless through her neck, cleanly shearing muscle and vein, whipping her head to the side so hard she was spun about and landed on the stone, facedown, her brown hair splayed out into the blood that quickly pooled about her head. Her small crossbow dropped from her fingers, but just before she fell a bolt had fired, aimlessly into the night.

Loch did not move. Even if he had wanted, it had happened too quickly. He remained still, his cold, dark eyes fixed on Satariel.

Darke screamed and launched his charger against the angel. He could no longer hold his rage, but it was another of the sons that rode to meet him. Rage and fury can make a warrior a terror in battle, but it also takes away focus, and this time a spinning, spiked morning star struck Darke's cuirasses in the chest before his sword could move. Darke's chest plate caved in, mangled, blood splattering. He was thrown from the saddle. He hit the limestone on his back, sliding. His sword clattered across the stone, knocked from his hand. He lay for a moment on his back, tried to turn to the side to get back up, but instead stilled.

The firstborn circled his horse back to Satariel's side. Loch watched as others joined them. The battle was finished below—this was what was left of the angel's sons. Loch did not know how many had landed on Ophur, but he guessed they had been thinned. Perhaps fifteen of them still alive, forming a semicircle to either side of the angel.

The angel studied him for emotion over Hyacinth or the captain's fall, but Loch's eyes remained cold and empty, like a wolf watching, centered only on Satariel.

"What is it about you?" the angel said, genuinely curious. "I have tried to understand, but I can only marvel that this is what Elyon sends in the final hour of turning—nothing more than a boy. I cannot fathom how you are to be the savior your frail prophets have written of for seven hundred years. Before you die, pray—can you explain it to me?"

"I never asked," Loch said. He gripped the hilt of the Angelslayer in both hands. It was calmly pooling blood sucked through his palms, from the pommel stone into the flange where it swirled through the glow of the crystal a rich, dark red.

"The sword of Uriel," said the angel. "Centuries since I have seen that glow. Do you even know what it is you hold in your hand?"

"Your end? Is that not what the frail prophets have told us?"

This seemed to irritate him a bit. "Yes, well, this has all been entertaining—pirates that can slay pure-blooded firstborn and a boy little more than twenty years carrying the sword of an archangel, even the sword that once guarded the East of the Land. Elyon knows I am a curious creature, but I am done with trying to understand any more of this madness. It has come time to die, boy. Let us finish it."

The angel's blade came to life, but it was Loch who moved first. He dropped to a roll, his cloak flaring. It was the move of a Shadow Walker, and for a moment Loch vanished, though the angel seemed to track him easily. When Loch came into focus, he was crouched, the sword poised to fire a blast of blue light that struck the angel in the chest. It had been swift, and when it struck, it exploded, bathing the plaza in blinding light. But Satariel had not so much as flinched. His horse had staggered a bit, back stepping, but nothing more.

Satariel remained calm, his blade humming, no longer crystal but now a deep, severe burn of white light. "That was it? This is mockery, nothing more than mockery. Make your last offerings, boy, your time is about to end."

To block the light of the angel's sword, Loch had to pour everything into the hilt of the Angelslayer and use its fire as a shield. The angel's strike bore down upon him like a wall of heavy stone, but the Angelslayer was able keep it from flinging him into the dawn's light. The cost in Loch's blood was heavy. A vessel blew open from the back of his hand, and the pain of keeping the Angelslayer lit surged through his head.

He then snuffed the Angelslayer's light and dropped quickly, letting the angel's blast pass over his shoulder, sundering the stonework behind with a gash that drove deep into the island's core. Loch rolled and was able to angle the sword quickly enough for a second strike, this time into Satariel's arm, which was bare flesh. It struck with such suddenness, even the angel flinched, which gave Loch time enough to slash the stream of light sideways and shear off the head of the angel's horse. As the horse's body crumpled, Loch ran—more than ran; as Eryian had taught him from youth, he flashed into a blur and then, aided by the cloak, he was able to vanish so completely, even the angel lost track of him for seconds. It was as though he had dived into a hole in the dim light of the dawn and when he appeared—he was behind Satariel.

"Father!" one of the Nephilim screamed.

With a war cry, Loch sank the Angelslayer into the flesh of the angel's neck at the edge of his armor, driving it downward, deep into the shoulder muscle—into what should have been lungs and vitals. He then fired the blade, letting it suck blood through the hilt so hard it was leaving him dizzy, his head spinning, light. A vessel burst open from his forearm, then another from his temple. Pain surged like he was burning alive, but he continued to funnel his blood and more—something of his soul—into the blade. Satariel's skin about the wound started to boil, the angel's blood spitting about the wound, a rich, lavish red.

With a snarl, the angel reached back, curled his hand about the flange of Uriel's sword, and yanked it out of his back. Loch could not hold on; the angel was too strong. Satariel threw the sword with a growl, and it hit the limestone—still alive, spinning, crackling, sending streamers of lightning that snaked across the stone until finally it came to a rest and slowly cooled.

The angel then grabbed Loch by one arm and flung him, as well, through the air to strike the shattered stone of the wall so hard he dropped to the plaza, almost unconscious and crouched on one knee, using one hand to hold himself up. He was breathing heavily; not only had the sword had taken everything from him, but the blow had nearly killed him. He felt crushed ribs, his shoulder dislodged. He was staring downward and the fine, polished limestone blurred in and out of focus. He noticed his own blood was dropping in splats. Pain was his entire world—a continual heartbeat of pain, sucking him in and out of consciousness. But somehow, he forced himself to focus past it and slowly looked up.

The angel, breathing through tight teeth, was also in pain. In fact, the skin of his face was reddened and he was sweating blood. He slowly stood up, watching Loch with black, empty eyes. Satariel's own sunblade was angled to the side, a soft white, like ivory. His sons were fanned out to either flank. One even started forward, furious.

"No!" warned Satariel. The Nephilim backed off. "Stand up, Angelslayer," Satariel commanded.

Loch could barely even hear his voice; it was as if the pain and blood loss had left him in a void at the edge of consciousness.

"I said, stand up! Or do you wish to die on your knees like the mongrel you are?"

Loch struggled. He had to brace himself against the stone, and it took effort, but he pulled himself slowly to his feet. And though he stood like a drunk, unsteady, using a hand on the stone wall to brace himself, he turned and faced the angel with the dark, wolflike eyes of the Shadow Walker. Satariel at last seemed impressed.

"Perhaps you are the seed of Uriel, Daath. A move like that—other than the scion of an Archangel, who could have moved like that? But the sad part of all this is you are no prophecy, boy. All that remains is your death."

Loch stared back uncaring.

There was a moan and Loch noticed from the corner of his eye that it was Darke. The captain wasn't dead. In fact, he had been watching, propped up on one elbow, holding his one hand to his crushed chest, blood spilling through his fingers. He was having trouble breathing, but his eyes were still strong.

"Should I finish the Tarshian, Father?" asked the firstborn that had brought Darke down.

"No, let him live. I want him to know your brother Arazach and five others are even now riding for the hidden cave, for the little ones and the women. I have told Arazach to kill them slowly—a slow burning over coals. For all my sons you have slain, Shadow Hawk."

Darke reacted, stunned.

"How does it feel knowing you end here, you, your people, your entire bloodline—forever and all time? Rather something of an anticlimax, is it not?"

Darke watched back with smoldering eyes. "I think you forget something," he said through tight teeth.

"And what would that be, Emerald King?"

"The Angelslayer is still standing." Darke rolled, ripping a crossbow from his back, swiftly coming to a crouch, and firing. The bolt struck the angel, even pierced his left shoulder, through the weakened skin of Loch's burn and out the back, but there was no reaction from Satariel—he seemed to have barely felt it—and the wound instantly began to close. But it made no difference; it was meaningless—a distraction. Darke had even thrown the crossbow aside. He was now holding the sword of Uriel.

"What is that line from Enoch I always liked?" Darke asked. "Oh, yes, Hyacinth read it to me—I was thinking of it earlier. 'Yea, though once you walked as sons of gods, Bene ba Elohim, you shall die as men shall die.' Darke threw the sword and Loch caught the hilt with both hands. The blade instantly flashed white-hot. The Daath looked pale and almost dead, as if he could barely stand, let alone use the sword once more, but still it came alive, simmering with a far promise.

"This time use it, Daath!" shouted Darke. "Use the damned sword, not your blood, and send this motherless bastard to creation's end!"

Darke then back stepped, leapt onto his horse, drawing up the reins and sinking his heels into the sides with a scream. The horse bolted forward into a heavy gallop—he was riding for the chosen—the last of his people, the last of his kind.

Satariel made no move to follow, nor his sons. The angel turned to Loch, watching him calmly. "Good advice, but you can hardly stand up, Angelslayer. I doubt you can even lift the sword, let alone light the blade once more. What exactly are you planning to do?"

"What the Tarshian said," Loch answered, out of breath, still unsteady. He tightly curled both hands about the hilt and eased into a back stance. "I think . . . I think I finally understand."

"And how can you possibly do more than you have? Please—I would love to know what you are thinking."

"I am thinking that it is not me. Not my blood—is it not the blade's thirst for blood that can kill an angel. Something else kills angels. All I need to do is let go and remember the home of this blade, the star from where it was born. Am I right, Satariel, Lord of the Choir of Orphanim?"

Satariel drew his lip back in a snarl. "Enough of this! It ends here; it ends now!" The angel's sunblade came alive, moving in a furious arc. It was blinding, searing. Loch had to avert his eyes, but he spun to the side as Satariel's fire cut a deep swath through the plaza's stone, sending chips of granite spinning past his cheek. Loch crouched, bracing himself, and brought the sword of Uriel over his head to catch Satariel's light, snagging it, letting it stream into the Angelslayer's blade. It came hot, intense, with a sound like lightning crackling.

The blast spilling over the plaza was so bright even the Nephilim had to shield their eyes. It continued, bearing down with more and more force, a sizzling, whirling blast, the heat of it burning Loch's face. But as furious as it was, it was being swallowed into the Angelslayer, as if the blade welcomed it. Loch was still losing blood. It was even flowing from the skin on his wrist in tiny streamers, like red strings. Loch knew he would soon black out; he felt his life draining, even his eyes were growing dim, but he lowered his head and leaned into it, continued to press into the stream of Satariel's fire.

And then—finally, he heard her voice. Her. Not Adrea, not his mother. On the beach that day, when Loch gave Adrea the ring of the Water Bearer, she had opened the eye of Daath. And it was her voice that whispered now. The mirrored image of the mothering star finally crossed the void, through a rift in time and heaven.

The light that pierced through to the small plaza in Ophur was not blinding, not like the severity of Elyon's wrath as the fire of the angel. It was merely the touch of creation; it was the *Light Whose Name Is Splendor.*

Although the light that burst through like a wave breaking seemed so bright and searing it should have blinded all of them, it did not. There was no pain to it, not for Loch. It was more like a wind spilling out, and Loch felt as though he were falling, that if he let himself go, he would fall into the sky, into this light, and reach heaven.

The fire of the mothering star came against the angel Satariel and his sons. It was the very word of the angel's song, which had once been his heart and his hope, that now struck the angel. Bathed in its light, he dropped to his knees, stunned, and lowered his head as the mothering light ripped through him like a howling wind. Satariel's sword exploded. Pieces of the blade spun outward in shards as if it had been no more than a crystal goblet.

The angel held his ground, though it seemed the light that passed through him hit like a hard rain pelting, like a fierce storm off the sea, almost flinging him into the rising sun of dawn behind his back; he continued to kneel against it. His sons, the gathered Nephilim to either side, dissolved into what seemed to be teardrops of shadow, and then they were no more, though behind them the green foliage of the conifers and the grasses were left untouched, unaffected.

The angel kept his head lowered into the blast, the wind of it tearing at him furious, screaming without sound—it was the feel of sound, a sad wail of a mother over a dying son, a cry of terrible loss. Satariel's cloak was shredded but stayed intact, though pieces of his oraculum armor shattered and tore away.

And then, as simply and mysteriously as it had came, the light ended, the eye of Daath closed as if the light in the plaza had been snuffed with a candle douser. Dawn's light fell over them in a bright, red hue and sound thinned to a quiet with far, soft flicker of fires burning below in Ophur. The Angelslayer was just a crystal blade, no blood swirling, no silver flashing.

Loch dropped forward, so weak he could not believe he was still conscious. He was on both knees, leaning against the sword for support, head hanging down. For a moment, he felt as if he were about to pass into shadow—and yet there was such peace in him, such a gentle, soft touch somehow slowly restoring his strength. He did not understand what had happened, not fully. It had filled him with a wondrous knowing—what was called the star knowledge—but even as he tried to comprehend it, he could feel it fading, slipping away. Faith was always a light that dimmed too quickly.

He set the tip of the sword against the limestone and drew himself to one knee, then looked up.

The angel was kneeling, head down. Satariel seemed confused, staring at the hilt of his shattered sword in utter disbelief. He finally tossed it aside, angrily. Slowly, he pulled himself to his feet, steadying himself. He had changed. Most striking were his eyes. Before they had been a terrifying black—threatening to spill the stars of the gods' wrath at any moment, but now Satariel's eyes were a clear, ice-blue—they were, in fact, the eyes of a human.

"Thou art mortal," a low, quiet voice said. "As mortal as the blood that has cried for centuries from this Earth, as mortal as the innocents you have slain all these years, Satariel."

Satariel turned. Loch knew the voice and looked to see Sandalaphon near the edge of the shattered stone wall just behind him—as if he might have been there watching all along.

Satariel glared at Sandalaphon, then looked down at himself. He held out his hands, turned them. His skin was different somehow, softer, merely flesh.

With the fingers of his right hand he ripped open his left wrist and watched, stunned as red blood flowed, spilled onto the stone. The wound did not heal as it had when Darke's bolt pierced his shoulder. He just continued to bleed. When he looked up, there was panic in his eyes, in his face. He brought his fingers stiff, forming a knife-hand, then staved it into his own chest and ripped out his own heart. For a moment, he stood there, staring at it in his hand, squeezed tight, blood spilling. He then fell to his knees, then onto the stone, facedown.

Loch turned to look at Sandalaphon. "How long have you been here?"

"Long enough."

"But you did not help? Why?"

"I am forbidden in many things. Time must unfold of its own. Heaven binds me. Not my heart, however. I bleed for you, Lochlain—but I am bound, and more than that, it is written, and so it must be, that the fallen must be made flesh by the scion of a Daath and the blood of a human. It is why Elyon sent the Arsayalalyur in answer to the cries of the Earth—that the blood of men would answer the death of their fathers; it is why the Daath have for centuries mixed their blood with their kindred, the Lochlain. But we are not quite finished. There is one thing left. Satariel must be bound. It is why I am here. Only the sword of Gabriel can bind them."

"You carry the sword of Gabriel?"

"He is my father. Close your eyes and cover your face—the light will blind you otherwise."

Sandalaphon drew the sword.

Loch turned away, but he heard the sounds, a thousand winds, the earth opening like a tree being split apart and then a rushing, like waters, and then something collapsing, closing with a thunderclap. When he could finally look up, there was a pale, green, glasslike circle impressed into the ground where Satariel had been lying.

"What happened?" asked Loch. "Where is he?"

"There is a prison fashioned for them. They will dwell there ten thousand years, until the coming of the lamb, until the Earth opens up its dead in the first lifting. Their prison is deep, bound on all sides by the pillars of fire that hold the form of the Earth, anchoring its heart." Sandalaphon then studied

Loch a moment with a look of concern. "You want to know, but I cannot speak of her, Lochlain. I care, I feel your pain, but there is nothing I can tell you. She is where hope still dwells—as the rest of us; she lives now by heaven's oath. The blood of the archangel is strong in you, but there is still anger, and the anger you feel is human—flesh continues to weaken you. This is not finished yet—it is only the beginning."

"What are you saying?"

"Satariel was the first to age, the first to actually fall from the grace of *the knowing*. There were seven prefects who swore the Oath of Binding upon Mount Ammon in the time of Yered. They were the seven Watchers of heaven, and six still burn with the star knowledge, the light of Elyon. Beyond them were the three, the lords of the choir. Even now, one of them, a Named, a lord of the Seraphim—the second of the three—come against your people. You will have to stop him, as well, before it is too late, before the chosen are lost to time and the Earth is swallowed by Aeon's End."

"Another? The weak one has left me all but dead, and you tell me there is another?"

"Another that is far more powerful than you or I can imagine."

Loch just stared at him; he had no words for this.

"I have a small ship in the lagoon," Sandalaphon said. "It light and shallow, but it is very swift."

"The captain—first I must help him."

"The sons of Satariel have become but spirits now, most of them lost and panicked. They are doomed to wander the Earth and plague mankind until the opening of the Earth. Those few left alive, the Tarshian will take care of himself. We must leave—time is thin, it grows thinner each second."

Loch just stared at him, winded, still weak. He wanted to scream at him, wanted to scream at heaven, but he was too weak, too tired to fight any longer. He turned to stare at Hyacinth, her long, curled brown hair snarled in the pool of her own blood that had formed to the side of her head and etched into the cracks of the plaza's limestone fitting. He walked to her, knelt beside her, and touching her shoulder, slowly turned her over. He stared at her face, half of it bloodied, but he took the time to smooth a lock of hair out of her eye.

"You cannot do what you are thinking," Sandalaphon said.

"I can and I will. She is coming with us." He lifted the Angelslayer, laying the crystal blade against the smooth surgeon's cut in Hyacinth's neck.

"Lochlain, if you do this—it will weaken you—like sin weakens a pure heart. It is against heaven."

"Giving life is against heaven? How could I not have guessed?"

"You must try to understand. Do this and a part of you will be lost that cannot ever be regained."

"She comes with us, Sandalaphon, and if it is of any interest to heaven, what harm it leaves me could hardly be more meaningless right now."

He closed his eyes and began to focus on the feeling that swam in the pommel's stone. He knew how to do this. Enough of the star knowledge was still in him, the knowing grace. He understood it was going to fade like dreams fade, that he would soon wake and it would be gone. Even the faith that it had ever happened would be gone. Like the face of his mother. He had tried to remember her, tried so hard, but the years took her face, her memory, her smell. But in this moment, Loch knew, he understood, and he let his mind open, let a trickle more of his own blood, through the palms of his hands.

"Amen-Omen-Diaman," he whispered—spell-binding words whose meaning he would soon forget. It would not matter—it was not the words, it was the understanding of them, the burning of starlight left in them. He then let a part of himself through the pommel stone into the blade, a part of his life, not his soul, more a part of his faith, of his inner light, something that would leave him weakened, perhaps forever.

The blade flashed softly—nothing like the fire of battle—and with a start, Hyacinth gasped, sucking in air as if she had just surfaced from almost drowning. When Loch lifted the sword away, her wound was healed, the skin smooth, no scars. She started to get up and he set his hand on her shoulder, helping her to sit up. She stared at him, startled.

"Loch?"

He nodded.

"Is it . . . is it over?"

"Yes."

"And the others—did any of the others make it alive?"

"They have been slaughtered, all but a few."

"The captain? Darke—did they kill him?"

"No. He will survive."

Her eyes searched his quickly; she then touched his neck. "Was I . . . did I die?"

"You are going to be weak for the next few days. Your blood loss was great; it will have to replenish before you have the strength to walk."

"You used the sword. You brought me back."

He didn't answer.

"You should not have done this, Loch. Not for one such as I—not for me."

Loch glanced over his shoulder. "This is Sandalaphon. I must return. You can stay if you wish, or if you choose, you can come with me, Hyacinth. Which do you wish?"

"What would you want me to do?"

"Come with me."

"It is not over, is it? All you must face—it has not ended."

"No."

"I have been in you, touched you—I may even love you. I will go with you, Loch. But you should have left me here, dead; you should not have weakened yourself. I am only a witch; I am no Water Bearer."

"I know who you are. Sandalaphon will carry you; I am too weak. We must leave now."

Hyacinth looked to the giant, but her eyes were sad, misted in tears.

Chapter Thirty-Nine
Cassium

Eryian stood on a knoll and from there he could see the bustling city of Ishmia, once a fishing village, now a trading port that could only be rivaled by the Mother City herself. Almost any ship bound for Etlantis from the south stopped here. Ishmia had grown fat and rich, but Eryian could only think of how many would die if Hericlon fell, if the named one of Du'ldu crossed and came north for Terith-Aire. Ishmia would lay between them, unwalled, a sprawling city impossible to defend.

He turned east to follow the ribbon of dark water that was the river Ithen. It flowed from the mountains east, from Hericlon's vale and once was much wider until the Galagleans, upriver near the vale, built a dam that tamed it. Still, as he watched its dark waters he felt something cold from them; he felt as if something had changed and it left an ill ease he didn't want to feel. He looked to the east, troubled.

It was said the Etlantians had built the massive gate of Hericlon long ago, when first the angels had come to teach the children of men. But the second to follow the Light Bearer, Azazel, fought with him over a woman, slaying her in the end, and to escape the Light Bearer's wrath, he sailed to the south. The angels themselves bordered on war and the passage through Hericlon divided all that was the death lords between those who sided with Etlantis and her king, the bringer of heaven's light. It was then the Etlantians built the massive gate of huge cyclopean blocks of black stone cut from the mountain and the massive portcullis poured of pure oraculum, the heaviest, strongest structure on the whole of the Earth. For all the centuries of mankind, Hericlon had stood as the might of Etlantis against the rogue angel who not only broke his covenant with the choir of heaven by swearing upon Mount Ammon, but also was the first of the angels to commit murder.

Staring to the east, Eryian knew something had changed. He could not let himself believe that the mighty gate had fallen, that the passage was open and the lord of death would pass through now like the shadow of a dark star. And yet it whispered to him, a cold wind that came down the river Ithen, a dire warning that all was not right, that the balance of the Earth had changed and nothing he could do could turn it back.

It was near sunset and Eryian searched the sky. He had returned from the spire. He carried at his hip the sword that was known as the sword of Righel—a sunblade forged of aganon, the metal of a distant planet that circled the seventh star, the mothering star whose name was Dannu, whose sister was her mirror image, the queen they called the Daath. And now, reaching Tillantus and the legions above Ishmia overlooking the Ithen, he saw in the sky the answer to the call he sent to heaven from the star spire. It was the herald, the talisman. At first, against the darkened sky of the west, it was a quick, brilliant flash, a pulse of light as if something had burst through the heavens. Many of the Daathan warriors gathered on the high ground above Ishmia looked up to see the sky briefly lit. Eryian then heard the caw of an eagle and he saw the circle overhead, a silver eagle, its talons arched. He followed its path, saw where it dipped one wing downward indicating direction. Then in an arc, the sun glinting off its brilliant wings, it soared and vanished into the sky. The signet of the seventh star. Eryian's call had been answered. Something inside him understood it all, what it meant, why it came, but his flesh still held back the memories of the spire and the sword and even the meaning of the talisman, though he understand to follow its signal.

Tillantus had been near Eryian at the time, and he stared upward, amazed.

"My lord, you see that?" he asked. "Thought it was an eagle, but it soared so high, it seemed to vanish into heaven. A silver eagle, never seen the like of that. Have you?"

"No, Tillantus. But you are right. It is a signal; it comes as herald."

"How do you mean that, my lord?"

Eryian turned his gaze north toward the coastline. He saw them. The bird had dipped its wing above the western shore, across the river from the city. It was there they would meet him, and searching he saw the tips of their masts, white masts against the darkening western sky, three ships sailing for the coast. It left a shiver across his skin. It was all real, the fog of memories that had lived hidden deep inside all these years, tangled memories, like the shadows of dream still left in daylight. *The knowing* in him whispered. If he wanted, he knew they he could finally peel back the veil, but ironically, he chose not to. The sadness that had struck him in the star spire, which had left him so overwhelmed, was not something he wanted to bring to life. These memories, whatever they were, however far back they reached, he would leave as shadows for now.

"Are you all right, my lord?" asked his first captain.

"I must ride north, Tillantus."

"Let me guess: alone."

"Not this time." Eryian pointed. "If you look, you can see their masts against the skyline."

"Ships!" Tillantus said, spotting them. "And tall, those are tall masts, my lord. Etlantian?"

"Yes. Once of Etlantis. Long ago."

"It is why you left the night the king was taken—to summon them. Am I right?"

"Yes, these ships have answered my call."

"And why, my lord, if I may ask?"

"I wish I knew, Tillantus. I knew to send the beacon, I knew when they would come, even where to find them when they did—but odd of it, I cannot tell you why."

"Perhaps it is a spellbound cast of the angel; perhaps they wait as a trap."

"I think not, but whoever they are, I will ride out to meet them." He noted Tillantus's disapproving glance. "You will hold here, on this high ridge. These are warships; their hulls are shallow enough to make passage from here to the vale. With them I can reach the mountain much quicker than our legions. And if they find the gate of Hericlon is still ours, trust me, those who come, the three masts you see against the horizon, they can hold Hericlon. They can hold till the winter snows seal off all passage through the mountains of Parminion, and that would grant us time."

"But, my lord, why should the Daath not march to follow, to meet you there in any event, the gate fallen or held?"

"If the gate is lost, the vale is low ground and offers no cover for your flanks. Here you are on high ground, the deepest part of the river below you. It is good ground to hold. It will cost heavily, the taking of this ridge against the legions of the Daath. The waters beyond widen to the sea and the port of Ishmia, and the death lord comes with the armies of Du'ldu. They are desert armies; they do not come with warships or galleys. They will follow the river and seeing the Daath gathered here, he will come for you. You will be his target; why venture farther when what he comes for waits here?"

"You speak, my lord, as though you believe Hericlon may have actually fallen."

"Perhaps it is merely a chill wind that comes down the Ithen I am feeling. They are not uncommon this time of year. Let us just say I will lead these ships upriver, not because I fear the gate is no longer ours, but in hopes to reach it quickly. Should it be that Hericlon has fallen, better it is they, those who come at my signal to this shore, meet the first wave of the Unchurians than to waste our legions trying to hold low ground with no barriers to our flanks. You would agree?"

"Aye, my lord. So then, Captain, it has come to this? That we even speak of Hericlon's fall? A gate that has held against the south for centuries uncounted. If that has happened, in Elyon's blessed name, what is it we face? What comes against us?"

"A Watcher, one who turned long ago. I choose this night not to name him, to leave him unknown, to give no honor. Prepare this ridge as I have instructed, give me three days upriver, as well as your prayers to heaven. You will see them pass, three white ships as we move upstream for the vale. They are Elyon's gift. I do not leave you without hope, Tillantus—they are our hope, our last hope against the tide. I may return, the gate secure, the winter snows locking her down, leaving her impregnable. That is why they have come, so honor them as they pass. Have our legions lift their swords in the sign that hope lives, that they come not to fall, but in Faith's Light. However, if by act of heaven, I do not return—"

"My lord, Eryian! Forgive me, but if you do not return, we are lost!"

"Until the last man falls, you have not yet lost, Tillantus. If one Daath still stands, you have not lost. And if I do not make it back, you will hold the ridge as I have instructed. Make the cost here heavy. If that fails, then pull back to the East of the Land. At its northern ridge, with the trees as your final barrier, make your last stand against them. Keep the chosen always to the rear, always protected. Nothing reaches the chosen; do you understand that?"

"Of course, my lord."

"And if that hour should arrive, Tillantus, that you make your stand with the forest before you, then look to the sea. Ships will come from the west, from Etlantia, a fleet of them. These you can trust; they will not fly the bull of Etlantis, but their sails shall be white. Hold the line against the East of the Land and ensure against all cost that the chosen reach the Etlantians. More than this, I cannot give you. I pray such hour never comes, that the final stand I just described never sees light. Yet, have we not learned in our day that Elyon often chooses His own path despite the prayers of the valiant?"

Tillantus studied Eryian, troubled, his eyes hardened. "Never believed in prophecy. Never listened to these wandering seers of Enoch or any of the legends passed down. If I am one of the valiant, my lord, I have not offered Elyon any prayers. Myself, I always believed in the haft of my axe and the spit on my balls."

Eryian smiled.

"You speak of legend, my lord," said Tillantus. "You speak of the winnowing war as if it lies at our doorstep. Tell me I am wrong."

Eryian did not answer.

"Then all those years," Tillantus said, "the gathering of the tribes—Argolis was not wrong. You were not wrong. And the hour spoken of in that long-ago day seems now to have arrived. If that be so, for myself, I do not see the silver eagle that soared into the sky just now. The bird I saw was the Raven of Aeon's End."

"You are the best warrior and the finest commander I have even known,

Tillantus. If it falls to you, save the chosen at all cost. I must leave now; I must meet the ships that sail from the deep of the Western Sea."

"Aye, my lord."

Eryian paused a moment longer, then reached his gauntleted hand and with a slap, Tillantus gripped his wrist hard, meeting his eyes in promise.

"If we do not meet again, Tillantus, Elyon's Light guide your path."

Tillantus stared hard, then nodded. "Godspeed, as well, my captain."

After crossing the isthmus of the Ithen where it spilled to the sea, Eryian led his horse off the boat, thanked his ferrymen, and sent them back with coin. The ferrymen had noticed, curious of the ships that came down from the west, but they had not dared ask Eryian from where or why.

Eryian rode south until he reached a long stretch of white sand. There he waited. He watched the tips of the white masts against the horizon. He had known they would come, he had known their count, three ships, but the rest of what he knew he left in memory's fog. Better that way, he told himself. He would learn what he needed when time came to know it. He calmly watched now as they drew up in order, closing on the beach. Though they were built as Etlantian ships, they were also built low and sleek—warships. As he had guessed, their sails were not marked by the bull of Etlantis. That was because they had not come from the Mother Island. He knew that; he understood that well. He had never seen white ships before, the hulls and sails were bright against the blue sea and dark sky. They could have been sculpted of ice.

Eryian rode through the sea grass at the edge of the shore, then along the sand where waves crested. They had seen him; they were going to shore their keels on the beach where he waited, and as he watched it seemed almost they were not sailing, but gliding, no wind against their full, billowed sails and no oars propelling them, yet they came on steady and certain. *Sky ships*, something in him whispered. They had not sailed out of the Western Sea; they had crossed from a far place, a place in the sky marked by the Seven Sisters. When they touched the waters, silver-white oars lifted out like feathered wings to dip into the sea, slowing them and letting the keels gracefully nudge into the sand.

Close up, the lead ship's prow post was a silver-white eagle with spreading wings. He saw warriors above the railings—giants. They did not wear the oraculum red armor or cloaks of Etlantians; their armor was silvered, their cloaks white. They all watched with more than mere interest; they were watching him with something like fascination.

A rope ladder unfurled, clattering against the white-silver planking of the hull. Eryian saw a woman's leg step over the white gunwale. Not a giant, as the warriors—this was a mortal woman. The first sight of her, coming down the ladder, took his breath. She wore a robe that was crystal blue, and her hair was white-gold.

Eryian dismounted.

She stepped into the shallow, warm sea waters at the edge of the sand and walked toward him. He was surprised she was barefooted. But there was something to her, the way she moved, and her face, her eyes, they struck him like a bolt from a crossbow. He knew her. But he kept the veil in place; he did not let memory break. He lowered himself to one knee, even lowered his head, for though he chose to keep his memories silent, he knew this was a queen.

She stopped before him.

"My lady," Eryian said quietly.

Surprisingly, she did not offer her hand. Instead, she lowered herself, dropping onto her knees in the sand before him, and there she waited for Eryian to meet her eyes at her level.

"You do not bow to me; it is I who bow before you. Have you forgotten?" She didn't wait for an answer; she found it in his eyes. "You have—you hold the veil, you do not know who I am, do you? Do you know even who you are? Do you know that?"

"I am Eryian, warlord of Argolis, king of the Daath."

The lips parted slightly, and she gasped. "You have buried them deep, the memories. Necessary, perhaps—but how it saddens me. Yet, it is your choice, my lord, and I will honor it."

Her eyes were ice diamonds; they burned with a light beyond human, but they were also kind, and seeing them this close, such a terrible sadness struck him, he felt his eyes sting. He knew her in a way that he wanted to hold her, but he restrained himself, just stared at her face, shaken. It was impossible to tell how old she was, for she looked pure, and her features were as fine and carefully cut as though her skin had been carved of ivory. It was a face filled with tenderness, as beautiful as any woman he had ever laid eyes on. Shivers ran through him.

"I . . . I know you. I understand that, but I must not yield, not now."

She paused. He thought for a moment her lip might have trembled. She bit it softly. She nodded. "Yes. You know me."

"Then it is why you have come—in answer to my call?"

"As you always knew we would," she said.

Eryian looked past her a moment, to the top of the white ship lined with rows of warriors.

"Three ships?" he asked. "How many men?"

"These are the thousand, Eryian, warlord of Argolis. These are the thousand sons of Righel."

The name startled him, and he realized that though her eyes were dimmed now, when she had spoken that name, for a second they had spilled light like the stars breaking on a clear night. The effect left him shaken. She seemed to expect more, and was studying him for a reaction. Finally, she looked down; almost as though she was hurt, but when the eyes lifted they were calm and assuring.

"I did not expect this to be hard . . . Eryian. Is that what you wish me to call you? Eryian?"

"It is my name here."

There were questions flooding him, but he did not ask them; he did not even think them through because the answers were already whispering all about, memories spilling—and it was only with difficulty he was able to turn them back. They were memories that threatened to overwhelm him, and he could not afford to be weakened. Emotions were weakness, and these were strong. Yet it was hard. Turning from their whisper was like turning his face from the light.

"Whoever you are," he said, "good lady, I thank you for coming."

She bowed her head and her hand brushed her cheek. It had been too quick to tell for certain, but she may have brushed away a tear. Still, when she looked back up, she smiled. Then she did something unexpected. She carefully touched his cheek, and when she did it was like quick current through him, something sad and far.

"For you," she said, "we would cross any sea—any night, any stars."

Eryian's mouth parted, stunned. That voice. He had heard it laugh, heard it sing, heard it weep. She withdrew her hand and Eryian was almost thankful.

"Should I have them disembark?" she asked.

"What . . ."

"Your priests, Eryian. Should they disembark here?"

"Priests?"

"Yes—these waiting on the ships, they are warrior priests. They were trained of a very powerful being. You have summoned the warriors of Righel—the thousand firstborn."

"Firstborn . . . these are Nephilim?"

"Like no others. They are not fallen, and they were born of Earth, but far. Their light is of a heaven, their home an ice moon that circles a planet near the seventh star. These are the sons of an angel who had never lost the star knowledge; they are pure."

Eryian closed his eyes a moment and forced the memories back. He would deal with it later. When he looked back up, he was sternly in control.

"Do we disembark, my lord?"

"No," he stammered. "No. I would like your ships farther in. This river is deep and your hulls are warships, shallow enough to sail far up its neck to the east. Far enough to reach a place called Hericlon's vale."

"The vale of Hericlon," she whispered darkly. "Yes, I remember. It is fitting; I suppose that if we are to meet him, it would be at Hericlon."

She studied him, and then, as though purposely, she let the star fire spill from her eyes a moment and Eryian spun with visions that bled out so swiftly he wasn't sure where it had spoken, or what it had been, but it seemed to have been the scream of dying souls, a scream of thousands. Eryian knew what it was; not memory, it was one of many futures. She knew, as well as he did, who they where about to face. There were stars that burned dark at the far end of the universe, stars that swallowed light and stole the fire of suns. Long ago, in the time of Yered, one of them had stepped from the sky to follow the Light Bearer, one of the firstborn of Elyon. And he was there; this being, Azazel, was waiting now in Hericlon's passage.

She stood and held out her hand. "Come," she said, "they have been waiting long to see you."

"Your warrior priests?" he asked.

She paused a moment, studying him. "I understand that you have chosen to hide. I cannot blame you. Perhaps it is even necessary. I remember how the veil was often a comfort. Very well, then. Come—Eryian, warlord of Argolis—meet the warrior priests of the seventh choir, the Choir of the Fiery Serpents of Elyon, the thousand Seraphim who are known as the Sons of Righel."

"And you, my lady?"

"You can't guess my name, Eryian?"

He could. He started to, but hesitated.

She smiled. "I am Cassium."

"You were his—Righel's. You are one of them. You are a Star Walker Queen."

"Yes, in a way I am. Righel taught me many things—he taught me the names of the heavens before the Earth was born, and the secrets of stars that burn deep beyond the rift of knowing, but also, before he left, he taught me of the *Light Whose Name Is Splendor.* But I am unlike the Star Walker Queens that are whispered of who dwelt in the time of Dawnshroud. I am not undead, merely aged carefully. And I do not hold the keys of turning, though perhaps I do remember a bit of magic." She smiled. "He changed me, but in a way he left me the same. That was his last gift to me."

"What gift?"

"My soul. If you had looked in my eyes in the age of Dawnshroud, you would barely have noticed it. But Righel laid hands on me and restored it; he did not let me turn."

She watched for his reaction, then smiled. The smile touched him. It was so familiar, the way it curled, the way dimples appeared; the quiet, half smile of Cassium, and he knew she could laugh with the thrill of a child. She was toying with him, letting memories spill like water over the lip of a glass. Eryian pulled himself sharply into focus, and though the smile remained, the memories drew back quietly.

"Come, Eryian. The Seraphim wish to see you."

As he followed her toward the ship, Eryian was grateful she had not pressed *the knowing* further. He knew the sword he had retrieved from the star spire off the coast was called the sword of Righel, and he knew that he was the Voyager of the seventh star. So not only did he carry Righel's sword, he was now about to take command of a thousand of his sons. Argolis had once told him Righel was a myth, a legend to inspire men to die, that the crypt in the tunnels beneath Terith-Aire was empty and always would be. Perhaps Argolis had known something he did not.

Eryian noticed as he climbed the ladder that the skin of the ship was more than just a brilliant silver-white, there was a oily light playing over it, reflecting darkly the purple waters of the Western Sea. He stepped over the railing onto the forecastle. He turned to help her over, as well. On this ship, from here to the stern, they all looked to him. One of them lifted his sword in salute, laying it across his heart, and bowed to one knee. Eryian was surprised, even stunned, when the rest of them bowed, as well, fists to their hearts in pledge.

"We honor you, my lord," said the first to bow. "I am Amathon, Commander of the First Century of Shieldbearers."

"Amathon," Eryian replied, nodding. "You may call me captain, or Eryian, if you prefer."

"Yes, my lord." The commander then motioned to an axeman beside him. "This is my second, my brother, Braemacht, who is commander of the queen's personal guard."

Even for a Nephilim, Braemacht was big. His axe had a back hammer and a killing spike on the pommel—built for close-in killing. If anyone ever reached the queen, they would face this one and others like him. His eyes, bright blue, met Eryian's briefly. "My lord," he said quietly.

In order, the others were introduced. The captains of the First and Second Century Horsemen; the thin, gaunt captain of archers, whose silver bow curled above his shoulder like the edge of a wing; the commander of the throwers; the spearmen; and two Century Captains of heavy sword.

"The Daath owe you all a heavy debt," Eryian said. "We are to sail east, up the neck of this river to a place called Hericlon's vale."

"Yes. We know of this place. It is the killing ground," said Amathon.

"Why do you say that?"

"It has always been known as the killing ground, from the time of Yered, from the days of the Dawnshroud."

"You say that as if you were there."

Amathon glanced briefly at Braemacht. "We were, my lord. We were there."

"For now, Amathon," said Cassium, "the veil protects us. For now we are going to let memories lie."

As the ships sailed up the Ithen, they glided through the dark waters much faster than oars or their strange gossamer sails could account for. There was wind in his hair as Eryian stood on the prow, watching the river unfold. The woman stood next to him. There was a smell from her, like the smell of fresh, pure, running waters. And even that, her smell, seemed to tingle a far memory inside him.

"What kind of ship is this?" Eryian asked.

"It is a warship," she answered.

"Not like any I have ever seen."

She smiled, saying something without really saying it. Eryian felt that if he wanted, if he let go, he could hear her with words. He turned, pointing.

"There," Eryian said. "The legions of the Daath salute you."

They turned to see a wall of shields and swords lifted high in the sun. A great war cry went up as they passed.

"You have trained them?" she said.

"Yes."

"They are warriors as were warriors of old."

She lifted her hand, pointing fingers to the sky. From amidships a cage was dropped open and a second silver eagle soared. Just beyond the ride, hovering in midair, the eagle arched its talons and screeched its caw, an echoing war cry. Then, as the other, it soared into the sky until it was only a dot and vanished from sight. A thundering cry went up from the Daath and the ship drew past, then continued east up the river, gaining speed.

Eryian glanced back to her. She was studying the river ahead of them, holding her cloak against the chill. She was smaller than Eryian, only coming to his shoulder.

"Do they know they are children of the seventh star? Did you teach them that?"

"Some believe, but warriors, after the blood slips from their blade from the first kill, stop bothering with scripture. Here, in this world, they must realize life is a matter of flesh and bone. They leave the rest, the secrets, to their women."

"It is said the Daath will be remembered as the Angelslayers."

Something in the way she said that gave him pause. "If they survive, if time allows, I believe they will," he answered.

"Yet you are not certain?"

"I am certain of nothing in this world, my lady."

"I was not sure when it all began, the things you did, the things you started, but now it starts to make sense. You stayed behind to teach them, to raise up Angelslayers. I can understand why you would choose to do so. In a way, their swords, in the final shadow of Aeon's End, shall also be your sword."

"How well did I know you, Cassium? The memories whisper, but I fear that flesh is too weak for memories, considering what I face due to the east. I hope you understand."

"I try. The world is such a perfect illusion, Eryian. Sometimes it is difficult to know what truth is and what is merely mist and shadow. Maybe, in the end, truth itself is only shadow. I hope not. It will come to you—who we were, who we are. The more you hear my voice, the more you look in my eyes. There," she pointed. "Hericlon's vale."

Eryian turned, startled. "We have reached it this soon?"

"These are not ships as you know in this world. They move swiftly. Do you choose to make landfall here, then?"

"Is there a reason I should not?"

"Hericlon no longer stands. You know that, of course."

He took a startled breath. He hadn't. Hericlon had fallen. There was nothing to turn back the armies of Du'ldu. The kindred of Dannu, the Daath, the ancient city of Terith-Aire, all lie before the armies of the south almost naked. Even these, mystic ships spilling with the light of stars, even these could not turn back Azazel. It seemed already lost, but that is not how Eryian had taught his men, and it was not what he let slip through his mind now.

"We are in the open here," Eryian said, concerned. "It is low ground, and our flanks are not guarded."

"You wish us to turn back?"

He paused, uncertain.

"I thought we had come to face him, Eryian. Is that not the reason you sent the beacon from the star ship? Are we here only for your Daath? Or did we come to find him?"

He had always known the spire that lay out to sea was a star ship, that the ceiling was not only a map of the night sky, but was also the ship's guidance. He thought for a moment to peel back the veil, but that was still dangerous, he was flesh, his emotions like a vapor near the surface, and with Hericlon fallen, he could afford no weakness. He had to keep these emotions at bay—if there was a past to be revealed, he had been someone else then. Here and now, he was mortal, flesh and blood. He scanned the vale before them.

"We could reach the center, that middle ground. We could face him there."

She nodded. "Does he know you are here?"

"He must see your ships; he must see the sons of Righel. Even standing from the mountain's passage he could see the river if he were watching. But no, he does not know of me. I am hidden from him. I have not revealed myself, and neither have I felt his probes searching. But looking south, I do realize you are right, Cassium. Hericlon has fallen."

"You did not expect that?"

"I had hope—that was all. Mere hope; a mortal's hope."

"Azazel would not make such an error. Of course you knew that, Eryian. You may hide, but you have not forgotten who he is. And he now moves in the shadow of Endgame. He will make no errors. He comes for your Daath, and you must know when he reaches them, he *will* slay them."

"There is yet a turn that even Azazel has not guessed."

She curled a smile, and after a moment he looked into the bright ice of her eyes. "You are still in there," she said. "I am sorry that I doubted at all. Forgive me, my lord."

"Forgive what?"

"Just that at first I did not know what to trust. It has been so long for me. I have not seen Earth in many years. Centuries. I have forgotten what it was like. We will take that central ground come the dawn—face him there. At last it comes, then; at last we end the book whose chapters have been so carefully written. Between then and now, if you would, Eryian, warlord of Daath, might we spend the evening here, along this beach? It is so beautiful here. The smell of Earth—the sky, the ridge of trees along that spine of the mountain. I had forgotten how beautiful, how splendid is the world of Elyon. I would like that, to camp here."

"Of course."

Close to her, he again felt a slight chill of her beauty touch him.

"I believe I understand you," she said. "Why it is you so carefully turn back memory. If you are not certain, then he will not be certain. Even Azazel would not think to search this vale for a memory that is no more than a shadow."

She lifted her hand, and that seemed all it took to guide the ships inward. He looked for a helmsman, but nothing on this ship was as it should be.

Eryian watched as the giants, the sons of Righel, laid out camp. Tents quickly lined the water's edge. He noticed they had captains among them who rode tall, white horses. One pulled alongside him, and when Eryian turned, he realized this was Amathon.

"Captain," Eryian said with a nod.

"This valley is cold with the south wind," Amathon said.

"Yes. I know I should be the one with answers, but tell me, Amathon, do you know their numbers? The armies of Du'ldu? What is your guess?"

"Numbers will not be what matters. My mother tells me we have not come seeking this army. They may number as the sand of the shores, but as someone once told me, someone whose word I have ever held close, when outnumbered, seek the head, not the body. If one severs the head, the rest shall fold."

"And who told you that, Amathon?"

"My father."

Amathon then pushed his mount forward, circling his fist to direct a disembarking column of spearmen. The shadow of the mountain was once again filled with Nephilim, high-blood firstborn who had not touched these shores since the time of Dawnshroud.

Eryian stared at the far ice spire of Hericlon against the dark horizon. Dusk had fallen and stars scattered, but the mountain itself snagged a dark cloud that obscured the sky. He knew it was not a storm cloud, that it held no rain or moisture. They were the whirlers, the thousand eyes of the angel. It was darkness boiling. Eryian wondered a moment of the Little Fox. If Hericlon had fallen, it could hardly be possible the Walker of the Lake still lived. He would not have turned from the gate, but then, in the gathering wars, Rhywder had surprised him more than once.

"Godspeed, brother," he said to the night, just in case Rhywder was out there somewhere.

He felt a whisper beside him and turned, finding Cassium. Her platinum hair brushed his bared shoulder, leaving a tingle.

"Seven centuries," she said. "One thousand prime of Righel's sons return to the killing ground. It will be as it was when the old ones fought here before the gate was ever built. It is war, but then it is almost poetry, the timing of it, the way the stars have turned and this movement has come to pass. Surely even the angel must know the shadow of Aeon's abyss closes on the Earth as we speak. Has living here so clouded his thoughts that he somehow believes he can escape it?"

She glanced at Eryian, but smiled as she realized he may or may not understand her. Yet, what he did understand were the dimples, there again, they left him a feeling of warmth and care. "But then," she said, "all that is just scripture, not something you have bothered with. There is one here called Enoch. Do you know of him?"

"Of course."

"He is called the Scribe by them, by the angels. They sent him, you know, to plead their cause. A mortal—they sent a mortal to stand before the face of Elyon and plead the cause of the sons of heaven. Such pitiful irony in that. When I learned of it, I did not know whether to laugh or weep."

Eryian noticed that the ships were pulling away, their keels slowly easing off the shore. "You are sending the ships back?" he asked.

She nodded. "I doubt once we find Azazel we will have further need of them."

They did not navigate the waters, nor was there any attempt made to hide their true nature. Their silvery bulwarks curled upward, like great wings, until they sealed the ships into sleek, narrow spears and the bulwarks smoothed until there was not a mark or a scratch. In one moment they were hovering above the waters and in the next, with a sudden brilliant flash, they were gone. They had moved with such speed, he had not been able to track their path.

She was watching for him to look to her for an explanation, but she offered none at all; she merely smiled.

"You are their queen," he said, "and they face certain death on the plains they so aptly name the killing fields. Yet it is your choice to stay, Cassium? Should you not have returned with the ships? Should a guardian's first duty not always be to ensure his queen be protected?"

She narrowed one brow over the icy eyes, almost in a gesture of anger. She stared at him a moment, and Eryian saw something spill from her eyes, as though in chastisement. They had scattered crystallized starlight against him, like ice drops. He suddenly felt foolish having said what he did.

"He may think he comes for the slaughter, Eryian. But he is wrong. You have, without choice, clothed yourself in flesh, but I have always been flesh. Now that you have taken me from the home you left me so very, very many years ago, the cold, almost lifeless ice moon I shall never miss, behold: I began to age. I would in time now grow old and die. You taught me that; you also taught me that it was a great and precious gift."

"I am afraid I no longer am keeping up, Cassium."

"It does not matter. What matters, you see, is that I have my soul. I am not undead. You, as well—we have our souls, Eryian! We should dance; we should scream to the night, throw off our shoes and run into the waters, singing. Great sacrifices you made to give us these simple gifts—the gift that we both may die."

The confusion in his eyes only made her smile that much more.

"You may not understand, but you saved me, at great cost, from Winternight."

"Winternight, yes, the curse of the Sky Walker Queens."

"They grow terrible from their knowledge; they take the blood of the innocent and the youth to keep their beauty. You spared me that, Eryian. I have not the imagination to understand how much I owe you, but remember my words—days from now, years from now, whatever may be, remember that I look in your eyes this moment and I offer you my thanks. Wait, here, look!" She grabbed his hand and laid hers over it. "The skin of this hand, though we do not see it, begins to grow old, even as we speak. In twenty, thirty years, it would grow wrinkles and age spots. If I were to live long enough, I would become an old woman, bent over and wrinkled. All my beauty would fade, my ice-eyes as you always called them, would fog with coming blindness, the cream color of my skin would wither to a gray mold, the white-gold hair would be left only white. And all thanks alone to you."

"It does not sound like something you should thank me for, Cassium."

"But it is! Oh, how it is. More than you are able to understand—given your veil." She set her hand upon his cheek, though he was left utterly confused. "Thank you, my love," she whispered. "You know what I thought so long ago when first they came, when I saw their streaks through the heavens. I was young, ten and two years, so young, so long ago. I saw them as they were when they stepped from the heavens and my father explained what was happening. I remember feeling such excitement that I leapt; I literally danced about. '*The angels are coming!*' I cried out."

She smiled, remembering, but then her eyes swiftly changed, growing dark and serious. "Mark this, Eryian, warlord of Daath; it is not Azazel who comes for the slaughter of these boys, the sons of Righel. My ships depart without me because it is I who have come for him! And if I accomplish nothing else with tomorrow's dawn, I will remind him of what he was before the Oath of Ammon was ever uttered. They have forgotten, all of them. In a different way than you—it is not a veil that blinds their memories; it is ego. But with just as much guilt on their souls as you or I, they have let Earth become their world, their entire domain. He comes from the south where he fled the Light Bearer over a woman. A woman, Eryian! Oh, if I could somehow make you understand how absurd that war! The Light Bringer, the most beautiful being ever created in all the universe, one of the very firstborn of our Lord and Father, Elyon; and Azazel, the second to fall, he was the reigning king of the celestial choirs. And what do they do within years of stepping from their oaths and their covenants with Elyon? They squabble like two children over the daughter of a man." She turned away, shaking her head with the absurdity of it. "He holds the mighty gate of Hericlon, does he?" she said, mockingly. "He comes now leading his *unnumbered armies*, his terrible warrior sons, in a battle that borders the very ending of time. And you, Eryian, you see the ships leave and you worry that these warriors of Righel should protect their queen by stealing her away back to the stars?" She half-chuckled at the thought and the sound of her laughter; he remembered that; it trickled down him as if her fingers were playing over the skin of his back. She grew serious and turned to touch a finger to his cheek. "Forgive me, of course. Forgive that I do not fully understand how different it is for you."

"I will, my lady."

"And do not call me that any longer! Love of Elyon, my name is Cassium. To you, from now on I am Cassium! Do you understand me? You can remain *Eryian, the warlord of the Daath*, but me, my name is Cassium."

Eryian nodded, tingling. Her words, her inflections, she was making it impossible to hide from her and she knew it. She knew her every word, every movement of her face, was cracking the façade he had erected to protect himself against the *real* Cassium.

"Tell me," she said, "did you know that it was my father who named the city of the Daath so many years ago?"

"I did not."

"He was a master mason; his teacher was a Star Walker. My father learned everything taught him, and I do mean everything. He learned so eagerly that he literally thirsted for knowledge, and in time, before his death in the days of Yered, there was no mortal on Earth who could match his talent. My father was named Terith. The final act of finishing the city was the erection of the spires, and he was fascinated by them. Just before their final erection, he would spend nights standing over them, running his hands along their smooth, unblemished surface. My mother pleaded with him, trying to explain that if he did not sleep, he might err in his construction, but he firmly put her in her place and told her than in erecting the spires, he would make not the slightest error—this his work would be perfect, unparalleled; even in Etlantis there would found nothing to rival it. He marveled over them constantly, how they were so immaculate and yet appeared so fragile, how they could reflect light like the most delicate glass and yet they were almost immortal. He begged and begged the angel who was his mentor to teach him how to craft them before they were erected high above the city where he could no longer study them. But laughing, his mentor told him he would require a substance not found on this planet and that the miles he would be forced to travel to obtain it were far beyond his lifetime and ten more. So my father named the city Terith-Aire, because the substance of its magnificent spires could be found only among the distant stars—that it could only be dreamed of. Not to mention, of course, his own boundless ego in including his first name, as well."

Eryian chuckled, realized how rarely he ever did so, that if Rhywder were here, surely it would be mentioned, the chuckle of Eryian.

She turned. One of the warriors had brought a horse and waited as Cassium took its reins. The warrior left. "Perhaps," she said, "this angel of death who allows the people of Earth to call him *Reaper* cannot be truly destroyed. Perhaps, like the spires of Terith-Aire, he is incapable of destruction, but I know one thing he may not suspect. I know that he can be turned."

"I am not certain I understand."

"His flesh, since he has lived here on this planet, so far distanced from Elyon and the hallowed palaces of heaven, no longer receives an essential nutrient required of a being of light, which once he was. He most surely has weakened—in fact, he weakens each day. It has been seven hundred years now, and it is just possible we can destroy this coil he shields himself in.

Whatever state in which he now exists, certainly he has weakened. We can only imagine the extent. But if weakened, he can be destroyed. Still, it does not mean that much. Even if we managed it, to bring down this coil he houses his spirit in, we cannot hope to destroy the soul of a member of Elyon's choir. Yet, think—if we can disrupt the coil he now inhabits, his soul will be thrown, turned. It would be cast from the body. He is not Uttuku, so he has not the capacity to wander the air and navigate the planet that spawned him. He was spawned of the mothering light of heaven and his soul would spin, out of control. It could cast mere miles, meaning nothing, aiding us little—or . . . or it could be thrown years into the sky, cast to the stars. It would take him a very long time to return should that happen. Amusing to imagine he would be lost out there, unable to even find his way back. Do you understand then, *Eryian, warlord of Daath*, if we can turn this being, this creature he has become, in essence, we sever the head from its body, and if—"

"If one severs the head, the rest shall fold."

"Yes. You heard that of Amathon, did you not?"

"I did."

"Those are the words of his father. He remembers all his father's words, no matter how insignificant."

"Then if we can turn Azazel, we gain time?"

"Exactly." Her horse danced a moment as she studied the dark skies over Hericlon. "Do you believe in them? These Angelslayers you have chosen? Do you believe in their hearts?"

"I do not understand what you are asking."

"Are they valiant?"

"They are. In fact, there are none so valiant on this Earth as the legions of the Daath, of that I have made certain. But why would you ask such a question?"

"I have my reasons. Knowing your answer, the conviction with which you speak it, would that not imply some knowledge of scripture, Eryian?"

"No, it would not. I have selected and trained them of instinct alone." He looked up, meeting her eyes, and a half smile curled across her beautiful lips, even that leaving the tiniest of a shiver across his skin. Who was she?

"Of course," she said. "That would suffice."

He was not sure of the implication, but did not press further.

"Would there be any harm in riding along the edge of these cool waters?" she asked. "Where I come from, these sounds—waters running free over their rocks as they fall for the Western Sea—there is no such sound. Or smell—the clean, clear smell of this crisp air, it stirs me."

"Of course we can ride its edge."

A second horse was brought for Eryian and both of them mounted. He felt the muscles of the horse's shoulders and sides, uncommon indeed. Such horses as these could fly as the wind itself. All their equipment, their shields and armor, certainly their ships, had no earthly comparison. When first he rode for them, near Ishmia, he thought they were from Etlantis. The thought now seemed foolish.

"Would you lead?" she asked.

"Certainly."

They rode slowly. Night had fallen, the stars spilled about them. Other than the dark and ugly swirls snagging Hericlon's peak this night, the rest of the sky was full and rich. It was the sky of harvest, not far from the equinox. For a long while, they said nothing, Cassium content to take long, deep breaths, smelling the richness of the air and the coolness of the night. Above them, what men called the star stream of the sky, a virtual river of stars that flowed each night overhead, was brilliant, and reflected itself against the wavering ripples of the river.

"It came into being with a Word," she said, marveling, "all of it, no time passing. I know that in Enoch's writings he speaks of seven days, but that is just his penchant for counting. If you knew him, if you ever read his writing, they are endlessly filled with counting. Each movement of the heaven, the length and carefully measured time of each season, of each day, of an hour, of a minute—the numbers of bodies that circle the heavens. He must spend all his time counting endlessly. If you were to journey up the streams of the Western

Sea and find his city, no doubt you would eventually discover him barricaded in some room counting and counting and counting again."

"You speak as if you know him."

"I follow the legends and the tales of this small blue planet. It hangs here in these dark skies alone, you know. In times beyond your own, should this Earth survive the shadow of Aeon's End that now closes over its horizons—for that matter, if you have taught well your Angelslayers and there is a future—mankind will acquire the means to search for life out there. They will build endless machines, even primitive flying machines to aid their search. They will profess no greater goal that finding the others—certainly they are not alone. Certainly there are others? If they reach that future, they will endlessly search, but all in vain, never knowing that their world, their Earth, was built on the very precipice of all creation. Beyond them lies the utter dark, nothingness, an endless nothingness. On the other side, never in Elyon's breath has there been life placed so far from heaven's light. It was almost, in your language, something of an experiment, to see if it was possible to survive this far from the source. We all live on an outpost, the very edge of the end of all things known. It is partly why the angels came in the first place, arguing that if the Earth was to be so far from the source of its light, with no life about it, alone in its shining black void—then surely they needed to step down from heaven and ensure its survival. And now you are gripped in a war that may threaten even that. When finally your Earth passes through the shadow of Daath, it will be the virtue of the hearts upon it that will weigh its futures, all of them, though they are unnumbered."

"You talk as if you are not a part of us."

"I suppose it is because of where you left me, Eryian."

"Where I left you? What do you mean?"

"I have spent almost seven centuries—do you know how long that is?—seven centuries on a small ice moon. It was beautiful. We were left everything we could possibly want or need—but there we waited. And waited. And waited."

"I am sorry. It sounds almost cruel."

Her eyes took a moment to testify it was no paradise. She paused and inhaled deeply of the crisp mountain air.

He paused abruptly. "Cassium, we are growing perhaps too far from your sons. Three are assassins in these trees. The past months along these ridges, there has been much terror, much bloodshed. We should be careful not to come too far."

"I have blessed our ride," she said with absolute firmness, leaving no doubt of her intent. "You need have no fear of assassins."

He nodded, understanding. For a moment as they rode, she studied him carefully, almost leaving him uncomfortable.

"When first I saw your talisman," she said, "my heart leapt and tears spilled so quickly and freely. I just let them fall, blurring my vision. You had remembered after all. You cloak your world in the veil, as well you must, as I no longer question, but to see your signet across the sky on such a far place as the ice moon near the seventh star of the Pleiades—it left me weeping. We may die tomorrow; you know that, of course. I need not explain. But dying is meaningless. It is but a crossing, and the planes and futures on its far side are as endless as these stars you see overhead."

She pulled her horse up and glanced back. "We have come far enough," she said. They were standing almost midstream. The waters were cool, but not so cold to cause the horses discomfort, for they were ankle-deep in the crystal dark waters.

Slowly, carefully, with her eyes trained on his, she lifted her hand and spread her fingers in what he now realized to be the universal sign of the word. It was more than a gesture of greeting; he had learned in this short time with her that it represented the very utterance that had brought all creation into existence. He did not hesitate to lift his own hand in response, to meet her palm, to spread out his fingers, touching hers one at a time. Something passed between them unspoken, without sound or sight. It was love. She spilled it like pouring an urn over his head; she held nothing back. There was a filter, memories were blocked as he would have asked, scenes and passages of time were strained as if through a fine meshed net, but the love she held for him, and in reflection the love he held for her, was unrestricted.

"It is important to protect yourself," she said firmly, "but I have crossed futures and stars for you, Righel of the Seraphim, and though we share but a sliver of time, as it closes on us, whispering away into the night so quickly—I touch my hand to yours and I return to you my love. Flesh is weak, I know. I am flesh, Righel. I am the daughter of a mason, a man. I see what comes with tomorrow's dawn and I give you your veil, but *not this*. Not our love! That part I let spill through my fingers like rain through a darkened night. Keep of your veil what you must, but I will not deny our love any longer, Righel. I have come too far."

The bright ice of her eyes bore into his now like no other he had known and for perhaps the first time in all his carefully hidden memories, in this life he held of Earth, Eryian suddenly wept. He had left her for seven centuries alone on an ice moon. How hard, how terrible must have been those years.

"I am so sorry," he whispered.

She continued to let the stream fall. He remembered her laughter, her running through fields of grass kicking up bare feet, her ponderings over the depths of the stars above them, her sorrow over the death of her father, her tears, her touch, her smell. He had loved her so. If only life were simple that it could be lived that way, for in all of its complexities, in its politics, in its wars of life and death, its forgiveness and revenge, its pleasure and its rage—this one thing alone among them made sense; all else was madness, there was only one perfection: love. He leaned forward, embracing her, and they both slipped from the saddle, dropping to standing in the river, wading to its edge where they fell to their knees, stripping each other of clothes as if there were only seconds to spare. With their flesh bared to the chill of the night, he ran his fingers through her hair, then the length of her temple to her hip, watching her carefully. He curled his hand over a tender soft breast. But in a second he remembered Krysis, but that was unfair; that was another world, another time, and Cassium deserved this. She had waited for him seven centuries alone. They fell back onto the sand and made love as love was ever meant to be.

Chapter Forty
Eryian's Dream

That night in a dream, with her body tight against him, both of them buried in woolen coverlets, the person who was Eryian finally revealed itself, using a dream to speak through the veil, to reveal who he was.

The veil was left intact, the memories now all hidden in a dream—but the dream could be remembered, as much as he wanted, as much as he wished.

It was a dream that might easily have been complex and tangled, and perhaps in the end it was, but at first it seemed only a simple dream, its images perhaps jumbled, and sometimes making little sense. Only when it was ended would he know all the meanings of what he had witnessed.

He was not a Daath, nor had he ever been one. That came as a surprise to him, but he saw it written out in the air by a swift finger: *"As them, you are not."*

There were stories of this first king of the Daath who was named Righel, and Cassium had referred to him using just that name. Indeed, it once was his. Eryian was one of the few alive that knew the tomb in the catacomb beneath Terith-Aire lay empty. Some came to worship it, to leave offerings, but it was as empty as the nameless many altars to gods and goddesses that existed up and down the coast, in the villages of the Pelegasians and the trading posts of the Weire. He had always known that, but in the simple words quickly sketched by an unseen finger, he understood without any further question that there was no more to worship in the tomb of Righel than the limestone shrine in Lucania dedicated to a god named Baal.

Unlike Baal, Righel, however, had been very real. Eryian saw him, a vague image of a man watching from the shadows and at his shoulders arched the splendid wings of an angel, feathered in a silvery gold, such beautiful feathers he found himself reaching for them, to touch them, almost envious. But the image was mist and as his fingers drew near, it folded in on itself.

The angel Righel, the dream told him, was no more—he no longer existed. At the same time, a voice whispered; once this angel had knelt each morning and each night before his creator, Elyon, vowing His grace, dedicating His cause, and renewing His covenants.

Righel was known. He was named among Elyon's children, and he was numbered among the host of the Elohim. His brother, his closest kindred and, oddly enough, his true friend, was none other than the mighty archangel Uriel. It was the reason Eryian looked so much like a Daath, the same pale skin, the same bluish tint, but he did not, as the others, come in the days of Yered with the ships that bore the Arsayalalyur and his kindred. He was singular; he was a lone traveler if ever there was one.

In his dream for a brief moment, he then saw the mighty archangel, standing at the fore of the eastern gate that watched over the garden of mankind's beginning. There was his sword, the fiery sword of Uriel. It was only an image of a brother who had once been his closest friend. How odd that seemed at first, but when the dream came to an end, he would understand why this bond existed. He had never even read the scriptures of the East of the Land or the blade that turned in all direction, guarding it.

"Warriors," he heard his own voice, Eryian's voice, echo, "after the blood slips from their blade from the first kill, stop bothering with scripture. The kill becomes their edge."

And then he saw the world of the Earth pale and become a gray fog. He realized this was because there were countless worlds, endless and beyond human imagining. And it was clear he would never know or comprehend in the course of a dream the world of an angel, its twists and turns. There were those who sang that angels were ever following their Creator, singing His phrases, and the gray before Him scattered in the wind as if angry any fool would even believe such to be the calling of angels.

Then he saw, as though swept past by the wind, a sun clock that bore no shadow, and he realized this represented the palaces of Elyon. The pillars and fountains and hills that were the realms of angels described of Enoch were places where there was no time. Time did not exist; it was neither a concept, nor an entity, nor even a feeling or passion. It simply was not.

Then he witnessed the burning fires that streaked across the sky. These symbols were even this day left etched in rock and carved in caves and painted upon the lintels of temples to represent the angels that had stepped from the heavens and had fallen to Earth. These, as well, were merely symbols that the human mind could conceive and understand, but in truth, the falling of an angel was not something a human could ever know or comprehend.

Then his dream became a day when Eryian was sitting beside his young scion, Lochlain, who at that time was only ten and one year old. They sat on the dock works of Terith-Aire, though in the dream they were hanging in space. It was a real moment, one from his memory. The boy's young face was drenched in sweat. Eryian, as always, had been working him harder than he should have. Why did he push the boy so hard? Why had he driven him so hard when Lochlain was only a child?

No answer came.

"Eryian," Loch said in his small, young voice. "I try not to anymore, but still at times I grieve for her."

"Your mother?"

"Aye. Sadness in me that she must wait."

"That she waits? How do you mean this, Loch?"

"Her fingers and mine were touching when her spirit left. I remember the very moment her soul slipped out of her, how her fingers fell limp. And I think I am haunted by how hard it must be that she waits there—wherever her soul is—to see me again."

He was so young, and yet his mind was far beyond his years. And what he had spoken was not from his ego—he understood she had loved him with all her heart, and she had, and his grieving was real, for she would be somewhere weeping, waiting to see him again.

Eryian wrapped one arm about Lochlain's shoulder. When he was a boy, it was easier then to touch him. Later things would change. He pulled the boy close. Lochlain resisted. He resisted all human contact, as if he were determined to walk every path alone.

"What I am to say may seem difficult to understand," Eryian told him, "but where your mother is, there exists no time."

He turned to Eryian, surprised. "No time?"

"None. It does not exist in that place. It is as if, from the moment her fingers grew limp and let yours go, in the very next instant, she will be sweeping you into her arms, welcoming you home, pouring her love over you once more. You might even be an old man, having walked many long and weary paths, but for her—for your mother—no time will have passed between those moments. Where she is, time is not. No tears, no hours to slowly pass or days to watch the sun rise and fall. Her touch leaves your fingers, and then she pulls you into her embrace."

"Welcome home, my son, my love," Loch mother's words echoed in his dream and Eryian was struck hearing her voice, Asteria's strange, whispery voice, strong and bold, yet as soft as if she might at any second be blown away by the wind.

He then saw himself, standing upon a ledge as if he were in space all alone, and below him was the brilliant blue sphere that was Earth, one of the finest and greatest of all Elyon's work, even though His works were without number or time or knowing. Earth was still the most magnificent.

Elyon was the limitless light. He had no names, nor could He be conceived or known of men in any form.

Eryian stood alone in space watching Earth and marveling of its work. Unlike any other, the endless, limitless, and numberless others, Earth dwelt on the outerlands, on the very edge that was between nothingness and the slim, tendril of light that held it to heaven. It was frightening, for the tendril looked so fragile, so easily severed.

Because the world called Earth was so far from heaven, it would become a place like no other. The nights would be darker, the evil more deadly, more appalling, more unthinkable than any evil known. It would be a place of constant and never-ending war and murder and terror. Earth was left too much at the edge of the outerland—that was what many of the angels thought. They were bold angels to question their Creator, but they spoke out loud and said Earth had been made too far from the light, that it was doomed to fail.

And then he witnessed once more the streaks across the sky. Those who came were not weak; they were the brave, the noble and good. They were in that day not the fallen; they were the mightiest of Elyon's sons. They feared that Earth had been placed too far away, that heaven's light was too dim here and mankind would need their help. They left risking everything, even their own salvation. They were not evil as later generations would name them; they were, in fact, the bravest. More than any, the Light Bearer spoke these words, that Elyon's sons should step down from heaven and risk all to help.

The Light Bearer was one of the greatest of Elyon's son's, one of two firstborn, twins, and this, the Light Bearer was born first—he came before the other. In all power and glory he stepped from heaven so that Earth would not be lost.

"My promise, Father," Eryian heard a dark and powerful voice echo within the gray and black of his dream, "from the heart and depth of my soul, my word and my covenant: my promise to thee, Father. I shall bring them home and not one shall be lost! Not a single soul shall fall! In all honor, in all glory, I will return and I will protect them, for I am become their messiah."

And again Eryian found himself studying the planet from his rock in the heavens and that was when he found her. He had not been looking for her; he had only been standing on his far rock, curious of the Earth, built as it was on the edge of the outerland. Would even its messiah, the firstborn of Elyon, be mighty enough to save it? Such were his thoughts that day his eyes unexpectedly were caught by a girl. What a strange twist. She was but the daughter of a man named Terith. Her beauty at first left him utterly breathless. For an angel to be struck of beauty alone—that was a sin, but she was so remarkable. Never had he seen such a creature. What Elyon had crafted in the stunning blue ball in the sky, such a beautiful thing, so, too, had He created upon its surface, creatures so lovely, so perfect, they took his breath. He stood for a long, long time on his rock watching her. Her name, he would learn, was Cassium.

And in the dream he now understood how it had come to pass that even magnificent beings such as sons of unimaginable glory had found themselves suddenly weak.

Alone.

In all of existence, there was nothing as terrible as being alone. Pain, death, horror, terrors of unspeakable imaginings, could not compare with this simple, ordinary word: *alone*. The outer darkness signified it. Righel, far out in space on his rock, watched in stunned disbelief, in utter silence, as the mightiest of Elyon's children broke their vows to their own Father for these creatures that were then called the daughters of men.

In secret, thinking themselves hidden, they made their pact upon Mount Ammon and Righel watched, horrified of all he knew or understood. It was as if for a moment, a crack in time had ripped the very fabric of the universe.

And all this terror was due to that one word—*alone*. The angels feared being alone. It was the first that struck them being so far from Elyon's Light. Perhaps an unreasonable fear, but it was loneliness that drove them to take the daughters of men, to ensure they would not be alone this far from heaven, or so Righel believed because he could think of no other reason, being an angel himself.

Though as yet he remained in the sky, he could longer look away. It was his first sin. He became a Watcher that day.

Then, later, on a day that may have otherwise been ordinary, a horrifying thing happened. He saw her—the girl he had been watching, the one named Cassium, in the arms of a most powerful being, a being he at that time believed to be full of grace and the light of Elyon. This was a being far more powerful than he, one known well of his Creator, Elyon, a brother much older than he, much wiser and far more aware of the songs of creation.

Azazel had taken the girl that Righel had fallen in love with from his rock far in the heavens.

For many days that even became years, Righel did nothing. It was as if he stood horrified, unable to move or speak. But Righel looked into the futures and what he saw left him chilled. Azazel would become an evil, a terror. A day would come that men would fear to even utter his name, and this would happen not by chance or mistake. He would be feared because he had become terror, he had become evil, he had turned against every vow, every covenant, every oath once spoken to his Creator.

Righel could only watch, paralyzed. Unable to move. How long did he stand on his rock not moving; how many years? Was it decades? Was it a century? How long did he watch his love in the arms of an evil that was slowly becoming something beyond all evils he had ever known?

At first, after the days of Ammon, after the angels had broken their oaths and tried to hide from their own Creator, they gathered their women and lay in secret places, hiding their sin, and they conceived many children with them. Spellbound, an angel could conceive hundreds, even thousands of children from a single daughter of mankind. They did this through magickal means, and they did it because they believed they needed to make time move swiftly.

Azazel had spoken a word in the day of Yered, and he had caused there to be among the children of men a thing called death. They would die. Even if they caught no disease or befell no peril, still they would grow old, a terror of itself. Their skin would wither. Their minds, the power of their thinking, would began to fail them, and they would turn to simple children and wet themselves and babble and finally die and become the dust of the Earth. The death Azazel had named was an unthinkable thing among other creations and planets of Elyon, but Azazel believed it necessary, and he made it terror. In other creations there was no such terror in dying. But here, on Earth, Azazel had began to delight in things evil, and *death* was his greatest word; it changed the course of all things on Earth forever. It was his first turning, what first made him begin a path of evil.

In horror the angels realized the daughters of men they had chosen, many of them deeply loved in the true light, would now become victims of this word Azazel had named. So they turned to Azazel himself.

"What do we do?" Eryian heard all the voices of the angels speak at once in his dream.

And that was when Azazel spoke a second terrible word, and with this one he created the Winternight. Now these chosen daughters of men would not wither and wrinkle, their minds would not become muddled, their beauty would not be lost. They would become Star Walker Queens, and the Winternight would spare them from death while others around them died in terror and horror. But to cross to Winternight, the daughters of men who belonged to the angels were forced to become beings of evil, a dark and profound evil. Some resisted, many were even destroyed for their resistance, but others were not in league with the angels and came willingly to this world of Winternight. They drank the blood of the living to restore their beauty, to never grow old or senile or wrinkled. Always they would be young and fresh, and their only secret hidden well from the heavens would be human blood.

Righel could only watch paralyzed with dread, unable to move or even to think. He knew what it meant to turn to the Winternight, and the time would soon come that his love, Cassium, would be turned by Azazel to an evil thing, and that—that was something he could not let happen. In the first day he had seen her he had first been struck by her beauty, but then, looking closer, he had been drawn to the purity of her heart. She was a loving and giving being whose heart was as pure as angels of the choirs and yet—she was merely human. It had touched him so profoundly that he had believed he now understood Elyon's aim. But Elyon forever confused those who in vanity believed they understood His will.

Righel finally broke from his spell of paralyzed dread. He worked quickly; he built an entire world for her. An ice moon. He made it beautiful; he filled it all with things he believed would make her happy, would even make it a home. But Righel's ice moon lay in the dark of matter, far out in space, far from the Earth and all the things Cassium had known her whole life. Still, the moon was bathed in the light of the mothering star, so she would not age. Just as those who were turned to Winternight, she would not fall to the horrors of death, the slow and terrible aging that Azazel had named for mankind. She would be spared, but not by becoming an evil being preying upon children and innocents. It would possibly take him many long years to purge her of the evils already staining her soul that came from knowing Azazel for so long, but he felt confident he could do this, given time—return to her the loving heart he had fallen in love with long ago.

The second thing he did was to teach himself stealth. Azazel was not his equal; Azazel would crush him without a thought. He would utter a word and Righel would cease to be, his spirit imprisoned for all time. So Righel created his own powerful spellbound illusion—what he named stealth. He called what he became a Shadow Walker, because he learned to walk the shadows and vanish into them with such agility that not even a being as powerful and terrible as Azazel would be able to track him.

The last of his dream was the night he stole Cassium from the Earth. It was a sad night. She did not know he came to help, she did not know him at all, and of course she was terrified and cried out to Azazel to save her. But Righel had planned well and with Cassium as his prisoner, he vanished that night. It was the very same night she and many of her sisters were to have been turned. But Azazel came to find that Cassium was not among them, and eventually he learned a thief had taken her—a thief that had come in the night and had vanished without a trace.

Of course Azazel was furious. For centuries he would scour every inch of the planet, which then, in those days, was mostly water. But Cassium was no longer on the Earth, and Azazel had sworn off his vows on Mount Ammon, so he could not follow Righel into space. He may have been furious, and he swore vengeance against heaven itself, but he could do nothing to bring back Cassium.

At the end of Eryian's dream he remembered a moment in time that was the saddest of all. By that day, Cassium had become his love. She hated him in the beginning, and indeed purging the evils left of such a being as Azazel had taken many long years, but slowly she had grown to trust him and eventually even learned what he had done, that he had stepped down from heaven, breaking his vows, only for her and her alone. No angel on Earth had done such a thing, and Cassium learned to love him deeply and with all devotion.

But Righel had broken his vows. It was the only way he could have taken her, a daughter of man. He had broken a covenant made with his Creator and the day he had done so he had wept bitterly, but he felt he had no choice, and once it was broken, there was no turning back. The vows of an angel were the most sacred of all the universe, and because of what he did, he was cut off from Elyon's Light.

Cassium had become his love. She bore him sons; as did the spellbound fallen angels of the Earth he had many children with her, and he taught all of them truths of light. He taught them of the star knowledge in its true form, and he taught them carefully, most of all, of the *Light Whose Name Is Splendor*. On his far ice moon, bathed in the light of the mothering star, he raised Nephilim unlike any known in all of Elyon's universe.

But Righel himself was cut off from Elyon's Light. As the years passed, eventually it was too great a burden; he could no longer endure being severed from the love of his Creator.

So the last of Eryian's dream was the day Righel brought his sins before his Creator. It did not matter his motives, his reasons, his purpose, or his love the day he had broken his vows. What he had done was unforgivable. He had broken oaths so sacred that heaven had no choice but to turn its face.

Righel came to the black rock from which he had so many years ago watched the magnificence that was Earth, from which he had so many years marveled and stood in awe. But this time, he knelt on both knees. From his shoulders he lifted his mantle and laid it out before him. In the dream, his mantle was the silver-golden wings of his covenants with God, and by lifting them off and laying them before Him, he gave up all that had been promised him. He became a mortal.

In the dark, cold wind of the ice moon, without his mantel, he would soon die. He knew this, and he even expected that to be the result, but he turned his eyes to heaven, or at least what once he remembered as heaven.

"Lord of lords," his voice echoed in his dreams, the memory of that far, sad day almost too much to bear, even though it was a dream shielding him.

"King of Hosts, Elyon, my Father, I come now before You and beg to be forgiven. My sins are great, for I have given up the pearls of wisdom and the powers and keys of Your Kingdom, precious and priceless gifts, and I have done this in sin. I have done all this for a woman; my sin is as great as any of those who laid hands upon the stone of Ammon. But unlike them, I do not send a human to plead my penance. I kneel before You in the cold and speak my own words. You are my Lord and my Creator, and whatever You answer shall be my answer, but I ask, with broken heart, to be forgiven, my Lord."

He lowered his head. The chill wind of the ice moon was fast taking hold, for now he was mortal, and soon he would die here. "In all humility I kneel before Thee. I ask forgiveness, Elyon. Forgive me, *Holy-Holy-Holy*! Forgive my trespass. I lay down my mantle before Thee and ask that You allow me to begin my trek once more. Though once I walked as Elohim, I surrender my gifts, my knowledge, and all my power. If ever I should find my way home, then I will do so now as a mortal.

"So ends my prayers for myself. For Cassium, I ask, Elyon, that she be forgiven. I have taught her all Your words, but she was deceived by one who was far too cunning and devious for me to overcome. I testify this night that her heart is pure, and I ask she be forgiven, and so ends my prayer for Cassium.

"As for my children, I have taught them only in the path of light; they believe you are their God, and they know no other. They are innocent but for my sin alone. If You find it in You, forgive them and lay what curse You wish upon me that I have brought them forth, for I knew it was a sin, and yet I wanted children and thus my vows were broken.

"If You wish, let this ice take me and do what You will with my soul, but so ends my words, my King and Lord, Elyon."

He then lowered his head and waited. It grew colder. The winds about him howled, but no answer came. In moments before death would have taken him, he felt a presence, and looking up, he found his brother, Uriel, kneeling before him. His one true friend.

"He sends me in answer, Righel."

Tears fell. Uriel had lifted the cold around them and feeling began to return to Righel's fingers and toes.

"If you turn away your anger, if you promise never to rise in rage and fury again, as you did against the angel Azazel, then I intercede on your behalf. Your sin is not forgiven, but it is unlike the others. You do not gather queens; you wait here, on your ice moon; you continue to pray; you raise up sons in the ways of the *Holy-Holy-Holy*. You leave your Creator baffled, for this night you lay down your mantel and surrender your blessings. Judgment, therefore, is mine to give.

"Leave now in your ship. Leave word with your sons and your woman that in a day to come from now they will see a talisman from Earth, and in that hour you will face the judgments of your actions. I pray the Lord of Hosts grants you penance, my brother. Many ask why you should be spared when the others are to be bound in prisons for ten of thousands of years and await the coming judgment of the son of women. Are you truly different from them, my brother?"

Righel had no answer; everything within him was drained.

"As them, did you not break the sacred vows created in the fires of heaven before the eyes of our Creator?"

Uriel stared a long time into the eyes of his brother. He wept, as well. He shook his head. "I always believed I taught you well, my brother. How has this come to be that your mantle lies at our knees?"

Righel had no more answers. He was still shivering from nearly having frozen. Perhaps it would have been fitting to be left on ice in the black night. But Uriel placed his hand on Righel's shoulder. "The covenant of everlasting is taken for you, my brother. You are left mortal, and should you find your way home, it will be a long and far path you must follow. But you will be spared the punishment prepared for the others who broke their vows upon Mount Ammon." Uriel paused a moment, his hand squeezing tight. "If I had the power, I would forgive you all. I know that all you did, you did out of love. Perhaps that is why you at least have been spared."

"Cassium?"

"She began mortal and remains mortal. She committed many terrible sins while she was a consort of Azazel, but her heart has listened to you, it has changed, and our Creator has given to all humans the right of penance. I believe she will be forgiven. She is good, she was born with a pure heart, and you have saved her soul. Righel, I bid you farewell, but also I honor you. I know of no greater sacrifice than that which you have shown this night. The feathers of an angel lie here at our knees for the sake of one soul, the soul of this girl. My brother, though I lose you as kindred this day—I will ever remember you, ever love you. Perhaps in eternity I will know you again as a peer. Perhaps one day you will again wear this mantle. Until then, go in Faith's Light, my brother."

"Thank you for forgiving her, that innocence may be hers once more."

"Thank not me, but your Creator."

"My children?"

Uriel hung his head. "They were born in blasphemy and they cannot be redeemed, not in this existence. I have pled for them; I have stood before Elyon and wept that they not be treated as the Nephilim of earth. He has listened. They will not be bound to Earth's dust; they will not be left to plague mankind as the others. But you will never know them. Your children have been taken from you, my brother. I am sorry, I could do no more."

The last of his dream might not have been a dream because he found himself staring upward in the darkness. It must be the last was not a dream, but memories. By dawn they would fade. He glanced to Cassium and smiled. She would not be his, she would be another's queen, but at least her soul was spared.

Chapter Forty-One

Song

At dawn the sons of Righel marched from the dark shores of the river Ithen toward Hericlon. The mountain lay distant, its icy spears resting against the dark underbelly of the black whirlers that marked the coming of the armies of Du'ldu. The Nephilim of Righel set out in columns, many on high horses. Eryian rode at the head of the First Century, with Amathon on his right, and to his left, Cassium. The deeper into the vale they came, the more the mountain's presence seemed to envelop them. Its foothills seemed to curl like waiting fingers about them, and the touch bristled against Eryian's skin.

By midday the sky was a slate gray. The clouds were thick, and from a knoll of yellow grass, the sons of Righel descended into a wide plateau. Hericlon's spurs now curled to either side. The battle once fought here, in times men no longer remembered, had left this ground named the Vale of Tears. Beyond, at the far end of the plateau, was an unkempt dirt road that wound a snaking path up through the glade into the passage that led to the gate of Hericlon.

Once the army had reached the plateau's center, the sky rumbled quietly. Amathon lifted the reins, slowing his mount and pointed south. Shadows moved across the sky, driven by more than wind. At first they looked to be plumes of the coming storm, lifting out of the dark clouds above Hericlon, but then they took shape and Eryian watched as they passed overhead. Minions, winged. Their passage spooked many of the horses. Cassium's mount lifted its front hooves, snorting, dancing a moment before she brought it in rein. The minions passed over without turning, as though they had no care of the warriors below, but Eryian noticed they were touching down in a pattern, some to the hillocks surrounding them, others vanishing without sound in the dark foliages that lined Hericlon's spurs. Then the fog came. It rolled across the plateau in waves, like the tide slowly coming in, gathering strength, and thickening. Amathon finally raised his hand and his captains called a halt. The gray fog was blurred only dimly by daylight.

Amathon glanced aside to Eryian. "I believe, my lord, we are being offered an invitation to dance—and this is his chosen field, the Vale of Tears."

Eryian searched, listening carefully. There were far sounds to the south, toward Hericlon, but soon they were also east, and west, until Eryian realized there was movement all around them; a shifting of sound, a low, steady rumble. There was no wind—the air had stilled, and the fog was carrying sound as though it were prisoner, as though they were in a great chamber.

"They have closed on our rear," Amathon said. "Their numbers are many. They use the fog to surround us." Amathon turned in the saddle, searching. "Take up weapons! Prepare your hearts for battle, my brothers!"

In a single motion, the sons of Righel drew weapon. Swords cleared their sheaths, and heavy shields lifted. The horsemen gathered inward, and the infantry began to circle outward to the flanks. Archers and spear throwers took up their positions.

A heavy, breathless silence hung a moment, and then a wind, low and chill, began to fall from Hericlon. It was winter wind, that kind that comes before a chilling frost, only this touched deeper, past armor and flesh, whispering against bone.

The fog was rolled back like skin peeling. Eryian knew they faced an army, but seeing them gathered, he still felt his breath taken.

As far as the eye could see, spanning the passage to Hericlon, lining the forest to either side, melting into trees and crawling dark about the far spurs and valleys, to the rear—in all directions—the land was thick with Unchurians and the dark red glints of their armor and weapons. The fog curling and falling away between them left the illusion they were materializing.

"Elyon's Light grace us," Amathon whispered, shifting in the saddle. "I suppose to guess their number is useless. It appears they have no number."

Eryian tightened his jaw. They were high-blood, firstborn of the angel. Between the sons of Righel and the armies of Du'aul were no fodder, no giants or miscreants. Azazel had sent in his finest warriors, and they held themselves as did the legions of the Daath. Eryian curled his forearm through the leather grips of his buckler and lifted it from his back.

"Good lady," Amathon said, "it would appear this trap has been well baited."

"Yes. But he has laid no trap. Our coming has not been a secret; he knew when he saw the ships sail up the Ithen to Hericlon's vale. It is not as if the angel has surprised us. We bear the surprise, Amathon. Azazel is out there, somewhere watching, and he senses something, the blade of aganon, perhaps, the sword of the Pleiades—he would smell that. But I have not felt his probe. He does not realize who waits here, who we are. He comes for the Daath, so perhaps he does not care. We are merely a puzzling inconvenience before he can move south for Terith-Aire."

Amathon circled his horse. "There is still a weakness in their rear," he said. He glanced at her. "If we broke for the river, I believe we could pierce through, but then I realize we have not come to prevail here; we have come to make the stand—as you have spoken all these years. The time has finally come. I will make the cost of our fall leave a mark upon this ground, my lady. Pray Elyon witnesses our sacrifice."

Amathon paused a moment, lowering his head, and Eryian wondered if perhaps he were sending his thoughts to the Blue Stars, to the heavens. When he looked up, his face was steeled against what they faced.

"It is more than armies," Cassium said. "It is time that has closed on us, Amathon. Sometimes a life is only answered in its final moments, in the clutch of last breath. We shall be what we have kept in our hearts. We shall die well, my son, more than that cannot be asked of us."

The giant slowly pulled his mount closer to her. He raised his hand and spread his fingers in the sign of the word. "Mother," he whispered.

Cassium met his hand, finger for finger. "Godspeed, my love," she said.

"Through your eyes and those of your brother's, the light of Elyon shines once more in the Vale of Tears."

Amathon then eased back in the saddle and latched down his cheek guards. His steel-dark eyes turned on Eryian. "My lord, I shall leave strength against the center as long as I am able. The last of us to move will be the horsemen. Braemacht and the queen's guard, of course, will remain until the last with her."

"As will I, Amathon," Eryian promised.

Still watching Eryian, Amathon reared his horse briefly and lifted a gauntleted fist into the air as a final salute; he did not intend to return to the center this day. He then turned the mount and began to move through his men toward the outer edge where he could command his troops. Eryian noticed that as Cassium watched Amathon pull away into the ranks, a mist crossed her eyes. She glanced at Eryian, noticing his gaze. "He was your firstborn son," she told him, and though Eryian still held the veil against his flesh to fight this final battle, he was stirred as he watched Amathon push his way toward the front. "He has always been their leader, their teacher. He was well trained in the days of the beginning."

As Amathon left them, the core of axemen tightened inward, surrounding their queen.

"This spawn before us," Braemacht said, backing his horse into position beside Cassium. "They leave their course scattered before they reach you, my lady. They may number themselves like sand, but they have not guessed the cost they will bear this day."

For a time the vale of Hericlon was quiet. In the center of the plateau, the circle of warriors with their white cloaks and silver armor shifted, making ready, their center tightening inward. The outer lines locked their massive shields into what looked a circular, impenetrable wall. The Unchurian were still, watching the movement below patiently. Many would wonder who these were, these warriors with their white armor and cloaks, their tall horses, if perhaps they had come of Etlantis, though nowhere was the red bull of the Mother City in evidence. Their shields bore a circle through which a silvered cross was emblazoned. It was a symbol they had never seen before, whose origin was a mystery to them.

For a moment, as though time had snagged, there was no sound in the vale of Hericlon. The quiet seemed an entity unto itself, as if offerings were being made from both sides. Then, a piercing cry shattered the stillness. From the north, toward the mountain, the Unchurians loosed a wall of arrows. It arched in a black shadow, curling. The shields of Righel angled to the sky. Eryian pulled his horse to the side and lifted his shield over both him and Cassium.

The arrows struck in savage rain, and though most of the bolts were warded off by iron shields and bucklers, many of the giants fell. Horses screamed, buckling. Any that dropped near the front were replaced quickly, bodies dragged back, and once more, silence danced.

Eryian glanced worriedly to Cassium. "They could do that all day; whittle us down hour by hour and never leave their hills and mountain spurs."

"But they will not. Their king will send them in to test their mettle. Only then will they realize they clash against the firstborn of an angel, though they will never understand he was one who chose light over life."

From all sides the Unchurians began a slow, steady beat of weapons against shields, their rhythm a heartbeat.

"Braemacht," Eryian said, "make the center hard to find."

"Aye," Braemacht nodded and lifted in the saddle. "Axemen, dismount!"

They did so in unison. Eryian dropped beside Cassium. The horses were taken by warriors and led to the outer ranks, and the queen's guard closed about her. From the hills, there would have been no sight of her in the center of the circle of warriors.

The heartbeat of the Unchurians began to increase, both in pace and strength.

"I do not know about you, my lord," Braemacht said to Eryian, "but the biggest problem for me this day shall be the wait. Our brothers will not die quickly."

Eryian glanced to the scabbard at his thigh. He had left the sword of

Righel sheathed, but he saw light spill about the lip of the scabbard, a pulse of it, in rhythm with the beating of the shields of the Unchurians. Eryian knew then the sound was in time with the heart of Azazel. He remembered years ago, even in the beginnings, many of the other angels called him the Reaper. Of all the Star Walkers who swore upon the stone of Ammon, he was the most unpredictable; his blood, even though he had walked as a lord of the choir, had always been hot.

Eryian glanced aside to Cassium. "Have you thought, my lady, that with your knowledge you should be the one to wield this sword? I have not lifted its hilt in battle in seven hundred years, and never have I wielded it as a mortal."

"Its touch would be acid against my skin, Eryian."

"I do not understand; you virtually spill the light of heaven from your eyes."

"No, Eryian. I seek the light, I seek that it will once more fill my heart, but I am still bound by the oath made upon the mountain of Etlantis that day long ago. I am unforgiven."

"I cannot understand what wrong you could possibly bear."

She paused. "Loving you," she replied. "And I would drink from the cup again if offered."

She stared back at him, her eyes attesting the truth of her promise. "Eryian, there is only one person who can light the blade of Righel, and that is Righel."

"Do you think he knows? That Azazel realizes it is not merely aganon he smells below, but that it is Righel's sword?"

She shook her head. "Not yet. You have hidden yourself too well—he is clever, but he has no reason to even dream that you have returned to the vale to face him. If I had not been summoned of the talisman, you may even have fooled me, warlord."

"It seems by rumor that some of them have grown weaker over the centuries, that some have begun to age, their skin like mortals, like old men. But not him. They whisper he has grown even more powerful, turning all his arts to darkness and the mastery of death."

"It is an illusion he casts. The star knowledge fails him as it does the others, but mortal seers do not realize. Since the day he broke his vows, as all of them, he has tried to hold to the light, grip it in his hand, but it spills between his fingers and seven centuries have passed. He is weaker than when last you knew him, far weaker. But for us, with you a mortal, his power is still beyond imagining. But I can promise, even Azazel is not immune, even for him the turning has begun. Your warriors, your king, have opened the eye of Daath and Azazel's weakness began to burn in him like fire against his skin. He feels it now like pain. To fall from the light is a terrible pain, I am told. You spared me; you did not turn me as many of the angels did their Star Walker Queens, so I will not know this pain. And yourself, you surrendered your mantel that you would find your way back as a mortal; thus it is spared, you as well. But I have heard it spoken of others that the pain comes deep from within, a burning in their soul like mortals feel a burning of the flesh. He walks proud still, but he cannot escape the passage, though he was once Bene ba Elohim, he shall die as men shall die, with a belief he has had to sustain, to believe that with the Watchers he can stand against heaven itself in the days of Aeon's End. Only a being as bright as the Light Bearer could ever have led him this far into denial."

"How long were you his?"

She turned, startled that he had asked. "You would want to know that?"

"I still protect myself through the veil, remember?"

She half-smiled. "Of course. A year, perhaps more. It was not long before you came to take me. I have always wondered of it, you know. That from the heavens you saw me, and found in me something that drew you so strongly you stepped down from the stars to spare me my soul."

"It seems not so hard to believe myself, seeing you again. Though I leave the memories fogged, I can understand why I came for you."

Suddenly, from all sides a great roar went up, shouts and cries. Swords and axes lifted high. Eryian could barely make it out, but up high, near Hericlon's passage, the Unchurians were parting to let a single rider through.

Near the edge of the southern front, Amathon took up ranks and remained mounted even though he became a prime target in the white cloak and the silvered armor. He would remain so for his men, to let his brothers know he was there, that his voice would guide them on. The horsemen were readied not far behind. They would choose carefully their moment.

Amathon circled his horse, watching the wall of men and shields from the ridge above lift and descend, like a wave breaking over the Earth. It seemed the air itself pressed against them, and Amathon heard more coming than the sound of their feet. He heard shrieks, whispered screams that passed through the ranks with cold slaps, and he could seem them, Uttuku, the dead of the giants. He and his brothers had not been born on Earth, and throughout his life, he had dedicated himself to the mothering light of the seventh star. Though they had never sung in the choirs of heaven, they still called themselves Seraphim, after their father. Yet still he wondered, if by fault of birth, there was no forgiveness, that his soul would be one those left wandering the Earth. He understood that Eryian had made a supreme sacrifice, that he had not turned their mother, as were most queens of the angels, into the walking undead of the Winternight. But they were Nephilim. Would even the sacrifice made by Righel be able to spare their souls? He felt heaven's light and he would die this day believing, but the shrieks of the Uttuku left a sinister dread in the deep of his bones.

The wave coming against them left the Earth trembling in its quake; their weight alone could crush ramparts. The air trembled. The old one, the second of the three who was called Azazel by the men of Earth, had amassed thousands, hundreds of thousands . . . more. He had brought sons unnumbered and had launched them against the brotherhood of Righel at full run, a torrent. The sons were not giants as Amathon had heard all firstborn of Earth to be; they were smaller than he and his brothers, the size of men, with night-black hair and skin a reddish hue. Azazel's blood must have been pure in the beginning, almost as filled with light as the archangel, for these Unchurians were much as the Daath. Of course, it would make no difference in battle; their numbers alone would eventually overwhelm the sons of Righel. Still, he wondered why they came, these pure-blood warriors, these first blood of Azazel, as if they had all been carefully selected.

The circle of white cloaks and silver armor facing them was left no more than a pebble, and the wave that surged came from all sides.

"Archers!" Amathon shouted. The archers of Righel readied themselves, but Amathon waited; he let the wave in closer. The arrows strained against their sinews. Amathon continued to wait. He could see the battle frenzy burning in their eyes as they charged. Many had streaks of silvered hair to one side, and he knew this was not cosmetic, that it was mark, like a mutation of skin.

"Fire!" Amathon finally screamed.

It was a brief shadow that passed. The missiles slammed into the charge and for a moment, the entire circle buckled, folding into the screams of those struck and of others trampled as the wave curled, broke, and continued forward.

"Load!" Amathon said, pausing this time only a second. "Fire!"

Again, from the Unchurian front, horses screamed, men crumpled, and a second wave broke over the bodies. The Unchurians grew excited, almost reaching their mark, almost to the wall of shields held before the giants.

"Spears!" shouted Amathon.

As the archers drew back, spearmen took a slight run and launched their weighted long spears in a straight drive that tore through the Unchurians heavier and more devastating against flesh than the arrows. A final circle of warriors crumpled as the spears slammed through them.

"Shieldbearers forward, lock shields, and brace!"

Thousands of them dead already, the Unchurians finally reached the front. Their timing was careful; they struck from all sides at once, the weight of the charge hammered into the Seraphim of Righel. The shields of Righel were staggered, in places were broken, but many of them held, lifting and throwing the Unchurians back, as if they had struck a wall of white stone.

"Horsemen!" Amathon cried. "Attack!"

Like gates swinging open, in places the shield parted, and cavalry, in tight groups of sevens, became like missiles, as well. They drove forward, lances lowering, and bore into the frenzied attack of the Unchurians like carving deep wounds. Many of the lances were shattered, others lodged in their victims, and while some horses fell, many turned and vanished back behind the lines as the shield parted and let them through to regroup.

"Elyon's Light, Elyon's grace," screamed Amathon. "Hold against them, my brothers!"

As many as they were, as mighty as the warriors of the Unchurians had been, the wall of white shields locked and for a time held. Between the shields, swords flickered like the tongues of serpents, taking flesh, dropping Unchurians on all sides in a slaughter.

Cassium touched Eryian's arm—a furious scream of dying from all sides now, screams of terror, screams of fury, the blows and thundering crash of swords, hammers, and steel. From where they were, in the center, they could see nothing.

"It is coming hard against them," Cassium said, listening. "Azazel has filled them with such fury, their hatred so raw it is like a living thing, as if their rage might rise up as a beast to fill the sky."

Eryian shifted. His hand curled about the hilt of Righel's sword, but her fingers touched his wrist.

"Not yet. Keep it sheathed."

"I feel I should move forward, engage, Cassium."

"I know, you are a warlord. It is your blood and your training, but for this once resist. What damage you would do would matter little. It is better we wait, Righel, hidden here in the center." She had stopped calling him Eryian. "He searches, I can feel his mind probing, but he does not find us. You trained me well to hide. All that you taught me in the days of Dawnshroud, I have remembered it all. You call your elite Shadow Walkers, well, I am, as well, a Shadow Walker, Righel," she said with a smile. "For you, in this world of yours, I suppose this is unlike any battle you have known. You wait. He smells the aganon of the sunblade and yet he cannot sense who bears it. It must be driving him mad."

"Can it slay him? Righel's sword?"

"If Righel wielded it, as he was when first he came, against the weakened being that is Azazel, yes, it would slay him, or at least it would destroy all but his soul. But you are human; I cannot predict what it will do. He is much stronger than you, warlord. Our greatest weapon will be surprise, but I doubt you can destroy him. Nor do I know what my magick will do against him.

You taught me to hone one skill above all others, and I have done so, but this is Azazel, the Reaper, the lord of death. We can only wait and hope."

"And what is the most we can hope for?"

"To turn him, to destroy whatever flesh he walks and fling his spirit into the void. It would take him many counts of the moon to find his way back. If Gabriel were near, he could be bound, but we face him alone; I would feel the sword of Gabriel if it were close.

"He comes for your Angelslayers, for all of them, every drop of their blood, their scion, their sons and daughters, all of them. For if they are no more, how can the prophecies of Enoch be fulfilled? Elyon sent the Daath, and all these years the angels did not realize why they walked the Earth. But now, the eye of Daath has been opened, and they know that the Arsayalalyur is here, on the Earth, that Elyon's wrath has already crossed the heavens. They have owned this world long enough to deceive themselves. They may believe they can defy even Elyon, destroy His Arsayalalyur. They are as fooled of this illusion as mankind. Even if somehow they were able to destroy the Arsayalalyur, do they not understand that the wave of Aeon's End would swallow the Earth into time as if the whole of this universe never was? I would think they would know that, but the Light Bearer has blinded them all by now. I only know because you taught me in a time when you knew all things."

Eryian tried to ignore the sounds of battle, to ignore that these were his own sons falling, but the feelings in him continued to build. They threatened to turn to tears of rage that Azazel was slaying them as if it were a feast.

"I can stand no more," he said, gripping the hilt of Righel's sword. It burned, stinging, tasting his blood. Cassium seized his shoulder and pulled him his hand from the hilt. He was surprised to see a stream of blood briefly cross from his palm to the hilt. There was a time in memory he had used this sword, but never had it taken his blood to do so.

"Your anger, Righel!" she said. "It is your weakness. Strike not in anger. If he is able to defeat you, all that you have done, laying down the mantle of your knowledge, returning in flesh to find your way back to heaven—if Azazel realizes that is what Righel has chosen, he will know the one weapon to use against you: that you strike in anger, that you let rage become what drives your blood.

You could lose all if that happened. He would collect your soul like he has so many before you. You must remember. If you die, die valiantly. Do not strike in anger. Remember that, Eryian, Righel, remember it, keep my words close, for that is how he will try to destroy you."

"They are being slaughtered, Cassium. How can I stand here and not let my blade join with them?"

"See your son," she said, motioning toward Braemacht. Braemacht watched back, met Eryian's eyes hearing his mother's words. "He waits. You must do the same."

"She is right, Father. He will come to us; we will answer him when that happens. Until then, though blood boils, we wait."

"They have waited seven hundred years for your summoning; they die for you. It is their honor. They know what is at stake."

At a roar, Eryian looked up. Wobbly, knitted calfskin sailed overhead, moments before the phosphorus powers ate through to the naphtha. The bags exploded, raining fire. Axemen screamed. Eryian pulled Cassium hard against him, covering them both with his shield as fire pelted in streaks. One axeman staggered past them, swearing, wrapped in curls of flame. The black smoke twisted with a thick smell. A horse was screaming, ablaze. His head was cloven by a blow of Braemacht's axe. Braemacht then turned to crouch near them as a stream of fire spilled from the face of his shield like water.

"Lady, are you hurt?" he asked Cassium.

"Nom Braemacht, I am unharmed."

Amathon stepped back from slaying, weary. He and a small knot of captains were surrounded by blood and bodies. The front had been lost; only the inner core still held. Knots of survivors were fighting, but they were being sectioned off and hewn down. The circle of death had grown smaller, but Amathon and his captains still held and behind them, Braemacht and the axemen of Righel were the last line. It was a line whose cost would be heavy to breach.

Amathon looked up, noticing that it was snowing—lazy, drifting flakes that seemed almost otherworldly as they floated downward to melt into the blood-darkened earth.

The Unchurians managed to clear the small ring of shields and leapt for him. He was still mounted, still visible, and they had sacrificed heavily to reach him. Amathon turned and slew with quick death thrusts. He warded off their attacks with the spiked face of his buckler while his sword opened flesh and dislodged heads.

The Unchurians were savage and fought well, but none could get past his sword. He and a handful of brothers were slaying all who reached them. And the cost of getting this close, of killing so many of Righel's sons, had left the battlefield piled in bodies and awash in blood.

Finally Amathon sensed one of power coming, not a common warrior, but one of their lords. He turned to see a dark rider making his way through the ranks. The rider was not human. The body was blackened bone, and wings arched from the shoulders, folded back. He cleaved flesh with a spiked morning star in a steady hum, shearing through shield, armor, killing the last of the footmen guarding Amathon's inner core of captains. This was a minion—one of Azazel's dark chosen.

Amathon threw aside his shield and gripped his sword with both hands. He high-stepped forward and broke into a run against the Uttuku with a low growl in his throat.

Beside Eryian, Cassium suddenly turned away, staggered as though she had been struck. Eryian was instantly at her side.

She used his shoulder to steady herself, and took a breath.

"It is Amathon," she whispered.

Braemacht stepped forward, watching. Cassium glanced at him.

"Azazel sent a slayer for him," she said. "Amathon has fallen."

Braemacht threw his head back and screamed. He shook his axe at the sky.

Cassium stepped forward to touch his arm.

"Now," he pleaded, "let me go out there, my lady. I will find the slayer! Let me avenge my brother!"

"No, Braemacht. Vengeance is not why we are here. We lay down our lives; it is not as other battles. We will not kill in anger. We will stand until the last, but our fight is valiant and cannot be otherwise, or the cause is lost us."

Braemacht paused, his jaw tight. He gazed skyward a moment, his hand wrapped tight about the axe. "Home had better be worth this day, good lady."

"It will be, Braemacht."

The giant looked at her, tears falling into his beard beneath the silver helm.

"Home is the heart of heaven," she added.

The sounds of the battle were growing closer now. The stiff, steady drone of the dying was drawing near. They were boring inward. The day had been long, but slowly the Unchurians were reaching the center. It would be over within another degree of the sun.

Eryian glanced to Cassium. "When he comes, when he finds us—do you have a plan?"

"I can drop him—stun him at the very least. Let him see me first, then light the sword."

Eryian glanced at the blade. The flange was no longer pulsing, but seemed to be waiting, resting. It was much as he remembered the sword of Uriel in battle with Argolis, a brilliant, white diamond, steeled through the center.

The sounds of battle were suddenly snuffed. It grew oddly quiet, a hush falling, odd, just like the snow that was lazily drifting from the sky.

Cassium drew close to Eryian's side.

"They will soon breach the inner circle," she said. "The last of us. But it seems they have stopped."

"These are Unchurians. They will bring in their highborn for the final kill."

The Unchurians had withdrawn, backing slowly into the trees, retreating to the hills encircling the vale. As the armies receded, the enormity of the death was left bare, and the ground could hardly been seen through the bodies that covered it. It was like a tide going out, leaving a mound of rich, red harvest.

The last of the sons of Righel tightened into a much smaller circle. All that was left was an outer core of shieldbearers, and toward the center, the queen's guard, the axemen of Braemacht.

Eryian heard voices, soft and far from the hills, singing in clear, careful Unchurian. He understood little Unchurian, but this he recognized this. It was a prayer.

"We are being dedicated," he said. "These are old words, the ancient words of Etlantis."

"Yes," she answered, "once the words of the choirs."

"Song," Braemacht swore. "Well, we can give them song, as well." He circled, looking at the others. "Sing!" he commanded.

"What?" an axeman beside him exclaimed.

"By Elyon's Light, give them a song in answer."

"What song, my lord?"

"I don't give a damn! Just sing!"

Braemacht banged his axe against his buckler began to sing in a high, loud voice.

Several more joined in, then all of them, banging their axes in rhythm and singing. Their voices echoed through the vale. But Braemacht had not chosen a prayer. Unlike Amathon and the others, the queen's guards were axemen, and they had chosen a tavern song, a drinking song, and their deep voices carried above the prayers of the Unchurian priests and swelled across the valley.

Chapter Forty-Two

Sorcerers

Rhywder was watching from a high knoll, atop a dark horse, amid the trees, Satrina beside him. Both of them were in disguise. They wore the robes of slain priests, cowls drawn up to cover their faces, the backs of their hands muddied.

"Love of God," Rhywder whispered. "They are singing a tavern song down there."

"But who are they?"

"I still do not know, but by Elyon's grace, they are glorious sons of bitches."

Satrina opened her eyes. For the past turn of the sun she had kept them closed. Now she gasped at the bodies below, mounds of them, like rolling hills of bloodied flesh piled one atop the other. She had never seen anything like it—a horrid, red stain that silently swallowed the falling snow.

"What is happening now, Rhywder?" she said weakly. "Why have they stopped?"

"The Unchurians are offering the last of these as a holy sacrifice. There must be someone down there, someone special."

"Why do you say that?"

"This prayer, it is a sacrificial prayer, but not for just any sacrifice. They claim they are about to kill a Star Walker."

"What is that?"

"A Watcher. A Star Walker is an angel—though I cannot guess why one has come here to fight against the death lord."

"There is an angel down there?"

"There must be, and the white cloaks that have fallen, the shields with their circled cross, they are his sons."

"He is going to destroy them all, the death lord of the south, is he not?"

"Yes. We should see him, the death lord. If it is an angel down there, he will come himself for the final kill. We must take care, Satrina. His focus will be elsewhere; there is little chance he will discover there are two priests not his own in the ranks, but we should remain quiet, hushed. It is odd we are about to witness one Watcher fall upon another; I cannot make sense of it. We have no choice but to watch him die. But he will die well, die strong. I sense someone powerful, someone strong, but the odd thing is that I do not sense a fallen. I have no feeling there is a fallen of the choir, but those are the words of the Unchurians; they believe they are about to fall upon a Watcher of Heaven."

"I am not sure I understand, but it sounds very sad."

Rhywder nodded. She glanced at him.

"You will not, in the last moments, choose to do some wild, crazy thing, will you, Rhywder?"

Rhywder didn't answer that; he just watched the small circle of survivors below.

"Promise me," she said.

"Of course," he answered. "Why would I?"

"Who leads these people, these Unchurians?"

"I will not speak his name, but he was once a creator, once a member of choir that sang the Earth into being; in fact, this one is the second of the three. There were three lords who touched the stone of Ammon, and he was the second. He is very powerful, Satrina, but we are not going to fear him or think on him."

"What, then, are we to do?"

"Wait. Continue to pretend we are priests of the Unchurians, and wait here, in these trees."

"And who leads them?"

"How could a creator be brought to this, to the horror of Lamech's village? How could that come to be from one who sang in the creation of the Earth?"

"I have never understand such a thing myself, Satrina."

"Well, if it baffles you, I should not be bothered that it troubles me. You know so many things, so many secrets."

"Sometimes, Satrina, I think by knowing more, I know less."

She nodded.

"Why did you nod?"

"Because that is a typical Rhywder answer, one that makes no sense whatsoever. I am getting used to them now."

"I can say one thing; my grandmother once told me—"

"Another grandmother saying. Some of these I like."

"Yes, well, once she told me that one cannot create from light alone, that creation also needs the dark, the shadow, and that not all shadow is evil."

"Oh, that was a good one, Rhywder. It is one of the most confusing grandmother sayings I have heard yet."

"I am glad I am able to please."

"Actually, Rhywder, I feel terrified right now."

"I, as well, Satrina." Rhywder lifted his reins.

"And those magnificent warriors down there—waiting to die—and no one to even help them."

"Whoever they are, they did not come to Hericlon's vale without purpose."

"But they are being slaughtered! It seems to me they have come here but to die."

"Yes, but have you noticed, they have kept a very tight center. I have been watching, and all through the fight, nothing has moved in that center. They are protecting something. I want to find out what that is. Let us move forward slowly, Satrina."

"Oh, no," Satrina muttered. "I knew it. Now we must move closer."

"Just a bit, keep your head up; remember you are a high cloaked priest of the Unchurian."

"Of course, how could I possibly forget?"

"Stay with me; we will move slowly."

Rhywder nudged the horse's side and began making his way slowly through the ranks of the Unchurians. Beneath his cloak, his hand rested on the hilt of his sword. Satrina looked straight ahead; for fear her hood might slip, so she kept her head very still and her back straight, doing her best to behave as a proper sorceress.

Rhywder then drew the horse to a halt. It waited, hide flinching, as Satrina drew alongside. Everything had paused, even the singing had stopped, and the gathered Unchurians were not making a move.

"Why have we stopped?"

Rhywder did not answer, hoping Satrina would get the hint to say nothing more. He sat erect, one hand on his thigh. He then pulled his horse tight against hers. Other Unchurians about them also moved to the sides. Passing among them, making their way to the fore, were high-blood warriors. They were mounted on muscled chargers, thick in weapons and the dark red armor. Rhywder had seen a few Uttuku in thorn armor bodies ride down into the battle during the day, but none like this. These were the angel's elite firstborn. That was the reason for the pause, to let the princes come forward for the last offerings. They were coming like lords for the prime meat after the fat had been cut away. They were encircling the vale.

Rhywder was forced to let them pass and not follow. There were no sorcerers among them.

Chapter Forty-Three
The Sword of Righel

There was more fury in the final attack than anything witnessed in the light of day. Dusk was low when the last of the sons of Righel began to die, slow at first, but as the lines weakened, bloodied, they began to die quickly. The warriors coming against them were the elite of Du'ldu, deadly at their craft, and even the sons of Righel could not turn them.

"Axemen!" Braemacht screamed, tensing. He took a tight grip of his axe. The last of the front was giving way; the inner circle of shieldbearers was finally being breached. All that would be left were axemen.

"Stand ready to protect your queen!" Braemacht screamed to the heavens.

He was answered in a resounding roar as the axemen of Righel lifted their weapons.

Eryian's hand was curled about the hilt of Righel's sword, and only with difficulty did he restrain himself from drawing it. If they came for her, if they tried to kill Cassium, he would unleash the light on them. It would no longer matter; he was not going to let her die easily.

"Prepare . . ." Braemacht said, watching as the final fury broke through the shields before them. He then leveled the killing pike of his axe forward. "Now!" he screamed.

The axemen rushed forward, huge, weighted in hard muscle; they were like stone monoliths hewing into the Unchurians, and even though they were the elite of the entire firstborn of Azazel, Braemacht and his axemen scattered them, cleaving horse and rider, cutting down everything in their path in a widening circle.

At the center of their circle were now only two. Cassium crouched beside Eryian. Eryian took battle stance, his hand on the hilt of Righel's sword, the tall oblong white shield covering Cassium's right. He watched with baited breath. The axemen were no longer cutting into them; they had gone as far from their queen as they were going to and now they drew together, their axes for a moment holding back ten times their numbers.

"Time narrows, my love," Cassium whispered.

"Time I cannot bear," he answered.

"Remember one thing," she said, touching his forearm.

Eryian paused. Her eyes studied him carefully. "We fight this day, and there is no doubt that evil has come against your sons and continues, but we will not turn on them in rage. Slay with your sword; never with your hatred. You are the valiant, Righel, hold to that part of you. Promise me. Even when he comes, promise you will not turn in rage."

He tightened his jaw.

"Righel."

"I promise, my lady."

A sudden, fiery bolt shot up Eryian's arm. It came without warning from the blade of Righel's sword, and he sucked in a breath as several veins in his hand exploded. Blood flowed over the cross hilts. Eryian was seized in pain.

Cassium stared amazed. "He is coming," she said.

Eryian swallowed the pain and continued to grip the hilt. His blood seeped through the pommel, and the scabbard against his thigh was hot.

He staggered as another vein rippled beneath his the skin of his shoulder as though in spasm. Eryian was nearly staggered by the pain. "Elyon's Light! This sword is sucking out life!"

"It is your flesh. You carry the sword of an angel, and it feels the lord of death draw near." Cassium drew away with a hiss. She crouched, one hand on his thigh, searching the hills.

"Focus, Eryian. Try to feed it your soul, not your blood. It knows you; remind the blade who you are."

Eryian tried to focus. He let a whisper of *the knowing* spill though him. It was like a cool balm against the searing heat of the sword's hilt, and for a moment the pain eased.

The axemen had begun to fall. One by one they were brought down. Their end was only moments away.

He saw Braemacht rock back, head twisted to the side. Something had struck the giant so hard, he was thrown. His huge killing axe fell in the muddied ground, and Braemacht slammed into the earth and slid to where Cassium knelt at Eryian's side. She half-cried out, seeing his head twisted to the side. The giant's hand clawed the earth and for a moment he struggled to lift himself, until his body finally stilled.

Cassium and Eryian were the only two left. About them, in a widening circle, like a strange wheel turned on its side, were a tangle of bodies, both the Seraphim of Righel and the prime of the Unchurians.

It was quiet. The surviving Unchurians, instead of closing in on them, were backing away, clearing ground. Snow drifted from the sky and was slowly covering the fallen, melting into the blood. Above, from the forest, a single rider started toward the center, his Unchurians parting to let him pass.

Beside Eryian, Cassium slowly stood.

In Eryian's hands, it was as though the sword had sight, for when the rider came into view, it pulsed, sharp. Eryian braced against the coming pain, but instead his skin shivered, and he felt a raw, unyielding power from the blade. It no longer took his blood; the hilt no longer burned.

Rhywder's horse snorted, restless, and he kept tight reign. He stared, amazed. He could hear his heart pound in the quiet snow. There was a woman left alive down there. The Unchurian prime had fought back a central core of axemen and guardians, to reveal a woman. A woman, and beside her—none other than the good captain Eryian. Eryian had been the Star Walker they had dedicated. His past had always been a mystery, but Rhywder had never imagined he had once been an angel. It must have been some manner of attempted redemption, though Rhywder could not believe such an act as betraying the holy covenant of life could ever be forgiven. It was sad, actually. Still, this was the captain, and

Rhywder would do whatever he could to in order to get him out of here.

"Captain," Rhywder whispered low. He started his horse forward, slowly, cautious. But before he left the shadow of the woods, he drew up sharp. It was the dark one—the Named.

Azazel passed close enough to take Rhywder's breath. If the angel saw him or sensed him, he did not seem to care. The Watcher was riveted solely on his prey. And once again this day, Rhywder found himself stunned beyond words. Azazel had taken on flesh! The angel had clothed himself in a human's body, as an Uttuku would have done. Rhywder was fascinated and racked his brain for a possible reason why. How it could possibly have made sense? As he passed Rhywder saw it was a powerful body, heavily muscled, young, handsome, a body in its prime. Uttuku could not take a Nephilim, and he guessed the same applied even to an angel. This was a human, perhaps once a king or a warrior of great renown. He was bearded, with long, dark hair that fell over his muscled shoulders, twenty and seven at most. Rhywder had not seen the eyes, but they would have been as those of an Uttuku, a damp mesh of dark with an inner glow, and since this was an angel, looking into his eyes would have been like looking into the night sky.

And then it made sense. Of course—Enoch's curse had taken hold. The angel of death had turned, had himself begun to die, and the very revulsion of watching his own skin wither was too much for him to bear. Rhywder had to actually suppress an impulse to laugh. It was the finest of jokes. Of course, he was terrified—because, after all, they were about to die—so it was a simple thing to suppress, but that is what he wanted to do, laugh and laugh. Azazel, the lord of the holy choir of the Auphanim, had traded an immortal body of divine light for a human's course. Death itself, it turned out, was terrifying to the very one whose word had spellbound it into existence. The mighty Reaper was horrified of his own creation. In the end, how Elyon truly mocked them all, those who had mocked Him by throwing away their most precious gift, the pearl, the covenant of everlasting, all for the mere pleasure of a woman.

Of course, the body would have been spellbound as no other. It was likely far more powerful and stronger than even the hardened wood of a minion.

Satrina pulled up beside Rhywder, and he waited until she was close, until her leg touched his.

"Ride for Ishmia!" he whispered.

He glanced at her. His face was in shadow, but through the cowl he could still see her eyes. Slowly, defiantly, she shook her head.

Azazel rode across the plain of bodies slowly, his horse high-stepping as though it were moving through deep snow. He finally reached the small circle of ground about Eryian and Cassium. His horse danced, spirited, and gossamer-mesh eyes studied Eryian from beneath the helmet. He had taken a human body—not even Unchurian or Daathan, a pure-blooded human. He would have made the flesh almost invincible, and if it weakened, he could always find others. He had chosen to live as a wraith. Enoch's curse had taken him; it was taking them all now. The eye of Daath was opened; the angels would begin to age, like men. This was flesh, except for the eyes. The eyes were hollowed out, coated in a mesh, and it was only through the mesh that Eryian recognized him, Azazel—the second of the three.

The angel's gaze then shifted to Cassium, a mixture of recognition and mild surprise. The rider urged the horse forward slowly, and circled about to the left. Eryian turned, following. The sword sparked, leaving trails of light that played out along the ground. If the demon noticed the sunblade, he didn't seem to care. He turned the horse slowly, facing them. The horse shook out its mane.

"If it isn't the two lovers," he said, his voice two voices, twain, one the voice of the angel, and a second that echoed beneath it, the voice of the human he had taken. "How moving. You have come here, to the Vale of Tears, to bleed once more? I am admittedly stunned. I knew your sons were mighty beyond measure, but I never guessed it was you they were hiding in their center."

Cassium snarled and dropped forward, crouched, and crossed her wrists. "By the Boundless and Limitless Light I speak, by the Son of Women I speak, by the mirrored shadow of the Creator I name you, fallen one: Amen-Omen-Diaman, behold the *Light Whose Name Is Splendor*!" From her palms streamed a wind of light.

The horse reared, screaming, and then seemed to dissolve, vaporized. Azazel landed on his feet and crouched. It seemed a hard wind tore at him, and he forced to turn to the side. For a moment it looked as if he were going to fall. He had been driven to one knee, face to the ground, crossing an arm to block the light, but then the wind stilled and the light faded. Cassium drew back. A moment the rider remained crouched, stunned, but slowly he regained his strength. He lifted his head. The meshed eyes were empty of light, black as if he were blinded, but still intact, they slowly turned on Cassium.

Cassium gasped, glancing to Eryian. She had paled, frightened. "That was everything!" she whispered to Eryian. "Everything I have—all I know. He wears the flesh of a man—it shielded him, Righel. It shielded him!"

A moment later Eryian caught her eyes, and he saw panic—that and a quick, whispered good-bye.

Eryian started to move, but Azazel moved his left hand, extending three fingers, and the warlord was thrown aside. It was as though the air itself had come against him, and he was slammed into the earth on his back. The sword was knocked from his hand. It lay just beyond his fingers; still simmering, snaking bolts of light from the blade, but Eryian could not move to reach it. The pressure folding in against him continued to increase, as if the angel were gaining strength, recovering. Eryian felt a rib snap with sudden, sharp pain, threatening to pierce his heart. Eryian hissed. He was being crushed by air.

The Unchurian slowly lifted his right hand. "Cassium," the twain voice whispered. "How well I remember you. How these many years I have missed you." His wrist turned deftly.

It was as if his hand had seized Cassium, she was lifted from the ground and hung a moment, her back arched, and she gasped in sudden pain. She began to spin, slowly at first, then faster, until her arms were thrown out, her hair whipping.

Eryian struggled with all he had, stretching his fingers. Cassium began to scream. A splatter of blood slapped across Eryian's cuirass. The air continued to crush him back; another rib snapped. His fingers stretched, closer, all his strength to reach the blade.

Blood began to stream from Cassium's pores, spraying outward everywhere, her hands, her arms, her face. She was spinning into a blur.

Eryian drew strength and with a snarl heaved himself to the side. He touched the hilt of Righel's sword and sucked in its power, drinking its light—giving it whatever it wished to take, flesh, blood, it did not matter. The pressure against him shattered. He was instantly on his feet, turning, and for a moment, an instant, it was not Eryian who lifted the sunblade. It was Righel.

Cassium dropped to the ground like a broken doll. Blood pooled about her into the dirt.

Eryian stared through Righel's eyes; he remembered her words, what she had said of anger, of rage, but he could not suppress it.

"Look familiar, star jumper?" Azazel said, amused. "Her blood across your breastplate? Her light was not pure enough. As I, as we, she is unforgiven. But be assured, her heart still beats—if you want to call what she now has inside her a heart. It will take days; it is a craft of death that took some time to perfect. It leaves astonishing pain, unendurable, I imagine, even for a Star Walker Queen." Azazel then paused, tipped his head to the side. "You are different. I have taken and perfected mortal flesh, like a new set of clothes. But look here, you—you are mortal! What is it you have done, Righel? Wait; let me guess—you think that by laying down your mantle and taking up a mortal's coil that somehow He will forgive you? You have wasted your time. A pity, my brother, but you have wasted centuries. Elyon turned His face; He will not look back, not for any of us. And now look at your pretty Star Walker Queen—she was once so beautiful. What a sad end, Righel. Tell me something—what exactly do you plan to do with that sword? It belongs to an angel, not a mortal."

Eryian threw all his conscious energy into the sword, feeding it, letting it drink not only his rage, but his soul. And Righel's blade responded, it swiftly drank his lifeblood, and moments before it would have killed him, Eryian brought the sword over his shoulder in an arc and flung it like a dagger, hard into the chest of the Watcher. It was a burning, molten white. It pierced Azazel's armor like cutting through lard until the hand guards slammed against the oraculum breastplate where it lodged. Azazel gasped, sucking for air. Apparently, his mortal body sustained pain. It may have been momentary pain, but he was obviously staggered. He dropped to his knees and the blade exploded in a brilliant starburst that pulsed outward, imploding with a deafening roar.

Eryian threw himself down, covering his head. He felt the wave of energy pass over him. Had it caught him, it would have destroyed him instantly, but he was close to Azazel and the wave passed over both him and Cassium's crushed body. It felt like a seething, boiling surge of heat, passing with heavy wind.

It annihilated everything in its path. Men and horse seemed to melt into acid shadows. The earth, laden with bodies, charred and curled upward, blown back. But Azazel's body remained intact, back arched, paralyzed in pain, flesh peeling away. His very body divided the explosion, and it streamed past him to either side, leaving a vee-shaped shadow that expanded from the point where he knelt. But everything to either side was vaporized the instant the light struck it, trees, rock, horses, bodies; all were being obliterated by the fire of a distant star.

Rhywder brought his horse about hard, sucking in a breath. He was far up the hill, but by the luck that always seemed to follow him, both he and Satrina were directly behind the angel. The blast streamed to either side of them, but they, and the Unchurian warriors around them, were left in the shadow, untouched. He saw the trees lying back like feathers, saw huge chunks of Hericlon's rock torn free and thrown into the air like pebbles. It was called Severity, the pure and unbridled light of Elyon, light without forgiveness, light that did not judge but simply destroyed everything in its path. Unchurians were vaporized, flashing into shadows that seemed to hang in the air for a moment before they vanished. Yet he and Satrina were protected by the angel's body. Rhywder had guessed it to be spellbound, and it was. It was nearly as invincible as the divine flesh it had been traded for. Rhywder believed both he and Satrina bore pure hearts, but the light of Elyon did not make judgments; it was light that was absolute. Had they not been protected by the angel's shadow, they would have become shadows of ash as the thousands of warriors to either side of them.

Rhywder threw his cloak aside and sank his heels hard into the ribs of the horse, leaning forward, clutching the reins in one tight fist, lowering his head, shielding his eyes from the blinding white of the heat flash as he raced for the crouched body at full gallop. Satrina, on instinct, followed. Rhywder did not really think he could take the bastard out, but by Elyon's grace, the Watcher's flesh, spellbound or not, had to have been weakened and he was gong to give it a try.

The explosion ended, though it seemed to leave a concussion reverberating through the air, like waves that rippled in and out of each other, but Eryian slowly came to his knees. He turned to see Cassium's mangled body lying in the dirt. It was as if all substance had been torn from her, even bone and organs, until she lay like a piece of bloodied linen, discarded, twisted to one side. He noticed her small finger twitch. Unbelievably, she was still breathing. Azazel was right; he had crafted the cruelest of deaths. Somehow, by some spell, she was still alive.

The Unchurian remained on his knees. His armor, his cloak, his flesh, everything had been torn from him and he was left only muscle and blood, his body glowing and fading in waves of red and white as if he were a fire still smoldering. There was no trace of Righel's sword; it had been consumed. Azazel's head was hanging, but he was clearly still alive, although stunned like a dazed bull. Blisters on his body oozed blood, but even then it was slowly beginning to heal. New veins were forming and snaking in and out of the burned muscle tissue, repairing it.

For a moment Eryian thought he heard the voice of Rhywder calling him. He slowly looked up. It *was* Rhywder, coming toward him at full gallop. He wore the garb of an Unchurian priest, a heavy axe spinning over his head, gaining momentum.

"Captain!" Rhywder screamed. "It is me! Rhywder! And you were right—they are Unchurians!"

Eryian gasped in disbelief, seeing the Little Fox flying toward him, and just behind Rhywder was a girl with long hair streaming back in the wind of her horse's gallop.

Rhywder dropped sideways in the saddle. Azazel may have only dropped to his knees, but Rhywder was going to guess his flesh was weakened, as well. It was a pretty fair gamble—that was one bastard of an explosion. He wouldn't have wanted to be at its center, even if he had been an angel. As Rhywder closed on him at full gallop, he saw Azazel slowly turn his head to look behind, to see what was coming. It was an oraculum axe and as Rhywder passed at full gallop, he sheared off the head with a resounding *chunk*. It spun high into the air, like a red ball. In Rhywder's memory, even high Uttuku found it difficult to live without heads, but the angel seemed little affected. He was still kneeling, his hands on his bloodied thighs. His body, apparently, was repairing itself. It just no longer had a head.

Rhywder pulled up sharply on the reins as his horse spun about, hooves digging against the dirt.

"Captain," Rhywder said, his horse dancing, but Eryian didn't look up; he was staring the slain woman beside him. Surely she was dead, but then he realized her eyes were still in her face, though it was flattened. They blinked, these beautiful ice-eyes. She was alive!

Satrina had circled her mount at Rhywder's side.

Eryian crawled toward the woman. "Leave me, Little Fox," he said, his voice weak.

"Rhywder," Satrina whispered, alarmed. Rhywder looked up. She pointed to the hillocks of Hericlon's spurs. Unchurians—lots of them. They were left in confusion, but were slowly regrouping. There seemed an endless supply of these Unchurians. Even more were coming from Hericlon's passage to take up formation along the ridge, and others, highborn, were beginning to descend toward the plateau.

"And there," Satrina whispered, even more alarmed. "Look!"

Rhywder glanced at the body that housed Azazel. Now he knew why the angel had taken on the body of a human. It was virtually invincible. A head of bone had already regrown on his shoulders, and muscle and veins were crawling across the white bone, groping, reforming. He was going to grow himself a new head.

"Elyon bless us," Rhywder whispered. "All sanity is lost." Rhywder turned in the saddle. "Captain!" he shouted, holding his spooked horse in tight rein, "we have mighty little time left, and damn it, I am getting you out of here!"

"Leave me!" Eryian said once more. "That is an order, Captain Rhywder."

"You forget, but you told me those days are over now. You are coming with me, Eryian, like it or not."

Rhywder scanned the ridge. Highborn. Lots of them, descending slowly as if they were putting on a show, but they were likely wary of another explosion.

"Damn it, Captain, I have followed you, fought for you, killed for you, but not today. Today, you are going to do what I tell you to do. We are getting out of here."

"No, Rhywder. My place is here—with these fallen."

"They are dead. I will grant they were damned noble, but it is over and they are dead, Captain. And you are not."

Rhywder dropped from the saddle. Eryian was weakened, probably with a few bones broken, and blood seemed to have been sucked through the skin of his hands and arms so that when Rhywder grabbed his arm, he was slippery. So the Little Fox gripped tighter and since Eryian was weakened, he was wrenched to his feet. He stared at Rhywder. Those dark blue eyes of the warlord, Rhywder had never seen the will taken from them, but they were empty now. They were only sad and resigned to one things, and he guessed that was to die here.

"I know as well as you," Rhywder said, "how there come times to die. But by Elyon's name, this is not one of them!"

The sound of hooves. The high-bloods were closing on them. And though Rhywder didn't look on Azazel directly, he knew that the muscle was in place now, the cheekbones and forehead were molding, even skin had begun to grow back in place. He was getting stronger by the moment.

"So the thing is, Captain, you can go with me willingly—or I can just take you. You are too weak to stop me. It is your choice, but you have got precious time to make it. What will it be?"

Eryian studied him carefully. He reached forward and suddenly wrenched Rhywder's short sword from his belt. Rhywder paused, not sure of the captain's intent, but then Eryian turned, dropped to his knees over the crushed woman. He met her eyes. Rhywder could not imagine the pain she was in. Eryian clutched the hilt of Rhywder's sword in both hands, then lifted it over her chest. Rhywder could not believe she still moved, but she did, she lifted her hand, a limp hand that seemed to have no bone, but still she spread her fingers in the sign of the word. She whispered something—Etlantian words, some manner of spell-binding. Rhywder felt something pass through them all, like a wind of light. It took his breath, clear and clean, a tender wind, like the touch of a warm, soft kiss.

The lady's small hand then dropped, and in the same moment, Eryian screamed and plunged the sword into her chest, though the heart. Her body jerked, and moments later Rhywder saw the light finally, mercifully slip from her eyes. Whoever she was, she had finally left for home.

"Godspeed, good woman," whispered Rhywder.

Eryian stood and handed Rhywder back his sword.

"Thanks," Rhywder said. "Now let us get out of here." He glanced to Her-iclon. The angel's high-bloods were coming at full gallop.

Rhywder suddenly realized it wasn't going to be easy outrunning them. "Time to leave, Captain," he said, vaulting into the saddle of the horse. Only then did he realize something was different. The horse was white. He glanced to Satrina, who stared back amazed.

"She changed them," Satrina whispered. "Her whisper, her last words—she changed the horses!"

Satrina's horse was white, as well, and more than that, Rhywder noticed—laid tightly against the flanks were the feathered humps of muscled wings.

Whoever she had been, she knew star knowledge. But even with these, time was thinning, the highborn were closing swiftly, screaming, weapons clearing, and the gossamer mesh of the Unchurian's eyes was knitting into place. Rhywder knew that once Azazel was whole, the mesh of those eyes would mold into the dark star of the universe—the might of his power. Rhywder sank his knees into the flanks and let the horse rear. He felt the wings unfold beneath his thighs. He gripped the reins in one fist and leaned in the saddle.

"Follow us, Satrina!" he screamed, then seized Eryian's wrist in a tight lock. With a shout he kneed the flanks, pulling hard up on the reins, and with a strong wing beat the animal soared, lifting into the darkening blue sky. There was a quick thunder beat of wings against the air, and with a surge they pressed into the wind of flight, wheeling ever higher. With the slightest twist of the reins, he was able to guide the mount toward the river. He glanced over his shoulder to see Satrina leaning forward, hugging the neck of her horse, concentrating as though she knew exactly how to do this, her bared legs tucked back to ride the muscles of the wing. With the next wing beat, they soared higher, so swiftly Rhywder could feel his stomach in his toes. He pulled Eryian upward, until the captain could grasp the horn of the saddle. Then they soared into the very clouds.

It was some moments before the body of the Unchurian stood, but finally the demon rose to his feet and looked up, watching the sky calmly. His wounds were still closing, meshing. The blood on his arms and face dried and fell away, ashen, into the wind. The highborn had reached his side, weapons drawn, and his armies, those deeper into the forests and high upon the fingers of Hericlon's spurs where they had survived the acid wind, began to gather toward him.

Staring at the sky, he smiled. "Still as lucky as ever," he whispered.

Chapter Forty-Four

Dreams

Eryian watched images dance among the flame of a hearth. He realized he was awake—but the afterimages of his dreams still burned in the lick of flames, and the far scream of combat seemed a faint echo. He didn't know where he was; only that he felt weak, and pain burned through him. Eryian slowly turned his head, a slight movement that spun the room unsteadily. He thought he saw Krysis, his wife, the light of the fire whispering off her golden hair and playing soft shadows along her high cheekbones. Her head was lowered.

"Krysis," he whispered.

She glanced up with a start and her liquid blue eyes searched quickly, the mouth parting slightly. "Eryian!" she whispered back. She was real. Her hand entwined his fingers. She knelt from the chair and laid her head against his arm, her touch soft—the dampness of a tear. "You are alive," she said quietly.

She lifted a cup of water to his lips and he drank.

"Krysis," he whispered. "How did . . . where . . ."

"When we heard that you had moved for battle I made them bring me this far at least."

"And this far?"

"We are in the port city of Ishmia. I was afraid I would never see you again. I could not bear that . . . never again to see your face. You can not die on me, Eryian."

He stared back, numbed by the pain, and suddenly her image bled out through the white sun-flash of the aganon blade and he saw a shadow of Cassium, spinning, arms whipping outward as she was being lifted into the air—and her tight, small scream of pain. For her, a Star Walker Queen, to have been forced to scream in pain—it must have been unimaginable.

Eryian arched his back, slamming against the headboard, thinking he had to reach the hilt of the aganon blade. But then the visions paled and died, and the quiet of the room closed back in. He found Krysis watching him, frightened, almost as though she had seen what he had.

"Sorry," he said, "dreams still spilling?"

"What happened to you up there, Eryian?"

He stared at her a moment, swallowed. "We died," he answered.

He drew breath and tried to get up, but Krysis set her hand against his chest, laying him back.

"You are not going anywhere. For once, you have no choice. You stand up and you will just fall back down. You have not enough blood in you to keep a sparrow upright. The physician said it was as though they were draining you of blood. I have heard they capture humans, cut them, drain their blood to drink in celebration—but you are only half-human."

"Apparently the half that bleeds."

For another moment her face drifted away as though she were receding. Images fogged. Braemacht's voice echoed, screaming as he waded into them, hewing bodies to either side. A catapult missile roared overhead and Eryian jerked. He searched, desperate, then drew back, confused, seeing only Krysis's soft eyes.

"Damn," he hissed. "No more—no more dreams. Battle shock, I have seen it. Never believed after all I have gone through that I would feel it myself."

He then focused, forcing the dream images out, letting the pain suck at reality. He looked around—stone and wood walls; thick, double doors.

"Where are we?" he asked.

"A think this is a merchant's castle."

"Where is Tillantus?"

"The legions are encamped outside of the city. He tells me to ensure you that he understands his orders are to hold the high ground, but you are *not* going to them. Eryian, for God's sake, I think you almost died, for real this time. You have passed out, and once you stopped breathing. It was the ranger, the Little Fox, that did something to you, pounded your chest and threw some powder over you, brought you back. He said you would live, but he made me promise you get enough rest to grow back some of your blood."

He turned to her.

"And your bones are broken, as well. But your high captain, that Tillantus, he spat aside. Tillantus did not believe you were going to make it. He told the Little Fox there was no witchery that could fool death. So when he brought you here, it was because they expected you to die, Eryian! Except . . . except for the Little Fox. He said you were going to live, *damn it*. He said otherwise he would not have saved your thin ass in the first place."

Panic played in the air a moment. Again, the far, lost cry of Cassium's pain. As he closed his eyes, the images of the battle played against his eyelids like living paintings, and then, for a moment, Cassium's eyes, the soft light that spilled from them, and he felt the sadness grip. It was good he had trained his life against emotion; it finally came in handily. He now understood that he had lost her twice. He had, in fact, lost her in all of time. He opened his eyes to stare at the quiet flicker of the hearth fire. He loved Krysis, which meant love was not singular, but that did nothing to dull the sadness of Cassium's eyes as the light went out of them.

"Do not . . . let me sleep," he said, staring blankly. He groped for her hand, and finding it, clutched it tightly, desperate.

"Eryian, my love, if you do not sleep, you cannot heal."

He stared at her weakly and shook his head. "No. I can stand no more dreams—keep me awake for a time. Keep reminding me you are here."

She studied him, and then lifted a wineglass. She tipped a small vial, then sprinkled powder into the wine and stirred it with her little finger.

"What is that?"

"With this you do not dream," she said. She offered the glass and when he hesitated, she added, "Trust me, Eryian. How do you think I have slept at night all these years without you? It is sleep, and you must regain your strength, but I promise from experience, you will have no dreams. You will heal more quickly. Do it; drink it."

He propped himself up, took the glass, and drained it. When he leaned back she pulled a hand through his hair, lifting it out of his eye.

"Where is Little Eryian?" he asked. "Did you bring him?"

"No. But he is the one that told me."

Eryian glanced to her. "Told you what?"

"What you were feeling. That unless Elyon moved His hand, you were about to die. He seems to know so much. He was right. And you were far, far from him. Believe me, you have no idea how hard it was to keep him from coming to you. He is under watch even now."

The wine worked surprisingly quickly. Eryian could feel it leave a soft burn.

"Tillantus—tell him to bring up the rear legions. Tell him to move to the shallows near Ithen's ford . . . tell him they will soon come . . . without number."

As Eryian drifted to sleep, his hand slipped from hers.

Chapter Forty-Five

Rescue

Ishmia was the trading and shipping center of Terith-Aire, watched over by an austere, aged magistrate of merchants. Docks cluttered its bay in a semicircle. The city had no standing army, but it did have a garrison of Daath, of which, in the courtyard, before the castle, Rhywder had assembled twenty. Rhywder knew that when the Unchurians swept north, Galaglea would be like an untended flock in their path—but they would also meet the onslaught with a full legion of hardheaded warriors. Enough to slow down even the armies of a thousand fires.

There was no hope for them—the Galagleans. He had sent riders, but he did not know if they would reach the city in time. But if Galagleans knew anything at all in this world, it was how to die well. For that reason there was a thin change, so thin it was like the edge of a surgeon's knife, but it was there. He could maybe reach this girl Marcian Antiope had spoken of. If the story were true, Elyon would aid them. Elyon chose His own time and His own purposes of intervening, but He did seem to want a Daath scion about, so for that reason, even if Rhywder rode down the throat of an army to save her, he would still believe there was a chance.

The Little Fox turned his horse and rode slowly past the twenty men he had picked.

Some of them he knew. He knew Rainus, their captain, a capable officer. He had fought with Rainus in the gathering wars; the man was brave and capable. As well, he was one of the best horsemen to be found, as were his men. It was odd, in war they were invaluable; in peace, Rainus and his men had been stationed here, to break up brawls in taverns and keep merchants from being robbed. But now they were about to come in quite handy.

"I have chosen you for speed," Rhywder told them as he rode down their line. "We ride to save one girl from the edge of Galaglea. We will stop for nothing, and we shall reach her or die in the attempt. I suspect, luck being as it has been, we will meet the armies of the Unchurian coming or going, and I suspect the most part of us will not be returning. Any of you wish to leave, I will understand."

"You," said Rainus.

"What?"

"You should leave, my lord. The Daath, their king . . . now their warlord . . ."

"I am not a sitter of Daath, never had skills as a milkmaid; besides, it is a Daath we ride for. The girl has a child. It is the child, by the way, that will take priority. Not the girl—the child. Are we understood? Certain you are all willing to come, chances thin as they are?"

Rhywder's horse danced a moment. He waited. None of them responded; they were all Eryian's troops, and Eryian knew how to train men to die.

Rhywder shifted in the saddle, brought the horse about, and then stopped and stared at one of the warriors—something had caught his eye. The warrior was mounted on a roan horse, watching from beneath a bronze helmet, cheek guards closed, visor lowered, the face mostly in shadow—but the large, green eyes were hardly hidden. Rhywder sighed and lowered his head, shaking it.

"Satrina," he said quietly.

The figure made no motion of recognition.

Rhywder looked up. "Satrina, I know you are in there. Take off the helmet."

The figure looked right, then left in question.

"Remove the helmet!"

Slowly, she grunted, disgusted, and unlatched the strap, then pulled off the helmet. Long, silken hair fell over her shoulders and Satrina batted her long lashes.

"What are you doing?" he asked.

"Going with you, of course."

Rhywder shook his head.

"Little Fox, I have saved your skin more times than you would want me to count! I am going with you! I want you back alive."

"You listen to me, Satrina . . ."

"Every time I listen to you, we get in trouble! I am coming with you, so do not try to stop me."

Rhywder looked around, then motioned. "Rainus!"

The warrior drew from the ranks mounted on a great black stallion. Rainus was a big man, broad-shouldered and powerful, but he was ugly beneath his plumed helm. A long, gray Daathan cloak fell over the flanks of his horse.

"My lord," he said, pulling up beside Rhywder.

"Take this bint and tie her to that pillar!"

Satrina gasped. She glanced to the pillar, then to Rainus. She backed her horse away slightly. "Rhywder! I am not your house-wench; you do not own me!"

Rhywder thought this over. "I am afraid you would make a very poor house-wench, Satrina. You cannot even cook."

"I can cook!"

"Really?"

As Rainus closed on her, Satrina glanced at him nervously. "You keep away from me!" she shouted, pulling the horse back. "You keep back or I swear . . . I will cut you."

Rainus lifted a line of hemp from his saddle tassel with a muscular arm and laid it over his shoulder. The eyes beneath the helm were calm.

Satrina drew the sword she had bought that morning. It was a short sword like Rhywder's. "Do not assume I cannot use this!" she threatened. "I have killed bigger than you."

Rhywder lifted a brow. According to the stories Antiope had told him, it was true. Even a thorn-skinned Nephilim.

Rainus pulled up beside her, grabbed her wrist, and then pried the sword loose and shoved it back in its scabbard. Before Satrina could make another move, she was lifted from the horse and dropped over Rainus's shoulder. His horse trotted quickly to the pillar and Rainus dropped from the saddle, her with him. He pinned her against the marble and started wrapping the rope about her.

Satrina kicked one of his greaves. Her boot left a ringing thud, and she hissed, having hurt her foot. Rainus was wrapping her from shoulder to knees.

"When are you going to learn you need me, Rhywder?" she screamed.

"Leave one of your men to look after her," Rhywder said as Rainus finished off the tie.

"Damn you, Rhywder!" she shouted, struggling against the thick rope.

"If faith holds, I will be home in less than a few days, Satrina, and since you can cook, I most like lamb in lemon pepper sauce. See if you cannot have that fixed for supper."

"If I did not love you," she said, "I swear I would utterly hate you, Rhywder!"

"Most women do hate me; it is only natural. Truth be, it is a puzzle, your fondness. But I love you, too, you lovely wench/cook/sword-wielding beauty."

He turned his horse. "Move out," he said quietly, and then led the warriors out of the plaza, hooves clattering on the polished limestone.

Satrina looked at the mounted warrior left to guard her. She smiled. "I think he tied these ropes awfully tight."

The warrior made no response.

"It would be nice if you loosened them just a bit." She waited—still no response. He might have been made of stone. "I could make it worth your time," she said in her sexiest voice. There was still no response; the warrior purposely did not meet her eyes.

Chapter Forty-Six

Snowfall

Lucian Antiope was in the upper of his father's fields, scattering hay from an irregular pile into wooden troughs. Though the pastures beyond stretched far, vanishing into the hillocks and trees, Marcian's horses would always gather for the feed at dusk, crowding about the troughs, snorting, nipping at one another, tails swishing. They were intelligent, as much as humans in Lucian's opinion, just choosing not to live in houses or talk in Etlantian. But he had names for them all, and when he lectured them, they would always listen. Not coming for feed, knowing he was here—it was more than odd; it was alarming. Something was wrong and he did not like the feel of it—something scared him.

But near dusk, as shadows grew long and the wind died to stillness, the herd did not come, not even a single horse. Lucian stood, waiting. He even tossed a few forks of hay upward, letting the chill wind scatter the scent over his shoulder.

The wind was from the south, colder than he could remember it ever being this early. Looking southward, toward Galaglea, he was startled to see a dark storm forming over the far peaks of the Parminion Mountains, so thick the spire of Hericlon was even visible.

Lucian finally mounted his horse. One last time he scanned the trees for a sign of the herd, then he turned, and a moment later he gasped, startled, turning back once more toward Hericlon. It was more than a storm; it was night-black clouds and there was something in them, something deep in them, spinning, whirling. It reminded him of stars sucked into a whirlpool at high sea, spinning about its edge, and strangely, as well, it made him think of eyes.

The longer he stared, the more his skin crawled and the more he shivered. He had never seen anything like this. Unlike a storm, it moved slowly; it did not pass ever closer; whipped by winds, it merely waited. It was somewhere south, over the Vale of Tears, and whatever it was, a storm it was not.

He noticed them, westward, toward Galaglea, a red hue, like bloodstains against the sky. It was dusk, but he could see the western horizon and the setting sun. This was something else, something that left a chill through him. The sky was an orange/red because Galaglea was burning. It was impossible. The gates of Galaglea, even during the siege of the Daath in the gathering wars, had lasted three counts of the moon. The finest warriors in the world had not breached her walls until the diseases set in. Not only that, but though Galaglea had sent its legions for Hericlon; four cohorts of warriors remained stationed in the garrison stronghold not far from the city. They were more than enough to contain a fire within the city, yet it seemed they were doing nothing.

Lucian turned his horse and rode first at full, hard gallop, for his brother. When he reached Antenor, tall and lean in the saddle, he found him searching the skies above Galaglea, as well. Of all Marcian's boys, Antenor looked the most like his father, having the same lean figure, the same long nose. The youngest, Lucian, on the other hand, was built like his grandfather, an axeman, big in the shoulders, and though only ten and six years, already burly. The reason they were even on the ranch was that they were young. Marcian's other four sons, horsemen all, had left with him days ago at the call of the king to ride for Hericlon.

Lucian pulled up beside him, circling his horse, almost panicked, but remembering his father had taught him that panic, in times of need, was a weakness. He set his hand over the half of his grandfather's axe, which he always carried in a scabbard at his side, and felt through it a warning.

"You see what I see?" Lucian asked.

"It is impossible."

"Yes, it is, but Galaglea is burning, and the fires grow stronger every second."

From the tops of the trees along the eastern ridge, not only was the sky orange and red above the city, but every so often tongues of actual flames licked upward; the fire was raging now.

Lucian shifted his gaze from the line of flame to the cabin, then to the hill above it. He winced. Shadows were coming, dust billowing, as riders wound down from the hillock. The roadway had only one possible destination, their father's cabin. Adrea and the child were there alone. Worse, these riders were not the blue cloaks of Galagleans, not even Daath—these were dark riders, as he had never seen, with night-black cloaks.

"Adrea," he whispered, and without even waiting for a response from Antenor, sent his charger at top speed for the cabin.

Adrea sat across the room from the hearth, a broth of herbs and roots bubbling slowly. She had grown suddenly uneasy and had even searched through the windows of the cabin for Marcian's boys. Something was wrong; someone was coming, she was almost certain. She felt things at times; she was unsure of her powers, but certain now she felt danger. When Sandalaphon had brought her to Marcian, he had told her that she would be left with mixed memories of where she had come from and of the events that had brought her there. As well, he had given her a box. In the box, he had explained, was a ring and the day would come when she would know to open it. Until then, she was to keep it always sealed, never to even look on it, so that her memories were left uncertain and jumbled to hide her.

"There are hunters who will seek you, always, but unless you take the memories of this ring, they will not find you. However, a day will come when you have no choice, when for some reason or another, the warriors who seek you out will discover you. When that happens, open the box and touch your finger to the stone of the ring within. You will bleed with memories, and quickly both your powers, your skills as a spell binder and the knowledge of who you are, who your child is, will flood you. I pray in that moment, you are able to find the help you need."

She glanced now at the box where it rested on a wooden dresser. Its edge was glowing, and she knew it was time. She needed to open it, to touch her finger to the stone; the days of hiding had ended. She suspected that it had begun when Marcian and his older boys were called away to Hericlon. Her memories were jumbled and confused, but she knew if Quietus was leaving for Hericlon with the legions of Galaglea, then time had grown thin. Someone was coming from the south, and she knew he came with dark and dread.

That night, the night Marcian left, she had wept bitterly when finally alone. She perhaps had never had a chance to love him, but she knew he loved her, deeply, and his sheer devotion and care had broken her heart when she realized that, of course, he would not return. The Enochian prophecies were unfolding like a rising blood moon, nothing wavering, just as foretold.

Whatever the Galagleans rode out to face, it would swallow them. Her knowledge of such things came in bits and pieces, but she was sure of it as she watched him ride away with his four sons.

After Marcian had left, the nights had become a terror for her. When the sun would start to go down, a far, whispering panic tingled, and she shivered with an unknown sadness, with thoughts of Loch, whose memory Sandalaphon had left with her. Though he had dulled these memories and the sadness that went with them he had somehow eased them, as well, as though she were drugged.

Oddly, Marcian's sons had been well trained and never questioned that he had brought back a girl who was nearly full term. Their father's business was his own, and they accepted her readily, though she found herself being treated more as a sister than as a mother, something for which she was thankful.

It was Marcian's youngest boy, Lucian, who had given her the greatest comfort. He was ten and six, and he was not ordinary. Adrea had always felt that a protector would come, *the knowing* in her always whispered it, but she thought it would be one like Sandalaphon. In the days after Marcian left, she came to realize that instead, her and the child's protector was to be this strange boy.

Once, the young, stocky Lucian had come to her and asked if he could speak to her alone before Antenor returned from the fields. She nodded that, of course, he could. At times he may have seemed slower mentally than the others, but that was just because he was so stocky, so large, and he looked far older than his ten and six years. At times, when she saw only his shadow, he was as large as a man, with broad, muscular shoulders. He had knelt beside the bed and spoke very carefully that day.

"I had a dream, and you should know of it," he said. "I know that you understand magick, that you could spell bind if you had to."

She started to speak, but he waved her off. "No denying, Adrea, you know magick. I have seen it in your eyes. In my dream I was told you are a queen. I know my father is not a king, and I am not sure I understand, but it was a strange dream and I could not question the things I saw, the things I now know. The child you bear, it is not Marcian's, I know that. My brothers do not, but I have learned through my dreams. Do not be angry with me and do not attempt to lie; I believe it is the light of the mothering star that speaks to me. I was told, as well, that when the child comes, I am to be its protector, both to protect you and him."

"Lucian—" she began, but he waved her off.

"I know I am young, only ten and six, not the age of a warrior; however, long ago I was given something of my father, and now I understand its meaning." He pointed to a crate in the corner of the cabin. "You should know that in that crate, wrapped in fine cloth, is the great axe of my grandfather, Moloch of Galaglea. Some weapons, just as people, are ordinary, but my grandfather was no common warrior and his axe grew stronger with each righteous kill he made. Each he made for the kingdom of heaven, and so many did he slay, so valiant did he defend the light and the peoples of the mountain, I believe with my soul that Elyon imbued his axe with power. And when he died, something of his strength was left within its blade. If Antenor were here, he would be shaking his head. He has always believed I am touched, but I think you understand the things I tell you. I have been touched, it is true; I was never ordinary, and this is why. All things for a reason, my father always told me that. My father also told me when I was young that he had been given to understand this axe was to be mine, that the time would come when I should take it out and that he would teach me how to use it. He is not with us, but I believe the sword itself can teach me, or so say my dreams. Does that sound strange to you?"

She did not know how to answer, but she shook her head. The dreams were a way the heavens spoke; it had been like that for Loch. She remembered that of him.

"I will speak of it no more, but I wanted you to understand, to know that it is me. I am the one that is sent. I know, as well, that just as the axe of Moloch is not ordinary, neither is the child in you. He will be born a savior."

She shivered. "Did you just call him a savior?"

"Yes. It means one who will save. And three or four times, I have seen over the cottage silver eagles. They are his signet. All this is between you and me alone, but I know I am to protect him, to guard him all the days of my life."

The son of Loch and Adrea was born on a hot afternoon, and she had borne him alone, sweating in the dark of her room, gripping the brass headboard with both hands until her knuckles grew white. The pain was severe and she believed there were times she had passed out, but when each surge came, she braced and tried not to scream. She did not want them hearing; they were boys and would only complicate things.

Near noon, lying naked in the shadows, streaked by the dusty light that slivered through cracks in the wallboards, delirious with the pain and weakness of pushing, she finally gave birth. She did not panic; she knew of birth, for she had been taught. There was a moment, just as the child came free, when the cabin was bathed in blinding light and she thought she was passing out again, but this time it was a different light. The child had been trying to cry, but it was covered with a pinkish covering, and was fighting for air against it. Seraphon had been born in a cowl. She quickly peeled away the tissue. Warm water soaked into the floorboards.

Afterward, as the brightness cooled, she could see beings, shadowy, ethereal, but there—watching, all around her. She did not move or try to touch them, but she did lift the child where they could see. They were beings of a choir, and she heard them naming him in the words of the seventh star, the choir of the fiery serpents, the Seraphim. He was born the seventh and last king of the Daath. In the scriptures of Enoch he was named the Arsayalalyur, who would come to answer the blood of innocents laid at the feet of the Fallen.

The Earth would, in his day, be enveloped in the first apocalypse of men.

Once the linens were changed and the blood and afterbirth had been washed away, she put on a light cotton dress and sat in the coverlets watching him. There was much of Loch in the tiny face, but she could also see herself in the high cut of the cheekbone. Since Sandalaphon had brought her through time, Loch's memory had faded somewhat, the sadness dimmed almost as though by some drug, but that day she had seen a tiny cameo of him, molded in his features, letting her remember what he looked like, and through the child, she remembered also his love, how it reached through the aeons.

"We will find him, little one," she whispered. "Somehow, we will find your father."

He looked far more Daath than even Loch, and no one who had spent company with Daath would have guessed this child for a Galaglean—but Lucian and Antenor were young; they had never even so much as met a Daath or seen a newborn. Lucian knew the child was not his father's, but Antenor did not know to question it, even though the child's skin held a pale bluish tint. For the longest time his eyes burned with the tendril of the light of the mothering star.

"Will they always be this way—burning like this?" Lucian had asked.

"No, they will turn. It is heaven's light you see. The veil is open and as long as he remains a part of heaven, his eyes will glow with its knowledge. In a few days it should fade."

"I will tell you the exact moment he was born," Lucian said. They were gathered about her, having come back from the fields to find they had a brother.

"I was in the field and the sun was exactly mid-sky and that was when I saw the eagles. You did not see them, Antenor?"

"What eagles?"

"Silvered eagles—the purest silver, their wings were fantastic, they were the color of mercury. They came streaking out of the eastern clouds. Seven of them—seven exactly. They circled the cottage and then soared into the heavens. I can even tell you what they were."

"Please do."

"Messengers. Heralds. They came to honor him."

"Do not worry of him, Adrea; he has always been touched. He talks to the horses, has given them all mythical names. Father is somber; I suppose he got it from Mother. She was filled, like him, with imaginings."

"Say any more of my being 'touched,' Antenor, and I will bloody your nose."

"Let us ask Adrea; she is bright, smarter than anyone I have known. Adrea, do you believe silver eagles came out of the sky to celebrate the birth of . . . of . . ."

"Seraphon, his name is Seraphon."

"Yes. So, do you? Came down from the heavens to honor Seraphon's coming as if he were born a king or a seer of some kind?"

Adrea paused. "I believe he is a very special child, Antenor—but all mothers believe that. As for the eagles—I was inside, birthing. I did not have time to study the skies."

Antenor stared for a moment, then turned and shook his head at Lucian.

"There is more to this world than you think, Antenor," Lucian proclaimed.

"I do not doubt." He pushed past Lucian, walking through the goatskin curtain over the doorway. Lucian remained alone with her a moment.

"Are you all right?" he asked. "Anything you need? Anything I can do?"

"I am fine."

"Just that . . . you look awful."

"Well, having a baby is difficult, Lucian, even if you are a veteran of it—and for me, this is my first."

Lucian stared at the covers as though he were frightened. "Does his name have a meaning?"

"It is from Enochian scripture, when translated it means Burning One."

"You are sure you do not need anything? Some food? Some wine?"

"What I need most is just rest, Lucian. Water if you would, a goatskin of water."

"Immediately, right away." He paused at the hanging in the doorway. "Should I bring anything for the little one? Or does he not eat yet?"

"Oh, yes, he eats very well."

†

Strangely, in the following days, the resemblance to Loch seemed to fade, and then was gone completely. Seraphon began to look like himself. His eyes seemed to soften until at times she could even stare into them. Whenever she did, they looked back as though he were mature, as though there were no secrets between them—he knew her as well as anyone. If he could talk, he would have offered comfort. Still, he frightened her. The air about him seemed quicker, as though it were too close, as though something unnamable moved about him. Sometimes she would feel him stir in her arms, and looking down, she would find him staring back, studying her, fascinated—searching through all her secrets.

Lucian never dared hold the child, but often for hours he would kneel by the crib Marcian had carved, playing. It seemed at times, when Adrea watched, that the child was amusing Lucian more than Lucian was amusing him.

Lucian had slipped a torque of pure gold from among his family's heirlooms, and with care and patience, had etched out the letters SERAPHON in bold Galaglean script. It would eventually be a wristband, but it was also fashioned of coiled silver bands and flexible enough that Lucian curled it about the tiny ankle, overlapping it.

"Someday he will grow into this," Lucian had said proudly.

On another night, Lucian had been staring into the crib for a long while when he said, "He does not look much like Marcian, does he? Or any of us—even you, for that matter."

"Babies sometimes look like themselves, Lucian," Adrea answered from where she was straining goat's milk over a bronze bowl.

"Perhaps he has his father's eyes," Antenor said, leaning against a far wall and whittling at a stick with his dagger, sweat and dirt smudged across his face from the day's work. "Though, truth be told, sometimes, those eyes scare me."

"It is because he knows," Lucian explained. He was flipping the bells tied over Seraphon's crib. The child was watching intently.

"Knows?" Antenor said. "Knows what?"

"He knows us. Who we are. He knows secret things."

"What in the bleeding world are you talking about, Lucian?"

Lucian looked up, his expression firm. "He knows, Antenor. He knows things we never dreamed of knowing."

"He is a few days old and he knows more than us? Your head is so addled, Lucian, I sometimes wonder if we should not take you to the blind woman who takes care of the infirm."

Lucian came slowly to his feet, facing Antenor.

"Elyon's grace save us," Antenor complained. "First the child was delivered in the talons of silver eagles with mercury wings, and now he knows—knows secret things, knows who we are." Antenor chuckled until Lucian tackled him at the waist. Adrea gasped; they were fighting again, and she started for them, but in moments Lucian had brought Antenor to the floor, straddling him, lifting a wide fist and hitting his older brother with a hard thud.

"He does know and you are going to say it!" shouted Lucian. "Say he knows things, Antenor! Say it and mean it!"

Blood pooled across Antenor's upper lip.

"Lucian!" Adrea shouted, and the boy paused a moment, realizing he had lost his temper again.

Antenor took the moment to knee Lucian in the crotch, then pushed him off and kicked him back against the wall. Lucian slid to his knees, groaning. "Ah, mother of frogs," he murmured through clenched teeth, "that hurt . . ."

Antenor got up and walked over to the washbasin. He spat out blood, then washed more from his face. "If he broke a tooth, I swear . . ."

Adrea lifted Antenor's chin and studied his lip. She pressed against the front teeth. "You seem to be all right, Antenor. A little better off than Lucian right now."

Lucian was hugged against the wall, doubled up.

"He will never learn," said Antenor. "I have kicked him between the legs at least ten times. He is dumb as an ox. He carries around that huge axe now as if there is some reason for it, as if he has become a great warrior, but he still falls for a kick in the nuts like he has since he was five." Antenor lifted a weft of cloth, and went out the door, slamming it behind him. Lucian sat with his back against the wall, his head forward.

"Anything I can do to help?" asked Adrea.

Lucian only shook his head.

†

When the riders came over the rise, heading for Marcian's cottage, Adrea had finally been drawn to step outside, to look up and see them. She knew they were not Galaglean and neither were they Daath, but she could tell by the way they rode, they had come with purpose.

Seraphon had been sleeping, nestled in a blue, woolen blanket in Marcian's crib. But suddenly he woke. He cried out. Adrea went to him, and when she looked into the crib, he stopped crying and his eyes bore directly into hers. In that moment she knew what was coming, almost as though he had spoken it. Searchers.

She went to the dresser and opened the box. Inside it was lined with black velvet, and lying in it was the ring. Seeing it, memories began to spill. She touched the stone and with a sudden gasp it all came back to her, everything, even up until the last strange moment that Sandalaphon the Nephilim had taken her through the rift of time. She slipped the ring over her finger and set its golden box in a pouch of her belt, buckling it down. She knew everything now. The riders coming for her were Unchurians, and they were coming to take her life, her's and the child's.

There was a thud on the porch and Adrea looked up. She turned. Marcian's wooden door was flung wide.

At the same time, the thick, opaque window glass shattered and a dark figure hurtled through it, tucked. He came to his feet and turned. He was tall, and his hair was a silvery gray, his skin reddish. He drew his sword with a swift, quiet hiss.

Another stood in the doorway. This one waited, his cloak drawn away from one shoulder.

Seraphon lay breathless and silent. Adrea shoved his crib back, into the corner, then stepped between it and them. She kept her eyes on the Unchurian with the sword. He but watched, quietly. He didn't move. He held the sword loosely in one hand.

Adrea then screamed and turned, quickly grabbing the bone-cutting knife and flung it, hard, the way Lamachus flung his axe. The Unchurian was taken by surprise. He caught the blade in his hand, but it sliced open his middle fingers all the way to his wrist.

A javelin through the open window took the Unchurian in the back. Adrea saw the tip tear through his chest. The Unchurian grunted, as though irritated, then dropped to his knees and fell forward. The second Unchurian, in the doorway, now stepped forward, drawing a dagger pinned in his fingers ready to sling it, only to stagger and drop. There were two arrow shafts in his back.

Antenor stepped over his body and turned, searching, an arrow shaft pinned in his bow. He shifted to a crouch and angled it through the doorway.

"More of them," he said. "Riders—did not get a clear count. Where is Lucian?"

Adrea saw Lucian's leg drop over the windowsill. He clambered in.

"You see others?" Antenor said to his brother.

"I saw only these two." Lucian answered.

"That was too easy," Antenor said.

"The others spread out; they will come. The surprise is over—they will know we are here, as well. Then we will find out if it is easy."

Lucian lifted the latch and opened the chest in the corner. He lifted his grandfather's axe. Its metal had been burnished to a black hue, but the edge was sharpened silver, flashing.

Adrea took the child in her arms. "We should try to reach the city."

Lucian shook his head. "Galaglea is burning."

Staring out the doorway, Adrea saw that the horizon was on fire. But these fires were much closer than Galaglea. "Not only Galaglea," Adrea gasped.

Lucian had been buckling on the axe belt. Seeing Adrea's expression, he leapt to the doorway. "Brushfire—that is dry autumn wheat—it will come down that hill like a wave of water."

Antenor lowered the bow tip. The field of wheat beyond the house was quickly becoming a sea of fire. It looked molten.

"Go for the horses, Antenor," Lucian said. "Harness the chariot for Adrea and Seraphon!"

Antenor hadn't moved. He could only stare, mesmerized. The fire seemed to be swarming toward them intentionally. "It is coming too fast," Antenor muttered.

"Antenor!" Lucian shook him until he focused. "Get the horses! Now!"

Antenor turned and broke into a run. Lucian glanced back.

Adrea was holding Seraphon against her. As she started for the door a voice whispered, "*You die.*" She turned. The one Lucian had killed with a javelin was sitting up against the wall. The Unchurian was dead, his expression pale and frozen, but the jaw worked slowly. "You die this day. Welcome to the dead, Daathan queen; we come for you."

Lucian glanced at her, then swiftly decapitated the already dead man. "He called you a Daathan queen . . ."

"There is no time, Lucian; get us out of here!"

He grabbed her shoulder and ran with her for the horse stables. Outside, the heat felt strangely benevolent, cascading in waves of angry wind. The flame left the bronze of the chariot watery as Antenor rode it from the shed, already harnessed. The horses twisted madly at the bar, eyes wide, nostrils filled with the scent of burning. One reared and Antenor reined it in. He then held the horses tight by their harness straps.

"Get in Adrea!"

Lucian had dashed into the stables, throwing open as many gates as he could, and then came out leading two horses. He held their reins and threw a saddle over one.

"You can manage a chariot?" asked Lucian.

"I can!"

Lucian climbed into the saddle, taking up the reins. Antenor still had to cinch down his straps. Lucian watched, amazed at how quickly the fires had reached the bottom of the hill and were throwing fingers for the cottage.

Antenor leapt into the other saddle. For a moment he had trouble keeping his horse from spooking; it was circling, shaking out its mane, snorting. Antenor stared in awe at the flames.

"It moves too fast! We will never outrun this!" Antenor shouted, somewhat panicked.

In the chariot, Adrea knelt, tying Seraphon against the inside front wall, using the carrier thongs to lash him. He was wrapped in his thick blue, woolen blanket, and he stared back with his cold blue eyes as though he understood everything that was about to unfold. His eyes offered her a strange comfort, as if telling her that though terrible things were about to unfold, it would be all right. In the end, it would be all right.

Adrea lifted the reins.

"Good enough, let us get out of here!" Lucian cried. "Take the east road to Ishmia!"

Adrea lashed the horses with a whip, clutching the railing of the car as it bolted. The horses galloped forward with wide eyes, sweating. Adrea leaned into a sharp turn about the side of the cottage. The wheels of the chariot sent a spray of dust into the red sky.

The chariot, with the two horses at its flanks, turned west, for the narrow, wagon-gutted roadway that snaked into the forest. Antenor galloped beside the chariot, but Lucian kept to the rear, riding in their dust, searching behind, to the sides. He held the reins in one hand, the axe in another. He had told Adrea he had only touched the axe of Moloch once or twice, but it was clear he had practiced with another, for it was loose and ready in his hand.

Antenor was consumed in panic; his face was flushed. He had seen fire before, but this was more than fire. It had life. It had turned when they turned, and he had seen fingers of flame leap from the top of the stables for the trees as they galloped into the forest—it was like a spirit of fire with eyes to follow them.

Antenor glanced to Adrea. He knew she was wise and kind, but he had never seen this part of her. She was fearless. She held the reins tight in both hands, guiding the chariot as it turned a bend in the road. It tipped to one wheel, then dropped back, but Adrea seemed unaffected, nor did she look back to the fire that seemed to be leaping from tree to tree behind them, almost like a creature following.

It had been sunset, but as they rode into the forest, it was dark, with only the firelight to guide them. A dark had settled down out of the sky and pocketed in the trees, leaving them almost black. The fire's flicker, following as fast as their horses could press, left everything wet and slippery looking. Antenor glanced skyward, feeling a sudden chill. Something had passed overhead. He hadn't really seen it, but he heard it—a swift wing beat, not a bird, not anything he had ever seen, it was leathery and heavy sounding.

Lucian kept his heels tight against the flanks as the big horse drove forward. Its eyes were on Adrea, as though the horse understood the danger. They were riding through a thickening cowl of gray smoke, and Lucian knew the fire was not natural. It was possibly Uttuku, for it leapt, flying through the trees with a sound like dragons following. Lucian was sweating in the heat. He heard a wing beat. Lucian gripped the worn, dark wood haft of his grandfather's axe for strength. Suddenly there was a powerful wing beat. Something had soared out of the sky and alighted on the side of the car, right next to Adrea.

Antenor was closest and when he saw the creature, he thought of nothing else but Adrea and the child. He twisted hard on the reins, driving his horse into the side of the chariot. A creature with clawed feet clung to the bronze rail of the car. It moved swiftly, at times blurring out of focus. Before he could react, it turned its eyes upon him and reached out with a fantastically long, powerful arm, shredding the neck of Antenor's horse. The horse reared back, and if Antenor had not been trained by his father to be the best of horsemen, he would have fallen, but he only slipped, clinging to the saddle, trying to pull himself back up and bring the horse in line at the same time.

Lucian thundered past. Antenor caught only a glimpse of his brother, long hair streaming wild as he leaned into Thunderbolt's gallop, his axe lifted, ready. He looked so much older, nothing at all like a boy, and he was screaming a war cry through clenched teeth.

As Lucian closed on the chariot, he grew furious. Whatever had dropped from the sky now jumped into the car beside Adrea, and before Lucian could reach them, the manlike creature had seized Adrea by her neck. She screamed, attacking with her nails, but his face was bony armor. Though he was smaller than Adrea, he easily lifted her, and with a grunt, flung her over the side of the car. She vanished with a shriek.

Lucian felt himself screaming, but he could not stop for her, could not turn; he galloped past after the chariot. The creature had taken the reins of the horses, and was now whipping them, urging speed. Lucian saw Seraphon, bundled and tied in the front of the chariot.

From the corner of his eyes, Lucian saw riders—nearly a score of them—coming from the trees. He knew there were others; the two that had gone for the cabin were just to slow them. Here, in the fire's fog, was where the riders intended to trap them. The riders parted, half of them turning for the spot where Adrea had been thrown. The others swung toward Lucian and the chariot, coming at an angle downward through the trees.

Lucian was at the chariot's side, not close enough to see the creature's face as it turned, glancing over its shoulder at him—but ignoring him as though he were just a boy, no threat posed. Lucian pulled himself to crouch in the saddle, and then hurled over the railing. His axe was heavy, swift. It missed the creature's back, as he had wanted, but did thud through the bone of the creature's shoulder. Losing an arm seemed to have little effect. He had wrapped the reins about the railing and now turned to deal with Lucian, reaching forward with his single arm to slam Lucian against the side of the car. He was amazingly strong. A dark wood-like hand shot out and clamped hold of Lucian's neck. Lucian could feel the fingers forcing their way through the skin. This close, the creature's eyes looked as though they were backlit by small fires. It was growling.

Lucian snarled, brought his axe in a low arc, and hard as the wooden armor was, he sheared though the creature's gut. Then he split open its head and hurled the body out of the chariot.

Antenor had managed to climb back into the saddle, and now he pulled his horse up sharp. It reared, screamed. It didn't want to turn—the flames were curling right for them—but Adrea was back there, and he was going for her. He galloped hard, then circled her body. She looked so broken, lying face-down. He turned, searching. He had lost sight of Lucian, and the smoke that stung in his lungs was growing thicker each moment. As he watched, it closed in about him like a hand, and soon even the trees just beyond were hidden, and it seemed, though the fire was burning all about them, that it had pulled back, leaving only the smoke. This much smoke should be choking him. He should not be able to breathe, but this was different. It was not so much smoke as it was darkness—a living kind of darkness that closed about them, even cutting off sound.

"Adrea!" he whispered, but she didn't move. He wondered a moment if she were still alive.

Riders were coming. He could not see them, the dark prevented that, but he could hear them—a drum of horse hooves.

"Adrea!" he cried, but she did not respond. Her hair was flayed out across the ground. Her wrist was turned about so one palm was upward. "Elyon, give me strength," he whispered, pulling his bow from off his back and dropped beside her body, crouching, quickly bringing the arrow's gut taut with an arrow. He sensed the beat of hooves, and then fired. A horse burst from the dark, but he had taken mark—it was riderless. He quickly pulled a second arrow taut. He could hear others closing. Antenor fired, but the bolt went over the rider's shoulder. Antenor ripped his sword from its sheath, preparing himself. The rider had slowed, was circling them. It was not human; it bore great wings of leather and its skull was a skeletal mask of hardened black wood that curled in a mock cheek guard and arched at the temples in spines. Its body was covered in muscular-shaped blackened armor, a kind of hardened wood.

The minion swung one leg over and dropped from the horse.

Antenor screamed as came at him, but it ended quickly. The creature's backhand blow hit so hard, Antenor heard the crack of his own neck snapping and his legs went out from under him.

The creature now stood over Adrea. It lowered itself to one knee. It tipped its head, studying her. With a clawed finger, it prodded her bared shoulder. It turned her, rolling her onto her back. It leaned close, studying her face. Its eyes were a mesh of dark webbing, but somewhere behind them burned a low light. It gently swept a curl of red hair from Adrea's cheek. It had no mouth, but phantasm lips moved, and a shadowy tongue flickered just beneath the transparent leather skin.

"Do you know what I love about war?" it whispered. Adrea's eyes were closed—she could have been dead, but she was still breathing, a light, fluttery breath, barely clinging to life. The creature leaned closer. "Plunder and rape. But most of all . . . rape."

Rhywder and the maniple of Ishmians had ridden hard the entire day, resting little. He had seen the fires from the distance, and he knew the Unchurians had reached Galaglea, for she was burning. The city left a stain against the setting sun and a pall of black smoke. He had spent time there, Galaglea; the people there, so many, the legion of Galagleans who must have fallen, it left a pain in him. But Rhywder was coming for two, the girl and her child, and that is where he kept his mind focused. They had ridden even harder, and now they should have been to the east and north—which, from the information he had gathered, should have been near Marcian's land. Ahead of them, across a clearing of dull green meadow grass, was a thick forest, and it, as well, was afire, flames curling mighty fingers into the sky, and the roar was furious. The road they were following snaked right into it.

Rhywder pulled up, circling his horse. Rainus and the others drew up about him. "You are not going to suggest we go in there," said Rainus.

Rhywder started to shake his head, then paused. A chariot and rider came out of the forest, right out of the flame. The chariot horses were at breakneck gallop, the car was flying, bouncing off the road, and the rider—which looked to be a boy of about ten and six years—continued to crack his whip, gripping the rail with one hand. He glanced behind, over his shoulder. Rhywder then saw why—there were riders in pursuit, assassins, twenty or more, pressing down on the chariot, cloaks whipping like wings.

"Save that boy!" Rhywder screamed, launching his horse and drawing his sword. Rainus and the guards closed quickly at his flank, then fanned out to either side.

A javelin arched over the boy's shoulder and almost broached his horses. He cracked the whip again. One of the assassins was closing, the horse in a low, pressed thunder. The Unchurian leaned sideways, almost out of the saddle, and seized hold of the chariot rail. He leapt, but the boy with a scream had kicked him back, and the Unchurian went flying. His body hit and rolled, swept beneath the hooves of the other assassins.

The distance was closing. The boy had seen them now. "You there!" he screamed. "Daath! Help me!"

Rhywder screamed, drawing his sword, and his horse launched in a pressed gallop.

Rainus and the others were soon at his flank. The distance between them and the chariot was fast closing, but the assassins were also closing their gap.

Another javelin soared, and this one took out one of the chariot's horses, through its back. It twisted, going down. The car was flipped sideways, snapping the harness, and it rolled, spinning. Rhywder's horse had to leap, clearing the chariot.

The Daath slammed into the assassins at full gallop. They met each other with powerful, shattering blows of mace and sword. Armor and shield were split open. Both Unchurians and Daath dropped as the two ripped past each other. Rhywder's blade ripped through an assassin's stomach, then another's neck. He wrenched back on the reins, turning the horse sharply.

"Take them out!" Rhywder shouted to Rainus. "Every damned one of them!" He then spurred his horse toward the chariot. As the others circled for attack, two assassins had split off and were moving for the overturned car. From behind it, the youth who had been the driver was on his feet. He held a killing axe, a well-used killing axe that smelled of blood, and he waited, staring, cold-blooded and calm as the assassins rode him down. He whipped the axe in spinning arcs—he knew how to use it. With one stroke he killed a horse; with another he sheared off a leg at the hip. As the horse went down and the second assassin turned with his sword for a strike, his head was severed with a scream. The boy fought as a born slayer, like nothing Rhywder had seen.

At full gallop, Rhywder lifted a crossbow from his shoulder scabbard. He heard Rainus and the city guard locked in battle, weapons ringing. The youth now drew his sword and angled it, crouched and ready—yet another coming, but Rhywder took out the assassin from behind with the crossbow bolt. As the riderless horse passed the chariot, the boy sheathed his axe, then leapt, catching the saddle of an Unchurian mount with one hand to pull himself up. Mounted, he twisted the reins and waited for Rhywder.

"There is a child beneath this chariot!" the boy shouted. "He is still unharmed."

"This is the child of Marcian's woman?" Rhywder asked.

"You are the one sent to protect him; you should know!"

"How would you know that?"

"I knew someone would be sent. I did not know who, but someone would come. Stay with him; I must find Adrea!"

He whipped the reins, setting his horse at a gallop straight for the burning forest.

"Boy!" Rhywder shouted, but the Galaglean didn't look back. Galagleans were blood-bred with head of solid bone.

Rhywder dropped out of the saddle and crouched, looking beneath the overturned car.

He was startled. A child wrapped in a blue blanket was watching back calmly—watching as though it knew his name, and the eyes were so alive, so quick, they sent a shiver across Rhywder's back.

Rainus and three of the Daath were riding slowly toward him. The battle had ended, and these were the survivors. Of the twenty city cohorts he had set out with, there were now only four left alive, and it was going to be a long road back.

Rhywder stood. Rainus was cut fairly bad, his cuirass was dented in at the stomach, and blood had washed over his thigh.

Rhywder looked to the forest. The boy had gone in, at full gallop, without hesitation.

"Ah, for the love of frogs," Rhywder muttered. He pulled himself into the saddle. "Rainus, with your life and more, protect that child!"

"My lord! What child?"

"The one beneath that chariot." Rhywder turned the reins. "And if this damn Galaglean gets me killed, head back for Ishmia and get that child to Eryian. The warlord will know who he is."

Rhywder could not believe he was riding into death once more, but he was; the forest was melting all about him. To the left a huge limb crashed down, long streamers of white fire trailing. The heat was searing, and everywhere flame licked. The roadway was the only clear path, and he kept the horse in tight rein—it was going to bolt any second, eyes wide and terrified. He had not gone far in when he saw them. It looked like something out of madness; the boy was going face to face with a minion. The boy fought savagely, screaming, and it was only his fury keeping him alive, for the minion was far too powerful. Each blow of the minion's hand staggered the young Galaglean, but he had refused to drop.

Rhywder leveled the crossbow, coming at them full gallop. The minion looked up just as the bolt slammed into its head, between the eyes, cracking the bone armor. At this, the minion screamed, furious, hand in fists. The boy hurtled forward like a mad dog. The minion reached a hand to tear the bolt free only to have the boy's axe open its chest like a crab's, with a crack, vitals spilled. And the boy did not stop there; he took off a leg, as well, the axe was sharp; it sliced quick and sure of its path. The minion reeled, wings arched to keep from falling.

Rhywder leapt from the saddle as he passed, taking the beast's head in his arms to bring it down. Rhywder hit the ground, wrenching the head to the side, cracking the neck. He also heard a wing-bone snap. But the minion was still alive, still able to reach back and grope clawed fingers for Rhywder's throat. Rhywder's short sword was already clear, and now he hacked out the creature's neck. As the head lobbed to the side, the body started to thrash in spasms, and this close, kneeling over the beast, Rhywder saw a pale semblance of a man soar out of the chest cavity like smoke, to be sucked upward in the ascending heat.

A huge oak fell with a crash, and its limbs exploded with a roar, scattering debris in a fiery rain about Rhywder like bolts from heaven. He turned. The boy was standing near the two bodies. One was a girl, and beside her another boy who lay on his stomach with his head twisted about to stare skyward. The Galaglean knelt to close the boy's eyelids—ignoring the fury of the fires about them.

As Rhywder approached, the youth pulled off his cloak and used it to cover the girl. Rhywder saw her tunic had been cast aside, shredded. The boy's face was streaked with tears that left tracks through the soot.

"She's alive," said the boy. "She is still alive. Help me, whoever you are; help me get her to safety!"

Rhywder glanced down. He wanted to tell the boy she was too close to death, she could not possibly survive, but he did not. The horses had fled—Rhywder couldn't blame them.

Rhywder moved the boy aside and knelt to take the girl by an arm and a leg. He hoisted her onto his shoulders. He had seen her face briefly, and it had struck him—she was the very image of Asteria. This was a Lochlain, a Lake Woman, most probably a Water Bearer. Marcian had told him truth; this was the last queen of the Daath. And the child . . . the child was the Angelslayer of Enoch's prophecy.

A limb crashed down, burying the hard-bone body of the minion.

"We will have to run for it!" Rhywder screamed, shifting the weight of the girl over his shoulders. He turned. "Boy!"

The boy paid Rhywder no mind as he risked his life to retrieve his axe, which was lodged in the hard-wood armor of the minion. The boy reaching right through the flame of the tree limb to seize the hilt and wrench it out of the minion's carcass.

Rhywder ran, with the girl over his shoulder. Rivers of fire were spilling through the trees. Living tendrils swept out of the sky to lick him, white-hot, but Rhywder kept running, dodging waves of heat just before they burst into roaring billows. He could hardly breathe; the smoke was not overwhelming—the flames were too alive here—but the air was choked in heat. Beside him, out of the corner of his eye, he saw the boy run through a rolling wall of fire that left the edges of his tunic and his hair trailing smoke.

Chapter Forty-Seven

Nursemaid

Satrina turned as a figure appeared in the doorway. She recognized him as the same that had bound her to the pillar, though his cloak and tunic were matted in dust and he wore no helm. His cuirass was gone, also, and his stomach and chest were wrapped in bandages. It was the captain of the city guard, Rainus.

Satrina had been taken to a house in the city, and she had been waiting the entire day for Rhywder. The waiting had been so long, had so eaten into her, that she could hardly react to Rainus, or to what he held in his arms.

"My lady," Rainus said quietly.

"What do you want? Did you bring your rope?"

"Your husband has sent me."

"Husband! Hah!"

"Your master?"

"In a pig's eye."

"Whatever he be to you, my lady, he has asked me to bring you something." Rainus strode in. Without his bronze helmet, silvered hair fell to his shoulders in thick curls. His face was blunt and ugly with thick lips. He extended the bundle toward her carefully. Satrina stared for a moment, then looked over the edge of the blanket. It was a child! With one finger she carefully lifted the blanket aside for a view. Smooth, unblemished skin—a faint tint of blue. This was a Daath, his hair black as night; a perfect, sleeping child, as beautiful as anything she had ever seen.

"He was nearly Unchurian plunder," Rainus said. "I lost sixteen men for this child. I hope there was good reason."

Rainus waited a moment, then urged Satrina to take the bundle. She tried to lift it one way, then decided on another, settled for a third—she had never held a baby. She stepped back, cradled it against her.

Rainus stepped to a round, oak table and laid a wineskin on it. "Milk," he said. "I was told by a merchant on the docks that this was drawn from a mother's breast. Possibly a mother goat, but it will have to do until we can find a wet female." He lowered his head slightly. "My lady." He started to turn.

"But—what am I to do with a baby?"

"You are a woman; you had ought to know," the captain said, stepping out the door.

Satrina hurried to the doorway. "What about Rhywder? Where is he?"

"In the service of his king, I would guess," Rainus said, now striding down the cobblestone roadway. They were in a housing district of Ishmia, and the sea was close.

"But I want to see him!"

Rainus was too far away to answer. He rounded a corner out of sight. Satrina was not alone, however; a tall Daathan guard was left near the side of the villa. He kept his eyes outward even though Satrina stared at him a moment.

The streets were quiet, hushed. Word had reached them that Galaglea had fallen, burned. It was expected the enemy would reach the ford of the Ithen by morning, and lay siege to Ishmia soon thereafter. The Ishmians had relied for thirty years on the Daath; most of them were Daath, traders, tavern owners. But Ishmia was an unwalled, sprawling port city, and it had never drawn standing armies.

The whole day people had been steadily leaving, north, for Terith-Aire, and Ishmia had begun to look deserted.

Satrina stepped inside and closed the door. The cottage had a small room with simple furniture, a bed, a table. It was the cottage of a warrior, for the only personal items were two swords leaning against the wall in a corner and an old buckler that hung from the bedpost. Satrina sat on the edge of the bed and stared down at the child. A tiny fist was curled against one cheek. She carefully unwrapped the cloak. He wore a chitin of white cloth. "I suppose this is the best Rhywder can do, considering."

She noticed a glimmer from one ankle. She lifted and turned the leg to read the etchings in the bronze torque. "Seraphon," she whispered. But that name had resonance; it meant something—Burning One. She tingled. No ordinary child, this. She reached down and let a small fist curl about her finger. "Whose child are you, Seraphon?" When the child suddenly opened his eyes, Satrina gasped. She had never seen eyes like this. They took her breath and for a moment she swore she could see stars through them.

Chapter Forty-Eight
Warlord

Krysis was awakened by a sudden crash that echoed through the hallway. She sat up with a start, frightened. Suddenly she understood why Eryian had not wanted to dream, for her own dreams still swam, shadowed and cold. She was so cold she was shivering. Then she realized it was not without reason; she could see her breath as a mist, even though the embers of the hearth fire were still glowing. At first she wondered if it were still a dream, for the light of the fire seemed unable to clear its hearth. Something was coming, closing in on them.

She found Eryian asleep beside her. He looked as though he had fallen unconscious, and she remembered his long hours of tossing, moaning. She could also remember the name he spoke. *Cassium*. He had spoken it with such pain it startled her. She knew that among the legendary lords of the Daath, in the days of the beginning after the angel wars, there had once lived a queen named Cassium—that she had learned from an angel the star knowledge, a Star Walker Queen. She wondered if Cassium was perhaps someone he had known when he was younger, someone from his past, but for some odd reason, perhaps the way he had spoken it, she believed he knew her. He knew the Star Walker Queen herself. Yet he had never spoken her name before.

Krysis carefully slipped from the bed, leaving the white bearskin to cover Eryian. The room was pocketed in uneasy shadow. She started for the window, and then paused, hearing a low, guttural moan.

Krysis backed away slowly, then caught movement—not from the door, but from the window. When she turned, a figure stood in the room with her, his skin painted, the flesh edged in ridges. His head was shaven and his face was ritually scarred down one side, the right eye melted away, the skin about it dark and mottled.

"You can tell your warlord his time is marked," the priest hissed, then pointed a long, curled, yellowed nail. "As is yours."

Krysis gasped, backing away. She started to turn for the door. If she opened them, four of Eryian's guards were on the other side, but as she moved for it, a chest soundlessly moved to block the path.

"No need to scream," the priest added. "They cannot hear you."

Krysis turned, backed against the chest. "Who are you?"

"I am the herald of the Salamander. He wanted to send greeting—to you actually—the mortal woman of the star jumper."

She glanced to Eryian, who hadn't moved, his head still to the side. When she turned, the priest was suddenly in her face. His tongue flicked across her lips. She cried out, shoving him back, but found he was strong, weighted heavy in muscle.

"Seeing you," he whispered, "I amd disappointed to be only the herald."

His hand shot beneath her tunic to seize the inside of her thigh. She tried to scream, but he had drawn fingers over her mouth and with the movement had stolen her voice.

His breath stank, an acid, bitter smell, and she saw between his teeth, which were filed to points, bits of tissue as though he had been shredding raw meat.

He forced her back, bending her across the chest, and his hand now slid up her thigh. She swiped at the side of his face that was still human, leaving cuts from her nails, but the priest only smiled. He was holding her against the chest with one hand and his fingers curled about her bodice, but before he could tear it, a hand curled from behind about his face. Krysis briefly saw panic in his single eye. The hand tightened, then jerked. She heard the neck snap. But Eryian had not broken it; he had turned the priest about and now held him by the face, studying him.

"If you have a message," Eryian said, "you can give it to me."

"I will save that for when you have joined us, warlord."

Eryian studied him only a moment longer, then withdrew his hand and quickly brought it in a snap that cracked the priest's windpipe. As the priest staggered, Eryian turned and withdrew a sword from a wall mount. He walked toward the priest almost calmly, then grabbed him by the shoulder and spun him around, shoved his face against the wall. Eryian now leaned close to his ear.

"I don't know if your master can hear me, but if he is listening, he should know that if he touches her again, and I will come for his flesh."

Krysis then screeched, turning away when Eryian shoved the sword into the priest's buttocks, upward, piercing through to pin the body face forward against the wall. The priest thrashed for a moment, arms flailing.

With the noise, the doors were forced open from behind, the chest shoved aside. Two of Eryian's men stepped into the room, weapons drawn.

Eryian stepped back, then turned to Krysis. He touched her cheek.

"Are you all right?" he asked.

She nodded, drawing a hand over her mouth against the foul taste of the priest's tongue.

Eryian glanced past her to one of the guards. "Bring my armor; prepare a mount for me."

The guard nodded and both left, closing the doors behind them.

"I'll have you taken somewhere safe," Eryian said as he pulled on a leather tunic. "I'll leave you with heavy guard—they will not get to you again."

"You are not leaving . . ."

"I must. They are close."

"But Eryian . . . you almost died. You need more rest."

"No time. Once they cross the river, there is nothing to stop them from reaching even Terith-Aire. Where is Little Eryian?"

"At home. I have left him well protected."

"I will send a maniple of my personal guard. It is time the Daath began to gather their children."

"For what?"

"Escape. If one Angelslayer survives, the demon will have failed—he comes with numbers uncounted, he comes sure of his path, but he will trip, he will fall. I cannot say how, but I feel it in my blood." Eryian latched his belt, then paused, seeing her eyes tear.

"Demon? This is Endgame. Is it now, Eryian? That which you sometimes have spoken of?" she asked.

He nodded. He reached forward to pull her into a tight embrace and a moment he held her, then turned, lifting his cloak from a peg.

"Who . . . who is Cassium?"

Eryian paused, turned, but didn't answer at first.

"You spoke her name."

"Someone I knew, Krysis. Once."

"Before me?"

"Before you—before memory's veil." He stepped forward and touched her cheek. "In this flesh, there was no one but you." He leaned to kiss her lips. "Take care, my love."

"Will I see you again?"

He stared at her, his deep, ice eyes misted. He tightened his jaw, then lifted his hand to take hers, spreading her fingers in the sign of the word. He then turned and threw open the door.

Alone, the darkness of the room seemed to close on her and Krysis broke into a sob.

Tillantus rode at the head of the first legion of Argolis's Shadow Warriors, the King's Guard, the Daath's prime. They spread out along the plains of Ishmia as they marched, slow and heavy. Behind them came the two legions of the Daath, the finest, deadliest warriors in all the Earth. They were arrayed in full armor, and the centuries of white horses rode at the fore, with broad, smoked cloaks.

The aged first captain, Tillantus, was still broad-shouldered and firm in the saddle. He studied the sky as he rode. It was a hard gray, with a cold, south wind. Most of the men wore thick, silver-white fur about their necks and shoulders.

The Daath had always taken breath on attack; there seemed almost a poetry of death in white steel. This time, however, Tillantus felt a dread, a knot in his gut. The air seemed unnaturally cruel.

The captain suddenly drew up his reins, lifting his sword high. His commanders called halt. They were spread out along the western ridge of Ishmia; the smell of the sea was strong in the air. Tillantus watched a long figure on a roan horse riding toward them. The figure turned out along the shore, then came at full gallop up the grassy edge of the ridge near the river.

Once he reached the head of his armies, Eryian rose in the stirrups, drawing his sword and lifting it high, rearing the mount. When he cried out to them, they answered, and a deafening roar, a cry of thousands as the legions of the Daath, the conquerors of the seven valleys, lifted their weapons in greeting to their warlord, the Eagle.

Chapter Forty-Nine
The Angelslayer's Queen

Loch watched the island carefully as they approached. It was first a far line upon the waters, a dark shadow.

It was near dusk. The ship they traveled in was a long, sleek Etlantian warship, dark in the waters. But there was no crew, only Sandalaphon, his hand on the tilling oar. The ship's oars were laid back, and it moved with unseen wind against a sail that glistened a gossamer mesh. The warship cut the sea so quickly, the island seemed to have the illusion it was growing as they approached.

Beside him, Hyacinth watched, standing near the hull work, gripping the edge.

"I wish to stop here, at this island," Loch said quietly to Sandalaphon. Sandalaphon stared back, almost as though he hadn't heard, but suddenly they had stopped. The keel rested against white sand. The horizon was a rust stain, and shadows were long, but the air was warm and windless. Loch studied the trees as birds called to him from the thick of a rainforest nestled in dark green and mist.

Loch turned to stare at Hyacinth. She was surprised at how different he looked. The face seemed sharper, thinner, the eyes darker. He looked to have aged years. He held out his hand and helped her over the gunwale.

The sea was warm, and waves curled low and lazy against the sand as he led her up the beach. Hyacinth wondered why he had done it, why he had brought her back. The touch of his sword had whispered to her from death's shadow and at first she didn't turn. She hadn't wanted to come back. The rest of them were dying all around; she could feel their lives wink out—Storan, Danwyar, and soon, she guessed, Darke, as well. But through the light of Loch's aganon blade she had seen his eyes, and though she wasn't certain he would ever love her, truly love her, she knew at least that he would need her and that his need was too strong to turn away.

There was a green hue to the island forest mist. The ground was wet in moss. They stepped through the warm waters of a stream, and on the other side, Loch paused beneath the wide, thick canopy of a cedar. Loch cupped her chin. He took her hand and slowly knelt, urging her to kneel beside him. He watched her carefully.

"Sandalaphon," he said quietly.

She was startled to realize the giant was just behind her. "My lord," he answered.

"Cleanse her—then bind us. Do it now; speak the covenant."

Hyacinth gasped. She watched Loch, frightened. The giant's sunblade—the same severe crystal as Loch's, cleared its sheath and the dark of the forest bled with quiet, blue light. The crystal blade first touched Loch's right shoulder, then lifted and touched her left. She felt a quick pulse down her arm, though it did not burn as the touch of the blade had burned before. With the light came a knowing, a different knowing than any of her magicks, any of her spells, like nothing she had ever felt, and for a moment it took her breath. For a sliver of time she could see the stars open. She could see suns beyond the sun, and she felt a brush of power unlike anything she had ever tasted. As the sword lifted from her shoulder, it faded, but the taste of it remained, and Hyacinth knew that all she had just seen could be found again, for though the sting of power had faded its pathway remained. She turned, but the giant was gone; they were alone. She looked back to Loch.

"What just happened?" she asked.

"I have made you a queen."

"Why do that? Why?"

"They will need you."

"Who? Your Daath? They do not need me, Loch. You make an error; I am only a sorcereress, a spell binder. I have no light to give them. Or you."

He shook his head. "It is not the Daath I speak of."

"Then who, Loch?"

"Your son and those he will save."

She shivered.

"My son?"

He nodded.

"And what of you? You have bound me to you, made me queen—what do you feel for me, Loch?"

"Sadness, thirst—love. Someone once told me love did not exist. They were wrong."

His hand had been resting on the hilt of the Angelslayer. He lifted the sword slowly and held its flange near his opened palm. Though his skin was unbroken, from the pores, a thin vapor of blood moved along his wrist, and then, with a shiver of quick, blue light, it was swallowed into the purple pommel of the sword's hilt and spilled red and rich into the crystal of the blade.

"I am dying, Hyacinth. With each taste the sword takes, I age, I lose more life."

She shook her head. "No. Tell your protector to heal you."

"There is nothing Sandalaphon can do."

"Then throw the damned sword into the ocean! You have done what they asked of you! You have done all your powerful Elyon could ever want."

"No. He wants more, my heart. I am to sacrifice it, and I have little time left."

"Loch, you can stop this, turn it!"

"It is my birthmark. But as someone told me once, time may be thin, but I will take it anyway. I will take the time there is left and use it now as I please. For once in my life I will speak my will, not the prophets'."

As he watched her a slight smile curled on his lips. On the hardened, aged face, it looked almost a glimmer of what he was, or had been. "The sky has opened. I see them now. They used to hide, just beyond, always in shadow, but now I see them plainly."

"See who, Loch?"

"The paths of futures. In this one," he said, touching her cheek, "in this one you are tender and giving, and strong. In this one your son steps into a rift of shadow when all else may have been lost. The hard in you is lost now; I see only loving in your eyes. I know I am not your love, you know that you are not mine, but for now, for this time left to us, we will cheat that. We will be for each other a light to follow, a strength to hold."

She paused, searching his eyes carefully now, and they frightened her, for there was something different just beneath their surface, only a whisper of it, but there. Stars. His eyes were opening to stars, just as the giant who was his protector—just as the angel's had. She knew when the heavens opened, the Loch who had held her the night they slept so close—the prince in him—the human, would never return.

"I will stay with you, Angelslayer," she said. And for once, for the first time, he did not flinch at the name. A tear fell across her cheek. "I will follow you; I will be your balm when pain strikes. I am yours."

He slowly leaned forward and pulled her into a kiss. She felt a sliver of panic. How many times had she dreamed of his touch, and now it seemed to come spilling with stars and the whisper of futures past. His hand pressed against her back, lifting her. Shivers spread along her skin as he laid her back. Hyacinth closed her eyes. As he took her, a cool, quiet rain fell against her face, which was good—it would hide her tears.

Chapter Fifty
Water

There was a mist upon the dawn like a shroud. Fog curled its breath along the banks of the Ithen as though time had been slowed. The legions of the Daath were formed beyond the banks of Ishmia, along the high ridge that overlooked its wide river mouth. If the Unchurians were to come, they would have to cross here, where the river, though broad, was still shallow before it opened to the sea. Eastward, toward Galaglea, the forests still burned, though their light seemed far. Across from them was the last finger of Hericlon's forest, and about its ridges and trails, Eryian had laced the ground with traps and acid pits—and hidden beneath false earth was heavy oil. Many would die here. How many sons the demon had spawned, he could not guess, but this stand would cost them heavily. Perhaps they did have a number, perhaps if he killed enough of them, killed them and killed them, they would thin to pale numbers and be forced back to their southern jungles.

Snow drifted; flakes vanished into the icy, blue waters of the river. Eryian rode along the north bank, pacing, watching the south as the low fog curled tendrils about the legs of his horse.

"Nice weather to slay Unchurians," said Tillantus, who rode at his side, one hand on his thigh.

Eryian nodded.

✝

Far to the west of where Eryian waited, the Galagleans had centuries ago built a dam to control the waters of the Ithen for irrigation. It still stood, had still been used, until Galaglea had burned the day before. In the wide, icy shallows before the dam, Rhywder squinted, scanning the still groves of aspen and birch along the south cliffs. The trees were cloaked in a hushed, white snow, but he knew everything south of the Ithen was now Unchurian.

The Ithen dam was a massive structure of wood and hard rock clay across the canyon mouth. Its limestone spillway was worn and blackened; it bore green scars of mineral and held back the waters of the mighty Ithen, forcing them deep and blue into the spurs of the mountains, where most of the year they were iced.

At the rocky shores of the river just below the dam, ice had formed in plates. Rhywder pulled his cloak tighter about his shoulder as his horse waded through the current.

Rhywder had come with a crew of engineers. During the night they had built a rampart intertwined with saplings and sandbags over the top of the spillway to slow the overflow currents. In the shallows below, they had brought siege craft—thick-beamed, towering catapults, in places glittering from bronze reinforcement plates. Three of them spanned the narrow ravine before the spillway like sentinels—only these sentinels were aimed at the center of the dam's spillway.

The legs and hooves of Rhywder's horse had been wrapped in leather and fur against the ice water. Rhywder circled the charger about a catapult platform, pulling up where an engineer was working the sinews, winching them tight. The catapult's bowl was laden with heavy, sharp-edged rock.

"This one higher," Rhywder said, gauging his sight line along the top of the spillway.

"Higher?" The man paused.

"A few degrees higher."

"But, if I sight higher, Captain, the missiles will miss the dam altogether."

Rhywder turned slowly, squinting one eye. "Higher," he repeated.

The man swore quietly and took hold of the winch lever, adjusting it back slightly.

Rhywder turned to study the spillway. He had gauged the other two for the weakest spots in the limestone face.

The captain of the engineers was riding toward him, his horse pushing through the waters. He was a shipbuilder; Rhywder knew the look, skin leathered and eyes dulled by the sun. A look much like a plodder. The lean, narrow Ishmian pulled his mount alongside Rhywder's and glanced about nervously. "Something is wrong here. My skin is pimpled."

"Perhaps you descend from some manner of bird," Rhywder answered, not turning.

The Ishmian narrowed his brow. He pointed a finger. "That catapult is chalked too far back."

"It is chalked where I want it chalked."

"You want it to miss?"

Rhywder leaned in the saddle, reached forward, and seized the man by his leather jerkin.

Rhywder's breath was a mist as he pressed it between his teeth. "You people seem to have a problem hearing what I say. Perhaps I should clean the salt out of your ears, shipwright!"

Rhywder shoved the man back. The Ishmian caught himself in the saddle, then straightened.

The Little Fox turned back to study the face of the dam. The catapults were anchored into the sandy riverbed with thick, wedged billets of oak, driven deep. Mooring lines had been lashed to hold against the current as long as possible once the dam began to give way. Mud still streamed from the edges of the billets as though from wounds. Rhywder studied each of the catapults once more.

"Looks good. This should be like punching holes in plaster. You and your men can move out."

"Move out?" the engineer said with a look of surprise.

"You and your people can leave the riverbed. Take position upon the north ridge. Provide me a line of archers."

"Against what?"

"Surprises." Rhywder studied him, his dark eyes daring another question.

The Ishmian backed his horse away, then circled it. "To the north canyon wall! Everyone!" He glanced to Rhywder. "Forgive one last question, but how do you propose the sinews be loosed?"

"I do not propose to loosen them," Rhywder replied. "I propose to cut them. I do not believe we will be reusing these particular machines."

"But there are three! And you are one man!"

"I know how many I am, shipwright."

The engineers were making their way to the north canyon wall, where ropes snaked up the side to the top.

"You try to cut all three sinews and you will not get out of the river alive!" The captain said, his tone earnest.

Rhywder didn't answer; he waited, still calm, one hand resting on the hilt of his sword.

The man studied him, then turned his horse and pressed it into a quick trot, splashing through the blue waters. He glanced over his shoulder to shout, "I think you are a damn fool!"

Rhywder chuckled.

Tillantus pointed south, his eyes cold beneath the bronze helm. "They come, my lord," he said quietly. Eryian turned.

From beyond the far bank, images stirred, dark shadows merging wraith-like from mist. Black armor stilled in a dull gleam. Gray cloaks were matted in snow. The horns of their helmets curled against the white of the sky.

The fog began to roll back, as though tide receding. The air was left cold and clean. When the fog had cleared, the valley was filled with them, quiet beneath the falling snow—Unchurians as far as the eye could see. The sons of Righel had thinned them, but they were still the most massive army Eryian had ever beheld. From the riverbank, they lined the hills until they melted to ants, then to bristled to fur. He wondered if they had been bred and kept young for centuries just for this, just for this one single moment in time, to wipe the Daath from the face of the Earth. The demon's plan. "You will fail," Eryian said, knowing somewhere he was heard. "By light and faith, you will fail."

"Mother of gods," Tillantus whispered. "What are they? How could there be so many?"

"Return to ranks, commander," Eryian said beneath his breath. "And we shall see if we cannot thin them out this day." He began to back the horse away from the river's edge.

From the opposite bank, a line of tall, muscular horsemen faced him, heavy with weapons. Steam curled from the nostrils of their armored horses.

Eryian lifted his sword in a gesture of greeting, then brought it back to touch the shoulder of his cuirass. "Azazel, you may have a queen, but never her. Let that sink into you now; let it be your thought as you feed me your sons."

He wrenched back on the reins, turning his horse, and set it at a gallop for his men, ducking low against the mane. No arrows followed—no javelin. The Unchurians waited, calm, then they came forward with thunder, churning the waters of the Ithen, and the ground trembled.

The legions of the Daath were assembled along the high ground of a wide butte beyond the river. It stretched seven miles, first from a gentle slope, then steeper near the top. Just before the flat rocky summit, the dirt was like sand. Eryian and Tillantus were galloping up the side. They rode through a long line of archers who crouched in the dirt, lifting silver arrows to their bows.

Below them, the blanket of snow stretching from the river was being churned to black mud by hooves.

"Archers!" Eryian cried, and along the ranks, his captains echoed the command.

As the Unchurians closed on the line of archers, a solid wall of arrows massed a dark cloud against the sky, and with a muscled grunt, the Unchurian attack crumpled. There were two thousand archers, and the Daath, when their arrows were spent, wielded long swords as their brothers; they were trained as slayers. The dark wall of arrows struck like a terrible storm—shields shattering, horses rolling, the dead vanishing beneath thundering hooves.

When Eryian and Tillantus reached the Daath's front line at the top of the butte, the glimmering smoke shields opened to swallow their lords. Now on center ground, Eryian turned his horse and shouted, "Release the first barrier!"

Out of the dirt, lines of rope jerked taut, and the torsion of thousands of steel-honed lances were released dead center before the heavy charge of Unchurians. The lances sprung upward, locked into place, and impaled Unchurian horseflesh with a hard grunt. Horses and men were sliced, thrown, then crushed beneath the armored weight of those behind. A wall of bodies and armor built upon the lance tips until it literally formed a long, narrow dune of bloodied flesh. Then, horsemen began to spill over as though through deep mud, leaping the last few feet, then charging forward on solid ground, armor and weapons ringing, hooves beating the earth to a heavy pulse. The pikes had slain thousands, but had caused only a moment's delay.

"Javelins!" Eryian cried, and his command was echoed down the lines.

Daathan javelins soared, quilling the white, morning sky. They struck with a scream of death, and the front of the Unchurian horsemen for a moment buckled, then spilled over and continued rolling forward, crushing the fallen.

"Release the first signal," Eryian said to Tillantus.

Rhywder paced, riding the shallows, at times glancing over his shoulder to the south where from a high ridge, tree shadows flirted with him. Bobbing on the water, lashed to ropes in a line stretching between the catapults, were wooden kegs, their planking sealed with wax.

"Captain!" a voice called from the north ridge of the dam. Looking up, he saw the Ishmian shipwright waving frantically. "There! My God! There, in the sky! It is the first signal, Captain!"

Rhywder turned. He caught the last moment's breath of a far, fiery dart, launched upward, into the white clouds, streaming a line of smoke. Rhywder unlatched his killing axe from the rear saddle tassels, then spurred his horse forward, galloping for the barrels.

Rhywder began to shear open the casks with strong swipes of the axe, shattering the planking. They bled. Oil oozed, then swirled upon the waters. He was careful to space the cuts until the river was swathed with a long, glittering stretch of naphtha film. It would have, in ordinary times, been a bane to smother fish and choke birds caught in it. But now it would be a cloak and in fifteen degrees' movement of the sun, this cloak would flow far enough downstream to reach the battle, which from here was a far, distant roar, a blunt and terrifying sound, caught in low clouds and amplified by the still air. The oil was so thick it seemed to tumble in long streamers.

Eryian lowered his sword and the command launched catapults that flung huge, wobbling bladders of naphtha, sown together so taut, they burst only on impact. Arrows dogged their flights, fired, and the effect was strafing explosions of flame that melted skin and left black smoke.

"More of your sons," Eryian whispered. He knew the demon heard each word, though silence was the only answer. "Before this day, even you must feel their loss."

But even fire seemed not to slow the Unchurians; it seemed they absorbed the rivers of fire and multiplied in the thick smoke.

Eryian ordered runners down the side of the butte where thick, aged logs of dried oak had been lashed in heaps and coated with pitch. Once lit, they burnt their ties quickly and rolled free, flames spinning. The Unchurians literally threw themselves into the face of the avalanche of fiery thunder, until the logs pummeled their way through, leaving blood and blackened flesh scattered in wide swaths. For a moment they had been stopped, staggered, but then, like insects, they began to scurry, trampling their wounded, until they surged forth with new energy. Eryian let them come.

"Elyon's breath, Eryian," Tillantus whispered beside him, "this has no pity; this is madness. He throws these men at death as if there were no thought of its cost."

"There is none, Tillantus."

The ropes of the boulders were then cut. Huge rocks with sharp-edged corners had been bored and caulked with black pitch and came like tumbling comets. The collage of horses and men on the slope became a circus carnage into which Eryian poured arsenals of arrows and javelins. When they struck, many of the boulders burst in explosion. The Unchurian advance was once more halted, halfway up. The ground below the butte was littered with a sheer mountain of dead and dying. The winnowing wars had been brutal, but never had Eryian seen this many die so quickly, so without ceremony. The Unchurian front had been decimated. Bodies coated the hillside, burning.

But more were coming, a new front fast morphing from the dead. They climbed and threw themselves over the rubble of their brothers' bodies. Horses struggled through the course of deep swamp.

Tillantus, beside his captain, watched from beneath the silver visor of his helm. "This is useless. We have slain more than our own number and yet they still come. Is there an end to them?"

"All things must have an end; it is a decree of heaven," Eryian said, watching without emotion.

Those coming up the hill now were savage, some half-naked, with painted skins and crude weapons. Eryian had destroyed an entire legion of the highblood horsemen. Before, his old enemy had fed the sons of Righel fodder to weaken the circle of shields, but this time he had had chosen to send in highblood firstborn in hopes of quickly breaching defenses. But they had died. There were still more, waiting beyond, but these had died hard. Had they been his own sons, Eryian's heart would be breaking.

Now the demon offered up jungle tribes—untrained savages. His first attempt to shatter Eryian's front had failed, but now he was simply filling in the void to keep forces coming as he prepared his next calculated assault. This was chaff to fill the gap. They were being fed to the dark arrows and spears of the Shadow Warriors of the Daath, and the dead were merely growing on the ridge where the legions of Eryian waited.

"Light the second pylons," Eryian said calmly. Tillantus echoed his order. More logs came from the ridge of the butte, crashing downward, spiraling flame as they gathered speed. Unchurians were crushed and skin was left burning with death screams. Eryian wondered—if he continued to slay, if he could slay for weeks, for a season of the moon, would that even matter? Azazel reveled in death with nightmare, with pomp and blood and fury.

Winds had begun to build, and the snowfall was being whipped into blizzards of wind and stinging snow. Eryian could no longer see the far shore, or the forests of Hericlon's vale, but he could still see the river where it came from the hills, and now it was streaked with a film of oil from Rhywder' casks. The naphtha would reach flesh. He let it thicken.

"Release the third barrier," Eryian said calmly.

The Unchurians had fought their way up nearly two-thirds of the butte; they came with savage screams, furious, struggling, but it was more difficult now—their angle was steeper, and the going more unsteady. This time, heavy-tipped lances were launched from buried torsion wires. They pummeled into the Unchurians with a sound of iron and sundered bone. Then came a second wave of javelins—then a third.

For a breath, the Unchurians were again stopped. Bodies rolled back down to the river. The carnage there was unfathomable. How many spirits left their flesh this day, the mounds and mounds of dead, now falling, rolling back on each other until they were heaped below like felled timber.

"Fire the river," Eryian said quietly.

Tillantus turned in the saddle and screamed at the archers. A new shower of fired arrows soared overhead, this time in a high arch, leaving a shadowy streak of smoke across the ground to mark their flight. The top of the butte was still white in snow; it left the Unchurian lines below stark and black and bloodstained. The arrows soared over them, then burrowed in, leaving thick streamers of smoke. The murky film of the river was waiting like dark pus.

The Ithen roared to life, becoming a surging wall of flame, and it spread, growing, fevered. It spread outward, and when it reached the shores, it did not stop. The night before, on the far side of the river to the south, Eryian's men had dug trenches into the forest marshes. With the Unchurian attack, the entire vale had become a heavy froth of oil and gas. The flames spread through it quickly, with the fury of a woman, upward, inhaling flesh in a wind of searing white and orange, spreading outward. Sparks began to soar, spitting at the falling snow.

In little time, the entire valley was awash in flame, bodies squirming, screams far and long. The land was like burning skin, rippling, heaving.

Tillantus stared, aghast. "If I were not as hardened as I am, I would be puking now, Captain, heaving out my guts. Never seen such as this. Those men, I even feel for them, what it must be like to burn with nowhere to run. I swear, in all war there has been no sight like this, nothing to compare with these pitiful souls being swallowed like ants."

The Unchurians on the Daathan's side of the Ithen, just below the Shadow Warriors on the butte, were stunned. The river had now cut them off from the main armies. Most had turned to the screams of their brothers. The attack had stilled in shock. Eryian lifted his sword high, then motioned forward.

The Shadow Warriors came over the crest of the butte with thunder, with a trembling of the Earth. The Unchurians before them were thrown into hopeless panic.

By mid-sun, the Daath returned to high ground, weary and laden with slaughter. Stretched before them, from the butte to the forests beyond the river, hundreds of thousands of Unchurians lay crushed and charred, sundered by catapult and landslides, then hewn down by the sword. It was thick and dark, but for patches of white where the snow managed to take hold.

Eryian was stained in sweat, blood was splattered across his breastplate, and his sword had been returned to lie across his thighs. Its silver was stained with a dark sheen of blood.

"Perhaps this is what it feels like to be damned," Tillantus said quietly to the commander, staring over the valley. "This much death wrought of your own hand."

"No," Eryian answered. "Damned is worse."

Rhywder waded his horse through the waters toward the far east bank, feeling more uncomfortable as he did. He kept watching south, where the rocky shores of the river met the trees. His skin was bristling. He stationed himself next to the first catapult. He expected company. When the Unchurians downstream began to burn, they would send riders east to search.

On the top edge of the dam, the ramparts the engineers had thrown up to block the overflow of the spillway were beginning to slip. Once in a while a sandbag would slide over the spillway to plunk into the waters below. The river was slowly rising, the current getting stronger. Rhywder leaned forward in the saddle to check the tension of a sinew. It was winched tight and seemed solid. When he drew his hand back, an arrow whunked through the center bones in whispering breath, nearly passing through, catching at the bristled feathers where it wobbled a moment. Blood spilled free, and the pain seemed to come as a dull afterthought. Rhywder cried out, jerking back.

"Ahhhggg! You sons of whores!"

Taking the reins in his teeth, he tore a buckler from his shoulder, sliding his forearm through the strap. He then took the reins and turned the horse hard against the side of the catapult. Arrows whunked into the wood bracing. He ducked as one whistled over his shoulder, nicking the edge of his cloak, and he caught a second in the face of the buckler.

"Unchurians!" the engineer screamed from above. "Unchurians! They are shooting at you!"

"Lord, but that man has an eagle eye," Rhywder hissed through clenched teeth as he slid from the saddle.

The arrows had come from above, from the ridge above the dam, and now, five riders were coming up the riverbank, their hooves splashing. Rhywder squeezed himself back against the catapult's beam.

"Take out those damned archers!" Rhywder shouted to the engineers above.

"Fire across the canyon!" the engineer commanded. Arrows began to interchange.

Rhywder took hold of one dark feather of the arrow and ripped it away in a quick jerk that sent pain sharply up his arm. "Damn!" he hissed. He then ripped the other two quickly, taking short, fast breaths. Gripping the bloodied shaft, he wrenched the arrow free of his hand and cast it aside. For a moment he leaned forward, letting blood drip into the water. He tested his fingers. They still moved.

"Riders are coming!" the engineer shouted from above. Rhywder swore between tight teeth. "Look behind you, Captain, riders!"

Rhywder quickly ripped a leather tassel from the saddle and used his teeth to tie off the ends, wrapping his hand. He could hear hooves splashing through river water, getting closer.

Rhywder lifted a crossbow from the saddle, then turned and gripped a side post to climb onto the catapult platform. He lifted the crossbow and dropped a bolt into the stock. "You bastards!" he screamed. "That was my drinking hand you put a hole in!" The metal crossbar of Rhywder's bow twanged, and a rider crumpled from the saddle. From above, an arrow thudded into the platform near the edge of Rhywder's boot. Four riders were closing a small distance between themselves and the catapult, heavy hooves spraying the cold water. Rhywder dropped another bolt in and fired. A second rider vanished over the flanks, soundlessly.

From the ridge above, an Unchurian archer fell with a scream. He seemed to bounce along the rocky shoreline.

Rhywder threw the crossbow aside and unsheathed his sword. He was better at close killing anyway. From the spillway, enough water was now flowing that it broke over the edge of the icy platform in a film, making the wood slick. Rhywder stepped forward and used the flat of his sword to block the slice of a jagged scimitar that came in a heavy arc as a rider galloped past. Rhywder started to slip. Scrambling for balance, he barely blocked the slice of an axe with his buckler, then his feet went out from under him. He slammed onto his back, losing breath, and slid.

An Ishmian arrow whispered past Rhywder and sank deep into one Unchurian's thigh, through the muscle, anchoring him to his own horseflesh. The Unchurian cried out, dropping his axe as his horse reared. Horse and rider careened off balance and slammed against the catapult platform, straining the mooring lines. One anchoring billet was jerked from the riverbed. Rhywder dove forward and thrust his sword deep beneath the horse's front shoulder flank, into the heart. The beast grunted, its knees buckling. It disappeared beneath the platform, dragging the Unchurian under water.

"Behind you!" the shrill voice of the engineer echoed from the ridge. Rhywder turned. He spotted a dagger lifted for the throw and barely had time to leap clear. It hissed over his side and thunked into the catapult's bracing beam. Rhywder landed on his belly with a slap. He slammed his sword into the wood to stop sliding—he hadn't guess the wet wood would be this slick, but muck and moss were pouring from the dam, as well. Just as he got to his knees, an Unchurian tackled him. They went over the edge of the platform, Rhywder struggling to keep a sharp-edged blade from his throat. The cold water seemed to seize muscle, and for a moment they wrestled, numbed. Rhywder came out of the waist-deep water on his feet. He grabbed the Unchurian's long hair and rammed the head into the platform edge. It seemed to crack. The Unchurian's eyes rolled up as he slipped beneath the water.

"The signal!" screamed the engineer. "It is the final signal! Captain, cut the torsion sinews!"

Splinters sank into Rhywder' palm as he clambered back onto the catapult's platform.

"Oh, Elyon save you, there are more riders coming, more of them! More, look!"

Rhywder didn't look. He really didn't want to know, but he could hear hooves against the rock of the river's shore, and this time they were hundreds. He wrenched his sword free and swung about, shearing the sinew. When the firearm slammed into the crossbeam, the entire platform was heaved forward, the back wheels lifting. Rhywder nearly fell, but he grasped a line of hemp and watched. The heavy catapult rock arched into the sky, spreading, and soared over the top edge of the dam, missing completely. The engineer had been right' it was too high—now everything depended on the last two catapults.

"Horse piss!" Rhywder hissed.

"I told you it was too high! I told you!"

"That bird-faced son of a bitch," Rhywder muttered, leaping onto his horse and spurning it forward. The horse struggled in deeper water, half-leaping, half-galloping toward the second catapult. A javelin spun past him and shot though the waters, trailing a stream of bubbles.

Once the flames died down and the cinders were still cooling, the Unchurians came for Eryian's butte once more, this time like an ocean rushing. Eryian had darkened the sky with arrows, javelins, and catapults laden with piecemeal flint that shredded flesh, but finally, the Unchurians were able to reach the butte—there was nothing left to stop them, only Rhywder's dam. Eryian had fired the last signal, but by then, the best of the Unchurians had begun to push through.

The ranks of the Shadow Warriors did not give at first; they held, they slew, and bodies were thrown back. But slowly, even against the terrible, battle-hardened blows of Daathan sword and axe, the toughest of the Unchurians managed a foothold on the top of the ridge.

For a time longer the Daath held, the sound of weapons harsh and bitter; the echoing cries of the Unchurian were the song of beasts. Horsemen reared and plunged with pikes, driving downward. Powerful hammer blows of dark axe sundered shields and men alike. Lances, buttressed by strong horses that struggled over the edge and came forward, pierced shields like chisels hammering stone. Foot warriors came with shield and buckler, sword, scimitar, axe. Flails and javelins soared into the air to plunge deep into the Daathan ranks. It was said in the days of Dawnshroud, long ago, that of the angels, it was Azazel who taught men warfare, how to fashion weapons, how to fight. The Unchurians were no mere army; they were masters of their craft, trained by the lord of death himself.

Eryian noticed an Unchurian warrior, tall in the saddle, wielding a spiked iron ball from the end of a short, roughly hewn haft. It shattered a shield, sending splinters, then knocked the helmet from a Daath.

"We will sunder flesh and spill your blue blood!" the Unchurian was screaming as he killed. He was highborn, and when the shaft of his morning star was shattered, he lifted an already bloodied war hammer. A heavy swipe of it tore away the shoulder of a Shadow Warrior.

"This day, we eat your children, true bloods!" the Unchurian screamed.

Eryian ripped a javelin from the fingers of a warrior beside him and flung it. The highborn with his quick tongue hissed, furious, as the heavy tip tore through his breastplate and crumpled him over the saddle. He joined the dead on the slope of the ridge.

Eryian could then see four minions, coming mounted, with terrible weapons, making their way toward him—the hard wood exoskeleton armor that was tougher than steel, the beings inside the harvested bodies that had lived for aeons. The warlord watched, shaken, as they cleaved their way through a line of solid locked shields. He knew they had been sent for him alone. The closer the slayers got to the warlord, the more enraged the Shadow Warriors became. The minions paid them no mind, pressing forward, but these were the King's Guard, and the minions did not scatter them. One had to pause, as, with a scream, a warrior leapt from behind, wrenched back the neck, and sheared open the throat in a cut that reached through bone. The minion tried to keep going, but it was difficult when his head lobbed back and hung against his cloak. Though the others had kept their eyes trained on Eryian, two were finally forced to deal with the Shadow Warriors who surrounded their warlord. Never expecting to be felled by mere Daath, they were nonetheless brought down one by one. The heads of minions were flung high to land deep into the mass of Unchurians—to remind them who they faced.

Tillantus drew his axe and wrapped a thick hand about its haft. "Captain, I believe the time has come this day to do some personal killing. I will be going in now."

"Stay back, Tillantus, you are the high captain; you will need to order your men."

"Sorry, Captain, but my axe thirsts and must be quenched."

Eryian would have followed, but the timing would be critical; life and death. His ribs ached with each breath, and a dull pain pulsed through his head. He had still not fully recovered from the battle in the Vale of Tears. He was weak. Too weak to chance a killing front, even though he watched his high captain wade in with fury.

The front lines of battle were a seething frenzy, blood rich. It seemed as though two awesome beasts were boring into each other with equal fury. Eryian watched Tillantus's wide axe shear flesh like a meat cutter in a shop.

He glanced to the west. "Where is my water, Little Fox?" he whispered.

Rhywder hugged the mane of his horse as it struggled forward, the stout muscles churning water that brushed the underbelly. He had chosen a high horse for high water.

Behind him, the waters were being frothed by a century of Unchurians. They were parting water like ships coming. Their weapons glimmered; their armor seemed to swallow light. A javelin skittered across the surface near his horse's right flank, and Rhywder veered away, cursing. He had reached the second catapult, mid-river, in the deepest current. As the horse struggled past, he leaned in the saddle and cut the sinew. Water swept in ripples over the catapult platform as its arm thudded hard into the crossbeam, so hard the back wheels were wrenched upward, pulling loose the mooring lines. A wooden anchor wedge was wrenched free and sailed past Rhywder's cheek like a missile.

Heavy catapult rock soared high, and loosed of the mooring, the catapult swung about in the current, its thick, oaken wheels rumbling. The rock struck the face of the dam, punching in holes and sending a web of cracked fissures across snaking over its face.

Rhywder spurned the horse harder, driving for the last catapult, the one that would crumple the Ithen Dam like a barn door. Behind him, a rider had reached the second catapult. He quickly grappled up, onto the crossbeam. He leapt for the Little Fox, arms outstretched.

Rhywder dropped tight against the horse's neck and slid over the flank, letting the Unchurian sail over the horse's back and vanish into cold waters, his scream cut short at high pitch.

"Bastards, as if javelins were not enough—now they throw themselves," Rhywder muttered, pulling himself back into the saddle. A dagger sung past his ear so close the cross handles clouted him in the side of his head. At this, he swore bitterly, clenching his teeth. There was blood in his eye. He was getting truly angry.

The dam trembled. A gigantic slab of limestone dropped from the top edge and rode the spillway like a child. Crevices split deeper, rippling up the face where water spurted through in wide, blue sprays of icy, deep waters.

Rhywder was nearly to the third catapult. The horse was struggling for all its worth against the current, steadily pushing forward, when suddenly it was struck by an arrow. It screamed, rearing back and Rhywder went under. He was ground into the sediment of the riverbed as the horse rolled over him.

He fought his way to the surface, breath sucked into the cold. He managed to grasp the lashing line of the catapult and crawled along it, hand over hand.

When he reached the edge, Rhywder leapt onto the platform. A javelin sliced past his leg as he spun from its path and in the same moment kept spinning, shearing the torsion sinew with both hands gripping the hilt of his short sword. He quickly sheathed the sword, turning as the heavy crossbar slammed into its beam, flinging a spray of heavy rock into the weakening face of the dam.

Rhywder smiled at those chasing him. "Fare you well, you unholy bastards!" Rhywder screamed, then turned and dove headlong into the surging current.

In his mind's eye he saw the barrage of stone soar, tumbling, almost in slow motion as it came against the face of the dam.

Most of the Unchurian horsemen stopped and turned to watch. There was nothing more to do now but die.

Rhywder swam hard. His muscles were numbed, he felt as though he were swimming without benefit of legs and arms, but he kept at it, kept lashing the cold waters, using the current to carry him, angling for a shale and sand beach just downstream, where the canyon wall opened into a vale. In seconds the dam would sunder completely.

It seemed almost impossible to make out which direction he was swimming; the waters were muddied; pebbles and stone were hurtling through it. One grazed his side. When his boots took hold of sediment, he burst from the water at a run, sucking air into frozen lungs. His legs were numb, and he ran half-stumbling at first, until he could force rhythm. He heard the dam give way behind him. It had a sound like gods screaming. As the lake broke through, it seemed to lift into the sky in a frenzied wall of crushed limestone and blue ice water.

Rhywder saw it only from the corner of his eye, but it left him breathless—it was a sight, unlike he had known, as if heaven itself were falling. Rhywder ran full-out, sucking hard breaths, his short, muscled legs working as powerful as a horse's.

He was running for a tree, one he had chosen the night before, a huge, magnificent oak, bowled, with naked limbs and hard, knotted wood.

The roar was deafening. The ground beneath him shook, threatening to spill open. The hair on the back of Rhywder's neck bristled; he could feel the fore-winds of the oncoming torrent; he could hear the earth ripping apart.

He climbed, then caught a limb and swung himself around it, hugging tight, pressing his cheek against the strong wood, gripping with legs and arms. He closed his eyes against a last vision of terrible white froth a mile high, spreading outward, ripping whole slabs of the cliffs away. Rhywder whispered the true name of God. It was another of those times—a time to die.

At the ridgeline, where Eryian and the Daath still held, the Unchurian high-blood finally shattered through the inner shields of the King's Guard, taking Eryian by surprise. The demon had sent in his finest; sensing the moment, he had sent in slayers as deadly as any Eryian had ever had to face. They were equally matched, but the inner circle of guards were outnumbered and Eryian guessed, as weak as he still was, he would have to fight.

They were killing Eryian's prime, fired with blood, frenzied—a wedge of them, boring through to the center, toward Eryian's white horse and silvered cloak. They were splattered in blood, and continually they dropped, horses crumpling, vanishing beneath those behind—yet more coming, tall, powerful warriors, firstborn prime, fighting with such skill and alacrity that even Eryian could not help but feel impressed.

The Daathan personal guard were fighting back savagely, they had never been bested, never been breached, and their weapons were cutting through plate armor, shearing horseflesh, chests, necks, cleaving limbs, crushing skulls. It was skilled, deft, savage fighting that seemed almost a work of art as it closed on Eryian.

Eryian prepared. He drew the silver sword, tightened his thighs on the horse's flanks.

Behind Eryian's guard, the first lines of the second legion were advancing, Daath rested and prepared to slay with fury, but if the guard broke, there would be a moment of thin blood between here and there for Eryian. He did not believe he would fall this way; his faith was firm, but his logic spoke otherwise.

Archers kept a continual rain upon the Unchurians, a steady darkening of the sky that almost seemed like cloud cover, leaving strange shadows, and sounds like insects boring.

Directly before Eryian, the center was finally pierced, and open fighting broke out. Tillantus had backed his horse to block Eryian and was killing from left to right.

"My lord, you must retreat!" Tillantus screamed.

"I stand here!" Eryian screamed, his face red. "Let the sons of demons do their worst. I will not turn away!"

From the rear, Daathan axemen came forward, wading hard into horse-flesh, their work quick.

Unchurians were still getting through—only Tillantus was keeping them from engaging the warlord directly. The high captain's killing was continual, unrelenting, and bodies were all about him, almost forming a wall.

"We will hold here!" Eryian screamed. "This line cannot give way before the waters come!"

An Unchurian seemed to hurl through the air for Eryian, as though launched by a catapult. Eryian used his shield to deflect him, hurling the warrior over his shoulder where he was quickly cut to pieces. Another broke past Tillantus on horseback. Eryian killed him quickly, a flicker thrust through his heart.

Eryian pulled alongside Tillantus and began to slay.

"Back, my lord, you are too weak."

"Not weak enough," he said, his sword a blur as each movement, each slice, was a killing thrust. The axemen of the second reached them now. They came with one purpose, to keep the warlord alive, and they hurled themselves into the fury. If their lord chose this moment to die, they would ensure the cost would be great, indeed.

Eryian ignored all pain, all thought. He slew with craft and skill, like a woodworker honing the finest furniture—it was not frenzy or fury that Eryian fought with; it was precision. The attacks seem to come from all directions. The Unchurians had found Eryian, and he was now their single target. Soon Tillantus, Eryian, and a tight core of horsed Shadow Warriors were hacking through a wall of bodies that came at them out of all madness, with screams that echoed through the coming night.

"I fear we are about to be outflanked, my lord!" shouted Tillantus.

"Rhywder will not fail; it is moments away," answered Eryian, shearing open a neck to a smooth white cut through the spinal cord.

A captain screamed beside him, then it seemed he spat, but it was the splatter of his tongue as an arrow tore out his cheek.

An Unchurian breaking through to Eryian reared his horse and cast a heavy javelin. Eryian dropped low, hugging the horse's mane as the javelin tore through his cloak and over the flank of his horse, impaling an Daathan shield-bearer.

A second spear sank deep into the shoulder of Eryian's horse. The beast screamed, thrown sideways. Eryian tried to leap clear, but the ranks were too tight and his horse came down upon him, rolling with a grunt, legs kicking. Eryian felt his thighbone snap with a grinding crack. When the horse rolled clear, he lay for a moment paralyzed in pain, sucking for breath.

The Unchurian hurled themselves for the kill, but with equal fury, the Daath drove them back, clearing ground about their fallen warlord.

Eryian saw the bone of his own leg torn through muscle flesh.

Warriors and captains lifted a wall of shields to protect him. The frenzy that came against them seemed inhumane, an animal fury. But the shadowy shields of the Daath held them back. Tillantus had dropped from his horse and knelt beside his warlord, breathless, his entire body, face, hand, all splattered in blood as if he had been showered in it.

"Bind my leg, Tillantus! Lash it to spear shafts!"

"Aye," Tillantus hissed and snapped a heavy shaft across his thigh.

One of the high captains set his boot against Eryian's right thigh, gripped the leg beneath the knee, pulled it straight, then twisted it about until it looked almost normal. Eryian reeled, drunken with pain. Two swords and a broken javelin haft were laid against the skin and quickly lashed with leather strips.

"A horse!" Eryian shouted, and was lifted by his arms onto his feet, then helped into the saddle. Mounted warriors encircled him. Eryian took the reins, then swayed and lunged for the mane. He held it in fists, breathing tightly. "Lash me to the saddle!"

"Why this, my lord?" shouted Tillantus.

"My people must know I have not fallen."

A captain quickly tossed leather saddle straps over Eryian's waist, then under the horse's belly where they were lashed from either side until Eryian straightened in the saddle. He turned. Behind him, a fresh century of Daath were closing to engage. The moment of truth was past—the best and mightiest of the Unchurian had gotten close, but they had failed to take Eryian and his high captains out. The fresh shields from the rear had reached the battered King's Guard and began to drive the Unchurian back.

Eryian lifted his sword. "Hard to the ridge! Push them against the ridge!"

Eryian heard the waters, even above the roar of battle. He looked west. A mountain of water was breaking through the forest, annihilating everything, uprooting trees, churning boulders. Panic was breaking out below. Seeing what was coming, the Unchurians on the ridge fought to hold their ground, but were being pushed back. The centuries of the second legions had reached them now, fresh, waiting behind the lines for their moment.

Thousands of Unchurians were below, either crossing the river or struggling up the ridge. The waters closing on them was as high as the ridge itself; whole elder oak and tall pine tumbled in the churning currents along with boulders the size of houses.

The foothold the Unchurians had on the ridge was being lost, panic had broken out, and they were falling back, slipping over the edge of the butte.

Below—madness. They had begun to scramble, helpless. The massive wall of water closed on them like a great hand, sucking them up like ants until the river Ithen was dark with skin and purple with blood.

This day, the Daath had survived. How many times their own numbers they had slain were uncounted, but many. They had dispatched an entire kingdom of armies. And yet, Eryian knew there would be even more.

Chapter Fifty-One
Firestorm

Many of the Daath crouched along the edge of the butte, leaning against sword and spear shafts, shields cast aside. Others were dying. Some held slain brothers. Below them, filling the valley from the butte to a south shore of high ground, waters churned, heavy. As it had been in ancient times, the river was once again wide and mighty, the icy waters of the mountain spurs. For a long time the waves were dark and rolling, until there was only purple and white froth, drifting with trees and debris.

There would be time to rest. The waters would be high and strong—impossible to breach without a bridge or crossing.

Eryian rode slowly among his men. The wounded that would live were being lifted onto litters. The dying were slain and laid upon the pyres being built. Eryian was amazed to find a weary, bloodstained Tillantus standing dazed, staring over the waters.

"Look there," he said, pointing his bloodied axe. Across the river, in the vale, Unchurians were gathered. Fires were being lit, dotting the land like stars, glittering in forest and along far hills.

"If not for you by my side, I would believe myself mad. How many more could there be? We've killed a kingdom of warriors this day!"

"It is a calculation the demon has nursed for seven hundred years. He has raised and honed these firstborn—the finest of them—since the oath of Mount Ammon. They have not aged, and they have been trained for centuries."

"Why? For what purpose?"

"Our extinction."

Tillantus glanced at him.

"Those are the Follower's words. Never guessed you for one of those Enochian tale weavers."

"I have been one, but now I wonder."

"Well, I will admit, this particular bastard is as powerful as anyone I have ever faced."

"More than even I, Tillantus—possibly more cunning, as well. For aeons he has bided his time, chosen his moves, all for a single hour. This hour."

"Then by logic our extinction is imminent. Our only possible next stand could be the forest of the East of the Land. That will slow them, give us time to reach the walls of Terith-Aire itself. If they catch us before the East of the Land, we will be sword against sword on open ground and we cannot prevail."

"Hold to Faith's Light, Captain."

"Never have known you to be a man of scriptures, my lord."

"I have not known myself to be one until these last days. Faith's Light, Tillantus, when next they come, when next we stand sword to sword against ten times our number, find in the center of your heart that place where light still dwells. It is all we have left us."

Eryian turned the reins and rode through the ranks west, toward the ports of Ishmia. It left Tillantus wondering. Eryian had never been wrong. If there was light of heaven, so be it. Though it was, admittedly, late in life for Tillantus, the aging high captain of the Daath, to be searching for that place in him where it dwelt. If these were the prophecies of Enoch unfolding, the world, in his view, had as little chance as a hare in an open field against a wolf pack. He turned and somberly started after the warlord. Odd, he thought, how the day had no taste left in him, that all the blood and flesh and bone that had been crushed of life held no taste, even little sorrow. No pity of the dead. Perhaps that was how prophecies unfolded. Elyon seemed to bear no sorrow of his loss, so why should those who suffered it? This god was not one for compassion; no one could argue that point. Perhaps He had heaven's purpose, but of sorrow for the suffering of men—none.

✝

It was night when Eryian reached the port city of Ishmia. The first legion had been hit hard, had lost perhaps a century of men, but they were still strong. The second legion had hardly seen bloodshed. Both armies were abandoning the ridge and would now form a barrier to the rear of the refugees as they fled along the King's Road for Terith-Aire. It was open ground, no cover, no defense. Eryian thought he had never really fought a war of defense. He had slain, that was all, he had burned and crushed and overwhelmed to achieve the gathering of the tribes, but never had he been on the wrong side of a siege, never had he been in retreat. But an ancient enemy, apparently, had been watching him long, knew his every weakness.

From the second legion, Eryian peeled off two centuries to guard Ishmia. The flood had effectively cut off the south bank, but he no longer trusted logic.

There were no ships in the typically cluttered dock of the city, and the buildings and temples and courts were vacant, empty. The women, the dancers, the noise of the bustling port were all gone. By now, nearly all of the civilians had been evacuated—they held a view of the ridge and the fighting from here. Any who wished to climb to the tops of buildings or hillocks could have watched the carnage. There was little resistance when the Daathan scouting parties came through the city streets ordering the inhabitants to leave their belongings, to take but the clothes they wore, their children, and loved ones, and press hard for the high walls of Terith-Aire. And so they did; they left their taverns, their shops, villages, left even their jewels and fine wares still waiting to be sold. It was a thieves' paradise, but even thieves had fled. The only tangible occupants left were the shadowy pockets of fear and terror. If any had doubts of what they faced, all they needed was to look upon the blood-darkened waters of the isthmus beyond the wharf, bobbing with the burnt and bloodied corpses of horses and men, like leaves scattered after a hard autumn wind.

Eryian was looking over the strange sight when a boy rode up beside him and bowed in the saddle. "I am the chemist's assistant," said the boy, "and you must be Eryian, the warlord."

Eryian nodded.

From a saddle pouch the boy lifted several small packets, wrapped with thin, green leaves, and offered them. Eryian took them, grateful.

"Send your chemist my thanks, boy."

"Aye, my lord, but it is our thanks to you. If you need more, the chemist shop is opened, unlocked—we are riding north with the others."

Eryian nodded. "Godspeed."

The boy bowed once more, then turned his horse and set off down the street, weaving between the warriors of the first and second century from the second legion.

Eryian had always ridden out pain, but this, the shattered bone in his leg, for this he gave in, stuffed a wadded leaf packet just inside either cheek, then put the rest of them in his belt pouch.

He leaned wearily on the horse, still lashed to the saddle.

"My lord," said a commander, pulling up beside him. "I have escort for you to rest with your wife. Your injuries are severe. We will watch the wharfs, my lord."

"I will stay for a time, Commander, satisfy myself against surprises in the night."

"Speak of them," said Tillantus, who reached his side. He had been riding hard, his horse sweated, and he was even a bit winded. Eryian could not believe there was more danger; at least the night should be sound—they had earned that.

"Elyon's grace has blessed us further," Tillantus swore, then grabbed Eryian's arm hard, nails biting. "Look there!" He pointed across the muddled bay. "Ships! They have a legion of damned fully armed ships!"

Eryian felt a shiver, which was rare for him. He must have kept them to sea or the flood would have destroyed them, and in fact, he noticed a flotilla closing on the southern shore even now from the west. He had outguessed even the flood, Eryian's last stab. It should have been complete, should have at least broken battle for a day or so, enough time to get civilians and what remained of his legions to the trees of the East of the Land. But now he stared across the darkened water in disbelief. The bay had risen; it had even swamped many of the wharf and docks, leaving it almost an inland sea. Here, on this side, any merchant ships, any galley still left, had been swept away, and some were even thrown up against taverns and shop faces, looking out of place lying on their sides and tops with crushed masts. Yet, on the far side, across the isthmus, untouched ships had gathered in the dark and now were fearless enough to light their stern and aft lamps for boarding. They were ships of all kinds, warships, merchantmen, heavy galleys with angled sails and tiered oars. Eryian felt a revulsion, a powerful hatred; he had been outguessed. No one outguessed the warlord of Argolis, and he imagined, none had outguessed his former flesh, the angel Righel. But this one saw futures so clearly, he had planned for each. Eryian remembered now the seamen's rumors: that the southern seas past the Daathan coast were cursed; that despite the riches in spices, gold, and slaves to be gained beyond the western seas of the Daathan coast, ships simply vanished; good ships, hardened captains, disappearing without storm or ice or any logic. They simply went south and never came back. Now it was clear why. They had been collected. The angel had looked into the future, he had seen this as possible, his first onslaught against Eryian a failure. If these ships could form a bridge across the isthmus, it would be possible for the Unchurians to catch the remaining legions of the Daath, as well as their protected civilians, in open land, with no defenses. Even after the slaughters of two insane battles, the vale, and the ride—the number of the Unchurian armies would still be an answer to the angel's prayers. Elyon's grace. Elyon's Light. He left His people like sheep before predators; He stole hope; He crushed hearts and trampled strength. Eryian spat to the side. He wanted to swear his anger to heaven. His fury simmered though him and even the words of Cassium, her warnings against hatred, held no boundary. It was not Azazel that now stirred his fury; it was Elyon. It was a God that gave His best and most pure hearts to hopeless futures. Why even fight on? Why not give the civilians a quick and painless death, then drive into this unstoppable wall of warriors, die well, and end the prophecies and all the hope of mankind. They were not human; it was never the Daathans' fight to begin with—even according to legend the ship named Daathan had left in the day of Yered to answer the blood cries of an Earth they had no place on, and true to form, the Daath had been outcasts for all these centuries. Feared by all. Even Etlantis had been careful to offer no offense.

"My lord, are you all right?"

Eryian did not answer. He curled a tight fist against his thigh, feeling his blood pump through the temples of his head as across the bay these ships scurried with their ants and insects boarding with weapons and catapult and fire.

"My lord?"

"How far the legions?"

"Two, three degrees of the moon."

"Then they would never reach us in time to do anything but die."

Tillantus did not know how to respond; he had never seen such a look on Eryian's face.

"Those ships," Tillantus said, "most look Etlantian. They could aid us, possibly. If the south takes this port city, not to mention Terith-Aire, it is not good for Etlantian trade routes."

"No, they are his, Azazel's. That is his name—why hide it any longer? The unholy bastard is outguessing every move we make," Eryian said, simmering in anger.

There seemed a whispered chuckle in answer, but it was indistinct; it could have been a whining timber of the dock, or a wind through the awnings of one of the taverns.

"But how?" asked Tillantus. "How so many ships? The Unchurians are not seafarers."

"No, these ships are Etlantian, Pelegasian, fishers of Ishmia. They are ships that made the mistake of sailing too close to the islands that lie to the far south of Hericlon where he had built his kingdom."

"It cannot be," Tillantus muttered. "This cannot happen. We have fought the dark itself this day—we need time, at least to catch our breath. They breach this isthmus; there is no time to even mount a defense."

"We have no choice; they are gathering their ships quickly. The campfires of armies left behind in the vale were merely to fool us. They are going to cross, and they are going to cross now, with nightfall. We will fight with what we have, give Elyon more lives, more souls, and when all is lost, perhaps then He will be satisfied."

"Moments ago you spoke of His Light, to find it, use it as our last hope."

"That was before He gave the demon an Endgame."

"You have any specific orders, my lord, any preparation?"

"Other than to die?"

"Yes, other than to die, my lord."

"Naphtha. Ships burn. Do we have catapults and naphtha?"

"Catapults are still being brought down from the ridge, too far to reach us, but useless if they did. Every drop we had was used in lacing the vale and coating the river to burn. There is naphtha in Terith-Aire in abundance, but of course, that does us little good here."

"The first and second legion have by now reached Lucania; they could never turn in time. So then, we have what we have—two century. Good men. We will make a stand here, a line along this wharf. It is crushed and mangled by the floodwaters; that will make at least a difficult landing. We can make a killing stand, even if it is in the end futile."

"Aye, at least that."

"Have your captains assemble shieldbearers along the line of this wharf, what archers we have, javelins, and when you have your orders given, press on, catch the legions moving north and press them at triple time, all they have. There will be weak civilians, old ones, young ones, unable to keep up, but they must be left behind. We cannot lose all our people, Tillantus. Hold first at the line of the East of the Land, using the trees to slow them—then prepare for the siege of Terith-Aire."

"Captain, I cannot leave you."

"It was not a discussion, Tillantus, those were your orders."

"But your leg, your injuries . . ."

"Go, now, there is little enough time to prepare."

"I will send a personal guard to aid you."

Eryian turned to him, studied him a moment. "It may be the last I see of you, old friend—brother."

Tillantus tightened his teeth and nodded. He lifted his hand in the sign of the word, as did Eryian.

"Despite what I said, go in Faith's Light, Tillantus. Godspeed."

"As you, my brother."

Tillantus turned the reins and started through the men, shouting orders that were then being repeated by captains of centuries and leaders of cohorts. The Daath swiftly began forming a frontal line, back from the wharf, close enough to damage by missile; far enough to gauge what came against them and prepare their last stand.

Rhywder's limbs slowly tingled with life, and pain, and when he opened his eyes, he fell. He had no reckoning of earth or sky and landed hard on his side in soft dirt. He rolled slowly onto his back, then stared upward. Night sky. He blinked. That was impossible, but indeed, there was a night above him. It was as though the torrent unleashed had even swept away the clouds and sunset. The stars were like ice shards. Rhywder felt as though he had been hammered out, worked like a sheet of bronze, and he imagined himself flat and crinkled. He sucked cold air into his lungs, and realized he was freezing, shivering, his wet clothes were icy. He leapt to his feet.

"Freezing! Elyon's grace, I am freezing!" he shouted, dancing, slapping his hands against his sides. He glanced up, still dancing. The huge oak lay above him as though tangled in the sky. It had ridden the edge of the flood until the forest snagged it, and that had saved them. The oak had held to its brothers like a grasping hand. Rhywder now ran for the trees.

Something living had to be in the forest. He needed something living. He fell twice; both times leaping back onto his feet, for if he stopped moving he was not going to last long. When he spotted a horse, he stopped, gasped. He glanced down. Most of his tunic was torn away, but not his sword; it was still lashed to the belt—he had done that, lashed it tight. Pity if he lost his clothes, but the sword he would need if he lived, and there it was. He picked up a rock, weighted it, cast it aside, then grabbed another. Balancing it, he walked forward. When the horse jerked up, he talked to it softly—using all his horse skills and feeling pity inside for what he had to do.

"Sorry about this, my good friend, but I need your blood."

Rhywder cracked the horse's skull. He grabbed his sword and quickly cut into the hide, fingers numbed; his skin looked almost blue as he worked. Finally he pulled the bloodied hide over his shoulders, then wrapped it about him and knelt, shivering in its steam until warmth began to seep into his chilled skin. He looked up. Beyond, the horizon toward the sea was stained a fire glow. It was Ishmia. They had failed; everything had failed. It looked, from here, as if Ishmia was aflame.

Weary as the Daath were, and few in number, being only two century, they braced for the promise that if the Unchurians forced a crossing this night—few as they were, with little missile launchers and barely any naphtha—it would still cost to take this dock. No matter where they fought, here, in open field, behind barriers—the Daath were going to make each engagement cost the Unchurian dearly. Other empires would have fallen by now, but no matter—Eryian's men steeled their faces against the coming onslaught as if this was just another skirmish.

Eryian watched the far southern shore. The armies of the Unchurian were moving quickly. They were going to stagger the assault, keeping the galleys and merchantmen deeper back, protected from any Daathan missiles. If it were Eryian, he would place his most savage and honed warriors in the sleeker, quicker ships, and he had no doubt that was precisely Azazel's move. If they were good enough at their craft, it would be possible to capture a foothold using the warships and their elite, then bring in the galleys and larger craft, creating a virtual bridge that would cross the isthmus.

The chemist's powders had numbed out his leg. They threatened, as well, to dull his thought, slow his decisions, but Eryian would fire his spirit past that. He burned with something, something he had never used as fuel before. Hatred. He no longer could say if he hated the choirs of heaven more than the demon he faced across the waters, but he could feel hatred burning in him. It was good fuel for killing. No wonder the frenzy of crazed warriors with nothing left to lose was so effective.

The ships launched. Behind Eryian a strong defensive line had formed. He noticed two bolt launchers and rows of longbows and crossbows. Shieldbearers were moving in just behind them, ready to step forward and absorb the first impact. It would take a degree of the moon, perhaps two, to make the isthmus crossing. The bodies and debris might slow the galleys some, but the sharp prows of the warships were designed to cut waves, and they would slice through the flotsam quickly, like minnows darting. He saw their oars rising and they launched. They were fast; they gained speed quickly.

Eryian turned to ride along the lines of defense. "Hold. Hold against the impossible; hold this night what cannot be held. Our brothers must reach the forest of the East of the Land before this army can close on their flanks."

A volley of screams and swords beating against shields came in answer.

"I will be here; look to me. If your spirit fails, look to me, and if we fall, my brothers, I will fall with you this night."

There was silence.

"But if we hold them back, then heaven is our shield. Let us pray and cling to that hope."

Eryian turned to look across the bay. As he had guessed, from between the lumbering galleys and merchant ships, warships surged like birds crossing air current, gaining speed, their oars flashing. They were closing much faster than he would have guessed.

"When they reach the wharf, the wood and stanchions weakened of the floodwaters will be unsteady. Wait until then to launch your missiles."

He glanced at the sky. Oddly clear; no broiling storm clouds. This had become a game of strategy; it was simple war the angel played now, as though he enjoyed it—throwing his honed slayers against the finest warriors the world had to offer. It was as much a game to him as it was his mission to destroy the Daath at all cost.

Eryian saw many of the warships had been fitted with fire throwers themselves. They began to launch now, high, arched, ready to plow deep into the city where they exploded in sulfur, naphtha, and splintering stone. The missiles soared over their heads and moments later the explosions could be heard. In little time, Ishmia would begin to burn.

"Come ahead," Eryian whispered, seething with fury, "bring what you have got. These two hundred will bring down ten times your numbers." Again, in answer, the whispering chuckle. *As if ten times two hundred would matter,* a voice played back in Eryian's head. He was listening, Azazel; he was somewhere across that bay watching the warlord, watching his eyes, his growing fury, and his answer was a soft chuckle.

They were swift, the front runners—the warships. Their prows cut through the flotsam of the isthmus like cutting through waves. The galleys, of course, were coming slow, just in case there were Daathan launchers in range. They were going to let the elite warriors in the warships take out the front lines. Most of them would be minions. For a moment Eryian wondered of the minions Azazel had created. His strongest, his firstblood, must have lost bodies over the centuries, but instead of letting them terrorize the Earth as Uttuku, he had taught his sons the craft of growing what were, though hardened as steel, plant bodies. They were almost impregnable and yet, in truth, no more than vegetables. Without minds to fight back, vegetable matter was easy flesh to manipulate and command, and should they wither or die—more could be grown. There were probably everywhere now fields of these creatures growing their armored, winged bodies. But why had the angel shed his own body? His own flesh? The flesh of an angel was said to be invincible, impregnable by even the fiercest fire. But Azazel was now only a spirit—stealing the bodies of men and making them slaves. Eryian wondered of this, because if there was an answer to it, it was a chance; it was a flaw he could use to bring the angel down. A single, fleeting weakness. It is what Cassium had meant when she said, "If we can turn him." If his flesh could be destroyed, for a time, as a spirit he could no longer command the elements of earth, perhaps not even these uncounted numbers of Unchurian warriors who were no more than extensions of his own mind, without wills of their own, just the driving will of the angel.

The warships came with oars flashing like wings, and Eryian could see mounted horsemen on their decks, waiting anxiously to leap the rails.

Fire rained from either direction. There were two or three bolt launchers with naphtha missiles in the Daathan ranks, dragged down from the ridge. They burst a number of the fast warships into flame, and even minions did not like flame. But then the bolt launchers were emptied; the missiles depleted. All that was left now would be the arrows of the bowmen, then the shields of the two hundred Daath. If nothing else, it should at least be quick. What crawled like fire beneath Eryian's skin was that he would not be allowed to face the angel once more. Even with silvered sword, with mortal weapons, that is how he wanted to die, with all his skill and might thrown at the fallen angel who once was Elyon's own chosen, the second of the three, Azazel, the lord of the choir of the Auphanim.

The clouded sky over the dark water was lit in watery streaks as the warships, hundreds of them, closed the last distance. Behind them, the few strikes the Daath were capable of had left crippled, floating pyres of orange-yellow flame.

The faster, more well built of the warships were coming in a wedge, coming like horsemen against footmen, formed in groups of threes and fives to pierce through like javelins cast, but they were not aimed for the shieldbearers. It was for the damaged wharfs they headed; the farther in they could breach the broken wood beams and planking, the more solid ground they would have for the waiting horsemen. The final surges of the oars were powerful and the rams of the prow posts lifted out of the water like sea beasts. Eryian held his horse in tight rein.

Eryian studied the warships—they had been reinforced, rebuilt; they moved faster than any Etlantians; their armor was thinner, lighter, but he was certain it was also harder to penetrate. They moved with astonishing speed, coming like a heavy wave in a spiked line toward the docks like the teeth of sharks.

"They will ram the docks almost to dry land!" Eryian shouted. "Prepare for horsemen and pikes; they are coming like cavalry!"

"My lord!" shouted one of the protectors left by Tillantus, his name, Eryian recalled, was Mammanon. "You must pull back; you are in open range of even crossbows at this distance!"

Eryian glanced at him. Death would matter little. It would end the pain, the anger, the fury. Perhaps it would not be so bad letting it come quickly. But he would lead these men to their last—he would hope for one more chance at the angel.

"Show my path, Mammanon."

Mammanon circled his sword to his other guardsmen, twelve in all. "Pull back; pull the warlord back."

Even as Eryian backed his horse behind the shieldbearers, surrounded by Tillantus's protectors, he watched the warships ripping toward them in perfect formation; they were going to utterly destroy the docking—drive their armor-piercing hulls deep into the broken wood to reach stable ground.

"Brace yourselves!" Eryian screamed.

The entire wharf, all along its structure, seemed to buckle. Planks were split, cast, timber snapped like bone, the heavy rams and edged prows of the ships cut deep, plowing through the broken wood like cutting into a ship broadside. They hit so hard, the Earth shook and even Eryian's horse staggered sideways.

He was right, minions, hundreds of them. Some leapt on horseback, not always successful, for the hooves broke through the weakened docking, but others leapt from warships that had plowed through all the way to the bedrock that met the waters of the isthmus. Still other minions did not bother with horses. They were not good at flight, but if necessary they could sail, their heavy wings bearing them up, and many were soaring over the front lines of the Daathan front to strike from the rear.

Soon. It would be over soon. Eryian's worst regret was that he was going to die at the hand of a minion. He would take several out, but weakened, his leg smashed, his blood already thinned, his death was imminent. It was not the death he would have chosen.

The horsemen of the highborn Unchurian hardly paused in their charge—over the railing of the low-built warship onto the ground of Ishmia, quickly forming to charge in small groups, piercing groups; phalanxes with lances anchored, they would break apart even locked shields like a knife through the ribs.

Missiles of the Daath soared nearly point-blank, dropping hundreds, thinning them considerably, but into other places, the horsemen came so swift, the Daathan lines were being smashed open, thrown into disarray, and once inside, there was open slaughter. The minions were quick, deadly slayers.

Eryian's guard forced themselves about his front, forming a shielding of their own. They would die before their warlord; it was their last duty and Eryian waited with dark eyes, his blood seething. Out across the isthmus were hundreds, perhaps more than a thousand heavy galleys and merchant ships. The Unchurians would soon be able to cross throughout the night, with nothing left to hold them back, and if they had fresh mounts and rode through the night, it was well possible they could reach the retreating Daathan legions and their civilians before the forest that was the East of the Land. If that happened, the thousands of Unchurian warriors would have open, clean, perfect killing ground.

Loch dropped over the gunwale and waded through the low tide onto the shore of Ishmia's northern bank. You could not see the city from here—there was a hill that blocked its view—but you could hear screams and you could see fire licking from the isthmus. It meant Hericlon had fallen. It meant Galaglea had been destroyed, and it meant the unwalled and almost impossible-to-defend port city of Ishmia was surely about to be slaughtered. There was a time that would have brought a terrible shock to him, a terrible blow—enough to take his breath. But Loch felt little in thinking of the slaughter, the dead and dying. It was as if something had gutted him of all feeling—he needed now only to understand what was to be done, what was next required of him by Elyon's grace.

Assembled on the bank were four riders. They were not Daathan or Ishmian. They might have been Etlantian, but they were not. They were giants, Nephilim, but the curse was not over them. These were sons of archangels, and their hearts, as Sandalaphon, were pure even now, even centuries from the light that spawned them. They were true Watchers. They saw what happened in this world, but as Sandalaphon, by edict they could do little.

Loch had seen these men once before. They were with Sandalaphon, and they had been there, in the shadows the day his mother died and when the others had left, when Loch was alone with her a moment, these same Nephilim gathered about the body of the fallen queen and bowed their heads, honoring her. He had heard once, of Sandalaphon, that Asteria was as pure as any queen he had ever known, that she was as white and perfect as even the mothering star.

Now the Nephilim waited, wrapped against the cold in leather and fur. They waited calmly until Loch, Sandalaphon, and Hyacinth were come ashore.

Three horses had been brought, a large one—an Etlantian mount, dark and bred strong— for Sandalaphon, and two smaller, one of them light, steady, swift—a horse for Hyacinth—and the last a warhorse—a charger for Loch, black and shiny.

They mounted. Sandalaphon took up his reins, then studied Loch a moment.

"Ishmia is besieged," Sandalaphon said. "Your warlord, Eryian, has little time left before his life is taken. He is outnumbered and will certainly die. As always, time is thin, Angelslayer."

"As always," Loch answered back.

"We cannot follow, cannot help," Sandalaphon said.

"I understand—the edict of heaven."

Sandalaphon turned and lifted a silver cage from the hand of one of the riders. He lifted the door latch and held it high, letting the silver eagle soar into the sky.

"Why this?" asked Loch.

"We have followers, Etlantians. It is their messenger. The chosen of the Daath—the children, including the scion—must survive at all cost. The legions of your people will, of course, fight to the death, but that cannot save the chosen. Thus our brothers will come with seven ships—sailing for the docks of Terith-Aire. They will be marked of white sails and silvered armor over their hulls. They are your final hope—but should they reach the chosen in time, they will press for deep water, and the Unchurian, even the dark one, Azazel, cannot pursue in deep water."

Sandalaphon paused a moment then. Sadness leaked through his eyes, even as somber as they always were, a mist that might even have been tears—something Loch had never seen in him before.

"My time is almost finished here—one last task, but that shall be quick. I know the weight of heaven bears down upon you, Lochlain. I know you have turned against trying to understand heaven's path and I can hardly blame you—but that aside, what I say now is personal. Something I have never spoken in all these years."

"And what is that?"

"I care for you. Even from your birth—across these two decades I have cared for you. Deeply. I see the pain in your eyes and I stir inside, but I know you will stay true to the course. I know who you are. More than I, perhaps, in aeons past—more than I. We may not meet again in this life, Angelslayer, so I bid you farewell. I leave you Elyon's grace, Elyon's Light."

He lifted his hand in the sign of the word. After a moment, Loch did, as well. It was Sandalaphon who pressed forward to touch his palm against Loch's. He then drew back and looked to Hyacinth.

"My lady, all blessings I give you," he said.

"And you, Sandalaphon. I regret I could not have known you better."

"Heaven's grace, in time we may," he said with a slight smile. He then glanced at the others, and took up his reins. "Godspeed, both of you," he said and the five riders turned, heading north and east, the hooves of their horses barely brushing the earth as they galloped, swift, so swiftly they were soon out of sight.

At the top of the ridge, Loch circled his horse, staring below. The entire bay of Ishmia was flickering fire. They might have been campfires in the waters, but they were ships. Many were burning, but many more were not, and these were sailing for the port. The docks and wharfs of Ishmia had been destroyed, and what looked Etlantian warships were embedded into their ruins like a line of spears, forming new docks, new wharfs. Loch could see that when the galley reached them, hundreds of thousands of warriors waited to cross. And perhaps his heart was not entirely hardened, for a line of Daathan warriors, mostly shieldbearers, were holding against minions and skilled firstborn warriors. The bodies in the bay held testament of the battle that had raged there.

He then saw a small number, six or seven of his father's personal guard, fighting alongside an injured, weakened Eryian. All of the Daath remaining were locked in death grips. It would be over in moments alone. The killing was swift; the outcome certain.

"Your people, Loch—they have not a chance," Hyacinth said, watching below, "and there, from the south, even more coming!"

Loch glanced to the southern bay. It was a mass of ships, thick with triangular sails, thousands, more ships than he had ever seen gathered before.

He slowly drew the sword. As the Angelslayer came free of its sheath, it was not crystal or silvered. It was a solid, harsh light that brightened the area all around them.

"When I am done with this, Hyacinth, take me to my people," he said, meeting her eye.

"I will," Hyacinth whispered.

Loch curled both hands about the hilt of the sword. The muscles of his neck were stretched taut. He set his teeth tight against the coming pain, and then he screamed, leveling the sunblade.

There was a sound, an imploding *whumph*. Blue lightning simmered about Loch and Hyacinth, crackling. It formed a barrier between them and what the sword was becoming. Loch closed his eyes, focusing. He was shivering, he looked weak, and when Hyacinth saw him, she screamed, for blood spilled out of him everywhere, one stream from his temple, along his cheek, another from his lip, still another from his eye, and every drop formed lines that quickly wove themselves into the pommel of the blade's hilt. Hyacinth was forced to throw her arm over her eyes when the starstream burst from the sword.

As the minions closed on him, tearing through the last of the King's Guard, Eryian heard a thunderbolt so powerful it swallowed sound, snuffed it out, and left everything in a numbed emptiness—almost the most profound silence he had ever heard. A vacuum of silence, the very fabric of dark space, and then, like a breath, the sky sucked inward and then burst with the fire of a sun. He recognized this kind of fire. He had seen it before, felt it. It had burst from Righel's sword when it exploded in the body of Azazel. But this light was not random. It was as if it had eyes to search. Eryian watched living tendrils of white air taking out the minions, striking down from the sky and selectively vaporizing them. And when their skeletal bodies flashed to ashes, each of their spirit shadows were sucked upward to join the rising brilliance that had become the sky. A sun storm. Creation's fire. He stared amazed as the very air above the Isthmus caught fire and with terrible heat, broiling, destroyed everything above water. Eryian's men had to look away, shield their eyes. He alone was able to watch as every bit of debris, every ship, every floating corpse, was vaporized and sucked into a vortex that streamed skyward, left of the horsemen in the stars—the stream of light soared for the Seven Sisters, the Pleiades. When he looked back at the isthmus, the water was boiling.

Then, with a shudder of air—as though heaven's door had just slammed shut—it was over. The quiet that followed was a deafening cowl of numbness. Steam misted. There was nothing left of them. No ships, no highborns, no minions. It was not the end of the Unchurians—for across the far water he could still see their armies in the trees among the southern hills. But for this day, it was over. Many of Eryian's men dropped to their knees beside him.

For a moment, Ishmia remained as light as day, and the air glowed, silvery. Then, slowly, the night sky seemed to bleed through its tissue, and darkness closed like a word of mercy. Eryian searched the hillside where the sun strike had come from. He saw two riders. One, he knew, despite the distance, was Loch, the son of Argolis, still wearing Daathan armor and cloak. The other, he did not know. Eryian felt a shiver. The blade that had just spoken was the Angelslayer. The boy had become more powerful than Eryian could ever have guessed, yet, at the same time he saw the sword fall from his hand. The rider next to him, a girl, caught it, slipped it, still glowing a fantastic white, into the sheath at Loch's hip. She then took the reins of his horse. Loch fell forward, barely conscious, gripping the mane of his horse to stay in the saddle. The girl was leading them down the hillside, and when she was close enough, he recognized her face: the little pirate whose poison had dropped even him.

Chapter Fifty-Two
Satrina and the Little Fox

It was night when Rhywder reached the city, breathless, weary, his lungs rasping. From the white spiral of light that had spun into the sky for the Pleiades, he expected to find nothing. That had been star fire, capable of vaporizing the entire city, and from the distance it had looked as though the sky itself had sucked Ishmia into oblivion. But as he got closer, he saw houses, a few hearth fires, life. As he staggered through the streets, his legs at one point buckled, gripped in painful spasms since he had run so hard and so long to reach here. Slowly he pulled himself to his feet, leaned against a stone pillar to rest.

He stared at the ruins of a burnt-out villa. It looked as though it had been struck by a comet; the roof was caved in, the door and one set of shutters lay in the street where they had been thrown clear by an explosion. The catapult rock still glowed amid the embers.

Rhywder turned and staggered forward. He began to search for the villa where they had taken Satrina. He knew the color, he knew about where it should be, but so many of the houses were gutted, it was difficult finding his path. The cobblestone was lit eerily in dying embers. In places flame still cast and unsteady shadow.

He staggered past a fish vendor's shop. The vendor, naked, lay dead across one of the counters, and fish were scattered, crushed and stinking. Rhywder stared a moment. Sitting sleepy-eyed in the corner, belly fat and fish heads littered about him, was a small minion. It looked to have eaten itself into a stupor.

Rhywder backed slowly away, then turned.

As he walked, fire weaved a tapestry glow against the sky. Doors and shutters of intact houses were lashed and bolted. Ishmia was emptied; there were only scattered Daathan warriors and the dead left now. He could not piece together what had happened. The Unchurians had reached the city, but for some reason, they had not held it. Ishmia, damaged as she was, remained in Daathan hands, and the fire stream he had witnessed came not from a Watcher's sword, but from somewhere else. There could be but one possible answer. Loch. He had been found or returned. The star fire could only have come from the sword of Argolis.

Rhywder knew he must be close to where Satrina was to have been taken. Parts of the street made sense. When he heard a noise from a villa he paused. He stepped onto the porch and knocked on the door. "I am Lochlain," he said. "Not an enemy. I need only direction."

The voice that answered sent a shiver along his skin. It was a woman's voice, parched as though from thirst: "Go away."

Rhywder slowly backed from the villa, then turned into the street. The deeper into the city he got, the worse it looked. He saw dead scattered, civilian dead, some already gnawed by dogs. He kept swallowing his panic. He paused before a horse trough and knelt to splash water across his face to keep focus. He stood dripping. The villa was just up this street, he was almost certain. He just wasn't certain he could go on. On the cobblestone just beyond the trough was a pool of sticky blood, a thick pool, clotted over with a film.

Something attacked. Rhywder spun about, his sword drawn, only to find a dog. It was a yapping, insane dog, and it seemed to unnerve him even more than a minion might have. The small, mange-furred animal shot under his blade, and before Rhywder could flinch, it sunk its jaws into his ankle.

"Ahhh! You little bastard!" Rhywder kicked the animal airborne. It slammed into the wooden side of a candle shop, then scrambled onto spindly legs, barking with obsession, a small, rattish creature so furious and active it seemed mounted on springs.

Rhywder sheathed the sword and continued on, but the animal dogged him with incessant, manic yelping, at times bravely shooting forward to nip at Rhywder's heels.

"This has become ludicrous!" Rhywder screamed at one point, spinning around and again kicking the creature into the air. It somersaulted and rolled—a ball of dirty fir. It went down behind a stone fence and for a moment Rhywder thought that was the end of it, when suddenly, it sprang back up, yelping with renewed vigor. At least it had guts.

Rhywder tried to ignore it. He turned, weary, feeling sick. His stomach was coiling in knots. He paused—this was it. This was the villa he had chosen for Satrina. In the street outside of the villa lay a slain guard. His bowels were spread along the wood porch.

"Ah, love of God," Rhywder moaned. If something had happened to her, he could not bear it.

The Little Fox leapt the stone hedge, then sprinted, ripping open the door, stepping inside. He stood, out of breath, panic gripping him as he searched. A table was overturned; a body was hunched over in the corner. Rhywder half-moaned as he continued to search.

"Satrina," he whispered, not yet daring to speak.

Panic was hot and quick, and then melted to a sinking feeling, a hopeless dread.

Slowly he sank to his knees, unable to search for her body, his nerve for once, failing. Tears came, spilling from his eyes uncontrollably.

"Rhywder," she whispered softly from the shadows.

He looked up. Satrina stood in a doorway, watching him, holding the child, still wrapped in its blue cloak.

"Satrina!"

She laid the child in a wicker basket, and Rhywder was on his feet. He stepped forward and pulled her close, burying his face in her tangled hair. For a time he but held her, let the warmth of her soothe him.

"There was fighting here, but we survived, me and the little one."

He stepped back, traced her cheek, then dropped against the wall and slid to sit with his head propped back, weary. She sat down beside him in the shadows and held his hand.

Rhywder's hand was calloused and hard and blunt, but the smell of him beside her was something she wouldn't have traded for anything in the world.

They both ended up staring at the creature in the doorway, bristled on skinny haunches, its dark eyes blinking through tangles of hair.

"A friend of yours, Rhywder?"

Rhywder drew back his lip in a snarl, and the creature was tripped into insane, manic yelping, bouncing on its paws. Satrina chuckled.

Chapter Fifty-Three
Water Bearer

When Loch opened his eyes, he had to search his memory to recall where he was. Ishmia. When he focused, the three captains within the room knelt, bringing their fists to their chest. A fourth quickly left, possibly to summon Eryian. Loch found himself in a great, oaken bed, a palace room thick in gray stone and warm from a full fire in the hearth. Beside the bed, Hyacinth stood, hands folded in front of her. She looked very relieved that he was awake. She sighed.

"We have assumed she is with you, my lord," said Mammanon from the doorway. Loch recognized him as one of the captains of his father's personal guard. A Shadow Walker lord.

"She is," Loch answered.

The big axeman nodded. He slowly brought his fist to his shoulder, bowing his head to Hyacinth. He then turned to Loch. "Eryian sends Elyon's grace, my lord."

"Have we turned them?"

"Thinned them out a bit, but if I were to trust my own fears, they would be spawning new numbers in the hills beyond the isthmus right now. There seems no end to them."

Loch eased back against the headboards.

"Anything I can do for you, my lord?"

Loch stared at him a moment. The axeman was weary, bloodstained from battle.

Endgame was like a smell here. "Any bloodroot about?" Loch asked.

"This is Ishmia; there is no shortage of bloodroot wine here. I will have a cask brought up." He gestured to a guard who turned with a flair of his shadow cloak.

"Galaglea?" Loch asked.

"Burned. We could not have reached them in time, not with the fall of Hericlon."

"Were there survivors?"

"Some, though they are few. There is a small camp east, near the sea."

Loch pulled himself forward and allowed Hyacinth to help him to his feet. "I'll need a horse, Mammanon."

"I will see to it, my lord."

Mammanon turned and lowered his head to Hyacinth, then strode from the room. His guards followed, and the door was closed.

Hyacinth turned to watch Loch carefully. "You are going to search for the red hair?"

"I must." He lifted the belt and sheath of the Angelslayer from the bedpost.

"I will wish, for you—that she still lives."

He buckled the clasp, then paused to study her a moment. "I have always felt her, but I feel nothing now. It is doubtful, but thank you for such words, Hyacinth. You have changed a great deal, do you know that?"

She nodded. "Death will do that to a person, I suppose. Still, I have not changed as much as you." She reached to touch a strand of silvery hair that curled past his temple. The night-black hair had begun to turn, as some of the elder Daath, into a silvery sheen. "It is aging you quickly now. I would think you could fire only once or twice more and you would reach your end. Please be careful, my love. Keep your palm from its hilt. It is like a beast to me, a beast hungering for you. It seeks more than your blood; it seeks now your soul."

"This palace is surely well guarded. You will be safe until I return."

"I can attest to that, Daath are everywhere, all around every corner. They make me terribly nervous, Lochlain. Are you sure I cannot come with you? You might need me—assassins, I can smell them."

He shook his head.

"I say again you might need me, my king."

"Not for this."

She nodded. "Just . . . do not leave me here long. Alone—with them. Promise."

"My word. But you need not fear them. You are their queen."

"The red-hair was their queen—I will not even be remembered, but I am your queen, Loch. I am yours until the end."

"Your Book of Angels speaks of the Water Bearer's son, but when I feel the futures, I feel two of them. Two that shall lead—one born of fury; one born of strength. I believe the Angelslayer shall bring the storm, but it is the other, the second, who will ride it. It is a future marked of two queens." He softly touched her cheek, then turned.

"Loch . . ." She started for him, but he was already gone. When the door closed behind him, she slowly slid down the stone to sit against it, curling her toes into the thick rug. She laid her head back and closed her eyes. What he had said terrified her. Partly because she felt it in her, and partly because she felt she could never bear a son like that, a son that could ride Aeon's Storm.

Loch rode slowly among the refugees. There were no more than forty or fifty—tired faces, sleeping children. Loch could feel their sadness. He had paused, tingling, seeing a girl whose back was to him. Long red hair spilled over white shoulders, but when she turned, she was far too young. She had stared at Loch openly, frightened. Loch stepped from the saddle, then came to one knee and offered his hand. She hesitated, her mother moving closer, and when her hand touched his fingers, he gently kissed it.

"Elyon's grace take your sorrow," he said.

He mounted and rode through the rest of the camp at a trot. She was not going to be here, in this scattering of broken Galagleans. Adrea was not among them.

Alone, Loch rode along the shore, watching the twilight bleed stars. Sensing he was being followed, he drew up the reins and turned the horse. It looked like a scout approaching, no silver armor, just dusted, stained leather and wild red hair. He recognized the figure instantly. He was only mildly surprised to find his uncle still alive. The Little Fox of Lochlain had always been hard to kill.

Rhywder drew up before his nephew and stared at him a moment, taken by the change in his face, his eyes. No longer a boy, no longer common at all. The Daath had a king, an able king, far more powerful than Argolis had been. "You have changed, boy," Rhywder said.

"Time has gotten thin—have we not all changed a bit?"

Rhywder paused. Even the boy's voice was different—edged and certain. "Aye," answered Rhywder, "that is has."

"How did you find me?"

"When I heard you were in the city, I guessed you would come here."

Loch studied Rhywder carefully, sensing what he was about to say.

"I know about the Water Bearer," Rhywder told him. "I know where she is."

"Alive?"

"In a way."

"How do you mean that?"

"Spellbound—one of the magicks I happen to know of." He handed Loch a small, leaden box. "The ring," he said.

"Why is it not on her finger?"

"To keep her hidden it lies in that box. It is lined in golden, spellbound foil—not mine, but gold of the Watcher, Sandalaphon. The ring cannot be seen even by those with shadow sight. I suppose it should be with the child, as it was with you after Asteria died."

"You speak as if already she is dead."

Rhywder did not answer. "Come, I will take you to her."

The horses danced outside of a simple, wooden cottage—ordinary, even poorly kept. A good choice for hiding—set in the center of a forest clearing, well back from the city. It was bared and bolted. Loch stared at it, though Rhywder could detect no emotion on his face.

"How bad?" Loch asked. "Does she suffer?"

Rhywder tightened his jaw. "She sleeps. It was a minion got to her. We killed it, but there was a lot of her blood when I lifted her."

"How does she survive?"

"I used a particular magick on her. Rare, few even know of it. It is Unchurian; I learned it of a witch. They know death, the witches of Unchuria, they learn all its secrets of their lord. This one gave this secret for her life."

"Explain this magick."

"There is a potion used by the Unchurian priests—usually for torture. They can cut you, peel the skin off slowly, for days letting the tissue beneath dry in burning pain. There is no finer torture because you do not die. I killed a priest back there in Hericlon, inherited his potions, and the powders needed were among them. It is meant for torture, but I have used it to keep her alive, adding a second spellbound herb that would leave her sleeping."

"Why go to such trouble if she lies so near death?"

"Let us say I guessed I might see you again and further guessed you would wish to bid her farewell." Rhywder reached in his belt pocket and pulled out a small crystal the color of dried blood. "When you break this crystal over her, the spell-binding potion will be neutralized. That should wake her—but when she wakes," Rhywder paused, "when she wakes, it is short time before she dies. Moments only. I am sorry, Loch, I could do no more."

Loch moved his horse closer and took the crystal from Rhywder's fingers. He curled it into his fist. "My thanks, uncle. You can leave me now."

"It is not safe, even here. We have held back the Unchurians for now, but not their assassins. They make their way through; they kill at random. We have lost many able Walkers. I should wait, watch over you."

"They find me—they welcome death."

Rhywder paused. "I suppose you have a point." Rhywder lifted the reins and backed the horse away. "Faith's Light, my king," Rhywder said as he turned the reins and rode away at a lope.

✝

Loch lifted the heavy bolt of the door and dropped it. It opened with a whine as he stepped inside. It was a hunter's cottage, lit only by moonlight. In the shadows, Adrea lay on a simple bed, a thick, Galaglean quilt over her body. Her hair was soft across the pillow, played out. She looked perfect, beautiful, her skin porcelain. Loch walked to her side, then knelt. He lifted his fist and crushed the Unchurian crystal, letting a vapor of dark blood spill over her.

Adrea's eyes flicked open and she took a breath as through breaking water. She searched quickly, frightened; she cried out in pain, arching her back, and Loch gently touched her shoulder.

She searched the darkness of the room, panicked. "Seraphon? Where is Seraphon?"

"You need not fear for him. He is well protected now."

At his voice she turned, startled.

"Lochlain . . ." she whispered. She lifted her hand, weakly, to touch his face, but the pain again seized her and she cried out in a soft whisper.

He let a soft pulse of blue light pass from his fingers to hers. When it did, Loch lowered his head, closing his eyes. Adrea slowly eased back.

"What . . . what did you just do?"

"Took your pain," he said. He sucked breath against the pain now in him. It was strong as it rippled through him. It was no wonder she had cried out. But Loch had gotten used to pain. He looked up through dark, Shadow Walker eyes.

"You have changed," she said. "You are so different from when we last touched."

"More than I ever wished, I am afraid." He stroked her hair. It was so soft, silken. "Adrea, I am sorry."

"For what?"

"Everything."

"As you once told me, Loch, we had no choice. If I have learned anything from you, from the ring, from the birthing of your scion, I have learned that all of it was truth. The path is marked of heaven's grace. It is all truth, Loch. All you have shown me, all you believed. Faith's Light, my love, and you will you find your way." She had to pause to take breath. Even without pain, breathing was difficult. "I am dying?"

He nodded.

"Seraphon . . . I will not see little Seraphon again . . ."

"Not in this world."

Tears fell. "Promise me, Loch, swear to me he will be cared for—more than protected, as you were, but that he will be loved."

"I promise."

She turned slowly to gaze at him. "You have aged. You look as old as your father."

"It is the sword."

She studied him a moment, searching his eyes. "Yes, that and taking her, bringing her back from death—the priestess."

"You know?"

"As brave as you are, you have one weakness; you fear to walk alone. Even though it is your path, still you fear it. But you will learn. You are the Voyager, my love; in the end you will understand who you are."

His eyes misted. It surprised him. He thought all emotion had been taken from him just as the blood sucked through the pommel of the Angelslayer, but suddenly it flooded him and he remembered the love he bore for her, the love they had shared through worlds he could no longer name.

She gasped—her breath short. She watched a tear run across his cheek and was able to reach up, take it in her fingers. "Sometimes . . ." she whispered, "when I was alone and frightened, there was a place I would go. A place where we reached the ship that day. We outran the assassins, and the ship sailed into the deep waters of the Western Sea where we found it, the island of Enoch, and there we looked into the eyes of God." She half-smiled. "Have you ever gone there? Have you seen that future?"

He shook his head.

"We lived long there. We learned to know each other's thoughts in this world's flesh, to love each other beyond merely our memories, and we changed. We grew old. It was a good thing, a good place, Loch. It was a life well lived—a long life."

Her breath was shallow as she lifted her hand, spreading her fingers in the sign of the word. He lifted his own to meet them, and then, as she had once before in a dream, she curled her fingers tightly into his.

"When it is ended," she said softly, "if Earth survives Aeon's End—you can find me if you wish. I will be there—that place, the place where the ship would have taken us—I will wait for you there, on the island. As long as it takes you to find me, I will wait for you, Voyager." The light from her eyes left quietly. Loch slowly lowered his head until it rested against her shoulder and for a long time, he did not move.

Chapter Fifty-Four
Bloodstone

Satrina was sitting against the wall, watching the child as he slept. She stared at him, fascinated. He seemed so beautiful, so peaceful. Sleeping, his eyes closed, he might almost have been an ordinary child. She crawled over to lift the blanket to his shoulders, and as she did, he turned, curling into it.

When there was a knock at the villa door, Satrina got up, walked to the door, and opened it without looking. She believed there could be no danger if the child was sleeping. If there would have been danger, he would have wakened and warned her. But she was startled nonetheless, and stared a moment openly. She knew without asking who this was. The face of the child—it was much like his. The dark eyes, the cut of the cheekbone.

She bowed her head and stepped back. "My lord," she said, but was surprised when he touched her shoulder.

"No, I do not come as your lord. I may never have been a lord, or a king. It was never my path. Please, just call me Loch."

His eyes were hard to look at directly, so intense, dark as night, and yet there was a ring of light about their edge that left a chill through her. She thought she could see through them, a different soul, far more tender than the Shadow Walker, a singer.

"I am Satrina."

"Yes, I know."

"Come," she said, and led him into the room where the infant lay sleeping. "This is Seraphon; this is your son. I suspect he is the reason you are here."

Loch stepped near the bed, staring, though the cloak hid Seraphon's face. Satrina started to pull it aside, but he caught her hand. When she looked to him, it startled her to see a single tear openly fall, even from the dark eyes of a Shadow Walker. It was a tear of the singer that had retreated deep within. He then took her wrist and placed the leaden box in her hand. He curled her fingers about it before she could speak. "When he is of age, you will know to open this and give him what is inside. Only he can find the one who must bear it. Until that time, keep it always on your person. I name you the Ringbearer, Satrina. Teach him. Teach him of the light and the splendor; teach him all you know, for his path will not be easy. His destiny will come with the rain of fire. You must teach him well, for he must walk the edge of Aeon's End."

"Yes, of course, but my lord, have you not made some mistake? I am no one special. I am a barmaid; my father a drunk, a gambler. I am not royalty, far from it. How can you name me the Ringbearer of a king?"

"I see your eyes, your soul. You will give him what his mother asked. A mother's love, it is in your eyes. You are the one."

He looked one more time at the child, and seemed about to say more, but suddenly turned. His cloak flared, and he left the door open behind him. He was gone before she realized he had moved. He had vanished into shadow as the Daath were said to do. Satrina looked down and opened her palm. It was a carefully wrought plain leaden box, small, the hinges tiny, but still she shivered. She could almost sense what was inside. She knew enough of the legends of the Daath, of their kings and their queens—this was the ring of the Water Bearer—the bloodstone of the Daath from the seven centuries they had dwelt on Earth. They had been sent as the protectors, and this was the ring of their last queen. Sensing movement, she turned to the crib. Slowly, she withdrew the coverlet. Seraphon was staring up at her, watching carefully, as if he understood perfectly all that had just transpired. She clutched the box tightly in her hand.

"Little one," she whispered, "I fear your father has just made a terrible error in judgment."

Chapter Fifty-Five

Ice

Eryian paused in the hallway of the palace, tingling with alarm. He was alone, using a bronze walking crutch. His leg was bound in a wooden cast, lashed with leather. The hallway before him was quiet; the wall brackets of the torches had been torn loose. The stone here was a sweating cold, frosted in the corners. There was also a smell, something vague but noxious, something that bristled his skin as he continued, making his way down the corridor.

He stopped before the dark hole of the chamber where he had last seen Krysis. The door was gone, but for splinters of wood at the hinges. In the hall were the bodies of two Shadow Walkers, both warriors prime, one thrown back against the stone and seemingly crushed into it, the other basically cut in half.

A chill left him numb as he entered the room. There was blood on the walls. Lines of it glistened where moonlight caught it still damp.

The bed had been pushed to one corner of the room and its center was caved in.

A hand dangled over its edge, small, white, with painted nails. Feathers and down from the mattress were torn and bloodied, scattered, some drifting with the cold wind from the window. He didn't want to know this; he didn't want to see more. He started toward the bed, forgetting to use the crutch, and fell, wincing in pain as the leg twisted. He straightened, pulled himself onto one knee.

Krysis's eyes were open, dulled, staring upward. She had died in a scream, her golden hair flung across the coverlet, her head to the side. There was a deep gash through her breast, cutting deep through muscle, and blood still oozed. Her legs were askew over the back of the bed. A bedpost had been rammed between them, still in place.

Eryian quickly turned away. He knelt a moment, taking quick, hard breaths, then he slammed his fist against the stone with a scream.

There was a whisper, a voice as quiet as soft wind.

"Time to come home, star jumper."

In the night, at the edge of an empty street, Eryian waited, leaning against the walking cane. He watched calmly as a warrior rode toward him from the cluttered villas beyond. When Eryian stepped into the light, the Daath warrior pulled up on the reins, startled.

"My lord," he gasped.

"Your horse," Eryian said. When the warrior hesitated, Eryian stepped forward, grabbed the man by his belt, and wrenched him out of the saddle. He mounted, drew up the reins, and turned to ride at a fast trot toward the dock, gripping the mane for balance when the horse broke into a gallop.

Near a lamp maker's shop, which was looted but still intact, he pulled the horse up, circled about, then urged the charger onto the wooden porch. He kicked in the door with his good leg, leaned forward, and rode in. Hooves clattered on hollow wood. He straightened in the saddle and searched. He kicked aside a table that had been displaying glass oil lamps, then pulled up near a wall of shelves and clay vessels. He scooped a handful of the thick oil paste, and smeared it first over his face, then his forearms and legs. He rubbed oil into his hair until the silver was matted and black. He then turned the horse and leaned forward as he rode beneath the doorway.

The horse pranced, spooked as it rode into the street, then broke into a gallop. Eryian's silver breastplate clattered across the stone when he flung it aside, then the back plate.

He rode toward the docks, and there, as the horse picked its way through the course, Eryian searched. He leaned in the saddle to pluck away dark Unchurian armor. He gathered weapons. The saltwater was soaked into the wood in places, and the bodies sloshed. Eryian found a boathouse still intact and rode into it, then rode out, dragging an oar boat. He pulled it to where the dock slid into the water and rode the horse until the water was up to its neck. Using his good leg, he swung over the saddle, then rolled into the boat. He now wore a dark cloak, cowled, and armor that swallowed the night. He straightened himself, then pulled the cowl over his head and took up the oars. He began stroking. Even deep into the bay, the water was ashen with a film that left the oars stained black at the tips. It was snowing, and the moon was against far, white clouds. The snow seemed to settle into the dark water as though it had never been there.

On the opposite bank, black water lapped about the edge of the boat as Eryian dropped over the gunwale and waded to shore. He had lashed the splints as tightly as possible, even cutting off blood flow to his foot, but that would no longer matter soon.

The snow was thick and lazy; it seemed to leave warmth as Eryian made his way through the trees that lined the shore. The entire shore was littered with the cindered husks of ships, dark against the white clouds of night. He made his way south, using his leg despite pain, and moving rather quickly, keeping always to the thickest wood. The priests rode the trees. In Hericlon's vale, he had watched their shadowy figures and realized the priests of Unchuria made themselves shadow, using a force of will to blend with the dark of forest. Eryian paused, pressing back against a thick, bowled cedar trunk. He could hear a heavy crunch of leaves, a horse coming from the left, riding slow. Eryian stilled as death was still, and watched as a figure rode through the white puffs of snow, searching. Suddenly it pulled the reins taut and froze, seeing Eryian.

This was one of the marked, a priest, cowl drawn. He watched Eryian with confusion, perhaps awe. He was trying to read Eryian, searching, but Eryian fed the priest only his pain. From the rider's saddle tassel hung a dulled, gray throwing axe. Nothing moved but the snow. Nothing breathed. The rider then shot his hand back and the axe was snapped from the tassel. The horse reared. Eryian calmly lifted his arm and a crossbow bolt ripped out the back of the Unchurian's cowl after driving through the face. It sounded as though the bolt had struck a water flask.

✝

Eryian rode cloaked, the Unchurian's throwing axe lashed to the side of his splinted leg. All his weapons were concealed. He rode slowly, the horse's hooves soundless in the snow as he wove among the trees, and Eryian *was shadow.*

He followed a dulled, aching vision in his mind of a tent, with staffs carved in salamanders. It would be centermost in the first Unchurian camp. He could feel the air now as though it were a living thing, something easy to follow.

As he rode from the forest, he could make out the dark shape of ramparts thrown up in a clearing. This was one of hundreds, of thousands, but it was here he would find the demon, the one lord of the high choir, now fallen, lower than the Earth. If Elyon's Light were with him, surely such a creature could be slain, but Elyon was far. Eryian had lost Him; he came with only his skill, his weapons, and a plan to use the one small weakness Azazel had exposed, to use it to the fullest. Eryian rode calmly beneath the manned archway, and the guards but glanced down as Eryian passed below. He rode for the center, in line with Hericlon's vale.

He rode quietly. None of the warriors in the camp even looked in his direction. Either they did not see him, or when they did, they took him for one of the marked ones, the quiet ones. Eryian never looked to the side. He rode calmly, one hand on his thigh, near the cloak.

An Unchurian warrior suddenly stepped in his path, but Eryian only veered the horse slightly, slipping past. Eryian turned his horse up a wagon-gutted roadway, then started up a slight hill toward the purple and blue pavilions on top.

Here the ground was soft in snow. There had been no tracks on this road since sundown, and the snowfall was heavy. Above, there were no guards near the pavilion—none were needed. An angel waited here, but even Azazel would not sense Eryian coming. Eryian was not there; he was only shadow—there were things in his time he had learned that were beyond human, and he was about to employ them all. The pavilion stood alone, in silence, firelight illuminating it from within. To either side of the entrance, staffs bore the emblems of the salamander.

Eryian pulled up on the reins. He had reached the crest, on a level with the tent. There was no snow here. Near the tent, the ground was dark and barren.

Eryian brought his leg about and slid off the horse. Above, he saw starlight. The clouds were thick; they had covered the night sky since he left Ishmia, but here a hollow pierced the cloud cover, high and centered.

He drew back the dark cloak and laid one hand on the ivory hilt of one sword. Eryian could see within the edge of the tent. Eryian took a step, then dragged his leg forward and took another step. More and more of the tent came into view. It was unadorned, empty, and the ground was dirt. The flaps were parted. The Salamander, the Reaper, the being who once stood before the face of God among the choir of the Auphanim, was seated in a throne of black iron, watching Eryian with smoked, mesh eyes, as still as stone. It seemed he was just waiting there with no look of surprise, no expression whatsoever.

Eryian took several steady breaths, then forced his mind inward, and with all his strength, in his mind he pierced through the veil of the meshed eyes, and with his sprit he spoke, not to the Reaper, Azazel, who had crafted death, but to the mortal coil of flesh he had taken as his shield in this last ploy against heaven. For all his power the demon had one weakness: he was not of angel's flesh—he had taken a mortal body prisoner, possessed it, and the human who once dwelt there was crushed somewhere inside. But Azazel would have chosen a strong one, even a king or a prince, a warlord; he could take any human he wanted, no matter their strength, so he would have chosen the strongest he could find. And Eryian, searching quickly, found his spirit, lost inside, imprisoned in a kind of mist of darkness and void. He had been devoted to his father, Azazel. He was, amazingly, truly a king. Azazel had taken the body of his own firstborn son, Menelagor, the king of all Unchuria, the lord of the south, the Given, blessed at birth by his father and the Star Walker Queen that was his mother, destined for all glory, now crushed into a dark cavern, lost and confused. Suddenly, Azazel realized what the warlord was doing, and for a moment, Eryian saw the meshed eyes flicker, uncertain. Eryian lifted his arm and fired the crossbow.

"Menelagor!" Eryian screamed, more than just words, a spellbound command to bring him forth, cast in the Light of Severity.

The bolt jerked the body, slamming deep into the chest, and the Salamander hissed between his teeth—as the same time something had flickered in the eyes, a moment's focus, the blinded Menelagor.

"Amen-Omen-Diaman, in the word of the *Light Whose Name Is Splendor,* I command your spirit forth, mortal, Menelagor, the king of all the southland, come, I command you to fill your skin!"

It would be a hard spell to resist, and Azazel would be forced to turn his mind to pushing it back, holding the prisonor inside intact.

Eryian continued walking, moving quicker now, casting his cloak aside. From his back he drew a second crossbow and destroyed the left eye, the blunt iron dart shattering the bone at the back of the skull. Eryian threw both crossbows aside, still walking.

"Stay with me, mortal—come forth, take your skin, and I will bring you the peace of death."

Menelagor moaned, a sick, dry moan, the shriek of a dead man. His spirit, for a moment, seemed to mold into the face, changing its shape and leaving the eyes dead sockets—the meshed, almost starry gaze of Azazel was for seconds gone, taken by a ploy he had not guessed. In all of the futures he could have foretold, this one the angel had not seen.

Eryian ripped the axe from its tie and flung it with a snap of his wrist. It anchored the throat against the wooden neck of the throne. The body jerked in spasm.

"Stay with me—look through my eyes, Unchurian! Menelagor, keep focus on my spirit, my eyes. Stay in your flesh, for I am about to deliver to you your freedom from the darkness."

Eryian passed through the tent flaps. From a back scabbard, with both hands he flung knifes. Menelagor seemed to welcome them as they pierced his lungs. He began to whisper; perhaps it was a prayer of his own—if this breed had ever been taught prayer. The half-human king was in his flesh now. He held his arms out in supplication, waiting to be delivered.

Eryian pulled a battle axe from a belt tie, snapping the leather. "Welcome death," he said, focused on the spirit now breathing through the gray flesh. Time was quick, time was slow, but as Eryian lifted the axe to cut the spine, time closed.

Azazel, with a scream of fury at being tricked, spilled through the hollowed eyes like a wind of the darkest winter. Eryian was staggered. The axe spun from his fingers into the night.

The Reaper pulled his throat free of Eryian's axe, though it tore out part of the neck.

"No!" Eryian screamed. He reached to his back scabbard and drew a second blade—this one white steel. He stepped forward, bringing the sword in an arc. The Salamander hissed, deflecting the blow, though it sliced through the tips of the fingers, shearing them off. A side of Menelagor's head was cut away, spinning off with a dark knot of hair flying.

Then it was over.

Something slammed into Eryian's back, knocking the breath from him, shattering bone. In a moment sight was gone, grayed, and then Eryian found himself on his back—he had been sucked into the earth. His arms were pinned. His leg split through the cast to reach stone. Eryian could no longer move. The earth about him shattered with a sharp crack, and a slab of stone slowly lifted upward, tilting, until Eryian could stare into the face of the his ancient nemesis. He had damaged Azazel once again, leaving his face almost halved, leaving him bloodied along one side, something watery from the wound in the skull. Azazel ripped out the crossbow bolt from his eyes and now, despite the blood, both eyes glossed over with the moist spider mesh of the demon. They instantly burned to life, black but light, somehow connected to the far dark star of the universe.

Azazel sucked away Eryian's breath.

"Clever, star lord," he whispered. "Almost you did it. Almost you turned me. And all by whispering Elyon's name and the mothering star as if her light still touched our heart. Worthy, my friend, I will give it that. A worthy effort, but in the end, we always knew whose name you truly whispered. You believe the death you have wrought leaves no mark on your soul?"

Eryian felt the blue light receding. It was lifeblood, it was the light of sunblades, and losing it was a lot like drowning—like his first death, when he fell to flesh and Daathan blood seven centuries ago. *The knowing* lifted from his chest leaving him empty, and that left tears in his eyes.

"You came in fury—that was your error, fool. She told you the secret of your redemption, fallen one, but you would not listen; the years have made you too proud. Much like me. It was not the name of Light, not the Splendor—it is the name of my lord that will now press against your lips. Hail, Light Bearer, hail, he who was prince of all heavens! The war has not ended, and Earth is its final killing ground. We stand ready for them—even the archangels. And besides, now you will join us. How can we fail?"

Eryian could hear them, the others, the thousands, the millions who had fallen, the Uttuku. They seemed to welcome him, and their voices were like ice.

Chapter Fifty-Six
Guardians

Rhywder filled his haversack with dried meat and bread cakes from the villa's pantry. Satrina stood by the door with the child bundled, held fast against her.

"Will you be with us, Rhywder?" she said.

"I will be close. In any event, the full Second Century of the Daath are sworn to protect you, the child, and the chosen."

"The chosen?"

"Always they have prepared for this moment. The strongest and brightest of their children. It is a sacred number; along with the child, it becomes seventy and seven, and you will be in their center, so I am certain you will not be lonely, Satrina."

"It is not loneliness I fear; it is you, off on some heroic last stand to die."

"I wish I could stay, my love, but I am afraid I must ride with my king. If it is true that he sends me on some heroic last stand to die, then yes, but our stand now will be these children, to get them to the ships of Etlantis that remains their only hope."

Eryian was missing. In one of his last orders, the warlord had sent the king's personal guard, all that was left of them, to ring like an iron fortress of armor and shields, the scion, the Ringbearer, and the chosen seventy and seven. A maniple of fine warriors they could not afford to lose had insisted on riding in search of Eryian, but Rhywder did not believe they would find their warlord. When he had heard what had happened to Krysis, he guessed Eryian's last move.

He was about to open the door when Satrina laid her hand on his wrist. She waited until he met her eyes. "I have been wondering, Rhywder, and I wish to ask you—what is going to happen to all of us? The Unchurians are just going to keep coming. Nothing can stop them, not even the walls of Terith-Aire or even the ships of Etlantis."

Rhywder stared at her a moment. "One thing I have learned. You live the battle when it comes, you take what is given you, and you fight for what you believe. You leave the rest to Elyon. In the end, the battle is always His. Let Him work out the details of how the sun shall rise in the morning." Rhywder lifted the latch, then drew open the door. He paused, a bit startled.

The street was filled with Shadow Warriors—the best, the finest. These were the first blood of the King's Guard; they had been well hardened of war, and even this last carnage had not shaken them. Bloodstained armor glittered stark in the sunlight; horses shifted. The first captain, broad-shouldered and weighted in age, Rhywder knew to be Tillantus. His eyes were stern. Rhywder knew the loss of Eryian was hard on him, but no pain would dull his resolve. More than the warriors, what surprised Rhywder were the children. Gathered in the street, surrounded by the Daathan guard, were children—some young, some older. There were girls in the flower of youth, young warriors barely fitted for their armor. Rhywder stared at them, amazed. They all seemed so beautiful, so beyond the terrors of the last days that they seemed misplaced, out of time here among the smell of blood and sulfur. There were precisely seventy and six of them. Seraphon would make them seventy and seven, make them scripture. Rhywder swore he had never seen so many tender, innocent eyes gathered in one place.

Tillantus urged his mount forward, drawing up beside Rhywder. "Little Fox," he said. "We meet again."

"How did you acquire so many children?" Rhywder asked.

Tillantus only smiled. It faded quickly. "All I know is that these little ones the Unchurian will never see, so help my sword, my lifeblood, and Elyon's grace. There is more of heaven's light in this plaza than is gathered in all the world, and these men will deliver them safely."

Rhywder shivered—not from the children, but because he knew this was the last move, the last spoken tactic of the final battle. The children would be taken from Terith-Aire and hidden for another day, another future, a generation where the true final battle of Earth and the crossing of Aeon's End would come. Just as written, all had unfolded. What was left gave even Rhywder a dark feeling that clawed at his chest, but he blunted it. Some things Rhywder chose to put aside, and prophecy was one of them. It spilled all over this gathering of the chosen, but he turned it aside. Knowing prophecy was a weakness when your job was the sword or the axe or the bow. It was not a warrior's place to read the future.

He turned. Directly before the door, mounted, holding two horses in rein was Marcian's boy. He knew the name now; this was Lucian, son of Marcian Antiope and grandson of the fabled Moloch of Galaglea—carrying, in fact, the axe of that legendary figure. Rhywder briefly wondered if this one, Lucian, might be the only Galaglean warrior left alive. Their entire legion had fallen, the city burned, though there had been a few refugees. The fight and fires of the days before had left their scars on the boy, had lifted all youth from him. He might just as well be a full-blooded warrior now, and he was named, of his own request, in fact, his demand—Lucian was the guardian of the child Seraphon. Nothing would deter him, so Rhywder had blessed the calling, as well, telling the boy it was now ordained, and telling any others that should know.

"Your horses, Captain Rhywder," the boy said. He had two horses in rein; one for him, one for Satrina.

"Still alive, I see."

"Yes, I am still alive. My bruises are healing, my burns still sting, but I am as able as ever I have been."

Rhywder smiled. "Well, boy, you are a damned impressive fighter, I give you that—and here is your liege, Seraphon, and this is his Ringbearer, whose name is Satrina."

"Satrina, yes, I know of you. They told me of you. Know that I am here to guard my brother's life, and by extension yours, as well. I will not fall, I will not drop of axe or sword or spear, and I will keep him alive from this day until some later year when my body fails me. But my faith is firm—those who pursue us, they will not take my brother. Not this hour, not this day—not this fight. He will survive." Lucian lifted his hand in a fist, then slammed it against his chest in promise. He now bore full Daathan armor, and when he pulled on the helm, there was no longer any boy; there was a blood warrior waiting with strong, broad shoulders and a dark, sure-hafted killing axe at his side.

"I have no doubt," said Rhywder in answer, "that should any Unchurian make it through the second legion and breach the King's Guard surrounding these, the chosen, that you will be there to make them tremble."

"What is your name?" Satrina asked from where she was watching on the porch.

"I am called Lucian. I have two mounts, good mounts." Lucian turned to the captain. "This one—this one is yours, Rhywder of the Lake," the boy said, leading a dark stallion forward.

Rhywder marveled, noting the smooth muscular flanks. "That is quite a horse."

"Much of my father's stock was in Lucania. This one my father was very proud of—the breed line of this horse stretches back to my grandfather and beyond. This mount will serve you well. You have my word that he will take you where you need to go."

Rhywder took the reins and pulled himself into the saddle. The horse snorted, as though it were ready to run a race. Rhywder patted its neck. He noticed Lucian watching with a slight grin of satisfaction. It was his father's craft, horses such as these, and this was obviously one of the finest.

A Shadow Warrior was helping Satrina and the child into the saddle of a light, roan mare, obviously swift and able.

"Lucian," she said, "I am grateful you will be with us. The strength of your spirit offers comfort."

Lucian nodded. "Thank you, good lady."

Rhywder leaned forward to kiss Satrina's cheek, then turned the reins of his horse. "Watch the sky, Tillantus," he shouted. "Move at hard pace for Terith-Aire, but watch the shadows and the sky. The fliers have thick wings; you can hear them. They are capable of a dive that could take out one of these chosen even from the center, so keep your bowmen alert."

"Aye, my lord."

Tillantus watched, somber, as Rhywder left them, riding slowly back toward the city.

"Satrina, I shall see you when next I do!" the Little Fox shouted last before he was out of sight.

At a harsh cry from Tillantus, the horsemen of the second legion started forward. Lucian led Satrina's mount as she held the child. Satrina stared at the children following all about them. They were young, their skin sometimes tinted with the blue ice of a Daath, sometimes porcelain as a Galaglean, sometimes with the golden hair of a Lochlain, but all seemed so beautiful, so perfect, some clutched against the darkened silver breastplates, others riding their own mounts. The group was about half boys and half girls, and it was strange—there was a smell of youth to them, literally a smell of fresh rain, as well as light. Light was all about them, not light one could see or read by, but more like a part of the air they breathed. The chosen, she thought: the seventy and seven. As they moved through the outer streets of Ishmia, they were ringed in a wall of powerful, armored horsemen. Surely no harm could reach them.

Chapter Fifty-Seven

Mist

Hyacinth pulled up on the reins and searched ahead. She had heard mention of the Ithen, but this was nothing like she imagined. There were yellowwood and oak as old as the Earth, vines and creepers, and shadows—many shadows. This was a sacred forest; she could feel the knowing of the trees. Clustered about her were prime Daathan warriors, among them the gray-haired Daathan captain whom Loch had called Tillantus.

"Could you stop here a moment?" she said aside to the captain.

"Certainly, my lady." He motioned the others, and they drew to a halt.

Below, beyond the ancient forest, there was a narrow valley of sea grass, weaving in the soft wind. Cutting through its center was a well-used, paved road that led to the walls of Terith-Aire, and from here, as well, a view of the high-walled, spired city. The road was thick with people, and to either side of them, warriors. All were filing toward the city's its alabaster battlements. The thought left Hyacinth panicked.

"My lady," the captain said. "Is there a problem?"

"Before I go any farther, I must see Loch."

"That cannot be done, my lady. I do not know the whereabouts of your king, but we have orders to deliver you to the city. The Second Century is just below us, and you are to ride with the chosen."

Hyacinth pulled her horse about, twisting the reins. "I can sense him; I will find him myself."

As she turned her horse, her way was instantly blocked.

"I cannot let you do that," the captain said. He reached forward to take her reins, and Hyacinth quickly wrenched open the cheek guard of his helm. The sharp nail of her little finger left a scratch across his skin before he could react. He snarled and reached to catch her arm, but before he could move, Hyacinth's dagger tip was against a vein in his neck.

"We should come to an understanding, Captain. I am not one of your milk women!"

The captain narrowed his brow, then paused, looking past her. Hyacinth turned. It was Loch. It seemed he had appeared from nowhere.

Loch nodded to Tillantus. "Have the men circle wide, Tillantus, and leave several to wait for her beyond the clearing."

"Aye, my lord," Tillantus said, snapping his cheek guard into place. "And to you, my lady," he added, bowing from the saddle.

He turned and motioned to the others, and his men began moving through the trees. She dropped her knife into its sheath.

"Do you really think the walls of Terith-Aire are going to protect them?" she asked.

"No, but it is their best chance."

"Well, I am staying with you."

"That is not meant to be."

"Do not give me any more of your futures, Loch! I am not one of them, these Daath, all cold to me, like they have ice in their blood. The Tarshians were hard enough to endure; I cannot live with these, not without you, and I will not be shut behind their walls. You're the reason I'm still here. I'm not leaving you."

He rode forward, pulling up beside her. He had become hard to read, but as he watched, his eyes seemed to change, as though he had stepped into them for her—they softened. The warrior had receded for the moment; this was the Lochlain to whom she had first been attracted.

"Are they taking care of you?"

"Where have you been?"

"There are things I needed to finish."

"And are they finished?"

He nodded.

"Why are you not with the others—leading these legions?" she asked. "Are these not your armies? And you their king?"

"I am not here to command armies."

"Then what?" The quick eyes were demanding. "What are you here for?"

"To stop him."

"Him?"

"You know his name; you sensed him as well as I. We can speak it here; he is close enough it no longer matters. I must stop Azazel."

She could only gasp at first, speechless. "Alone?"

"How else? You believe armies are going to help?"

"How can you possibly stop an angel that has prepared for this moment, the taking of the Daath, for seven hundred years? How, Loch?"

"It is much as with Satariel, I do not know precisely how, but I sense it; I feel something drawing me. I believe I can find a way."

"Here? In these trees?"

"This forest is as ancient as life on Earth. It is the East of the Land; there is much magick here, much power, and none of it belongs to him. If I am to make a stand against this creature, this is my place of choosing."

She scanned the trees, realizing what he meant. "The East of the Land, the forest that borders the place where Elyon first touched His finger."

"Yes. These trees were witness. There is also an ancient structure here, a ring of stone, and something else; I believe it to have been a temple. One the first ever formed on Earth."

Her eyes then locked on his. "You knew even when you brought me back, you knew then you would come here—did you not?"

"No, I had a sense of the future, but until now I did not know."

"And so now you know and now you are planning to die here. Tell me that is not true."

He didn't answer.

"And you think I am going with them? I have no place with these Daath, Lochlain! I cannot stay with them. If you choose to die here, then in the name of your god, let me choose the same, with you, as I said I would be. What else have I to live for? What reason should I follow these horsemen and these warriors who mean nothing to me?"

"You have forgotten so soon?"

"What?"

"Your child."

"My . . ."

"You already carry him, Hyacinth. From the night on the island."

She paused, startled. She shook her head. "If I were with child, I would know! That was merely a signet of love; that was not taking your seed for a child. I could not have been fooled in that!"

He studied her, waiting, and suddenly Hyacinth realized that somewhere, inside, she did know. She had chosen, the light rain that night, the touch of him, somehow, far and away, she had chosen. "No," she whispered, "no. This was not supposed to be. I died—with them, on Ophur, and you should have left me. Loch, you should never have done this! I am not a bearer of children! I am not supposed to be here. I was never part of your prophecy! Enochian, all of them, their scriptures, their high words—I am no part of that!"

"I am sorry, Hyacinth, but you are. More than you know. You bear inside you a child, and you no longer have a choice of dying with me. Your place is in the center of the Second Century, with the chosen, for your child, as much as you might deny it, is one of their protectors. He must survive."

A tear ran freely along Hyacinth's cheek, and she made no move to stop it. "You tricked me."

He lifted his hand, touched her tear, and took it. "Perhaps. I have also loved you, without restraint, as much as her, as much as the red-hair."

"Damn you."

"Good-bye, Hyacinth."

"No . . . no, Loch. You cannot do this! No."

He slowly backed his horse away. "Do not try to follow. The child, Hyacinth. If you follow, it will be lost, and that cannot happen. Find the center where they keep the chosen, stay with them. If you do, your child will survive this day. Few others will, Hyacinth. So you have no choice."

"You bastard! Loch, you cannot leave me here!"

He held his hand in the sign of the word, but she did not respond. Instead she spat to the side. "There, that is for your god!"

"My love," he whispered finally, "farewell, little one," and then turned the horse.

"Nooo! You cannot leave me!"

The last she saw of his face, the warrior had returned; the eyes had darkened like night closing without stars. He quickened the pace, and his horse started moving swiftly, deeper into the trees.

"Loch!" she screamed and started to follow, but then paused, drew back. Tears streamed down her face, and never before in her life had Hyacinth felt her heart shatter so completely. She paused, glancing back toward the valley where Tillantus had left the cold Daathan warriors waiting to escort her. When she turned back, he was gone. The mist of the forest had swallowed him or he had vanished into his Shadow Warrior twilight.

"Loch!"

Only the forest answered.

"Damn you!" Hyacinth screamed, tears spilling unhinged.

Chapter Fifty-Eight
Star Temple

Loch's horse stepped through heavy mist between the ancient trees. The forest had swallowed all sound, but he could sense a steady rumble, growing closer now. The Unchurians would soon close on the forest of the East of the Land, and somewhere among them, the demon Azazel was searching with all his power for Loch, for the one that had lit the sunblade the night before. The sunblade sucked blood and life and aged him quickly, but it also gave back knowledge. Loch had cloaked himself like the dead of night. Even the angel Azazel would not sense him or the Angelslayer that hung at his hip.

He paused, searching, then turned the horse to step through the trees into a clearing. He had been here before. The standing stones. There was soft, quiet light to them. He understood it now. It focused unseen light, for though the forest was dark from the thick, overcast sky, and the light of the stones cast no shadow, these stones were still connected by a thin tendril to the moon, the mirror of the light of the mothering star, the eye of Daath.

He looked around. This was it, this was the place, and if you were to bring an army straight through to Terith-Aire, you would not veer westward and choose the King's Road, you would bring them through here, through these trees. The city had been built in line with this circle of stone. It had once, when the Daath were younger, centuries ago, drew power from this circle, fed off it like drinking from the purest lake. But centuries dim the light of flesh, even if it is mixed with that of an archangel. Men, flesh, it began to believe in its own, weave its own fantasies of faith—the illusion of this world, this earth, cloaked in its veil, was too overcoming, too complete. Few humans ever managed to hold to Elyon's Light, and few ever would. But sometimes, in some moments, a few were enough.

He swung a leg over and dropped from the horse. He lowered himself to one knee and closed his eyes, feeling the stones that surrounded him. There was a presence of aged air, the witness of time, but there was more . . . and suddenly he could see it, through closed eyes, as it once was—more than a temple, a city had been here. They had touched down on this spot when the ship called Daath left from the Blue Stars, when it came in answer to the cries of the Earth to its Maker, that the blood in its soil was too fouled with sorrow and suffering.

Loch's eyes flicked open. The ruins. The mound of earth he had often studied. He knew there was something beneath it; he could see in places where the earth and vine broke through a smooth, almost unblemished surface. But he had not realized quite what it was until now. Until the knowing of the sword gave his the wisdom of an old man.

Looking up, he saw a spark, a far blue light from the tip of the mound that rose from the forest foliage. It sparked into the sky. Perhaps to the Blue Stars, no, no, not perhaps, it was real, all these things, they were real. A spark of knowing had just flashed homeward. He stood, feeling his skin shiver. It had spoken like stars, and it touched with the same acid light of the Angelslayer.

He heard a far trembling and glanced back toward Lucania. Adrea's home. Once her simple home, her harsh father, her giving mother, her small kid brother that held such tender memories in her heart. A brief sadness passed through him and then he realized how close they were, that the far trembling he had just felt was the armies of Unchuria closing. They were moving slow and steady. Many of them had already entered the shadow of the forest called the East of the Land. Most would not know or understand how ancient, how sacred it was. But some would. He would.

Loch watched until he could see shapes beginning to merge from the dark of the forest. Fog had begun to curl along the ground about the stone.

Loch slipped the bridle off his horse, then slapped its flank, letting it leave at a high trot.

He moved quickly to the edge of the clearing, and then began his ascent of the ruin, using the vines and creepers that wrapped the side. The edge was steep, covered so thick in dirt and vines it seemed no more than a mound of earth. But every so often there was a glimpse of the smooth skin below. The ruin's age was almost equal to that of the trees that had swallowed it, but whenever the surface broke through, it was unblemished.

He moved quickly, and as he reached the level of the treetops, he paused to look down. The armies of the Unchurians were moving slowly through the mist below, crossing the clearing and the ring of stone in a straight line for the city. As he guessed, they had ignored the King's Highway; they would cut through the forest at its center line and break into the open field where the second legion was now crossing for Terith-Aire. What was left of the first legion, battered and thinned from the battle of Ishmia, would be forming a line against the northern edge of the forest, but the Unchurians in their numbers believed they could shatter that line, perhaps before the others could gather inside their walls.

Since the sword had begun to teach him, Loch had learned to see the light of souls beneath the skin. Some, like Hyacinth, burned so intensely they were almost white. But many of the riders below moved with a darkness that swallowed light—they had been given power through blood. They were covenant bearers and their lord, who had devoted all his knowledge and faith to the killer star that waited at the far end of the universe, seemed to not even possess souls, as though they were merely skin and bones of killing machines.

He turned and continued climbing. At times he used his dagger in crevices and vines. He soon pulled himself above the rich canopy of the East of the Land, and this high up, the air was a mist that still bore the taste of fresh rain. The surface of the temple broke through more often now, but it also became more difficult to climb. Where dirt and foliage gave way, there were no handholds, only a smooth surface that looked like finely polished silver, burnished a bit, like the armor of the Daath. He knew what this metal was; it was aganon, the same that formed the metal of the blade of the Angelslayer; only in this form it was solid and always this color, a darkened silver. It was stronger even than the famed Etlantian oraculum. But Loch was surprised that the whole of the temple was sheathed in it, an entire skin of aganon. He began to think now, as he climbed, that it was more than a temple. It was a star ship, and then he knew, he understood. This was it, the Voyager; this was Daathan, sheathed in aganon, to sail even stars and the dark matter of heaven's fury.

Using a single vine he was able to reach the base of the capstone. He was high enough that even the treetops now looked far, and he realized he had climbed far more quickly than he could have without help. Perhaps he was not entirely alone; perhaps there was some aid, some pity left for him. He spread his palm along the skin of the star ship and the comforter whispered like a tender touch. *Home*—it remembered home as if it had left only that morning. The skin of this temple ship was somehow a part of the Blue Stars of heaven, the cluster that men called the Pleiades—fashioned of it, built of it. Where his hand touched, it began to grow warm, soft, and Loch finally let go of the vines. An opening appeared, and Loch was able to kneel onto a ledge of the capstone. It faced the rising sun, and had been the source of the light he had seen below, a small niche in the side of the temple. It seemed to welcome him with a touch that was tender, spoken. He had only felt this touch once before, when he was young. It had once been Asteria's touch—his mother's. As Loch lowered to one knee in reverence, the opening closed, swallowing him into the star temple that was Daathan.

Chapter Fifty-Nine
The Light Whose Name Is Splendor

The alabaster of Terith-Aire's walls glittered. The survivors of Ishmia and those gathered in the retreat were reaching the gate. Beyond the clearing, the tightened second legion of the Shadow Warriors of the Daath were slowly coming out of the oaken forest that was the East of the Land, and before them, encircled by the King's Guard, the finest warriors in the world, were the seventy and seven chosen. It was believed by some that once behind the walls of Terith-Aire they would be protected, walls that were built by a race so long ago and so close to Elyon and the light of the mothering star that even the sunblade of a demon could not shatter the spired walls and gates of the city.

Rhywder pressed his way, with his men, to the center of the chosen, to the children, and among them he found Satrina and the Galaglean, Lucian. He caught up with Satrina, glanced for a moment to the child in her arms.

"Rhywder!" Satrina exclaimed. "You are back!"

"Passing through, my love. One more task north of the city—Eryian's boy, I need to ensure he makes it to safety. It seems odd, this."

"What is odd?"

"It seems too easy. The gates of Terith-Aire in sight, and from the knoll above, I have seen the masts of ships. They are the Etlantian galleys—seven by my count, just as Loch promised would come."

"Then what is odd?"

"We have been pressed as if by the fury of a woman scorned, but if these children reach the seven ships coming for them—they will fast vanish into the deep waters of the Western Sea, to the islands of the prophet—perhaps even the city of Enoch itself. Where are the fires and the brimstone and the unnumbered Unchurians? What is it he waits for?"

"Perhaps even this demon you speak of, the one I saw myself, perhaps the burning of Loch's blade has disrupted his plans, slowed him."

"I cannot believe that. He sees futures. The fires of Ishmia were merely more amusement for the bastard. Something is wrong here; this is too quiet. Still, I will put my skepticism aside and take comfort that you should soon be at sea under full sail. Even this one, Azazel, even he cannot follow into the Western Sea of Enoch."

"I should be at sea? What about you, Rhywder?"

"I will be where I will be. Unlike some, I do not plan ahead that often."

"Ah—a Rhywder answer."

He suddenly looked about, alarmed. "Wait—something, I feel something . . ." He glanced down. "The Earth! Mother of frogs, you feel that?"

"What?"

"The Earth is moving! It is coming, the final blow. He has not been slowed; he comes just as he planned."

"What do you mean?"

Rhywder grabbed Satrina's arm. "If anything happens, stay with these men. Stay with the King's Guard, you understand? They will remain here, in the center with the child."

"What is happening? What are you going to do?"

"Reach Eryian's son. I have a feeling the future will need him."

"Wait!"

He pushed past her, drew up alongside one of the Galaglean. "Godspeed, boy," he said, gripping Lucian's wrist, then pressed forward. He turned in the saddle just before he broke into a gallop and shouted to Satrina, "I will be back, love! Fear not!"

Satrina watched him go, worried. She noticed a group of axemen make their way through the outer warriors to leave a girl among them—or what looked like a girl. Closer up, Satrina realized she was older, just small, and oddly she was dressed as a seafarer, a pirate, in a dark tunic and cloak, and leathers. Her breasts and hips were riddled with rows of daggers. But she was beautiful for a warrior, her hair twisted in dark braids that fell over her shoulders. She did not look up; she rode quietly, her head down, and Satrina could feel the sadness in her. It made her wonder, someone so beautiful, yet a warrior, and yet so saddened Satrina could sense her broken heart. Satrina that knew somehow this woman was connected to the king that had come to her, to the Daathan king with his handsome face and dark, impenetrable eyes. His. She was his.

Tillantus had broken off from the second legion and now rode along the front of the first legion, even the first shieldbearers of Shadow Warriors forming a wall beyond the borders of the great forest of the East of the Land. It was a forest thick enough to slow those who came through it, and Tillantus had reinforced the lines thick with archers who were also as deadly with the sword and axe. Once their missiles were out of range, their shields and weapons were as effective as any shieldbearer's. They were especially trained, even expensively trained, for only the ablest warriors were chosen to make up their ranks.

What was left of the decimated first legion of the Shadow Warriors were the last of the Daath to emerge from the forest. The second had gone before them, leading in their center the seventy and seven chosen. Tillantus was pacing, looking for any sign. What was different from any other battle he had ever faced was that there was no warlord to follow. Eryian for once was not with them, and beyond even that, no king. This king, this Lochlain, he had turned back into the thick oak and disappeared, leaving only the standing order to hold the line of the forest as long as possible and to protect the inner circle of the chosen at all cost, delivering them to the Etlantian ships that should come before nightfall.

He wrenched his horse about hard and faced the forest. He could feel them in there, like one might feel bugs crawling beneath a mound of dirt. They were coming all right. And himself, he would stand here. He had sent the last of his men, his closest brothers, the axemen of the King's Guard with the dark-haired so-called queen. Perhaps she was a queen. She came with Loch, their king, she was obviously his mate, but she seemed an odd queen to lead the Daath.

This was the rear of the retreat. He expected to engage, but what made his back bristle was that it would come this quickly. The Unchurians were cutting through the center of the legendary oaks of the East of the Land. He had hoped that would slow them, awe of their sacred spirits, but then again, the Unchurians seemed trained and groomed for killing alone. It should have been no surprise they would cut through the center of the most ancient of land, once guarded by the fiery sword of Uriel the archangel himself.

No matter. The shieldbearers were in order. He could wish for more time. He would like to see the chosen well inside the city and they were now in open ground, halfway across the fields between here and Terith-Aire, but though the first legion had taken hard blows, though their numbers were thinned, they would hold here. Hold here until winter froze the passes and left the Western Sea iced, he swore beneath his beard.

They were quick, these Unchurians; they were unhuman in the way they moved and the way they fought. Why be surprised they had crossed the isthmus, crossed the lands of the villages such as Lucania, cut through the thick, most sacred center of the ancient oak? Why be surprised of anything they managed?

His first commander, Mannamon, pulled up beside him. "Anything wrong, Captain?"

"I can smell the bastards," Tillantus muttered.

"This soon."

"Damned swift, these bastards. Not only are they without number, they move like wind."

"But that is impossible—the fires destroyed all their crossings."

"Nothing seems impossible any longer to me—a demon leads these men."

Mannamon looked over the forest line. "Are you certain, Captain? I see nothing."

Tillantus searched the trees, determined. There were shadows among shadow, and then, everywhere, in all direction, the trees came alive with warriors, blossomed with them, readying for a charge as though the trees themselves were shifting.

"Where is the king?" Tillantus shouted. "Where is Loch? He has remained in that forest—gone in there to die, that is what, and in doing so leaves us without a warlord and without a king!"

"He had left us with you, my lord, that is good enough for me, and for the men that form your ranks. Looks time to take the lead, my lord. I see them, as well."

"Lock shields!" shouted Tillantus, and his order echoed down the line. "Sound the battle horns, by Elyon's grace, we are about to engage!"

The horns sounded all along the Daathan ranks and the armies shifted, turning; shields were lifted, slamming with a unified clank into a solid wall.

From the trees, the Unchurians came. Most were horsemen to the front, big warriors mounted on powerful chargers, staggered in piercing phalanxes to break the lines. They emerged, but did not attack immediately. It was insane. Tillantus stared in disbelief as the Unchurian horses danced. A highborn rode forward, before his people, and in the space between the two opposing armies, the Unchurian circled about, his eyes trained on Tillantus. He was a firstborn and of them, he was equal in rank to Tillantus.

"This day!" the Unchurian shouted. "You Daath shall fall by the sword and the arrow and the spear! You, your women, and your children—even your seventy and seven chosen! Behold, you shall fall this day until the Earth is quenched by the last drop of your blood! And in the ages that follow, you shall be no more. You shall be but a shadow of a memory long forgotten."

Tillantus drew up in the saddle, lifting his sword, designating himself commander, and shouted a single word in answer: "Pigshit!"

He drew his sword swiftly downward, a signal that let the arrows fly.

The last battle of the Daath of Terith-Aire, the final stand of the tribes of the seven valleys of the Dove Cara, began.

Arrows soared over the locked shields and brought down hundreds, the whole line of warriors that had paused for their speech. Tillantus thought it the simplest damn lunatic tactic he had ever witnessed.

But even as the front lines of the first Unchurians dropped, an even greater number of horsemen poured from the shadows—these all firstborn, all high warriors. Perhaps the first line had been fodder for the arrows and now a staggering line of powerful chargers and unflinching warriors surged from the trees in staggered lines like sharks' teeth about to bore into the line of Daathan shields.

Within ranks, Rainus, the Daathan captain of the Ishmian guard, had been left with the chosen by Rhywder, as their captain, since commanders had dropped on the battle of the ledge. He circled his horse, startled, and looked above to see the horsemen of the Unchurians breaking through the great oaks of the East of the Land. It was not to have been this soon. Even at full gallop, Terith-Aire, though in sight, was too far for comfort. The first legion, all that was left to hold the line against the trees, had been winnowed considerably in the battle of the ridge. They could hold, but for how long? Rainus feared not long enough to get the chosen safely behind the walls of the city.

Even then, as he saw the onslaught above, he felt a shivering tremble through the ground beneath him, and looking down, saw a wedge in the earth the size of a ditch snaking its way through them as if searching for something. The onslaught from the trees was savage, the screams inhuman. But moments before, when they had been pushing through the tall grass, thinking there had been time, there was silence, only a soft wind, and now madness this quickly was reaching through to them, and it seemed, though Rainus dismissed the thought, that the madness knew where to hunt, that its eye had found them already—the seventy and seven. He could see the expressions on the King's Guard about him, the deadliest warriors on Earth, and they seemed to be thinking the same.

"Forget the city!" Rainus screamed.

"My lord?" questioned one of the guards.

"We will never reach it if the first legion breaks, and already its front is being shattered. Send a rider and plant white flags on that far sand shore just short of the walls. We might not reach the gates of Terith-Aire, but we can reach the sea. The ships are Etlantian; supposedly they are keen enough and quick enough to understand the signal."

"Aye, my lord," the guard shouted. "Aramour—use cloaks for flags and pike for their pole—erect a signal on the far beachhead below."

"Done, Captain," the guardsman said, galloping forward.

"Keep the chosen inward, tight about them, and move in formation for the beach. Not double-time, we do not wish to be singled out—but move in a steady, slow gallop!"

"Slow gallop!" echoed a guardsman, and the surrounding warriors dedicated to keep a hard center about the chosen also spread the command.

"Follow my lead!" Rainus shouted.

They turned in the grass and began to head for the shore. What worried Rainus the most was the earth splitting. The angel's eyes tracked them. It was more his magick that Rainus feared than the fury of battle all along the line of the trees of the East of the Land. Another crack, but again it seemed as if it was searching. He was far, this demon; he was not close enough to sense them with surety, and perhaps riding for the sand of the shore instead of the heavy gates of the city would not be a move he would quickly guess, though Rainus wished it was Rhywder here with them instead of him.

"Keep your head," Rhywder had told him last. "Ignore fear, ignore magick, use your instinct. It is why I have chosen you."

Hyacinth kept a tight grip of the flanks, realizing they were suddenly turning, no longer making the run for the city, though the streams of civilian refugees of Ishmia and many of the warriors leading them were doing just that, breaking into a pressed run for the gates of Terith-Aire.

If not for the child in her, Hyacinth would never have come this for, let alone any farther with them, not for a shore where no ships were in sight. But she could not deny that she carried. Only days old, there was a powerful being within her; she felt its light. That was the new knowing Loch had pressed through her from the sword. All her magicks were gone. She could not even skin walk now—it was all something else, a knowing of stars and futures and an understanding of light. She much preferred her old magicks, but they had been cleansed. What was she now? An Enochian? The thought chilled her. She had cherished the books and the teachings, she had never doubted them, but to follow the light of their word—it seemed something she would never had tasted in her own lifetime, and indeed, this lifetime was not her own. It had been stolen from time.

As to her path, she was given no choice. Hemmed in on all sides, these children, as beautiful as any she had ever seen, children like a gathering of soft light, might just as well have been surrounded by solid plate armor. They moved where the horsemen of the King's Guard and the outer shell of the second legion's First Century of Shieldbearers willed them to move—and their will was suddenly to separate from the others and abandon flight to the city. She noticed one woman, clutching a child wrapped in a blue blanket, and this knowing left in Hyacinth, this gift of the Angelslayer's sword, whispered to her that there, in that woman's arms—that child was the scion of the Daath. The child of Loch, just as the one inside her. And she remembered Loch's words, that they were connected. They moved at a quick trot, almost a gallop.

Hyacinth then gasped, seeing the sky. Beyond the mighty trees of the East of the Land, quickly sweeping what was a blue sky, coming from the south, were clouds that broiled, spun about one another—like dark snakes circling in and out of each other. It was the same sky they had seen over Satariel, only this one was much more sinister, not as loud or as showy—but moving deft and with purpose. She knew what was within the circling snakes—the angel's eyes. She knew it was the anger, the ethos, the searching mind of the one named Azazel. He would assimilate knowledge from the weak, and she was certain, already, that this storm was looking for them, only for them, this small pocket of young ones. This was his target. Azazel cared nothing of the legions of the Daath, cared nothing of Terith-Aire; he had come from his shadows of the far south where he had ruled for centuries to find them this day and this hour. They were the promise of Enoch; they were the ones that would behold the terror and glory of Aeon's End, and Azazel intended to end it here, to destroy the scions of prophecy on this ground. She tingled at the thought, but now Loch had made her a part of it all, as if he had written her into the books of the angels. He named her as bearer of this child she now carried, and she steeled herself with the thought. If nothing else, her knives, her poisons, would protect this child in her, for now that she had accepted it, she would protect it with all the fury of a cornered lion.

†

Rhywder glanced behind him. It was impossible—the Unchurians had broken through the trees of the East of the Land—already. However they had managed to cross the isthmus, they had also crossed the open ground between here and the scar of earth below Terith-Aire, the Dove Cara, in a wink, in a blur, faster than horses could move, faster than armed men could possibly have traveled. She should have had a day or more at least, but then, they faced no ordinary army; in truth they faced but one being. The demon. If any of the angels had fallen to the dark star, it was this one, Azazel, and he had fallen so far, so quickly, that the dark was his light; the dark was his teacher, and he had become more powerful perhaps than any of the others who struggled to hold to their fading star knowledge. He had given over his soul without question. Perhaps that is why he had shed his own holy flesh for a spirit able to take any flesh he wished, the strongest, the quickest. No human nor breed could possibly resist him. In the back of his mind, the thought had troubled Rhywder since the Vale of Tears where he watched the muscles and veins of a man's head form from the demon's barren shoulders.

They had struck already. If the Daath had managed to reach their city, with ports to the sea, even unnumbered Unchurians would have been hard-pressed to breach the walls. They were holy walls, build seven hundred years ago, and the breath of an archangel had sealed them. Even a demon's blade could not burn through them once the gate was closed and the signet of Uriel dropped as the crossbar lock that would seal up the city in spellbound light.

He had hoped that would be their chance; he had thought that was the opening Elyon would grant them, to reach the ancient spired city, built not as cities of Earth, but of a home far across the skies. Terith-Aire was and always had been a city of the Blue Stars of the Seven Sisters. There would be refuge here. But only the civilians had crossed, and the second legion was still shepherding in the rest. The chosen, Rhywder knew, were centered, hidden by the shields of the second, and he doubted the remains of the First Century could hold the line at the edge of the forest for that long.

He was tempted to turn about, make sure the chosen struck instead for the shoreline south of Terith-Aire. But Rainus would have reached the same conclusion, at least that was Rhywder's prayer, for even if he turned this fine Galaglean steed about and raced for the center, he would never reach them in time. The demon would use magick now. He would unleash all he had. Time had become as narrow as a needle. It could be possible. Azazel could do it, destroy the seed of the Daath long before the Earth passed through the gates of Aeon's End. If he did that, the dark of his heart alone would drag them to the blackest hole that existed anywhere in the universe, the very eye of Daath. It was necessary to pass the Earth through the abyss that was the eye of Daath, but without the light in the hearts of men to keep the planet riding the crest of its outer wave, nothing could save them.

Rhywder had always been a Follower, a believer of the Enochian books—even that there was an island in the Western Sea where the city of Enoch harbored its prophet. He believed, but he also had never trusted in Faith's Light alone. It was not Elyon's way. Prayer. Instead, it would ever be the deeds of men, the light of their own inner hearts, the works and actions of the elect of men and breeds that would turn the final hour. Nothing more, not hope, not faith. But for once, just this once, he had no choice, and he left a whispered prayer: *Protect the chosen; protect the seed and the scion; and Elyon, Lord of all, Elohim, Master of all gods, protect Satrina.* A selfish prayer—his love he prayed for, but it was the only damned prayer Rhywder had ever sent of his own heart, the only time he had appealed openly to heaven, and that must count for something.

He paused near the gates before moving on. Panic was everywhere. The civilians and refugees were dropping all they had and fleeing for the gate, the second legion had tightened about them to protect them as they were herded in, but then Rhywder noticed, with relief in his heart, that a core of riders, those he recognized as the First Century and the King's Guard, had turned. His choice in placing Rainus as their captain was sound—he was leading them for the shoreline, ignoring the promise held by the gates of the city.

Briefly, only briefly, Rhywder glanced at the line of warriors holding back the Unchurians at the forest. The fighting was savage, unlike anything he had ever seen, both sides boring into each other with equal insanity. But it would not last much longer. The weary First Century of Argolis, once the proudest and most capable army on Earth, was breaking; the frontal shields were being shattered by heavy horsemen and open fighting was breaking out within the ranks.

No more time now, Rhywder had come this far, and he believed in the purpose of his coming. He turned the reins and rode at a hard gallop through the gates of Terith-Aire for the northern edge where Eryian had chosen to build a simple cabin and dock and surround it with a common fence, as if he ever could pretend to be a plodder. The boy would be there, heavily guarded, and most probably being searched for by Unchurian scouts as earnestly as himself.

It was midday and the sun had shone moments before, but now the sky darkened with a storm, no simple storm, but angel's eyes, the whirlers with their thousand eyes. The killer angel men called the Reaper was about to play his most desperate gambit.

Once Rhywder had passed beneath the gate, sweeping about a line of refugees now fleeing in all direction, panic ruling like a fever spreading, Rhywder chose a thin cobblestone street that veered north between shops and stacked apartments, his horse's hooves echoing. Where other horses might have stumbled on the cobblestone, this one was able to gallop full-out—it was everything Lucian had promised. It even held ground when the Earth itself rippled in a shock wave sent slithering beneath the city. Rhywder had to twist the reins hard to avoid a sudden crack that split open in the street like wood cracking from beneath. It was at first a split, but then it became a full-fledged chasm opening to the ancient rock of Terith-Aire's foundation. From afar the angel was spell-binding Earth shakers, and they would swallow many before the day was finished.

Rhywder sank his heels hard into the flanks, gripping the flanks with his knees as the well-bred charger veered from the chasm's path and quickly broke into a gallop still northwest, for the docking that would lead to Eryian's simple cabin.

Behind Rhywder, the sundering cracks continued splitting open the Earth. The walls of Terith-Aire were only spellbound once the gates had been closed and sealed with the archangel's signet. Azazel had decided that was not going to happen. He was going to shatter the wall now, while they were still unprotected—he was madly searching for the chosen, that was Rhywder's guess, and he was going to leave nothing to chance. One chasm split open the Earth like a mouth gaping and struck the side of the Daathan's spired eastern wall with a crack that shook the whole city and sundered a huge section of quarter granite mined from Dove Cara itself centuries ago. The ancient rock was swallowed into the Earth.

The refugees and the civilians who had managed to reach the city now were wailing, screaming in sheer panic. If the walls of Terith-Aire were falling, what could possibly stop the unnumbered armies pressing against the far line of the first legion? The city was going to be no protection whatsoever.

Suddenly, almost directly before Rhywder, a huge section of limestone ripped upward, shattering, then slipping sideways to vanish into a chasm. Amidst the screaming and panic, there now was a smell of sulfur and fire that savagely licked out of the wounds in the Earth.

A big plodder, his eyes overwhelmed with panic, suddenly tried to grab Rhywder's reins in an attempt to steal the horse. Rhywder sneered and kicked him back so hard, he vanished into the chasm that had brought on his panic.

The Little Fox gripped tight as the fearless charger soared over a handcart, its owner ducking to cover his head. The horse almost seemed to know the correct direction before Rhywder turned the reins. If only he'd had a horse like this before instead of now, when his life was once more about to end. He reached the dock and veered sharply north, straight along the line of the wharfing. Ships out there, he saw briefly. The tall masts of Etlantians, just as Loch had said. He hoped Rainus knew to signal them away from the city. If the seven Etlantian ships were to sail for Terith-Aire, by the time they reached the docks, the city would be aflame.

Rainus reared his horse, but too late. With an entire front section of his men, he dropped away into a chasm mouth that tore through the Earth to swallow half the Daathan shieldbearers of the second legion surrounding the chosen.

The ground had simply ripped open—there was no time to react.

The Earth's crust was peeled back at the edges as the chasm continued to ripple outward, wedging its way nearly to the sea. The city was now cut off from the chosen and what was left of their surrounding shell of warriors. A quake heaved beneath them, and men and horses went down. Fire roared from the crevice, licking the sky.

Hyacinth screamed and hit the ground on her side, barely throwing herself clear of a horse-warrior that rolled past, caught beneath his mount. She scrambled to her knees, then watched, stunned, as another crack in the Earth slithered past her leg like a serpent searching. The ground beside her then heaved upward. Hyacinth was thrown. She saw the woman and child—the special ones—hauled from their horse and protected by a tight gathering of warriors in smoked armor and silver-gray tunics who seemed impervious even to earthquake. When she was on her feet, she watched fire rip upward, furious. She stared, amazed.

Fire began to slither over the edge of the cleft, and Hyacinth watched as even the green meadow grass began to burn, melting. The fire crept toward them slowly, white-hot, liquid—almost as though it were alive.

"Move for the sea!" one of the men left standing shouted. He pointed his sword. "All of you! Grab these children and move for the sea!"

She mounted a horse and paused, waiting. The Shadow Warriors were gathering up the children, mounting their horses. She could see that if they bore due west, they could reach the shore. The sea waited, blue and rippled, and she saw the ships—with the triangular sails of Etlantians—six maybe seven. She took up the reins, then lifted her hand to a young girl with dark braids, pulling her into her saddle. Even with the ships within sight, as the Earth shivered and fire warmed her backside, although close, in such chaos they still looked a long ways off. The demon, the second of the three, came for the Daath. This day came with the fury of the sky, and she wondered, briefly, how it was Loch was going to stop such power.

†

The skies were dark over the painted ships. Cintex, the captain of the Etlantian flagship, stood upon the forecastle of the lead galley. The other six were in phalanx formation to either flank. They were moving for the ports of Terith-Aire, but Cintex could not believe what had turned in the past few moments. He was now staring to the west, dizzy, amazed. Behind them, the sky seemed to have boiled up out of the sea and risen into dark-black clouds, massed like a beast. It was stealing the light of day. Patches of dull, quick lightning ignited here and there among them. The clouds came so fast, they seemed to literally be swallowing the sky. Cintex turned away from it, then stared with equal amazement at the city. Terith-Aire was in flames. It looked as though she had been hit by the siege fire of the gods. An entire corner had dropped away, castle and all. There was but agony beyond. Most of the docking was already aflame. People were leaping from the stoneworks, beginning to swim for Cintex and his ships.

Cintex then looked beyond the city, to the high forest.

"There!" one of his men shouted.

He looked toward the shore. Single white flags that were cloaks had been mounted on pikes. The Shadow Warriors, the Daath, were holding back an impossible number of enemy warriors at the line of the trees. The fighting was savage; from the distance it looked like two incredible beasts snaking across the valley, in total deadlock, boring into each other with fury and blood. But the shoreline was still protected, and a gathering of prime warriors were moving toward it. The chosen he had heard of must be protected by them. They would ward off considerable attack, but if the weakening front along the forest broke, there would be no hope.

"Name of the Goddess and all that is holy," Cintex swore. He gripped the forecastle rail. He glanced to his second, a tall, stone-faced captain who watched the shore without emotion. "A moment ago," Cintex screamed above the roar of battle and quakes, "there was clear sky, calm sea. Now the valley is swallowed in flame . . . and the sky! In Elyon's name, something hard comes against them!"

"Whatever comes here, my lord, comes not in Elyon's name." The first officer then pointed south.

"Hail our men and the other ships. We change bearing, move for that shore, the markers, the white markers . . ."

The second shouted the orders. They were echoed and, by signal, sent out to the other ships.

"Look!" shouted the second. "There on the horizon! You see it? A longship! I knew I saw something last night—trailing us! That is a blackship! A Tarshian!"

Cintex squinted his eyes. The sea was getting difficult to read with the coming storm, but his officer was right. South, far upon the horizon, the triangular sail of a pirate cut against the sky. It was full oared and moving swift. Then, slowly, as the sky darkened, the longship seemed to melt back into the sea. "Where did the bastard go? He disappeared!"

"He is a blackship, my lord—I have fought them before. They strike at night, and now, as the sky darkens, he vanishes. We will never track him through this storm, we . . ." The captain paused, looking to the sky. His mouth dropped open. For moment he was struck speechless.

Cintex was shocked to see fear in the eyes of his second; the man was a veteran of the fires of Hades itself. Cintex turned, looked skyward, searching, feeling his skin shiver.

"Minions," the second whispered, stunned. "There, my lord, minions of the Salamander—hundreds of them." He pointed.

Cintex thought at first they were birds, a huge flock of birds moving from the great forest called the East of the Land, then sweeping out to sea. The sky was soon covered with them. They were obviously coming for his ships, for the Etlantians, and as they closed, they looked more like bats, sometimes visible, sometimes swallowed in dark clouds. It was like trying to trace shadow against shadow.

"Take up arms!" Cintex shouted. He ripped his buckler from his shoulder. "It appears someone does not wish us to reach the shore."

Cintex's second unlatched his sword hilt and drew his weapon. Its blade was hard, polished oraculum.

As they closed, the minions looked to be coming out of the sky like black comets, swift. They never slowed. They came at full flight, living missiles. One hit the forecastle decking and smashed through the timbers, then struggled where it was lodged. What could possibly be the purpose? Such a strike would break even the bones of these creatures, weaken them. But then Cintex saw the beast lifted a flint stone and realized he was coated in black pitch.

"Goddess save us, he is going to burn us!" Cintex screamed, leaping forward, lifting his sword to try to kill the thing before the flint struck a spark. But he did not make it. The spark was slight, tiny, and the creature, coated in a thick paste, exploded. Cintex gasped, reeling back, but not quick enough, for the flames engulfed him. He turned, off balance. His skin was actually peeling away, burning. Cintex sucked a blast of molten fire into his lungs, then staggered. The sky was filled with enough of these to take out every Etlantian warship that had been launched in answer to the Daathans' plea.

Off the port bow of his warship, Darke could see flames everywhere. The ports of the city of Terith-Aire were burning, and now, even the Etlantian galleys coming to rescue them had begun to burn. Something was destroying them. They were being pummeled by some kind of siege missiles, but unlike any he had ever seen before. He lifted a seeing glass from his robe and brought it to his eye. The sky was almost night-black now. Though it should have still been day, this was an angel's storm, and its whirlers and dark clouds had swallowed the sun. He scanned for the missiles. Anything that could take out an Etlantian warship might be able to take his blackship out, as well. He gasped at what he saw—creatures were hurtling through the sky, and some were setting themselves aflame just before impact. He lowered the glass. All seven ships of the Etlantians had been hit—all of them were burning, the sails were going up in streaks of fire. Apparently, someone was even better at killing Etlantians than he was.

The angel's storm had moved swiftly, but there was more, for the land itself had erupted, the sea was beginning to rage, and sprays of cold water slapped across him.

"Shields!" he screamed, seeing the horizon. A tight swarm of the same minions that had taken out the Etlantians were now coming for him. He was amazed at their speed—they were large, winged beasts, but were moving like hornets. He quickly turned and shouted to the hands amidships.

"Light your arrows!" he screamed. "Be quick! Fire your arrows!"

Pitched arrows were quickly drawn, the heads fired. Pelegasian archers lined either gunwale, all along the ports.

"Hard starboard oar!" Darke shouted. A Pelegasian helmsman echoed the call, and Darke's ship turned its prow dead into the swarm, offering them the prow of the ship, its narrowest target.

"Give way! Hard oar! Hard oar!" the Pelegasian screamed. The oars surged, and the prow began to lift from the dark waters.

"Drop the mast!" Darke cried. "And stow that sail!" The sail loosened, then fell. "Archers! Those creatures are coated in naphtha. We are going to light them like festival candles before they reach us! Take your aim and wait my command!"

Darke watched their approach, feeling them, feeling the distance close. The clouds were almost black, and against them the creatures were all but invisible, but even against the storm's rumble, he could hear the leathery beat of wings.

Finally, he pointed the tip of his sword to the horizon. "Now! Fire!"

The arrows soared, brilliant streaks against clouds, and where they struck their mark, beasts erupted in the sky and dropped like comets streaming, writhing as they burned. They started to hit the sea before Darke's ship, exploding in flame and sprays of steamed water.

"Keep firing! Keep it steady!" Darke screamed.

A second volley of fire arrows, and more of the creatures burst into flame against the black clouds. But now they were getting too close, and even though they were ignited, they were streaming inward, wings folded back, making a dive for the ship, coming like unholy rain. He would be damned if he had sailed this blackship through deep water and even hidden it from an angel, only to burn at sea.

"Lay back oars! Lift a shield cover!"

At the command, the entire decking bronzed in a carapace of oblong shields lifted to form a cover, rising to a spine along the center.

Darke dropped against the prow post. The minions came out of the sky with screams. The oars were folded back, locked beneath the brazen shields. The fiery missiles of the minions began to strike the water about the ship. The creatures were heavy, almost like catapult stones, and though many were grazed off, in places they shattered through the carapace, destroying shield and men, sometimes breaking through the planking. Those that struck the prow were destroyed by the heavy, slicing blade of the ram. Darke's warship was cutting through the fire blast like riding a storm.

From a port, Rat watched, trancelike. The skin of his face was blackened and hard, he had no hair, and his eyes were furious amidst the scar. He gasped as a flame creature streaked past his gun port, warded off and ripped open by the prow blade. It plummeted into the cold sea with a spray of steam and a sound of snuffed flame that took Rat's breath. It was one of the most beautiful sights he had ever witnessed.

As he galloped about a narrow corner, the hooves of the Galaglean warhorse Lucian had given Rhywder sparked on the stone. Suddenly Rhywder was forced to pull up. The roadway before him was broken wide. Two shelves of stone were balanced narrowly over a gorge, and fire flickered about their edges. It was wide, but there was no way around it.

Rhywder hesitated, then pulled back on the reins, backing the horse. When he had distance, he hugged tight with his knees and leaned forward. "I know you have no wings," he whispered to the horse, "but it is has come time to fly!" He slammed his heels into the flanks. The horse bolted, galloping hard, hurtling, then soared. Rhywder felt flames lick his boots. On the other side, the horse landed on one upturned stone, stumbling, nearly going down. The stone started to slide for the crevice, and Rhywder kept his heels dug tight against the ribs. "Come on, boy! You can make it!" They barely leapt the edge to firm ground as the slab of stone dropped soundlessly into the fiery cleft behind them. Rhywder pulled up on the reins, then glanced over his shoulder. The chasm had been wider than he guessed. The slab of stone had been deceiving. This horse was one piece of flesh, that was certain.

Rhywder turned and rode at a gallop. There were bodies here; crushed beneath rubble that Rhywder steered around. If Eryian's boy was alive, it was meant to be, for the dead were everywhere. Rhywder rounded a bend, then pulled up. His horse danced. Before him were horsemen—not Daath, not Galaglean—these were minions. Seeing him, once of them let a smile curl.

Rhywder twisted the horse's reins, turning him about. He sank his heels in, galloping back toward the chasm. "You made it the last time," he whispered into the horse's ear, "and you can do it again, trust me—I never lie to horses."

Rhywder kept pressure with his heels, leaning as they rounded the sharp bend. They started down the roadway toward the chasm at a full, furious gallop; the horse was panting, preparing to soar.

Rhywder dropped tight against the hide of the neck.

Behind him, he could hear the minions coming, hooves heavy.

The fires of the crevice blazed even higher now, curling like tendrils. Rhywder glanced over his shoulder.

One of them was screaming through tight teeth, lifted onto its haunches.

They were almost to the crevice. Rhywder lifted the crossbow from his shoulder, pulled on his buckler, keeping the reins in his teeth. He drew a tight breath, timing the moment carefully, then wrenched back on the reins. The horse reared, spinning about, screaming. It had understood his every move so far, but this confused even this fine beast. The horse twisted about so hard, he almost went down on his side, sliding backward. Rhywder twisted in the saddle, leveled off the crossbow, and buried the blunt-ended bolt into one of the minion's chests before they passed him at a gallop. None of them had guessed the move—they had no choice but to keep galloping, and Rhywder's sudden hesitation had thrown them into confusion; none would reach the other side. He was able to turn in time to watch them drop into the fires of the crevice.

Rhywder circled the horse, patting the neck. "Sorry about that," he said sincerely, "but if you were not going to believe we would jump that crevice, neither would they. Come, boy, we are almost there."

Rhywder turned and pressed on at a gallop. He rounded a second narrow street. Here the villas were taller and stronger. At the end, near the harbor, Eryian's villa was still standing, though one side hung off balance, torn away. There was blood in the courtyard of the villa—and bodies, both Unchurians and Shadow Warriors, lay slaughtered. Rhywder guessed assassins had come against the house of Eryian, but on the porch, between columns, bloodied, and still clutching their swords, were four hardened King's Guard—four of Eryian's captains.

Rhywder galloped forward, then clattered onto the porch. One of the guards drew aside, and dropped to one knee, exhausted, leaning into the hilt of his sword, his own blood dripping.

"My lord," he said, recognizing the Little Fox.

"Is the boy alive?" Rhywder cried.

The guard only motioned to a tall young warrior in a white cloak, holding a silver bow. The last time he had seen Little Eryian, he had been only four, and even then Rhywder had been unnerved by the white eyes. Now a lad of ten and five, he was tall, even formidable.

Rhywder stretched forth his hand. "You are needed, boy!"

"Needed where?"

"At Aeon's End! The future! Now, come with me."

Tillantus fought in the front lines, his axe slaying in steady, powerful hammer blows, his great shield protecting his left.

The sky itself seemed to boil. From the north, clouds had spilled until a shadow covered the Earth like the hand of Elyon, and on the ground it seemed almost as dark as night, lit only by the fires of the ancient city of Terith-Aire burning, and farther, on higher ground, there were firefly naphtha strikes amid the forest of the East of the Land. It left the sky an eerie, bloodred hue, though the air seemed crisp and cold. The demon had done all he could to create a canvas of terror for his final strike.

Tillantus had fought for hours, fought until the muscles of his arms coiled in spasm and pain, until he could no longer lift his axe, and then he had no choice but to turn and fall back. A Daathan Shadow Warrior took his place with a fierce war cry, bringing his shield up to block the thrust of a spear. The weary, pummeled first legion of the Daath still held, held where no other army on Earth could have made a stand, held against blood fury unmatched since the angel wars of Dawnshroud so long ago. But the Unchurians had not been able to breach the line, and even though the city was shattered and burning, between its crumbled walls was the prize, the single target, the seventy and seven chosen; and the demon named Azazel, still behind the lines, was unleashing his final furies in order to reach them. They were the key to the future; they were the final warriors that were by myth fabled to stand in the last day against the dark of Etlantis and the mightiest of the fallen angels of Ammon's Oath. If they could be destroyed now, the futures where mankind survived would be swallowed in a single breath.

A moment later Tillantus dropped to one knee, lowering his head, completely exhausted. Blood dripped from the inside of his helmet. A slash near the temple had broken through and mangled flesh.

Seeing his own blood spill down his forearm, Tillantus realized this was the final battle of his generation, for that matter, of the people they once were. This day, the Shadow Warriors of Argolis and Eryian would die. Even if the children got out alive, it was over; it was going to end now, and that seemed to be a sad thing. He even questioned the purpose, but then he thought of the children he had looked over earlier in the plaza, the future, not just of the Daath, but of all the Earth, for if the angels were to prevail, though they knew not, the Earth would be swallowed into the dark of never being, of having never existed in this universe or any other.

He looked down the line. Fine men were holding back the impossible, knowing their task, but they were being destroyed. They were going to break, and time was narrow, too narrow to ponder.

Tillantus took a breath, then pulled himself back onto his feet and mounted. He gazed about, stunned at the madness. Before him, the Unchurian front was a terrible screaming—weapons, men, shields ringing against steel.

But while his lines had been fighting without breath to stop, the Unchurians had been rotating, sending fresh warriors to the front.

He glanced behind. In the valley before the city, the chosen had been divided by a deep cleft in the Earth that looked to have been cut by sword. In that moment hope failed him, and it stabbed like a knife—where were they? Had they reached the city, they would be burning. Had they not, there was only a moment before the Daathan line gave way. Then he spotted them, a small, tight core of the Shadow Warriors of Eryian, the prime of the King's Guard, still shielding the little ones. They were pressing hard, not for the city, but for the shoreline. He looked farther, out to sea, and almost cried out, overwhelmed. It was impossible, but the ships of the Etlantians were no longer coming. They had been halted, turned into burning husks about to go down off the shore of the Western Sea.

It would be for nothing. There could be no possible solution, no possible way out of this. He could think of no tactic to save the seventy and seven, and Argolis was dead, and Eryian had perished, and even the young king had vanished. It was on his shoulders that after seven centuries, the Daath would fall. Their enemy had simply been too cunning, too strong. How could Elyon have expected the Daath to have survived? What did heaven ask of them!

He looked up there, to heaven, his hand in a fist, a tear against his cheek. "What more!" he screamed. "We have done the impossible! What more?"

Tillantus heard a cry from the forest. The Unchurians finally smashed their way through the Daathan front before him, all of them, the defenders, especially here about the last commander, had been the elite, warriors he believed could never fall no matter the fury of the battle, but they broke, their shields finally dropped, and the Unchurians now began to pour into the gap like water breaking a dam. To the west, toward the sea, the Daath still held. The Unchurians had been after the head of the Daath first. That, at least, was an error. The children were fleeing for the sea, and the edge of the mighty forest called the East of the Land was still held there, a thin line, still struggling, but not yet breaking.

When the wave of fresh Unchurians reached him, Tillantus slew with tight screams, each blow a terrible swath of flesh and blood flung. Each blow was a death mark, and bodies fell to either side of the mighty veteran. He circled, killed to the side, then reared back, crushing a skull with his buckler, and then turned it, using its sharpened edge to shear open another neck. How many necks had he opened that day? How many had he killed?

When he turned back for yet another, a sword impaled him, cutting through his chest plate. He sucked for air that didn't come.

The hard, sea-worn captain of the Pelegasians seized Darke's shoulder with a clawed hand. They were the best men he had been able to find, killers of Etlantia, grizzled of the sea for all their lives and fearless as wolves, but they seemed now to be sailing into the throat of a enveloping beast.

"This is madness!" the captain shouted. They were on the forecastle and just below them, embedded amidships, was the burned-out corpse of a monster, twisted into the decking like a corkscrew. They had put them out. The blackship had taken damage, but the minions had been extinguished and now dotted the decking in disfigured and grotesque corpses.

"You expect to beach here?" cried the Pelegasian. "You are out of your mind!" He pointed his darkened, long-nailed finger to the edge of the forest. The Daath close to the sea still held, but it was a line about to break, any seasoned warrior could see that—it was a wearied, bloodied, tremulous line of still-furious fighting. Darke knew what the Daath were fighting for, and he knew they would sink even him should they have seen a darkship, a pirate, cutting through the frothing waters of the Western Sea—but he also knew he had guessed right. He was their last hope. Lochlain had done this much for him, and Darke was not a man to leave favors unanswered.

Beyond the shoreline the battle raged, insane, but the edge of sand was still a tiny, brief safe harbor. It was all they had left, and all around it was a circus of death.

"We must turn back," shouted the Pelegasian. "To go in there is suicide!"

Darke grabbed the captain by his purple tunic, then slammed him against the bulwark—slammed him hard, knocked the breath from him. "Listen to me!" he screamed at both the captain and crew. Beside Darke, two youths—young Tarshians, not yet twenty—crouched, wielding bows. They were the only Tarshians with him. The crew was entirely Pelegasian.

"Only I can get you out of here!" Darke screamed at them, holding the captain against the bulwark. "Your captain here could never outguess this storm, and if you turn for deep water now, it will take you because these are not the clouds of a storm you have ever known. Look at them! Look close, any who doubt, and you will see the dark circles, the snakes that swim in and out of each other! Look closer, and you will see the eyes of the demon that has caused the insanity you see raging about you! So look to the sky! And look to the Western Sea whose waves began to build like hills rolling. I know you have followed your captain these years, but right now, in this time, at this moment I am the only one alive to get you out of here with your skin still on your bones! Now do what I say, listen to my words, and we will see another dawn, that is my promise to you. I am Darke, the Emerald King of the Tarshians, and you know me; from word or from fear, you know who I am."

"You may be him," shouted the Pelegasian captain, "but you have tricked us, sailed us down the throat of a sea demon! Bastard! You said the Etlantians were sailing for gold and plunder—you lied!"

"I did." He looked in the captain's eyes; he looked over the crew. "I lied. However, once we have gotten free of this, you will be well paid—I will give you your gold and all that was promised. That is my given word. I may lie on occasion, but I am still a man of my word." He narrowed his brow and looked deep into the captain's eyes. "Now," he said quietly, "you tell your crew to obey me, or I am taking you by the throat and throwing you into the flaming deep you so fear. Your choice; make it quick; I have little time."

Darke waited, his eyes firm.

"I will!" gave in the captain. "All you command, Shadow Hawk, but get us out of here."

"I have already told you I would. I do not wish to repeat myself."

Darke shoved the captain to the railing of the forecastle where he could look over his crew. The captain straightened his robes, drew himself erect. "We listen to the Tarshian! He is our captain and he will guide us out of this madness. Agreed?"

They shouted back their approval.

Darke stepped high, up the edge of prow where all could see him. "Row for the shore!" he shouted. "For those heralds of white flags!"

His orders were echoed, and as the oarsmen below quickened the beat, the oars shifted, turning the prow for the Daathan shore.

"Full oar," shouted Darke. "Every muscle you have into it and then ten times more!"

The Pelegasian at the helm shouted over the side, "Give way full oar!" The pacekeepers' drum echoed hollow with the surge of the oars.

"Lift the mast!" Darke cried.

At command the mast lifted into its crutch, the pulleys whining.

"Raise the Etlantian sail!"

The Pelegasian captain stepped forward. "We will be seen for miles!"

"Which is why we are raising it, Pelegasian. We come to rescue them. If they think we are pirates, why should they trust us? Raise the white sail with the red bull of Etlantis! They need to see us now!"

One of the Tarshian archers, a boy, laid his weapon aside, leapt over the forecastle railing, then sprinted to the mast to help the Pelegasians play out the white sailing, stained on its foreground with the image of the crimson bull of Etlantis.

"Hard into it!" Darke cried. "If you want out of here alive, pour all you have into the stroke! Hard! Harder!" The oarsmen stepped up the pounding heartbeat. The white sail, risen, quickly caught the wind, whipping out taut. The bull's head of Etlantis, in its glittering oraculum sheath, caught the light of the fires along the shore.

"Light the throwers, Rat!" Darke shouted.

From belowdecks, the fire jets roared to life and spilled fire across the waters. Darke's ship looked to be sailing out of a sea of flame and could now be seen for miles, with its serpent's prow lifting out of the waters from the speed and boring down upon the white swath of shoreline.

✝

In the street, Rhywder's powerful mount staggered, then went down on its front knees. Young Eryian was behind Rhywder, holding tight. Villas were collapsing. An ivory column rolled past them. Rhywder kept a tight rein as the horse quickly regained his feet. When the quake stilled enough to gallop forward, the horse leapt the crumbled side of a villa, then clattered across its wooden floors, over debris, and crashed through the timbers of the back porch, landing on a dock work.

Rhywder paused, searching. The boy held tight, his head tucked against Rhywder's side. The docking swayed as a wave slammed into it, washing over. Rhywder looked to sea and gasped. An Etlantian galley was sailing for them—but it was entirely aflame, the oraculum plating the only thing keeping it afloat. The oars were long broken free, the masts had crumpled, not a living being was left in control, but the ship was still gliding heavy and true for the port; the prow cutting white billows of steam to either side was going to crush a hole in it the size of a house. Rhywder looked over his shoulder.

"Hold on, boy!" he shouted, then slammed his heels against the flanks. The Galaglean horse raced forward. Planks bounced as the hooves clattered. Some broke away, but Rhywder guided the steed along the right edge, near the strongest bracing. As he galloped, wedging nails were being torn loose. Rhywder could hear the ship closing, roaring in flames as if with a hundred screaming voices, and the reflections of it left the waters below the dock bright and swimming.

Rhywder swore—the docking posts at the end were giving way. The whole structure was buckling. Any second the huge warship would impact. The Little Fox screamed and rammed the spikes of his boots into the warhorse's side and the horse surged forward as if it understood—it must either make this jump or die. They soared over purple waters and then there was a hollow thud as the hind flanks of the horse hit the stone edge of the far landing. Rhywder heard the horse's bones crack. Rhywder and the boy were thrown. Behind them, the ship collided with docking, exploding. Spinning chunks of hull planking soared overhead. The powerful Galaglean charger rolled to one side and seemed to have been sucked back into a sea of flame, but he had gotten them across; they had made it clear.

"Run!" Rhywder shouted, seizing Little Eryian's wrist, and they ran along the edge of a stone docking wall. Looking over his shoulder, he saw the rest of the Etlantian galleys still out to sea. The entire armada was aflame. He could not believe it. There would be no ships! What were they running for? There was no hope—and then he saw it: a single mast, a bull's head, full sail billowed out, smart enough not to even attempt the city's docking, but driving at full oar for the sandy beach north of the city.

When he reached the edge of the landing, he took the boy by his waist. Beyond, over the edge of the landing, was a canal, and beyond that, the stretch of sandy beach the ship was headed for, and on it, signal flags anchored, white cloaks. "Swim for those flags, boy!" he shouted, throwing Little Eryian into the sea, then dove in after him.

From where she galloped—tight within the center cluster of Shadow Warriors, with beautiful children who rode, terrified—Hyacinth could now see the shoreline. For a moment her breath was caught. It was an Etlantian sail, glittering full-out with the bull's head of Etlantis, always their enemies, but beneath that sail were the fire jets of Darke's own blackship peeling white sprays of the sea from either side of the prow.

Hyacinth lifted herself up in the saddle.

"That way!" she screamed to the warriors. "There! An Etlantian ship!"

The last warriors of the Daath surrounding the children saw her motion and turned, driving in a hard run for the shoreline where the ship was gliding toward them. Just above, the last of the Daathan's First Century still held a line against the western edge of the forest, but it was sundering and moments would soon become seconds before even Darke's ship could not escape this madness—but it was him, it was the captain. She could not see him, but who else would sail through a firestorm to repay a debt?

Satrina rode with one hand beneath the saddle and with the other she held the child tight against her. She could feel him breathe in tight, quick gasps. She searched for Rhywder, but there was no sign of him. Everywhere, there were fires. Fires crawled like living things across the grass.

Toward the forest of the East of the Land, only a thin line of battered and bloodied Daath still held. Beyond them, the Unchurians raged insane, driven to utter frenzy. She heard a Daathan captain screaming, "Hold! Hold, you bastards, for your children are behind you! By Elyon's Light you will hold this line!"

But as mighty and determined as they were, they were being massacred. The flank above them, east, had been overwhelmed, and they were hopelessly outnumbered. Though the beach was before them, though a ship sailed to reach them, the last of the Shadow Warriors were falling now, and when their line gave way, the Unchurians would overwhelm them all. Only a miracle could spare them time to reach the shore. Only the word of Elyon Himself could save them. But Satrina believed. She had not struggled with the Little Fox of Lochlain all this way for it to just end in massacre. Someone, someone would intervene. That was her faith, and she held it as tightly as she held the child that was the scion of the Daath against her.

The one they called Azazel, once the lord of the choir of the Auphanim, and his followers rode slowly into the circle of stone within the ancient forest of the East of the Land. It was a sacred path, this, one used by those who came called of Elyon. It passed through the East of the Land, along its border, and this ancient circle of stone still held a tissue of the power that had created the world called Earth.

Beyond, the battle would soon be ended. Azazel was riding to watch over the final moments, following the pathway ironically once cut of the Daath themselves, those who were to have been saviors of this age of men, the first age. The rest, the next aeons, would belong to them, to the oath takers, and this moment was choice above all moments in his long life that stretched through stars;

through many worlds, this moment would shine. Azazel was about to witness the fall of the Daath, their armies, their might and mystery, and most of all, their chosen, their fabled seventy and seven that were said, by the weak prophecies of Enoch, to stand in the last hour of the first apocalypse of men.

Azazel had managed to shift time, to kill futures by flinging them from the sky, until now only his future remained. There was no hope left to them. Even if the young king showed up with his sunblade, the outcome of that meeting would be far different from when the boy had faced the weak and febrile Satariel. Why he had vanished, this scion, Azazel could not guess, but nor did he care. The sword called the Angelslayer meant nothing to him; he could destroy it with thought alone if need be.

His skin was the flesh of a mortal already, and surprisingly, strengthened by an overlaid multitude of spell bindings, it was stronger than his own given flesh—as was proven when the mighty Righel tried to use a sunblade to cut him down. Azazel could withstand the Angelslayer, Uriel's sword. In fact, given the time left the Daath and their king and their fabled blade of Uriel, it was over, for there was no chance, no possible future to which the Daath could escape. He even knew of the blackship of the Etlantian killer, Darke, the Tarshian. He knew all; his eyes had searched the sky and the land; his eyes had seen all there was to see. Except, curiously, this strange scion named Loch, who had utterly vanished—it was a mystery, but sooner or later it would resolve. Too late to change what was now going to take place.

Azazel moved slowly. He would emerge from the forest with a splendid view from high ground just in time to witness the slaying of the children—that was the moment of ending; that was when time would alter forever. The Earth and all it offered would become the breeding grounds of those who had performed the Oath of Binding so long ago on Mount Ammon. It had come full circle. Elyon's world was ordered and maintained by law and edict, by oath and by light, and Azazel, following his one given leader, the Light Bearer, the first to step down from the sky and lead his brothers against heaven, had used those very edicts, those very words that formed worlds of star matter, that formed universes of dark nodes as tiny and infinitesimal as a grain of sand. He had used them to bring about a future in which his sons and the sons of those who swore their oath seven hundred years before would own the Earth, would guide it past the eye of Daath and leave it strong, poised at the edge of all living matter where a heaven of their own would begin to form. Those who had come here in that day, in the day of Yered, they were Elohim, and they had sung in the choir of the first speaking, the *Holy-Holy-Holy,* which formed this existence—and they would soon bind it as their own.

In fact, it seemed already done, already finished, for Azazel could feel it now, all of it. He could feel the Earth; he could feel the sky like a part of his being. It was about to end, this prophecy of the crippled one, the one called Enoch. Azazel had plotted this moment for centuries, and he could taste it, feel it in the depth of his acquired skin.

What Azazel did not feel was the sword of the Angelslayer above him as its hilt notched against the capstone of the queen's temple—the hidden, cloaked star ship named Daathan, which, as brilliant and knowing as he was, Azazel had not sensed rising through the trees above him. He had not felt it there because it was cloaked in a skin of aganon and blessed of the light of the far mothering star, Dannu. It was invisible to his thousand eyes. Neither could Azazel feel the eleventh scion, the boy king named Lochlain, who now took his last breath as he angled the sword and set its tip against his heart where he knelt on the capstone of the temple.

"Amen-Omen-Diamon," Loch whispered, then let his weight fall forward, let the tip of Uriel's sword pierce his flesh, then deep, into the richest of his blood, the very center of his heart and there it drank full, lighting as it had not ignited in centuries.

The forest below Loch, especially the sacred ring of standing stone that funneled the light of the mothering star, came alive in both the giving light of a mother and the terrible Light of Severity that was Elyon's eye. The Light of Severity struck even the trees and melted them away, stripping the plaza and bringing to life the two smaller ships that had long ago set sail from the seventh star and had moments before been hills in the surrounding oak. They, too, were coated in aganon. The entire plaza came to life. The Unchurians about Azazel screamed as they were ripped into shadows with terrible pain, and even the demon himself screamed. It was true, his spellbound flesh, designed to withstand the light of sunblades, was maintaining, but much of it was stripped away, the legs, the arms, until but a burnt and agonized torso writhed in the lighted, brilliant circle of stone, living now with the light of the mothering star, the *Light Whose Name Is Splendor.*

His eyes were seared, his pain unimaginable, but Azazel still looked up, and before him stood the son of Uriel, the one named Sandalaphon.

"Even you, Azazel, so loved of Elyon that He gave you all power, even you stand now before the words of Enoch. The boy has crippled you, left you human. Now the sword of Uriel shall bind you in the Earth. Face now the prophecy of Enoch. Though once you walked as angels, yea, now you shall die; even as men shall die, so shall you. Beneath this sacred ground has been prepared your prison, the fiery columns that shall bind you for ten thousand years, until the coming of the one."

Sandalaphon drew his sword from its ornate sheath.

Through his damaged eyes, Azazel watched as the sword lit, striking the ground all about him with the divine Light of Severity and opening in the Earth a pit that would reach deep, almost to the Earth's heart. There, where the falls of fiery columns moved continually, the prison that would be Azazel's prison was formed, and the cores he had chosen to clothe himself in tumbled to the depths. Behind him it closed, sealed over, closing in the heat of burning that would continue beyond all endurance, even for one such as Azazel, for the next ten thousand years.

At the capstone of the star ship named Daathan, Sandalaphon gently lifted Loch's body back, then withdrew the sword. His back had arched in the last moment, dislodging his back plate and splitting open the leather of his tunic. The wings had torn through and spread outward in a magnificent silver blue, full and rich. He had become, in the final moment, the lineage of his bloodline. He lifted Loch in his arms, letting a single tear fall, for in his day, Sandalaphon had loved this boy. Lochlain, the son of Asteria, had accepted his fate from the time he was only a child and he had done it with grace and dignity. Sandalaphon turned, lifting the sword and its sheath, which he would give to the Presence inside for keeping, to the Lady of the Waters who was once a Star Walker Queen. She would hold it until the time when the last Daath, the ones who would face Aeon's End, would come for it. They would know the place, and they would know the time. As Sandalaphon stepped through the smooth, unmarked doorway, he seemed to just vanish, taking with him the limp body of the Daathan king, already drained of all blood, along with the sword and sheath of the Angelslayer.

Darke searched, tingling—something had happened. The sky was cleared, the angel's storm had simply vanished in a blink, and what was a quiet dusk fell over the still chaotic coastline of the Daath. The quakes had stilled. The fires burned, but instead of moving like fingers over the land searching for prey, they now burned lifeless. The thunder and quaking had ceased in a single motion, and the only sound was of dying, above, on the ridge, at the line of forest where the Daath still held back the Unchurians. The Unchurians had sensed something, for they had suddenly been driven to complete, unabated rage—and it was not the rage of tactics or warfare, or of any purpose—they had gone utterly insane. Darke stared amazed, because the Unchurians were now not only killing the last of the Shadow Warriors—they were now killing everything in sight, even each other.

"We must get out of here," Darke whispered to the Pelegasian captain.

"I will not argue that sentiment."

And then it dawned on him. Darke guessed the cause. Somehow, somewhere beyond, above, Loch had just spared his people a last sliver of time. It was a thin sliver. Had he not been here at this shore, the number of purely insane, raging Unchurians would still have overwhelmed them, and would surely do so by day's end. But the sliver of time would allow the Shadow Warriors leading the children to reach him, and should Darke reach deep water, there would be no finding him. He would escape even angel's eyes should they reemerge. But they would not; he was certain at least of that. The boy that they all had doubted so had just killed a second angel, and unlike the struggle with Satariel, this one had been snuffed quickly.

The prow post of Darke's ship hit the sand. The throwers were snuffed and oozed black pus.

Darke watched from the forecastle. Galloping toward him were a tight core of Shadow Warriors; he could tell by the look of them they were the elite, chosen for this one task, to deliver the flowers of the Daath to shelter. Within their ranks, Darke saw youth. It touched his heart, for the Daath were bringing no others, just the children, some riding, others clutched in the saddles against warriors' shadowy armor. They knew they died this day—the protectors that brought them, but they also knew this was the seed, and Darke could guess their number from the words of the Book of Angels, the Book of Enoch—these were the seventy and seven.

"Prepare to take on boarders!" Darke shouted. Rope ladders were thrown. As the Daath reached him, warriors splashed through the warm waters and surrounded the ship on either side—winded, sweaty horses; darkened, silver armor watery in firelight. Children were being lifted from the saddles and handed up. Darke stared as a young girl of perfect beauty and rich curls of red hair was lifted by a strong hand and pulled up by a dirty hand of one of the Pelegasians.

Then he paused, and a moment he felt his heart stop in his chest. He almost cried out. Below, Hyacinth was watching him. She was seated atop a roan horse, her long dark braids flayed by wind, tears in her eyes. He saw her whisper, "Captain! Oh, Captain!"

Darke gasped and leapt over the railing. He used a swifter rope to climb down the side of the hull. He dropped in the water, then turned, striding, and as Hyacinth dropped out of the saddle, he caught her, pulled her tight against him, and as he held her, his eyes stung with tears. In his life, Darke had never shed tears, but now he did. She was alive. Hyacinth was alive!

Satrina searched, beginning to panic. She looked to one of the Shadow

Warriors, one of the King's Guard that would have known the Little Fox, looked through the visor of his helmet and caught his eyes.

"We must find Rhywder!"

"We must get the youth aboard this ship, my lady. It is all. You and the child will go now."

"No, we have to find Rhywder! He has to come! Do you not see, he is supposed to be here! We must find him!"

"Wrong, my lady, Rhywder must find us—and if not, he had done for king and these children all he could. And you, Ringbearer, you will sail without him. Now, board the ship. We cannot risk the child."

Lucian pulled up beside her. His big, dark brown eyes offered an understanding gaze.

"Lucian!" gasped Satrina. "Take the child! I must find Rhywder!"

She started to hand Lucian the baby, but he seized her arm so tight it was painful. "No!" he screamed at her, furious for some reason. "No! You are his mother now! You are his mother, damn it!" Tears blurred the boy's eyes. "If he cannot believe in you, then who? Who will be his protector, his mother? Who?"

Satrina swallowed. He was right. She did not yet love this child as a mother, but she felt a bond, even now. Of course, though he was a boy, he was right—in this moment, wiser than her. Weeping, she urged the horse forward, and with Lucian guiding her hand, she took hold of the ladder and started to climb. To either side, Shadow Warriors were climbing the swifter ropes beside her—not to board, but to hold oval shields over her and the child—guarding against any possible attack, any missile, any sudden strike from the sky or elsewhere. Then she thought she heard Rhywder's voice. She turned, searching over the edge of a shield.

"Here! Over here!" screamed Rhywder. He was running up the white sand beach, holding a boy's arm, jerking him along in a stumbling, flying run.

"A horse!" Rhywder shouted. "I bring the son of Eryian!"

Several riders bolted from the ranks and sped along the sand toward Rhywder.

✝

Rhywder threw Little Eryian to a horseman, who immediately wrenched up on the reins, rearing the horse, turning, then thundered back for the ship. Above them, on the ridge of the East of the Land, unbelievably, there was still a thin line of Shadow Warriors fighting bitterly to hold back what was utter madness, utter insanity. They were about to fall, they were being overwhelmed on their eastern flank, and it was becoming a brawl. A good captain could have smashed through the line of Daath, could have gone for this ship, but then Rhywder, stunned, realized the fighting was simply sheer insanity. He saw the skies, the land no longer splitting with chasms. The angel was dead, and the boy had done what he was born to do; he had given the children a sliver of time that was impossible, that could never have been and yet was.

Above, it was over now. The last few standing of the first legion of the Daath were now being hacked mercilessly to pieces. The Unchurians killing them were not satisfied with mere death; they were hacking the Daath into bloodied pieces of flesh.

Any second they would pour toward the ship and the shore of the Western Sea in a flood of uncontrollable rage.

Rhywder leapt into the saddle behind a Shadow Warrior, one of Argolis's protectors—a man he knew, his name was Mammanon. They galloped hard toward the ship.

"I must find a mount!" Rhywder shouted. "A spare horse!"

When they reached the ship, for a moment, Mammanon turned in the saddle, met Rhywder's eyes.

"Godspeed, Captain," he said, then took his arm and flung Rhywder from the saddle. Rhywder landed on his side, hard in the sand.

"Farewell, Little Fox!" another of the king's guard shouted. "Faith's Light, my lord!"

The Shadow Warriors that had escorted the children to the shore were now turning, drawing weapons. A pure, frothing, insane number of Unchurians were pouring toward the shore. The Shadow Warriors drew weapons and in a single shout, galloped forward, heading into the heart of the charging Unchurians, even though they were but a handful, no more than ten or twelve riders.

"No!" screamed Rhywder. "A horse! Someone give me a horse!"

He leapt to his feet, searching frantically.

"Turn back, you bastards!" he screamed at the top of his lungs. "I command you to give me a horse!"

But they did not turn; they did not even look back. They were a tiny dot about to be swallowed into madness.

Rhywder stood gripping his short sword in a tight fist.

"Rhywder!" he heard a scream.

He looked back. Satrina was on the forecastle, shouting over the side, the child clasped to her breast.

Pirates muscled into the prow, pushing the ship into deep water where the oars could catch and quickly pull her from the shore. Watching Satrina, Rhywder began to back step up the beach slowly. He then turned and started at a run for his men.

"Give way the oars!" Darke shouted from the prow, Hyacinth beside him.

"We have to bring him, Captain."

"Looks as though he has chosen otherwise, my lady," responded Darke somberly.

The oars swept, then dipped, taking a backstroke that sucked the darkship into deeper water where she could turn.

Satrina screamed. She threw herself against the railing and screamed, red-faced.

"Rhywder! You little bastard! Rhywder, you have to come with us! Rhywder!"

Rhywder continued running for the others, for his brothers, sword drawn—time to die. Once more, time to die. But then, reaching the top of a dune, he paused. He watched them, tingling, the small band of Shadow Warriors looking insignificant as they were engulfed, swallowed. They had vanished without effect, and the Unchurians were all that were left, still coming, furious.

"Give way port oar!" Darke's voice echoed.

Rhywder looked back over his shoulder. The ship began to swing about, pointing her sharp prow to the sea, and as the ship made its turn, Satrina was at a run down the decking, clasping the blue cloak that bundled the child against her, but running for all she was worth. "Rhywder! Run! You can make it!"

When the ship had turned, Satrina was topmost. She had reached the stern and leapt onto the decking, and now she was leaning over the railing, screaming. Even from here, Rhywder could see the tears streaming over her cheeks.

"Rhywder!"

The oars lifted for a stroke.

Rhywder glanced once behind. The Unchurians were rolling like a wave, coming for him.

Rhywder finally swore and flung his short sword. He turned and sprinted down the side of the dune in a hard run for the sea.

"You can make it, Rhywder!" Satrina screamed. "Swim!"

He tore free his cloak, cast aside his crossbow, his scabbard, the killing axe, all but his jerkin, and dove headlong into a wave. He came out of it stroking hard.

From the prow Darke watched. "Hold the oars," he said quietly.

"What!" shouted the Pelegasian captain.

"I said, hold the oars and throw out a line."

It was one of Darke's youth, a Tarshian, who responded. He grabbed a coiled grappling rope, then ran, and when he reached the railing he threw the coiled rope high over the stern. It played out and dropped to the sea. Rhywder lunged for it, missed. Its cork bobbed just before him and he took a deep breath and lunged again. This time he caught it and began pulling himself hand over hand.

"Give way oars," Darke shouted. A moment longer and they would have been within range of fire arrows.

Rhywder was wrenched forward hard when the oars took hold; he had to cling with all his might. He fought through a swiftly curling wall of seawater as a wave crashed over him. He continued to pull himself along, until he reached the stern and used the rope to walk up the side of the dark hull, clamber over the stern railing, and fall to the deck. Satrina dropped beside him, still clasping the child. Slowly, Rhywder turned to her, and Satrina pulled him against her with a shriek.

✝

The blackship of Captain Darke sailed into the night, into windswept sea, and vanished into the deep waters of the Western Sea. Aboard his ship were the last of the Daath alive in this world, the last of Uriel's seed—those who, in the final days of the first apocalypse of men, would be called the *Angelslayers.*

K. MICHAEL WRIGHT

K. Michael Wright grew up near an Assinaboine Indian reservation in Montana where he first gained a deep appreciation for Native American culture, which later led to extensive travel and research into Mesoamerican myth and history.

After picking up a BA in History, he earned a Master's of Fine Arts degree in Creative and Critical Writing from Brigham Young University, during which time he won the Kennedy Center Award for Excellence for his play *Outrun the Night*.

After graduating, he moved to LA and worked in production companies and as a screenwriter. He also wrote scripts for the Canadian Broadcast Company in Vancouver. He eventually "did time" in New York as a consultant and technical writer for companies like Comedy Central and Bank of New York. *Tolteca* is his first novel.

Mr. Wright lives in an historic 1630 house in New England and also spends time in Utah. Among his hobbies are building wooden model ships, online computer gaming, and karate (SKA).

For more information
about other great titles from
Medallion Press, visit

www.medallionpress.com